Won't Let Go Of You
The Latch Trilogy: Book Two
Copyright 2026
Independently published by Briar Townsend
All rights reserved

No portion of this work may be reproduced in whole or in part without the express permission of the author. If referenced in another work, credit must be given. This work may not be used to train or inform artificial intelligence or related technologies. All rights remain with the estate of the author upon their death, unless and until the copyright expires.

Won't Let Go Of You is a work of fiction. Any references, resemblances to, or mentions of real people, places, or things are either coincidental or fictionalised, and not intended as a realistic depiction or representation of said entity. Any copyrighted and/or trademarked material referenced does not belong to the author, and all rights related to referenced material(s) belong to the trademark and copyright holder(s).

Cover art and design: Hannah Christensen
Edited by: J. Brighton and E. Hardman

Print ISBN: 979-8-9923066-6-8

Won't Let Go Of You

*The Latch Trilogy:
Book Two*

By Briar Townsend

Content Guidance

Won't Let Go Of You - as well as the entire *Latch* trilogy - contains allusions to, and mentions of, transphobia and homophobia.
There will also be instances of sexual assault, attempted sexual assault, doxxing, outing, a coercive sexual relationship, ableism (specifically in relation to autism), childhood bullying, racism, classism, familial rejection, grief, death of a family member, funeral, illness (influenza), and interactions with police.
This may not be an exhaustive list, and is provided as general guidance. Not all content listed will be mentioned in all three books, but will be found throughout the series as a whole.

One of the main characters lives with PTSD. The other main character is autistic. Along with the other identities portrayed, including multiple gender and sexual identities, these are written as individual perspectives and not intended to be understood as universal experiences. While Theo, Emir, and their friends offer one narrative of their identities, they are not representative of entire populations.

This book contains explicit sexual content. My style has been referred to as "comfort smut" and "homonormative." Be that as it may, if PG is your cup of tea, I am not the barista for you.

While I intend to handle these topics with both care and honesty, it's possible that reading about them may be uncomfortable or potentially triggering. Please take the space you need before, during, and/or after reading to look after yourself.

CHAPTER ONE

Auditions for the Roseborough University dance programme's winter show start on a Tuesday afternoon, just days after the autumn show finishes. The dancers are still recovering from a long two weeks, including four *Alice in Wonderland* shows each weekend and tech in between. They're tired but they're happy, every dancer in the programme exactly where they want to be. They've bonded as a group now that the first production of the year is behind them. The students intermingle between audition slots, first years chatting with third years, soloists with the corps, and friend groups opening up to make room to merge, a venn diagram of young adults who have learned to work together over the past few months.

There are new relationships too. Theo and Emir's is still the one that people seem most invested in, likely due to their past antagonism and their unofficial leadership of the other dancers. But there's also a few second year couples who got together at their end of show party, first years Sam and Esme who had their first sort-of date on Monday, and Lili and Jordan who still are very much not out, but who seem to be alright with everyone assuming they're together and loosening up a bit, at least around their peers.

Overall, the air in the audition is filled with healthy rivalry as they all try for openings in the winter show, where everyone will have a spot, but the solos are completely up for grabs.

The autumn show, *Alice in Wonderland*, was a proper ballet, with a series of call backs and formal roles that needed to be filled. And the spring show will be *Sleeping Beauty*, essentially the same process except without a majority of the students, with the second years abroad. The third years will be focusing on their dissertations, so it's tradition for the leads in the spring show to be first years.

But the winter show is where they're all on equal footing. There's no hierarchy, no traditional ballet, the entire thing much more free form, which suits the shortened rehearsal time. It's currently Friday evening, the first of December, and the show will be the last two weekends of February, with a lengthy break around Christmas in between. That's nearly a month of rehearsal time lost compared to the ballets.

Emir's always loved the winter show the best of the three. It's a bit of variety, a compilation of styles, each of their instructors offering at least one piece. There's modern, jazz, contemporary, really anything the choreographers are feeling inspired by. As a natural result, the dancers for each piece are chosen as much for chemistry and movement style as they are ability. Where the ballets they perform the rest of the year prepare them for life as a professional, the winter show helps them grow as true artists, trying their hand (or feet, rather) at whatever is new, fresh, and exciting.

Emir should be exhausted from the last two weekends of *Alice* shows, but this is what he lives for, more than anything. The last few days of auditions have had him constantly smiling, giddy as he finds Theo during every break and excitedly tells him what he's enjoyed about each piece they've auditioned for.

Theo also loves the winter show, but for predictably different reasons than Emir. He loves pushing his boundaries and learning about styles he's much less familiar with. He likes that it comes with research and he enjoys working with dancers he otherwise would barely see since they're in different years. It also helps Theo flex his choreography skills, the professional choreographers usually asking for input from the students as they go and allowing it to be a very collaborative process. Theo adores it.

He feels more at home choreographing than he ever imagined as a younger dancer, and the more time he spends crafting stories through dance, the more sure he is that choreography might be his path forward. When Emir finds him between auditions, cuddling into his space with an almost manic sparkle in his eye, he listens to all of Emir's excitement and adds his own, talking about how he hopes the stories weave and which dancers he thinks work best for each piece.

The winter show is also their first audition process as boyfriends rather than rivals. Maybe people would assume they'll be more distracted than normal, that they'd let their relationship get in the way of their focus or work ethic, but it's quite the opposite. They've never been happier as individuals, and they've always pushed each other to be their best as dancers. The difference now is that it's through encouragement and a genuine understanding of the other person rather than competition.

When Theo mentions to Emir that he should tilt his head a certain way in one spot, Emir nods and takes the note, seeing how it immediately changes his shape to be perfectly asymmetrical. And when Emir reminds Theo to loosen his torso for one of Sean's auditions, he smiles and agrees that he's using too much of a ballet posture. They aren't critical, they're helpful. And yes, they both adore watching their boyfriend dazzle and show off and breeze through the auditions, but not as a distraction. With their relationship becoming what it has, they find inspiration in each other as much as through their own work, and it only adds to their talent.

By the time the auditions are finishing up Friday evening, all the groups have been sorted and assigned to each choreographer, and while Emir and Theo aren't going to be in rehearsal together as often as the fall show, they both leave Tech Hall with satisfied smiles and their arms around each other as they head into the dressing room.

They wisely decided to take yesterday and today off from work on their dissertation, recognising that it'd really be pushing their physical limits so soon after *Alice* ended. Instead of more time in the studio, Emir is taking Theo on a date tonight. It's not a surprise, because Theo doesn't really like surprises, but it's still going to be special. Emir's been planning it all week, giving Theo as much say as he likes to make sure he's spoiling his princess correctly. They'll stop back at Emir's flat first to get what he needs to spend the entire weekend at Theo's flat and to shower, and then they're on their way to their romantic evening.

"See you tomorrow?" Sam, a first year that Emir's befriended, stops on his way out of the dressing room to say goodbye. He's really opened up the last few weeks since Emir chatted with him at the *Alice* pre-party, and tomorrow morning is the first time he'll be joining Emir's queer book club.

"Definitely." Emir grins at Sam while tucking his technique shoes into his locker for the night. He's been looking forward to tomorrow's meeting for days. "Finished the book a while ago. I can't wait."

Theo sidles up behind Emir with a sigh, hands hugging around his waist as he sets his chin on Emir's shoulder. He holds on tight, waiting until Emir's finished getting ready before detaching himself (only mildly hindering the process), leaning in for a chaste kiss and holding his hand out for Emir to walk him home.

Holding hands with Emir is one of Theo's favourite things, and he's not even sure he could explain it. Since they started being friends, then eventually more, Emir was so physically comfortable with him in a way that showed a vulnerability and trust Theo hadn't yet earned. Holding hands now is a reminder of that trust, Emir saying 'I know you won't hurt me' and Theo answering 'I know you won't leave'.

"You happy, princess?" Emir asks once they're outside in the cold, winter air. He wants to debrief the auditions with Theo before they go on their date so they can really focus on each other tonight. "You were incredible in that last section for Margaret's jazz piece. I didn't even know you could do a death drop."

"I haven't done true jazz in years!" Theo swings their hands between them, still glowing from the high of the auditions. "And she said it's going to be a Michael Jackson medley, but I think I convinced her to add at least one Janet section. Can't ignore Janet."

"It might be weird not having all of our rehearsals together." Emir pauses while they both think quietly for a minute. Their conversations tend to follow a natural rhythm of back and forth, sharing their thoughts as easily as breathing, no rush of information unless something is truly urgent. "But I'll be so proud to see and hear all about it. Promise."

"I'm glad she gave you the solo for her contemporary number." Theo squeezes Emir's hand before leaning over to kiss his cheekbone. He sees Lili and Jordan far ahead of them, clearly heading back to their flat, and if Theo remembers correctly, settling in for a quiet night at home. "It's really going to show off your artistry. Your acting and your character work were incredible in *Alice*, but this is going to be a more raw side of you. And you'll get to wear that creepy mask, which I already know you're going to scare me with at least once."

"How very dare you. I would *never*." Emir giggles despite himself because he absolutely was already planning to hide it in Theo's dance bag next week.

Emir lets them into his building and keeps a hand on Theo's lower back while they walk into his flat together. It's still early in the night, but he's desperate for that shower, hoping the hot water will rejuvenate him and bring some life back into his tired muscles.

"How were the auditions?" Laurie asks from the sofa, T laying on top of him while they watch the telly together. He has his hands in T's curls, playing with his fiance's hair while they relax together at the end of a long week.

They were both involved in *Alice* as crew members, Laurie helping with sets and stage managing, T with the costumes, and they're working a show for the theatre programme this weekend. There's never really a week off for them, but it's paid work, even if it's just enough to cover the basics and save a few pounds for their wedding.

"Brilliant!" Theo answers, walking over to bump fists with Laurie and lay a gentle hand on the top of T's head. "We're just here to shower and grab Emir's things and then you'll have the place for the rest of the weekend as promised."

"No rush. We're going to bed early tonight. This little dove already beat me to it." Laurie answers through a yawn, stifling it behind his hand. T is being suspiciously quiet, and it takes Theo a moment to realise it's because they're fully asleep. Laurie gazes fondly at T draped on his chest then looks past Theo to ask Emir, "Say goodbye before you leave?"

"Always will." Emir grins, taking Theo by the hand to bring him away from the living room and towards his bedroom. He turns around, pulling Theo by the shirt and through the doorway, collapsing on his bed with an exhausted groan. Theo falls on top of him with a smile, easy in Emir's space. It's always so easy with him.

"Can't fall asleep, Emi." Theo nuzzles his way onto Emir's chest, wrapping his arms around him and kissing the underside of his jaw. "But we can cuddle for a minute."

"And then shower? Together?" Emir sighs and settles under Theo. How they've managed to go the entire day since this morning without a cuddle is unclear. Theo cuddles are a very important part of Emir's life; it re-centres him to be quiet with his boyfriend and relax in the safety of his arms. He's never known comfort like this before.

"If you like." Theo hums happily as Emir rubs a hand along his back under his shirt. "But no sex. We have a date to get to."

"Tomorrow, maybe?" Emir asks, grinning because he knows that Theo's already looking through his mental calendar and trying to pencil it in.

Maybe some people would find it odd that being spontaneous doesn't really work for Theo most of the time, likely because many people see sex as a response to the heat of a particular moment. But Emir finds it both endearing and attractive that Theo likes him enough to plan to be intimate together, that he's intentional in their relationship and considerate to both of their needs and desires. It's honestly hot as fuck to know that Theo both remembers their past moments (he's found the notes on their shared calendar of first kisses and first hand jobs and etc) and clearly looks forward to what's next for them. There's still spontaneity and even when it's planned there's always consent, but knowing Theo looks forward to being intimate with him has been surprisingly comforting. Emir knows he's fit, but Theo reminds him that he's so much more than that, loving the rest of him at least as much as his body.

"Either in the morning when we wake up, or after we go to the studio to work for a few hours." Theo doesn't really have a preference, and they haven't done anything too physically involved yet, but he likes the pace they're going. They're steadily progressing to more intimate sexual encounters at a rate they're both comfortable with. Emir's never pushed him to do anything, happy to share his experience with Theo without making it awkward. Theo's completely new to sex, but with Emir, he never worries.

"Both?" Emir hopes, but he's not going to ask for more than Theo's ready to give. He would really like to get his mouth on Theo's gorgeous dick soon though. "Soft sleepy morning cuddles that turn into snogging and then hand stuff could be fun."

Theo groans at the thought, subconsciously starting to rub himself off against Emir while finding his mouth for a heated kiss. He opens his lips, letting Emir play with his tongue and get him worked up with the suggestion of more. They're both too tired tonight to do anything properly naughty, but his dick is definitely interested, and he doesn't want them to get too distracted and miss their date. "Hand stuff before your book club, then more later if we're up for it."

"Feels like you're up for it now." Emir shifts them so he can fit a thigh between Theo's legs and tease him while they keep rubbing against one another like kindling. "Kiss me and then we'll shower. I won't let us be late, baby."

True to his word, Emir stops them after only another minute of dry humping on his bed, giving Theo one last, lingering kiss before nudging Theo up and out of bed and stripping him of his clothes.

Per Theo's preference, they wash each other's hair and soap their bodies, kissing every inch of skin they come across like they're anointing one another in preparation for their romantic evening. It's a perfect start to their date and Theo has never felt more safe with anyone in his life. He hopes it's reciprocal, that Emir can feel the care that Theo puts into every touch, the thought he put into his outfit for the evening (his green jumper because Emir says it brings out the hazel in his eyes and it's warm for cuddling), the love that he tries to convey with every moment they're together. And if Emir's adoring stare as they finish getting ready is any metric, Theo thinks he's done alright.

***

Emir drops Theo's hand to open the door to the King's Herald pub and usher him inside, walking in behind him and crowding into his space while they approach the host. Squeezing Theo's waist before stepping forward, Emir trails his fingers along Theo's back to say, "Reservation for Shah. Just the two of us."

Theo glows beside him, hands in his pockets while he waits. He rather likes being treated like a gentleman, Emir holding doors and planning dates and, now that they're at the table, holding his chair out for him with a wink that brings a flush to his cheeks. This place isn't too posh, but it's certainly nice and definitely a step up from a traditional uni student's haunt. Emir gave him a few options for their date, but Theo's never been here, and he likes trying new things with Emir.

"You still want what you already decided on?" Emir asks Theo, glancing at the menu while hooking his ankle around Theo's beneath the table. He didn't get nearly enough cuddle time earlier and he likes having those little points of connection.

"Definitely. You?" Theo always spends time looking at menus before going anywhere new, especially since not everywhere has vegetarian options for him. And now that he's with Emir, he needs to make sure there's halal food. Emir's not religious anymore, but he's told Theo that he still feels odd eating certain things. It's not up to Theo to decide any of that for him, so he's made it a rule for himself to only go places that give Emir that option, unless Emir specifies otherwise.

Emir nods in reply, already setting aside the menu because he doesn't actually need it.

This is nice. Really nice. Tonight is their first real date as a couple. Sure, they had their *Cinderella* film night that Emir planned, they've had romantic evenings at home, they've gone to events together and met each other's families. But this is a traditional date night, something Emir supposes most couples would've done early on and not a month into the relationship. But he and Theo aren't most couples, and if anything, he appreciates it more because they're still choosing to do this even when it's not a societal obligation of courtship.

"You're thinking." Theo trails a fingertip along Emir's hand where it rests on the table to get his attention. He doesn't ask it as a question. He knows Emir well enough by now to recognise when he's deep in thought.

"Of course. You make me think, princess. About everything." Emir catches Theo's hand in his own for just a moment before releasing it and sitting back in his seat. "I like us together...I think we made the right choice to do this. The date and the relationship. All of it. I was so scared to let myself have this because I wasn't sure, I didn't want us to get hurt."

"I remember." Theo leans forward and sets his chin in his palm, gazing softly at Emir. There's no romantic candles atop the table, but there may as well be with the golden light in Theo's eyes. "Hard to believe it's been a month, either tomorrow or in three days, depending on how you count. I suppose we're celebrating our anniversary, then, aren't we?"

"I think we should celebrate on the fourth, that way it can be the same every month." Emir answers, thinking practically. "You're much better with schedules than I am, but if it's always the same day I'll remember."

"It's on the calendar, but this can still be our one month celebration. Even though you kissed me on the third, you waited until the fourth to make it official. Don't worry, I forgive you for making me wait fourteen hours." Theo grins at Emir, both of them startling when their waiter reaches the table and introduces themself, asking for their drink order. Since neither of them feels like drinking tonight with their bodies so physically tired, they ask for water, and Emir orders them a goat cheese bruschetta starter to share.

"I wasn't sure you'd say yes." Emir gets back to Theo's comment once they're on their own again. It seems a bit ridiculous now, but he was worried for good reason. They have so much history that led them here, and he couldn't be sure he hadn't fucked up his chances despite their new trajectory.

"And I was worried to ask you myself." Theo laughs, eyes crinkling while he stares at Emir. It's hard for him to remember there's anyone else around, all of the noise of a busy Friday evening fading into the background like radio static. When he's with Emir, he's all Theo wants to see. "I wanted it to be your decision. I didn't know what you were ready for."

"Ready for anything with you." Emir shrugs, as if that's not a huge deal, but he looks at Theo with so much more than love. After his last relationship imploded, he didn't know that he'd ever want something serious again. But Theo had more than shown him that he could be safe in this, that they could build something together on a strong foundation of trust. And now he can't imagine any other way forward.

Just as Emir's about to continue their reminiscing, he stops himself, staring with a smirk at the three people he just watched walk through the door. He should've known when he saw Alfie scurrying out of the dressing room in a rush.

"Look who's here." Emir whispers, tilting his chin to get Theo to turn around. But Theo doesn't get that Emir's being subtle and he waves animatedly at their friends, making Emir giggle and bite his tongue. So much for gossiping in private with his boy.

Ciaran's holding open the door for Gabe and Alfie, the three of them waving back immediately when they see Emir and Theo off to the side by the windows. Gabe speaks to the host briefly and the three of them follow to their own table on the far side of the pub. Emir and Theo glance at each other, both with about a dozen questions, suitably distracted from their conversation. It's unusual they run into their friends away from uni, especially when they're out on a specially planned night of romance.

"What are the chances they picked the same date night place as us?" Emir asks, amused by the coincidence. They're in London for fuck's sake. There's ten restaurants on every street. And, more surprisingly, the three of them could've had the flat to themselves right now with everyone else out, and for some reason they aren't taking advantage. "We've never even been here before."

"You sure it's a date?" Theo asks, tilting his head in confusion. The trio look happy from what he can see, joking about something with Ciaran throwing his head back and touching Alfie's forearm while Gabe grins beside him. "I thought they were just casual."

"Only one way to find out." Emir smirks again, standing up and gently grabbing Theo's wrist to follow him. He gets on Laurie's case for meddling, but he does enough of it on his own. Emir *is* the one who set up T and Laurie in the first place, even if everyone forgets that detail.

"Emir!" Theo almost trips as he follows along, finding his feet with Emir's help before Emir detaches himself.

Emir knows they're in public, and they don't really need to attract attention. It's London, but there's still bigots hiding in plain sight, and he doesn't want to give them a chance to ruin their evening, even if it's just for existing as queer where they can see it. But Emir brushes the thought away when he feels Theo's hand accidentally graze his own, and he knows he would die rather than deny their relationship. What they have is too important to him.

"That was quick." Ciaran snorts, dropping Gabe's hand to run it through his own hair as they reach their table. Theo hides himself behind Emir, peering his head around to be part of the conversation, but trying to be slightly less intrusive than his boyfriend.

"Two questions - " Emir starts, grinning at Ciaran because he knows he'll be the easiest to rile up. Gabe's too zen and Emir doesn't know Alfie well enough to be a pain. Not yet, anyway.

"Three." Theo interrupts. "Sorry. I thought of another one."

"Go on." Gabe's the one who answers, Ciaran still too busy rolling his eyes. The codependency is borderline clinical for the six of them, and he should've expected they'd want a chat the second they recognised each other from the doorway. They haven't seen each other since family dinner Wednesday night, so maybe it was overdue.

"How'd you end up at the same restaurant as us? There's no way that's a coincidence since Theo and I have been planning this all week." Emir reaches behind and tickles Theo's side, waiting for him to giggle before stopping with a satisfied grin.

Alfie watches them interact, laughing into his hand and trying to pass it off as a cough. He's more than happy to let Ciaran deal with the questions since they're much more his friends than they are Alfie's.

"Ooooohhhh." Gabe looks genuinely surprised, like he's just discovered something. "I knew I heard someone talking about this place. Sorry, this one's on me. Couldn't decide where to go and I remembered someone mentioning King's Herald."

"So I get to blame you for the interrogation?" Ciaran squeezes Gabe's leg beneath the table, making sure he knows he's teasing. He doesn't actually mind, but he's as surprised as Emir and Theo that this is how their night transpired.

"Right, well that explains the location." Emir takes the fourth seat next to Alfie that's left empty at their table, Theo standing behind him, still unsure what to do in this situation.

Theo wants answers too, but Emir just seems so comfortable teasing their friends. He would spend ten minutes deciding what to say before he could ask, but Emir's much more bold at this sort of thing. Leaning forward, Theo kisses Emir's temple because he loves how Emir is so quiet and shy, but also a bit of a menace when he wants to be.

"You three on a date?" Emir holds Theo's hand on his shoulder, rubbing his thumb across his knuckles. The back of Emir's mind is still focused on how, only a minute ago, he was worried about showing affection for Theo in public, but this is something he feels comfortable with. It's a quiet way to acknowledge what Theo means to him: the most gentle, precious soul he could ever love.

"Take your best guess." Ciaran snarks, holding out a hand to Alfie this time, grinning when he accepts and flushes to the tips of his ginger hair. Alfie's been out as gay for years, but he's not used to having so many queer friends who just...act like this with each other. It's nice, if a bit chaotic.

"Just checking. Last I heard it was casual, and I want to be sure I'm acknowledging Alfie appropriately if he's your boyfriend now." Emir shrugs. He doesn't actually mind one way or the other as long as they're happy. "More teasing involved."

"What Emir said." Theo looks between them, waiting for an answer. The three of them have been sleeping together for a while, so maybe he and Emir should've realised sooner. "Alfie, you can stay over if you like. You're always welcome at ours."

"Thanks, butt." Alfie squeezes Ciaran's hand before letting go and setting his hands in his own lap again. He's learning to relax into this the more time they spend together. Alfie's never had an open relationship of any kind before, but it's been easy with Gabe and Ciaran. It's not serious, but they enjoy each other, and they're good people.

"What, we can't take him to dinner before we fuck eight ways to Sunday?" There's a cleared throat to the side of their table, which Ciaran waves off, literally. He doesn't have time for bigots. They're in a pub. That was barely even inappropriate.

"Not what I said, Heathcliff." Emir laughs, leaning back into Theo while Ciaran scoffs at the ruination of his family name. With the name Ciaran Heath, there isn't much creative space for the many nicknames that Emi likes to give people. At least Heathcliff is literary. "You must have a busy weekend ahead if you're planning eight orgasms before Sunday..."

"It's a date." Gabe steps into the conversation, knowing Emir and Ciaran could gay banter for ten minutes before getting to the point. "But we're not exclusive. Alfie can date whoever he likes and so can we. Ciaran's my partner, Alfie's our friend that we go on dates with."

"Simple enough." Emir stands up again, ready to head back to their own table and their own date. But Theo hasn't moved from his spot behind Emir's temporary chair. After a moment looking at Theo, Emir remembers he wanted to ask something himself. He tilts his head, inviting Theo to ask his question before they leave their friends alone again.

"I just...wanted to make sure people are being nice to you. That was my third question." Theo bites his lower lip and reaches for Emir instinctively to set an arm around his back. He feels like he's putting his friends on the spot, but since they're already having the conversation, it's a good opportunity to verify their casual open relationship isn't being met with bigotry.

"We haven't really told many people. Just Laurie and T, technically." Ciaran gives Theo an understanding smile, because of course he would be worried about that. There's no one else who cares about their friends being respected like Theo. He gets downright stroppy if someone's homophobic when he's nearby. Since Theo's incredibly articulate in those situations, it's embarrassing for whoever chose to be ignorant in front of him.

"And Laurie didn't make any jokes?" Theo asks, knowing that Alfie may not understand Laurie's vibe yet. He's the most supportive person anyone could ask for, but he does take the piss more than some people are used to.

"He tossed me a box of condoms and told me to play nice." Ciaran laughs, remembering the way Laurie had found the three of them at it on the couch a few weeks ago, ignored them to walk into T's room, then came back with the projectile protection suggestion. "We're good."

"Do you not want people to know?" Theo realises he actually has a fourth question that he probably should've asked first because their relationship should be as private as they choose. He feels Emir's hand move along his back and settle to rest above his bum, a gentle reminder of his presence. The perfect boyfriend.

"I don't mind." Gabe says, looking to the other two to speak for themselves. He's probably the most laid back of their entire group, and his friends and family have always been overwhelmingly supportive of his queer identities. He doesn't have any worries about people knowing their relationship status, as casual as it is.

"I don't really want it broadcast, but I'm not embarrassed or anything." Alfie looks between Gabe and Ciaran making sure they know any hesitation on his part is not because of them. They've had this conversation before, but Alfie hasn't had to really explain it to anyone else. His own friends don't actually know more than the fact he's been seeing someone, and he's not entirely sure how they'll react to him dating more than one someone. "I suppose if we decide it's more serious I'll have to think about it more."

"We'll just keep it to our group then?" Theo clarifies, looking up to catch Emir's eye and getting a kiss placed at the side of his head, nestled among the curls.

Emir adores that Theo made sure to check their boundaries before ending the conversation. Always so thoughtful.

"Probably for the best. You know what the world's like." Ciaran puts his arm around the back of Gabe's chair possessively. He's not had a terrible go of the whole coming out process, but things haven't been great with his brother Lochlan since Gabe entered the picture. Ciaran doubts Lochlan would be open minded about a poly or open relationship of any kind.

"Back to your date then, and we'll go back to ours." Emir reaches out to touch Alfie's shoulder, giving it a squeeze as he steps away. "But if you follow us to the cinema I'm locking you out of the flat."

"So what you're saying is you'll be gone for a few hours and the flat will be empty?" Gabe clarifies hopefully as they walk away.

Emir stops to laugh in response as Theo answers, "I'll text you on our way back."

***

The food at the King's Herald is incredible. Theo and Emir devour their starter in under a minute, eagerly awaiting the main courses they ordered: for Theo, a watercress salad with a hearty cauliflower soup (he loves cauliflower), and for Emir, a plant burger as he's not had one before.

They spend most of the meal talking about nothing, ignoring uni and work and instead discussing telly and books and their friends. Because they're so comfortable with each other, they'll fall into silence while they eat, staring fondly at one another without needing to fill the quiet. Theo keeps bumping his toes into Emir's under the table since their hands are busy and cuddling isn't an option right now. Emir's just so *charming* and he feels like he has a crush, which is maybe ridiculous because that's literally his boyfriend he's mooning over but he's just so *wonderful* and Theo is more in love than he knows how to be.

Too full for dessert, and with a film to get to, they decline the waiter's offer and ask for the check. But when it's brought to them they have their first true disagreement in months, both of them reaching for it and looking offended that the other assumed otherwise. Luckily, the waiter shuffles away to help another table so they can have their domestic in private.

"I'm taking you out, princess. My treat." Emir lays his hand on top of Theo's, unclear why Theo would expect anything else. He'd planned the date, known how much it was likely to cost, and assumed he was paying for it. That's how this goes. It's not a gender thing, even, it's just how he's always known dates to work.

"It's my turn." Theo furrows his brow, trying to brush off Emir's hand for the first time he can remember. "Just because you planned this doesn't mean I expect you to pay for everything. That'd hardly be fair."

"How is it your turn?" Emir doesn't budge, more confused than ever. For a moment he thought Theo was just trying to be nice, but no, he actually wants to pay for their meal. "It's our first date, so it's no one's turn."

"You paid for lunch. I remember because I offered to split it and you said no." Theo frowns, sincerely not understanding the confusion. They've only been out together twice, once as friends and once as boyfriends. That adventure in Cookham was a very special day for Theo, and he doesn't know how Emir could forget any moment of it.

Emir pauses instead of answering right away because this isn't worth a proper fight. He can tell when Theo needs space to explain and this seems like one of those times. Emir notices when others talk over Theo and he retreats into himself, sometimes even telling Emir whatever it was later because he can't stop thinking about what he needed to say long after the conversation is over.

He doesn't want Theo to feel like that, especially in their relationship. So Emir drops his hand and sits back, opening the conversation. "Right. I don't know what you're talking about, but could you tell me? I don't want a fight, I'm just confused."

Theo's shoulders relax and he readjusts in his seat with a nod. He doesn't want to argue either. "When we went to Cookham, we had lunch and you paid for it. I told you I would cover the next time and I meant it."

"I don't mind, princess. It's - " But Theo shakes his head and Emir pauses again. He wasn't done and Emir must've cut him off, which he told himself he wasn't going to do. "Sorry, continue."

"I want us to be partners, like equals, but I don't like how that phrase gets used. Equitable partners is better, I guess. This matters to me. This partnership." Theo's trying to explain why this specific thing is so important to him. Money is a sensitive topic, and he knows he grew up with more of it than most people. Theo's aware of the imbalance that introduces into his relationships, including his relationship with Emir. "I don't want either of us to ever feel like we're expected to pay for the other person. We have to talk about it instead of assuming. Part of being in a queer relationship means we don't have to follow the *rules*, right? I want us to go on dates, but I never want it to be a source of discomfort or insecurity for us. I want to be honest about money before it becomes an issue. I've seen it happen and I don't want that for us."

"It matters to me, too." Emir offers his hand across the table, glad when Theo grasps it. He's starting to appreciate where Theo is coming from.

Theo's right that they don't have to follow the standard date expectations, even if Emir assumed they would. Theo consistently challenges his assumptions, both in their relationship and about things in society that everyone just accepts, which Emir is grateful for. Allowing Theo space to explain himself usually results in an incredibly well reasoned response that helps Emir better understand the world.

"We're both artists. We probably won't make much as professionals, at least not for a while. And I don't want our dates to revolve around posh activities and fancy outfits. I'm equally as happy walking in the park or going for a drive or whatever else we'll be able to afford." Theo stares at their joined hands on the table, the connection calming him down while he keeps talking. Emir hasn't gotten angry or upset, which is a good sign. "So what I'm saying is if we go on dates or do activities together that cost money, I either want to take turns paying or split the cost. It doesn't have to be fifty-fifty because that wouldn't be right either. But nights like tonight, when it's my turn, I'd feel better if you let me pay for it."

Emir waits another moment, processing Theo's explanation and realising that it's more than fair. He wanted to pay for tonight, but Theo's correct. If he wants to take turns paying for things, that seems like a very sensible thing to do...and he's already planning for a relationship with Emir well after graduation.

"Would it be alright for me to cover the cinema tickets and snacks?" Emir hopes that's a fair compromise.

Theo thinks, gazing at Emir and appreciating that he didn't push back against his explanation. It genuinely is important to Theo that they think about these things and don't expect anything from each other that they don't discuss at least broadly.

He nods, happy with Emir's offer. "That'd be alright. I don't want to, like, keep a running tally or anything. But when it's something like this meal that's relatively expensive, I'd feel more comfortable if we share the cost. Is that...will that work for you?"

"Definitely. I'm glad you brought it up." Emir looks around for a moment, then leans across the table and kisses Theo on the cheek. It's not platonic, but it's also not too much for him. Settling back in his seat, Emir adds, "And we can revisit the topic if either of us is uncomfortable. I think you're right to think of these things and stop them before they become an issue. I'm just...I'm lucky to be with you, Teddy. You don't do any of this by accident and it makes a world of difference. Thank you for being honest with me."

Theo's flushing, both from the conversation and from Emir giving him a gentle cheek kiss where anyone could see. They're not very into PDA, especially away from the safety of uni, but that was just...sweet. He's still not used to having someone listen to him as generously as Emir does. Maybe it's because they spent so long intentionally misunderstanding each other that now they're deeply invested in open communication.

"I'm sorry if I made a scene, but it's important. And, um, thanks for listening. I didn't want to fight either." Theo clears his throat, trying to regain his composure.

"We're figuring it out as we go. And you didn't make a scene, shehzadi." Emir grins across at Theo, hands still resting together on the side of the table near the window. "We used to fight over the stupidest things. But now, look at us. We're learning!"

"I like learning with you." Theo's bashful, but not because anything's wrong. He still feels nervous with Emir. It's been a few months of learning about each other, but their relationship is still new. When they test boundaries like this, decide where they compromise and how their values and beliefs align, it's something he's still adjusting to. But Emir's right: they're figuring it out.

"Looking out together in the same direction, yeah?" Emir reminds Theo of their conversation last Sunday, where they sat under their tree and talked about the future. Theo was honest with him that night, and that's really all he's ever been. His honesty is a gift that Emir's still unwrapping, finding the joy in every earnest smile and genuine thought.

"So...I guess I'll pay and then we can go. We shouldn't need to rush and we'll have time to get popcorn and chocolates, or whatever we want." Theo wishes he could hug Emir right now, but he can wait a minute. They'll be cuddled up at the cinema soon enough. Sitting forward, he whispers, "Are we allowed to kiss during the film?"

Emir leans in to hear his question, grinning and giving Theo's hand a reassuring squeeze. "I don't see why not. You look very kissable tonight."

Theo bites his lip as his eyes crinkle in a smile, thinking Emir must have no idea how perfect he looks. Kissable? That's just the beginning. Emi's wearing a worn burgundy jumper and dark wash skinny jeans, warm and soft and gorgeous. Theo could stare at him all night. But the staring might be interrupted by kissing him until his lips feel raw.

The waiter returns, Theo offers his card, and that's the last they speak of it for now. They wave at their friends as they leave, a brief goodbye while they go their separate ways for the evening.

***

"Watch the movie, baby." Emir giggles against Theo's lips, breaking their kiss because Theo keeps trying to peek at the screen to make sure he isn't missing anything. It's adorable, knowing Theo could recite this film from memory but kissing Emir is distracting enough that he keeps leaning over to do just that.

Theo whines, pressing his lips against Emir's for another taste, closing his eyes tight to focus on his boyfriend. But barely a moment later he's reopening them when he hears one of his favourite lines coming through the speakers. He's torn, wanting to watch *Pitch Perfect* (even though he's seen it a dozen times) and needing to kiss Emir. If it was anyone else, it'd be so simple. But Emir is his person and he's more than worth missing one of his comfort films.

"We have all night." Emir doesn't care much about watching since he's seen this movie at least as many times as Theo has. They're at one of those extremely low budget, two pound per ticket cinemas that only show films that are at least a decade old, where the popcorn and the snacks are half the fun, and only people around their age hang out. Which also means he's not self-conscious snogging Theo in the back corner late on a Friday night.

"But you're so…" Theo turns back to look at Emir with a pained expression while trying to decide what to focus on. Emir's sitting there, effortlessly handsome, smelling like heaven, and tasting a little bit like chocolate. But Theo also loves singing along to this film. He tries to stop himself since there's other people in the room, but it's hard not to at least hum and dance a little bit.

"How about this…" Emir gently turns Theo's face back to the screen, whispering in his ear and moving his hand to the inside of Theo's thigh. "We'll split the difference: You watch the screen and I'll pay attention to you. I'll tease you and rile you up and do whatever you're alright with while you watch, and by the time we leave you'll look like you're wrecked, hard in your trousers from being so good for me. If you really want a kiss, I'm more than happy to snog you into your seat. But if you're good and watch the movie while I tease you, I'll give you a surprise tomorrow."

Theo groans as Emir starts a love bite on his neck. His favourite spot is still right next to Theo's birthmark, but now he's behind Theo's ear, high enough it might be hidden by his curly hair as it fades. Emir's tongue barely touches Theo's skin and he shivers as he feels his barely there stubble scratch his neck when Emir presses his mouth down to start a mark in earnest. It's a new spot, but the tingles it sends through Theo's body are just like all the others. Emir's mouth is perfect, plush and warm, stinging just the right amount as he uses his teeth to make Theo shift in his seat and palm himself through his jeans.

"No touching." Emir pauses to whisper, putting his hand over Theo's and intertwining their fingers. Theo nods, doing his best to focus on the screen. The movie's only about half over, which means he'll have to figure out a way to make it through almost an hour with Emir being the most delicate menace.

Theo can't keep as quiet as Emir needs him to, so he pushes his index and middle finger into Theo's mouth to keep him occupied while he works on another love bite, this one closer to his jumper collar where he can smell the delicate cologne that Theo wears, warm with the heat of his flushing, butter-smooth skin.

Emir doesn't stop with love bites, using his fingertips to whisper over Theo's chest, tracing beneath the fabric of his clothes, kissing his jaw so delicately it feels imagined, letting his hands wander everywhere except his dick, careful not to cross a line while he keeps Theo flushed and hot. Theo's "watching" but he barely notices the film, Emir keeping his attention even more than when they were snogging before, and all Theo can think about is whatever surprise he gets for being good and quiet like Emir asked. Maybe he'll finally get to be tied up while Emir has his way, something he's been asking to try for weeks.

***

They've been back at Theo's flat for ten minutes, and nine of those minutes have been spent with Emir on top of Theo, kissing him into the mattress. They managed to make it through the movie and the entire walk home, holding hands much harder than was strictly necessary as they barely contained how wound up they were from Emir's experiment at the cinema. But as they walked, they calmed down, a bit of that energy dispersing into the night as they shivered in the cold. Not every moment of heat needs to end in an orgasm.

"Can I have my surprise tonight?" Theo asks, holding Emir off of him with a gentle hand and batting his eyelashes. "I only bit you once."

There came a point where Theo grabbed Emir by the back of his neck and kissed him so hard that his teeth got involved. But instead of pushing him away, Emir leaned in, kissing him just as fiercely, like it was the only natural outcome in that moment. Theo's been figuring out what his body likes, and while whatever Emir wants to do is welcome, when he gets rough, Theo feels another part of himself engage, trusting Emir to keep him on the edge of pleasure and pain and getting more out of it than just a physical response.

"You weren't supposed to bite me at all." Emir laughs softly, hair falling in his eyes while he gazes down at Theo. It was agonisingly delicious, but being in public certainly put a damper on the response he was able to give. That was the most fun he's ever had at the cinema, and Theo's been flushed and half hard for over an hour thanks to Emir's teasing.

But Emir also knows they're both too tired to really do anything more tonight, so he brushes Theo's hair off his forehead and leaves a kiss in its place, rolling off of him and standing up from the bed. "I'm not saying no because you didn't earn it. I just want to wait until tomorrow for other reasons. I'll explain then."

He holds out his hand to Theo expectantly, but Theo just lays there and pouts, making grabby hands. When Theo's tired he's extra needy, and Emir tries not to literally melt into a puddle at those pleading eyes. "Come on, pumpkin. Pyjama time."

"No shirts?" Theo asks. He'll consider getting up and getting ready for bed, but only because he's so tired he had to stop kissing Emir to yawn a minute ago. Even if his body wants an Emir-mediated orgasm, it'll have to wait.

"No shirts, extra blanket?" Emir counters, waving his hand around and holding it out to Theo again, even more dramatically than last time. Theo finally takes it with a smile, pulling himself up and falling into another kiss against Emir's lips.

"Baby, you're exhausted." Emir holds him by the waist and leans away, using most of his available willpower to stop things from going further tonight.

Theo sighs loudly, slumping against Emir instead and making him hold up his dead weight.

"I really like you." Theo mumbles into Emir's chest, getting sleepier the longer Emir rubs his back while keeping him upright.

Theo's only had two first dates, but they aren't even comparable. His chemistry with and affection for Emir has nothing to be weighed against, but that doesn't make it any less wonderful. Tonight was special and easy and fun and important, and he doesn't want it to end just because he needs rest.

But the benefit of having waited an entire month into their relationship to have their first date is that he gets to cuddle up on Emir's chest and fall asleep to the rhythm of his heartbeat, rising and falling while he breathes beneath Theo. So there are some perks to giving up and listening to Emir's suggestion of bedtime.

"Good. Because I more than like you, even when you're a sack of potatoes." Emir grumbles, dragging Theo backwards and towards the loo so they can brush their teeth and everything else they need to do before sleep.

"What was that?" Theo turns his head, not bothering to stand up properly and letting Emir manhandle him the entire way across the hall. He takes a moment to admire Emir's arm muscles where they bulge from moving his weight around, which is about to make him all hot and worked up again if he doesn't avert his eyes. When did he become some delicate Austenian heroine?

"I said you're a sack of potatoes." Emir tugs Theo back up to standing, reaching for his own toothbrush that he keeps in Theo's drawer.

They have a set of toiletries at each other's place by now, which their friends teased them about the appropriate amount for an entire week after Laurie noticed. It's sort of a miracle that this bathroom holds enough cosmetics for six gay people, and that Emir's flat holds enough for four.

Wetting his toothbrush and popping a toothpaste tab into his mouth, Theo garbles, "I know what I heard."

He nudges his hip against Emir, a flutter in his chest when Emir's cheeks turn just the slightest bit pink. Theo doesn't have any sort of timeline where he expects Emir to be ready to say that he loves him out loud, but it seems he's getting closer to it.

A few minutes later, they're bundled up in bed, Theo shifting around and trying to get comfortable while Emir flips through his book for tomorrow's book club, reminding himself of his favourite parts. Emir can't read with Theo flopping around and huffing, so he sets his book aside and reaches into Theo's bedside drawer. Theo has a hard time settling when he's overtired, in complete contrast to Emir who goes from feverishly awake to practising for his dirt nap in under a minute.

"You need your mask?" Emir carefully removes it from the drawer before resituating himself in bed. He pulls Theo onto his chest, handing him the mask and waiting for him to adjust it over his eyes. Theo pouts his lips for a goodnight kiss, which Emir gives him gladly, Theo finally settling where Emir holds him.

He runs his fingers through Theo's hair, kissing the top of his head and humming softly, some sweet little melody that might be *Titanium* adjacent thanks to their recent movie choice. Theo breathes deep, one hand warm on Emir's chest above his heart, the other tucked between their bodies, his legs wrapped between Emir's like he needs to be anchored to his boyfriend to fall asleep. Emir starts reading again until he feels Theo drift off, not quite ready for sleep yet himself.

As quietly as he can manage, Emir sets his book aside and reaches for his sketchbook instead. He has to sit up, but since Theo's asleep, he shifts him to his lap so that he can start drawing. Emir honestly has no idea how Theo sleeps like this, but they do this almost every night.

It takes Emir almost an hour, but he finishes tonight's portrait with a satisfied sigh. He drew Theo from his own view at the restaurant, across the table from him and glowing with that warmth he always shares. Emir makes sure that the dimple at the crest of his cheek is there, subtle but perfect. Theo's birthmark peeks out above the collar of his jumper, just like Emir noticed a few minutes into their meal, and Theo's eyes are crinkling while he smiles, a true happiness that Emir loves more than he may ever be able to say.

Flipping the page over to the blank side, Emir writes in Urdu, "You looked gorgeous tonight, princess. Thank you for a perfect first date."

He's taught Theo a few different words and phrases, things he commonly says to him that he can practise. Early on, Theo told Emir that ever since that first thank you note for the tea, he feels like it's extra special if Emir writes him something in Urdu. He said it's like Emir's sharing a deeper part of himself, and he feels lucky to get to know him so well. Emir can't argue with that. He's never had anyone outside of his family care enough to learn Urdu for him, or ask what it means to him to acknowledge that part of his identity. So Emir writes his note and quietly gets out of bed, wandering over to Theo's desk and hiding the drawing beneath his laptop for Theo to find tomorrow morning.

Sliding back under the sheets, he turns off the lamp and helps Theo to resettle on his chest. Now that it's dark, he gently removes Theo's mask and tucks it back into the bedside table, running his fingers through Theo's hair for his own comfort as much as Theo's. Emir falls asleep with Theo warm on top of him, curls tickling at his bare chest, their bodies breathing together in the quiet night.

CHAPTER TWO

Theo's alarm wakes him at 6:45, a weekend lie in of about an hour, but his body wouldn't have let him sleep much later anyway. Carefully, he reaches around to turn it off before snuggling back into Emir. This happens so often that it's part of his routine. He starts the night laying on Emir's chest, but by the morning he's the little spoon with Emir holding him close, nuzzled into him like they're glued together. Theo stays there for a minute, gingerly rolling his ankles and waking his body up before turning around to face his boyfriend.

"You sleeping in, Emi?" Theo mumbles, running his fingers through Emir's hair in an attempt to wake him just enough to get an answer. He has a strong feeling he already knows.

"Mmmmmm." Emir groans, pulling Theo in close and hiding his face against Theo's chest before relaxing again. Theo thinks of all the times that Emir's mentioned how adorable he is when he's sleepy at night, but it can't possibly compare to grumpy morning Emir who's always desperate for a cuddle. Emir's intrinsically comforting, cuddly nature is how Theo started to fall in love with him in the first place.

Theo smiles with his eyes closed, rubbing Emir's back and settling in for a few more minutes with him. He tries to keep his routine the same every day, with only slight changes, but Emir's weekends are a lot more freeform compared to his weekday mornings. If Emir wants to stay asleep, Theo is happy to go about his morning routine before waking him up in a few hours.

Climbing out of bed with a soft kiss to the corner of Emir's mouth when he fusses at Theo's absence, Theo wanders across the hall and into the loo to start his Saturday. He's always the first one awake on the weekends, even when the flat is full. There's something magical about a quiet weekend morning, knowing his favourite people are peacefully asleep in the other room while he tiptoes around the flat. Theo's always the first person awake on holidays, too, wanting to settle into his morning without disruptions, when he can just exist and think and move around until the rest of the world catches up.

On his way back to his bedroom, Theo stops to get a glass of water from the kitchen, noticing an extra pair of shoes by the door that he assumes belong to Alfie. He'd put their coincidental interaction from last night out of his mind while he focused on Emir for their own date, but he's glad to see his invitation to have the three of them stay here without judgement was already accepted.

Theo's always wanted people to know that he has a welcoming, warm space for them to visit when needed, and it gives him a secret joy to look after people, to make their favourite foods or play their favourite song or watch them light up when talking about their passions. He gets to do all of that and so much more in his own relationship. Emir never tells him it's too much or too intimate or whatever, letting Theo spoil him with attention and love whether it be breakfast in bed (maybe Theo should consider that for tomorrow) or adding Emir's favourite songs to his playlists for time in the practice studio.

"Emir." Theo kneels next to his sleeping boyfriend, pulling back the blanket that's tucked over his head for just a moment. The way Emir nests himself into whatever bed he's in each morning is so soft and endearing, and Theo would never disturb his sleep for longer than necessary. One of Emir's hands is settled near his face, and Theo notices the distinguishable pencil marks that usually mean Emir stayed awake and worked on a drawing after Theo fell asleep. He should've known. Emir's always extra sleepy when he stays up late to work on his art.

"Too early." Emir mumbles, bringing that same pencil covered hand up to shield his eyes from the soft sunlight filtering into the room. There's absolutely no way he's waking up right now, but being marginally awake means getting to see Theo, so he squints his eyes open just enough to get a glimpse of him washed gold in the early light. Gorgeous and somehow, remarkably, his.

"I know, sunshine. I'm just telling you that I'll be back in a bit so you don't worry." Theo leans forward and nuzzles their noses together, smiling when Emir's fingers reach out and pull Theo in for a warm, slow kiss in response.

But only a moment later he's pushing gently at Theo's chest and dragging the blanket back over his head, hiding away in his cocoon of warm sheets while Theo starts looking for whatever drawing he hid away. He finds it beneath his laptop, one of Emir's go-to hiding spots when he's very tired and can't be as creative with his surprise locations. The fact that he still tries, leaving little presents around for Theo to find, will never get old.

Theo stares at the picture of himself, the radiant smile that crinkles his eyes and deepens his dimple, and he knows he must have looked at least as heart-eyed as the drawing suggests. Emir draws him like he loves him, like he understands his mind and protects his heart, and Theo doesn't know that anyone else would notice the tiny details that Emir makes sure to include, but they mean the world to Theo. When he sets it with the other art from Emir, a collection that's grown to cover almost his entire bookshelf display area, he notices the note on the back, deciding to translate it later when he has the time to focus. Learning Emir's second language is a serious endeavour, and he's making slow but steady progress.

Theo slips quietly out of the flat and puts himself through his usual morning rotation: a brief bit in the studio to warm up, an hour in the gym to do some muscle group training (today is mostly chest and back work), then back to the flat for a green juice (pre-made each Sunday and labelled with the date, of course) and to Emir.

Adding Emir to his routine has required so little adjustment that Theo had initially wondered if Emir was just…pretending to make it work. But it seems he understands Theo's need for structure and schedules and all the rest, and since Emir needs to spend time alone and he has his own sort of training situation, Theo stopped worrying much after their first fortnight together. Sleeping with Emir every night has been so easy, easier than he imagined, and it all just feels so wonderfully domestic and nice, comforting. Theo's never had a boyfriend before, but he knows it's not usually this natural.

The flat is still and quiet when he returns, so he closes his bedroom door softly behind himself, smiling fondly at the lump of blankets that he knows contains his favourite person.

"You're my best mate." Theo mumbles as he shimmies himself back into his own bed, wearing only his boxers, so they can stay in bed together for a little while.

He can tell that Emir's awake, but that doesn't mean they're any closer to leaving the sheets. Emir stirs as Theo's chilled toes meet his sleep-warm calves, reaching out for Theo and humming happily once Theo settles against his front.

"Careful. Laur gets jealous." Emir stretches his back before relaxing down again, pressing a kiss to Theo's curls and wrapping around him like velcro.

Theo smells incredible: warm and natural with a hint of his deodorant that Emir's come to be familiar with after months in each other's space. There's no way Theo understands how *good* he smells. Emir wishes he could bury his nose in that spot where Theo's neck meets his hairline and stay there until the end of time.

"He'll get over it." Theo answers after only slightly too long, getting a bit lost in the sensation of Emir. And now that Emir's hands have started...roaming, he's also remembering what they tentatively agreed to for this morning. "Um...Emi?"

"Pumpkin?" Emir asks, innocently dragging his fingertips beneath the hem of Theo's boxers. He's just so warm and pliable and perfect after he goes to the gym, and Emir has to stop himself from latching on like a fucking vampire every weekend morning that he gets to have Theo like this.

He hasn't had the pleasure of tasting Theo on his tongue yet, but whenever Theo's ready he will literally drop to his knees, mouth open. But, like, completely calm and totally chill about it, of course.

"Did you still want to...like..." Theo moves so he's laying on top of Emir instead, letting Emir control his hips so they're gently grinding together under the sheets. After all that time spent winding each other up yesterday, Theo's more than ready to get off together.

"More than you know, princess." Emir takes one of his hands off Theo's bum to hold him by the chin instead, laying a sweet kiss against Theo's lips. Theo melts on top of him, arms relaxing around Emir's shoulders while opening his mouth to let Emir in.

"Boxers off?" Emir asks between kisses, fingertips already fiddling with Theo's waistband while waiting for an answer.

"Yes, oh my god, yes." Theo tries to keep their mouths connected while shuffling out of his boxers. With a giggle, Emir puts a hand on his lips and stops them so they can both get naked without a potential injury. Once their boxers are tossed off to the side, Theo lays himself back on Emir with a groan, biting near his neck and moving on top of him with a distinct purpose.

"I mean this in the least judgemental way possible," Emir gasps before groaning as Theo starts a mark on his collarbone. Fuck, Emir has to remember how good he is at taking notes and knowing exactly how to get Emir hard. It's not even a game because Theo wins so very easily. "Do you actually have a thing for biting?"

"What?" Theo kisses the mark he's started before pulling back to look at Emir, processing his question with a furrowed brow. He hadn't really thought about it, but when he does... "Actually..."

Theo sits up, the sheets pooling beneath his bum as he sits astride Emir's lap, their dicks *almost* touching. "Maybe. Would that be weird if I did?"

"No, I've just sort of noticed. Like just now and last night at the cinema, and you didn't seem very bothered when I chomped your shoulder before our first kiss." Emir bites at his own bottom lip, remembering how delicious that moment was, closely followed by every moment since. It was embarrassing, but it got them here. And if Theo actually does have a thing for it... "Come here, princess."

Emir buries his fingertips in Theo's hair, pulling him close for another messy kiss, humping up against him until they're both starting to sweat and groan in a way that makes Emir very glad that Theo remembered to close his bedroom door. When he thinks that Theo's focused in the moment enough to forget the conversation, Emir brings his mouth down to Theo's chest and bites at the fullest part of his pec, hard but not enough to break the skin. Theo *moans*, an obscenely loud and deep sound that has Emir grabbing at his bum even more than before, as if they could get inside each other by osmosis rather than penetration.

"Yes. That's a yes. Add biting to the list." Theo gasps as Emir kisses the spot he bruised, shivering at the way his lips feel against the now overly sensitive skin. Why does that feel so *good* and how did it take him this long to realise it? Thank fuck for Emir.

"You're fucking incredible, baby." Emir *really* wants to find out what would happen if he involved Theo's nipples in the biting equation, but he doesn't think they're ready for that just yet. But he will absolutely add biting to the list of options if it makes Theo act like this, whimpering with each gentle kiss across his chest, as if anticipating the next bite.

"Can we - hands - " Theo's starting to get frustrated, both of them very hard while they get off together in Theo's bed. "I like when we - both of us in your hand."

This happens to Theo every time they're intimate together. He knows what he wants, or at least what he likes, but he has a really difficult time putting it into words. It's like all his mental energy is already being used because he's so focused on all the sensations: the smells and the tastes and the *touch*. Trying to form sentences is asking too much.

"Lube?" Emir asks, because last time they tried frotting they were in the shower, and while water most definitely isn't lube, it's better than nothing. Theo told Emir more than once that he has the basics, even if they haven't had occasion to use any of it yet. No time like the present.

"Oh..." Theo slows down, laying his sweaty forehead against Emir's shoulder to catch his breath. "Just a moment."

Theo rolls himself out of bed with a soft flop onto the floor, Emir laying like a starfish in his absence, watching Theo peer beneath his bed until he re-emerges with an actual shoe box. Emir keeps his smile to a minimum, not wanting to make Theo feel embarrassed, but honestly that's so fucking cute. He literally has a little box of sex stuff under his bed, as if they haven't fully walked in on everyone they live with having sex more than once.

"Is, um, will this work?" Theo kneels beside the bed and holds up a small bottle to Emir with a shrug, worried that he bought the wrong kind or did something else weird or incorrect because of his inexperience.

Theo did his research, and he only bought a few things, but lube is essential for their bodies' combined anatomy in a sexual relationship. So he waits with the box open beside him, each second feeling like an eternity while Emir squints at the label.

"It's perfect." Emir holds out his free hand to Theo, waiting for him to put the box away and join him back in the bed. Really any lube will work for frotting, but the kind Theo gave him should work with toys and condoms, so they'll be good to go for a while. Water-based won't 'last' as long as some of the others, but it's the most inclusive option and they can always add more. Plus, Emir has his own supplies back at his flat if needed.

"Yeah?" Theo hasn't moved, still kneeling beside the bed and making sure that Emir isn't just saying that. "There were so many to choose from, and I didn't want to ask Laurie or the others. If it's wrong we can do something else or, like, stop or whatever...sorry."

"Shehzadi..." Emir sits up, setting the lube beside him in the bed and reaching a hand out to cradle Theo's cheek.

How does Theo always manage to do this? He makes Emir feel so protective and in love in the middle of sex every single time without fail. Loving Theo is deep, engaging all of Emir in a way he never knew he needed. He's better for loving him, his world expanding by experiencing it by Theo's side.

"You picked exactly right. It's good for this, and if you wanted, we could use it on some of the toys I have. And I don't know what sort of condoms you bought, but this will work with basically everything. You can always ask me if you have questions, alright? We'll learn together."

Theo watches Emir's expression, making sure he doesn't miss any hint of teasing or hesitation. But he doesn't notice anything besides love and maybe even adoration in Emir's eyes, so he relaxes his shoulders and nods, closing the box back up and sliding it beneath his bed before climbing in beside Emir.

"Will you - " Theo pulls at Emir's waist to bring him close again, their bodies gliding together with ease. "Take over, please?"

Emir grins, kissing Theo deep and getting them back into the moment they were in before he interrupted them for a lube stop.

"Give me your hand." Emir picks up the bottle from beside him and waits for Theo to lay his hand palm up . Dripping about a teaspoon into Theo's open palm, Emir closes the lid again and sets it aside. That's plenty for now. "Hold it in your hand for a moment to get it warm. If you'd rather play with temperature, we can try that another time."

"Can we - kissing?" Theo noses along Emir's jawline, already missing Emir's tongue. It's very talented. Emir nods, bringing their mouths together and guiding Theo's hand down to his own dick.

"Coat yourself, princess. When you're slick, get me wet too, yeah?" Emir keeps them laying sideways facing each other. He has an idea that requires a freedom of movement that being stacked on top of one another won't allow.

Theo takes himself in hand, groaning and rubbing against Emir while pulling himself off. He didn't know that lube could be used for anything besides penetration, but adding a glide to this feels incredible. Emir is so smart. Theo should remember to tell him later when words are easier again. But he doesn't want to get himself off, so he stops, opening his hand and waiting for Emir to drip a bit more onto his fingers.

"That's enough for both of us. Don't forget we'll be sharing." Emir glances down, nudging his dick into Theo's and smirking when Theo gasps and closes his eyes. He loves how sensitive Theo is, so responsive to every little touch, especially when they're naked together.

After a moment of collecting himself, Theo nods, trailing his fingers along Emir's dick before coating him. He loves making Emir come, in any way, watching the effect he has as it ripples through Emir's body. It makes him feel special, powerful even, to get to be with Emir in this way, to know the trust it requires. It's like a superpower, making Emir feel *so good* that he physically releases in more ways than one.

"Theo! - fuck." Emir arches as Theo does much more than just coat him in lube. For someone who only started giving handies a few weeks ago, he's incredible at it, knowing every trick that Emir's ever taught him, and so, so much more. "Can I - Theo wait."

Theo drops his hand and sits back, staring at Emir with a question while panting from how aerobic things have become. "Stop? You alright?"

Looking Emir up and down as if he could detect a wound, Theo keeps his hands to himself, watching Emir shake his head calmly and open his eyes. Emir trails a hand along Theo's front, a whispering touch over Theo's gorgeous body while he catches his breath.

"Can I touch your bum?" Emir asks, staring deep into Theo's eyes to make sure he gets an honest answer. He doesn't want Theo to feel pressured to say yes just because he asked. "You can say no."

"Touch whatever you want, but, like, only on the outside because we have to work later, and I'm not ready to be aware of my actual arsehole while we dance." Theo lays his head back against the pillow, heart racing at the thought of Emir's delicate fingers exploring yet another part of him. His quickened pulse is from excitement and anticipation, not fear. He knows Emir would never hurt him.

Emir laughs, hiding his face against Theo's neck for a moment. He loves that they can laugh together, that they communicate openly and never for a moment feel unsafe. It's a gift to be so trusted and to give that trust right back, in sex and in life.

"I completely adore you, you know that?" Emir nips at Theo's nose, teasing him a bit before kissing his gorgeous lips.

"I do, but I like when you remind me." Theo kisses Emir back, tilting his head as an unspoken question while holding up his dirty hand. Words are still a challenge, but when Emir asks him directly it's easier to find his answer.

"Use your hand to get us off, princess." Emir murmurs in Theo's ear, pulling their bodies closer and guiding Theo's leg to sit across his hips. This was exactly why he needed them to be laying facing each other, so he could open up access to Theo's bum if he was comfortable with it. "And tell me if you need me to stop."

Theo pushes his tongue back into Emir's mouth, chasing Emir's until he can pull it into his own and give it right back. He's learned so much about snogging the past few weeks, and it's quickly become one of his favourite activities. Theo is so engrossed in the kiss that he barely registers the sound of Emir adding lube to his own fingertips. But then he feels a smooth, warm glide across his hole and he shivers, catching his breath and pausing their kiss to experience the new sensation.

"Baby? You alright?" Emir asks, hand still after the faintest of touches from tailbone to taint, not wanting to overdo it right away. But then Theo is nodding, hiking his knee further up Emir's side to give him deeper access while biting at Emir's collarbone again as he takes both of their dicks in his hand.

"I need a yes, Theo." It's hard for Emir to concentrate when Theo is literally writhing against him, but consent is a rule, not a guideline.

"Emiiii." Theo groans, mouthing at the bruise he'd been working on before moving his lips off to whine. "More. Yes. Touch me."

And that's all he can get out before he's back to fucking up into his fist against Emir's own dick and continuing to suck a deep mark into Emir's favourite sore spot like it's his purpose on earth.

"You look so fucking fit right now..." Emir groans as Theo finds an especially sensitive spot on his dick to move against, and Emir honestly didn't know that he could enjoy this kind of sex as much as he does with Theo. Everything's so different with him in the best way.

Emir lets his hand find its way back to Theo's bum, starting to move his middle finger gently around Theo's rim and flushing at the way Theo shivers and moans in response. He's the most incredible partner, and if he had any idea how he looked and felt and smelled and sounded... Sex with Theo is a workout and a poem, and it never lasts as long as he wishes. "Fuck, baby, I'm already almost there."

Theo can't do more than whine his agreement, moving his head to kiss Emir as deep as he can while keeping his hand busy between them. And then Emir presses directly against his hole while simultaneously biting quite hard on Theo's bottom lip and Theo loses it, his eyes screwed shut while he yells in pleasure (only slightly hindered by Emir still holding his lip in his teeth) and shoots his release onto both of their dicks. His whole body shakes with the force of it, Emir following moments later, the sensation of Theo's cum added to their already slick skin more than enough to bring out his own orgasm.

"I can't - how did you - fuck - " Theo's trying to catch his breath, now fully laying on top of Emir in a sweaty pile of limbs and spunk, pressing lazy kisses to any inch of Emir's skin that he can reach. His boy is so very, very talented and precious and he needs to tell him but his entire body is so heavy. "Emiiiii - you're so - I need - "

"Shhhh, I'm right here, baby." Emir wraps himself around Theo, calming them both down and replaying the last several minutes in his mind because holy fuck that was incredible. But Theo *needs* cuddles after sex, whereas Emir just prefers it, so he strokes Theo's back, dirty hand not any filthier than the rest of them, burying kisses on the crown of his head and mumbling praise to his gorgeous, remarkable, inspiring boyfriend until they're both half asleep in Theo's bed.

"Should shower..." Theo mumbles, picking his head up to look at Emir before giving up and flopping back against his chest. He's *exhausted* and they were only shagging for about ten minutes. "Sleepy."

"We'll shower, but another minute of cuddles first." Emir kisses Theo's sweaty temple this time, Theo humming happily in agreement, knowing that Emir will take care of him. He always does.

***

"Samwise." Emir grabs Sam's elbow gently as their book club concludes, pulling him aside while the others start mumbling about their weekend plans and whatever happened at last night's parties. Jordan winks across the room at Lilibet while continuing her conversation with one of the visual artists in their group.

"Emu." Sam answers with a grin, trying on the dozenth nickname of the past few weeks on his quest to find the one that annoys Emir the most while still making him laugh. Emu got a small chuckle, so it's in the running.

"Just checking how that went. Are you glad you came?" Emir drops his hand, eyes darting over to where Theo is sitting with Lilibet in another section of the library, both of them waiting for their partners to be done. Lili and Theo's friendship is one of Emir's favourite things to observe, the way they fit so easily together, mirroring language and posture and mannerisms, but also pushing each other's buttons like annoying siblings. The fact they've found partners with similar interests shouldn't be a surprise.

"Definitely! I know I'm shy, but it's not so bad with only a few people." Sam shrugs, leaning against the bookshelf and crossing his arms over his chest. It's the first time Emir's seen him outside the studio, and his wardrobe impressively has both academia and athlete vibes: a tailored buttoned shirt, rolled at the sleeves and untucked, corduroys cuffed at the ankle, and a cardigan with elbow patches tied around his shoulders, all below Sam's tightly coiled sandy hair. "And they're all very nice."

"They are, yeah. I don't, like, spend time with them outside book club, but they always invite me to stuff. Usually interferes with dance, though." Emir tucks his copy of *House in the Cerulean Sea* back into his rucksack, knowing it will likely stay there for several weeks until he gets annoyed enough with the clutter to clean it out again, or until he asks Theo to find something for him and Theo does it automatically.

That thought reminds Emir that he still needs to thank Theo for organising the shelves in his wardrobe when he gave up and flopped on his bed twenty minutes into the process. Emir watched him happily sort and fold and label all while softly humming and leaning down for kisses every few minutes. Theo is so incredibly wonderful.

"I haven't heard of the book you picked for next month. Have you read it before?" Sam asks, his own copy of today's book borrowed from the library. He'll return in a few days, after he has time to go over a few bits again following today's discussion.

"*Two Boys Kissing*. Yeah. Read it a few times. It's a quick read, but it hurts. Like you have to really spend time with what it does to your emotions." Emir pushes his fringe out of his eyes, mirroring Sam's posture and not really in a rush to get out of there. They finished just on time, and he knows Theo factored in at least a ten minute overage given how the meetings usually go. "It's different from what we usually read for the club, so I thought...why not?"

Sam nods, eyes drifting over to the same area of the library that Emir recently tore his gaze away from. When a subtle flush creeps into Sam's cheeks, Emir glances over with his eyebrows raised before biting down a smile and clearing his throat to quell a laugh. "You and Esmerelda have plans today?"

"Oh...um, sort of." Sam looks back at Emir, his flush deepening while he scratches at the back of his neck where his hair is shortest. "I think we might be dating?"

"You're not sure?" Emir asks, not even a hint of judgement in his tone. He knows what that's like well enough, and as Theo teased him just last night, he made Theo wait an entire fourteen hours before making their relationship official.

"I think I forgot to ask." Sam stares at Emir, eyes wide as if he holds the answer to whatever Sam's worried about. "Was I supposed to ask?"

"Were you?" Emir glances over at where Esme has joined Theo and Lili at their study table, the three of them talking in hushed voices. They are still in the library, after all. "Depends on your relationship, but you should probably ask. Best not to assume."

"Right, but like...how?" Sam's trying to look cool and nonchalant, but this is very much new territory for him. He hasn't dated anyone officially before, and he really likes Esme.

"What do you two have planned?" Emir isn't great at this whole relationship advice thing either, but he knows about communication. "Maybe ask her today? It might feel awkward, but it'd be worse to wonder."

"We're, um...at my place...because everyone will be out." Sam flushes the deepest red yet, eyes staring fixedly at the ground as if Emir would possibly judge him for planning a casual shag. Before Theo, that was essentially all Emir ever did.

"Sam." Emir reaches out a hand to Sam's shoulder until he finally looks up to meet his eyes. "I mean this in the kindest way possible: you need to ask her before. I don't know if you've already...you know. And I don't need to. But if that's where things are, you don't want anyone getting hurt, physically or emotionally. You're both better than that, and I know you don't want to hurt her."

"No! I would never!" Sam reacts immediately, his flush quickly falling off his face to be replaced with a look of panic. "Oh god, you're right. I need to ask like...right now."

"Well, not literally." Emir gives him an understanding smile. "But I'll walk over with you, if that helps. Theo's waiting for me anyway."

"Yeah, alright." Sam sighs, standing up from his lean against the bookshelf and running a hand down his face. "I can completely do this. It's just words. I know how to do words."

Emir chuckles with a hand on Sam's shoulder while they walk over to meet their people, Jordan trailing behind them as she says goodbye to the rest of the book club. Emir tosses himself into Theo's lap, Theo catching him around the waist with a huff of surprise, but holding him there without hesitation. Emir tilts his head in Esme's direction while smiling at Sam, a subtle encouragement.

"Babe?" Theo starts to ask what's happening, but he's cut off by Emir's careful fingertips on his lips. He pouts until Emir runs those same fingers through Theo's hair instead, Sam nervously asking Esme to chat with him for a minute before they head out. The two of them shuffle over by the windows, Sam so pink that Emir honestly feels bad for him. Being young and in love is never easy.

"What's happening with the first years?" Jordan asks, mirroring Emir's spot but in Lili's lap instead. Lili squeaks, not used to Jordan being so comfortably in her space in public.

The last week or so Jo's really loosened up around their friends, even outside the flat. Since Lili is willing to be as open as Jo wants, she relaxes after a moment and holds Jordan around the waist, the four of them looking like some bizarre musical chairs scenario.

"Sam's asking Esme what their situation is." Emir mumbles, leaning back to leave a gentle kiss behind Theo's ear where no one else will see and whispering, "Missed you."

"I was only a few tables away." Theo answers, finger brushing under Emir's chin while they stare at each other.

It's always nice to know he was missed, and Emir reminds him so openly, with his words and with how he folds himself into Theo's space as soon as it's an option. If Laurie was around he'd definitely throw something their way to break it up, because who looks that infatuated in the middle of a library on a Saturday?

"But too far away for cuddles." Emir pouts, Theo giggling and pulling him in for a hug. They have to leave to go work in the practice studio in a few minutes, but they can stay and chat with Jo and Lili for now.

"You two in the studio all day after this?" Jordan asks, putting one arm around Lili's shoulder while facing the boyfriends. Lili's staring at Jordan like she's a work of art, and Emir thinks about teasing her before deciding he'll save it for later. She's probably still sensitive about how they look together in public.

"Only for a few hours. After this weekend we'll probably need to focus on choosing our music before going much further with the choreo." Theo answers, one hand holding Emir at the waist, the other warm on his knee. He's usually the one on Emir's lap, but he certainly doesn't mind this arrangement.

"I'm thinking I might go work on mine for a bit later. Let me know when you're done?" Jordan stands up from Lili's lap, getting ready to head home together. They don't spend nearly as much time in the studio as Emir and Theo, but they're also in the midst of their dissertation work. But unlike them, Lili and Jordan are working alone, as are the rest of the third year dancers.

"Easy enough." Theo smiles at her, but the rest of their goodbyes are cut off by a loud squeal from Esme. The four of them turn to look just in time to watch her hold Sam's face in both of her hands and give him a very excited kiss. Sam startles, barely managing to catch her at the waist before she pulls back and grabs his hand instead.

"Bye!" Esmerelda waves at them, clearly in a rush to get some privacy with Sam. Emir laughs, leaning into Theo as Sam looks to him and mouths a *thank you* before being dragged out the front door.

"That was quick." Lili comments, the four of them staring after the first years with slightly stunned expressions. Sometimes it's hard to remember how it felt even a few years ago, still new at uni and excitedly sharing a kiss with your crush like you have all the time in the world.

"She's liked him since they started." Jordan adds with a flip of her hair. She's very proud of the way Esme came to her for dating advice. "Esme was just waiting for Sam to figure it out."

"Sounds like someone else we know…" Lili turns her attention back to Emir and Theo with a smirk, Jordan tugging on her arm to get her to follow her out of the library.

"Two someones." Jordan clarifies, blowing the ballet boyfriends a kiss before following Sam and Esme out into the early winter sun.

Emir watches them leave with a scoff, settling in Lili's vacated seat but linking his fingers through Theo's to hold hands between their chairs. Theo leans back, head against the top of the seat and gazing at Emir with all the love in the world.

"You were so cute our first year." Emir admits, watching that pink flush that he adores creeping across Theo's cheeks. There's so much to compliment about him, and yet he reacts as if it's the first time he's been admired every single time. "Your hair was even curlier than it is now. And you would get so excited in class...still do, but it was brighter then, I think. I used to watch you and Lili laughing and having the best time together. I was so gone for you and I didn't have a clue."

"Neither did I, though." Theo squeezes Emir's hand, his eyes catching the sunlight in Emir's hair like gilding on a painting. Emir's undeniably gorgeous, even on days like today where he's in joggers and a hoodie and he's barely styled his silky hair. He's the prettiest person Theo's ever seen. "Do you think we would be here now if we knew back then?"

"No." Emir sighs but his smile stays bright. As much as he wishes they'd had two years together already, he wasn't in a good place. Even if he and Theo hadn't been fighting and arguing all that time, they would've imploded so quickly. "I wasn't ready for us. You? You're perfect, princess. But I was healing. I still am."

"Yeah...you're so smart." Theo turns his attention to the table when his phone chirps, reminding him that it's time to head across campus to the practice studio together. "Ready to leave?"

"Sure. I'm excited for today, actually. I think I want to solidify using that Max Richter string piece for the first song, if that's alright with you." Emir swings his rucksack over his shoulder, keeping their hands connected until Theo drops it to gather his own things. He didn't have any homework he needed to do, but he brought his laptop for some research. Like his secretly nerdy boyfriend, Theo is constantly learning, well outside the realms of a classroom.

"Definitely. I think we just have to decide how long. The song's like six minutes or something." Theo pauses Emir with a warm hand on his elbow, holding out a jacket to go over his hoodie. Emir rolls his eyes but accepts the jacket by leaving a kiss on Theo's cheekbone, knowing he really should bundle up even if it's just across campus.

When they're both sufficiently warm, Emir leads Theo outside, holding the door open for him and grabbing onto his hand again as they make their way along the pavement. Theo glows in his presence and asks, "Did you have a nice discussion in book club?"

"We did. Sam really opened up while talking about Arthur's character. I'm glad he came." Emir gives Theo's hand an appreciative squeeze, grateful that Theo genuinely cares about his interests. He's so lucky to be in a relationship with someone so attentive and thoughtful, and he hopes he returns as much of that as he can. "What did you and Lili get up to?"

"We were both doing research." Theo heats slightly, remembering what he had been spending his last hour learning about. "Lili needed to look in the library archive for a few videos for her dissertation. She might want them playing on the screen behind her while on stage, if possible. And I - "

He clears his throat, still shy talking about these things, even though he knows he's more than safe with Emir. "I looked up my, um, my biting thing. It's called odaxelagnia. It's a sort of oral fixation kink."

Emir stops their progress, stepping to the side of the path and bringing Theo with him. He can usually tell when Theo needs a moment to process, and this seems like one of them. Theo wouldn't have brought it up right this second if he didn't. Something's bothering him about it. "Did you want to tell me what you read?"

Theo shrugs, dropping Emir's hand to shove his in his own pockets and drag his toe through the dirt. "I didn't like a lot of what I saw. There wasn't much to read outside of like Reddit or Twitter, not even on the like paraphilia sites. It's not that rare but..."

Emir watches Theo, sees his hunched shoulders and downcast eyes, looking like he's embarrassed or upset, or possibly both. With a grimace, Emir wraps his arms around Theo's shoulders, holding him tight in a hug because Theo shouldn't feel anything like that. There's nothing wrong with having sexual preferences. Emir knows if he gives Theo time he'll keep talking, explain what he's feeling and let Emir in. He focuses on being patient and steady and letting Theo process in whatever way he needs.

"It's just...people were saying it's like violent or something. Like I'm some sort of animal. Aggressive." Theo sniffles, holding his arms folded against his body while Emir keeps him in a hug. It helps. "I'm not going to hurt you, Emir, I swear. But like I can also ignore it. I don't want you to feel like I - like you're scared or - like I know those people are probably ignorant or just being mean because they don't understand human sexuality, but it made me feel really small and like I'm a bad person or something. Like there's something wrong with me for getting off on that."

"Baby, no! You're right about those people being ignorant." Emir kisses the side of Theo's neck, snuggling into his space even deeper than before. He's not going fucking anywhere until he helps lift this hurt from Theo's shoulders. "Biting is nothing to be worried about. I know you won't hurt me. You're not a bad person and it's not dangerous. You're the softest, sweetest, squishiest man I know. About as dangerous as a marshmallow."

"The minis or the regular? I hear those can be a choking hazard." Theo asks, sniffling again but feeling better with Emir's reassurance. He knows going online to learn about sex isn't always the answer, but where else is he supposed to learn this stuff? It's not like he could've expected it in school growing up, nevermind the fact his bullies literally focused on him because of his queer identity (among other reasons). Even if he did properly learn about sexuality in school, he wouldn't have brought up any questions in class out of self-preservation. "You promise I don't scare you? Even if I like biting?"

"Not in the slightest. I was already thinking of ways to explore that with you, if it's something you wanted. I'm not scared, shehzadi. It's actually incredibly sexy. And so are you." Emir's staring at Theo head-on again, his arms loose around Theo's shoulders to keep him close. He watches as a shy smile grows in Theo's eyes, so he'll count that as a win. "Now, am I allowed to make a dick joke, since you've definitely got a jumbo sized marshmallow and I'm looking forward to choking on it?"

"Emir!" Theo looks up at him, half in shock, but laughing despite himself. He always manages to comfort Theo's worries and bring out a smile, all without making him feel embarrassed or unintelligent or naive. And if Emir says it's alright to have a biting kink, well...he trusts Emir, because Emir doesn't lie to him. "It's not that big."

"It is, princess. I've seen like every size and yours is going to *ruin* me." Emir winks, Theo flushing *scarlet* and looking a little horrified until Emir reminds him, "Don't worry, I've had plenty of training."

"Oh god." Theo hides his face in his hands, shoulders shaking with laughter. Emir is such a contradiction, comforting and intelligent and lovely and also really fucking funny. He's so underrated, everyone praising his looks and his charm, but that's only a fraction of him. "You're a menace, but I'm glad you use it for good instead of evil."

"Maybe just a little bit of evil." Emir pinches his fingers together and squints at the nonexistent space between them, making Theo laugh and fall into him again. Emir loves when Theo laughs so hard he can't stand upright, overcome with joy. It's so fucking cute. "Time for the studio?"

"Yeah. Time to work." Theo sneaks a quick kiss as he stands back up and takes Emir's hand to continue on their way across the grounds, his mind clear and their afternoon back on track. "I'm just glad it's with you."

***

The haunting string melody of *On the Nature of Daylight* has been playing in the practice studio on and off for almost three hours now, Emir and Theo so immersed in their work that they've barely taken a break except for a drink from their water bottles while reworking a particular section. They're fully in agreement about using this song for the opening of their dissertation, the part where they're dancing through their separate stories before they come together, before they meet and share space and eventually so much more. They've tried a few different songs for this portion, knowing it sets the tone for their entire body of work, but this is the option they keep coming back to because it's beautiful but sombre, just like the story they're trying to tell.

For the past few hours, they've been debating about how long to use the piece for. Do they use it into the beginning of the character's intersection? Cut it off as soon as they find each other? Since they haven't decided on a second song they don't know what it needs to flow into. But what they're both slowly realising is that it fits perfectly, their bodies reacting as if it was meant to be, and that cutting the song off to start another when it almost exactly matches the amount of choreography they have for that section would be the wrong choice. The full six minutes are staying and they're leaning into it.

"Think we should film a run through so we can watch it back tomorrow and make sure it looks how we want?" Theo asks, about a foot away from where Emir is catching his breath with his arms over his head.

"If you don't mind." Emir smiles, stopping to leave a kiss to the corner of Theo's mouth before setting his phone up to get the fullest angle possible in the small studio. Well, not small, but not as large as the stage will be. "I think we should call it a day after that."

Theo nods his agreement, pausing to drink his water and holding Emir's Hydro Flask up so he'll do the same. It'll give them a small boost of energy before running through the section one last time. Since Emir and Theo both start off stage, they shuffle to opposite sides of the room before Emir presses play on the song and starts into his first solo portion. He has about a minute and a half to himself, Theo watching him in wonder because Emir's his favourite dancer and even this mostly pedestrian movement is enchanting.

But then it's Theo's turn, Emir walking back off stage in time for Theo to start his own part of the story. About halfway through the song they're both on stage, and will be for almost the entire rest of the piece, but they're not interacting. They're moving around and without and occasionally in sync but never together. It's ecstasy for Emir, knowing how this is going to play on stage, that the moment they finally interact will be like a sigh of relief for the audience.

They can tell this is it. They never once catch each other's eye, because they're not meant to, but the energy is exactly right. They're both finding their moments precisely as they need to and even without watching they know they're working in tandem. Reviewing the video tomorrow will confirm and help them decide any slight changes in angle or distance, but sometimes you just know as a dancer. You can feel the other person like the air is water and you're sharing the waves as they come.

When the song finishes just as the two of them touch for the first time, they're both filled with a sense of contentment and surety. *This is it.*

Emir waits until the song ends before jumping in celebration and into Theo's arms, both of them talking loud and excited, animated in a way they wouldn't be around anyone else. Emir wraps his legs around his partner, Theo catching him happily and giving him a spin with his head tucked into Emir's shoulder while he tries to catch his breath. They both know they've created something beautiful, and that it's truly only the beginning.

Theo sets Emir down and captures him in a kiss, only breaking it when he feels Emir smile against his lips. It's a special moment for them, knowing they're going to succeed for the first time since starting the project. This work means so much to both of them individually, and allowing them the freedom to love the other during the process has made all the difference. They're their most authentic, open selves and it shows.

"You're remarkable. The best partner I could've ever hoped for." Emir traces his fingers through Theo's sweaty curls, only now remembering the camera and stepping away to turn the video off. As he's standing back up with his phone in hand, he feels Theo's warm fingertips sliding his headband off to start massaging his scalp. Emir groans, falling back into him with his eyes closed and letting himself be loved on. Theo's always doing this, treating Emir sweet and soft and gentle whenever he can. "You ready to go home, princess?"

Theo drops his hands from Emir's hair and wraps them around his waist instead, holding him in a cuddle from behind and moving them together while their bodies calm after several hours of intense dance. "We need to stretch and cool down first."

"I'm so lucky to have you." Emir doesn't move out of Theo's arms, wanting physical intimacy after the emotional intimacy they've been building the past few hours. "It's early, but we should make food when we get back. Relax the rest of the night. I think we've earned it."

"Already planned for it." Theo confirms, turning Emir around in his arms so he can rub his hands along Emir's back instead, tossing Emir's headband to the ground. He loves how Emir easily sinks into him, sighing happily and trusting Theo with everything he is. But they really do need to stretch before they get lost in another moment or they'll regret it tomorrow. "Come on, babe. Stretch with me."

Emir pouts, but he knows Theo's right. They settle on the floor, sipping their water and stretching out every muscle group they can think of. It's warm and intimate without being anything close to sexual, just two people spending their quiet moments together.

"Did you know that song was written as part of a protest against the Iraq War? In, like, 2003 or 2004. Max Richter recorded it about a week after a huge protest." Theo stretches out his hips with a grimace, knowing they'll need extra attention tomorrow. "We aren't telling a story about a war, but...we kind of are. Just not a militaristic one. Well, maybe sometimes...it's complicated, I suppose."

"I don't know anything about the song other than I like it." Emir's leaning forward in his splits, restretching both of his legs deeply before doing some gentler, calming stretches. No one gets to be as flexible as he is (or Theo, for that matter) without a consistent stretching regimen. "But you're right. It's a war for love and for escape from the marginalisation of multiple communities. It's a fight and the casualties are significant. Like how many people died of AIDS before anyone decided they gave a fuck? Or how many trans women get murdered just for existing?"

Emir sighs and switches to his other side, Theo nodding in agreement and looking solemn as they both fall into silence for another minute.

"I wonder if I should talk about our music choices in the written portion. I hadn't planned on it, but that could be an interesting thing to include. Write a bit of history on the songs and why we chose them." Theo knows he's mostly done with the written requirement for his dissertation, and has been for months, but he's reworking it anyway to include Emir, so why not add another section?

"I think I will, but you can write about it too." Emir lays back on the studio floor to start rolling out his back, silently asking Theo for the foam roller near him with an open hand and a tilt of his chin. "Sean said my outline was fine, and I had that included in the section about performance choices."

"You're so fit when you sit there all focused in your glasses and your blankets while you type away. I like when you're in nerd mode." Theo decides he's mostly done stretching, laying next to Emir instead and waiting for his turn with the foam roller. "I know we're relaxing the rest of the night, but if you wanted to get some writing done tomorrow I could...distract you while you do it."

"That so?" Emir turns his head, rolling off and away from the foam and letting Theo take it. "If I knew bedhead and glasses was what it took to get you, I would've thrown away my contacts and hair products."

"Don't do that!" Theo laughs, kicking Emir's toes with his own before focusing on rolling out his sore back. Emir's just laying on his side staring at Theo and not at all subtly scanning his sweaty body with the eyes of a siren. "You need your contacts and I like when your hair does the swoopy thing. And when just, like, one or two strands fall across your eyes...But you could also look however you wanted and my mouth would water. You're, like, unfairly fit."

"Keep talking and I'll have to get myself off before we eat." Emir teases, pushing himself up to sitting now that Theo's done and ready to leave. "But I'd rather we get our energy back so I can give you that surprise I mentioned yesterday..."

Theo fumbles his phone from where he was opening a text to Jordan to let her know they're done and she could come use the space. It's a shared studio for all the students, but for this kind of work it's easiest when you have the place to yourself. He barely remembers to finish the message and tuck his phone back into his bag before Emir is tugging on his waist band and sliding his fingers around Theo's neck for a heated kiss.

"I want my surprise, please." Theo murmurs after Emir brings their foreheads together again, pressing their bodies flush because Theo's delicious when he's all sweaty and warm from dance and Emir wishes they were home already and he could do something about it.

"Alright. Suppose you've earned it." Emir kisses him once more, bending down to pick up his bag and taking Theo's from his hand. It's become a habit to carry Theo's things, but Theo still flushes every time he does, as if Emir treating him like a gentleman is a surprise. "Just know it's taking a lot of willpower to wait and not just get us both off the second we're at your flat."

"Duly noted, babe." Theo slides his hand down Emir's back and grabs his arse before stepping away, taking Emir's hand instead to walk out of the studio together. And if they take a five minute detour in the dark alcove in the hallway? It's the weekend and they're in too good of a mood to care.

***

Theo: Laur, Emir and I dropped off dinner for you two at the flat.
Theo: It's in the fridge. One of Emir's mum's recipes.
Theo: It's delicious, I promise.
Emi: it's called kitchari
Emi: should be good for after a long day of work
T: YOU TWO ARE AMAZING
T: Thank you sooooooo much /crying emoji/
Theo: We were already cooking anyway, and I know you have a long weekend.
Laurie: Teddy I could kiss you on your entire mouth right now
Laurie: We're literally starving and we're stuck here for hours
Emi: theo said i'm the better kisser /painted nails emoji/
T: But how can we be sure?
Theo: I think all four of us have kissed at some point?
Theo: Wait, no. I haven't properly kissed T, I don't think.
Emi: i think you'd enjoy it
Emi: they kiss the way you like

Theo: ...I have a kissing type?
Laurie: Yes
Emi: yes
T: Yes
Theo: Was this a thing I was supposed to know?
T: No I've just watched you kiss both Laurie and Emi enough to notice
Emi: to be fair you seem to like every way we kiss, but you have favourites
Laurie: How did we end up here?
T: This is literally your fault Laur. Stop snogging everyone
Laurie: What? They're fit
Laurie: You're still my forever /heart emoji/
Laurie: And you like being jealous
Emi: as a fellow capricorn, so do you lawrence
Theo: Wait...
T: I'll teach you, Theo. It's an art
Emi: don't teach him too well
Emi: you two are way more open than we are, at least for now
Theo: Aren't you two like...busy right now?
Laurie: They don't need us much in the first act
T: This is more fun
T: Also we're on opposite sides of backstage so I'd be texting Laur right now anyway
Emi: we're almost back to theo's flat so.......bye
Emi: we'll be busy for a bit
Theo: OH
Theo: Bye have fun and don't shag backstage
Laurie: Are they about to.......
T: Probably
Laurie: So maybe we should.............
T: Later /wink emoji/
Gabe: I can't believe we missed all this
Ciaran: We were BUSY
Ciaran: I guess we're all taking turns
Gabe: How does the flat ever smell like anything other than hormones and cum? Especially on weekends.
T: I like scented candles so there's that
T: I have one that smells like Laurie for when he's busy and i miss him
Gabe: Do you think they make a Ciaran candle?
Laurie: T knows so much about candles. I'm sure they can help you find one
T: I bet the ballet boyfriends want candles too
T: But they're BUSY

Ciaran: Aren't you and Laurie literally at work?
T: Laurie's lesbians have it covered
Laurie: They could take over the world without help from anyone else
Laurie: I'm so gay proud of them
Gabe: Is the gay in that sentence necessary?
Laurie: I'm gay. They're all gay. Therefore gay proud. Also I could never be proud in that withheld boring way the straights are.
T: You can't do anything straight /rainbow emoji/
Ciaran: True, even his cock curves.
Laurie: Stop staring at my penis and calculating angles
Ciaran: It was right there!
Laurie: Not for the purposes of geometry /eggplant emoji; mouth emoji/
T: Sigh. And he wonders how we end up in these conversations
Gabe: Has anyone seen my lucky guitar pick?
T: Under the fruit bowl on the counter.
Ciaran: How did you possibly know that?
T: I found it there Thursday but didn't want to move it in case it was there for a reason
Gabe: I need a new designated spot for it...I'll ask Theo when he's done with Emir. He's good with those things.
Ciaran: I love our weird gay family

***

"I know we just - *ngh* - this morning but - *ouch* - I'm ready for - *Emir!*" Theo can barely get a few words out at a time now that they're back in his flat and stumbling across the common area to get to his room. Emir is taking full advantage of Theo's newly discovered biting kink to leave a fresh love bite at the base of Theo's neck, using his teeth more than in the past now that he knows he can.

"Hm?" Emir detaches his mouth and stares at Theo with all the innocence he can find, which to be honest isn't much. He's fairly preoccupied.

But now they're in Theo's room so Emir brings his lips to meet Theo's instead and walks him back towards his bed, carefully laying him down and climbing on top of him all while maintaining the kiss. It's a talent he's sure Theo is appreciating based on how he's started to lose himself in Emir's hands, pliant and warm and a bit loud. Emir is so far beyond in love with him.

"You're so pretty." Theo mutters, bringing a hand up to caress Emir's face, holding his own bottom lip between his teeth like he's embarrassed to admit it. But Emir is every word for attractive that exists, and right now he's *very* pretty, bright eyes and soft hair and cheeks a bit pink from the short walk to his own flat and back.

"You ready for your surprise?" Emir lays himself on Theo's chest and stares up at him as best he can, fiddling with Theo's free hand in his own.

He knows Theo's in the mood for sex of some kind, but maybe he just wants to do something he's already comfortable with. But then Theo sits up, bringing Emir with him and covering his own eyes with his hands, as if waiting to open a present. Maybe Emir should've wrapped it. "You don't have to hide, princess. Just let me get my overnight bag."

"But - " Theo keeps his eyes covered, feeling the bed shift as Emir climbs off and in the direction of Theo's wardrobe where he tossed his weekend bag. He's thought about clearing actual space for Emir to use in more than just the loo, but he also doesn't want to bring it up and scare Emir with more commitment than he's ready for. "I *want* it to be a surprise."

Emir glances back at Theo, hand clasped around what he'd hidden away between the folds of a jumper, hoping that Theo wouldn't find it by accident that way. Theo doesn't usually like surprises so Emir figured this was more of a *hey let's try this together* gift of sorts. But if Theo wants it to be a surprise, he can work with that.

"Alright." Emir mumbles, climbing back into Theo's bed and across his lap. "Keep your eyes closed but hold out your hands to me. It's not that special but you seemed interested, so..."

Theo lays his hands out palms up and holds his breath, hoping it's exactly what he's been waiting for. Ever since that first joke about Emir and rope and being tied up, it's been on his mind every single time they've gone further than snogging. He craves that feeling, of putting himself in Emir's hands and knowing there isn't a safer place in the world.

Emir's fingertips meet his own and Theo feels something set gently across his palms before Emir curls Theo's fingers to hold it properly. It has a bit of weight to it and if he's not wrong it sort of feels like...

"Go on, then." Emir encourages, kissing Theo on the forehead and waiting for him to open his eyes. He's not nervous, but he's also doing his best to take things at Theo's pace. They haven't reached the point of blowies or any form of penetration yet, so he may be skipping a few steps. But Theo has not-so-subtly hinted at wanting this multiple times, so worst case, they talk about it and try it later.

"Finally!" Theo shouts, staring at the bundle of rope in his hand and bouncing in place before pulling Emir into a very tight hug that turns into a bit of a wrestle. Emir keeps tickling at his sides and Theo's too excited to do anything except squeak and laugh and try to bat his hands away, all while keeping his eye on the rope as if anything could possibly happen to it with them thrashing around like this. It's rope. It's meant for thrashing. "I knew it! Wait -"

Theo suddenly stops, flopping back against the bed and throwing his arms up so they're beside his headboard. Emir laughs at the sight, Theo closing his eyes and holding completely still, like Emir's going to just tie him up, fully clothed and without any conversation beforehand. As if.

"I'm ready. Tie me up please." Theo squints his eyes open, like he isn't sure if he's supposed to, but Emir's still laughing, holding his stomach and staring at Theo with heart eyes. "What? Isn't it for tying me up?"

"It is, Teddy, but not like this." Emir stops his laughter with a hand over his mouth, taking a few calming breaths. Theo's just so fucking endearing, so excited and flushed and completely ready for whatever this means. But Emir's never been able to actually use rope before so it's really not that simple. Also, he only brought three metres. "Could you sit up for me, please?"

Pouting, Theo sits with his back against his pillows, but he reaches out and brings Emir to sit with him instead of on the other side of the bed.

"I would like to be tied up and have you do naughty things to me. In case consent is what you're worried about: you have it. All of it. Tie. Me. Up." Theo kisses Emir between each of his last few words, still eager and ready to get back to the heated snogging they were in the middle of when they returned to the flat.

"Give me a minute. This is a big step for us." Emir moves so he's between Theo's legs, hands on his thighs while he strokes them soothingly. God, Theo's so fucking strong. Emir knows his own body is like one limber muscle, but Theo is just so...he's getting distracted. "I only brought enough for your wrists because I figured that'd be the safest place to start. What do you think?"

"Literally right now. I've been thinking about it for *weeks*." Theo picks up the bundle of rope in his hands, turning it over and thinking about all the ways they could use it. He's looked shibari up briefly since he knew using rope could be an option, but he wants him and Emir to explore it together, too. "Why red?"

"Oh, well..." Emir flushes and runs a hand through his hair nervously. He was hoping the rope would be distracting enough that he wouldn't have to explain this. The colour choice was very intentional, and of course Theo noticed. Emir's a visual thinker, connecting his emotions to colours and shapes and all the rest, which is part of why dance is so expressive for him. "It's sort of...your colour. Like, to me, you're red."

"Oh." Theo's eyes widen because he actually knows what that means to Emir. He's never spelled it out exactly, but Theo's learned Emir's colour system by now and red is love. Whenever he uses it in his paintings or says it's his favourite, it's because he's feeling love as his primary emotion. Which means this isn't just fun, this is...Emir loves him. Emir thinks of him and he thinks of love. Which Theo knows, and he also knows Emir isn't ready to say that explicitly. So instead of expecting an explicit declaration, Theo just nods and slides forward with his eyes fluttering closed to brush a kiss against Emir's angel lips. "I like red."

"Not too much?" Emir asks, keeping Theo close and running his nose along Theo's before meeting him in another kiss. He knows that Theo understands the connotation based on his reaction, and as always, he appreciates Theo not pushing him to verbalise something that he just...can't yet.

"Definitely not too much. It's perfect." Theo keeps kissing him, laying down further on the pillows and bringing Emir along. But this isn't the heated intimacy of a few minutes ago, this is soft and slow and full of meaning. "I'd really like you to use it now."

Emir breathes a small laugh against Theo's mouth, giving him one last kiss before sitting up again. The two of them are always a rollercoaster of emotions, but in contrast to the first few years of knowing each other, it's almost exclusively positive now. "In all that thinking you've done, what did you want me to do once you're tied up? I need to know what's off limits."

"I've been dreaming about your mouth." Theo stares up at Emir where he's straddling his hips, actually glad they're both still clothed for the moment. It helps slow things down. "And, um, I don't want to be tied up the first time you blow me but I was wondering if maybe...when you were touching my bum earlier, I was thinking that maybe, like...rimming?"

"You want me to eat your arse?" Emir asks with a tilt of his head, grinning at Theo because yes, he can definitely do that. He's been looking forward to it at least since their first shower together when he realised just how sensitive Theo can be. "I'd want you on your front facing away from me and hands bound behind your back."

"*Yes* - I mean, yeah, I'd like that." Theo flushes, in an almost constant state of heated skin when he's with Emir. It's not embarrassment exactly, more an awareness of his own eagerness and inexperience, and more than a little excitement. "I *really* want that. If it's not asking too much."

"Definitely not, pumpkin. I'd love to. Just one suggestion then: how about you go get yourself undressed and wipe down a bit? I sincerely don't mind, but I know you get self-conscious about being between showers when we're...you know." Emir fiddles with the waistband of Theo's joggers, meaning every word of what he said. He *really* doesn't mind. "I actually sort of like when you're all musky and sweaty after dance, but I want you to be comfortable."

"I didn't know you noticed that." Theo smiles softly up at Emir, understanding that he's genuinely suggesting it for Theo's own comfort.

Theo has definitely noticed that Emir gets off on Theo being sweaty from a workout of any kind. He's not subtle, clinging to Theo and literally breathing him in, nose tucked up against his sweaty hairline or damp shirts like Theo's the best thing he's ever smelled. But Theo just can't handle knowing that he's not properly clean, especially when he's sharing his body with another person. It's gotten better with time as he grows more comfortable with Emir, but it's sort of automatic for him to need at least two showers a day. "Give me like three minutes. Do whatever you want in here. I want you to be comfortable too."

Emir helps Theo off the bed, sending him across the hall and into the loo with a pat on his bum and a wink. Closing the bedroom door most of the way, Emir strips himself down completely, setting the rope on the bedside table and fishing the safety shears out of his bag. He'd be shocked if they need them, but it's good practice and he wants there to be zero anxiety for Theo about actually being trapped.

Emir folds back the sheets and turns off the overhead light, leaving just the lamp and the twilight that's peeking through the curtain as mood lighting. Just as he hears Theo leave the bathroom, Emir starts one of his playlists, wanting a touch of ambience that they didn't have earlier when they were busy not-so-dry humping with the sunrise.

Theo comes up behind Emir and hugs him close, kissing his neck before stepping away and dropping his dressing gown so they can both be naked.

"Alright, babe. It's time." Theo flops onto the bed with a little bounce, holding out his hands like he's about to be handcuffed. "Ravish me."

"Baby." Emir laughs again, straddling Theo easily, but changing the mood to something softer. He likes being playful, but he wants this to be more than fun. "Did you want to pick a safe word or use the colour system or what works for you?"

"I have a hard time with words when we…you know." Theo won't meet Emir's eyes, knowing that it's always a lot for himself to process, but he's not been ready to have that conversation with Emir yet. It's one of those big ones, along the lines of those words Emir can't say, or at least, it is for Theo. "Could you just, um, keep checking in with me? And I can remember to say stop. It's just the one syllable and it's literal, so I think I'll be alright even if you get me all worked up."

"I plan on it." Emir brushes Theo's curls away from his face and caresses his chin with his fingertips, guiding Theo to meet his eyes again. "I know you'll want to see how it's done, but I'll need to tie you behind your back this time. I'll show you in front another time so you can learn. I promise."

"I'd like that." Theo sighs, relaxing again and waiting for what comes next. He actually doesn't think they'll need to talk much. It's only a feeling, but he can tell when Emir wants quiet, when he's showing Theo his love with his delicate fingertips and sensitive touch. As Emir turns him over, Theo can feel it in every lingering graze, every kiss left behind as he moves to a new spot on Theo's body.

Emir takes his time, bringing Theo to relax on his stomach, making sure his head is comfortable and he can breathe easy before holding his palms together to rest above his bum. Theo moves so responsively, trusting Emir without hesitation, making his happy little noises each time Emir can't help but kiss Theo's butter smooth skin as he goes about the scene.

He hasn't had a chance to actually tie anyone up before, but Emir's practised, and it only takes him a minute to secure the rope around Theo's wrists and finish it with a box knot. Emir checks the tension with a finger beneath the cotton cord. Satisfied, he leaves a kiss on Theo's fingertips.

"You're all tied up, shehzadi. I'm going to use my mouth now, start all over your skin and make my way to your bum, alright?" Emir lays himself on top of Theo, the vision of him restrained like this already making him wonder about what else they can try together. Theo's so much kinkier than he imagined, but he loves it, knowing that there's a whole world of sexual fun to explore.

"Please. I feel all tingly but like…relaxed. I feel happy." Theo's eyes are closed and he looks completely blissed from what Emir can see.

Emir gives Theo a soft kiss to the side of his mouth before moving down and to his back, reminding himself to give Theo a few bites along the way. Theo squirms beneath him, groaning and giggling in equal measure because Emir keeps alternating the kisses down his back with tickles to his side, keeping Theo in the moment and anticipating each new movement. Theo never once tries to get out of his bondage, his arms held uselessly behind his back, but he's never felt more secure.

After a few minutes of kissing and biting and teasing, Theo's starting to move against the bed in a way that's more pointed, and Emir knows it's time to give Theo exactly what he asked for. He trails his fingers down Theo's sides once again, stopping at his hips to pick them up and push Theo's bum into the air. Theo doesn't hesitate for a second, spreading his knees and opening up for Emir as if they've done this a dozen times already. Emir smirks, nipping playfully at Theo's right bum cheek and enjoying the way Theo's breath catches in response before shoving his bum back towards Emir. As if he needed another invitation.

"You're perfect, princess. If you get overwhelmed just ask me to stop and I will. I promise." Emir rubs his palms around Theo's bum in a massage, waiting for him to nod his agreement before going further. Once he has it, Emir uses his hands to carefully spread Theo's bum apart and press one careful, delicate kiss directly against his hole.

Theo's whole body shivers as he shoves his face into the pillow, his hands twitching for the first time since they were tied as if he needs to grab onto something. Once he calms, Emir teases his tongue gently from his taint up, Theo feeling like his whole body is on fire and he can't wait to burn. Every inch of his skin is covered in goosebumps, Emir's hands soothing them away wherever he can reach while he keeps licking and sucking around Theo's arse.

"So...fucking...*good*..." Theo has no clue if Emir can hear him since he's basically yelling into a pillow, but he feels a small laugh against his bum cheek when Emir turns his head and lays it there for a moment, hands smoothing along Theo's ribs to give him a moment to catch his breath.

Emir's having the time of his life, watching Theo squirming and moaning and shivering like his body literally can't contain the pleasure it's feeling. And he did catch Theo's little outburst. He's pretty sure it was loud enough that their friends will hear it from rooms away. The more into it he gets, tasting Theo so thoroughly and carefully biting where it's safe, the more Theo's legs start to shake until Emir has to physically hold his hips up.

He doesn't want Theo to be properly sore tomorrow since he needs his legs for literally everything he does, so Emir decides that's enough for tonight, taking his mouth away from Theo's arse and shifting up to be near his face again to ask, "Alright if I get you off with my hand, baby?"

"Hand and - " Theo pauses to take a deep breath, feeling tears on his cheeks from how much he's been experiencing. So many things to process in such a short amount of time. "Mouth, please?"

"Since you asked so nicely..." Emir wipes away the tears pooled beneath Theo's right eye and kisses the side of his mouth, Theo leaning into it like he wants a taste of himself.

Emir moves back to where he was, using his left hand to hold Theo's hips up and letting his right move around to take Theo in his hand. And wow, he is *wet*, probably a combination of pre-cum and sweat as he's been writhing on the bed trying to get himself off, anything to keep feeling this. Emir enjoys being serviced, because who wouldn't, but he's never felt like this. Theo is made for it, his mind and his body following his heart and letting himself experience every moment of their sexual encounters in a way that Emir will have to learn. It's incredible to witness.

What finally gets Theo to shout his way through an orgasm is a firm bite to his bum after a minute of pulling him off. Emir keeps stroking him through it, kissing gently at the base of Theo's back just below his bound wrists until Theo finally collapses, panting and smiling and completely worn out.

But when Emir goes to untie Theo's wrists, Theo's eyes open and he mumbles, "Wait, want you - on me - on my back."

"You want me to cum on your back?" Emir asks, and yeah it won't exactly take him long, fully hard from eating Theo out and the occasional tug on his own cock to relieve the buildup.

Theo nods, his head falling back against the pillow, a satisfied smile on his face. So Emir does exactly as requested, taking himself in hand and running his unoccupied fingers along Theo's beautiful legs, his toned abs, any inch of skin he can reach, Theo honest to god *purring* in response like Emir's touch is a balm to his soul.

Aiming carefully once he's close, Emir lets his spunk fall across Theo's bum and his bound hands and whatever he manages to see between squeezing his eyes tight while groaning Theo's name over and over and over and over until he's finally through the crest of it.

Emir falls next to Theo on the bed, shaking hands untying his wrists and tossing the rope off to the side. It'll have to be cleaned and reconditioned before they can use it again, but Theo would probably want to learn all that anyway so Emir isn't even close to bothered. He snuggles himself up to Theo, the big spoon to his happily sedate, needy boyfriend, both of them warm in the afterglow.

Theo's so overwhelmed but Emir's grounding him with his legs across his hip and his body as close as possible behind him. That was incredible, so much more than Theo imagined it would be, and he's exhausted, completely worn out like he danced a whole ballet twice through and forgot to take a break. He swears his body is humming, glowing, shimmering with a deep contentment.

Steady breathing and gentle, infinitesimal snores let Emir know that Theo's drifted off. Emir lets him sleep for a minute before cautiously disentangling himself and shuffling across the hall for a flannel to clean them both up. It's too early to really go to sleep, but a nap sounds perfect. He slides himself back in behind Theo, messy sheets and all, kisses the tip of his shoulder, mumbles something that sounds suspiciously like *I love you so fucking much*, and lets his own joy carry him off into sleep.

CHAPTER THREE

"Why the pout?" Emir leans over to kiss Theo on the cheek, knees knocking as they sit side by side on the sofa, enjoying breakfast together.

Theo's been quiet since they sat down, and not his usual happy quiet. His soft lips have been frowning even while he spoons perfectly spiced oatmeal into his mouth and pretends to look for something to watch on the telly.

"Don't laugh." Theo glances at Emir, cheeks pink while his hands cradle his favourite bowl. He knows he shouldn't be disappointed, but, "I wanted to make you breakfast in bed, but you didn't sleep in this morning."

Emir stares for a moment, waiting to see if there's more to it, but Theo just keeps looking down at his lap.

"You had a plan for it, didn't you?" Emir asks, gentle fingers reaching out to brush one of Theo's curls behind his ears.

He knows how much it matters to Theo to get to be thoughtful, to show his loved ones his care through things like meals and special moments. Even if it wasn't intentional, it sounds like he took that away from Theo this time.

"Yeah." Theo sighs, shoulders curling in on themselves while dejectedly stirring his half-eaten oatmeal. "I wanted to finish cleaning while you were asleep and then make a healthy breakfast for us and wake you up with a kiss. You get so grumpy-fond when I wake you up, and it's one of my favourite things because you're too tired to hide your smile, and I can tell how happy you are to see me. And then I'd surprise you with breakfast and we could cuddle in bed while you wake up. Something like that."

"That sounds perfect. Maybe next weekend?" Emir would obviously love what Theo just described, but they went to sleep together last night, and they woke up at the same time today. Theo takes Sundays as his day off from his morning routine, using that time to do his weekly cleaning tasks instead. "Honestly, I wasn't that tired this morning and helping around the flat sounded like a good way to start the day with you."

"You didn't have to help. I appreciate it because it's nice to have help and you don't make fun of my checklist, but I don't expect you to." Theo sets his head on Emir's shoulder, leaning into him like always.

"Seems only fair since I helped make the mess." Emir kisses the top of Theo's head and nudges his breakfast to get Theo eating again. He went through all the effort of making it on the stove, and Emir doesn't want him to miss out.

Theo and T both loving to cook perfectly balances how Emir and Laurie have barely touched the kitchen they share. Except for the rare instances where Emir misses his mum's food and needs to make one of her recipes, or when he wants to impress a beautiful, sensitive boy with some homemade desserts.

"It's not really about the mess though. You usually contain that to your place." Theo smiles, thinking about how Emir does his best to respect Theo's flat, always tidying after himself and putting things back where he found them. It's so thoughtful, and Theo notices it every time Emir goes out of his way to preserve Theo's space, in stark contrast to the artistic mess that is the flat he shares with Laurie. "I just...wanted to do something nice for you this morning."

Emir thinks it might be a bit of a losing battle to get Theo to start eating again, but that's alright. He sets his own bowl down on the coffee table, gingerly doing the same with Theo's and noticing he doesn't get any resistance.

"Princess..." Emir moves to sit across Theo's lap with his knees on either side of his hips, hands taking Theo's face and waiting for their eyes to meet.

"But we're on the sofa?" Theo asks, confused about what's happening. He didn't think they were in a sex mood, but maybe Emir changed his mind. Straddling him is a good indicator that Emir's about to attack his neck, but they usually do so privately in one of their bedrooms. Theo tilts his head in the direction of Ciaran's bedroom where he and Gabe are still asleep. "And I'm sure those two will wake up any minute."

"Not now, baby. Later, if you want." Emir gives Theo a soft kiss before sitting back on his lap and waiting to see Theo relax. It takes a moment, but his warm, crinkle-eyed smile grows the longer Emir patiently waits. "Do you think this wasn't thoughtful too? I know it's not breakfast in bed like you wanted, but you still made us breakfast and brought it out here to cuddle on the sofa together. When I got cold you brought me my favourite jumper that I always borrow because I like how it hangs over my hands. And when I almost used the wrong thing to clean the shower you took the time to show me the labels you made and helped me finish cleaning the bathroom and never got upset that I got it wrong, even though I would've made the tub all sticky. When you made breakfast you used the spice mix I showed you for when my mum makes kheer back home because you know I've been feeling homesick off and on all week. You're the most thoughtful person I've ever known."

Theo trails his nose along Emir's and gives him another kiss, letting his arms move around to hold him in a hug. "I just really like you and I want you to know. You're my favourite person. You deserve breakfast in bed sometimes."

"I know, Theo. I always know with you. I've trusted you since long before we started dating because you're never anything less than honest." Emir leans down to kiss Theo's birthmark at the base of his neck, one of his preferred places to give special attention. "You're my favourite person, too…but don't tell Laur. He's sensitive."

Giggling, Theo lets his hands move beneath the jumper Emir's wearing to slide over the smooth skin beneath, fingertips kneading away the tension as they move. "Thank you."

"What for? You're the one who did all those nice things." Emir closes his eyes and relaxes against Theo's chest while Theo keeps rubbing his back. He's not sleepy, but it settles part of him when Theo's gentle and sweet with his hands, like he's absentmindedly pressing his love into Emir's skin just because he can.

"For noticing. You always notice." Theo kisses behind Emir's ear, not wanting to move out of their cuddle even to kiss him properly. "You draw attention even when you don't want it, and I disappear into the background sometimes, but you never lose me. You could resent it, but instead you just focus on me and ignore all the staring. You have Theo vision, I think."

"Mmm…Is that my super power?" Emir teases, tickling gently enough at Theo's sides that all he does is sigh and nod against Emir's shoulder.

"It is to me." Theo admits. It's not that his friends and family aren't wonderful, because they absolutely are. But Emir notices Theo and notices things he doesn't even realise he's showing. Emir's said before that he feels seen by Theo, and it's more than reciprocated. "Maybe I should get you a cape. I bet T could make one."

Emir laughs, leaning back in Theo's arms before pressing their foreheads together. "Only if you get one too."

He kisses Theo once more before ungluing himself from Theo's lap and sitting beside him again. "Now, breakfast before it gets cold and then we can go on our morning walk."

Theo just smiles, taking the bowl that's passed to him and smushing himself into Emir's side while Emir finds something for them to watch on the telly as they finish eating. It might not be the morning he planned for, but it's full of light, and he can be alright with that. It's a different sort of comfort, but just as meaningful as what he intended. Emir has this way of reframing things that Theo has a hard time processing until they make sense again. Theo was only mostly kidding about the cape.

***

Laurie: *I know you said we could have the flat all weekend but we'll be working the matinee all afternoon if you need some alone time*
Laurie: *Even if we weren't away you know you can always crawl into your Emir cave as needed*
Laurie: *But T and I do have celebration plans after our long week so maybe sleep at Teddy's tonight as planned unless you want to be slightly traumatised and/or turned on by our activities*
Emi: *nothing you two do could possibly shock me at this point*
Laurie: *Is that a challenge?*
Emi: *fuck no you two don't need my permission to try out every new kink you come across*
Laurie: *True*
Laurie: *But seriously if you need a break the flat's open you can head over whenever*
Emi: *it's alright you know being alone with theo isn't the same as being with other people*
Emi: *he's quiet and cuddly and makes me happy*
Emi: *theo's in the kitchen making his green juice for the week and he's literally so cute writing on those little labels so i had to draw him with his tongue sticking out concentrating on the jars with his forehead all scrunched up*
Emi: *also gabe and ciaran are busy gay fighting over a sports thing and basically we miss you and T*
Emi: *how could anyone be anything less than in love with theo? his eyes are this amber hazel colour and his lips get all pouty when he's thinking about something and his cheek dimple might end me one day*
Laurie: *Ugh i did not text you to hear your vows*
Laurie: *But like I'm glad you're happy. It's nice to see you two together. I've never known either of you to be so...content*

Emi: *please my vows won't be anything like that*
Laurie: *Oh so you've thought about them*
Emi: *fuck off*
Emi: *maybe*
Laurie: *Well i could use some help with mine*
Laurie: *Since you're part of the wedding i think you owe me*
Emi: *honestly ask theo he's incredible at that sort of thing, but of course i'll help if you want me to*
Emi: *you and T are soulmates. i'm gonna cry through the entire ceremony*
Laurie: *Obviously*
Laurie: *I need to actually work for a while. Flat's there if you need it and say hi to the others for me*
Emi: *say hi to T for me*
Laurie: *No*
Emi: *istg lawrence*
Laurie: *Love you*
Emi: *love you too*

***

"Remember that it's just the first section and we still have a few months and it's not completely polished yet." Theo is sitting beside Emir on Lili and Jordan's sofa, nervously managing his expectations before they show their friends the video they took in rehearsal yesterday.

"But, like, we sort of need a second opinion before we keep working, and you two know what we're trying to do. Also, you're some of the best dancers we know." Emir has one arm around Theo's shoulders, essentially spooning him from the side.

He could pretend it's so the four of them can all fit on one sofa, but Lili's mostly in Jordan's lap with her feet across Theo, so Emir doesn't *need* to be quite so cuddled. Every time he moves an inch away, Theo follows, and Emir's heart softens into putty, so easily moulded by the look in Theo's eyes.

"Just play it before I regret saying yes." Lili nudges Theo not-so-gently in the stomach with her toe, waiting for him to lean forward and press play on his laptop.

Jordan smiles but otherwise leaves them to it. Lili and Theo exist in their own found family bubble that truly only makes sense to the two of them.

Theo brought a notebook so he can make his own observations and so that he'll remember what their friends offer as feedback. They plan to send Sean the video tomorrow, but it was important to both of them to include Lili and Jordan as they go, knowing they'll give honest criticism where it's needed and necessary encouragement. Theo and Emir will of course do the same for their respective dissertations when the time comes.

Emir's already watched the video twice since they filmed it yesterday, needing to process it on his own without Lili and Jordan's input. As he watches the first few minutes of his solo, he's slightly annoyed at the step he takes just out of cadence, then at the arm he needs to raise three inches higher. These are the tiny details that will literally make or break their performance. But it's like Theo said: they have months. This is the time for him to be critical and invested in those details so that they can move forward on a solid foundation.

Theo makes a few notes, mostly staging concerns about needing to be more symmetrically placed when they're sharing the floor or angling their bodies differently for the intended effect. But like Emir, he reminds himself that they have time and that some of those changes may need to wait until they're finished choreographing the entire piece.

When the six minutes are up, Theo lets the screen go dark, turning his gaze between Emir and their friends while waiting for their reaction. Emir kisses the top of his shoulder and tussles his hair with the hand still around his back, thinking that Lili and Jordan probably need a moment to gather their thoughts before they share. They've been silent for the entire viewing.

"I think…I think I should quit." Jordan finally looks over at them, partly confused and a little overwhelmed. She doesn't look angry, just thoughtful. "That was only the start?"

"Yeah, just the first part until we get together." Theo confirms, notebook poised to jot down any comments. He's not sure what to do with that one.

"I didn't know that you…Theo, what the fuck?" Lilibet's staring hard at him, as if waiting for some type of explanation. "You've never danced with me like that. Not once. That was…"

"Haunting." Jordan finishes the sentence for her, Lili nodding in agreement and laying back against her. "Beautiful, but…it hurt something in me."

"In a good way?" Theo asks, staring back at Lili and trying to figure out what she means.

Of course he's never danced with her like that. Everything's different with Emir, and this is their own choreography. Dancing with Lili has always been someone else's story and movement. As well as Theo and Lili work together, it's not the same.

"I think so." Jordan answers, tapping at her lips with her fingertips, chin in her hand. "But, like...that could be finished. You two could pack it in and present that in May. The rest of us may as well give up now."

"There's no competition. It's just for uni." Emir grins, their reaction better than he anticipated. Sometimes they get so close to their own work it's hard to see it from an outside perspective. "And we have so much more story to tell. We don't want it to end there."

"Did the narrative read well from what we've told you?" Theo writes a quick note of *haunting and it hurts in a good way*, not sure why, but feeling like he needs to write *something*. He was expecting more questions, or at least a few technical notes. "Like, if we hadn't already filled you in, do you think it would make sense?"

"Definitely." Lili pauses for a moment before punching Theo on the shoulder then squeezing him tight in a hug. For someone so tiny, she manages to knock the wind out of him. "You've been holding out on me, you twat."

"Ouch?" Theo mumbles, his face squished against her shoulder as he slowly brings his arms up to hug her back.

Lili has a unique way of showing support, but he knows she loves him as well as his family, and could certainly tease him just as efficiently. This is basically her way of saying she's really proud of him.

"You're an idiot. The both of you." Lili lets Theo go, gently shoving him back in Emir's direction. Emir catches Theo easily and holds him close to his chest with a grin. Lili rolls her eyes because, somehow, it took them years to figure out that they belonged in each other's arms. "Can't believe you didn't want to work together."

"I thought my dissertation idea was alright, but...I think I should start actually working on it and soon. I need to decide if I'm casting other dancers and if I still plan on it being a large ensemble. The four of us are all performing the same day since we're with Sean..." Jordan pulls her hair up and into a messy bun, her long blonde fringe falling out and into her eyes at the last moment. "Let's hope you two go last."

"Honestly, though. Mine will be great, but it's not going to be *that*." Lili tucks Jordan's loose hair behind her ear and snuggles into her space, bringing her legs up onto the sofa so the four of them are facing each other in spooning pairs. "You two should use that clip as part of your audition tapes for after uni."

"So you really enjoyed it? Like...genuinely?" Theo asks, poking Lili with his toe just like she always does to him. His notebook fell when Lili squish-hugged him, but it can stay on the floor for now. He's in Emir's lap and he's not planning to move away unless absolutely necessary.

"It's significantly more than I imagined. I know the two of you are talented but..." Jordan sighs, her eyes drifting to stare off into the middle distance for a moment. "This isn't at all what we're talking about, but I don't think I want to be a dancer, like, not properly. Now that I'm almost done here it's, like, I'm so grateful and happy with studying dance, but I don't think it's my career, and I'm not really sure what to do about that. I see something like what you just showed us and I get this feeling, like I know deep down that you're meant to share that with the world and I'm meant to do something else. I just...don't know what."

Lili turns to look at Jordan but otherwise seems unsurprised, so Theo thinks it's likely they've discussed this before privately. Jordan has only been getting closer with Theo the past few months, so her opening up like this is new for their friendship.

"I don't think anyone can decide that for you, Jo." Theo offers, holding Emir's arms across his stomach like a safety blanket. "But if that's how you feel, I get that. I feel like that sometimes. Maybe not exactly the same, but I don't know what my future looks like either. Like, I see Emir and Lili and I know they're meant to be on stage. But I'm less sure about myself."

"I'm, like, ridiculously privileged of course, with my family's money and status and all the rest, but I don't have a backup plan, you know?" Jordan tucks her chin on top of Lili's shoulder and sighs. "I think that's part of why I'm so scared to come out to them. Besides the obvious terrible reaction I expect, I don't know what to do without that safety net, especially if my degree is basically just a fun pastime and not a path towards my career."

"You don't have to decide right now. We still have until summer." Emir adds gently, mirroring Jordan's posture with his head beside Theo's. "And you have us, if no one else. You'll come out if and when you're ready, and if it goes like you think it will, you know where to find us. I don't, um...I don't really talk about it, but I had a pretty terrible coming out experience a few years ago. I'm not saying *it gets better* or whatever the fuck, but I wasn't alone, especially once I got to uni. And now I have Theo, so like..."

Emir feels Theo's hands holding tighter, an acknowledgement of what it must take for Emir to even bring this up without making him mention more than he's ready for. What a gift it is to have Theo in his life.

"If you ever want to talk about it, we're not just dance friends. Lili is literally my mean twin sister, so you're basically my sister in-law." Theo jumps when Lili tries to kick him again, making him thrash around and squish even more into Emir.

Within seconds, Lili and Theo are play-wrestling on the sofa between their partners, Lili going for Theo's tickle spots with practised precision and Theo basically just trying to pick her up to hold at arm's reach. Emir and Jordan intervene when the two of them almost fall over onto the coffee table, Emir throwing his arm out to catch them and Jordan pulling Lili back by the waist.

"That's enough out of you two." Emir can't stop laughing, Theo crossing his arms and pouting while Lili aims one more tiny kick in his direction. Theo turns to Emir looking for backup, but Emir just kisses him fondly and runs a hand along his chest before settling the both of them on the sofa again. Laurie play-fights with anyone nearby that he considers a friend, so Emir is pretty used to this sort of thing by now. "Jordan, didn't you want to talk through some ideas for your dissertation before we leave?"

"Only if David and Alexis Rose here can behave for five seconds." Jordan teases, reaching over to grab her iPad and scroll through her notes.

She's planning this really interesting group piece where she recreates some of the classic dance scenes from film and television, but overlapping and reworked to tell a story about the media's portrayal of dancers. She's still in the phase of gathering scenes and deciding which are the most important, and she could really use their input while she tries to prioritise. The idea doesn't feel quite right, but it's all she has and she can't wait much longer to start.

"Wait, am I David or Alexis?" Lili asks, standing up from the sofa to refill her water glass and kissing Jordan on her way. The entire dance programme was obsessed with watching *Schitt's Creek* during this group's first year, and this specific sibling comparison for Lili and Theo has lived in Jo's mind ever since.

"You're David." Theo and Jordan answer together, Emir hiding a smile against Theo's neck. Emir's hair falls forward and tickles at Theo's bare skin, sufficiently distracting him for a moment until Jordan starts talking again.

Theo never knew his weekends could be like this and he wouldn't trade them for anything. He's so lucky to have found a boyfriend who fits in perfectly with all the most important people in his life, while remaining completely distinct in the most incredible way. Emir is the light of Theo's days and it's hard to remember his downtime from before.

When Lili rejoins them in the living room, Theo turns around to whisper to Emir, "I like being your boyfriend."

He says it as if he hasn't told Emir the exact same thing a hundred times over the past month. But Theo just needs to know that Emir *knows*.

"Yeah?" Emir brushes his fingers through Theo's hair again and kisses under his jaw before whispering, "Me too, princess."

They stare at each other, soft smiles and twinkling eyes, caught up in a moment together until Lili tosses a cushion at them and steals their attention.

"Eyes on me and hands where I can see them." She grumbles, sitting on the floor by Jordan instead so they can all have more room to spread out while they chat. "Feet too."

"Feet?" Theo asks, laughing and tucking his legs beneath himself while leaning back against Emir again. Just because there's more room now doesn't mean he has to use it.

"I don't know what you're into, and I don't intend to learn." Lili fake retches, Emir flipping her off but he's grinning wide. It's been a really great day.

***

"What are you smiling about?" Theo's reclining on the ground on one of the blankets they brought with them on their walk, peeking his eyes open to find Emir grinning down at the painting he's been working on for the past half an hour. They're beneath their tree, sheltered from the drizzle that's tapping at the glass of the lake like so many notes on a piano.

"Never you mind, shehzadi." Emir feels his cheeks heat, focusing on mirroring the lake's surface on his paper, trying to capture the way the sound translates into colour: dreary but calm, greys and blues with an undertone of pink. He's been caught daydreaming about coming here in the spring, watching Theo delight in every flower and ask about each new leaf as if Emir was his guide in discovering their world. "You sure you aren't cold?"

Theo shrugs, rolling over on his front and laying his face on top of his arms so he can watch Emir easier. "I'm bundled up. But aren't your hands cold without the gloves?"

Emir stripped them off as soon as they settled under the tree, knowing their interference would make any art he attempted useless and clumsy.

"A bit." Emir switches to a finer brush to work on a few of the stray branches near the water's edge.

They fall back into silence, Theo watching Emir while Emir keeps imagining their future under the guise of capturing the lake in early December, insistent that he needs a new painting every few weeks to have a complete collection. The rain on the water has Theo drifting off into that space before sleep, where dreams and reality feel less like cousins and more like mirrors. His eyes fall shut again, relaxed near Emir with one hand reaching out to lay against his leg. Emir doesn't dare move, sleepy Theo the sweetest sight he's ever known. He'd fight wars to preserve this peace, to keep Theo safe and relaxed and *happy*.

"D'you want me to head home? Give you some alone time?" Theo mumbles, startling Emir who thought Theo was actually asleep, but apparently not yet.

"I'd rather you stay, baby. I'm happy exactly as we are, staring at your pretty face while I paint the water." Emir pauses, setting aside his sketchbook to press their hands together. Theo's warmth can be felt even through the fabric of his gloves, a reminder of the ember that he seems to keep just below the surface, easy to excite into a gorgeous flush.

"You're sure? You haven't had alone time in days." Theo takes Emir's hand, linking their fingers together awkwardly and resting them on Emir's knee. He's still got his eyes closed, but if Emir needs space he's fine to walk home.

"You sound like Laur." Emir says after a moment, running his thumb along the top of Theo's hand in a pattern that matches his mind, a give and take like waves against the shore. Why do they keep asking if he needs alone time? He doesn't feel that typical need to get away that he does when it's been too long, that itch under his skin to sit with his thoughts and ignore the world. Should he feel that? "Thank you for checking, but I'm alright. You?"

"Hmmm...happy." Theo yawns, letting his hand drop out of Emir's but still on his knee. It's comforting to know that Emir is right there, just below his fingertips, Theo's favourite person watching over him and letting him be.

Emir soothes away Theo's worries about talking too much or too little or not understanding the joke or needing a moment to find his words or being over-sensitive or under-sensitive or too quiet or too loud or needing guidelines where everyone else can just guess. He doesn't have to *try* all the time with Emir, he can just exist. Emir sees and understands the truest version of him; Theo doesn't mask around him. The energy that saves and the trust that builds between them is something Theo never expected to find.

Theo yawns, covering it with a gloved hand to say, "Happy all the way through my toes."

Emir chuckles, bending down to kiss the top of Theo's head through his beanie before going back to his painting. Maybe he'll need alone time later, but not at this moment. For now, he's exactly where he wants to be.

***

The problem with Emir ignoring his need for solitude is that it always starts to creep in eventually. He should've learned by now that if he doesn't pre-emptively give himself space, by the time he can, it's past when it was needed. Like overdoing it during a workout or holding a wee on a long drive, it builds and builds until he loses control.

It's hard for him to explain to people, this need to be alone and find his grounding. He's lucky that his family has always understood. Even when he was a baby, he needed alone time to play with his toys and babble to himself and understand the world around him, in many ways the opposite of most toddlers.

Emir's been introverted and shy since he was old enough to talk, his mum and baba telling stories about how he would love spending time with his friends or at the park, but start getting very frustrated if he didn't get to go dance or play on his own once he was home. It just takes a lot of energy to be social, and especially after everything that happened around his genderqueer coming out - or rather his genderqueer being outed - it got harder to feel safe in social spaces. Not being able to trust anyone or any situation has made solitude a necessity so that he can recharge and recentre himself.

But...Emir doesn't know *why* this time. Why is he feeling this way now? He's been feeling the best he ever has, content and creative and happy. Emir thought he was finally moving past that need, that he'd healed whatever broke inside him two years ago.

Theo is safety and warmth and joy and love and Emir doesn't understand why he's starting to feel that familiar itch in this exact, perfect moment: with Theo asleep on his chest while Emir stares up at the dark ceiling, well past midnight, as he waits for Monday to dawn cold and achy.

Emir had a wonderful, productive, gentle weekend full of Theo and friendship and dance and all of his favourite things. He spent time doing his art, he and Theo had incredible sex, they went on their first date and made memories he'll be thinking about for years to come. Just a few hours ago, they watched the play that T and Laurie worked on with Ciaran and Gabe in the seats beside them, another one of their family traditions that Emir is grateful to be part of. And he didn't feel drained or like any of it was too much until about an hour ago.

He can usually identify where he pushed himself too far, but not tonight. He's never been happier. But now, awake by himself while Theo cuddles him in his sleep, Emir feels like he needs to go for a midnight run, to sprint until his lungs burn and his muscles give out.

That would be irresponsible, Emir reminds himself. He's in the middle of a dozen different things, between regular classes and the first week of rehearsals for the winter show and their dissertation work. Opening himself up to that type of injury is something he's supposed to be too mature for now. He's learned his lesson about pushing his body to the point of breaking.

But what if staying put means he's pushing himself towards a different sort of break? What if it's his mind that gets worn out until he snaps and doesn't have a choice but to give himself space?

Theo startles in his sleep, looking scared for a moment, like he's having a bad dream. Emir shushes him, rubbing his back over his shirt and burying his face in Theo's hair. Theo mumbles nonsense, holding tight to Emir like he's the hero of his nightmare, turning his fears into pixie dust with his soothing.

Emir knows immediately that he isn't going anywhere, not right now, and not for as long as Theo will have him. He's just falling into old patterns, expecting himself to need space because he has before. If he really needed a break he would know it, and Laurie and Theo are just fussing because they care about him.

It takes another hour, but with his body surrounded by Theo's warmth, Emir finally falls asleep for the night. He dreams of birds, of flying and falling and surfing the air like he was born for it. Distantly he thinks of a mate waiting for him back in his nest, arranging bits of twig and debris until it's just right, a resting spot for when his wings are tired and he's ready to go home. It's a beautiful dream, one that he forgets the moment he wakes up to Theo's gentle smile and a good morning kiss.

***

Theo doesn't know what's off, but Emir's been distant all day today. Not cold or rude or anything like that, just…Theo can tell something is wrong. But when he asks, Emir assures him he's fine, happy even. They go through class together, spend lunch on a walk before the weather turns cold later that day, and then they're in separate rehearsals until it's time for dinner. After eating leftovers, they head to the practice studio together to start deciding on the music for the rest of their dissertation.

Sean watched their video of the first completed part of their work and he'd mostly raved about it, while also sending a few quick notes with questions about connections to later in the piece, things they've already accounted for but that they're glad to have as confirmation that they're on the correct path. It's motivated them both to get back to work and create the next section.

"You sure you're alright?" Theo wipes his forehead while chugging water down. They've been going without a break for quite a while, and this section has more than a few lifts, with Theo primarily acting as the supporting partner, so he's starting to get tired.

"Course." Emir scratches at his headband, wondering why Theo keeps asking him that today. That's at least the third time, and he can see the genuine concern sitting behind his eyes. "You need to rest for a few minutes?"

"Yeah, my arms are getting sore." Theo fans himself with the front of his vest, the fabric almost see-through because of how much the two of them have been sweating (but mostly Theo). Someone must've turned up the heat in this part of the building, which always has the shittiest temperature regulation, anyway, because it's just a spare studio and not for classwork.

"How'd you feel about that last song?" Emir puts himself through a few held positions, studying himself in the mirror to get them just right. His arabesque is definitely not high enough today, so he makes a mental note to dedicate extra time for stretching each morning this week. He didn't think he'd been slacking, but his technique suggests otherwise.

"Not sure it flows well enough from *Daylight*, if I'm honest." Theo sits, using the floor to stretch his arms before laying down on his back and taking a few deep breaths. "I actually had an idea for the second section but I wasn't sure how you'd feel about it. Also, we'd have to ask and they could say no."

"Ask who?" Emir pauses, not sure where Theo's train of thought is headed, but knowing if he's bringing it up he's already put consideration into it and it's likely a good idea.

"I was thinking about asking Gabe to sing something a cappella. Have Ciaran record it for us and do the production." Theo feels Emir sit beside him, so he reaches out a hand with his eyes still closed and places it on Emir's leg. "I can imagine how it would sound. Something angelic, almost. Those high notes he carries so well. Soft, though, like the first sun on a spring morning. I'm thinking two to three minutes long when our characters are first discovering each other."

Emir links his fingers with Theo's and gives them a squeeze, letting them fall into silence while they both think about it. He's not sure exactly what Theo is imagining, but they could certainly ask. Gabe is more than talented enough to make something incredible, and Ciaran knows everything technically required in the recording studio to make it flow well with the rest of their music. They'll likely agree because they can both add it to their portfolio for after uni.

Honestly, it's surprising neither of them thought to ask sooner. Emir sighs as his internal thoughts become external. "I think it might be nice to ask them. T and Laur are already helping. Sometimes I worry Ciaran and Gabe feel left out since they're not as involved in our world, like, we spend so much time in rehearsal and at the theatre, and those two are in a whole separate place doing their art...the more I think about it, the more I like it."

"Mmmm...me too." Theo turns his head to smile at Emir, blinking his eyes open with a happy sigh to match. Emir may be tired after a long day, but he's still the most wonderful person Theo's ever known. "Help me up?"

"I've got you, princess." Emir kneels, holding one hand out for Theo to use to leverage himself up. Once Theo's on his knees, Emir traces his hand around Theo's neck and pulls him forward for a kiss. He loves that he can have these moments with Theo and still work incredibly hard together to make their work the best it can possibly be. "You're so smart. Beautiful brain underneath all those curls."

Theo looks down at the marley, shy while receiving the compliment. He's spent a lot of years wishing his mind worked differently, that it processed more the way that everyone else's seems to. But Emir is always saying how brilliant he is, helping him feel more accepting of his own intelligence in a way he hadn't expected from a relationship. "I like when you say that. Like...when you like my brain. It's...thank you."

"Look at me?" Emir brushes his fingertips beneath Theo's chin, waiting to see those hazel eyes shining back at him. Theo's still flushed and sweaty and a bit tight from being in the middle of their rehearsal, but when their eyes meet, Emir knows his own face relaxes into the honey-sweet smile that he saves just for Theo. "Your brilliant mind is one of my favourite things about you. It's the reason everything changed."

Theo tilts his head, letting Emir cup his cheek instead as they stay kneeling on the floor. It's a perfect visual for their work, but Theo doesn't realise it in the moment.

"I thought you said it was because I had such a big heart?" Theo's not fishing for compliments, but he always appreciates hearing what Emir loves best about him. Of course he does. But he's also just trying to follow Emir's thought process.

"That first week when we agreed to work together, when you sent me your written portion, or when Sean did, I suppose," Emir presses another kiss to Theo's warm lips, pausing to breathe him in for a moment. "I read it and I realised how wrong I'd always been. That's the morning I apologised because I knew you were so much more than I judged you to be. And it was that window into your brain that gave me permission to find your heart...Does that make sense?"

Theo nods, their foreheads pressed together, leaning forward for another kiss. He doesn't know what he's supposed to say to that because it was so lovely and exactly what he needed to hear. He'll keep this moment next to all the others with Emir, a cherished collection of memories that tend to happen more organically than the movies ever prepared him for. He never knew love could be like this. "Should we go home? Maybe we should rest and get back to this tomorrow?"

"Might stay a bit longer by myself. There's a few things I want to work on." Emir stands up, bringing Theo with him, then stepping away to grab his own Hydro Flask.

"But, um...aren't we staying at yours? Or do you...where should I...?" Theo hasn't walked home by himself from the studio in months. Should he stay and watch Emir while he keeps practising? It'd seem strange to go back to Emir's alone, even if he knows he's always welcome there. He's never done that before, unless he was there to see Laurie. "I can watch?"

"Sure you can. Stretch those arms some more." Emir winks at him, setting down his water and walking towards the middle of the studio. "You can pick the music for me. Something slow so I can work through an adage. My extensions need work."

"...Should I go? It's alright if you need space." Theo fiddles with his phone, ostensibly finding music like Emir asked, but actually just mindlessly scrolling through his options without paying any attention. He's not sure if staying or leaving is what Emir needs, and he still feels like something might be off with him.

"Give me thirty minutes and we can walk home. I just need to focus on my extensions." Emir bends into a fondue, right leg seamlessly moving into a developpe derriere while he squints at the angle in the mirror. With a concerted effort, he straightens his knee further without dropping any height, lifting out of the position before carefully ending back in fifth. "You think I've been wasting time on my turns lately? I spent entire hours on them during *Alice* for my solo."

They keep talking like this while Emir works, blowing through that first thirty minutes and ending up at the studio for a full hour past when they stopped to have a chat. Theo mostly stretches but helps Emir when asked, offering a hand as support while he finds the placement he needs or overstretching a position while Emir attempts to hold it on his own. Eventually, Emir admits he's done what he can for the night and they walk back to his flat with their hands linked, Emir carrying both of their bags, like always.

Despite their time in the studio, Theo still thinks Emir's slightly different than normal, but he tries not to read too much into it. After all, he just gave Theo that wonderful speech about how much he enjoys his mind, so maybe it's something else entirely. Maybe something with his family he doesn't want to talk about or something he's processing internally. And he's allowed to have days where he's less than 100% without needing a reason. Whatever it is, Emir is still lovely and kind, just…different. The vibes are off. And Theo wishes he wasn't so painfully aware because he can't stop worrying.

But if Emir says he's fine, he needs to take him at his word. So Theo leaves it be for another day, cuddling up on his chest after they shower and falling asleep within minutes.

***

Tuesday morning inevitably dawns and Emir wakes up knowing he's at his limit. He's grumpy and grouchy and downright unpleasant, and his thoughts feel like they're fighting through static. Emir snaps at Theo over literally nothing, throws a pillow at Laurie when he makes a joke about his bedhead, and even glares at T for not leaving enough hot water in the kettle for his morning tea before class. Emir knows he's the problem and he knows what's caused it, but he doesn't see a simple solution.

Emir's rushed the entire day, Tuesdays through Thursdays are, by far, his busiest in the studio. Between classes and rehearsal, Emir barely has enough time to take a lunch break. He's already impatient to get back in the practice studio and fix his placement in those extensions that he was barely achieving last night. Emir knows better than to allow his hips out of alignment to get an extra inch of height in his arabesque, and yet there he was, trying to cheat like an amateur. Emir's in his head and he's being a miserable presence to everyone nearby and he doesn't know how much longer until he snaps but he can feel it coming, like a rubber band held tight for slightly too long.

Theo notices, of course, as do T and Laurie, who avoid Emir until they're out of the flat for the morning. When Theo holds Emir's hand on the way to tech hall, there's space between their bodies that's usually non-existent, but Emir doesn't seem to be aware of it. It's like he's pushing Theo away but he doesn't want to, and Theo has no clue what he's meant to do.

Emir's *grumpy*, and when anyone has said even a single word to him all morning, he snapped in a way that Theo hasn't seen since the beginning of the year, when they were unable to tolerate sharing the same room without interference. And when they reach the empty studio (because they're always the first ones there) Emir lets Theo go to his spot across the room with barely a peck of a kiss, Theo trying his best not to take it personally. He knows it's not him, but...he feels small. Theo doesn't know how to help Emir feel more himself and he tries not to feel slighted as Emir pulls away in more ways than one.

"What's up with Emi?" Lili asks, incapable of subtlety as she joins Theo at their spot at the barre a few minutes later. She just tried to greet Emir and was completely ignored. Not even a grunt of a hello.

"Think he just...needs space. He's not having a great day." Theo answers, darting his eyes over to Emir and seeing him obsessively stretching and watching himself in the mirror. Emir's eyes are stormy, his forehead wrinkled while he fights with himself, paying zero attention to the other dancers as they start to file in for class.

"You alright, Teddy?" Lili pauses her warmup after watching Theo for a minute, leaning over the top of the barre with her arms crossed, invading Theo's space. "You seem sad."

"I just wish I knew what I should do." Theo shrugs, worrying at his bottom lip and standing still with his arms at his side, frozen with indecision. Does he insist that Emir take some time off? Leave him to figure it out for himself? Where's the boundary?

Lili surprises Theo, sneaking under the barre and attaching to his front in a very tight hug, face buried against his sternum. He sighs, wrapping his arms around her and hugging back, glad that she knows him well enough to understand that sometimes he doesn't need advice, he just needs a cuddle. Theo doesn't think he's going to find an answer anytime soon, but it helps to have Lili always there if he needs her. The hug helps too. He feels less conflicted with Lili's unspoken acceptance of his dilemma, still worried, but thinking he can probably get through class alright.

They do make it through class, Emir still very much in his head the entire time, but he's usually quiet, so most people don't even notice. Pas de deux class is next, Jordan unable to get much out of Emir besides a few mumbled words as they work together. Lili and Theo are both preoccupied with how quiet the space beside them is where Emir and Jordan usually banter good-naturedly throughout the hour. Theo sidles up to Emir when class is over, offering a hug that Emir falls into, hiding his face in Theo's neck, but otherwise standing still like he forgot how to cuddle.

"What did you want to do for our break?" Theo asks, still holding Emir and knowing he's more fragile than Theo is comfortable with. Like Emir, he can feel something building, but he doesn't know what.

"Ngrh." Emir groans, no other words making their way through his mess of a subconscious at the moment. He doesn't have any answers.

"Walk?" Theo asks, nodding to Lili as she and Jordan pause before leaving to make sure they're good. They stare between him and Emir for a moment until Lili nods back, understanding that Theo has it handled. "Let's take a walk."

Emir doesn't argue, unable to think of a better alternative because his schedule hasn't cleared up in the slightest since he woke up. Theo guides him to the dressing room where they both get bundled up to take a walk outside, Theo for once very much in charge of making sure the two of them actually make it.

Luckily, the walk does seem to help. Emir feels significantly better (though not his usual self) after an hour spent in the cold, and Theo's grateful to feel him slide his hand around Theo's back when they return to the dance building, tugging him forward for a kiss for the first time all day. It's tentative and brief, but it's true, and Theo accepts it gladly. He feels like he misses Emir, even with him right in his space.

"Lunch?" Theo asks, neither of them having spoken for the entire hour. They don't always need to talk when they're together, something they both appreciate about their relationship, but Theo doesn't like the colour of the silence today. Usually it's warm and soft, rather than sharp and fragile. He was hesitant to break it in case he broke something else in the process.

"Not hungry." Emir answers, shrugging in response to Theo's concerned look. That look had disappeared the last few minutes, then returned with a vengeance.

But Emir's really not hungry. It's only spending time with Theo the past few months that has improved his habits. Before Theo, Emir would usually remember dinner, maybe and a snack or two throughout the day, but he'll easily admit that his routines are much healthier with Theo around.

"We could go hide in the student lounge? First years are in Modern with Margaret, and Sean's about to start Choreo with the second years. Should be empty." Theo tilts his head, reaching out a hand to run through Emir's hair. He'd taken his hat off a few minutes into their walk like it was interfering with his experience of the cold.

"Yeah…" Emir leans into Theo's touch, still avoiding his eyes, but he really is grateful for how gentle Theo is being with him. The walk helped, but he's still minutes away from everything being too much. "Thank you for…"

"Of course." Theo leans forward hesitantly, pressing a kiss to the side of Emir's mouth before guiding him back inside the building and up to the lounge. While Emir huddles in the corner of the sofa, Theo traipses back down the stairs to where he'd stored the lunch they'd packed last night, grabbing it from the dressing room with the extra blanket that Emir keeps in his locker. It's not much, but it'll do.

They eat in silence, Emir with his blanketed legs across Theo's lap, chewing his salad while staring at nothing at all. He's still pushing back against himself, trying to feel better without just shutting down. And Theo isn't pressuring him to do or say anything, but Emir knows he's worried. Emir wonders vaguely if Laurie has texted him after how he acted this morning. Probably. He hasn't checked his phone all day.

"Walk you to rehearsal?" Theo asks when they're done, holding out his hand hesitantly, like he's worried Emir will crumble if he asks for too much.

Emir hesitates, holding Theo's hand but not standing up right away. He's not in a good headspace. He knows that. But Emir can't skip rehearsal, and he wants to get back in the studio with Theo after and keep working on their dissertation. They've been making incredible progress and he'd feel selfish stopping that momentum so he could have a night off.

So, after a few extra moments of Theo waiting patiently, Emir stands up and lets Theo guide him back downstairs, slowly, as if he knows Emir needs the extra time to adjust back to the environment around them.

***

"Really, a night off wouldn't - " Theo gets cut off before he can even finish the sentence.

"I said I'm fine. Could you all stop fucking asking me?" Emir snaps, glaring at Theo for about three seconds until he recognises the hurt in his boyfriend's eyes and immediately regrets it. He knew he was acting rumpled today, but he shouldn't be taking any of it out on Theo. "Shit, fuck, Theo. I'm sorry. Just...let's get this over with, yeah?"

"I don't know if..." Theo doesn't finish his sentence, leaving *this is a good idea* to remain implied. Also, get this over with? Since when has Emir ever said that about dance? Or thought that about time with Theo? The second question is the one that bothers Theo, because it feels more possibly true than the former.

Theo knows he can be a bit much sometimes, and regardless, Emir doesn't seem to know what he needs. Without any point of reference, Theo isn't any closer to knowing how to respond to Emir's current mood. "So...should we skip the second section until we can sit down and talk with Gabe and Ciaran?"

"Yes." Emir says, letting out a heavy breath and feeling grateful that Theo's agreeing to get to work. Dance, he knows how to do. Navigating his personal life? Still a work in progress. "Let's see about the middle section where we separate."

"Oh...alright." Theo tries not to read into that choice too far, but with the way Emir's acting the past few days, it feels suspiciously relevant. He hopes he's very wrong, a fresh sort of panic crawling deep down in his gut. "I was thinking about trying Chopin's *Prelude in E Minor*."

"Play it for me?" Emir knows he will, but he's trying to...he doesn't know what he's trying to do. He would say act normal, but nothing about today is normal.

Theo nods, finding the song on the playlist he's created of potential music choices and pressing play. Emir closes his eyes, arms resting on top of his head while he lets the music flow in and around him, feeling it as much as he hears it. Theo watches Emir process the song, having already analysed it himself multiple times. It might be what they need here. It's haunting, a bit, which would match what Lili and Jordan had said about the first section, so that would tie together nicely. And the song is well known but not overdone, so that also fits the choreography they're creating, a mix of classic movements with their own queer additions.

The music fades out after almost three minutes, Emir needing a moment once it's done to re-open his eyes. Theo really is brilliant because if Emir tried to describe the emotion needed, that song would've been it. "I think it'll work well. Could you play it again and I'll try to move with the music, see how it feels with some of the ideas we've already come up with?"

"Want me to record so you can watch it back?" Theo asks, already reaching for Emir's phone because he knows his habits by now. The amount of cloud storage that Emir keeps so that he can have his hundreds of studio videos is admirable. Theo understands the process, even though his own is different, it's no less important or specific.

"Thanks, princess." Emir gives Theo a fleeting smile, moving to a random spot in the room and sitting down, not sure where else to start since they've skipped the section before. Choreography certainly doesn't have to be done in chronological order, but without something to flow out of, he has to guess.

The music starts up again and Emir lets the first few measures pass without movement. But then it starts, that impulse flowing through him, his body understanding where to move and what to do and how to convey what he's feeling. Fuck, this is cathartic as hell. The music builds, Emir's internal friction rising along with it. He penchés into a somersault and lets his heart fall with the roll of his body.

Emir's movements show the defeat he's feeling, turning and falling and seeking something that's out of reach all while he's finally giving in to what he knows he needs, what he's known for days, but tried to stubbornly ignore. The piano notes fade away as Emir finishes dancing, staring at what would be offstage like he's frozen in time. He stays there catching his breath until he feels Theo walking over, the gentle hand that grazes his fingertips bringing him mentally back into the studio and the situation at hand.

"That was brilliant, Emi. Could we maybe try together? I won't record, but I'll sort of follow along, mirroring you maybe?" Theo doesn't expect Emir to turn around, but he knows he's listening, his pinky finger wrapping around Theo's index to acknowledge his presence. Since Emir doesn't want to take the night off, Theo's not sure what else to offer.

"Alright." Emir finally agrees, moving back to the centre of the room because he has no plan for how to do this. He doesn't know how to remove himself and get the space he needs without being destructive in the process. Emir can't look at Theo right now because he knows what's coming and it's his own fault. How could he have been so stupid as to end up here? They all tried to stop him before it got this bad, recognising the signs before he was willing to acknowledge it himself.

But, back to dance. Always back to dance, no matter what mood Emir's in or dilemma he's trying to navigate.

Theo has a gut feeling of dread, but he pushes through it. He doesn't need to record this time, so he leaves Emir's phone face down, using his own to replay the song for the third time, wondering if choosing it was a mistake.

Emir's different again, more settled, but now he won't even meet Theo's eye or participate in any of the automatic ways he normally reaches for Theo. No brush of a hand on his waist in passing, no fingertips through his curls, no kiss under his jaw before they get back to work. It's like Emir's removed himself from the room and from Theo. Somehow, he's never been further away, and Theo thinks his own heart might be breaking. He doesn't know what he's meant to do.

As Emir starts again, trying to follow what felt right the last run through, Theo keeps his physical distance, both because of what this section of their work is meant to convey and because he's not sure what would happen if he reached out for Emir like he so badly wants to. He wants to comfort Emir, to wrap him in his favourite blankets and fix his tea just how he likes it and somehow make whatever's happening alright. Theo would do whatever Emir needs, but when he asks he gets pushed away, further and further until he doesn't recognise the distance between them.

This is worse than before they were friends, before they were more. That, Theo could deal with. That was before he loved Emir and he thought Emir loved him. Emir always has this light, but Theo can't see it tonight, like it's hidden from him and maybe from the world, too, and Theo feels helpless to do anything about it.

Halfway through the song, their dancing brings them within breathing distance. Emir turns abruptly, shocked to find Theo there because he had almost forgotten he wasn't dancing alone. Emir has to throw out a hand to catch himself, his fingers landing in the centre of Theo's chest while they both freeze, standing still and breathing heavily.

Theo doesn't dare to move, Emir's fingers like daggers on his skin. He's never felt uncomfortable with Emir's touch before. This is the first time it's felt like a barrier.

"I can't do this. I need a break." Emir is finally the one to speak, letting his hand drop from Theo's chest and stepping back until they're several feet apart. He can't fucking breathe. He needs to go run in the cold as immediately as possible. He needs...he needs...to shatter. Something has to give, and he knows what comes next. Emir can see it crystal fucking clear and he hates himself, but he's already cracking around the edges from the pressure, and Theo's about to be collateral damage.

"Oh..." Theo stays put, still stuck in place and waiting for whatever's coming next. He knows. Somewhere deep in his heart he knows. He needs to cry, but that would only make this worse. If this is what Emir needs, then Theo has to accept that. He tries to be casual, to pretend this is about dance, to pretend he isn't about to shut down completely. "Should I go refill our water? Give you a minute?"

"No, Theo. No. I need a *break*. I need to be done." Emir tears his headband off and tosses it to land by his bag near the front of the room. "I have to go."

He walks past Theo, carefully avoiding being within his reach, and starts gathering his things. Emir's phone is the first thing into his bag, followed by his Hydro Flask and his speaker and, if it were possible, his entire being, because he just needs to be carried away right now. Anything to get him away without imploding.

Theo still hasn't moved. He doesn't know what he's supposed to say. Does he push for some sort of conversation? Just watch Emir leave? Fight for him to stay? Beg him to? Emir's almost to the door, shoes in hand, before Theo lets out a sob, not even realising he was crying, but unable to hold it back anymore. Emir stops at the anguished sound, slowly turning around and finally meeting Theo's eye.

"Are you..." Theo has to at least ask. He deserves an answer, even if it might break him in a way he doesn't know how to fix.

Emir takes a tentative step back into the practice studio towards Theo, drawn in by the pain he sees written so clearly across Theo's face and felt in that broken sob that brought Emir out of his chaos for a moment.

"Are you breaking up with me?" Theo falls to his knees, crying into his hands and trying to stop because he doesn't want to make this about him.

Somewhere in the back of his mind, he knows this is about Emir, that he's been off for days. But that doesn't make Theo's question any less relevant, with the space that

Emir's been wedging between them and the way he looks straight through Theo like he isn't even there. That's not a healthy relationship, even if it's not his fault.

Emir kneels in front of Theo, torn because he meant what he said: he needs to go. He *has* to leave before he gets worse and does or says something he'll truly regret. And Theo doesn't deserve to be treated the way Emir's been acting. Theo also doesn't deserve this: to be heartbroken on the floor when he's done nothing wrong.

But they're here and Emir can't think of any other way. All he can think about is getting outside and running until he can't run anymore. "No, baby, not unless you want to. I just...I have to go. I need to be alone for a while. I don't need a break from you, I need a break from *everything*."

Sniffling and wiping at his eyes, Theo looks up at where Emir is kneeling in front of him. He's earnest, his eyes pleading with Theo to be understood and believed, so Theo takes him at his word. His heart is broken and he's confused and maybe a little lost and so fucking tired from the stress of today, but hearing that Emir doesn't see this as a break-up helps. But Theo also can't stop crying now that he's started.

"Okay. I'll..." Theo clears his throat, trying to find the words he needs Emir to remember while he's alone, because this might be it for a while. Emir needs a break from everything, including Theo, and he doesn't know how long that could take. Theo can already feel himself closing off, hiding himself away from Emir, and by extension, everyone else. "I'll miss you."

Emir hesitates but leans forward and kisses Theo, trying to tell him *I love you and you're the most remarkable man and I'm sorry for what you're going through and for being the reason and I love you and please wait for me because I don't know how long I need but at least a few days maybe longer and I love you and it scares me and I just need some room to breathe.* He's not sure that he succeeds, but he still has to go.

Emir pulls away from the kiss, tracing a hand down Theo's face to remember how it fits in his palm before standing up. He leaves Theo without another word, picking up his things by the door and literally running out of the building, Theo listening to his hauntingly familiar footsteps until the exterior door shuts and leaves him in complete silence.

Theo can't move. He can't think. He reaches for his phone, knowing he needs help to get home and that he only has to ask. Just a few more words.

He listens to it ring three times before Laurie picks up. "Alright, Teddy?"

"Come get me, please? I'm at the studio." Theo knows he's monotone, unable to focus on putting any emotion into his voice and hearing the moment that Laurie notices the change.

"I'll be right there." Laurie doesn't hang up, but Theo lets the phone drop to sit on the floor beside him before he starts crying again, sitting cross legged in the abandoned studio while the tears are pulled out of him by painful sobs. Alone.

CHAPTER FOUR

Emir's entire body is on fire. There's ice in his veins and phantom needles piercing every muscle. After he left the studio, he sprinted to his flat, dropping his bag without pausing to wonder why it was silent. And then it was straight outside again, running circuits around the university until he forgot everything except the pain in his body, his mind clear of static for the first time in days. Time isn't real when he runs, the sky as black now as it was when he started, seemingly alone in his night-time spiral.

When his body physically can't take it anymore, he finds his way to his tree beside the lake, collapsing beneath it on his back while catching his breath. He feels cleansed, like he's just worked through a barrier. One down, dozens to go.

It's been weeks since he was last alone under this tree, no longer really just *his* anymore. And he shared it with Theo intentionally, but right now he's not thinking about any of that, his mind completely blank except for the sounds of his own laboured breathing and the occasional gust of wind across his cheek.

Emir eventually finds his breath, hauling himself back up to take a walk around the lake. If he was in a better, more aware frame of mind, he would realise that a solitary walk near a body of water, alone in the middle of the night, is significantly less than safe. But as he's preparing himself for another run, the walk isn't for reflection. If he stops moving for longer than absolutely necessary, Emir doesn't know that he'll be able to start again.

With a groan as he rounds the edge and reaches the tree again, Emir picks up his pace, starting with a jog and quickly working his way back up to a full sprint. He runs back around the campus, past his own flat and then the one Theo and his friends live in, around the dance building, up and down the path, keeping to the side of the walkway so he's not ruining his body by running on as much concrete. It's not a conscious choice, just a habit after years of throwing his body around.

Hours and hours later, when he can't run for longer than a minute without feeling like he's about to be sick, Emir jogs back into his building and to his flat, letting himself in and shuffling around until he's in his cave of a room. He kicks off his shoes, throws back the sheets - he vaguely remembers Theo making his bed this morning - and faceplants on his bed. He should be stretching, rehydrating, showering, any number of things to compensate for what he just put his body through.

But instead, he falls fast asleep, pushed so far past the point of physical exhaustion that his mind is blank and his body has given up. The only option he's left himself is defeated rest, a sleep so deep and fitful that, on top of his inevitable body strains tomorrow, he'll feel hungover, like running a marathon while drinking his friends under the table combined.

Emir doesn't dream so much as he ruminates, replaying saying goodbye to Theo like a tormented film reel on a loop. Whatever he feels tomorrow, he deserves it.

He sleeps like he's fighting, and though his mind was blank while he ran, its defenses have broken down now, thinking about Theo and how he's definitely never going to forgive Emir. He's remembering how, weeks ago, he told T and Laurie that he wouldn't hurt Theo, and that if he did, it'd be worse than being the one who got hurt.

Is this some twisted karma for what happened with his ex? Is he cursed to hurt people who dare to love him? Emir wounded the person his heart chose, the man he tried to push away because he knew if he let himself feel anything for Theodore Palmer, it'd be end game. And yet, he fell anyway, so deep that he dragged Theo down with him.

If he could experience his so-called sleep from outside of himself, Emir would hear himself whimpering, calling out for Theo, for his mum, for Laurie, pleading them to forgive him and crying that he loves them. He's apologising for the way he's too often taken them for granted, how he's waited too long to tell Theo how he feels, for forgetting to call his mum more than once, for not making sure Laurie knows what he means to him: a brother, a best mate, family.

Emir loves his family, his friends, he loves *Theo*, and he shouldn't have let that love become a weapon. He knows better and he still let himself get to this place of hurt because he wanted to prove some sort of point. He ignored his well established boundaries until everything broke.

But Emir doesn't hear any of that. He thrashes through it while he sleeps, tangling himself in his sheets and wetting the pillow with his tears. His eyes are closed but he doesn't rest. Emir's night is darkness all the way to the core, his own light hidden even from himself. He ran until he broke his stubborn internal defences, and now he's stuck in the rubble, deciding if he puts the wall back up or builds a bridge with what's left.

***

Emir's alarm startles him awake, forgetting for a minute where he is and what's happened and why his bed is so empty. But it all hits him with a groan as he turns it off, only having had about three hours of "sleep," but knowing that he won't be able to rest even if he turns his alarm off and tries again. Emir pulls himself out of bed and gets ready for his day, alone and not enjoying the solitude like he used to.

He stumbles his way through his morning until it's time for class, wondering what's going to happen when he sees Theo. Will they fight like in the past? Will Theo give him *that look*, the same one he gave him last night, like Emir had physically removed his heart and tossed it away? Or will Theo ignore him completely, waiting for Emir to apologise? That thought makes Emir physically cringe, a reminder of how many times he's had to do so, Theo always patient and forgiving of Emir's carelessness. Theo deserves better...better than Emir.

But Emir never finds out because Theo's not there. He's not in tech hall early like he's been for three years. He's not in class at all, but Sean never asks where he is, so it must be an excused absence. Emir glances at Lili but she won't look his way.

He's never been this distracted in class before. Emir falls out of his turns, stumbles his extensions, and it's not from the way his muscles are literally shaking from exhaustion due to his late night run. Is Theo alright? Is he so angry with Emir that he's removed himself from the equation? Is he hurt? Emir gave himself space, but he never wanted it like this. He wanted quiet, but it wasn't supposed to be empty.

Emir keeps to himself the entire day, spending his lunch at the lake beneath his tree, chewing on some snacks that Theo made with him this last weekend, yet another reminder that he should've taken care of himself before things got this fractured. Without Theo he doesn't remember to eat, to rest, to take care of his mental space. And that's unfair in so many ways.

Theo's not his parent, he's his boyfriend. He shouldn't be the only reason Emir doesn't fall apart, because as it turns out, he wasn't doing so well before they started dating.

Emir thought he was fine. He had his commitment to dance and his art as an escape, he spent time with friends and visited his family. But he knows now what a sham that life was. He was never truly happy, and it wasn't just Theo that showed him that truth, though Theo's love has transformed his life entirely in just a few months. It was the way Theo guided him to look after himself, showing him what he deserved from life, believing in Emir in ways he would never ascribe to himself

Fuck, he needs to go back to therapy. But Emir shoves that thought away for now, his immediate regret and ennui too close to think about the future.

After his last rehearsal of the night, Emir forces himself sheepishly to wander over to Lilibet, wanting to make sure that Theo's alright. The way she's avoided him all day tells him she knows at least a bit of what happened. Lili still won't look at him, retrieving her things from the front of the studio with Jordan just a few steps behind. Emir knows once she's out of the room, he won't get another chance to ask.

"Have you heard from Theo?" Emir's voice shakes, but he knows she heard him, her back stiffening as she continues picking up her discarded warm up clothes. You'd think he was a ghost with how completely she ignores him.

"Lili, *please*. I just want to know if he's alright." Emir tries again, not even caring that there's multiple other people in the room who can hear him. He's a private person, but knowing if Theo is sick or hurt or just ignoring him overrides that.

"She's not talking to you." Jordan sets a hand on Emir's elbow to get his attention, giving him a sympathetic smile that he's not sure he deserves. Emir had guessed as much, but now he has confirmation. Lili's like a sister to Theo, so he shouldn't be surprised.

"Neither are you, Jo." Lili's voice is like a wall, and Emir realises he's never heard her truly angry before. They've always gotten along, even before he and Theo were friends and then more. But now, it's like he's dead to her, not even worth acknowledging.

"Emi's just worried." Jordan answers, letting Lili storm past them without even a glance in Emir's direction. When she's through the studio door, Jo gives Emir the only answer she has. "He'll be alright. Laurie and the others are looking after him."

"I fucked up." Emir admits, his voice low even though they're alone in the studio now. Everyone else is eager to go home for the night, to rest before another long day tomorrow. But Emir is grateful to Jordan for sharing what she knows, giving him even a minute of her time when she could easily be acting like Lili has been. Jo may be a newer friend to Theo, but she respects him and how much his friendship means to Lilibet, which should put Emir on her shit list.

"I know." Jordan gives his elbow a squeeze, tentatively dropping her hand and giving him a hug instead. She can tell he's doing terribly, from the way he looks physically to the lack of his usual spark. Jordan's never seen him look less...alive. "He'll be alright. You'll figure it out."

Emir hugs her back, realising that his friendship with both Lili and Jordan is also thanks to Theo, and that he would be entirely alone in this moment if Theo had never brought them all together. When he remembers that, Emir hugs her back properly, hoping she understands his gratitude. "Thanks. And I'm sorry."

"I know." Jordan repeats. They understand each other better than the others sometimes, even if most of it goes unsaid. He wishes he'd let himself get to know her years ago. He should have gotten to know her and so many of the wonderful people in Theo's life that have let him in recently, too. Quietly, she suggests, "Maybe check your phone."

He wonders how she knows that he hasn't so much as looked at it since last night except to silence his alarm this morning. Emir still has a complicated relationship with his phone, even if it wasn't a direct trigger this time. He wasn't sure that he was ready to read texts from all of their friends yelling at him, telling him exactly how badly he fucked up, because he already knows and he doesn't need the reminder. Last time his phone scared him, he ran to Theo, who welcomed him with open arms, even in the middle of *yet another* fight. Jesus fucking hell. Why had Theo ever agreed to be with him?

"Give it some time." Jordan steps away from the hug, grabbing her own things from the floor to go home with Lili. She can deal with Lili's annoyance at her breach of the stalemate just fine, knowing that she'll get over it. "Lili's just being protective and Theo's had a rough day."

"Should I - " Emir starts to ask, biting at his lower lip and realising it's already chewed raw with no memory of having done so.

"No. Not tonight." Jordan pulls a jumper over her head, needing to stay warm for the walk home before she can ease her sore muscles with a very hot, steamy shower. "You have to get your own head right first, Emi."

Emir nods, watching her go until he's alone again. But he doesn't want to go home, knowing he'd either run into Laurie and get flayed alive for what he's done, or be alone with his thoughts which...aren't great right now. So, he leaves the rehearsal studio and walks to the opposite end of the building, setting himself up in the practice studio to work through what they blocked in rehearsal all afternoon.

All he wanted was to be alone, and now that he is, he's never been more miserable.

One pirouette turns into ten, one run-through into a dozen, Emir spiralling, pushing his body even further and ignoring that it might break. Dance is the only way he knows how to think, his foundation while everything else is crumbling. Jordan's right that he's not in a place to try to fix anything after just a day. He's still working through too many internal obstacles to have any hope of making things right. Theo deserves him to be his best self, or at least on an intentional path to getting there.

If Theo forgives him, he doesn't want it to be after an empty apology. When Emir promises Theo it won't happen again, he wants to mean it. And he has a lot of thinking to do to make that true.

***

"Theo?" T knocks softly on Theo's bedroom door, pushing it open and slipping inside without turning on the light.

It looks like Theo's asleep again - or maybe still - huddled under his blankets with his sleep mask hiding his eyes. He's been wearing a few of Emir's things all day, another anomaly, because he slept in dirty clothes last night after Laurie brought him home from the studio. Theo's very particular about showering before bed and having that transition time, and foregoing it was a sign that he wasn't doing well. But this morning he'd crawled inside Emir's hoodie after his shower and that was that, falling back asleep after only a few minutes, his body and mind needing all the rest he can get.

Walking up to Theo's bed, T lays beside him, carefully brushing his hair away from his face while laying mostly on top of him, letting Theo be the little spoon. When Theo has shutdowns, he needs as much comfort as possible to go along with the extra rest and tranquillity. He's warm and sleepy, and if it weren't for the three others waiting for them, T could fall asleep beside Theo until Laurie inevitably, reluctantly wakes them up.

T can feel Theo slowly leaving sleep behind, nuzzling into their gentle fingers and shifting around under the sheets. They give Theo a minute to adjust before asking, "Did you want to get up for family dinner?"

T cautiously removes Theo's sleep mask, letting his eyes calibrate to the semi-darkness of his bedroom. The only light is the small bit sneaking beneath the door that T closed behind them.

Theo rubs at his eyes, turning himself around to hide against T's broad chest and letting himself be held for a minute. He's still exhausted, but he hasn't eaten anything since the reheated soup Laurie brought him around lunch time. Theo tries to focus on anything besides his need to sleep, his stomach grumbling as if it knew what T was asking. He's suddenly ravenous, the need hitting him all at once.

Slowly, Theo nods, still hidden in the safety of T's chest.

"Alright, let's get you up then." T presses a kiss to Theo's forehead, checking his temperature to make sure he doesn't slip into an illness while still going through a shutdown. "No need to get pretty for the lads. Let's just get you across the hall for a wee."

Theo sits up with T's help, yawning and stretching his arms before falling back onto the pillows. He does want to see his friends, but his arms are like lead and his eyes could literally close again at any moment. But then Theo's stomach gurgles again, reminding him how badly he needs to eat something.

"You want your headphones for dinner?" T asks, already hauling Theo up again and to the side of the bed. Theo shakes his head no, leaning heavily on T, glad they understand what he's going through. Laurie does too, of course, just not from the inside like T does.

With T aiding him every step of the way, Theo gets out of his room, blinking against the harsh light of the rest of the flat, and into the loo, neither of them shy as Theo sits to have a wee. Standing is too much work right now. He tucks himself back into his boxers and fixes his joggers, shuffling to the sink and cleaning his hands.

With a nudge, T splashes some cold water on Theo's face, which is honestly an incredible idea. Leaning into his sensory needs is the best way through this. So Theo rinses his face with cold water, the effect rejuvenating while making his skin tingle in the best way. He's awake now, and all he can think about is how hungry he is.

"Teddy!" Ciaran trips as he runs into the table, trying to get to Theo for a hug. He makes it eventually, bruised hip forgotten, squeezing Theo extra tight, as if worried he'll disappear back into his room. "You alright?"

Theo shrugs, giving Ciaran a half smile, which is already more effort than he really planned on. He loves these people and he's doing his best. All the sleep helped, but he's not up for small talk, really. Gabe seems to read his exhaustion, hugging Theo silently once Ciaran's done with him, then letting Theo take his usual seat at the table.

But the problem with Theo's usual seat is that it's directly across from Emir's usual seat, which means he's left staring at it like a beacon of pain, an obvious reminder of last night and the days that preceded it. Emir's gone and Theo doesn't know when or if he'll be back. Theo's been thinking about it whenever he's awake, and they'll need to talk, but he just wants Emir to be alright.

Maybe they've become a bit codependent, or at least Theo has, because when he thinks of every moment of the past few months, every smile, every laugh, every morning and night, Emir is there. It's hard to remember before, and maybe what's happened is as much Theo's fault as Emir's. Or maybe it's no one's fault. He hasn't actually reached a conclusion yet and now isn't the moment, surrounded by his friends at the dinner table.

Laurie fills Theo's plate with pasta without having to be asked, overloading it as if preparing him for hibernation. T smiles, adding a side plate of sauteed veggies, Theo already digging into his food. Who knew sleeping for almost an entire day could be so exhausting? And like the unofficial dad that he is, Laurie gets them all chatting as usual. Theo mostly tunes out but catches the occasional update.

Ciaran and Gabe are busy in the recording studio this week, both of them working hard on long term projects that they hope to use after graduation. They still haven't decided if they're moving to New York, and it seems like a sensitive subject, so none of them ask follow up questions tonight. Laurie and T have a slow week of work, with no shows this weekend or next. Laurie's family is coming to visit soon, so they're trying to catch up on their sleep and their social lives and plan their wedding. From what Theo can gather, they've decided on most of the important aspects, but the small details still need to be sorted. It's a lot for two uni students to manage on top of everything else. But Laurie and T insist on doing everything themselves, wanting their wedding to be *theirs* in every possible way, which makes sense. Theo's never really planned a wedding for himself, his imagined future vague and far away, though it's become more focused lately, both because of Emir and because of their dissertation work.

"Done eating?" T asks Theo, looking between his empty plates and the food left to be shared in the centre of the table. Theo shakes his head for a moment to clear it so he can be present, but that only confuses T who reaches to refill his plate for him. Theo shakes his head again, this time to let T know he's good and not to worry.

"I'm full." Theo mumbles, pushing his plate a few inches away from himself as if to prove his point. T just nods, snuggling up against Laurie while they continue eating. Theo hadn't noticed how quickly he was shovelling down his food, but the rest of them still have half a meal to finish, which unfortunately leaves him stewing in his thoughts without the task of eating to occupy him.

He's staring at Emir's empty seat, wondering if he's alright, hoping he's been able to get the space he needs. Laurie and T decided to stay here for the next few nights, Theo not having told them much, just that Emir needed a break. The crying probably clued them in on the rest. He's checked his phone twice, and all he's missed is a few texts from his family that he decided not to answer until he was feeling better and had a few more "spoons" to dedicate.

Laurie texted Lili to give her an idea of where Theo was and not to worry, so he has a few texts from her as well. And this morning, T helped Theo type a short email to Sean letting the dance professors know that he was ill and wouldn't be in class for a day or so. Theo had an email back almost immediately telling him to take his time and to rest as long as he needs.

But nothing from Emir.

Emir's probably not on his phone. He likely has it turned off entirely if not ignored at the bottom of his dance bag or discarded in his room. Even when things were good, Emir wouldn't spend much time on his phone compared to the rest of them. And with how contentious technology has been in Emir's past, Theo wouldn't be surprised if he's sworn it off entirely until he's taken the space he needs.

Theo's hurt, massively confused and trying to figure out a way forward, but he knows Emir didn't hurt him intentionally. He's important to Emir, and he loves that Emir values his relationships with his family and friends (and hopefully Theo) above everything else. If he got to the point of cutting everyone off, Theo knows he's not doing well. But, he also can't do anything to help, especially when he's in his own state at the moment.

Should he go back to class tomorrow? Will Emir be there? If he is there, do they talk? Or would that interrupt the break? He's almost positive Emir's in class even if Theo needs a day off. Probably two days. The more Theo thinks about it, the more sure he is that tomorrow would be too soon to be back in class. But Emir needs dance like he needs oxygen, and skipping class wouldn't help him. Or at least, Theo doesn't think it would.

But if Emir's in class, why isn't he here tonight? It's family dinner. Is he busy in the studio? What is he working on? Did he remember to take a break to eat first? Maybe he's just at his own flat, drawing or painting or some other outlet to process his feelings. But why isn't he here?

Theo's not missed a single family dinner in more than two years, and neither have the others. Even if they're sick, they lay on the sofa and let their friends worry over them until they're sufficiently coddled. It's what it means to be family. And even if they're on a break from each other, does that mean Emir thinks he has to avoid all of their friends too? Should Theo tell him somehow that he doesn't have to choose, that Theo will keep to himself and not interfere? Would he be able to handle seeing Emir less than a day after being left behind like that? Why did Emir leave him all alone? He knows why, but *why*? Why is he able to go to class but can't sit through dinner with the people who care about him most? Where is that hurt hidden inside of Emir and why won't he let them help? Theo's his boyfriend, shouldn't he be there right now?

But Emir asked for space, and Theo respects Emir's agency, even when it hurts.

"Theo?" Laurie's voice gets his attention, along with the hand placed over his own where it's curling into a fist, over and over again, tensing and releasing, wrist on the table. Laurie carefully relaxes Theo's hand with his fingers, giving him his own hand to squeeze instead, reminding him he's not alone.

They're all looking at Theo in concern, four sets of worried eyes assessing him from head to toe as if they could figure him out. But it's not that simple, especially with Theo. T would have the best chance but the others just see that he's upset. They don't understand that it's like physical pain, that his body and mind completely gave up when it became too much, when he stopped being able to process *anything* and had to focus on the literal basics of survival: rest, food, and water. Everything else is out of reach.

"Theo." It's T's voice this time, much closer as they've walked over to hold him around the shoulders while he cries. Theo isn't sure when he started crying, but it makes sense given the way they're all looking at him and the weight he's feeling. It's similar to last night, when he was so overwhelmed that he didn't realise how his body was outwardly processing because all he could feel was his inner pain.

"He should be here. Emir should be here." Theo wipes at his eyes, frustrated that he can't explain it properly right now.

It's not just about his physical presence, it's about all that space Emir created even before last night. It took three days, at most, for Emir to push him and everyone else away. And the worst part is, Theo knows that Emir didn't want to. He knows he's in pain too. But how does Theo explain that when all he wants right now is to be in his bed, cuddled and safe and rested, waiting for both of them to recover enough to talk it through.

"He's probably still at the studio. Laur - " T knows that Theo won't be able to rest properly until he knows. They decoded at least a portion of what Theo's worried about, knowing he'll be hyperfixating and reasonably anxious about the person he loves most. It's happened with T and Laurie before, if not to this extreme.

T is pretty certain that Theo is struggling with the boundary of respecting Emir's space while also focused on concern for Emir, his comment about how Emir should be here having as much to do with his own emotions as with his concern about Emir's wellbeing. Because if everyone's here, who's taking care of Emir?

"I'll go." Laurie and T share a look, able to communicate more than should be possible in a single glance. Without a second thought, Laurie grabs a Tupperware and starts putting together dinner for Emir to take along, positive that it'll be needed.

"You tired, Theo? You want to sleep or do you want company?" Gabe asks, hand held in Ciaran's under the table. He and Ciaran haven't ever broken up or anything similar, but he understands what it's like to miss his person. They're on separate continents for months sometimes, and feeling like your other half is missing isn't easy, even if you rationally understand why.

"Cuddles and Batman?" Theo asks, leaning back into T for the comfort of their familiar hug. He can't focus on anything and he's not tired enough to fall back asleep yet. But he definitely doesn't want to be alone if there's another option. Theo just needs rest, his comfort items, and his comfort people. And time.

"I'll get the sofa cushions." Ciaran grins from the seat beside Theo, his constancy a reassurance that they're all grateful to have. He's never fake or insincere, and Ciaran's always there when needed. His heart is pure gold, covered in fairy dust and stronger than Irish whiskey. It's no wonder almost everyone falls entirely in love with him from the first moment. And if Ciaran says he's getting the sofa cushions to create a makeshift pillow fort in Theo's room, it's happening. He'll do whatever Theo asks without hesitation or question, one of the most loyal people any of them know.

"Let me clear the table." Gabe adds, because Theo usually takes care of that without having to be asked, and he doesn't want Theo to worry about it tonight. Theo nods his thanks, letting T guide him away from the table and to his room again, appreciative of their support even if they don't really understand what he's feeling.

"Cartoons or one of the modern eras?" T asks, knowing Theo has both readily available. Laurie pauses them to give T a quick kiss, tilting his head towards the door to let them know he's leaving to go check on Emir. Laurie also gives Theo a kiss to his temple for good measure, glad that he and T have been able to step in and help Theo out while he looks after himself. He knows Theo would do the same for any of them, and then some.

"Cartoons and my weighted blanket." Theo answers, turning to smile at Laurie as he walks away.

He can relax again because Laurie would literally walk through fire for Emir, even if he's a little caught in the middle of them right now. If there's anyone who can handle the situation with grace, it's Laurie. Knowing someone he trusts, especially Laurie, is going to check on Emir means that Theo's mind can calm back down and refocus on resting.

***

Laurie: *I know you aren't checking your phone but just in case*
Laurie: *I'm coming by the studio, so consider this a warning if you want to run*
Laurie: *But please don't*
Laurie: *I'm just making sure you're alright*

Laurie knows where to find Emir. When he's happy he goes to his tree, when he's tired he hides in his cave of a bedroom, and when he's in pain he goes to the studio, throwing himself around until his physical state matches his internal conflict. It's not healthy. Emir knows it isn't healthy. But it's what he's always done when things get to be too much. Laurie knows Emir intimately after so many years sharing space, his habits, both good and bad, like second nature to his own.

As expected, when Laurie enters the empty dance building, there's only one light on at the end of the hall, music able to be heard even over the sounds of the outdated structure as it moves and settles beneath his feet. It's a long hallway, giving Laurie plenty of time to think about his approach to the conversation. But as he makes his way to Emir, he supposes it depends what he finds when he walks in the studio.

"Fucking shit, Emir." Laurie stands in the doorway, hands full and staring at his best mate in shock. He looks undone, bruises on both knees where they show beneath his bike shorts, hair completely ruined and held back by a headband, Emir's vest soaked through with sweat which shouldn't even be possible. Without pausing to think, Laurie drops what he's holding and walks to Emir's speaker to turn it off. Standing upright again, he opens his arms to catch Emir as he collapses into Laurie the moment he's in reach. "Shhh it's alright, love. It'll be alright. I've got you."

"I ruined *everything*." Emir cries into Laurie's shoulder, holding him tight as all the exhaustion he's heaped on his body hits him at once. His joints turn to jelly and his muscles unwind, only standing because Laurie's holding him up. All those walls he's been breaking through since yesterday have left him vulnerable and unstable, everything flowing out of him the second he saw Laurie in the doorway.

"It's not ruined. We'll figure it out." Laurie's dealt with crying sisters his whole life, crying T when someone intentionally misgenders them, even crying Theo a handful of times, including last night. But crying Emir breaks his heart.

Emir feels this need to forcefully separate himself when he's struggling, to hide away and never expect help. But the moment someone reaches out he cracks, finally losing his desperate hold of the situation. And this is the worst time that Laurie can remember.

"I hurt Theo." Emir may be in acute physical pain, but he's overwhelmingly worried about Theo. All he can think about is the mixture of hurt, confusion, betrayal, and love that he saw last night as he walked away. It's all he's been able to think about the entire day, from the moment he woke up and forced himself out of bed. "I fucking hurt him, Laur."

"We've been looking after him. He's alright." Laurie reassures Emir, ignoring how sweaty and gross Emir is and letting his fingers brush through the hair at the back of his head. Emir shivers, still holding on to Laurie to stop himself from collapsing.

"Why don't you hate me?" Emir didn't expect Laurie to show up this time. Theo's his best mate and Emir's the fucker who crushed him. Theo didn't even show up for class today, which means he either hates Emir and can't stand to share a room with him, or he's so upset he stayed away from the thing he loves most.

What happened the past few days is exactly what Emir was worried about before they started dating, exactly what he cried about to T and Laurie that night before they became official. Why the hell would Laurie show up to comfort Emir when he's the problem?

"I don't hate you. I could never hate you." Laurie keeps massaging Emir's scalp with his fingertips, his other arm brushing along his back, up and down and up again as Emir's breathing evens out. "I know you love him. You didn't mean for this to happen."

"I just needed to breathe." Emir tries to explain, not making excuses, just agreeing with what Laurie said. He does love Theo, so much it scares him. And he never wanted to let himself get to this point. "I didn't listen to you or to Theo or to anyone. I let it get bad. It's my fault."

Laurie takes a break from talking, focusing on letting Emir relax back to a functional level, waiting for his panic response to subside. Emir loves and appreciates Laurie so fucking deeply, the two of them looking out for each other like siblings separated at birth. If Laurie hadn't shown up tonight, Emir's not sure how much longer he would've kept spiralling, how much further he would've pushed himself, how injured he could've gotten.

This sort of self-loathing, self-destructive behaviour is what he needs to fix and it shouldn't have gotten this bad before he realised it. And beautiful, kind, perfect Theo got caught up in his mess this time, which is making every part of this worse.

"Brought you food." Laurie finally releases Emir, giving his shoulders a firm squeeze before letting his arms drop. "How about we get you home and have a chat?"

He watches as Emir wipes at his eyes, clearing away the tears that didn't soak through Laurie's jumper.

"Yeah, alright." Emir acquiesces, sighing and removing his headband so he can run his own fingers through his hair, wincing at the state of himself. He's filthy and sticky and probably smells like a barn. "Could use a shower."

As a bonus, the idea of a steaming hot shower sounds like heaven to Emir's overworked body.

"You said it, not me." Laurie gives him a small smile, nudging their toes together, Laurie's covered in blue and white striped socks, Emir's bare, blistered, and in need of a rest. "Come on, then. Haven't got all night."

Emir barely returns his smile, groaning when his muscles protest as he packs away his things and tosses a hoodie over himself for the walk back to the flat. "Thanks, Laur."

***

Laurie: I took Emi back home. I think i'll be staying here with him tonight
T: Good because I think I'm Theo's cuddle buddy for the evening
T: /picture of themself and Theo curled up in Theo's bed, Ciaran on Theo's other side/
T: Not enough room for all four of us or I'm sure Gabe and Ciaran would spend the night too
Laurie: Is he doing alright?
T: Yup, but not going to class tomorrow either. He still needs to rest
T: He's loads better than yesterday, or even this morning
T: How's our Emi?
Laurie: Not great, but I've got him
Laurie: I hate seeing the both of them hurting like this
T: Me too /three crying emojis/
T: They'll figure it out, but we can't fix it for them
T: It's hard to watch
Laurie: I love you T
Laurie: Nights like this remind me that you're exactly the kind hearted, caring partner I always hoped to find
Laurie: I knew I needed someone to braid the girls' hair and let me be dramatic and be mates with mum and care as deeply about the world as I do
Laurie: We're both caretakers by nature
Laurie: I can't wait to marry you and make it official /wedding rings emoji/
T: Not soon enough :(I wish we could just be married without worrying so much about the wedding

T: *I still want us to find a middle ground somehow*
T: *I'm yours and you're mine. Why isn't that enough?*
Laurie: *Taxes, mostly*
Laurie: *And the kids we don't have yet <3*
T: *Is Emi alright enough that I can tell Theo?*
T: *He's really worried now that he's awake and more rested*
Laurie: */selfie with Emir/*
Laurie: *Freshly showered and cuddled on the sofa together while he eats*
Laurie: *Tell Theo he's in good hands*
T: *The best*
T: *Love you*
Laurie: *Love you, babygirl*

***

Laurie inhales deeply before passing their shared joint back to Emir, fingertips brushing. Emir takes it gladly, unsure where coping with weed fits on the healthy choices matrix, but it's the most stable he's felt in days. Most of that likely has to do with Laurie and the pasta he got Emir to eat, preceded by a remarkably hot shower. But the weed is playing its part.

"You want to talk tonight or are we just..." Laurie gestures vaguely at the smoke in the air, Emir following his hand like a lure.

Fascinating, the way Laurie's hands manage to look gay at every moment, like his queerness is so inherent that it flows through him. Emir's mind wanders, wondering if that's part of why they bonded so quickly: seeing so much of themselves in the other subconsciously, like their own secret language.

"Dunno." Emir shrugs, handing back the joint and turning his face to Laurie, both of them sitting sideways on their sofa.

He's glad they still share this flat, even with Laurie and T being engaged and everything else that's changed since they initially got thrown together their first year. None of the others would light up in the middle of their flat in the midst of an emotional intervention. Also, it's just nice to have him around. Laurie was the first friend Emir made after his life imploded, and the bond they have will always be stronger as a result.

"You get any sleep last night?" Laurie asks, already knowing the answer based on context clues and shared history.

"Some...not enough." Emir sighs, watching his feet as he stretches out his toes. They're more blistered than usual, which is quite a feat. Emir winces thinking of trying pointe in the next few days, knowing it would be torture. "I think I should take tomorrow off."

"Yeah?" Laurie grins at Emir, his eyes mostly closed over a glimmer in his smile. Sometimes Emir understands how T fell helplessly in love and never looked back. They're all a little bit in love with Laurie, especially when he's all soft and happy and bright. "Good for you."

"Mental health day. I think I need it." Emir feels himself heating, not used to admitting that he's struggling, but given the circumstances it sort of goes unsaid. Acknowledging it aloud *is* quite a step for him though, and he's glad Laurie's a bit high with him. It makes it easier to verbalise. "I think I'll walk over to the counselling team tomorrow and see if they've got room for one more."

With surprising grace, Laurie scrambles across Emir's lap and takes his cheeks in his hands, joint held off to the side to keep them in a green haze. After a moment of staring at each other, Laurie leans in and instead of kissing Emir like he was expecting, Laurie blows a raspberry right across his lips, loud and wet and obnoxious. Emir splutters, pushing at Laurie's chest and laughing for the first time in days. Who the hell is Laurie Tempest and why is he like this?

"Ugh, that's disgusting, Laurie!" Emir swats him away, Laurie leaning down to smack another raspberry to his cheek, unrelenting in his attack. Emir starts to flush with annoyance and Laurie cackles with pride. "You're so gay and loud!"

"WHAT?!" Laurie shouts, switching to even him out on the other cheek, even sloppier. He leaves a wet mark behind, Emir's few days of stubble glistening with it as he pulls back. "COULDN'T HEAR YOU, MATE!"

"Laurie!" Emir laughs so hard he feels tears in his eyes, his abs clenching while he tries to catch his breath. Laurie is absolutely ridiculous and Emir loves him with his entire heart. How did he get so lucky to find a best mate in Laurie completely by chance? "Laur, I can't breathe."

Emir's laughing and smiling and feeling like a *person*, all thanks to his messy gay angel of a flatmate.

When Laurie finally seems satisfied with Emir's reaction, sitting back on his heels but still in Emir's lap, Emir asks, "What was that for?"

He leans his head back against the sofa, hands still on Laurie's chest so he can't restart his slobbery antics.

"Proud of you." Laurie shrugs, licking his bottom lip and winking before climbing back off of Emir and settling at his side. He holds the last semblance of the joint up to Emir's lips, waiting for him to finish it off before putting it out in the ashtray T made for their flat early last year in a pottery class. Apparently, if they were going to smoke in the flat, they needed proper equipment. "I don't love the circumstances, but I know how hard it is to reach out."

"Haven't done it yet. But I will. Can't keep going like this." Emir sighs again, hand coming up to cover his eyes. He's so unbelievably tired, but he can't go to sleep yet. His mind is still -

"You want to know how Teddy's doing?" Laurie asks, somehow always able to read him.

What Emir keeps forgetting is that he's only ever cared about one person the way he does Theo, and it's crystal clear to everyone around him. Laurie saw their connection years ago, the tension below their bickering, the gravity that kept them close. And now that they've both gone and fallen in love, it's even more obvious, the two of them going through their own struggles at the moment but still indelibly linked.

"I shouldn't have left him." Emir leans forward, face in his hands as he groans. "I should've walked him home before I ran away. Anything but just fucking *abandoning* him in the middle of the studio."

He's had time to examine the events of the night before and this is what he keeps coming back to. Emir needed space but he shouldn't have imploded like that, making Theo collateral damage. Theo's told him before that what he worries about most is being left behind or forgotten, that he'll be too much for Emir to handle, and that's exactly how Emir made him feel. He made one of Theo's worst fears a reality.

"You're right. That wasn't the best." Laurie puts a hand on Emir's back, rubbing between his shoulder blades consolingly. He won't lie and say what happened was alright, especially as he's been watching the aftermath since last night.

"I was just...panicked. Couldn't think straight." Emir's hands are in his hair now, tugging at it until he feels Laurie stop him and pull him back upright instead.

"To be fair, you've never been able to think straight." Laurie gives him a small smile, hand on his knee while waiting for the joke to land. When Emir gets it he scoffs, leaning his shoulder into Laurie for a cuddle. Laurie isn't wrong about that.

"I won't let it get that bad again, I swear. Theo's too important. If he even wants me back." Emir remembers that heartbreaking moment, when Theo thought Emir wanted to end their relationship, as if it wasn't the best thing that's ever happened to him. As if Theo isn't the moon, the stars, and the entire night sky of Emir's world.

"He didn't go anywhere. He's just...processing what happened in his own way." Laurie chooses his words carefully, wanting Theo to be the one to explain what he's going through in his own words rather than putting the situation through his own lens and speaking over him, even to Emir.

"But he's alright?" Emir looks up to meet Laurie's kind eyes, his own pleading for an answer he isn't sure he deserves. "He'll be alright?"

"He'll be alright." Laurie nods, pulling out his phone to show Emir the picture T had sent a short while ago of their little group curled up in Theo's room together. "T wouldn't let anything happen to him. They're spending the night just to be sure, but Theo's already feeling better than this morning."

"He skipped class. He's never skipped class." Emir gingerly takes Laurie's phone, this picture of Theo something he needs to examine and memorise. It's been an entire day since he's seen those kind eyes, that curly hair, a whole day since he had Theo's beautiful laugh and warm hugs. And Emir needed the space, but he's got to find a balance. No more of this all or nothing bullshit he's been going through the past few years.

"He was shut down. Slept almost the entire day." Laurie takes his phone back to show Emir another picture instead, this one of Emir and Theo from last weekend. It's a picture that Emir didn't even know existed, with Theo in his lap and the two of them laughing at something together with stars in their eyes. "But he loves you, mate. Like...an unreal amount. Maybe more than you love him."

"Impossible." Emir says a little too quickly, flushing at the look Laurie gives him, a combination of understanding and exasperation. "He's who I want, more than I want anything. I love dance and my art and all the things that make my life beautiful. But Laurie..."

Emir looks down at his hands, his fingers fiddling while he tries to find the words. "He's shown me that life is so much more than that. Those things are important, but one day of separation and I realise it'd be empty without...everyone. Theo and you and T and my family and the rest of our friends. I thought if I just shut everyone out, I'd find some mysterious peace, but all I found was pain. I need both. I can't expect to be happy without the balance. And I don't think I would've understood that without Theo. He's like...wicked smart. His heart is just..." Emir makes a vague sound of admiration, Theo beyond words.

"He's a pretty special person." Laurie confirms, fingers moving through Emir's hair again to give it a ruffle. "But you know something?"

Laurie drops his hand back to his lap and waits for Emir to look up at him with a question in his eyes. "So are you."

Emir thought he was done with the crying for today, but apparently not. He sniffles, tugging Laurie into a hug before the two of them collapse in a pile on the sofa, Laurie offering Emir company until he falls asleep. Gently, Laurie wakes him up and gets him into his room, both of them huddling under the sheets of Emir's bed. They used to do this often their first year, when they were both barely adults, sharing gossip and fears and joy after nights out, talking about the world and their families and their hopes for the future. It's so different now, years of life shared in between, but they're still like kittens curling up beside the fire for a winter nap.

They sleep facing each other, hair messy on the pillows and breathing even, safe from the storm together. Laurie watches over Emir so he can rest safe in the knowledge that he'll have support while he figures this all out. Maybe Theo isn't the only one afraid of being left behind, and maybe that's part of why everything fell apart so dramatically.

Emir doesn't cry through his sleep tonight, instead dreaming of what could come next, playing out scenarios for his apologies and more than anything thinking of the future. A future that includes Theo, god willing, so clear it's in 4k. Theo's the sky and he's Theo's earth and if he makes this right, they can get back to building that sunrise.

CHAPTER FIVE

Theo wakes up on Thursday without his alarm, feeling refreshed and peaceful as his eyes flutter open. Immediately he's aware that T spent the night, curled up beside him and snoring gently, their body not as accustomed to such an early wake up time. Theo feels a combination of emotions flow through him at the sight: lingering sadness that it's not Emir spooning him, then gratitude for T and the way they support him, even in this. Before they fell asleep, T showed him a picture of Laurie and Emir back in their flat, assuring Theo that Laurie was spending the night there, which gave Theo the peace of mind he needed to rest.

Starting to squirm around under the covers, Theo wonders how similar the two of them spent their night, a few buildings apart. Maybe Emir sought the comfort of a friend and is on his way to feeling better, too. Theo's awake and calm and missing Emir, but he's alright with it. He just needed the time to process and let his heart settle. Now, he waits.

As with any morning, Theo stretches around in bed to urge his body awake, pointing and flexing his toes, rolling his ankles, arms pushed above his head while he yawns wide. Compared to the last two days, he feels like a new person. It's not that everything's fixed or magically better, but he can tell he's finally rested, no longer overstimulated or shut down. Theo's still not ready to go to class, but he's stable. He needs today to reset, reschedule, and sit in his peace before going back to his usual routine.

"Teddy?" T mumbles around a yawn, their green eyes squinting at him in the early morning light. "Done sleeping?"

"Yeah. Done sleeping." Theo smiles, facing T and watching as they rub at their tired eyes. He thinks T is asking about more than just sleep, wondering if Theo's done needing to hide in his nest and reset. Either way, his answer is the same. "You stay here and sleep, alright? I'm just going to do my normal Theo stuff."

"Normal Theo stuff." T repeats, burrowing back into the sheets with another yawn. They reach out a hand and ruffle Theo's hair with their careful fingertips, barely awake but distracted by Theo's bedhead. "Fluffy."

"So are you." Theo does the same to T, tousling their curls with another smile. The way he is with T is how he always imagined it would feel to have a younger sibling. He's got his older sisters of course, but he never got to be a big brother. "Laurie's hair never fluffs like ours. Emir's does a bit."

"Laur's a kitten." T's eyes start closing again with a relaxed grin while thinking about their fiance. "Emi and Laurie are kittens. Grumpy little gay kittens. Squirmy, too."

"Yeah." Theo giggles when T starts snoring again, barely able to stay awake, even to talk about Laurie. They must truly be exhausted.

With a deep breath in, Theo gets up from his bed, careful to tuck the sheets back around T so they can get a few more hours of rest. It's later than Theo usually sleeps on a weekday, and he's not ready to be back in the dance studio yet, especially the practice studio. But the gym sounds nice, just his usual morning workout to get his body moving after a day of rest. So, after having a morning wee and brushing his teeth, Theo dresses himself in his usual gym attire, adding Emir's hoodie on top for comfort before leaving his flat to walk across campus.

It's sort of nice, spending a day like this. He's still awake earlier than most people, but the sun rises while he's on the treadmill for his ten minute cardio warmup and he watches it with a renewed appreciation. It's London, so the sunrise is mostly just the gradual ability to see the outdoors. But the way it reveals the world slowly is reminiscent of how he always opens his Christmas presents, one millimetre at a time, careful so he doesn't miss a single detail. That's what Theo loves about having the sunrise accompany his morning routine.

What eventually distracts Theo from the serenity is exactly the sort of surprise he wants to take his time with.

Outside the gym's wall of windows, Theo sees a familiar figure on their morning run, silky black hair buried beneath a borrowed grey beanie, hands covered in well-loved homemade mittens, their eyes tired but bright. Seeing Emir like this, completely by accident but at a distance, is the perfect way for Theo to process the moment. He doesn't have to think of what to say or how to act. Theo can just let his body run along his unmoving track while Emir mirrors his actions in his own way on his own path.

Emir looks alright, from what Theo can tell. Tired and contemplative, but more like himself than he has been for days. And he's wearing Theo's beanie, just like how Theo's been wearing Emir's hoodie nonstop since the other night.

Emir doesn't see Theo, too focused on keeping to his path around campus. But for fifteen glorious seconds, Theo gets to appreciate Emir from afar, allowing himself to process everything he's feeling and let it pass through him, a trail of love and contentment left behind as he gives up on running to start his weight training instead. He's still sad about how things happened, but the sting of that night is gone.

Theo's always been able to do this, if given the time and space he needs. He can contextualise and see the larger picture, even if all he can feel in the moment is overwhelming emotion. It's definitely part of being autistic, at least for Theo, and understanding that when he was a teenager, when everything was just too much all the time and he knew why the bullies were targeting him even if they didn't, gave him the mental space to process that experience.

This situation is nothing like that. Emir hurt him, but it wasn't intentional and Theo knows there was as much love behind what happened as there was Emir's own need for solitude. Emir pushed himself too far because he loves Theo, not in spite of it, and seeing him this morning, at a literal distance, puts that into very clear perspective for Theo.

Maybe changing his routine isn't always bad. Maybe he needs more room for whimsy, like Emir had once suggested. Maybe he should spend the rest of the day thinking of all the things he's always wanted to try and never allowed himself the chance. It's a new day in more ways than one, and Theo's actually excited about it. Another gift given to him by Emir that he wasn't aware of until this moment. Christmas is overrated, he decides. Maybe next year he'll celebrate the fourth of November instead. Hopefully with Emir by his side.

***

"Tell me I can do this." Emir stares straight ahead at the wooden door in front of him, the task of walking inside suddenly insurmountable. Once he's inside, there's things he has to say. Questions to ask. Decisions to be made.

"You can definitely do this." Laurie sets a hand on Emir's shoulder, letting him do things at his speed and in his own way. "I'm just here to remind you of that."

"What if they say I'm fine? What if they think I'm being dramatic and wasting their time?" Emir still can't make his arm move to open the door to the student resources building. The knowledge that the student counselling office is inside has him stuck outside instead, feet no longer cooperating with forward movement.

"They won't say that, love. And you're not fine." Laurie reminds him, hand giving his shoulder a squeeze but not leaving. "You're my best mate, but you're not fine. Remember what you told me last night."

"It's just - how do I - " Emir turns to look at Laurie, glad they chose to do this first thing in the morning before Laurie has to head to class, because if he'd walked over here alone, he would've kept right on walking, past the building and back around until he got home. "I'm not used to - and, like, what if they're homophobic or some shit?"

Laurie isn't quite sure where all of those half-finished sentences were headed, but he understood the vibe. "Then we find you someone new. They're professionals. They'll understand if you ask to speak with someone else who might be better for you."

"I don't know how to do this." Emir tries again, chewing on his bottom lip which he has a habit of doing when he's nervous. He doesn't just mean he doesn't know how to go about making the appointment.

It's the asking for help, admitting he can't handle everything on his own, letting people in, because he's learned that makes him vulnerable. His circle of trust is less than ten people, and adding another person is a huge ordeal.

"You're doing fine. Today's just making the appointment, yeah? Getting your name in their calendar." Laurie smiles when Emir nods, staring at his feet and falling quiet to internally talk himself into doing what he knows he needs to do.

Emir thinks back to that awful moment in the studio, the way Theo had collapsed, the look on his face when Emir left, the way it hollowed Emir out to hurt Theo while feeling like he didn't have any other choice.

That's enough for Emir to sigh in acceptance, reaching out to open the door and letting Laurie follow him inside. He feels an encouraging hand in the middle of his back steering him in the correct direction. Emir's been standing in the doorway without actually getting anywhere because he's still seeing Theo's crumpled, crying face in his mind's eye. Never again.

"Right. Over there then." Emir's feet finally start moving.

Laurie nods, hand still warm on Emir's back so he's less tempted to run. But if he truly isn't ready, Laurie would walk back home with him. There's no point in Emir being here if he isn't at a place to ask for the help he needs.

"I don't like that sign." Emir mumbles to Laurie once they reach the office, a poster next to the entryway full of bright colours and abstract figures posed as if having a conversation.

It's probably supposed to depict what happens inside these offices. But it's pedestrian and mass-produced and everything Emir avoids. Sure, it's technically art, probably made by a person and not AI, but it doesn't have any life. What the fuck is the point? Just don't display anything.

"We can't all be undercover artists." Laurie laughs softly. The sign is a bit juvenile, but not outright offensive. Just boring, maybe. But Emir gets moody about this sort of thing, refusing to pass it by without a comment, no matter where they are. It's sort of hopeful to Laurie, that Emir's alright enough to notice and point it out as they walk inside. "They look nice. Try starting with them."

Emir looks where Laurie's indicating, some sort of receptionist or assistant watching them walk inside with a smile. He tries to send one back, but it probably looks painful based on how forced it feels. This is more difficult than he anticipated, but that's why he has Laurie here.

"Can I help you?" The person asks as they get closer to the desk. Emir glances down to see that their name plate reads *Dylan*. They must be accustomed to nervous visitors because Emir's apprehension doesn't seem to phase them in the slightest.

"I was sort of wondering if - I mean, it's alright if you can't - but I think I might need an appointment?" Emir brushes his hand through his hair, watching them expectantly for some sign of judgement or reproach, but it never comes. Dylan just nods and clicks something on their computer before answering.

"You're in the right place. Is it an emergency or should I be looking to plan around your class schedule?" Dylan has this serenity that immediately calms Emir down, a sort of grey-blue vibe that permeates the reception area. He understands why they're the one greeting students who come in looking for help.

"Um, not an emergency. But I was hoping maybe tomorrow? Or next week?" Emir looks at Laurie to confirm. He gets a gentle nod in reply before Laurie wanders off to examine the desktop water fountain a few foot away, giving Emir privacy without leaving him behind.

"Just for you, or will the both of you be needing an appointment together?" Dylan clarifies, already opening something on their computer that Emir can't see. Probably a schedule for the available counsellors over the next few days if he had to guess.

"Just me. Laurie came along to make sure I made it through the door. I'm a bit nervous." Emir admits, smiling at Dylan. It's small, but honest this time, and he's glad to see Dylan smile back.

"I get it. I still bring my partner to the dentist with me. Never quite outgrew the fear of that place." Dylan shrugs, their acceptance of Emir's anxiety putting him more at ease. "Can I have your name? That way I can see your uni schedule and compare it to the counsellors on campus tomorrow."

Emir gives Dylan his name, student number, and area of study, taking the time to look around at the space and get used to it. If he's going to be here for regular visits, he supposes it could be worse. There's comfy chairs scattered around and the hallway to the offices has a few skylights that keep the place lit without the stark overhead lighting of most of the other areas of campus. It's very zen in a way that he would find infuriatingly dull in other contexts. But here, it works.

"Do you mind sharing a bit of what you're hoping to see someone about? There's a few people available tomorrow because it's Friday." Dylan removes their hands from their keyboard and lowers their voice a touch in case Emir doesn't want Laurie to overhear. They're otherwise alone since it's still early in the day.

"I sort of had this breakdown the other day. Like, I'm alright, but everything was just too much and I have a bit of, um, a bit of trauma from a past relationship. And...yeah." Emir fiddles with the cup of pens in front of him just for something to do with his hands. "I saw someone after it happened, but it's been a few years."

"I'm sorry to hear that, but thank you for sharing. I'm sure it must be hard to talk about, especially with a stranger." Dylan waits for Emir to glance at them again before continuing so that he can tell that they mean it. "Do you have a preference for the gender of your counsellor? Or religion or that sort of thing? All of our counsellors are happy to meet with anyone, but it's normal for students to have preferences."

"I hadn't really thought about that. Sort of just...showed up and didn't plan past that." Emir gives Dylan another small smile. "Anyone's fine."

"How about tomorrow morning during your free hour?" Dylan glances at the calendar again to double check that it's available.

"Yeah, that's...yup. Tomorrow, then." Emir looks at Laurie, silently asking him to come back and comfort him again now that it's more real. Of course Laurie understands immediately, walking back over with his hands in his pockets. "Do I need to do any sort of paperwork or anything?"

"I'll send it to your student email. If you don't have time before tomorrow, that's alright." Dylan types a few things while Emir waits, Laurie putting an arm around his shoulders and giving him a squeeze. "If you need anything before then, you know where to find me. Otherwise, I'll see you tomorrow morning."

"That's it?" Emir tilts his head, chewing on his bottom lip again and shoving his hands in his pockets, mirroring Laurie subconsciously.

"That's it." Dylan confirms, giving him another of their tranquil smiles.

"Thanks, I'll just, um..." Emir looks at Laurie, surprised it took him less than two minutes to get over this seemingly mountainous obstacle. He just had to answer a few questions and Dylan took care of the rest. "Tomorrow, then. Thanks, Dylan."

Laurie waits until they're outside again to pull Emir into a hug, arms tight around his back. He's such a good hugger, and Emir appreciates it most in moments like these. Laurie's voice is warm when he asks, "Weren't too bad, yeah?"

Emir nods, still holding tight to Laurie. He releases any lingering nerves with a huff, relaxing and enjoying the fresh air before letting him go. "Think you could walk over with me again tomorrow? It's alright if - "

"Don't even start with that shit. I'll be there." Laurie nudges him with his elbow before pulling him into a headlock. "Now, let's get you back to the flat so I have time to swallow my fiance's cock before class."

"Didn't need to know that." Emir shoves Laurie away before taking off at a sprint to race home, Laurie right behind him.

***

Theo's having a really nice morning. He went to the gym, then back home to indulge in a large breakfast of french toast and eggs, with one of his green juices to balance out the sweets. And now he's wandering around campus, an entirely different experience at this time of day. Usually, when he and Emir go on their walks, it's afternoon at the earliest, usually evening or on the weekends because of their long days in the dance studio. He's seeing the full breadth of the student population at this time of day. He knows a few of the students he walks by, people he hasn't seen much because they have different areas of study, but there's a friend of Gabe's and a classmate of T's and others he recognises from more than two years spent at Roseborough. It's humbling to remember that his own experience here is just one of literally thousands, that he and his closest friends are peripheral to almost everyone here, in the same way they are to them. Sometimes, it's refreshing to feel part of a whole rather than the main character.

He stops occasionally to take pictures of different plants and creatures that he sees, wishing Emir was there to tell him what they are and what they do and all his interesting science facts that he knows. Emir being a nerd is one of Theo's favourite things about him, especially because Theo loves to learn deeply about anything and everything he can. Theo knows that Emir's told him about this tree before, but he can't remember what it is. The Latin names are harder for Theo to remember, but he loves hearing Emir sound them out for him, even when he knows Theo won't retain it. Over the course of his walk, Theo collects about a dozen pictures to ask Emir about, keeping them for when things are settled and they're talking again. He doesn't think he's supposed to text him while he needs space unless it's something important, and this can wait.

Just as he's rounding the corner back to his flat, Theo sees Laurie leaving his building. He hasn't seen Laurie since family dinner last night, so he must've stopped by to say hello to T before class.

"Laurie!" Theo jogs to catch up to him, hoping to borrow a moment of his day before he leaves.

"It's good to see you out and about." Laurie lets Theo fold him into one of his bear hugs. So many cuddles for Laurie this morning, between Emir and then T and now Theo. Maybe he should circle back and join Gabe and Ciaran in bed, because somehow the two of them managed to have no morning classes this year and they get to sleep in as late as they want. The well rested bastards.

"I feel better today." Theo steps out of the hug, tugging the fabric of his shirt away from his neck. He's still wearing Emir's hoodie and he notices Laurie's eyes flicker down to it with a knowing smile. "Just wanted to see you before you leave for class."

"Course. I'll always have time for you, mate." Laurie pulls on one of the hoodie strings before tossing it at Theo with a grin. "What's your plan for your day off?"

"Mostly...this." Theo shrugs, hands tucking themselves away in the kangaroo pouch of the hoodie to keep them warm. It's not actually *cold* today but it's chilly. December isn't exactly summer. "Emir, um, he told me once that I don't indulge my whimsy. Like, those exact words. And he was right. I need to make time for that when I can, try new things just for fun, so I'm just sort of..."

Laurie watches Theo closely as he mentions Emir, but he doesn't see any of the overwhelming pain from a few nights ago. Maybe a bit of hesitation, but mostly Theo seems to have his Emir face, where he gets all squishy and smiley and giggly just thinking about him. "He really cares about you, Teddy. I know things got a bit fucked but you're in his heart so deep you're at his core."

"Is he alright?" Theo asks, staring intensely at Laurie so he can properly gauge his answer. Seeing Emir through the window this morning was a nice surprise, but it wasn't enough to satisfy his worry. He knows exactly how sensitive and hurt Emir can get, especially if one of his loved ones is also hurting. He's surely been going through it at least as badly as Theo.

"The two of you, honestly." Laurie shakes his head, reaching out to ruffle Theo's curls fondly. "Both of you keep asking me about the other, which is dead sweet, but it's just so..."

Laurie sighs, surprising Theo by darting forward to kiss him on the temple. "I'm not worried about the two of you. You've always been so connected, even before you started in with all the boyfriend stuff. And yes, he's alright. Just taking some time to get himself right before he comes back to you."

"So he's, um, he still wants to do...all the boyfriend stuff?" Theo uses Laurie's phrasing to ask. He knows that Emir said he didn't want to break up, but he's had a few days to think and that could've changed.

"Definitely, definitely. He wouldn't string you along like that." Laurie watches Theo's shoulders relax at the confirmation. As if Emir would ever voluntarily let go of his princess. "Just give him a bit more time. And focus on your whimsy or whatever the fuck you said earlier."

"Alright. Thanks." Theo leans forward for another hug. He's had plenty of cuddles from everyone while he hasn't been feeling well, but he still feels a little extra needy, especially for human connection. There's one person's presence he's acutely missing, but he loves his friends, too. Not a day goes by that he isn't grateful for them, especially after growing up with hardly anyone outside his family willing to get to know him. "I'll see you tonight?"

"Probably. We're staying at T's flat again to give Emi alone time. Your flat too, but you know what I mean." Laurie steps away, ready to leave for class. "Do something gay today, yeah?"

Theo laughs, because of course Laurie would end their conversation on a gay note. "Bye, Laurie."

With a middle finger flipped over his shoulder, Laurie leaves Theo to finish his walk and get on with the rest of his day.

***

Emir's been busy in his kitchen since noon and it's approaching five in the evening. It's such a strange feeling, for it to not be a weekend and to knowingly not be in the studio, an entire day abstaining from his life's purpose. He had, of course, let Sean know that he was taking the day off, and he received a very kind, concerned response about taking his time to rest and to let Sean know if he needed more than a few days. But Emir's sure he'll be back in the studio tomorrow, so he relays that in his reply, grateful for Sean as both mentor and advisor.

Faffing about in the kitchen was Emir's attempt to get out of his own head, to be creative and use his hands and, for once, not rely on his visual art. He loves to cook when he has the time, but he never really has that time because of dance. So far this afternoon, he's made cham cham (because he absolutely plans to offer it to Theo in a few days) and kheer for desserts, and he's still working on vegetable samosas and paneer masala as savoury options. He'd usually make both meals with chicken, but Theo's vegetarian and he's started to adjust by proximity. Emir really doesn't mind, his favourite dishes delicious either way, and able to be shared because he's cooking enough for a family of about half a dozen.

Maybe missing family dinner last night is floating through his subconscious because it wasn't even planned, but he noticed the quantities when he was halfway through his preparations. He hadn't realised how important those weekly meals had become, but missing last night's was hard, on top of everything else.

As comfortable as Emir is in the kitchen, there's only one person he can call to make sure he's getting everything right, from the consistency of the kheer to the dough for the samosas, and who can also be a sounding board for everything else in his life. So while he's still working his way through his savoury dishes, he dials the home phone, hoping his mum is doing the same thing a few hours north in Shipley.

"Emi!" It's not his mum who answers, but Saima, his youngest sister having picked up after only two rings when she recognised the caller ID. "We miss you! I saw a dog today and it was so tiny. It was, like, the size of Buddy's paw! I got to hold it and it licked my cheek!"

"Wow, Saima. That sounds adorable." Emir can't help the smile that splits his face while he stirs the spices into his vegetable mixture that's simmering on the stove. Saima is at that age where everything is a miracle, and maybe that's not such a bad thing. It's nice to have the reminder. "I miss you too. You have a good day at school?"

"The best! I had double art class because Miss Florence was out sick." Saima's voice moves in and out of focus, so she must be running around or doing something that keeps her hand jostling the phone. Emir can only guess based on how hyper his sister can get after school. "I'll have mum text you pictures. I might even be better than you."

"I'll bet you are. You've always been good with art." Emir sets aside his stirring spoon to lean back against the countertop and focus on the call. "Is mum home?"

"Muuuum!" Saima yells right next to the receiver, quite loud if Emir's being honest. Their house is definitely not large enough for that level of shouting, but she's a kid. He remembers those years. "Emi wants to talk to you!! - She's in the kitchen, one sec."

And then the sound cuts out entirely and there's a clatter, so he assumes she must've dropped the phone on the counter for his mum to pick up when her hands are free. And sure enough, "Hello, my sunshine! This is a lovely surprise."

"Hi, mum." Emir's overcome with emotion at the sound of her voice. There's an ache for a childhood he's left behind, where he could hide away in her embrace until the world stopped being scary or the problems too big. But he's not a kid anymore, and he's just glad he can still call her and have a chat. "If you're busy I can call back this weekend or whatever..."

"I always have time for you, Emi." Natalie's voice is soft as velvet, a reminder of home and comfort and so much that he's been missing. "Aren't you meant to be in rehearsal?"

"Yeah, I sort of, um, needed a day off. I'll be back tomorrow." Emir turns to the stove and lowers the heat when he hears the unmistakable sound of boiling liquid. Boiling is about ten degrees too hot. "Spent most of the day in the kitchen. Reminds me of home."

"Is everything alright? You not feeling well? I can have Safiya bring you something." Natalie is immediately concerned. She knows beyond a shadow of a doubt that Emir wouldn't skip dance if it could be avoided.

"I'm alright. Or...I will be. Mental health day, like." Emir sighs, running his fingers through his hair and pulling a chair over into the kitchen so he can sit while they talk but still be able to monitor the stove. "I sort of let things get bad and needed a break. But it's good to hear your voice."

"Did you want to talk about it? Food's in the oven, so I have plenty of time." Natalie sounds like she's settling in at the kitchen table, the familiar noises of the kettle being turned on and a chair being pulled out audible in the background.

"I just pushed myself too far. Didn't give myself space. You know how I get. I'm a monster when I don't have my alone time. Especially since...well, you remember." Emir sighs again, standing up to search the cupboards because a cup of chai sounds incredible right now. "But I'm actually going to see someone tomorrow. Made an appointment with the uni counsellor."

"You're not a monster, love. You just need space to breathe. You always have, even before. And you know what the last therapist told you." Natalie knows what to say to calm Emir's mind. She's understanding without being patronising. He really wishes he could cuddle up to her on the sofa right about now and have a cuppa together while waiting for the others to show up and join them. Nowadays, that only happens around

Christmas, and maybe once or twice during the summer. "It's not always rational, the way your body is going to react."

"I sort of…imploded. At Theo. Well, Theo was there. He tried to warn me. So did Laurie. They both know me better than I know myself, I think. But…yeah. I *never* want that to happen again." Emir takes his time getting out his chai and measuring everything he uses to make it just right. Green tea is his usual choice, but a double spice masala chai is what he needs sometimes, his mum's handwriting on an old scrap of paper a reminder of love even if it's not needed for the ingredient list anymore. "It made me realise how much I miss you and the girls. Baba too, of course. Is he home?"

"Not yet. On his way, I expect." Natalie is so patient with Emir, letting him share what's on his mind and in his heart without interruption. Emir might be biased, but he thinks she's the best mum in the world. "You said you're in the kitchen? What's on the menu?"

That's how the call goes for the next hour. Emir tells him mum about what he's already made, gets her advice for his samosas to make sure they puff up perfectly, and in between, he shares what's been weighing him down and how he plans to move forward. By the end of the call he feels another 10% more like himself. Each piece of him is falling back into place, between Laurie and his mum and making an appointment for the counsellor. Tomorrow he'll be back at dance, and maybe he'll even see Theo. Emir's not sure what to do when he does, as he tells his mum, and she reminds him to just follow his heart because it won't steer him wrong. It's cheesy, but she has a point.

Natalie passes the phone to her husband with a final reminder of love to Emir, letting the two of them catch up as well. He doesn't get into the details with his baba, but he lets him know the general situation, getting similar reassurances as he had from his mum. His parents truly love him unconditionally, and Emir knows that's an incredible gift that he will never take for granted, especially after everything that happened with his ex. Some people have to find their family, and Emir certainly has in his little gay circle here at uni. But he's lucky it was a choice and not a means of survival, that his parents and siblings have been his biggest support in everything, especially when things were bad.

Emir should really schedule these calls home into his week somewhere. It's not that he doesn't talk with his family, but it's not nearly enough. Maybe when he's talked things through with Theo, he can ask for his help building a new schedule to include family time and alone time and everything else. Theo's so brilliant, Emir in awe and in love with him and wondering again how he ever convinced himself to be anything else. There's so much Emir still has to learn about being a person, and he knows that Theo would patiently show him whatever he asks.

By the time his phone call is over and he's talked to both his parents and once more with Saima, Emir's food is done, ready to be eaten and shared with the others. He packs away enough for himself for a few days before placing the rest in Tupperware and stowing it in a tote bag in the fridge to have Laurie bring to the other flat for everyone else to enjoy. He keeps the sweets here for now, wanting to save those for just himself and Theo, hopefully this weekend. Theo is honey and cinnamon and cream and rose and everything good, and he deserves every treat that Emir can dream up.

Emir thinks back to their *Cinderella* date, when he'd seen Theo's face light up in a way that was entirely new to him. He was full of wonder, excited and nervous and overwhelmed at the gesture. Knowing he made Theo that happy was one of the highlights of Emir's life. It's a miracle he didn't kiss Theo senseless the moment that look appeared. But the way they've both been patient with their relationship, understanding of the other's boundaries and needs, it's so much better than any pre-emptive kiss. Emir still has personal healing to do, but he can't wait to get back to Theo, to give him cuddles and kisses and to pet those soft curls and hold him on his chest. He's so in love he can taste it.

***

Thursday evening, Theo finds himself at the nearest pottery painting store. There's two unpainted mugs and a pile of tools in front of him. He's a mixture of nerves and excitement. This is Theo indulging his whimsy, but he's not used to being spontaneous. Sure, he has his trips to get lost and find himself, like he'd shared with Emir a while back. But this is doing something just for fun, without any planning ahead.

After running into Laurie this morning, Theo made himself a list. He wrote down everything he could remember that he'd wanted to try, but never made the time. Theo gets intimidated by new things. There's too many unknowns, especially if he's unable to bring a safe person along with him. The list kept growing throughout the day, including pole dancing, karaoke, drag, that painting technique where you throw darts at balloons that he saw in *Princess Diaries* and never forgot. And of course this: pottery painting. Making pottery someday was also on the list, but this was the only activity he found that he could accomplish today, near Roseborough, and without spending much money.

Theo let his flatmates know where he'd be, but they were all busy and he had to come alone. It's not that he minds alone time. He loves it, actually. But when he's in a new environment and there might be a lot of loud people and potential overstimulation, he likes to bring someone along. Luckily, he called the pottery studio, and they said Thursday nights are quiet and that he'd likely have the place to himself for a while.

Theo arrived around four, letting himself in the front door and glancing up when he heard a tinkling bell sound through the shop. He was greeted by the same employee he'd spoken to on the phone, a young person not much older than him who was currently wiping what looked like mud on their apron as they approached with a smile. Theo was, in fact, the only one there, and the employee was kind enough to walk him around, show him all the things he could paint, the different types of paints and glazes, all the brushes and sponges and stencils and more things than he could remember. It's so much more than he imagined, but when he flipped through the stencils he found a *Batman* logo and settled in with his plan.

So here he is: his hands covered in a bit of paint, his back hunched over the table while he works determinedly on his mugs. They're nothing special, just standard round mugs with a sturdy handle, but plenty of surface for him to stencil on the design before painting it in.

Before he started, Theo decided to make one for himself and one for Emir because he still wants to make breakfast in bed someday, and having matching mugs seems very boyfriendy and domestic. The mugs won't be twins, but they'll be similar enough that they're a set. Theo has plans for the colours, gay plans, plans he hopes will make Emir laugh and flush in that way he tries to hide but that Theo always catches.

Hours of painting and detailing later, Theo stares at the two mugs with a grin, taking pictures of both to remember what he made before signing the bottom of each. They won't be ready until next week when he'll have to come back to pick them up, but that's alright. This excursion was as much about the process as it was about the result. Theo had no idea time could pass so quickly doing something like this. He barely finishes his mugs before the place closes at eight and he has to drive back to uni and put himself to bed.

Theo plans to go to class tomorrow, fully rested and ready to face his routine again. It's almost the weekend, so he just has to make it through one day before he can get extra decompression time if needed. But as he sits at home that night, he looks at the picture of the mugs, then across his room at his collection of art from Emir, and he smiles. Maybe Emir won't be the only artist in this relationship. Maybe they can do art together more often.

Even if they don't, Emir's suggestion is what gave him the idea to go, and he's glad of it. While he sat there and painted careful lines with muted colours (the employee had explained the difference between the look now and after the pieces were fired) his mind had felt so open, free to think and wander and focus only on the task at hand. He can't wait to do it again sometime, maybe make little creations for all his friends and family, something that both nourishes his creativity and allows him to give something to his favourite people. It's a wonderful combination he's glad to have accidentally found.

***

Emir sets his shoulders as he walks into the dance building Friday morning, taking even longer than usual to make his way to tech hall. He's positive that if Theo is coming to class today, he's already there warming up his body. No one else will show up for another few minutes, so it'll be just the two of them together. Emir wants to see Theo, so badly it's like he's gasping for air, but he doesn't know what to expect when they reunite. He hasn't heard from Theo since Tuesday night, but he's almost positive that's due to Theo respecting his space and not being ignored. Theo doesn't play games with emotions. If he was angry with Emir, he would communicate that very clearly.

Theo hears Emir before he sees him, that familiar tread in the empty hallway that he's come to know as well as his own. He stands up from his spot on the floor where he'd been gently stretching into his body, ready to see Emir for the first time in days. He's already holding himself back from literally sprinting out of the studio to meet him halfway, not sure where Emir's at mentally or emotionally. Theo only knows that he misses his boyfriend and he's glad they'll get to see each other in private before everyone else shows up. He doesn't even expect a conversation, just a moment together would be enough.

Emir flows through the doorway and it's like reality suspends itself, gravity and inertia tilting to pull them together the instant they're both in sight.

Without thinking, Emir drops his belongings and walks straight up to Theo. He's standing still with open arms, waiting to collide. There's a harmony to their movement, an inevitability that the second they touch they're embracing one another like two halves of a whole.

Theo tucks himself into Emir's hold, hiding his face away against his neck and squeezing tight with his arms around his back. Emir lets one hand find its way into Theo's hair, the other strong around his waist with his fingertips pressing in as if testing that Theo's real. They sigh in tandem, settling into the familiarity without breaking the moment and just letting themselves be held, finding that comfort and love that they've both been missing.

Not wanting to overwhelm Theo, Emir goes to pull back, but Theo grunts in dissent and holds him tighter, Emir smiling and falling back into the hug. He's not ready for it to be over either.

So Emir breathes him in, his perpetually warm body, his Theo smell that's a combination of his soap and something else unique to him, the sound of his breath so near Emir's own. And Theo lets himself be inhaled, brought into Emir like they're sharing one body, re-centering the longer they hug. They're grounding themselves, planting their roots together again, if only for a few minutes before class.

"I've missed you so much." Theo mumbles against Emir's neck, muffled, but he's not moving away yet. Being back in Emir's arms is too important. "So, so much."

"I'm sorry, baby. I've missed you too." Emir turns his head to kiss Theo on the cheek before laying his face down on Theo's shoulder, eyes closed tight. "Never again. I promise."

"I'd like that." Theo releases a half laugh, burrowing further into Emir's neck before finally pulling away from the hug. It's incredible how a few days without the comfort of these arms makes him appreciate it that much more. "How are you feeling?"

Emir drops his gaze for a moment, trying to contain his fondness for this beautiful man. It's a bit overwhelming being in his space again. "I'm alright, princess. Getting better. You doing alright?"

Theo leans down until he can meet Emir's eyes with the way he's tucked his chin, his smile growing when Emir tilts his head and knocks their foreheads together instead, so similar to that moment before their first kiss. God, Emir missed that smile, those crinkled eyes, that cheek dimple. Theo's so genuinely beautiful and full of warmth.

Without overthinking it, Emir gives Theo a tiny kiss, just a peck to the corner of his mouth before standing upright again and waiting for Theo's answer.

"I'll be fine. I know you didn't mean to hurt me." Theo's fingertips find Emir's as he holds their hands between them. "We don't have to talk right now, I'm just glad to see you."

"Yeah. Suppose we have class." Emir sighs, leaning forward for a real kiss, pressing his lips to Theo's, not caring who might walk in. "I'm not, um...I'm not all the way ready yet. I actually made an appointment for this morning with a counsellor. Someone to talk to about all this. I said never again and I meant it, yeah?"

"I'm not in a rush." Theo means it, too. He can be patient and keep giving Emir time if he needs it. Just getting to see him and hearing the start of an apology is enough for this morning. He understands Emir by now and he knows he'll come to Theo in his own time. "We'll get through today, and maybe we can talk sometime this weekend. You know where to find me."

"I do." Emir drops Theo's hands to grab his face for another kiss. He keeps it short and sweet before pulling Theo into another hug. He owes Theo more than the sentence of an apology he's so far been able to offer, but it really helps knowing he's not being rushed and can take his time finding the right words. "I think I still need to spend today by myself, if that's alright. Not like...you don't have to avoid me. But, like, lunch by myself and I think I'll stay at my flat again. Might depend on how things go with the counsellor."

"Alright." Theo flops down on the floor and starts stretching again, Emir joining him after a moment with a look so fond he's positive it would make Laurie retch. He can't help it. Theo is too wonderful for words. "I'll see if Lili wants to get lunch. I haven't had friend time with her in a while."

"I'm sure she'd love that." Emir grins, remembering how fiercely protective Lili was the other day. Even if he understood why, it was quite something to be on the receiving end of. She's a force of nature.

They stretch in silence for a minute, hearing other dancers enter the building through the far door and head into the dressing rooms across the hall. They'll only have a few more minutes alone before everyone else starts showing up, but it's sort of nice to spend the time just being together, not trying to force anything besides companionship.

"It really helps me when you give me specifics like that." Theo adds, realising he should communicate that to Emir as one of his needs. Most people don't usually understand how helpful it is to have things clearly laid out and with context, so he should probably mention it. "Like, I know you can't always, but letting me know what to expect so I can think ahead really helps me. I don't need, like, a minute-by-minute breakdown, but just knowing I should plan to be alone tonight, that means I don't have to worry about it the whole day until it happens. I'll know the plan, and then if something has to change it's easier to adapt. Does that make sense?"

Emir takes a moment to make sure he actually does understand before nodding, bumping his toe against Theo's shin since it's the closest thing he can reach as they stretch. "I'll remember that. I think I might be up for a chat tomorrow, if that sounds good to you?"

"Let me know in the morning? I don't have plans this weekend because we have the master class next Saturday. Just sort of hanging around the flat, that sort of thing, but...yeah." Theo reaches out and tickles the bottom of Emir's feet. It's basically his only tickle spot and he's delighted to hear the tiny giggle that accompanies Emir's scoot out of his grasp. He's so ridiculously cute.

"Oi! What's all this then?" Lili's annoyed voice gets their attention from the doorway, storming over to where they're seated in the middle of the studio. She's ready to throw herself between them if necessary.

"It's alright, Lili. We're good." Theo gives her an easy smile, letting her stare back and assess the situation for a moment until she believes him. He knows how she can get when someone's mean to him. He'll never forget when she found out about his sixth form bullies, ready to march to Stafford and put them in their place all by herself. "Actually, I was hoping we could get lunch today. Do you have time?"

Struggling with herself for a moment because she's in full protective mode, Lilibet thinks a few hours ahead and nods her head yes, slowly relaxing with Theo's reassurance but still ignoring Emir for now. "Just the two of us?"

"Just us." Theo confirms, standing up and letting his hand graze Emir's shoulder as he does. "I was thinking we could head to yours? But if you have plans we can do something this weekend instead."

"No, Jo's busy anyway. We can make something at mine, that's fine." Lilibet's eyes dart over to where Emir is still stretching just beside them. She leans in towards Theo and whispers, "Am I mates with Emir again?"

"Of course." Theo answers in a hushed tone, pulling her into a side hug until she squirms away. Lili studies Theo for another moment before squatting down next to Emir and tapping on his shoulder to get his attention. He looks up at her then glances across at Theo who's staring back at him with a bright smile while clearly holding back a laugh.

"Don't hurt my boy again. Or else." Her arms are crossed over her chest and she definitely looks like she could take him in a fight despite their size difference. Emir more than understands why she's mad, so he makes sure she knows that he's taking the situation seriously, nodding and meeting her angry stare.

"I won't." Emir promises, glancing up again when Theo giggles and blows him a kiss. He's ridiculous, but it makes Emir flush, so he looks away and goes back to stretching. Emir has a feeling Lili wouldn't appreciate them flirting so brazenly in front of her in the midst of her stern reproach. "If I do, you have my permission to feed me to the ravens."

"Good. Glad we understand each other." Lilibet stands back up, throwing herself at Theo for a hug which he gladly accepts. She hasn't seen him in days either.

"Sorry if I scared you." Theo mumbles. He had Laurie text her Wednesday, but he's barely been in contact with anyone all week. "I just needed some time."

"Want me to fight him?" Lili turns them so she can keep Theo in a hug but glare at Emir. Multitasking.

Theo laughs, shaking his head no and dragging her away to their usual spot, moving the barres into the studio space and away from the far wall. "Thanks for always having my back."

As if to prove his point, Lilibet thumps him quite hard between his shoulder blades. A sign of rough camaraderie, as if she needs to remind him of just how much she has his back and always will. They warm up in their usual way, Emir and Theo catching glances as the rest of the class files in. All through tech hall it's secret smiles, an occasional hand graze when it's time to work in centre, even a chin hooked over a shoulder during their stretch break. Sharing space again comes so naturally. It's like they never stopped.

***

Emir spends half of his counselling appointment just trying to keep himself together. He hasn't been in this type of environment in years, not since his ex outed and doxxed him and he lost every single friend he'd ever known. Being back in any form of therapy is a bit triggering by association, and he doesn't exactly trust people on sight. So, while the counsellor that Dylan made him an appointment with is incredibly kind and understanding, he's spent almost thirty minutes giving one word answers and anxiety spiralling in his seat. It's a comfortable seat, but he's been sitting on the edge of it and fidgeting the entire time.

"It's alright to be nervous." His counsellor, Amanda, reassures Emir when he misses two of her questions in a row. "You don't have to talk about anything you don't want to. We're just meeting for the first time, so I don't expect your life story or anything like that, yeah?"

"Sorry, it's just…I sort of have trust issues. Because of my ex." Emir messes up his hair again, running his hands through it and twirling loose strands between his fingers. "I'm trying, it's just…the last time I was in one of these rooms, it was because of what he did."

Emir watches her reaction at his use of a masculine pronoun, looking for anything negative. He's carefully avoided mentioning his queerness so far because he never knows how safe someone is.

"Did you want to talk about him today?" Amanda doesn't seem phased in the least, no reaction besides an encouraging tilt of her head. So, probably not homophobic then. Or at least not outright. That's something.

"No. *Fuck* no." Emir laughs before covering his mouth. "Shit, sorry. *Dammit -* " A groan, because apparently he can't stop. "Suppose I shouldn't be swearing."

Amanda laughs too, pushing her glasses further up into her hair and crossing her legs at the knee. "Don't worry about anything like that. I'm not bothered by a bit of language. I won't allow outright bigotry or racism or anything of that sort, but we all use a dash of colourful language in our everyday."

"Right...I don't really know how to do this." Emir scoots back in his seat until he's about halfway, a marked improvement. "Like, I've done this before, but I was a different person then."

"Let's just have a chat to see if this is a good fit, I suppose. There aren't really any rules here." Amanda gives him an encouraging smile and waits a moment before continuing. "Let's stay away from anything heavy today, unless there's something specific you need to chat about."

"Not really...I had a bit of a breakdown this week, but it'd been a long time coming. I sort of...like, something in me just breaks if I don't have alone time, and it's not because I don't love my boyfriend and my friends and my family. They're wonderful, I just...I need to be with my thoughts and have time to do my art and that sort of thing to keep me grounded and in the present." Emir sits on his hands because he's still nervously fidgeting and he doesn't want to be. This is really fucking hard for him, even if Amanda's nice and he *knows* he needs to talk to someone. "Like, I'm an introvert, but if I ignore my need for space, I spiral really fast. And I suppose that's...why I'm here?"

"You mentioned your art. Is that separate from the dance you study?" Amanda has her chin in her hand, looking genuinely curious and not like she's asking just to tick a box or distract him.

"Erm...yeah. I like to paint. Draw. Sometimes watercolours are nice, and I really like using charcoal as well." Emir breathes easier because he can talk about this. His relationships? That's a sensitive subject. But art can be conceptual as much as it is personal.

"What do you like about those mediums?" Amanda's still listening intently, and Emir visibly relaxes while thinking about how to respond. He has so much to say.

He tells her about how he chooses colours, how he decides what to paint and draw, how he frames his scenes, how he likes the mess of charcoal and the fluidity of watercolour, how acrylic has never appealed to him on canvas, only on wood. Emir talks about art and how he uses it and when he turns to it, and before he realises, he's got his legs crossed in front of him in the armchair, talking a mile a minute with Amanda occasionally asking a clarifying question.

If this is how seeing Amanda might go, he can do this. Emir won't be pushed into talking about anything before he's ready, but he's alright with getting comfortable and knowing he can go deeper when needed. It feels like a start.

***

"How long have we got for lunch?" Lili unlocks her flat, letting Theo step inside before closing up behind them and toeing her shoes off by the door.

Glancing at his phone, Theo calculates, "An hour and thirteen minutes."

He always answers with exact numbers, Lili counting on him to be the time keeper since early on in their friendship, her own chaotic ways often leaving behind the concept of linear time.

"God, you're a remarkable man. I hope Emir appreciates you." Lili sighs, reaching up on her toes to ruin Theo's hair then sauntering into her kitchen, knowing he'll follow.

Theo smiles down at his phone at her comment, thinking about how often Emir reminds him just how much he appreciates Theo and how he's never felt more loved. He never expected smooth sailing in his first relationship, and the past few days were just an obstacle for them to overcome.

Theo's lockscreen is a picture from their first official date last week, when he'd convinced Emir to take a selfie in the cinema just before the lights went down. Emir looks bright and happy and he's smushed up against Theo like he's trying to steal some of his body heat (he probably was). Sometimes it's hard to remember how new they are to this whole relationship, but that perspective also helped Theo get through the past few days. They're only at the beginning. "He does. I promise."

"Enough of the heart eyes. Come help me." Lilibet is standing in front of the open fridge, hands on her hips with a furrowed brow. "I should bring something to Jo, too. She's in a meeting."

"Posh cheese toasties? You have pesto leftover and we could add cheese with spinach and tomato. It's not gourmet, but it's something." Theo reaches past her for the water pitcher, ready to pour both of them a glass to go with whatever they make. "And, like, just the one pan to clean."

"I didn't know my best mate was a chef." Lili teases, but she gets out all the ingredients he listed off because that actually sounds delicious. "This is nice. Just us. It's been a while."

"Yeah. I think I let myself get a bit...codependent. I love Emir, but we need time with other people too." Theo finds the correct size pan in the cabinet, having a bit of a struggle locating the accompanying lid. He moves a few things to the side, but it's very clearly not there.

"Here." Lilibet takes the lid in question from the drying rack and hands it over as Theo stands back up from where he was kneeling to search.

"Why...?" Theo takes it from her with a tilt of his head before turning to the stovetop.

"No clue. Jo said she wanted to see if she could be a drummer, so all the lids and most of the pans were on the floor last night. Her parents called after rehearsal, so there was coping happening." Lili shrugs, watching as Theo dollops a teaspoon of butter into the pan and turns on the hob. "I get that way with Jo sometimes. Codependent. Hard not to when you're, like, in love and shit and your person is right there. She's my favourite, so why wouldn't I want to spend all my time with her?"

"Exactly!" Theo holds his hand out for the cutting board, already knowing Lili will be handing it over any second. She'll help along the way, but he's better at certain tasks. "Emir's the most wonderful person, and he's safe, you know? I can be myself around him and he doesn't drain my energy. It's so rare to have someone like that and to be the same for them. But...yeah. I know everyone thought Emir was the reason for what happened, but it's a little bit my fault too."

Lilibet sets the tomato on the chopping board just beside his hand, the spinach already chopped with precision while Theo shared his thoughts. She knows he learned how to cook from spending time with his mum in the kitchen growing up, but he's so comfortable doing this, and Lili smiles to herself watching how in his element he seems. "We should have mate dates like this. Nothing fancy, just..."

"Yeah? I'd love that. I always feel weird asking people to plan stuff with me, like it's asking too much, but if you're sure." Theo stops halfway through slicing the tomato to look at Lili, seeing a soft look in her eyes that's rare. She's so rough and tumble around everyone else as a defence mechanism, whereas with her friends and Jordan, she allows her gentler side to take a turn...occasionally. "I'm a bit worried about next year. After all this."

Theo gestures vaguely around them, trying to encompass the entire situation of their final year. Uni, living in the same building, getting to see one another whenever they like. Everything's going to change, even if they're still in each other's lives.

"We don't know what's going to happen yet. Jo's started really considering not pursuing dance professionally and finding something else to do in whichever city I land. Maybe I should be terrified of the commitment involved, but I'm not." Lili reaches for the container of mozzarella, opening the seal so they can add it to the rest once the bread's in the pan. Any moment now.

"I want to dance, but, like…I don't know. I just have this feeling. Like there's more to it." Theo turns back to the hob, adding two slices of bread to toast for a minute before flipping them to add in their filling. "The past few days got me thinking. There's so many things I've always wanted to try and never had the chance. Like yesterday, I went to a pottery studio to paint. Just went on a whim. I didn't plan ahead or anything, just showed up and gave it a go."

"Wow, that's…" Lilibet stares at Theo for a moment, choosing her words carefully. She knows she has a tendency to put her foot in her mouth. "That's sort of a huge deal for you. You went alone?"

"Yeah, it was…weird. But a good weird. Like, it wasn't busy and it was new, but not overwhelming, and the employee I met was nice." Theo carefully arranges their ingredients atop the freshly toasted bread while the other side browns in the remaining butter. "I think being with Emir is making me braver."

"I think so too." Lili lets him finish what he's doing before hopping on his back like an annoying sibling trying to get in the way. "But if you want company on some of these adventures, I'll stow away in your suitcase."

"You'd definitely fit." Theo laughs, turning around in his spot and trying to dislodge her. She has a surprisingly firm grip. "You're pocket-sized. I'm surprised Jordan doesn't just carry you around in her dance bag."

"You take that back." Lili swats away his hands, Theo careful to stay away from the hot stove, but otherwise laughing and twirling in place while they bicker in the kitchen. "I'm not a purse dog."

"A chihuahua, for sure." Theo gasps for air after that because Lili aims for his tickle spots until he drops her back to the ground. She doesn't stop, wriggling her fingertips against his sides with a gleam in her eye as he flails around and squeaks. "Alright! I give up! I take it - I take it back!"

"Good. Now flip the toastie. It'll burn." Lilibet lets him go, handing him a spatula and getting a plate ready to set their creations on. "Love you, you know. You're a himbo sometimes, but I still love you."

"Love you, too." Theo laughs quieter, never having been called a himbo before, but if it puts him in the same category as Kronk and Ken from *Barbie*, who is he to complain? "Pass me the garlic?"

***

Emir stops outside his flat on Friday evening and turns to Theo before even searching for his keys, letting himself be backed up against the door to receive a soft, lingering kiss. "Thanks for walking me home, princess."

"Thanks for letting me." Theo grins, kissing him again and winding his arms around Emir's shoulders. He's missed this. "First time for everything, isn't there?"

"I'm still walking you home and carrying your bag. Try and stop me." Emir draws his nose along Theo's and bites his upper lip, heart fluttering at the gasp he gets in response. He's so far gone in the best way. "See you tomorrow?"

"Please, god, yes." Theo softens into the next kiss, pressing forward and savouring it like the last spoon of custard. Emir is his favourite flavour in more ways than one. Having him here within reach, able to be held and loved, it's perfect, no expectations or agenda, just a bit of snogging in the corridor.

Emir kisses back, smiling every few moments at how gentle Theo is, caging him in against his door but making it perfectly clear that Emir can move away at any moment. Humming a happy little noise, Emir licks into Theo's mouth, along the inside of his bottom lip then just against the tip of his tongue before separating from Theo with a sigh.

"Goodnight, handsome." Emir pecks Theo's lips one last time before nudging him away, laughing when Theo turns to wave just before he's out of sight. It's the same adorable goodbye wave he's been giving Emir since they stopped all their fighting and decided to work together, like he doesn't want to leave without one last glance.

Emir's so glad they were able to chat and laugh and kiss and be in class and rehearsal together, but that he was still able to go to his appointment and that they went their separate ways for the night without it seeming like the end. Today's starting to give him that balance he was so sorely lacking.

Just as he's getting his keys out of the side pocket of his rucksack, Emir hears a bark from inside his flat. They don't have a dog. Unless Laurie...

He stops, stares at the door like he's losing his fucking mind, then hears another bark and he thinks it sounds...familiar. "What the fuck?"

Emir lets himself in, and before the door's even fully open, he's flattened to the ground by about forty kilos of canine fluff.

"Buddy!!" Emir can barely breathe, the wind knocked out of him when he hit the floor. If dog cuddles are how he goes, there are worse ways. But if Buddy's here, that means -

"Get off him, you lump. Buddy, come here!" Safiya's smile comes through clearly in her voice, even though Emir can't see her through all the fur. Theo once called Buddy a polar bear, and Emir isn't sure he was wrong. There's a lot of animal currently clambering off of him in response to Safiya's command, and if he didn't know better, he'd think an arctic creature found its way inside.

"Yaya, what're you doing here?" Emir pushes himself to his feet, dance bag abandoned while he shuts the door and hurries right up to his big sister. She's on his sofa, but the closer he gets, the wider her smile grows, already knowing what's coming. And sure enough, Emir plasters himself to her in a tight cuddle, Buddy joining in only a moment later while trying to get their undivided attention on himself instead.

"Apparently you call everyone except your big sister when you're stress cooking now? I was feeling a bit left out." Safiya messes up his hair and kisses the side of his head fondly.

He's the only little brother she's got and she's appropriately protective of him. Since she and her husband Mihir live in the city, Safiya's hoping Emir will settle here, too. But she knows that this may be the last few months they're only a tube ride away from each other. It's bittersweet to know her brother is destined for great things that may take him far away. "Was that Theo I heard?"

"Of course." Emir grunts, shifting Buddy to their laps instead of letting him push the two of them into the sofa cushions. Buddy licks his face before finally settling down.

He's not a very loud dog, but he's very heavy, especially when he wants cuddles. Emir's always thought he makes an excellent weighted blanket. "Teddy walked me home."

"Hm. So things with you two are...?" Safiya isn't wasting a single second, apparently.

Emir rolls his eyes, but he's so happy to see her he'll let it go. For a moment, Emir wonders if it was his mum or baba who told her, but realises it was almost definitely Saima. It's not like it was a secret, but he also wasn't broadcasting the struggle he's been dealing with this week.

"We'll be fine. I wasn't taking care of myself and Theo was collateral damage, but I'm working on it." Emir buries his face in Buddy's fur, scratching along his sides with both hands and enjoying the comfort that only a giant dog can provide. "But actually, how are you here?"

"Laurie." Safiya shrugs, scratching Buddy beneath the chin while letting Emir continue to get his dog fix. Sometimes, dogs understand in ways people never will. Cats, too. "I knew you'd be in rehearsal and I wanted to surprise you, see if you'd be up for some sibling time. Maybe food and something mindless on the telly?"

"Can we stay here? I'm not really wanting to go out." Emir looks up at her, fully leaning on top of Buddy and fluttering his eyelashes. He knows how to get what he wants. "But I'm glad you're here."

"You're glad *Buddy's* here." Safiya teases, already pulling out her phone to order takeaway for the two of them. "Pizza?"

"Pizza." Emir grins, leaning over to settle his head on her shoulder. "Thanks, Yaya."

Without getting up, Emir reaches for the telly remote and turns it on, flipping through the channels until he finds something they'll both like. Between talking to his parents, cooking his favourite family recipes, and having Safiya here tonight, it's like all the best parts of home have found their way back in. He's not glad for how this week happened, but he's grateful that he's been able to grow through it and remember what he wants to hold on to.

He loves Theo, he loves his family, he loves the friends he's made here, and maybe he's learning to love himself in a new way, too. If he's a product of those he loves, then he must be pretty fucking special. The people who make up his world are strong and patient and kind and intelligent and everything he would ever want to be.

"Love you." He adds as he finally settles on watching *Gogglebox*, sighing and letting his hands fall into Buddy's fur again.

A moment later he feels Safiya kiss his temple and cuddle closer beside him. "Love you too, nerdlet."

***

Emi: had a surprise visit from safiya and buddy :) :) :)
Theo: Oh! That's great! (send me a selfie with Buddy?)
Theo: I know you've been homesick /heart emoji/
Emi: /selfie with Buddy, his eyes crossed and tongue out while Buddy smiles and looks off to the side/
Theo: YOU TWO ARE THE CUTEST THING I'VE EVER SEEN
Theo: /heart eyes gif/
Theo: /fainting gif/
Emi: are you having a nice night at home?
Theo: It's pretty quiet since everyone's out being social, but I don't mind.
Theo: I'll probably go to bed soon. I had pizza for dinner since it was just me.
Emi: ME TOO
Emi: yaya ordered from some place nearby i've never been to
Theo: I made my own from scratch /shrug emoji/ Not nearly as exciting I suppose.
Emi: you know how to do that? why have we never had a pizza night for family dinner?
Theo: It takes a bit of time to let the dough rise and all that but we can definitely make it together sometime /pizza emoji/
Emi: you're the coolest boyfriend in the world
Emi: i maybe sort of miss you
Theo: I maybe sort of miss you, too.
Emi: it's been weird sleeping alone
Emi: don't sleep as well without my favourite cuddler heater lover boy beside me
Theo: You're welcome to reinstate sleepovers whenever you like /snore emoji/
Theo: You know where to find me /heart emoji/
Emi: not sure if Buddy's staying the night, but i'll think about it
Emi: thank you for giving me space
Emi: and for not hating me
Emi: i know we said we'll talk tomorrow but i just want to apologise again and remind you that you were never the reason for what happened. it was all internal this time
Emi: i want to tell you about my appointment, too. i think i'll keep going and i already learned a bit

Theo: I'm so glad it went well! Amanda sounds nice from what you told me earlier.
Theo: If you ever need space, just let me know. I don't mind. I just want you to be happy.
Theo: I hope I make you happy, but I want you to find your happiness on your own, too /heart emoji/
Emi: i'm so fucking lucky to have you and your dozens of heart emojis per conversation
Emi: safiya's making fun of me because i'm smiling at my phone instead of watching the telly
Emi: apparently i'm "sappy and ridiculous" but to be fair
Emi: /picture of Theo, laughing while sitting on Emir's lap, Emir smirking because he'd just tickled Theo to make him giggle/
Emi: you're sort of incredible
Theo: You're sort of incredible, too.
Theo: Shower time.
Theo: /shirtless selfie from the bathroom/
Emi: THEODORE THIRST TRAP PALMER
Emi: شہزادی
Emi: YOU CAN'T JUST DROP THAT AND BE AWAY FROM YOUR PHONE WHILE I HYPERVENTILATE
Emi: FKDSJFLKDSJFLKDSJFKLSDJ
Theo: /smirk emoji/
Theo: Goodnight, Emi /kiss emoji/
Theo: /snoring Batman gif/
Emi: goodnight pumpkin /kiss emoji/
Emi: see you soon /three kiss emojis/

***

Safiya and Buddy left after a few hours of pizza and chilling because they have an early morning with Mihir's family on the other side of London. But Emir's alright with that, the surprise visit leaving him a tad socially drained, so he's looking forward to some alone time before bed.

Since he hasn't had time to draw all day, Emir gets out his watercolours, inspiration striking him for a very specific picture that won't work in charcoal or graphite. He needs reds and yellow and oranges and pinks. A perfect brick red for the details and a smooth butter yellow for the background. He knows it's Theo he's drawing, just in another form. Or rather, it's Theo inspired, both by his words and his aura, everything about him warm and sunny and bright.

Theo is red because Theo is love, that love at the very centre of who he is and the warmth he radiates. Emir's mum used to tell him stories all about his own light, but he knows he's found his equal in Theo, the two of them brighter together than they've ever been apart. That's essentially what their work together on their dissertation has been about: how two people live separately in their own way until they collide, and suddenly they realise how much happier they could be with each other.

When Emir imagined his dissertation the past few years, he didn't expect it to become what it has. But he's so proud of the evolution, of how he and Theo have combined their best qualities to create something truly special. It's something they'll be proud of for the rest of their careers.

It takes Emir several hours to finish his painting, lost in a world of colour. He takes his time, knowing exactly the vision he has in his mind, his emotions flowing into the shapes and patterns as easily as breathing. Once he's done, he takes a picture on his phone, just to be safe in case something happens to it. This one feels special.

The painting has to finish drying for a minute, and while it does, Emir paces his flat. Now that he's done with it he's restless, craving time with Theo in a way that he hasn't in days. The separation is catching up to him, and he doesn't want to be alone anymore. Didn't both Amanda and Safiya remind him that he should listen to what he needs?

Theo did say he was welcome to restart their sleepovers at any time...

Scribbling an inscription on the back of the now dry artwork, Emir bundles up to brave the early winter night, carefully tucking his painting inside his hoodie for protection before leaving the flat. Maybe he'll just hide it in Theo's room for him to find in the morning. Maybe he'll slide it beneath his bedroom door and text him it's there. Or, maybe he'll gently wake Theo up and ask to join him, the comfort of sharing a bed such an underrated aspect of their relationship. He wasn't lying when he told Theo he sleeps best when they're together.

On instinct, Emir detours to the lake to spend a minute beneath his tree before visiting Theo's flat. It's very out of the way, but it calls to him at night even more than during the day, the chance to see the moon reflected on the mirrored surface like a siren call he's helpless to avoid. Will he find somewhere like this wherever he ends up next? Will he have a new special tree? A new treasured walking path? Will he get to share all of those with Theo, or will their careers take them to different places, out of reach and alone again?

Regardless of the answers he can't find on the lake's surface, he doesn't have to be alone now. More sure than before, Emir takes the picture out to check it's still alright before finally heading for Theo. He's had his space and now he just wants to be with his boyfriend, sharing breath, stealing warmth, giving love. Emir doesn't know what comes next, but tonight Theo is just a short walk away, and Emir's closing the distance.

CHAPTER SIX

Emi: *you awake?*
Laurie: *Of course*
Laurie: *It's only just after midnight*
Laurie: *Everything alright?*
Emi: *let me in?*
Laurie: *What do you mean let you in?*
Emi: *the flat*
Emi: *it's not as if there's a spare key lying around*
Emi: *i need to drop something off*
Emi: *please laur i'll leave if he doesn't want me here*
Emi: *it's just a painting*
Emi: *fuck should i go home?*
Emi: *i would've just walked over and asked theo to let me in but he's asleep*
Emi: *i won't wake him up*
Emi: *okay i might wake him up*
Emi: *i just...he likes surprises*
Emi: *he likes some surprises*
Emi: *is this a bad surprise?*
Emi: *i want him to wake up to a sunrise*
Emi: *so i made him a sunrise*
Emi: *i can just hand it to you if you think that's better*
Laurie: *Are you done?*
Emi: *that depends*
Emi: *am i stranded in this corridor for eternity?*

"You are absolutely too far gone." Laurie grumbles as he opens the door to Theo, Ciaran, and T's flat, bed hair and smudged glasses accompanying his pyjamas. "You know the others are awake, too. Could've just knocked. It's a Friday night. Only Teddy turns in this early on a weekend."

"Thanks, Laur." Emir kisses him full on the mouth, both hands grasping the side of his face before stepping past him and tossing his shoes to the side. He makes it three paces before turning around, putting his shoes neatly in the shoe holder by the door, and resuming his trajectory. Not his flat, not his rules (or lack thereof).

"Oi, what was the smooch for?" Laurie calls after him, but not too loudly. He doesn't want to wake Theo either. It's been a long week and he needs his rest. Luckily, Theo's bedroom is furthest from the front door.

"Because I love you, my messy gay angel." Emir turns around when he gets to Theo's hallway, saluting Gabe and Ciaran on the couch where they're laying with Alfie beside them, watching *Derry Girls* at a low volume. Emir gets the briefest glimpse of T sprawled out in their bed across the flat, waiting for Laurie to come back to them. "Pass it along to T for me?"

"Course…" Laurie watches Emir go, removing what he assumes is the surprise painting from under his shirt. It must be raining, then. He can usually tell the weather by Theo's preparedness, and apparently, that now extends to Emir. Love is so clearly visible, sometimes, its effects obvious to those who pay attention.

Pausing outside Theo's bedroom door, Emir carefully sets the painting down and strips out of his hoodie, not wanting to get the rain soaked fabric on anything important. He'll just set it on the floor once he's inside and Theo can borrow it if he likes. Theo definitely has a *thing* for borrowing Emir's clothes at every opportunity. It makes Emir's chest hurt in the most spectacular way every time Theo borrows a hoodie or fills out one of his oversized t-shirts.

Not bothering to knock, Emir opens the door as carefully as he can, finding his way through the dark by habit. He has so many memories here to guide him, so many nights sleeping next to Theo, safe in their love and the peace they've built together. He can barely see Theo under the sheets by the light of the corridor, closing the door behind him again and walking not to the bed, but to the bookshelf where Theo keeps all the art that Emir makes for him. He doesn't want to rearrange anything already there since he knows Theo has a system, but he needs the new one front and centre. Emir wants Theo to see it first thing in the morning when he wakes up, a sunrise in his own bedroom, one that won't fade into the day and disappear.

Once the painting is situated directly across from the bed, Emir finally approaches Theo. He's turned toward Emir's usual side, one hand on the vacant pillow and the other tucked beneath his cheek. He's gorgeous and Emir hates to disturb him, but he can't just climb in without asking. Sitting gingerly by Theo's side, Emir runs his fingertips through Theo's hair, tracing his curls and admiring the man he loves. He needed the time he took by himself, but there's nowhere else he's supposed to be right now except here with Theo.

"Mm?" Theo doesn't wake at first, just scrunches his face and leans into the touch. A few caresses to his cheek and Theo turns over, hiding himself against Emir's side instinctively while smiling at the petting. An actual puppy, Emir thinks, a cuddly, warm, loving puppy.

"Princess…" Emir leans in, laying a kiss against Theo's temple and trailing his hand down his neck and to his arm instead, gently squeezing his bicep. "Wake up, Teddy."

"Emi?" Theo's eyes are still closed, curling himself into a ball against his boyfriend as if confused to find him outside the sheets. Sighing, his face relaxes again, clearly asleep, and Emir has to stifle a laugh. He's too perfect for words.

"Babyyyy…" Emir sings it near his ear this time, another kiss along his hairline while he finds Theo's hand, moving the sheets to do so. He interlaces their fingers, wanting to wake him up as gently as humanly possible.

"Mmmm." Theo grumbles, blinking his eyes awake. Emir can see the exact moment Theo realises he isn't dreaming. His eyes open as wide as they can go and he jolts upright to shout, "Emi!"

Theo throws himself on Emir, literally, arms around his shoulders while the blanket falls to his lap.

"It's me, baby. It's your Emi." His heart might start leaking, the sound of Theo's honest excitement at his presence like a knife that's cutting through the scar tissue on his heart that's steadily dissolving. Emir rubs his hands along Theo's back through his shirt, letting Theo nuzzle into his neck and breathe him in, his excitement drooping into contentment. "I'm sorry I woke you up."

Theo shakes his head, still clinging to Emir. He's here, in Theo's bed, smelling like boy and laundry and moonlight and Theo's so happy. He's so wonderfully, earnestly happy. "Are you here for sleeping?"

Words are still hard. Theo only woke up ten seconds ago, so he figures it's allowed.

"I would like to be here for sleeping." Emir separates himself from the hug, carefully laying Theo back down against his pillow and returning his fingers to his hair. "But it's up to you. I know it's late."

Theo huffs, throwing aside the sheets in one dramatic flourish that leaves his torso exposed, then tugging on Emir's wrist until he falls across him, legs still dangling over the edge. "In...please."

"You're sure?" Emir rolls onto his side, looking up at Theo with his softest smile. He feels like warm butter, malleable and thick with emotion.

Theo grumbles this time, yanking Emir up and into the bed by force until Emir is laughing and Theo is satisfied. Emir ends up diagonal, face beside Theo but still above the sheets. They stare at each other for a moment, Theo still half asleep and Emir still in his joggers.

"Hi." Theo chews on the inside of his cheek, eyes sparkling. He's more than alright with this turn of events.

"Hi." Emir moves in slowly, giving Theo plenty of time to turn away if he wants. But he doesn't. Theo just shuts his eyes and pouts his lips until the two of them meet in a puckered kiss. They end with their foreheads together, smiling, laying like that for another minute until Theo is almost asleep and Emir forces himself to move and get out of the bed again.

"But - " Theo pouts again as Emir stands up, one hand reaching out to him.

"I just need to get out of these clothes. I got rained on." Emir takes Theo's proffered hand, squeezing it then letting it drop back to the blankets. "Can I borrow something?"

"Yeah, just um..." Theo thinks back to what he did yesterday morning, moving some of his clothes and rearranging so there was space for Emir to keep a few of his own things here if he wants. But he hasn't exactly been able to show Emir yet and he's too asleep to have that conversation right now. "Maybe naked sleeping?"

Tugging his own shirt off, Theo tosses it at Emir to distract him, Emir giggling and catching it easily. "Sounds perfect."

Emir strips out of his own clothes while Theo gets out of his boxers and tosses those to the ground as well, Emir making sure all their dirty laundry ends up where it belongs and not strewn across the floor, then grabbing an extra blanket from the wardrobe.

"Now, can we please sleep?" Emir asks as he folds himself into the spot beside Theo, kissing him between his eyebrows and getting settled.

"But my fit boyfriend just climbed into my bed naked in the middle of the night." Theo smirks, leaning into Emir for a real kiss and wrapping his arms around him.

"Just sleep tonight, pumpkin. We're both exhausted." Emir knows Theo's just teasing, but he also always tries to remind Theo that he's not only here for the sex. He's here for Theo and everything that they are together.

Theo steals one more kiss before turning himself around to be the little spoon and taking Emir's arm to fall across his waist. "Happy."

Emir kisses his strong shoulder, one leg thrown over Theo to keep him as close as possible. He's going to sleep so well tonight. "Me too, baby. So happy."

Pressing three more kisses to the back of Theo's neck as an *I love you*, Emir waits as Theo drifts off to sleep. It takes a few minutes, but his breathing slows down, their chests moving together, hearts aligned beneath the sheets.

***

Theo found his sunrise immediately. He's been holding it in his hands for seven entire minutes, finding every individual colour used while admiring Emir's work. Careful to treat it delicately, he removed it from his small gallery of Emir art and brought it back into bed with them so he could snuggle up to Emir while he looks at it. Theo uses his finger to trace the patterns within the sun that remind him so instinctually of the art he'd seen on Emir's hands in the days following his sister's wedding. He wonders what it means, because he's done a bit of Googling, but that won't tell him if that's what Emir intended to say by including it.

The painting is *gorgeous* and the first thing Theo thought of was that conversation they had back in early November. He had been high for the first time, Emir sharing his smoke until they floated between the earth and sky together. And Theo had said he wanted to invent the sunrise with Emir...which Emir followed up with an admission about wanting to marry Theo someday.

And Theo's trying not to read too much into the painting that Emir brought him in the middle of the night, but it's a sunrise and there's potentially wedding related imagery contained within, and the inscription on the back made him want to cry. It's written in

Urdu, of course, because Emir has very patiently been sharing his second language with Theo.

I won't ever leave your side, scrawled three times, one above the other like a poem, in Emir's signature smudged charcoal. He thinks Emir probably meant it as an *I won't leave you* or the closest translation that Google will provide to Theo when he looks it up. Theo keeps flipping back and forth and back and forth and looking over at Emir's peaceful form beside him and wondering how much longer he has to let him sleep.

He wants to wake him up, but he knows Emir needs the rest. That was so clear yesterday, when Theo had seen him for the first time in days. The dark circles and the exhaustion that he tries to hide were definitely present, and Theo can always tell. Even before they were friends and then more, he could always read Emir.

Is Emir thinking long term? This sunrise definitely seems to suggest it. There's no way it's a coincidence, because Theo is positive that Emir not only remembers that conversation, but also the feeling they found together that night. Emir says he won't leave, and more importantly, Theo believes him, despite everything. Despite his past, and despite Emir leaving him behind the other night. He knows when Emir is being sincere, and his apology (more than one) yesterday had definitely been true.

He won't leave Theo. He wants to stay. Neither of them knows what's going to happen in a few months, but Emir *wants* to stay.

Theo needs to talk to him.

Setting the painting aside on the bedside table, Theo snuggles in closer to Emir, trying to wake him up in the gentlest way possible, returning Emir's caution from last night. A hand on his cheek. Toes gliding along his calves. Kisses against his shoulder.

"Whaswrong?" Emir mumbles, eyes scrunching together as his arms reach out to circle Theo, pulling him to his chest. Always so protective, and Theo goes gladly.

"Um...how do I say it?" Theo kisses Emir's bare chest, wondering if he can even hear him, muffled as he is.

"Hmm?" Emir gives him a squeeze, eyes opening reluctantly to blink down at Theo's messy curls. He's so gorgeous in the mornings.

"On the...my sunrise. How do I say it?" Theo asks again, turning around in Emir's arms to reach for the painting, careful not to bend it. He looks at it lovingly, Emir watching his soft eyes trace the red pattern before turning it over so he can show Emir the words. As if he could forget what he wrote. "I don't know how to say it, but I looked up what it means."

"Mein tumhara sath nahi chodunga." Emir mumbles, watching Theo try to fit his tongue around the sounds. He repeats it back and forth with him, one word at a time, kissing his temple between each recitation until Theo gets the hang of it and smiles up at him, waiting for his approval. "You've got it."

"And, um...how would I say..." Theo sets the painting across their hips over the sheets and settles in. "I won't hurt you. Because I won't. Not ever...okay, maybe sometimes, like, if sex is happening and that's a thing we're into but, like, not your heart and - "

"Shhhh." Emir grins, tilting Theo's face up for a gentle kiss. He's barely awake, but he doesn't mind the conversation, and Theo has nothing to worry about. "Mein tumhe kabhi dard nahi pahunchaunga."

It's a long phrase, much more than he usually teaches Theo, but Theo wants to reassure Emir in more than one language. He actually sees Emir, more than anyone else ever has, and Theo knows it will mean more this way.

"That's how I say that I won't hurt you?" Theo waits for Emir to nod, then tries it himself, Emir gently correcting him until he's got it right. He still stumbles over certain sounds but Emir appreciates the effort, knowing he'll keep trying and improving over time. "Will you show me how to write it?"

"Later." Emir grins, taking the painting and setting it out of the way again. He doesn't want to get up anytime soon. "Too early."

"But...I missed you." Theo curls back against Emir's chest, Emir's fingers trailing through his curls, listening to Theo hum happily as if being here is all he's ever wanted.

"Need sleep, princess." Emir yawns, hiding his face against the top of Theo's head and holding him as close as possible. His precious angel boyfriend. "But you can get up. I don't mind."

He'd mind a little, but he knows Theo will be back. If nothing else, the past few days have taught him they need alone time.

"Maybe I'll go to the gym?" Theo doesn't want to move, except he really does. His body is awake, even if laying here with Emir is maybe the best thing that's ever happened to him. Except for every other moment they've shared.

"Mmmm yes." Emir rolls onto his back, pulling Theo along with him to keep him on his chest. "You are *delicious* after the gym."

"Oh?" Theo flushes, as if he hasn't noticed Emir's ill-disguised interest when he comes home sweaty after his morning exercise. "You want a taste?"

"I want a whole fucking meal." Emir groans, pushing their bodies together while he stretches out his back. "But I need more sleep first. Wake me up when you get back?"

"Keep the bed warm for me." Theo shifts himself up for a kiss. The gym can wait a few minutes.

***

"That was a very productive shower." Theo sits cross legged on his bed, skin pink and hair damp, cosy in his joggers and a beige henley. He loves Saturday mornings.

"Could've tried biting you again but someone was just so sensitive this morning." Emir winks at Theo, clambering up beside him until they're facing each other. He takes Theo's hands in his own, pressing a kiss to the back of his knuckles. They'd gotten off together in the shower, of course, and there was so much emotion involved after their heavy week that it was all very enthusiastic and over much sooner than Emir usually prefers. Luckily, they have time for round two later today or tomorrow.

"My body likes your body." Theo shrugs, grinning at Emir in the mid-morning sun that shines through his bedroom window. He'd spent about an hour at the gym and came home to a bleary-eyed, bed-headed Emir curled up inside his sheets, as if he hadn't woken up once already. "Couldn't wait today."

"No complaints. Literally zero." Emir drops Theo's hands and leans back on his own instead, staring at his beloved boyfriend with a sigh. He's his favourite person in every way. "Is it a good time for us to talk?"

"Yes, please." Theo leans forward for a kiss, hands on Emir's shoulders to steady himself. Emir smiles against his lips, nudges their noses together, and kisses Theo's forehead before he shifts away, mirroring Emir's posture. "I have a few things I want to share too, but you first."

"Alright." Emir agrees, taking a moment to stare at Theo and truly appreciate him for all that he is. "Last apology and then I'll leave it be. I am sorry, Theo. I ignored both you and Laurie and I pushed myself too far. I was self destructive, but this time I almost took you down with me. And I definitely should not have left you alone at the studio like that. I regret that moment more than anything. I won't put you in that situation again. I swear. Even if I get to a bad place again, I won't just run away like that."

"Thank you." Theo knows that Emir's already apologised, more than once, but the fact he's already taken steps for his apology to have credibility gives Theo no hesitation in accepting and moving on. "And I realised that I was at least partially to blame. I let us get a bit too codependent, you know? Like, of course I want to spend time with you, but we need time apart, time with our other friends."

"But I still shouldn't have let myself get that bad. I shouldn't have needed the wake up call." Emir knows he's already making progress to being a healthier person, both on his own and in his relationships, but it's a long road ahead. The last few years have been a study of patience and self reflection while he processed his trauma from being outed, and this is both a continuation and a new path. "I was just…so into you and our relationship. I've never been happier or safer in my life and it felt like I was failing for needing space, like I shouldn't because of where I am now. Like…I know that's not true, but it still felt that way."

"We all need space sometimes." Theo sits forward enough that he can set a hand on Emir's knee. He likes the physical connection and he knows Emir appreciates it too. "I'll, um, I'll tell you a bit more later, I think, but sometimes I need to be alone to…decompress. But you've never overstimulated me, somehow. You always know when I need quiet. I just don't want you to think that either you're the only one who needs space sometimes or that me needing space is because you've done something wrong. It's normal for us to need time by ourselves."

"Let's talk boundaries? And plans I have to work on balance and being healthier?" Emir lays his hand on Theo's where it rests on his knee, letting just the tips of their fingers interlock. "I remember you said that it helps you to know what to expect, so I thought I'd tell you what I've been thinking?"

Theo beams at him, like literal sunshine, because Emir really listens to him and values what he says. "I already started working on a schedule that gives us both alone time and time with our friends and family, but I want to talk about it together, like, have your input too, even if I'm the schedule boyfriend."

Theo turns pink when Emir giggles and squeezes his fingertips. That sound will never stop being like butterfly music, making Theo's heart beat faster. He's never known love like this, and he spent years worrying he'd never have it. But here they are.

"If you're the schedule boyfriend, what am I?" Emir teases, tracing his eyes along Theo's flushed face and appreciating it more because of their distance this week. He's so fucking pretty.

"I indulged my whimsy, like you said." Theo answers, in his own roundabout way. "I took myself to paint pottery on my own because I remember what you said that day in Cookham. And you were right. You know me really well, babe. It's good for me to try new things, but, like... on my own terms and only sometimes. Baby steps. But, um, I think that makes you the inspiration boyfriend."

"And what is it I've inspired?" Emir flops down on the bed now, arms above his head, waiting for Theo to lay beside him. They can chat laying down, and he hasn't been dramatic in about twelve hours, so it's overdue.

"Basically my entire life. I kept a list of all the animals and plants and stuff I saw this week so I could ask you about them because I love how you teach me things on our walks. And you share Urdu with me, which I know is really special to you. Even if I'm shit at it." Theo huffs, laying with his head on his palm, elbow holding him up while he faces Emir. "You make me brave. Even Lili thinks so."

Theo laughs at Emir's grunt of disbelief, using his free hand to boop him on the nose. It's just so cute, and it's right there needing to be booped. Emir crinkles his face and laughs along, biting the air near Theo's hand until he retracts it. "I based an entire section of our choreography on the patterns from your mehndi..."

"You what?" Emir sits up again, hands finding their way to Theo's chest to press him into the pillows so he can straddle him, one knee on each side of Theo's hips. He can feel his eyes widen with surprise. Just the thought of Theo being so enamoured that he incorporated an ephemeral pattern into their work together is enough to make Emir's stomach fall through the floor. Theo, like, properly loves him, and he has for so fucking long. His sister's wedding was months ago. How does Theo even remember the art on his hands?

"Didn't you say you wanted to talk boundaries and plans?" Theo flushes much deeper, almost maroon from Emir's attention. He's not embarrassed by his love, but he'd sort of been keeping that specific detail to himself, not wanting to make a big deal of it. He knows that Emir loves him, but he still doesn't want to scare him away. Maybe that's his own internalised issues with abandonment. Which...he'll get to that later.

"Right, those." Emir sighs, laying briefly on Theo's chest and breathing in near his neck before rolling back over to the side so they can face each other. "I think I need at least thirty minutes each day to myself, a full hour on weekends. And I think studio time alone is really helpful for me. We're making incredible progress on our dissertation, so I was thinking I could have one night a week that's just me in the practice studio? Four or five days a week working together should be enough. And I don't have a set appointment time with Amanda yet, but I'll start with once a week and go from there. Oh! And I was hoping you could help me find a time to call my family to make sure I don't forget."

Theo plays with Emir's hand while he talks, absorbing his ideas and already mentally fitting the boundaries Emir's mentioned into the schedule he'd been working on yesterday. "What about sleeping?"

"I want to sleep with you every night. I don't care where or for how many hours, just...I sleep better with you. I love waking up to you every morning. You're the best start to my day." Emir reaches out to hold Theo's face delicately in his fingertips, leaning in for a press of a kiss that Theo sighs into.

"But, um..." Emir blinks his eyes open again and scoots back to his own side of the bed. It's easy to get lost in Theo and forget their conversation. "What about you? What do you need, princess?"

"I want at least one thing a week with Lili. Could be lunch or something gay, I don't care. I think we see Laurie and the others plenty without having to plan it, especially with family dinner." Theo grins when just at that moment he hears the unmistakable sound of T and Laurie in the flat's kitchen, laughing about something together while T makes their morning tea/pancakes/whatever they have the ingredients for. He's so glad to have this little found family, knowing they'll always make time for each other. "And I also prefer to sleep together every night. You're...safe. I sleep fine on my own, but I still want to be your little spoon, if you'll let me."

"Mmm." Emir hums happily, scooting towards Theo until they're hugging properly, laying on top of Theo's made bed. He rests their foreheads together, sliding his arms beneath Theo's henley and drawing patterns on his soft skin with slow hands. "Warm, angel baby. You're so perfect for cuddles. We fit."

Theo smiles, eyes crinkled shut while Emir adores him. It's hard to believe that yesterday at this time, they were still on their own, unsure of what their reunion would bring. But even with the drama of the week, they know each other's foundation. They used to spend their energy finding ways to antagonise and annoy one another, and in the process, they found out all the tiny details about each other: all their favourite things, all their pet peeves, all the idiosyncrasies of a human life. So while they may only be a month into an official relationship, they know how to communicate. They learned in an unconventional way, but their understanding of the other is well established.

"Didn't you say you wanted to tell me more about your appointment yesterday?" Theo remembers while thinking about communication.

"Oh, that." Emir keeps Theo close, fingers in his hair and a kiss to his cheekbone before he continues. "She thinks I may have synesthesia. It might be part of why I need alone time, because I'm processing more sensation, or, like, layers of it. I already knew I have PTSD, so that wasn't new. Amanda said we could talk about that more another time. She's really nice about letting me take things as slow as I need. But, yeah...seems I associate feelings and music and concepts with colours and that sort of thing. Amanda used the word associative, which makes sense. I see shapes in movement and my brain just...makes connections, apparently. It's part of the reason I can memorise choreography so quickly, or at least, it might be a factor. So...synesthesia. I'll have to learn more about it."

"That, um...yeah, that makes sense actually." Theo watches Emir as he shares this new thing he's learned about himself, not surprised because he knew there was something going on there beyond just artistic talent. Emir gets something important from his time spent working on his art, both his dance and his visual art, like painting and drawing. Theo noticed months ago that Emir links colours to emotion automatically, and that red always means love. Which makes his surprise sunrise this morning even more important. "I didn't know about your PTSD, like, not officially. That diagnosis was from your last therapist?"

"Yeah, the one I saw after what happened. I saw her during that summer and the first few months of uni over Zoom." Emir holds Theo closer for a moment, appreciating his ability to absorb new information and love Emir exactly the same as before. "I don't talk about my PTSD because it was shit, but...still is I guess. Or at least, if I don't take care of myself or get triggered. You saw what I was like that time."

"I was so worried when you showed up that morning. I didn't know what was wrong, but I knew I wanted to help." Theo remembers every moment of their day in Cookham and what led to it. It didn't matter that they had fallen out. It didn't matter that he was waiting for an apology after their fight. He'd known immediately that Emir was dealing with something well beyond a standard level of anxiety or panic.

"You always help." Emir guides Theo's face so their eyes meet, fingertips gentle as he feels Theo's Saturday morning stubble against his skin. He waits for Theo to smile before giving him another kiss, tickling under his chin as he leans away. "You didn't even know what was happening or why and you still dropped everything. You're always so good to me."

"I emptied out space for you." Theo blurts out, instead of the *I love you so much* that was at the forefront of his mind. But really, the reasoning is the same. "Sorry, tangent, just like...I rearranged my wardrobe and moved some stuff around. In case you want to keep a few things here and not have to always worry about an overnight bag."

"You reorganised for me?" Emir asks, breath catching as he searches Theo's face. The thing about Theo's room is that everything has a specific place and he has a system and the flat is small because they're uni students. But Theo took the time and effort to make room for Emir in his sanctuary. "This week? After I was horrible to you?"

"You hurt me, but it wasn't personal." Theo won't deny the pain he was in, but it's been a few days. He's processed it. "I wasn't sure if it was too soon. That's why I didn't want you looking for clothes to sleep in last night. I didn't want to surprise you when I was half asleep and couldn't talk about it."

"Does this mean I can't wear your clothes anymore?" Emir teases, but on the inside he's filled with light, chest tight with the joy it's trying to contain. "I like stealing your hoodies. It's like wearing a Theo hug."

"You can wear whatever you like...or as little as you like..." Theo bites on his bottom lip, trying to focus and not immediately be distracted by how attractive Emir is in any amount of clothing. They both have a thing for the other wearing something of theirs. "I just wanted to make space for you. Because, like...it's sort of your flat now, too."

"At the rate we're going, Laur and I will only use our flat for weed, sex, and storage." Emir laughs, glad to realise that he doesn't feel anything even remotely resembling panic with the confirmation of a new type of commitment from Theo. It feels right, like Theo found the perfect time to offer this. "And with Alfie here more often, we're at seven gays in one flat. You sure there's room for me?"

"I'm sure." Theo laughs along, happy that Emir's accepting his offer to share the flat, seemingly feeling as right about it as Theo had yesterday when he made it happen. "I think we both needed a few days to figure out what it is we want, even if the way we got that space wasn't great. But, like, if we add the things you asked about into our weeks, I think we'll have more time with our own thoughts, which we need sometimes."

"I didn't bring anything with me to leave here." Emir traces a hand through Theo's damp hair before sitting up and rolling off the side of the bed. "Maybe we could pick a few things up later? How much space did you make?"

"Half of the second and third drawers." Theo watches Emir open the aforementioned drawers, smiling as he turns back around to Theo.

"Same side as my side of the bed." Emir notices, always in awe of how neat and organised Theo's belongings are. He literally folds everything, from his socks to his boxers to his dance attire. And Theo even put in little drawer dividers so they could keep their things separate, probably knowing that Emir's will stay a bit of a mess, even in this much neater bedroom.

"And a bit of space in the cupboard." Theo watches Emir move around his room, appreciating how he waits for Theo's permission before snooping around, even in this context. It's his now, too, but it's an adjustment for them both.

Emir thinks about how many of his things already reside here, and vice versa, how they both keep toiletries at each other's flat, how they share hoodies and hats and tee shirts, how Emir has extra blankets at both flats, how Theo keeps an eye mask and headphones at Emir's tucked away in a drawer, just in case. What Theo's done is essentially formalise a decision they've already been making together, turning momentum into intentional growth. He's spectacular. "Let's go on an adventure tomorrow."

Theo sits up at Emir's suggestion. He's turned around again, facing Theo with bright eyes and hope in his posture. "What sort of adventure?"

"Well, we have the master class next weekend and Laurie's family will be here visiting, so we can't go then. It's been a while since we ran away together." Emir sits sideways on the bed, taking Theo's hand and bringing it to his lips. "Like that day in Cookham but with a happier start. Let's get lost together and find our way."

"Yeah?" Theo grins as Emir stares at him with a bounce in his movements, like a kid excited for a trip to the zoo. He loves Theo so much, so happy at the idea of an adventure together. "First thing? Well, not first thing because I need to do my weekly chores, but that should only take an hour or so, and you can sleep through that anyway, and we can get breakfast on the way somewhere so we don't waste time on it here, but where should we go? Because I don't want to drive too far, but it's meant to be random, so maybe just picking a time limit would be best - "

"Hour drive or less." Emir presses their lips together, tackling Theo as delicately as possible, even if he still gets the wind knocked out of him a bit. "Opposite direction as before. I'll bring art supplies this time, because I'll definitely want to paint you wherever we end up."

"That sounds perfect." Theo lets himself be kissed for a minute, the security of this morning so gorgeous in his mind. It's as if he can physically feel the safety that he and Emir represent for each other. He won't hurt Emir and Emir won't leave him, and other than that, they'll figure it out. "I'll call my mum this afternoon so I don't miss our weekly chat."

"You're literally the best: best boyfriend, best son, best mate, best dance partner, just..." Emir sighs again, kissing Theo's forehead where his curls have left an open spot. He'll do all of the difficult internal work necessary to keep their relationship healthy and stable. Emir doesn't want to lose this. "Did we talk about all the things so we can go annoy our friends while we very loudly make something to eat until Laurie throws something at us to make us stop kissing in the kitchen?"

"Well, um..." Theo swallows past the sudden lump in his throat. He was sort of hoping this would come up organically, but it hasn't. Theo decided this weekend would be when he shares this with Emir, this vulnerable part of himself that he doesn't want to feel like he's hiding anymore. And he's never felt safer, so it's definitely time. "There was one more thing I wanted to talk about."

Sitting up, Theo takes Emir with him. Emir tilts his head, touching Theo's hair and kissing the underside of his jaw while Theo situates himself with his back against the headboard. He stares at his collection of art, the tangible reminders of Emir's presence in his life, an important piece of himself that he's shared with Theo the past few months. That collection is Emir's love for him made visible.

"Go on then. I'm listening." Emir waits for several more seconds, giving Theo plenty of time. There's no rush. Theo seems to be deciding on the right words, his brow scrunched while he chews on the inside of his cheek.

"I'm autistic." Theo darts his eyes over to Emir then back down to his hands where he still has one of Emir's held in both of his own. Especially after his shutdown this week, he'll feel better if Emir knows and they can talk about it together. He's not ashamed and he wants Emir to know all of him. "I have autism, but I prefer to say I'm autistic."

Emir waits longer, wondering if Theo needs to keep talking or if he's listening for a response. He doesn't seem scared or worried or anxious or anything, just…Theo glances at him again and Emir realises he's asking him to react somehow. "Tell me more?"

Theo releases a sigh of relief, a smile relaxing across his face. Of course Emir wants him to share in his own words rather than being invasive or making assumptions. Emir knows that T's autistic, and it's never once been an issue, but sometimes it's different person to person. Theo's his boyfriend and the person Emir spends the most time with, and Theo's been told before that he can be…complicated.

"I've known, like, my whole life. Since I was a kid. But it's hard for me to share with people because of, um, all the bullying when I was younger. And still sometimes now, unfortunately. People don't understand and they don't listen and there's all sorts of bad information that gets spread around. And, like, I'm just one person, and I don't enjoy spending my life correcting people's harmful opinions about it just so I can exist, you know?"

Theo pauses for a moment, finding his train of thought from before. Emir's been quietly soothing him as he gets worked up, which makes Theo even more glad to be telling him.

"In some ways I'm sort of lucky for knowing my whole life because I was able to get some support, even though it wasn't all good, but…anyway, I wanted to tell you because it's not, like, a secret, but I was worried...I didn't want you to see me differently or anything, even though that's sort of inevitable." Theo finishes with a small huff of relief at finally having shared this.

"You're my Theo, baby. I know your heart. You've always been honest with me and you get to decide what parts of you are shared, with me or with anyone else." Emir cradles Theo's face in both of his hands, sliding his thumbs along Theo's cheekbones and holding the weight of the moment in his hands. "But I should tell you that I've sort of known for a while."

"Who...?" Theo runs through the list of people he's told, wondering if it was T or Laurie or Lili, because none of them seem likely. And no one else at Roseborough explicitly knows, not even Sean.

Although, he's positive plenty of people know he's neurodivergent in some way or another, and he's pretty sure Ciaran figured it out years ago and just sort of went with it. But Theo's also high masking and dance is one of his special interests where he can stim in a lot of his preferred ways, so some people don't even notice.

"Your mum accidentally told me." Emir watches Theo for a reaction. He didn't think he should hide the fact that he already knew. It didn't change anything when he found out besides further understanding certain things Theo says, especially about his past. "The night I met your family after *Alice*. She made a comment like she assumed I already knew. And I wasn't going to ask you about it, knowing you'd tell me in your own time. I wanted to hear your experience from you, but only when you were ready."

Emir knows what it's like to have your truth shared without your consent, though of course their situations are incredibly different.

"That's...thank you. I don't usually get that chance." Theo tugs at Emir until he settles beside Theo and he can hold him again. He lays his head on Emir's shoulder, arms going around him from the side while he gets comfortable. Theo's so glad Emir is as tactile as he is.

"I noticed a few months ago that I don't mask around you, at least not anymore. When we used to fight all the time I did, but I tend to mask with basically everyone else. Because of how things were as a kid, I repress a lot and it's exhausting. But once you saw me, like, really *saw* me, it just...fell away. I don't stop myself from stimming or asking for what I need, and, like, our energy is really compatible. When I need time to decompress, you need quiet for your introvert time, or whatever you call it. And when

I need hugs or my weighted blanket, you cuddle up with me like it's as easy as breathing. So I wanted you to know because sometimes I need to talk about things and I want to be open about it with you. My brain isn't like everyone else's, and that's alright, even if it can be difficult living in a neurotypical world. Being autistic is part of me, like my accent or my sexuality or the colour of my eyes. There's things I could do to hide it, but I don't want to hide from you."

Emir keeps stroking Theo's hair, pressing occasional kisses to the top of his head while he talks. He knew they'd have this conversation at some point and he can't imagine any other way but this: alone in Theo's room, cuddling through their calm back and forth. "Can I ask who else knows? I've never heard you talking about it with the others, but I guess you wouldn't if you're keeping it private."

"T was the first person I told, probably for the same reason you told them you're genderqueer, right?" Theo turns his head to ask, Emir nodding and staring back with soft eyes. Theo couldn't love him more. "Laurie sort of figured it out and just asked me one day. Not in, like, a rude way, of course. He'd already known for months about T so it wasn't really anything new to him. He was mostly just confirming and I trusted him. Always have."

"Of course." Emir grins because Laurie is a natural at being blunt but respectful, never crossing a line and always clear with his intentions; he's the most supportive person in the world. The past week has been evidence enough of that.

"And Lili. I told her last year when I had my first shutdown around her. Well, I told her after." Theo isn't used to talking this openly about his autism except with other neurodivergent people. It's nice to share this part of himself with Emir and defog the window into his mind that he assures Theo he loves. "I lost speech for a few hours after a particularly rough day of trying to push through burnout and had to sort of hide away and rest for a while. She was concerned and it just felt like the right time to tell her. I let her in, since she was already basically family. Like Laurie."

"I, um, I remember in those first few weeks of us getting to know each other, earlier this year...I used to notice you sort of, like, code switch from being relaxed to, like, having some sort of front. I was worried you thought you had to act a certain way around me. And I didn't mind, I just...noticed." Emir hopes this isn't going to make Theo uncomfortable, but the goal is for Theo to know that Emir loves all of him, especially his soft, squishy, vulnerable heart. He doesn't want Theo to ever feel like he has to hide around him. "I hoped maybe you were getting more comfortable with me but couldn't trust me yet, which is totally fair after the history we have."

"That is actually what happened. Like, quite literally. I would stop masking around you and only notice occasionally and at first I was sort of panicked." Theo presses his face beneath Emir's jaw, closing his eyes and letting himself be held. He'll try to explain his sensory seeking later since it's part of all this.

"And a lot of the time I don't mask consciously because I'm just trying to fit in and anticipate reactions, to avoid being laughed at or bullied. Like, there's this horrible thing that happens, similar to when you meet a new person and you're trying to find out if they're safe to come out to, but you're worried about their reaction. Sometimes I'll let my guard down and unmask just a tiny bit, like bounce when I get excited or ask a bunch of questions about one of my interests, and it's only because I felt safe around them for a second. But I can tell the moment they decide I'm 'not normal.' They think they're being subtle but they're not. There's this expression they get, or worse, they, like, verbally point out how weird they think I am. And it fucking hurts. It's like I think I've made a new friend, but the moment I'm even the tiniest bit my actual unfiltered self, they *know* and they think of me differently. And then I have to continue like nothing happened and pretend I'm fine and then go home and process it all on my own and probably cry about it and decide to keep that person at a distance for my own sake because they're *not* a safe person. And I'm reminded all over again that people can be cruel, and it's like I'm four years old at the park, wanting to show my favourite dinosaur to the other kids, but they think I'm weird or talk funny or make strange faces and they tell me I'm scary or call me an alien and they don't want to play with me, and I wish it didn't still hurt but it does. It hurts so bad. I don't want to feel ashamed of myself, but sometimes people are fucking cruel when I haven't even done anything wrong. I just...I get excited or overwhelmed or happy and I just react. And spending so much time hiding is really exhausting."

Emir knows that people are cruel, he's seen evidence enough in his own life, but to hear about it like this, knowing how vulnerable and kind and generous Theo is only to have people treat him that way is genuinely sickening. "Baby...I hope I've never made you feel that way."

"You haven't!" Theo sits up immediately, because he's sharing all this with Emir as part of his experience, not trying to make him feel bad for something he's never done. He's reminded of that night his family was visiting, when Emir found out how badly he'd been bullied growing up, and Theo needs to make sure that Emir knows the difference.

Putting his hands on Emir's shoulders, Theo wipes his teary eyes on the sleeve of his henley. "Not once. I wouldn't have even talked to you unless I absolutely had to if that was the case, for self-preservation. Even when we were fighting or being awful to each other, you never did that. It's one of the reasons I trusted you, even then. You were never cruel, babe."

"Alright, just wanted to make sure. Because I'd like to personally fight every single person who does that, to you or to anyone else like you." Emir kisses the tip of Theo's nose, smiling as he settles back in against Emir's front. They take turns being the little spoon, but sometimes Theo likes to be surrounded by cuddles. Like now. "I'm glad you feel safe enough to tell me all this. I don't know what it feels like in the same way, but I know it's hard to talk about things that hurt. T tells me stories sometimes, but I'm sure it's just like with everything else, how each person has their own experience, yeah?"

"Yeah. Lots of different ways to be autistic." Theo sighs, wrapping Emir's arms around himself until it feels just right. Somehow Emir reads his mind and sets his chin on Theo's shoulder so they're as close as possible. "T and I are different in a lot of ways, but sometimes, when it's just us and all the boyfriends are away, we joke that we have the neurodivergent flat. Like, Ciaran has his OCD, even if it's generally less noticeable, and T and I are autistic, and it's sort of like queer people, how we tend to find each other. I feel really lucky to have the two of them as flatmates."

"We have the best friends." Emir kisses Theo's cheek and gives him a full body squeeze before relaxing back against the headboard. "And *I* have the best boyfriend. You're my favourite person in the entire world."

"The feeling is very mutual." Theo sits quietly for a minute, enjoying the peace of a morning in his room with Emir while the vague sounds of their many, many flatmates filter under the door. He's going to miss this next year, with everyone off on their next adventure, an indeterminate amount of space between them. Theo squeezes Emir's arms at the thought, hoping he'll get to keep holding him close wherever they go next.

The following hour passes in much the same way, Theo sharing more about his autism with Emir, Emir sharing his own stories that Theo hasn't heard. They could stay here for hours without realising the day has passed them by, never running out of things to talk about. Their natural comfort is part of how they got into the situation they're working their way out of. When it's this easy to be together, it's harder to remember that time apart is needed. But that's why they both have to be intentional about it.

When they look at the schedule Theo created to make adjustments, Theo tells Emir how he was taught to think of his calendar like a colouring book: the lines and general structure are defined, but he can colour it in however he wants; he has his routine, but there's always room left for quiet time or walks with Emir or a last minute change (even if those are still less than desirable). Emir praises Theo's ability to schedule, his own mind barely able to keep track of the time most days, and he brags about how he's shared Theo's calendar with his mum and Safiya and how they use it to know when they can call him or, in Safiya's case, stop by for a visit.

Emir takes the opportunity to talk to Theo about how he wants to focus on taking better care of himself, and part of that is having more routine. He thanks Theo for showing him by example, and teaching him more about real self care, the less fun or aesthetic, but truly necessary parts. Like how Emir needs to feed himself even when he's busy, or how he gets more regular sleep with Theo in his bed. But Emir doesn't want to rely on Theo and put that burden on him, he just appreciates the example Theo sets. Maybe they're both the inspiration boyfriend.

Theo talks about how when they had their *Cinderella* date, he'd told Emir he worried he was hard to love, too difficult or complicated. And at the time he'd come out as demi to Emir, but that was only half the reason for what he said. That date and their huge fight the week before both hit Theo in a particularly sensitive spot: he'd been told by society and the media that he was unlovable for being autistic, that no one would ever want him, and even if they did, he'd be *too much* and unable to ever have a family or know romantic love. Theo's parents had always been the antithesis of those messages, reminding Theo of the beautiful person he is and giving him the confidence he never would've found elsewhere.

But that doubt stuck with him, like a shadow over his head anytime he did develop a crush, or even a desire for friendship with someone new. And Emir apologises again for leaving Theo behind when he needed space, for feeding into his deepest insecurities, albeit without meaning to. They share a tender moment of acceptance, a different sort of apology and forgiveness than earlier. The new phrases that Emir taught Theo first thing this morning, reassurances that Emir won't leave and that Theo won't hurt Emir, are sealed with a kiss before they decide to get out of bed and spend a few hours with their friends, then head to the studio to work on their dissertation for the first time in days.

On Sunday, they find their way to Farnham in Theo's car. It's much colder than their last adventure, both of them bundled up against the chill as they walk down the main road, making new memories together for another day. Over lunch at a spot called Veena's Kitchen, Theo shares his list with Emir, all the creatures and plants he wanted to learn about during their days apart. Emir tells him as much as he knows, Theo making notes on a borrowed piece of sketch paper from Emir's art supplies.

Emir uses his phone to show Theo a bird called a bearded reedling, because it's so fluffy and round and he knew Theo's eyes would go wide and bright the moment he saw a picture. He hands Theo the phone and starts sketching, needing to capture Theo's light. Spending the day getting lost might be the best idea Theo's ever had, and Emir's so happy to be included in one of Theo's secret joys.

By the time they're back home from their adventure, they need an hour apart to recharge before spending their evening together. After their alone time, Emir brings a bag of his things to keep at Theo's while he picks him up to walk back to his flat where they're spending the night. Theo helps him decide where to keep everything, joggers and dance clothes and two of his hoodies to share.

After a meandering walk around campus, cuddled up the entire distance, they're in Emir's flat for the night, showered and bundled under many blankets in Emir's bed, talking about the week to come and thinking as far as the upcoming holiday break that's sooner than they're ready for. They still need to work on finding balance and following their plans for a healthier path forward, but this upcoming week feels significantly more promising than the last.

CHAPTER SEVEN

"Are you sure we have enough time?" Theo looks around at his friends with concern as he finishes setting the table.

Unlike their standard family dinner, this week's tableware is accompanied by novelty party hats and whatever decorations the five of them could throw together to celebrate Laurie's birthday two weeks early.

"Plenty. He's being actively distracted at work for at least another ten minutes." T smiles at Theo from their spot in the kitchen where they're putting the final decorative touches on a small, round cake. They managed to frost it in red and black swirls, Laurie's current favourite colour combination, with *Happy Birthday Laurie* in cursive icing across the top.

"And we're sure about the balloons?" Gabe asks, holding up the sad, leftover bag of gold rejects from some forgotten party in their first year that T had found tucked away in their decor box.

"They'll pop if we even try." Ciaran takes them away from Gabe, tossing them back in the box and handing him a present for Laurie instead. "Help me wrap. I forgot we were doing that this year."

"He deserves a nice party, and since he refused a proper one, he's getting this." Emir sneaks up behind Theo, hands finding his waist to pull him into a hug, Emir's front to Theo's back. He sets his chin on Theo's shoulder and smiles as Theo's arms cross on top of his own, inviting him to stay in his space. Without needing to look, Emir knows Theo has his eyes shut, a peaceful smile growing by the second. Things have been really good the past few weeks, like the calm after a storm. "Need any help?"

"Nah, almost done." Theo sighs happily, turning himself around in Emir's arms for a kiss and a cuddle. "Think he'll like it?"

"Mhm." Emir starts swaying them on the spot, arms around Theo's shoulders with their foreheads pressed together. "I like the little name plates. Very sweet. Thoughtful."

"I thought they'd make it feel more like a dinner party." Theo mumbles, pressing another kiss to Emir's lips while being gently danced around the side of the table. "And then I thought about their wedding and how soon it is. Only a few months away."

"You ready for it, Mr. Best Man?" Emir slides his nose along Theo's and tucks away a sideways smile. "Started on your speech yet?"

"Have you?" Theo surprises Emir by squeezing his bum, making him startle and swat him away before pulling him right back into his arms. Laurie and T asked both of them to act as best man, with Gabe and Ciaran as unofficial bonus groomsmen. Their wedding party is so far from traditional, with both fiances sharing a mixture of Laurie's sisters and their uni friends, with T's sister Lucy as their officiant.

Barely twenty seconds into their heated kiss, because how could they possibly not when they're in each other's arms and talking about weddings, a cushion sails from across the room and thumps them both on the side of the head. They groan and break apart. Emir scoffs, leaning down to retrieve the projectile and launch it back at Ciaran who dodges, meaning Gabe gets hit in the centre of his broad chest. Good thing he's tall.

"Sorry, New York. Collateral damage." Emir calls over, taking Theo by the hand instead and leading him to the kitchen to help T get everything plated. Gabe only laughs and lets Ciaran fuss at him for a moment before finishing wrapping the box in his hand. This one contains Laurie's favourite hair mousse that Ciaran bought to go with the new dopp kit he's getting as his Christmas gift.

To compensate for Laurie's birthday being just after Christmas and often overlooked, they were all very firm that there are birthday gifts to be opened when they celebrate together at uni and then there are Christmas gifts that they all take home and open Christmas day (or in Emir's case, whenever he wants over break). No cross contamination of presents allowed, and no expectations that anything be expensive or even cost money at all, most of their favourite gifts being homemade or fungible. They'd decided years ago over family dinner that what matters to them is the thought, remembering each other for important dates and celebrating together when possible.

Just as Theo and Emir are carrying dinner to the table, containing all of Laurie's favourites, the front door to the flat opens and T squeals, rushing at Laurie and covering his eyes as quickly as they can.

"You were supposed to be busy for four more minutes." T keeps a hand across Laurie's eyes, letting him squirm his way out of his shoes and coat while hindered by his fiance. He's used to this sort of thing with T by now.

"Whatever you all are up to, you shouldn't have." Laurie grumbles, finally disentangling himself from his coat sleeves and tugging T forward instead.

T lets their hand drop to kiss Laurie hello but immediately covers his eyes again as if they knew he was just trying to get a peek.

"I knew Risa was trying to slow me down. I can't believe you roped my lesbians into this, you devious little minx." Laurie tickles at T's sides until they have to drop their hands entirely. He pulls T into him and smiles around at his friends.

"Um...surprise?" Theo shrugs and steps away from the table with a half hearted flourish, Emir rolling his eyes and walking over to pull the (almost) birthday boy into a hug. Why any of them ever thought they could pull a proper surprise over on Laurie is beyond him, but birthday hugs are necessary even if they didn't get to complete the whole hiding in the dark behind the sofa bit.

"You're lucky Gabe helped me wrap or I'd shove you back in the corridor until we were done." Ciaran stands up from the floor where he and Gabe have just finished Laurie's presents, but the evidence of their last minute attempt is still on the coffee table. It'll have to do.

When Emir lets Laurie go, Theo's next to hug Laurie, arms firm around his back, the two of them holding on for several seconds longer than they normally would. It's that time of year when they're halfway through and they're all starting to realise that this is...it. It's their last few months together before everything changes. Their last holiday break before they leave uni and each other behind, possibly forever.

"No weeping, Teddy. I'm older, not dead." Laurie grins when Theo lets out a wet laugh because he had, in fact, started to cry. He's so damn grateful for Laurie and he doesn't know what any of them would do without him. He's the roots of this found family tree.

"I just sort of love you, alright?" Theo wipes at his eyes, cringing when Laurie gives him a very loud kiss on the cheek and pushes him towards Emir instead, who gathers Theo into his space without hesitation.

Emir brushes Theo's hair off his forehead and kisses the tip of his nose, joining their hands between them. He's been feeling extra affectionate the past few weeks, as if making up for those dark days of lost time.

"Ciaran." Laurie's the one to grab Ciaran, messing up his hair and clapping him on the back several times while accepting his mumbled birthday wishes and at least one filthy joke that makes Laurie laugh properly and step away again.

"Happy birthday, man." Gabe's last in the line of embraces, his hug warm and genuine, and Laurie thanks him while holding him close. The two of them don't spend much alone time together, but that doesn't mean they aren't just as sentimental and important to each other as the rest.

"Well since the surprise is ruined…" T lets out a long suffering sigh that has Laurie turning back to look at them. T's dimple shows as they catch sight of Laurie's bright smile and gorgeous blue eyes that they fell in love with about a week before being all in on the rest of Laurie. "Happy birthday, Laur. We love you."

"But you most of all, right babygirl?" Laurie gathers T up into his arms for a passionate kiss, dipping them and earning a few laughs from their friends.

Their engagement last year had been a surprise to no one, announced just before most of them left for their time abroad. There'd been a ring box hidden safely inside T's favourite overcoat pocket, Laurie loving the thrill of never knowing which moment it would be discovered, but always prepared for the event. It was unseasonably warm and took four days of eagerly waiting before he heard the excited squeal and was able to finally propose. They're so in love it's unfathomable that they only met a little over two years ago, thanks to Emir's match making.

Laurie strokes T's hair from their face and cradles them in his hold with practised ease. "Thank you for my little party, love."

"They helped." T credits their friends, blinking their eyes open as Laurie guides them back to standing. "You said no party, but this doesn't count. It's only a few decorations at family dinner…and presents after."

"I also said no presents." Laurie looks around at all of them, faux stern with his reproach. As if they were ever going to listen to that. "We'll be getting loads of gifts at the wedding. You didn't need to do all this."

"Shut up and let us love you." Emir groans, pulling out Theo's seat at the table and waiting for him to take it before sliding into his own chair across from him. The other four follow a moment later, settling into their usual spots and putting on the party hats T had insisted on. "T spent hours on your cake and we all helped cook. You will sit here and eat your birthday dinner and your birthday cake and open your birthday presents and let us make tonight about you for once."

"What Emi said." Theo nods his head, already passing around the pizza that he'd made, knowing it's one of Laurie's favourites. "You're always so busy taking care of us and everyone else. You said no party, so this is just family dinner with a Laurie theme."

"We even agreed to watch *Grease* after presents to make it a proper Laurie appreciation night." Ciaran adds, readjusting his party hat to rest behind his quiff. He's not normally one for musicals, but he'll make an exception for Laurie.

"And we're singing you *Happy Birthday* and you're blowing out candles. We'll know if you don't make a wish." Gabe grins when Laurie grumbles and covers his eyes with his palms. "*And* T will be taking pictures. We don't have enough of us all together."

"Seems I've been outvoted." Laurie drags his hands down his face and reaches for the pizza that T is holding out to him, taking two slices for himself and trying very hard not to cry. It's really nice to feel appreciated for once, even if he pushes back so hard against it. "I'll allow you tonight, but no more fussing until the wedding. And even that should be directed at my fiance."

Laurie nudges T with his shoulder, well aware that he's going to cry once they're alone together that night. T sees all his softest, squishiest moments that are too private to share with anyone else.

"We'll be fussing over *both* of you." Theo counters, knowing that Laurie sometimes needs a push to let himself have nights like this. He can't always be the caretaker. "Now, who's starting tonight? Gabe?"

"Ooo yes. I totally killed it in the studio today." Gabe starts his story with excited eyes and a kiss to his cheek from Ciaran. He's always proud of his boy, listening to Gabe's update with his full attention and showering him with praise when he's finished sharing, as if he hasn't already heard of all this and then some.

The rest of the night goes exactly as they plan: dinner shared along with their usual weekly updates, presents opened and appreciated, *Grease* watched and sung along to. It's one of those nights that feels nostalgic even as it's being spent, where they settle into their respective bedrooms at the end and store away the memory of it in the safest parts of their minds.

T softly sings another *Happy Birthday* to Laurie as they drift off, Emir and Theo cuddle up and swap stories of past birthdays that they've spent apart, both vaguely alluding to spending the next few together, and Ciaran and Gabe talk quietly about next year, if they'll be able to make it back for things like birthdays or holidays, if their plans to move to New York are truly what they want when they look ahead.

The future and the past both seem unknowable tonight, this little family celebration helping them understand why now is referred to as the present. This young life together has been such a gift, one that none of them are quite ready to move beyond just yet.

***

"It's so quiet. Almost...spooky." Theo looks at Emir across the pillows of his bed, the flat empty and most of the building with it. The Christmas holiday has officially started with almost every single person abandoning the campus and the student flats earlier in the day, all of their friends included. Lili and Jo joined them for dinner, but even the two of them are now on their way to their respective homes, leaving Emir and Theo to the peace of the empty building, alone.

"You glad we decided to stay tonight with everyone else gone?" Emir asks, drawing shapes across Theo's chest beneath the sheets then pressing a hand above his heart. "It was weird working on our dissertation in the middle of the afternoon with rehearsals cancelled so everyone could head home."

"I like being alone with you. We have the whole flat to ourselves." Theo finds Emir's feet with his toes, tangling them together under the sheets. Somehow, Emir's feet are cold even after the warm shower they just left. "And...I'll miss you. Three weeks seems like such a long time and no time at all."

"Yeah...three weeks." Emir doesn't correct Theo, because he has a surprise planned that he absolutely does not want to ruin. Especially if it doesn't work out. "It's still early. Did you want to go to sleep? I can entertain myself if you need the rest."

"Actually, I sort of want to talk about...sex." Theo flushes, eyes drifting away from Emir's face to stare at his chest instead. They're already naked, or rather naked still, since they've already showered after a few hours together in the dance studio followed by dinner with their friends. Being all alone in the flat means they don't have to worry about flashing anyone, so they'd taken the opportunity to revel in their comfortable nudity together.

Emir moves his hand to graze under Theo's chin, rubbing gently at the stubble there until Theo looks back up at him. "What have you been thinking?"

Theo gets so shy sometimes, even when it's just the two of them, but Emir always wants to hear what Theo has to share.

"I think I'm ready for…more. Not like *sex* sex yet, but I've been dreaming about - " Theo flushes deeper, hiding his face against Emir's chest. His dreams have been incredibly vivid the past week or so, and he even came in his sleep once. Honestly, Theo's not sure how it didn't wake Emir up because he was probably moving around and making…sounds. But Emir was still asleep when Theo cleaned himself up in the bathroom before rejoining him for a few more hours of rest.

Emir kisses the top of Theo's head, hugging him close and waiting. He knows that sex is different for Theo, for multiple reasons: Emir's the first person Theo's been sexually intimate with, he's demi, and he's explained to Emir how, because of his autism, he's both sensory seeking and sensory avoidant, depending on the environment and about a dozen other factors.

Emir has never loved anyone more than Theo. He doesn't wish they were doing more or moving faster, very satisfied with the sexual experiences they've shared. "I wonder if your dreams are anything like mine."

"You've been having dreams?" Theo asks, words muffled because he's still cuddling up into Emir. It's just so comfortable with his face pressed to Emir's chest, his scent and his heartbeat and his *everything* surrounding Theo like a safety blanket.

"So many dreams about you, baby. Some of them are about sex but there's…others." Emir would never admit it to anyone else, but Theo is literally the man of his dreams, the perfect partner for him, the person he loves more every single day.

Emir used to think Laurie was daft, talking about how he knew T was his person from the first few weeks of dating, but now he gets it. Emir's not being unrealistic, he knows that life may pull them in opposite directions, but what matters is that he *wants* to choose a life with Theo, something he never knew was in his future.

"Others?" Theo peeks up at him, staying in his arms but meeting Emir's kind eyes. "What others?"

"Nope, you won't distract me that easily." Emir grins, running his fingers through Theo's curls. His hands always find their way into Theo's hair. "Tell me about sex, I'm listening."

Theo nods and starts to ramble, all of his thoughts tumbling out with barely enough space in between to breathe.

"Okay, well, first: I want us both to get tested for everything before we have, like, all-the-way sex, regardless of who's bottoming or whatever. I know you went this year and neither of us is having any symptoms, but I've never been before and I'm nervous as hell, and I know we aren't doing anything with increased risk yet, but maybe we could go together because doctors can be scary for me - I mean, I guess they're scary for a lot of people - but I don't like not knowing what's happening, and sometimes they won't explain what they're doing which makes me anxious because I just want to understand, but they think it's annoying or like I'm weird and - " Theo's ramble gets cut off by a soft kiss. "Oomf."

"I've been to the uni health clinic a few times and they won't mind you asking questions." Emir presses his lips against Theo's once more, waiting for him to relax before he leans away again. "We can go together, but they probably won't let us be in the room together. Confidentiality and all that."

"Oh...I'll have to think about that." Theo's brow furrows because he was sort of hoping Emir could hold his hand through the appointment, or at least be there just in case he needed to be comforted. "I know we need to go, so I'll just have to...prepare. Know what to expect."

"They're closed for the holiday, but we could make appointments when we get back in the new year, or just whenever you're ready. We don't have to call or anything, just book online." Emir's used to the process. He's been sexually active since before uni, and the student health centre is very busy with sexual health screenings. "They give you free condoms, too."

"Oh, I already bought some for us." Theo bought a collection of things once he and Emir got together: lube and condoms and a proper douche, which he hasn't tried yet but knows he'll feel more comfortable with than some of the other options he's looked into. He's done a significant amount of research, both before and after making that purchase. "And we're like...similar sizes."

"Nah, you probably measured yourself and needed large since you're *thicc* and I fit just fine in the standard, but we don't have to worry about that tonight. I have my own stash. They're rainbow." Emir grins, knowing he's more than prepared for whenever Theo feels ready to take that step. Or, if he never does, there's plenty of ways for them to be intimate, even if anal sex isn't something Theo ever wants.

"Of course they are." Theo rolls his eyes, teasing while leaning forward for another kiss. By this point in their relationship, they're both quite fluent in conversing while kissing, pausing to make a point then back to getting off. "Should've known you would use rainbow condoms."

"I would hate to be confused for a heterosexual." Emir kisses Theo deeper this time, Theo's lips always so plush and soft that it's a small miracle Emir ever does anything else.

He lets himself get lost in Theo's kiss for a minute, hands in Theo's hair or caressing his back, legs tangled together, Theo kissing him back with equal enthusiasm. Emir could do this for hours, and sometimes they do, snog and caress and moan and enjoy each other without the need to take it any further. It's one of Emir's favourite things about the ways they love one another, that sometimes they stop here, sometimes they go further, and either way, neither of them feels any pressure or disappointment with the outcome.

Theo loves the way Emir loves him: the care, the intensity, the gentle hands and firm hold, the way he feels adored and wanted in equal measure. It's so easy with Emir, so beautiful and warm, like building home with each new kiss. Theo's body has never come alive because of another person before. He's never felt this strong of an emotional bond to even develop this sort of sexual desire.

They've been dating almost two months now, officially, and Theo can only imagine how much better this can get, but… "I want to try new things."

"Mm?" Emir hums his question because he's not sure what Theo means by new. Their evening has already heated up significantly in the past few minutes, bodies moving together, kisses deep, tongues exploring, and hands everywhere they can reach.

"Blowjobs." Theo answers, still kissing Emir because he's very in the moment. He's just also ready for more, and he knows he has to say something to make it happen. Emir will *never* assume what Theo wants, so as hard as words are when they're intimate together, "I'm ready for - want to try -"

"Hold on." Emir pulls himself back, panting slightly and putting a hand on Theo's chest. Maybe this is what Theo meant to bring up earlier before they both got distracted. "Talk to me, princess. What is it you want?"

Theo whines, leaning towards Emir and stealing a tiny kiss, but Emir's hand holds him off from going any further. "That's what I've been dreaming about. Blowjobs."

"Oh. Right." Emir's eyes fall to Theo's mouth, lips wet and darkened from their rough snogging. The number of times he's imagined that mouth on his body, sliding along his dick, rimming his arse (which he's done for Theo more than once, but not the other way around yet), there's just a world of possibilities to explore. And if Theo's kissing is any indication of technique, then things are about to get incredibly interesting. "Giving or receiving?"

"Both. Definitely both." Theo notices Emir's fixation on his mouth, the way he keeps trying to look at Theo's eyes but is drawn back over and over again in the space of only a few seconds. "Is that, um, could we try that?"

"What, like right now?" Emir finally does focus on something other than those pouty lips, meeting Theo's equally beautiful eyes instead. "You're...are you sure? I don't want you...just because I'm - and we're leaving tomorrow morning - "

Emir's suddenly worried about half a dozen things, but he's not really sure why. Theo's the one who brought up this topic.

"Woah, babe." Theo's calmed back down enough to have a mostly normal conversation again, noticing the slight panic in Emir's face and guessing the reason. "You haven't pressured me into anything. I'm ready. Really truly completely ready. I've been wanting to ask for a week at least, but we've been busy with uni and Laurie's birthday party and everything else."

"You promise? That's sort of a new level, you know?" Emir drops his hand from Theo's chest and lets it fall to his waist instead, running softly up and down Theo's side. His skin is incredibly smooth. "I'm ready for anything with you, I just...I know taking this step means something to you that's well beyond physical."

Theo's heart may melt right through his toes because Emir is almost too lovely. It's not only the consent, which is both mandatory and continual, but the understanding of Theo's heart and his mind in a way that informs all of Emir's behaviour with him. He doesn't push, he doesn't assume. Instead, Emir asks and he talks with him, giving Theo the voice and the agency that they've both had taken from them before. "The past few weeks have been even better than before. I was already on this road with you, but now it's definitely...more. So, yes. I'm ready for the physical and the other stuff. I'm there, babe."

Emir doesn't say anything right away. He can tell that Theo's being sincere, that he is ready. Emir just needs a moment to understand that, between the mention of penetrative sex earlier and Theo wanting to try oral sex tonight, they're entering a new phase of their relationship.

For some people the sex comes first and the other aspects later, but with Theo it's all tied together, interwoven and inseparable. Theo's committed to him and to their relationship, and Emir already knows that, but this is just another reminder. His PTSD makes him hesitant to accept this information even though he knows he's safe with Theo. Several weeks of counselling have helped Emir understand himself and his reactions better, so he recognises why he's feeling a bit caught off guard. It's not Theo, rather it's Emir not trusting himself.

"Are you ready, though?" Theo asks after several moments of Emir continuing to hold him close without responding to his reassurance. He's ready for more, but there's two of them in this relationship and in this bed, and both of them have to be on board with everything they do. Just because Emir has experience doesn't mean he's automatically going to want to do every sexual thing that Theo imagines.

"What?" Emir looks up into Theo's eyes again, hoping his silence hasn't been misinterpreted as discomfort or disinterest when it's almost completely the opposite. He's so invested in Theo, so physically and emotionally attached that it scares him. "Oh, baby, you have no idea. I'm very ready. I was just...reminding myself of a few things."

Theo nods, rolling onto his back and pulling Emir against his chest. After settling in, he repeats that phrase Emir taught him a few weeks ago, a promise that he won't hurt him but in Urdu. He says it twice before Emir sighs and responds, promising that he won't leave.

They take turns pressing kisses to each other's skin, their cheeks, necks, shoulders, noses, foreheads, all while trading those promises until they're giggling together, any anxiety gone. Emir tickles Theo's sides and Theo laughs and squirms beneath him, thinking about how wonderful it is to be in love.

"You still want that tonight?" Emir asks, stopping his tickle attack in favour of playing with Theo's hair instead. He adores this beautiful boy, this kind hearted man, and all the delicate sides he gets to see. Theo isn't like this with anyone else, this unguarded and free. Sometimes Emir can't believe that he's the one who gets to know him so completely.

"I still very much want that, yes. I was wondering if maybe you could like...show me?" Theo circles Emir's waist and brings him closer until their bodies are flush again. It won't take long to work back up to the intensity they'd found a few minutes before. "I don't know what it feels like or how to make it feel good, and I swear I'm not being a pillow princess - "

"You can be a pillow princess if you like." Emir grins, the side of his smile tilted but true. He'll never forget Theo admitting he's probably a bottom like it was some sort of secret at the very start of their relationship. "I don't mind spoiling you."

"I know." Theo smiles back, always grateful for the reassurance that Emir accepts him in his entirety. "And sometimes I want to be. But I like doing things for you, too. Just this time, I think maybe I need to know what it feels like before I just, like...slobber on your cock."

Emir laughs, eyes falling shut before he covers his mouth with his fingertips and twinkles a smaller smile at Theo. "There is a lot of slobber involved, like, just to be clear."

"Does it hurt?" Theo asks, unable to stop his curiosity. His friends certainly enjoy the act and, like, films and the internet make it seem like the best thing that could happen to a person with a penis, but he's never been in this position before.

"For which person?" Emir doesn't mind talking Theo through this before they actually do anything. He knows it makes Theo more comfortable, but it also helps Emir think about things he's never really considered before. He had his first handjob at fourteen, first blowjob at fifteen, returning the favour not long after, and for him, it was just a hormonal decision with someone he was into. When Theo asks him questions, they help Emir process his own experiences in a new way.

"Oh, um...both. I was thinking of the person giving, but I guess there are...teeth." Theo loves the sound of Emir's giggle. He knows Emir isn't laughing at him, just at how odd sex sounds when laid out in more clinical terms. He can usually tell when he's being teased, and Emir has never made him feel small for his inexperience.

"It could hurt for both people, just like anything else with sex. Yes, there are teeth, pumpkin. If the person blowing doesn't know how to, like, keep them out of the way, it can be uncomfortable, or even painful, but I've only had that happen twice." Emir shrugs, thinking back on those times. It was mostly a combination of inexperience and trying to rush through things, and since he knows the attention and focus it takes, he hadn't faulted those people. "And, it can occasionally be painful for the person giving. Sometimes your jaw gets sore, even if you go slow and take breaks. If we're talking something like throat fucking, that can definitely be painful, and it's not for everyone. Some people have, like, TMJ or something similar, and blowjobs don't really work for them, or maybe they do sometimes, but not always. And depending on the position, like on your knees or if the person you're blowing wants you to hold still so they can face fuck you, it could mean tense muscles or bruises, that type of thing."

Theo nods along, cataloguing the information to add to what he's found on the internet. He's read Reddit threads, Tumblr posts, watched videos, looked through as many varied sources as he could. But most of them essentially said that experience was the best teacher, that he wouldn't be able to understand the feeling until he did it himself, either the giving or the receiving.

"And, um, do you have, like, preferences? I know people joke about the swallowing thing, and apparently there's a lot of techniques that some people like better than others. But then some people don't like them at all?"

"I like oral, but I'm not always in the mood. Like, you know how I want you close, yeah? Blowjobs are great, but I don't always expect or even want them." Emir shrugs, hoping he's answering Theo's questions adequately. He tries to think what it'd be like to be new to all this again, and he imagines it's a lot of information and sensation, especially for Theo. "And I don't care about the spitting or swallowing or just getting me wet and finishing me with your hand. I'm happy for the attention, and if it's not your thing, I don't expect you to do something you don't enjoy just because I want my dick wet."

"Do you like giving head or just getting head?" Theo asks, hand low on Emir's stomach, fingertips scratching at the hair that leads to Emir's cock. It's not sexual, but it's intimate. Something about the way Emir engages his mind and his heart as well as his body gets Theo so incredibly turned on.

"I love going down on anyone, if the situation is right. It's this incredible feeling, dropping to your knees or crawling down under the sheets, knowing they trust you with the most intimate part of themselves, and that you can make them feel absolute bliss with just your mouth and hands, it's…" Emir pauses to think for a moment, Theo's hand making his stomach jump every few seconds. He's not even teasing, just caressing, and Emir loves it. "And I don't like the taste of spunk much, but I swallow when people are into it. Watching the face someone makes when you take what they give you is so fucking sexy. Or, it is to me, anyway. Like I said, you might not be into it, but I am."

"I want to find out…tonight." Theo leans in for a lingering kiss, hand sliding from Emir's stomach to his thigh and pulling his leg across his hip so their dicks fall together. Emir kisses him back, smiling into it until Theo's hand shifts to his bum and gives it a squeeze, turning his smile into a moan as he presses forward. Theo is fucking delicious and Emir can't believe he's about to taste even more of him than before.

"Could kiss you forever, baby." Emir rolls himself on top of Theo, taking his time to get them into position for what Theo's asked for.

Giving head is much easier in bed than any alternative, especially for Theo's first time. Emir wants Theo to focus on only this: enjoying and learning and exploring in the safety and comfort of his own bed. Gently, Emir takes Theo's hands in his own, interlocking their fingers and pulling Theo's arms above his head. By now, he knows exactly what Theo likes, and Emir being in charge is top of the list.

Groaning, Theo starts to grind against him, wrists held in one of Emir's hands while they continue to kiss, messier and less coordinated by the moment. Emir does this thing sometimes, this combination of a press of his hips and a body roll, and it drives Theo absolutely wild, ready to climb a tree, or in this case, his boyfriend. But he can't because he's being carefully held in place and it's all making him very heated and excited and squirmy. Theo feels Emir's teeth at his neck, that spot beneath his jaw, then down near his birthmark, coming back up to kiss Theo soft and sweet before surprising him with a hard bite to his shoulder.

"*Fuck*, Emir!" Theo's eyes fly open, hands ripping themselves from Emir's grasp to grab him by the hips and thrust up into him. Emir's dick is hard on his thigh and Theo can't stop thinking about what it will taste like and how, if he's lucky, he'll know soon enough.

"You want me...lower?" Emir asks, tugging at Theo's hair to bare his neck, leaving a small mark just next to the one he was born with and watching Theo shiver. He'll never get over how responsive he is.

"I want you *everywhere*." Theo holds Emir by the back of his neck, kissing him hard and sliding them both further down the pillows. "But *yes* lower would be - I think if - blow me, please?"

"Well since you asked so nicely..." Emir grins, kissing Theo's rose petal lips once more before making his way down his body. He kisses and bites and slides his hands between Theo's thighs to make more room for himself, Theo opening like an automatic door at the lightest touch. Emir gets where he needs to be and waits, holding Theo's legs apart and pressing his lips to the inside of each of his knees. "I'll be using my hand, too, alright? There's...a lot to it. Just tell me if it's too much."

Theo nods, biting at the inside of his cheek and trying not to do something obscene like he wants to. They're alone in the flat, but if he starts out at a level ten, there's not much further he can let himself fall.

That restraint disappears when Emir takes Theo's dick in his hand and guides it to his lips, starting with just the head inside his mouth. Theo swears he intended to be decent, but the sound he just made was decidedly feral, like a cat in heat or some type of desperate bird. The desperation definitely tracks because after one second with a fraction of his dick in Emir's mouth, Theo forgets that anything outside of this room exists.

Emir moves his mouth further down, lets his tongue get involved, and his lips are the smoothest fucking thing in the entire world, like silk along Theo's shaft that ebbs and flows. Theo rolls his body, trying not to move too far, just follow the pull of Emir's mouth and go where it leads.

And then Emir's mouth is gone again, replaced by the familiarity of his hand instead, just a sample of things to come, and Theo has no idea where that leaves him.

"Alright?" Emir watches Theo, sees his brow scrunched like he's thinking far too much for someone who should be blissed out and in a haze. He knows he's good at this, but technique doesn't matter for shit if Theo isn't ready. "We don't have to do this."

"I want to do this - *fuck* I want to do this." Theo groans again, biting hard on his bottom lip and staring at Emir's mouth. Now he knows what it feels like on his dick and he can never unknow that. He doesn't want to ever forget, not in a thousand years when he's less than dust, just energy redispersed, the electricity of this moment somewhere in the ether, waiting to reform. "It's just...what do I - with my hands?"

"You're alright, baby, I've got you." Emir takes Theo's right hand and moves it down, placing it into his hair. It's a start. "Now the other, put it behind your head. Under the pillow. Use it to move."

Theo does exactly as he's told, the fingers in Emir's hair starting to caress him as Emir's hand keeps a steady rhythm on his dick.

"So soft..." Theo mumbles, watching the way his fingertips disappear in Emir's beautiful hair then getting distracted by Emir's hand. Familiar doesn't mean boring, Emir's way of pulling him off as incredible as always.

"Want me to keep going?" Emir loves seeing Theo like this, when they're alone and he's unguarded and letting Emir love him.

He's familiar with Theo like this by now, how his skin shines as he gets more into it, the sounds he makes during sex, the way his eyes go from as wide as possible to scrunched closed when he comes. Theo's the only person that Emir's learned this way, the only person he's known this intimately. Emir's done so much more with many other people, but this is different. Theo's his baby, his princess, his boyfriend, and Emir...he's so far beyond infatuation, walking headfirst into a real, lasting love with Theo's hand held tight in his own.

Emir's taken out of his thoughts again by Theo's response, a groan and a thrusting of his hips that seems to be agreement.

"I need words, shehzadi. Is that a yes?" He's noticed that Theo has a hard time talking when they have sex, so they'll need to chat about that before they do this again.

"Yes, please...so soft." Theo watches as Emir licks his lips, wondering if his mouth is getting dry. There's so much for him to learn, but he's supposed to be enjoying himself and not analysing to quite this extent...yet. "Could you, um, take breaks like this?"

"Of course." Emir grins, kissing the inside of Theo's thigh, wondering what exactly Theo thinks is so soft. He's said it twice now. "You taste nice, you know."

Emir isn't even lying or just saying that to make Theo flush (which he does). Theo is so meticulous about being clean and smelling good and since that extends to every inch of his body...

Theo's glad Emir told him what to do with his hands because otherwise he'd probably be waving them around trying to find purchase. Emir knew to give him anchors, one hand on Emir and the other trapped beneath his head, because Emir's brilliant like that, understanding Theo and his needs even while making *noises* that somehow sound hot even though there's a lot of saliva happening. Which, to be fair, Emir did warn him about.

But Emir's hands seem to be *everywhere*: on Theo's back, his stomach, tickling at his thighs, and more sensitive areas too. Theo didn't know that hands were so involved in a blowjob, but it's hard for him to focus on those talented fingers because there's so much *pressure* around his dick, and it's so *soft*, and Emir is giving him breaks just like he asked, but Theo still doesn't know what to do with them besides try to collect everything he's feeling into some semblance of a thought.

Every once in a while, Emir lets his teeth just graze along Theo's dick, and for some reason it's doing something to him, something deep and maddening, like Emir could do whatever he wanted and Theo would thank him for it. It's not pain just...sensation. So much sensation for Theo to experience and decide if he wants to chase it or leave it be. And it's all incredible.

Emir's been trying to take it easy, to slow himself down and let Theo process everything, because when he imagines what it'd be like in his place, Emir can understand how overwhelming this is. It's overwhelming for *him* and he's had dozens of blowjobs. But he still wants Theo to enjoy himself, to come apart a little and melt into the mattress once he's done, to have that wonderful, unique feeling of being completely free and happy. God he's pretty, flushed and moaning and caressing Emir's head as if to remind him he's good. He's perfection, brilliant and kind and warm and fit, and he's Emir's to love and romance and fuck. What a life.

Theo has no idea how long Emir's been going down on him, but he doesn't think he can stand it much longer. It's not just his orgasm, which is steadily approaching, but he thinks about what Emir said, about how they're not as in each other's space, and he wants Emir closer. He doesn't want to finish on Emir's tongue tonight, though he definitely wants that some other time. Theo needs Emir's mouth back on his own, craves Emir's body pressed against his, he wants to hold him while falling apart.

"Emir - babe - " Theo removes his hand from beneath his pillow and uses it to guide Emir's shoulders back instead. He knows what he wants.

"Need to be done?" Emir wipes away the fair amount of drool that's collected along his mouth and chin, letting himself be tugged upwards to Theo's chest instead. He could keep going for quite a while, the feel of Theo's heavy dick on his tongue something he's been dreaming of for months. The trust and the patience it took for both of them to be in this exact moment isn't lost on him. Also, it's just really hot to watch Theo and know that he's the one bringing these sounds and reactions to the surface.

"Need you here." Theo closes his eyes the moment their lips meet.

Emir tastes different, his lips are puffier and hot, and it takes Emir a moment, but he falls into Theo who savours the proximity. Guiding one of Emir's hands back down his stomach, Theo tries to communicate what he wants without breaking the kiss. He *needs* this kiss.

Emir gets the message, shifting himself to the side enough that he can finish Theo with his hand. It shouldn't take long with how close he can tell Theo already is. He pushes his tongue into Theo's mouth, grinds himself along his thigh so Theo can feel how hard he is, uses the leftover spit from his blowjob to jerk Theo off. Emir listens and waits, feels when Theo's abs clench and his arms tighten around Emir. And just as he's about to let go, Emir bites hard at his bottom lip, Theo shouting into his mouth when he comes on Emir's hand as he guides Theo through his release.

Emir's kisses turn softer, his hand slowing down while Theo pants and falls back against the pillows like he's gone limp.

"Emiiiii." Theo whines, unable to move but wanting a cuddle. That was a lot. Not too much, but decidedly more than he's grown used to, and he needs to be held while he puts himself back together. He needs Emir.

"I'm right here, baby. You're so handsome, so brilliant, yeah?" Emir quickly cleans Theo off with the flannel at the top of the bedside stash and tosses it to the floor. He could use some water, tea even, though he didn't even approach using his throat this time, thinking it may be too much for tonight. But Emir can worry about all that in a minute. "You did so good."

"Hold me, please?" Theo can't open his eyes. They're too heavy.

After a moment, he feels Emir's arms gently moving him into place, Theo's face on his chest and one leg between both of Emir's own, as surrounded as he can be in their current circumstance. Perfect.

"You alright?" Emir asks, stroking Theo's hair and holding him close. Theo's always so warm, but after he comes he's like a spent comet, all residual heat and energy without the fire. His own release can wait. They're in no rush tonight and they both love to cuddle.

"So soft." Theo moves his arm from Emir's chest to his face, resting his fingertips against Emir's lips and smiling when Emir pouts them forward for a kiss of acknowledgement, finally understanding what Theo meant. "Didn't know...strong but soft. Not like kissing."

Emir laughs quietly, still passing his fingers through Theo's curls. "No, not like kissing at all. You like it?"

Theo nods, cuddling his face against Emir's chest and moving both arms around his back instead, holding him tight. "*Loved* it. I could tell you were holding back. Thank you."

"I didn't want it to be too much." Emir sighs as Theo pulls away enough to lay beside him, their noses pressed together and their bodies aligned. Sometimes, Emir wonders if they're like that story Theo told him, about one being separated into two bodies. It was from Plato probably, and maybe that's why they fit together so well. Theo told him that story a week before their first kiss...maybe Emir should've been paying closer attention.

"You're my boyfriend." Theo presses forward for a kiss, grinning when Emir's fingertips tickle at his side. "And I'm your boyfriend."

"That news to you, pumpkin? Did I steal your memory through your cock?" Emir teases, tickling Theo with more intent until he's squirming and swatting Emir's hands away with a laugh.

"I just like it. I like being your boyfriend." Theo's hand drifts to Emir's stomach, once again caressing the hair there and wondering if he can save giving Emir head for another time. He doesn't think he's ready to translate what he's experienced into any sort of useful technical skill yet. "Sometimes I just want to shout about it. Tell everyone: *look at my boyfriend. They're the most amazing partner and they're all mine.* But shouting is usually frowned upon, so instead I'm telling you like this."

"That's...the first time you've said that." Emir clears his throat, his mouth suddenly much drier. Damn, he really needs that glass of water that he decided could wait. Next time he'll have it ready before they get started.

"Hm?" Theo's still curled along Emir's body, settling back into his own before they do anything else. He really really loves Emir and he can't wait until it's time to actually tell him those words out loud. Theo knows they're getting closer.

"You, um, you used a *they* pronoun when you meant me. For the first time." Emir worries he may cry. It's a bit overwhelming and entirely unexpected.

Last time he was in a post sexual situation and discussing his gender with a partner, his entire life had been torn apart. He knows that's not at all what's happening right now, but it's an adjustment. Here's his PTSD showing up again, but at least Emir can recognise it and try to calm his racing heart, focus himself on remaining grounded before anything spirals.

"You said only in private, and I'm not usually talking about you in the third person when we're together." Theo feels the tension in Emir's body but he doesn't understand why. "Would you rather I didn't? I didn't mean to upset you, I just remember what you told me that day in your room. You said that you use he/him, but that in private you're alright with they/them, too, and, like, femme terms sometimes. Unless I misunderstood - shit, I did, didn't I?"

Theo pulls back to lay on his own pillow and sets a hand on Emir's cheek to hold his gaze. "I'm sorry, I shouldn't have said that."

"No, baby, it's not that." Emir scoots over to where Theo's pulled himself away, kissing him on the forehead, between his brows, the tip of his nose, then full on the mouth. "I'm just adjusting to having a boyfriend who listens and remembers. I told you that months ago, and I sort of thought you'd forgotten."

"How could I forget? That night was really important to me." Theo searches Emir's face, glad to see that he's smiling even if his posture is still tense. "It just...hadn't come up yet. But in my head I use neutral pronouns for you sometimes, at least since you told me about being genderqueer. So...I didn't fuck up?"

Emir shakes his head no, wondering if Theo will ever stop surprising him. He's a kaleidoscope of a person: one minute he's experiencing his first blowjob, the next he's validating Emir's gender identity in his post-orgasm bliss. "Thank you for seeing me."

"I could say the same." Theo places a hand on Emir's chest, but not to push him away, just to feel that gorgeous skin again. "I don't think I'm ready to blow you tonight. Is that alright?"

"Of course that's alright." Emir would never expect Theo to do something he isn't ready for. That's like rule number one of being a decent person. "You mind if I go take care of this, though?"

Emir glances down at his own dick, still half hard because it's only been a few minutes since it was last receiving attention.

"I was thinking you could - I wouldn't mind if - " Theo flushes maroon and follows Emir's gaze. It's not that he doesn't want to have Emir's dick in his mouth, just not tonight. And there's other things he wants that don't involve that. "I like feeling used. Like, when you get off because of me."

"Oh?" Emir takes the hand that Theo has on his chest and intertwines their fingers. His boyfriend is a man of never-ending intrigue.

"And I like the attention. So, um…" Theo swallows hard, trying not to be embarrassed by the filthy things he wants. Sometimes he surprises himself. "I was thinking you could get yourself off and make a mess of me?"

"Can I touch you while I do? Come on your chest?" Emir asks, very interested in this idea. They've played a bit dirty before, but Theo is getting braver in his exploration of what he likes, inviting Emir along on the journey.

"My face, if you don't mind." Theo knows he slips into this overly formal pattern of speech sometimes when they're intimate. But Emir seems to find it charming rather than annoying, so. "And I'd like you to touch me and move me however you want, within reason. Nothing inside my mouth or my bum but…you can touch."

"Question." Emir sits up, straddling Theo's lap and sitting back on top of his heels instead. "How do you feel about the idea of me sitting across your chest and teasing my dick at your mouth and around your face without it being inside? Maybe get you warmed up to the idea of blowing me without the act?"

Theo nods before Emir even finishes his question. He's pictured this before, Emir slapping him with his dick, running it along his lips and teasing him, shooting hot and sticky across his face while Theo teases at his bum and begs him to keep going. The dream he had about it finished with Emir in his mouth, but it's the perfect middle ground. Emir really has no idea how incredible his understanding of Theo is. "Now, please."

"That could be arranged." Emir sparkles a dangerous smile at Theo before diving in for another kiss, wanting to get himself warmed back up before essentially sitting on Theo's face.

Theo slowly slips into what might be subspace. He's still not entirely sure, but his mind goes fuzzy and his body gets warm and relaxed, all while Emir does exactly as promised. It's a delicate whirlwind that ends with them both exhausted but satisfied.

After releasing across Theo's face, Emir finally gets up on shaky legs for that glass of water, bringing Theo one of his own and cleaning his face with a damp flannel, despite the protest.

"You're dirty, princess. I'm not going to let my spunk dry all over your pretty face." Emir kisses Theo's parted mouth, getting a bit of his own cum on his lips and licking it away, easy as anything.

"But I like it." Theo whines again, trying half-heartedly to stop Emir's careful hands. He's still a bit floaty after all that. "I'm...marked. Yours."

"How about I leave you with a decent sized purple love bite on your neck instead, hm?" Emir offers, playfully nipping at a spot near Theo's shoulder as he finishes cleaning him up.

"I suppose." Theo pouts, he actually pouts, and Emir can't believe his life. It's been a long, incredible night.

"Tomorrow. Before breakfast." Emir hands Theo his water, glad that he takes it and starts drinking immediately. They're both definitely dehydrated after all that. "I'm too tired to do it properly tonight."

"Can I give you one too?" Theo asks, yawning as he sets his now empty glass aside. "You get all hot and bothered."

"Of course. Mark me, baby. We belong to each other." Emir knows he's being a sap, but it's a side effect of being in love with Theodore George Palmer and all his glorious multitudes.

"We belong to each other." Theo repeats, asking Emir how to say the same but in Urdu. It's like second nature now, to have Emir translate so they can communicate their love and care in another language, one that means something very personal to Emir.

"Now, sleep. I will not be responsible for sleep deprived driving tomorrow. Your mum would be very disappointed." Emir laughs along with Theo, reaching across to turn off the lamp before Theo settles on top of his chest.

"Night, Emi." Theo yawns again, moving around until he's comfortably settled in his favourite spot.

"Night, pumpkin." Emir kisses the top of his head, closing his eyes.

It's so quiet in the flat tonight that Emir can truly focus on the soft sounds of Theo's breathing, the way it slows and evens out from his spot on Emir's chest. All Emir can see is red: blushing, crimson, ember red, filling the room and coating every inch of where they touch. He mumbles an *I love you* into Theo's soft curls just before he joins him in sleep.

***

Laurie: *Everyone home yet?*
Emi: /selfie with Theo on their uni flat's sofa, Theo's head on his shoulder/
Theo: *We're leaving soon, just spending a few more hours together before I drive Emi to Safiya's flat and then myself to Stafford. We decided we weren't in a rush this morning, so it was breakfast in bed and now cuddles on the sofa. All packed, of course.*
Emi: *you and T settled in darton then?*
T: /selfie with Laurie's younger sisters at the Tempest home/
Laurie: *We're good :)*
Laurie: *Staying at my dad's place for the holiday, but we'll be seeing my mum every day since she's not far*
Laurie: *And we'll go to Suzanne's house the week after Christmas to see her and Lucy and probably talk more about the wedding*
Laurie: *Dean should be there for a day as well, but he's a bit busier so we'll see*

Emi: why didn't we all talk about this before?
Theo: Family dinner was focused on Laurie this week, as it should. /shrug emoji/
Laurie: Anyone heard from Ciaran or Gabe?
Theo: I think they're both still at the airport?
Ciaran: Unfortunately, Teddy is correct
Ciaran: /selfie with Gabe on the floor of a terminal at Heathrow/
Gabe: Both flights delayed because of a storm :(
Gabe: But I should be on my way to New York in a few hours
Ciaran: And I'm staying until after his flight leaves. I don't mind the delay and I don't want Gabe stranded
Ciaran: Short flight to Dublin, then mum is picking me up and driving me back to Kildare
Ciaran: Our last holiday break.....
Laurie: Don't you start
T: ITS OUR LAST HOLIDAY BREAK BEFORE WE HAVE TO BE ADULTS
Laurie: Sigh
Laurie: Now T is crying
T: I am not
T: Alright maybe a little
Gabe: So weird that you'll all be an ocean away next year
Gabe: I've gotten so used to our little world together
T: It's not too late to decide to stay in London
Laurie: We aren't even going to be in London though
Theo: ...what do you mean you won't be in London?
Theo: What happened to the Tempest-Brooks newlywed London plans? The three story walkup in Soho with a rescue dog and a sewing corner?
Laurie: Fuck
Laurie: /three running emojis/
Emi: lawrence get back here
T: Laur wasn't ready to tell everyone yet but i think he got distracted by Ruby styling his hair oops
T: Mine's already braided obviously. She put tinsel in it :)
T: But I've just been told I have permission so...
T: Sara is pregnant again. Twins.
T: She told Laur when she and the girls visited us earlier this month
T: Surprised you lot didn't notice she's quite literally glowing
Theo: Christ.
Laurie: Yes, quite
Emi: you'll be the eldest of SEVEN?
Laurie: somehow yes
Ciaran: So what does that mean?

Laurie: It means we're moving to Darton after uni and not sure if or when the Tempest-Brooks Soho flat is going to happen
Laurie: We're having the wedding there anyway
Gabe: And when are the new babies due?
Laurie: /three running emojis/
T: I told you your mother already had enough on her plate and that was before the news about the twins /eye roll emoji/
Laurie: We figured out the venue situation it's fine everything's fine
Laurie: She's glad to have us even with the twins
Laurie: I asked. You were there. It's fine
T: The babies are due in late June but will probably be born sooner because twins
Theo: Lawrence William Tempest.
Theo: Your wedding is at the end of June, just after uni ends, and she's hosting all of us the night before. Your mother will have newborn TWINS.
Theo: That new husband of hers better be a saint or we'll be having words with him.
Theo: But I see why you've decided to stay there, at least for a while.
Emi: but what will you two do for work?
T: We'll figure it out. I have some ideas
T: We have time to plan, it's just really important to both of us to be around to help Laur's family for at least a year or so
T: My sister's older and my parents are more than fine (and not far away, just a train ride) and my mum and Sara spend practically every weekend together anyway
Theo: Suzanne and Sara are best friends by now, this is true.
T: Actually my mum plans to help Sara with the new babies two days a week in the beginning since her work is flexible
T: And you four still haven't decided where you're headed so London wasn't a must anymore. We were going to break the news after the holidays. Didn't want to ruin the mood.
Ciaran: Fuck. This is like...real. This is all almost over
Ciaran: We won't be sharing a flat after June
Ciaran: Suddenly I don't want to get on this flight
Gabe: We're still deciding what we want to do, but we have to be sure soon
Gabe: And every day, I'm less sure that we belong in New York with my family
Gabe: I love them. With my whole heart. But that doesn't mean C and I should move there.
Gabe: I just...I don't know
Theo: Emir and I will be sending audition tapes along with applications in Spring, but we won't know until like just before the end of uni.
Emi: might not know for sure until your wedding, and that's assuming we get contracts
T: But...you're moving somewhere together?

Theo: I'm following Emir to whichever company he ends up with.
Theo: Fuck, we really do have a lot to talk about when we all get back from break.
Emi: teddy thinks he won't get his own offers, but i know he will
Theo: We'll see. Either way, we've talked about it and yes, we're planning to go together when we leave here.
Ciaran: When did we grow up?
Ciaran: This is like proper adult shit
Gabe: If nothing else, we'll be there for your wedding :)
Gabe: Wouldn't miss that for the world
T: :)
Laurie: Let us know when your flights get rescheduled?
T: And text us when you get home safe and all that?
Emi: we're leaving the flat now :(it's so empty and sad i can't imagine what this is going to feel like in June
Emi: /sad minion gif/
Theo: /picture of him and Emir pouting with the soon to be abandoned flat behind them, front door open/
Theo: Six, sometimes seven people to a flat, and I'm not sick of you all yet.
T: We're family /crying emoji/
Laurie: Oi enough with the water works
Laurie: Love you all, but we've still got time
Emi: i'll remind you of that when you're the one crying in a few months
Laurie: /eye roll emoji/
Laurie: /group hug gif/
Theo: Have to drive. Text you all when I'm home <3
Emi: what theo said
Gabe: /selfie from the same spot in the airport, peace sign at the camera and kissing Ciaran's cheek while Ciaran frowns at his phone/

***

"You head home next week then?" Theo asks, car powered off as he faces Emir in the passenger seat. They've arrived outside Safiya's flat, so this is goodbye for a few weeks. It's their first real time apart since they started dating, and Theo knows it's good for them, that they're both excited for family time, but he also isn't sure what to expect.

"Should be there on Wednesday. We don't really celebrate, but my little sisters are sort of into it because of their school mates." Emir shrugs. He's staying with Safiya before they drive back to Shipley together, her husband Mihir staying at their flat with

Buddy. She'll leave Emir in Shipley for the rest of the holiday break until his parents drive him to uni again. "You want me to call you on Christmas Eve? Or is it more family time for you?"

"You can call me everyday. I'll miss your voice. And your face. Probably best if you FaceTime." Theo reaches for Emir's hand over the centre console, rubbing his thumb across the top of Emir's knuckles before giving it a kiss. "I'll give you space, I just like talking to you."

"We'll text, and I'll FaceTime you everyday as long as we aren't busy." Emir won't be too busy. He might teach a few classes at his old dance school, but otherwise he'll mostly be spending time with his sisters, and a potential few days elsewhere… "I won't be a stranger. You'll see me again sooner than you think."

"But three weeks seems so long." Theo pouts, unsure why Emir looks like he's up to something. He gets that same look before tickling Theo or pulling some prank on Laurie.

"It'll be over before we know it." Emir smiles, using the hand not caught in Theo's to brush through those beautiful caramel curls, memorising the feeling for when Theo will be out of reach. "You sure you want to be stuck with me next year?"

"Very sure." Theo answers easily. They've already talked about their plans for after uni, then reaffirmed them again during their drive across the city because of the text conversation with their friends this morning. "We'll figure it out. I have a meeting with Sean soon, too."

"I should schedule one of those." Emir sighs, letting his hand drop from Theo's hair and back into his own lap, not quite ready to go yet. "Remind me?"

"I already have it in the calendar." Theo grins, glad for the way Emir doesn't just accept, but actively supports his routines and schedules. "Kiss me again before you go?"

Instead of leaning across the console, Emir fully crawls over and straddles Theo's lap, honking the horn with his arse before he gets settled and making them both laugh.

Taking Theo's face in his hands, Emir kisses him slow and sweet. He's gentle, like Theo is a precious angel in need of cherishing (he is). Theo's hands find his waist and Emir couldn't care less that his knees hurt in this position or that anyone could look through the window and see them. He's kissing his boyfriend goodbye and he'll be damned if he dampens the mood for any reason. This moment is sunshine and honey and cinnamon and a summer breeze, right here in central London on a cold December day.

"Hm?" Theo asks, not having understood whatever it is Emir just mumbled against his lips. It sounded like Urdu, but not any of the words he's learned. But to be fair to himself, he was sufficiently focused on the earnest passion of Emir's kiss and may have missed something.

"I'll tell you someday when we're watching the sunrise." Emir kisses Theo's nose, his forehead, the top of his hair, still cradling his face with both of his hands. With a sigh he adds, "I should go. Buddy's waiting."

"Give him a cuddle from me?" Theo pulls Emir in for the closest approximation to a hug he can get with them cramped in his driver's seat together like this, but he likes the semblance of privacy it gives them to say goodbye.

"Help me get my bag?" Emir tilts his head and waits for Theo to nod before untangling himself and getting back on his own side to exit out the passenger door.

Theo walks around to the boot, opening it and lifting Emir's suitcase one-handed with ease while Emir fits his rucksack over his right shoulder, leaning his hip against the brake light.

"You really are a sight, baby." Emir whistles softly, watching the way the flush creeps up Theo's face in response. He tugs him into his front by a belt loop, Theo falling against his chest and dropping the suitcase beside them to hold Emir instead.

They hug and they sway and Theo kisses the side of Emir's neck as he breathes him in, trying to get his fill. Three weeks. He can't wait to see his family and celebrate the holidays, but he's going to miss this. He'll miss Emir's laugh and the way he sips his tea. The pencil marks left behind on his hands after a late night of drawing while Theo sleeps. He'll miss their early mornings and their long evenings in the studio together. It'll be three weeks without Emir's lips and the honest way he kisses, without his hands and the magic they summon. There's not a thing Theo won't be longing for, but they'll be fine. They'll talk and they'll flirt and they'll have even more stories to share when they reunite in the New Year.

"Text me when you get home safe?" Emir finally extracts himself from the hug when he feels Theo's arms loosen. They're both sniffling, Emir using his thumbs to wipe a few tears away from just below Theo's sparkling eyes, ignoring the solitary tear that slides down his own cheek.

"Of course. Should be just a few hours." Theo looks around but doesn't see anyone nearby, so he leans in for one last goodbye kiss. Emir smiles with his eyes closed, sliding a hand into the hair at the back of his head to kiss him deeper and nip at his bottom lip before softening it again.

"Bye, princess. I'll see you soon." Emir leaves Theo with a kiss to his cheek, picking up his bags and heading towards the front door of Safiya's building. He wasn't lying about Buddy waiting for him, Safiya promising that he could take him to the park within the hour. He'll have to send Theo a selfie with Buddy to enjoy when his drive is over.

Theo watches Emir go and waits for him to turn around one last time as he heads inside, waving until Emir disappears. With a sigh, Theo retrieves his keys from the pocket of his jeans and slides back inside the car, suddenly so empty without his companion. He turns on a podcast that he knows will make him laugh, texts his mom that he's on his way along with his ETA, and pulls away from the building to head home, realising his true home isn't only a place anymore. His heart lives within Emir as much as it ever has any physical house, and he sits with that feeling all the way to his parent's driveway where he tucks it away for later so he can greet his parents at the door.

CHAPTER EIGHT

"Emi?" Saima knocks quietly on Emir's open bedroom door, peeking around while trying not to disturb him. It's early on Christmas Eve, and he and Safiya just drove up to Shipley last night.

"Alright, Saima?" Emir looks up from his drawing to give her a smile. He's sitting on the floor in the middle of his childhood bedroom, putting the finishing touches on Theo's Christmas present.

"Can I do art with you?" Saima has always asked to paint and draw with Emir, ever since she was a toddler. She's a tween now, but she still loves spending time with her big brother, even though she does art on her own when he's away.

"Course you can." Emir pats the ground beside him and watches as her eyes light up when she walks over, sitting next to him with her legs crossed. "Can we have quiet time? I need to focus, but I've got plenty of stuff for you to try. Look at these new colour charcoals mum bought."

"Oooooo." Saima reaches for them immediately, opening the small case of pencils and holding her hand out for a sketch pad. Emir grins and leans to the side to find an empty one for her to take. He had a feeling she'd like the bright colours. "Did you use these on that one over there?"

Emir looks where she's pointing, another of Theo's presents waiting to be finished after the one currently in front of him. "Nah, just my old set. I think this new set is meant for you."

Tweaking her nose, Emir watches fondly as she gets settled before going back to his work. He's been able to draw most of each piece over the past few weeks after Theo fell asleep, but the final touches that require daylight had to wait. He wants these to be as good as he can make them since they're being given for an occasion and not casually like his usual drawings.

Saima and Emir draw together in silence for almost an hour while the sounds of the house float through the open door. Their baba and Safiya are in the living room catching up while ignoring the telly in the background. Amina is still in bed because she stayed out til dawn with her friends. And Emir's mum has just gotten home from a last minute trip to the store, buying everything they'll need for their feast tonight. It's a familiar comfort that Emir's missed, even though he loves his life in London.

"I like Theo." Saima's bright voice brings Emir out of his reverie.

He's just finished and set the drawing aside, Theo's face staring back at him. Emir knows he'll never perfectly capture him, but he plans to keep trying. Saima must have been waiting for his concentration to end so she could interrupt, knowing these drawings mean a lot to him.

"Yeah? Me too." Emir carefully lays blank pages over each of the drawings, hoping to minimise any smudging before they're delivered to their intended recipient.

"Do you, um, do you love him?" Saima's been working on an intricate mandala using every colour in her new pencil set, staring at the spirals while waiting for Emir's answer. "Like properly?"

"I do, yeah." Emir reaches over and brushes a strand of hair behind her ear. He can't believe how much she's grown. Her toddler years were basically yesterday and now she's almost a teenager. "I love him a lot."

"Have you told him?" Saima shades one of her green sections carefully, Emir watching her small hands with admiration.

Sharing art as a hobby has been their thing since she was little and he's watched her grow and evolve into her own style. Emir gets to see her quiet, creative side that most people don't, distracted by her (at times overwhelming) energy and extroverted tendencies. They couldn't be more different, but of the four siblings, they get along best, never having a fight in twelve years.

"Not yet, but I will." Emir sits back on his hands, legs stretched out in front of him. "I'm still working on some things. Some inside my heart and my head things. You might have been too young to remember, but a few years ago I loved someone, and they hurt me really deep."

"I remember." Saima looks up at Emir with wide eyes, setting her pencil aside, back in the case. Her eyes are so much like their mums, just younger and slightly more tempestuous. "That's why I like Theo. He's nice. He won't hurt you."

"I'm sorry you remember." Emir glances down at his own feet, rolling his ankles absentmindedly. He hasn't been able to dance in almost a week, not properly, and he's starting to get fidgety about it. Thinking about his ex doesn't help. Emir wishes he could have spared his family from the worst of it, but his ex made it their problem as much as Emir's.

"He hurt you and he made everyone come after our family. Of course I remember." Saima scoots closer to Emir and pulls her knees to her chest. She may be growing up, but Emir can't get over how small she still seems, as if her time as a toddler and her future as a grown woman are clashing while she processes the memory. "And I remember hearing mum and baba talking about you at night when I was supposed to be asleep. Almost every night, they'd stay up worrying, but they didn't want us to know. They were really scared something bad was going to happen to you."

"I know. I was too." Emir mirrors her posture, sitting beside her with both of their backs against the side of his bed. In some ways it was a blessing that he left for uni shortly after everything happened. It gave him an opportunity to get away, but it also gave his family space to breathe while the community moved on. "But that's why I, um…why I need to be careful this time and not rush things. Not because Theo would ever hurt me, but because my brain still looks for the danger. Even though I'm safe and Theo is…Theo, my body still panics sometimes. Does that make sense?"

"What happens when you get scared?" Saima's toes tap against the floor, one foot then the other, a quiet heartbeat of a rhythm that Emir follows as he thinks how to answer.

"Honestly, I haven't been handling it well." Emir doesn't want to lie to his sister. She's old enough now for at least the general overview. "I tend to not take care of myself and sort of spiral a bit. Like, if I was in your picture: imagine being trapped inside and it's dark and cold and far away from help."

Emir pauses as they both look at her artwork. "But I'm talking to someone about it again. I had a therapist back when it first happened, and I have a new one now. Her name's Amanda. She helps me find better ways to react when I'm scared…Theo helps too. He's really patient and he understands that if I panic it doesn't mean he did something wrong. And he reminds me to look after myself, just like Laurie does. Mum and Baba too. I'm lucky. Not everyone has so many people who love them, you know?"

"Is Theo going to marry you?" Saima asks, and Emir's not entirely sure how that's her follow up, but she is twelve, so. She's at that age where she starts really considering crushes and dating and grown up things like that.

"Maybe someday. We've talked about it a bit." Emir shrugs, putting his arm around Saima's shoulders and giving them a squeeze. It's really good to spend time with her, just the two of them. "First we have to figure out what happens after uni."

"I don't want you too far away." Saima admits, looking up to Emir for only a moment before wriggling out of his grasp and going back to her drawing. She picks up a marigold yellow pencil and gets back to work, her stormy eyes focused and confident.

"I don't want to be too far either." Emir pulls himself up onto his bed instead, sitting cross legged and checking his phone for the first time in hours. He has a few dozen missed texts between all their group chats, of course. "But even if I'm far, I'll always come home and visit."

"Promise?" Saima meets his gaze again, her expression firm. She's not often serious, but when she is, it's important. She's a bit like their dad in that respect.

"Promise." Emir lays back on his bed, phone in hand while he scrolls and reacts and replies where applicable. It seems everyone is having lovely family time back in their various home towns, except for Jordan, who says she's one argument away from needing a rage room. He can't blame her, with the way her family is. "I'm gonna go help mum in the kitchen soon. You want to come?"

"Uh, no." Saima wrinkles her nose, smudging one of her heaviest lines with her pinky finger to give it a gradient effect. "I think I'll go visit Tahira for a few hours. Haven't seen her since last week even though she's close. She's been busy."

"Tahira still your best mate or is that Sarah now?" Emir loves getting all these updates about his sisters' lives, letting them talk about whatever's on their mind and in their heart. It's a talent he learned from his mum, to ask a simple question and let them loose, giving them the freedom to just breathe out their thoughts.

"She'll probably always be my best mate, but Sarah's alright. She's really sporty, like, and I'm not, but the three of us have fun at school and sometimes we get together. But Tahira's just like...we have all these jokes and I know her favourite foods and the ways she likes to braid her hair, right? It's just...different. I've known her a lot longer." Saima holds her drawing up for Emir to assess. He tilts his head and indicates that she should rotate it upside down. Once she does, a new idea overcomes her and she starts adding shading to a different area before talking again. "Tahira's mum is having another baby."

"That so?" Emir lays back on his bed, eyes closed while Saima keeps talking for another thirty minutes.

Once Saima's done with her drawing, he finally heads downstairs to see his mum and help her in the kitchen. True to her word, Saima swaddles herself in her warmest coat and bright orange mittens, promising to be back before it's time to eat as she rushes away to her friend's house down the street.

"When did she get so grown up?" Emir asks his mum, coming up beside her at the stove and giving her a kiss on her cheek. There's nothing in the world like walking into this kitchen that he's known for years to find his mum already there waiting for him, the scents of his childhood rich in the air.

"Last Tuesday." Natalie answers with a grin, handing him the apron she'd already set aside, knowing he would make his way to her eventually. Kitchen time is sort of their thing, when they can talk, or not talk, and share more than just the recipes.

"Catch me up?" Emir ties the apron and nudges her out of the way with his hip, taking over what's already simmering on the stove so she can start on something else. They don't celebrate Christmas, but with everyone off work and school, it's the easiest time to get them all together. Hence the feast.

Emir stays in the kitchen with his mum until everything is done, the two of them talking and laughing, making a mess and cleaning it up together. He loves learning all these recipes from his baba's family that Natalie has inherited over their many years of marriage. The rest of the family drifts in and out from time to time, sniffing and sampling and being shooed away, told to wait and have a snack if they're hungry.

When it's finally time to eat, Emir sets the table, Safiya walking over to help him with a hair ruffle and an understanding smile. They light a dozen candles, turn off all the overhead lights, and set everything in the middle before calling the others into the room to join them.

Emir spends the meal thinking about family, what it means to him, how important they are, and automatically imagines Theo by his side. It's as if he's really there, smiling at Emir and listening hard for all the words he's learned, double checking with Emir about pronunciations and then laughing along with everyone when he catches a joke. Mihir had blended seamlessly when he first came to the house with Safiya, and Emir's positive that Theo will be the same. They all already love him just from one post-show dinner and they've come a long way since then.

Saima was right to remind him not to move too far. Emir doesn't want to lose this, to give logistics and circumstance the opportunity to interfere with family too often. London already seems far enough, and it's the closest his career could be. He's glad to have tonight and this break from uni to realise what's important as he gets ready to embark on his next chapter. His priorities have never been more clear.

***

"Is it possible you've gotten more handsome since yesterday?" Theo asks over the FaceTime call, staring at Emir with stars in his eyes. This has become their holiday routine: FaceTiming each other just before bed to catch up on their day.

"It's the mood lighting. The candles were so nice at dinner that I brought a few up here." Emir leans back on his free hand, watching as Theo settles himself in his bed a few hours away.

"Nope, it's you." Theo sighs, holding the phone above his head, closing his eyes and trying to get comfortable before staring back at the screen. He's feeling restless, but happy. "But the candles do give you a warm glow."

"You have a nice Christmas Eve?" Emir asks, tracing each centimetre of Theo's face with his eyes like Theo's a sculpture he plans to replicate from memory. He really, truly misses him, their daily video calls just enough to hold him over.

"The best! We won't see my sisters and the kids until tomorrow, but mum and dad still did all our usual traditions. They said it's the last year I'll be home for them so they wanted to make sure we got to everything." Theo readjusts on the bed again, still trying to get comfortable. If only he had a warm boyfriend to cuddle into. "We had pizza and watched *Polar Express* and mum took a picture of us all in our Christmas pyjamas with hot cocoa in front of the fireplace. Bruce wouldn't look at the camera, of course. It had to be a selfie this year but it's still nice. Oh, and we left a carrot for the reindeer, out in the garden. I like having traditions, even if they're a bit silly."

"What time will Barbara and Jayna get there with the kids?" Emir asks, as if he doesn't already know tomorrow's schedule like the back of his own hand. He could listen to Theo talk for hours. "And the husbands, I suppose."

"Early! Half nine. And they're leaving again early afternoon." Theo finally finds a comfortable spot and stops fussing, watching Emir's smile in awe. He really is ridiculously pretty and Theo gets to see that smile first thing in the morning most days. "We're planning our roast for around noon. I helped mum get everything ready while dad finished decorating today. They've been so busy this year that everything's a bit last minute, but it came together."

"Sounds really nice. I'd like to see it all someday." Emir can't help how bright he smiles. He loves seeing Theo so happy. He'd literally kicked his feet excitedly like a school kid while looking at the pouty selfie Theo sent just a few minutes ago, Bruce cuddled up next to him on the sofa in his own set of matching dog pyjamas. "You're so cute in your little outfit. Very squeezable."

"Maybe next year? I know you said you have plans until after New Year's and it's not as if you can just walk here." Theo tosses a curl away from his eyes. His hair is growing a bit longer than usual, but he'll get it cut again before class starts back up in a few weeks.

"Yeah. Going for a drive with my parents tomorrow while the girls stay home to spend some time together." Emir yawns, covering his mouth with the back of his hand so Theo isn't just staring at his tonsils. The rest of his face is much prettier. "I'm teaching a bit the next two weeks while all the usual teachers have time off and the kids still want classes. I don't mind. It's decent money and keeps me in the studio."

"Where are you driving to? Anywhere fun?" Theo asks, thinking back to the two small road trips they've been on together. Those trips have been some of the highlights of his year.

"It's a bit South of here. We've got a whole plan. I'll send you pictures. There's this house we want to go visit. The roads are always empty on Christmas and everyone's got their decorations up and we like to look at the lights." Emir gestures with his hand, being as generic as possible without outright lying. "Mum still likes all that and I just want to spend time with my parents. Hardly enough time together anymore, but I did get to cook with mum most of the day."

"I would love to cook with your mum someday. I mean if she invited me, of course, I wouldn't assume - I just - " Theo flushes, still not sure how far into the future he's supposed to be planning. They've talked about living together after uni and joked about getting married, but still. And if they do get to that point, Theo definitely wants to know how to make all of Emir's family recipes.

"She'd love that." Emir stops Theo before he can panic properly. There's absolutely no need, especially since the idea of Theo and his mum bonding in the kitchen is like a dream come true. "And so would I. Hopefully I'll get to know your family more, too. You know, since we're in this long term committed relationship and all that."

"Yes, that." Theo chews on the inside of his cheek, still staring at Emir because why would he want to look away? "I was thinking about you today…"

"Yeah? About what?" Emir pulls one of his blankets up to his chin, cocooning himself and imagining cuddling Theo. Soon.

"Just you being here. Wearing matching pyjamas and playing with Bruce in the garden and helping my dad decorate and stealing me away for kisses in the hall. That sort of thing." Theo shrugs, but his cheeks are slightly pink. Emir wants to kiss them until they're red.

"Next Christmas Eve, I'll be there. Matching pyjamas and stolen kisses at the ready." Emir loves the effect his words have on Theo, the way his eyes crinkle when he smiles, his shoulders relaxing against the pillows. He wants to spoil Theo with every love language, finding ways to share their family holidays and create a life all their own from their separate foundations. "Mum already invited you to Eid, but I think I maybe forgot to tell you…"

"Yes, you definitely forgot." Theo's eyes widen immediately, suddenly worried about a hundred things all at once. Being invited to Eid is a big deal, a commitment *situation* that he can't just show up to and hope for the best. "When is it this year? I don't have anything to wear. I'll have to learn a lot more Urdu before then and do I bring something? For Christmas people bring something. Shit, I don't know anything about Eid but I know it's not like Christmas. Why did I even bring that up? You mean Eid-ul Fitr, yeah? I learned there's more than one Eid, but I should've done more research."

"Baby, it's alright." Emir tries to calm Theo as best he can through the phone. "I'll take care of all that. You just have to show up and be Theo. It's in April this year, a few weeks before our dissertation. We'd be allowed the day off uni to travel, but we shouldn't need it since it's a weekend this year."

"Isn't it like…your whole family? Like cousins and everyone?" Theo runs his hands through his hair, tugging on it slightly. He's so nervous already, and according to Emir, he's got a few months to figure it out. But it's just…a lot to figure out. Emir's not religious anymore, but the family traditions and holidays are still important to him. Theo has to get this right.

"Yup. I'll introduce them to my wonderful boyfriend." Emir probably should've mentioned it a few weeks ago when his mum told him to invite Theo, but he genuinely forgot. Her invite was extended while they were taking their break, and in the getting back to each other process, it wasn't at the top of Emir's list. "Don't worry about learning all the traditions or the language. We have time and I'll make sure you know what you need to be comfortable. I want it to be fun for you, too. It's a celebration, a day for family and community and you belong there. With me."

"Have you ever, um, brought anyone with you before?" Theo asks, sitting up in his bed and wondering if it'd be too rude for him to pull out his laptop and start Googling while still on the phone. Probably.

"Laurie, once. He's family, too." Emir shrugs, wishing he had waited just a few days if he was going to forget this long anyway. Now Theo's all distracted and it's supposed to be bedtime. "Princess, I can see you panicking. Is there any chance I can help you calm back down and reset so you can get some rest? I didn't mean to upset you."

"No! Not upset. Just...overwhelmed. I don't know how to be your boyfriend around your whole family and what the rules are. I don't know how to marry into a Desi family because I respect your culture and it's an integral part of you but I didn't grow up with it so research can only get me so far. I don't know enough Urdu yet. I don't know the customs or the jokes or the clothes I need to wear or any of it. I definitely need to learn more about the history, especially if it's your whole family we're meeting. There's nicknames and ways to address people and I only know your immediate family. I'm so fucking stupid and ignorant and my world is so small. I need to be better about that. Why don't I know any of this? I should know about Eid, it's your favourite holiday!"

Theo drops the phone between his crossed legs and holds his head in his hands, covering his eyes to drown out the light. One less sense to focus on. One less stimulus. There's just too much right now. "I want to be with you so bad I just don't know how. I don't want to fuck up. I don't want to hurt you or your family."

"Teddyyyyy. Baby, angel, princess, pumpkin." Emir coos, seeing the slightest hint of a smile beneath Theo's hands as he rolls out the pet names. "You wouldn't be invited if you didn't belong there. I promise. And maybe you could chat with mum? She knows all of what you're worrying about and has been nothing but graceful while navigating all that. And she likes you. A lot."

"She does?" Theo asks, hands still covering his eyes while he listens to Emir's familiar, perfect voice. It's like a memory of his hug to hear his soothing presence so close.

"She thinks you're brilliant. Saima likes you, too. She told me this morning." Emir confirms, glad to see that Theo's shoulders are slightly less hunched. "Safiya and Amina are incessant with the teasing, which means they like you. And my dad would've invited you himself if my mum didn't do it first. You're very welcome here, Theo. Them inviting you isn't a test, it's a show of love and acceptance that you make me very happy."

"Could we talk more about it soon? Like maybe not tomorrow because you'll be in the car and I'll be with everyone here, but the day after? Or even next week maybe? And you can tell me what to research?" Theo takes his hands away from his eyes, but he still squints. He should've used his lamp instead of the overhead light. "I don't want to fuck this up. You're important to me. Your family is important."

"Definitely. I want you to feel comfortable and I don't want you to come to Eid if it's too much." Emir really wishes he could be comforting Theo in person right now. He'd cuddle and kiss and soothe away every anxiety and answer all three dozen of his burning questions because interest in his family and his traditions is more than he allowed himself to hope for when he was younger. Theo's taught him to expect a full love, and Emir plans to return it in equal measure.

They sit in shared quiet for a minute, Theo thinking and wondering and sorting through his scattered emotions while Emir waits patiently, finding something in his photos. Theo makes a mental list of what he needs to learn and do, planning to make an actual list after they talk about it. Knowing he has time helps. Sitting on the phone like this isn't so different from being together except for the physical component. Theo misses Emir's presence like a piece of a puzzle. It still works and you can see the picture, but you notice the absence.

"Check your messages." Emir's voice brings Theo's heart back from longing, reminding him that Emir might be a few hours away, but he's also right here with him.

"Oh, it must still be early in New York. Gabe looks good in his ice hockey gear." Between their group chat with Lili and Jordan and the other one with their flatmates, Theo's phone is never short on notifications. "Bet Ciaran's enjoying that one."

"Your other messages." Emir giggles, laying back on his bed with one arm thrown above his head. Theo's adorable. "Your boyfriend sent you something."

"Oh. Was that picture from a few years ago? You look...younger." Theo winces and he knows it's visible. It's just that Emir looks so...small. Not physically, just like he's shrinking and sad and dim. So different to the Emir he knows now.

"It was just before we met, actually. But that's not why I sent it." Emir doesn't look back at these pictures very often, that time in his life like a flood crossing his path rather than the firm ground he's now walking. "I thought you'd like to wear that to Eid. I have a few and that one should fit you. It's always been a bit big on me, so it should fit your broad shoulders that I like so much."

"Are you sure? I'll wear whatever you tell me to, as long as it's alright. Like I said, I don't know the rules." Theo zooms in on the picture before minimising his messages so he can see Emir again. Present Emir, not haunted Emir from the past.

"The rules are that you have to completely adore me and have fun. And yes, I'd like you to wear that." Emir can't wait to kiss that handsome face again. It's only been a few days, and it's been a wonderful few days, but right now, he could really do with getting all up on his boyfriend. Just being in his space would be perfect. "Does that help?"

"Yes, definitely." Theo sighs, finally laying back on his bed again, his posture a mirror to Emir's. Even in separate beds they leave room for their partner. "You think I should let Bruce in for Christmas Eve cuddles? He's down in the living room with my parents."

"I think you should absolutely do that right now, yes." Emir can't believe that Theo usually has a *no Bruce in his bed* rule, because if Emir had a dog to cuddle, he'd be giving them their own pillow right beside him. "You call Laurie yet?"

"First thing this morning. I figured I should get to him before the next few days get busy, especially with all the kids." Theo watches as Emir runs a hand through his hair, and it shouldn't stop his train of thought, but it does. Emir's ability to distract him is everlasting. "You?"

"Tried earlier, but he was busy. T said I could call tonight, so I'll try to embarrass Laur with a nice *Happy Birthday* song when we're off the phone, even if it's a few days early." Emir grins, so excited for Christmas in a way he's never been before. Tomorrow is going to be a wonderful memory.

"It's alright if you don't have time to call me tomorrow. But once everyone leaves, I'll just be around the house with my parents, watching telly and eating junk food. It's weird not having Grandad around, but he's busy helping his sister this Christmas after her surgery." Theo shrugs, his holiday plans nowhere near as full as Emir's. Essentially, he'll be at home unless his parents decide they want to go out somewhere. And he'll be visiting the gym most days but that's about it.

"I'll see you tomorrow, don't worry." Emir winks, but he's not sure that Theo catches it. He's busy fidgeting with a seam on his pillow to avoid letting Emir know how badly he wants to talk tomorrow. Even if Emir was busy, he'd be able to find a few minutes for Theo. "Text me another selfie with Bruce? You know how I swoon for that."

"You're too easy." Theo teases, already getting up from his bed to go call the dog up the stairs. He turns on his lamp on the way, already reaching to switch off the overhead light. "I could send you a blurry accidental picture of the ground and you'd compliment my photography skills."

"Only easy for you, baby." Emir waits for Theo to groan and roll his eyes, but he also smiles so big his cheek dimple shows, so Emir considers it a win. "Happy Christmas, princess."

"Don't forget to call Laurie." Theo waits for Emir to blow him a kiss and hang up with a fond goodnight.

Opening his bedroom door again, Theo listens to make sure he isn't interrupting a moment for his parents before calling out for Bruce. The dog trots obediently up the stairs, waiting outside Theo's door to be invited in, seemingly not believing his luck when Theo carries him up and into the bed.

"You get to cuddle with me tonight, Bruce. Christmas present for both of us." Theo scratches behind Bruce's floppy ears, holding him close and unlocking his phone for a selfie. He won't actually let Bruce sleep overnight with him because Bruce is a bed hog and Theo wants his rest, but they can cuddle and watch something on Theo's laptop for a few hours. Give his parents some privacy downstairs and himself some destimulation time. "Now, how would you feel about the *Schitt's Creek* Christmas episode? Perfect, right? Yeah, that's what I thought."

It takes Theo a few minutes to navigate to the episode he's looking for, but once he does, he and Bruce settle in, Bruce's head on Theo's lap, Theo sending a selfie to the group this time and getting a flurry of responses in return. He feels so lucky to have two families, the one he grew up with and the one he grew into at uni. Bruce sighs and moves further into Theo's lap, waiting for a hand to start petting his side. Theo's had some wonderful Christmas Eves during his life, but this might be his favourite one yet.

***

Jordan: Happy Christmas /three christmas tree emojis/
Lili: Or in emir's case, happy friday /yellow heart emoji/
Emi: i don't mind being wished a happy christmas but thank you
Theo: HAPPY CHRISTMAS
Theo: /gif of Buddy the Elf screaming excitedly/
Theo: The kids are on their way and Bruce is very excited. Look.
Theo: /picture of Bruce wearing a candy cane striped bow tie on his collar/
Jordan: That's adorable :)
Emi: wish i could be cuddling bruce right now :(
Theo: What about me?
Emi: yes obviously you princess
Emi: the both of you
Jordan: I'll have to get off my phone now. Christmas here is a bit of a to-do and requires my attention, unfortunately.
Lili: Ugh money people
Jordan: Yes, dear. My family.
Emir: i'll be at home for a bit then in the car but i'll send pictures when we get there
Emir: it's so warm and cosy and even though i don't get the christmas thing i do get that
Theo: THE CHILDREN ARE HERE AND THEY DEMAND UNCLE TEDDY ATTENTION HELP ME
Lili: Put in those ear plugs you got
Lili: The real subtle ones that are purple and help with the overstimmies
Emi: THE OVERSTIMMIES /skull emoji/
Theo: That helped, thank you /purple heart emoji/
Lili: My brothers woke me up three hours ago but at least Nathan made coffee
Emi: when does he have to leave to go back to japan?
Lili: Not for a few weeks :)
Lili: And Christopher and my parents go with him this time for a visit
Lili: I'm the only one who can't go because of uni but Nathan promised I get a chance next year as a graduation present
Theo: Wow. I forget what it's like to be a kid on Christmas morning. These two already had presents at their own homes this morning, but showing up here, you'd think it's the first time. Double Santa, double the excitement apparently.

Emi: you'll be such a cute christmas dad someday
Lili: He'll take the Father Christmas thing very seriously
Lili: Probably that stupid elf too
Emi: what stupid elf?
Theo: THE ELF ON THE SHELF
Theo: Babe, we have to have an Elf on the Shelf. We'll give it a name and everything.
Theo: I help Boo and Jayna with ideas every year. It's so much fun!
Emi: i have googled and pumpkin i am not going to be posing a vaguely haunted doll around the house every night for a MONTH
Theo: Well, no, you won't be. I will.
Theo: But you could maybe help. It's a lot of work for one person.
Emi: could we maybe train the children to believe in a slightly less involved fictional creature?
Theo: Nope :)
Theo: Also, I don't think we're meant to be training the kids like they're dogs. I'll have to ask mum if that's a thing.
Lili: Oi what's all this about children?
Theo: You know I want kids, Lilibet. Always have.
Lili: Well yes but
Emi: and i want to be a baba someday so
Lili: Happy Christmas you two are having a kid?
Theo: Obviously not! I can barely handle my two niblings and they're on their best behaviour. It'll be years before we even talk about that!
Emi: should probably start with getting a dog /side eye emoji/
Theo: Or a cat. Might depend where we live.
Lili: Omg please get a cat and let me cat sit and bring it toys and you should get it one of those cat treadmills
Theo: Whatever animal we get, it will be spoiled and very loved.
Emi: just give me a fluff to cuddle i'm not picky
Lili: Clearly I mean you cuddle Theo and he's only fluffy at one end
Emi: i cuddle theo for many reasons but yes he is very much a teddy bear
Emi: i love when his hair is all floof and soft
Theo: This is nice teasing, right? I'm not being made fun of?
Emi: no, princess, not being made fun of /kiss face emoji/ we're busy adoring you
Lili: Adoring is a strong word
Emi: be nice to my teddy
Lili: /eye roll emoji/
Emi: about to leave the house :)
Lili: Did you decide what to wear for your drive....?
Emi: i did ;)

Theo: *Wait, I want to see the outfit. Selfie?*
Emi: *i'll send one later can't get a good picture right now*
Theo: /selfie with the kids, a Santa hat on his head and one nibling squished against each of his cheeks/
Theo: *They wanted to say hello and Happy Christmas!*
Lili: /selfie with two very annoyed older brothers/
Lili: *They didn't want to say hello but I made them do it anyway*
Emi: /picture of his trainers on the floor in the backseat of his parents' car/
Emi: *tell everyone i say hello :)*

***

"You enjoying your new book, sweetheart?" Caroline wanders into the living room where Theo is relaxed into the corner of the sofa, spending his time reading after the chaos of having the rest of the family over.

Theo looks up at his mum and nods, moving his bookmark to save his page so he can set it aside and pay attention.

"You have any plans for the rest of the day?" Caroline asks, sitting near his feet and running a gentle hand along his shin. It's one of those things mums do, where they learn to give their grown kids space but still want to cuddle close and keep everyone safe no matter how big they get.

"I might FaceTime Emir tonight. Been texting all my friends, but everyone's mostly doing this." Theo sets his new book in his lap and runs a hand through his hair. Everyone gifted him at least one book from his list, along with a few other small things. Now that the three siblings are grown, presents are more practical. but no less appreciated. "I thought I'd just sort of relax and cuddle with Bruce, read my new books, maybe take a nap."

"Your dad and I are going to take a walk. You want to join us?" Caroline glances over at her husband as he walks from the kitchen to stand near them in the living room instead. Their Christmas roast was a few hours ago, so a snack is warranted.

"It's alright if you need a break after all the excitement, we just wanted to offer." George sets a familiar hand on Theo's head and gives his hair a fond tussle. The two of them and Bruce are currently wearing matching snowflake jumpers, a gift from Jayna and her husband. Caroline has her own jumper to match the grandkids, a jolly snowman stitched across the front.

"I'd love a walk!" Theo has always appreciated taking walks, but since Emir entered his life as more than an antagonist, it's a part of his routine that he misses on days when he doesn't take one. "Could I have a few minutes of transition time? Put my book away and get my shoes and all that? Or do we need to leave right now?"

"Is five minutes enough time?" Caroline gives Theo's ankle a squeeze as she stands up and moves away towards George, letting Theo get up from the sofa.

"Can one of you get Bruce ready? If not, I'll need a few more minutes." Theo moves his book to the coffee table, ready to continue reading the sappy gay romance after the walk. Or, if his parents want to watch something on the telly, he's happy to do that as well. Christmas is one of the few days of the year where he's alright without a schedule.

"On it." George sets a hand on Caroline's back before stepping away to do exactly that, knowing that Bruce needs his harness and matching leash, and this time of year, his little boots to keep his paws safe from the cold. It's a whole process, but Bruce has gotten more used to it over time. He doesn't even gnaw on his covered paws after the first few minutes anymore.

"Thanks, mum." Theo surprises her with a hug, falling into her space and holding her tight.

"For what, sweetie?" Caroline holds him back, always so glad when her youngest is home for a while. She's still adjusting to the empty nest, even almost three years on. Having Bruce helps.

Theo sways them in the hug, letting himself relax in the safety of his mum's embrace. "For all of it. I'm glad you're my mum."

Caroline pats him softly on the back, appreciative of how sweet and kind he is. She's lucky to have her kids and to know they've grown up into adults she's very proud of. "I love you, Theo. I'm glad you're my kid."

George drops the leash and harness to the side, Bruce waiting patiently at his knee, then fits his arms around his wife and son to join the hug.

***

Laurie: /group photo of Laurie with all his sisters/
Laurie: /couples photo with T, T wearing a bright red jumpsuit and Laurie in a matching red jumper/
Laurie: /photo of Laurie with his mum, showing off her growing baby bump/
Laurie: /photo with everyone, including T's parents and stepdad, sister Lucy, all of Laurie's sisters, Laurie's mum, stepdad, and newer stepdad, Sara's parents and their two dogs/
T: /selfie with their mum and stepdad, all pulling faces at the camera/
T: /picture with their dad and Lucy, T in the middle as the tallest of them/
Laurie: Sorry I haven't texted much today. We've been in a state of absolute chaos
Laurie: No idea what the hell we're going to do with two more next year but I'm sure it'll be brilliant
T: I can't wait until we have the little babies to look after <3
Emi: honestly i'm amazed everyone fit in the house
T: It helps that my mum and stepdad are staying with Sara
T: Lucy and my dad are driving back to Manchester soon so they were only here for a few hours
Theo: It was a lot for me to handle with just the two kids, I can't imagine how you're still standing!
Ciaran: /selfie with his dad in a pub, Guinness in hand/
Ciaran: Merry Christmas, ya filthy animals
Gabe: Still morning here /sun emoji/
Gabe: There's snow as tall as my knees and I miss every single one of you
Gabe: /family photo with his sister and parents in front of their very tall Christmas tree/
Emi: i'm almost done with my drive :) :) :)
Laurie: Send us pictures when you get there?
Emi: of course :) :) :)
Theo: My parents and I just got back from a walk :) The weather is so perfect for Christmas. It's chilly and grey but not freezing and I got to run with Bruce the last few streets home.
Theo: /selfie with Bruce, both still in their matching jumpers, Theo flushed and smiling/
T: We should probably go but we'll make sure to check in later
T: Emi don't forget.....
Emi: i won't :)
Gabe: Awwww we're just opening presents and you all are too sweet
Gabe: Thank you for the beanie and the ornament and all of it
Gabe: And thanks for making sure everything fit easily into my suitcase /laughing emoji/
Ciaran: Call me when you're done with opening presents?
Ciaran: We're still at the pub but I'll step out to talk

Ciaran: I miss you, angel
Emi: /excited minion gif/
Theo: Are you there yet?
Laurie: He should be in just a minute, yeah
Theo: How do you know?
Laurie: Just called him of course
Emi: our pre-birthday call got cut short last night so we had to find time today that worked with the busy Tempest schedule
T: Excuse me someone tell Laur to get off his phone and help me with the gingerbread. There's about to be a small mutiny
Theo: Laurie, go help your fiance entertain the weebles.
Ciaran: I miss you all /crying emoji/
Ciaran: I'll be smooching each and every one of you when we get back in a few weeks
Gabe: What Ciaran said
Gabe: I fucking love New York but it's enough to be back a few times a year
Ciaran: Everyone should come to Kildare for Christmas next year or whenever we can make it happen, depending on where we all live.
Ciaran: I want to share it with you all
Theo: I would love that! Maybe in a few years?
Emi: /gay screaming gif/
T: Have fun :)

***

Theo is back in the living room, sitting between his parents on the sofa with his feet up on the coffee table, watching a rerun of last year's *Great British Bake Off Christmas Special*, when the front doorbell rings and gets his attention away from the Technical challenge. It's late afternoon, almost evening, and as far as he knows they aren't expecting anyone. They have all their decorations up, fairy lights and bauble laden tree visible through their picture window, so it might be a neighbour stopping by on their own walk to say hello.

"Oh, that'll be Mrs. Alderman. Her kids are away this year, so I invited her by for a cuppa." Caroline stands up to answer the door and gets Theo's attention to ask, "Could you go and put the kettle on?"

"Tea actually sounds perfect." Theo smiles at his mum and gets up as well, heading towards the kitchen while she walks to the front door. George pauses their show and follows after Caroline to greet their visitor. Theo's known Mrs. Alderman since he was small, and she's always been very kind to him and his sisters. It's nice they can offer her some company while she's spending the holiday alone.

Theo fusses around the kitchen, getting down four mugs from the shelf and filling the kettle. He's absentmindedly humming Christmas carols as he paces about the kitchen, spinning and dancing to his own little rhythm while waiting for the water to boil. Maybe he should get out the biscuits as well? Might be nice to have them.

There's quiet voices coming from the front door, a few excited barks from Bruce, and Theo smiles to himself before gracing the empty room with a twirl just as the kettle clicks off.

"Shame I left my favourite mug at uni. Could really go for a cuppa right now."

Theo can't believe what he's hearing, and then believes even less what he's seeing as he almost falls out of his twirl in shock.

Emir's standing in the entryway to his kitchen, cheeks pink from the cold and beanie pulled tight around his ears, hands in his pockets while he leans against the doorframe and smiles his perfect smile right at Theo.

"Emir?!" Theo quite literally launches himself across the room, colliding with his boyfriend and bringing them both down to the floor in a tumble of joyous limbs.

Quieter he repeats, "Emir," and nuzzles into his neck.

Theo is pretty sure Emir can hear the pure joy placed in that one word. He's so happy he feels his heartbeat in his fingertips, a rush of adrenaline and love so strong he wouldn't be able to stand up right now even if he wanted to.

Emir huffs from the impact but holds on tight, unable to withhold the surprise a moment longer even though watching Theo dance around was very cute. Theo in his own little bubble is so sweet and free, but Emir didn't think he could go unnoticed for very long.

"What are you doing here?" Theo slides his arms beneath Emir's jumper so he can hold him closer. Why must they be in the kitchen where he can't climb into Emir's skin like he wants? He's been without his cuddle buddy for days, and now Emir's right here, in his home and in his arms, unexpected in the best way.

"Surprise." Emir mumbles, the wind more than a little knocked out of him.

He was hoping Theo would be excited, but this is even better than he expected. Emir's currently being hugged into the floor, Theo's arms so tight around his back it's like he's testing if Emir is real. If only he knew that being with Theo is the most alive Emir's ever felt, the most himself, the most grounded and whole. This is all so beautifully real.

"But your drive?" Theo still doesn't quite understand how Emir is here right now. He's meant to be spending the day with his parents and he said he was busy until after the New Year. Did something happen? No, Emir would've called first.

"Told you it was a bit South." Emir didn't lie, but he did want to keep this a surprise if at all possible. He's been plotting with Caroline and their friends for weeks to make this happen. Theo squirms on top of him, but his face stays glued to Emir's skin. "I just…didn't specify which house we were driving to visit."

"But Mrs. Alderman?" Theo asks, and surprisingly that makes Emir laugh. Oh how he's missed that sound, feeling the way it moves through Emir's body and fills the air with his light.

"Your mum and dad are going over to see her later tonight, don't worry. We needed a cover story to get you away from the door, so your mum fibbed a bit." Emir finally gets to see Theo's face again when he pulls back enough to give Emir quite a hard kiss. But he's snuggling back into his neck again almost immediately, needing Emir's presence more than just the sight of him. He's seen Emir's face every night since the holiday started. It's Emir's everything else he's been missing.

Emir could melt into the floor, happy and warm in Theo's arms, but they're not entirely alone, even if the parents have been wise enough to give them a moment before intruding.

"Is that Bruce?" There's a sniffling somewhere nearby and the sound of a collar, so Emir assumes Bruce has come to see what all the excitement is about. He'd left the dog back at the door with both sets of parents so he could surprise Theo on his own, but Bruce is even cuter in person than all the pictures that Theo's shared.

"Oh my god, you haven't met Bruce!" Theo sits up immediately, pulling Emir with him but not getting up from the floor. He's been waiting for this moment for months, knowing how deeply Emir loves dogs and needing to watch them bond. "Bruce, sit."

Bruce sits. There's a tail that won't stop wagging and a whine at wanting attention, but he sits.

As an aside to Emir, Theo badly whispers, "Ask him to shake and tell him who you are."

Emir giggles but does as Theo requests. Holding Theo around the waist with one arm, Emir offers his right hand and asks Bruce to shake, taking his paw to add, "I'm Emir, your big brother's boyfriend. It's nice to meet you."

Bruce pants, his bright eyes shining, and he waits only a second longer before knocking Emir back down on the ground, very gently attacking his face with kisses. He's not so different from his human brother.

"This a family trait, then?" Emir teases, letting Theo laugh and watch as Bruce steals his boyfriend for a cuddle. They're really going to have to adopt an animal together once uni's over. "For a border collie, he's quite strong."

"Bruce, down. Come here." George calls from the other room, giving Emir the chance to recover and focus on Theo again. Bruce scampers off and sits obediently beside George, waiting for the chance to go sprint around in the garden and run off some of this extra energy.

Theo gives Emir another tight squeeze, still sitting on the ground, then glances behind Emir to see Saleem and Natalie chatting with his parents and hanging up their coats near the door. "Your parents are here."

"Yeah, they drove me. Your mum said it was alright." Emir kisses the side of Theo's neck and breathes him in. He's so glad he decided to do this. "She said she'd like to get to know them, and my parents were excited too. They like being involved in our lives, and you're an important part of mine."

"Are they staying for tea?" Theo sits back, crossing his legs and taking both of Emir's hands in his own. There's no signs of recent artwork on his sculpted fingers, but he's sure that will change soon enough. Emir never travels anywhere without at least a sketchbook and some pencils.

Sitting here on the floor with Emir in his space, this is the best Christmas Theo's ever had.

"Definitely. But they're having a posh night at some hotel in town before they drive back home tomorrow. It's just you and me for a bit tonight and then time with your family tomorrow." Emir also crosses his legs, facing Theo and laughing when Bruce comes and works his way into both of their laps. He'll have to be let out soon before he sprouts wings.

"Wait, does that mean you leave tomorrow?" Theo pouts, his eyes still shining, but his posture sad. Now that Emir's here, he's not ready to say goodbye again so soon. If the Shahs leave tomorrow, that means less than twenty-four hours together for the next two weeks.

"Nope." Emir grins, darting forward to kiss Theo where his dimple should be. Theo smiles at the kiss, and there it is, right on time. Emir doesn't think there's anyone more stunning than a happy Theo. "You and I are staying here until Sunday, then we're driving to my parents' in Shipley to spend a few days there. We're meeting up with the lads in Darton for New Year's. Well, not Ciaran and Gabe, but T and Laurie. It's all planned and scheduled. We'll be staying the night at the Tempest house, but we'll have to share a floor mattress. Laur said it's not bad."

"Really? You've planned all this?" Theo genuinely can't believe it.

This surprise is so much more than Emir showing up on Christmas. He didn't have anything against a quiet holiday at home with his family, but now it's like he gets the best of both worlds. Does he start singing the song? Emir is a miracle.

"As long as it's alright with you? If it's too much or you'd rather not, I can go back with my parents tomorrow. I know it's a lot all at once. Me and Laurie have been conspiring with your mum for almost a month. You'll still get that last week at home so you don't miss out on family time, and your mum said that your Grandad Robert will be back and her parents are coming to visit the day after New Year's so you'll be around to see them, but I really wanted to surprise you and we thought it'd be nice to go visit Laurie and T and get to see the wedding venue and all that." Emir takes one of his hands back to give Bruce a bit of attention. He's being very well behaved for an excitable dog who has three new people in his house to sniff at. "And I can show you around my place a bit. Make some...happier memories there with you."

"Emi!" Theo tackles Emir again, Bruce falling to the side and running back to the others who've now settled themselves on the sofas, chatting away like old friends. They'll go join them in a few minutes. "It's perfect! You're perfect. I'm gonna kiss you now - if that's allowed?"

Emir laughs again, guiding Theo's lips to his own with a soft hand in his curls, waiting for their mouths to meet for their first proper kiss in days. Almost a week, actually, but who's counting? They keep it chaste, just a few soft brushes of their lips, Emir's hands on Theo's back and in his hair, Theo's still hugging tight to Emir's shoulders. There's nothing that compares to a kiss of reunification between the sky and the earth, both shining so bright it's ultraviolet.

"Gotta get up, buttercup." Emir grins and pulls back after a few kisses, eyes still closed with Theo's forehead pressed against his own. They have time for much more of that later. "We have tea to make for everyone and we should spend some time with our parents."

"This is the best present I've ever gotten." Theo presses forward for one last kiss before standing up, holding out a hand to help Emir up as well. There's something so lovely and domestic about the two of them preparing tea for their parents, mumbling quietly to each other and brushing hands and stealing kisses until the water's boiled again. Their every interaction is home, full of warmth and joy and love.

"Theo?" Emir pauses Theo with a hand on his waist before he can pick up the tray and carry it into the living room.

"Emi?" Theo falls back into him, as easy as breathing. Emir's arms are where he belongs, his heart the warmest welcome he could ever receive.

"Happy Christmas." Emir brushes the hair away from Theo's eyes, pulling him forward to kiss him in front of the sink. Their parents can't see them from where they are, so they're allowed another moment alone before joining the conversation happening in the other room.

Theo smiles and kisses him back, pressing Emir against the counter and holding him like the gift he is. Having Emir here, in the home he grew up in, it's everything he could've hoped for but never thought to ask. It's two halves of his life joining together, Emir offering him the opportunity to be his tour guide before taking his own turn in Shipley. Two days from now, they'll be having a similar moment, only in Emir's home instead. Every hour of this surprise has been planned as thoughtfully and carefully as possible.

It's so rare to have a perfect moment, a spot in time that's only joy, only love, entirely light. Theo kisses Emir through it, absorbing every particle of space and time as it collides, the taste of Emir's lips and the feel of his skin better than any photograph. He'll be looking back on tonight for the rest of his life.

CHAPTER NINE

Early morning on Boxing Day, Theo traipses quietly downstairs and into the kitchen, wiping the sleep from his eyes and stretching his arms over his head. The windows are frosted over but the sun is catching on the wood floor in softened streams. This early in the day, there's a quiet that Theo loves, a soothing sort of calm that blankets the house and settles under his skin.

"Dad." Theo isn't surprised to find his dad already downstairs, having his morning coffee and scrolling the news on his tablet. The two of them both like their routines and keep to a regular sleep schedule, which means sleeping in isn't likely, even on a holiday.

"Morning, kid." George sets his iPad down and opens his arm for the side hug Theo offers, briefly wondering when the hell Theo got so tall. Surely he's not still growing? "Sleep well?"

"Perfect." Theo yawns again, reaching for his *Power Rangers* mug then filling the kettle from the tap. "Mum up yet?"

"She's having a lie-in. I think the grandkids wore her out a bit yesterday." George watches Theo move about the kitchen with pride. Having his youngest at home is a better present than anything they unwrapped yesterday. "Emir?"

"Oh, he's tough to get up in the morning. I struggle to get him out of bed most days, especially on weekends." Theo grins, looking down at his sock covered toes and rolling through his ankles out of habit. "Thanks for letting him stay and all that. I know some parents…especially because we're…just…thanks."

Theo glances up at his dad, hoping the words he couldn't quite say were understood. His family is pretty good at decoding his thoughts by now. It's not as if he thinks his parents are under any illusions about his relationship with Emir or anything like that, but some parents still have a hard time accepting that their adult children are in romantic and sexual relationships, especially in their own house.

"He's a good person and he makes you happy." George clears his throat, bringing his coffee to his lips for a sip while returning Theo's stare with sincerity. "I'm glad to have a welcoming home for you and your partner, Theo. I hope you've never doubted that. Same as your sisters and their partners, though if I'm being honest, Emir might be my favourite. He's certainly your mother's."

Grinning, Theo nods, running a hand through the front of his hair and marvelling at the tangled mess he encounters. He'll need to sort that out before waking Emir up. "You and mum have been great. Like, I didn't quite know what to expect since it's my first relationship, so I was just...I knew you supported me. I've always known that. But there's still that worry, I suppose. And Emir's...he's not just some person I'm dating..."

"I know." George uses his foot to slide out the chair across from him, tilting his head to indicate that Theo should sit. "You're not a kid anymore, Theo. It's time we chat about a few things."

"Oh, Dad, that's...I mean it's a little late...like, I'm in uni and – " Theo flushes, turning around to pour the now boiled water into his mug, glad to have something to distract himself from *that* conversation. If he didn't want to talk to his mates about sex, he certainly doesn't want to discuss it with his parents.

"Not that, Theo. I know you're up to date on sexual health." George laughs, a sound very similar to Theo's but a fraction more gruff. "No, I think we should talk about the other things: how to be a good partner, build a healthy relationship, what it's like to have kids, if that's what you want. I taught you how to change a tire and how to shave, but there's still a few pieces of wisdom I've been saving."

Theo finishes fixing his tea and calmly takes the proffered seat, hands around his mug and legs crossed in the chair in a way only a dancer could manage. If that's what his dad wants to talk about, he's open to it. His parents have been happily partnered for three decades and then some. He could use their advice.

"I think Emir's it, Dad. He's so special, like, he's brilliant and kind and gentle, and he understands me in a way I didn't know another person could. I sleep better when I know he's there. I feel safe when we're together. He makes me laugh and comforts me when I cry. And...I don't have to hide from him. It's..."

"Freeing? Validating? Comfortable?" George tries, pushing his iPad fully away to the side of the table. There's time to catch up on the BBC homepage later.

"And so much more." Theo sighs, blowing the steam off his tea while leaning forward on his elbows, deep in thought. "I know we've only been dating a few months, but we've already been through a few phases. We communicate well and we have all the same priorities, which is like...it feels so right. I don't have to try to love him, I just do. It's not like he's perfect or anything, and I have plenty of my own issues, but when things come up we work through it together. We learned that lesson the hard way, but we're better for it."

"It was the same with your mum. We met and we dated and I knew from that first week that she was my someone. I think for people like us," George pauses, readjusting in his seat and scratching at the stubble growing on his chin, "We know ourselves better than most people, so when it comes to finding a partner, or multiple partners…"

George pauses again, waiting for Theo to acknowledge his acceptance of a potential open or polyamorous relationship, "We know what we need, what we want, what we value. Emir may be your first relationship, but that doesn't mean he can't be the person you'll grow old with. If you're happy and healthy, and you look after each other, then that's all I need to know."

They sit in stillness, listening to the sounds of the refrigerator and the wind against the windows, both processing their thoughts before they continue. Theo's mum is all gentle affection and earnest excitement while his dad is sensitive conversations and open dialogue, both with more than enough hugs to offer. Caroline's chatted with Theo since the beginning of his relationship with Emir whenever he's sought reassurance or excitement, but his talks with his dad have been less involved. Supportive, but Theo and George are more reserved together, and Theo likes that he gets different types of support from each of his parents.

"We're going to get a flat together after uni." Theo thinks his parents probably figured as much, but he hasn't actually said it in so many words yet. "We don't know what city or really any of the specifics, but we've talked about it, and we want to stay together. Build a life, wherever we land. And family is important to both of us, so hopefully not far."

"You promise to let me help you with that? Don't be too proud to let your family love you into your next phase, alright?" George reaches across the space, giving Theo's wrist a squeeze before going back to his coffee mug. "I hope I'll be invited to the house warming, but if you need help building furniture or anything else, you know where to find me. We just want to be in your life, but we'll give you your space. Spread those wings of yours, but remember you can always fly back home, yeah?"

"Thanks, Dad." Theo rubs at his eyes, taking a sip of his tea to clear the lump in his throat. He feels so lucky to have the parents he does, the most accepting and supportive of all his many identities and facets. Theo struggled with friends and school more than most kids, and he knows it was hard on his parents, and even his sisters. But they never resented him or were anything other than loving, even when he threw tantrums or was having meltdowns or needed to process all the bullying in his own way. And now that he's happy and has solid friends and an eye on the future, he's glad to invite his family into the joy that they helped him find.

"Now, let's talk about buying your first home in a few years. It's quite a process and you may want to take notes." George nods his understanding when Theo literally gets up to do just that, retrieving a notebook from the living room where he'd been watching dance videos and reading his new books last night with Emir.

Theo likes his lists and his references, depending on an organised calendar on his phone and a search engine at the ready. George isn't much different, though his notes tend to be more scattered about the house. Being autistic certainly runs in their family as true as their physical features, but like their outward appearances, it looks a bit different for each of them.

"Could we maybe also discuss radiators? They're very confusing." Theo resettles in the kitchen chair, pen and notebook ready to absorb the generational knowledge about to be passed along. "And, like, secrets to a successful marriage would be good, and also, I may ask for your help in a few years when we start considering kids."

"Probably too much to cover this morning, but let's see where we get before the others wake up." George stands up to fix himself some breakfast from the leftovers in the fridge. He can talk while he reheats. "First thing you'll need to decide for the house is the location, both the city and the neighbourhood. Everything else grows from there."

***

Late morning finds Emir and Theo sitting beside the Palmer's Christmas tree, both in soft joggers and oversized jumpers while they face each other on the floor.

"You don't mind us old folk hanging around while you open your gifts?" Caroline asks from her spot on the sofa next to George, Bruce sprawled out on the other sofa as if he owns it.

"Course not." Theo gives his mum a smile before turning back to Emir. "Is this weird for you? Like having Christmas presents and all?"

"Nah. Wouldn't have brought you gifts if it was, princess." Emir holds up the parcel nearest him and gives it a little shake to prove his point. "Who's first?"

"You!" Theo crawls across to the box he'd lovingly wrapped and left beneath the tree. Even though he didn't know Emir would be here, it felt right to place it there until he could give it to him, and now he doesn't have to wait until January. "I chose plain paper since I didn't want it to be Christmassy. I promise it wasn't because I didn't want to decorate it or anything."

"It's perfect." Emir brushes a curl behind Theo's ear and cups his face before reaching down and taking the box from him. It's surprisingly heavy, a clothing box of some sort. And while Theo explained why the wrapping is plain, it's clearly lovingly done and there was effort involved. There's even a tiny rainbow sticker holding the paper closed.

"I had it shipped here so you wouldn't see." Theo fiddles with his hands and chews on the inside of his cheek while waiting for Emir to unwrap and then open the box in question, hoping it's not too little or too much. They haven't really exchanged proper gifts before, even though they're constantly sharing art and snacks and tea and clothes. This is different.

Emir lifts the lid off the box to find a fluffy, oversized pale heather grey crewneck jumper. Theo knows Emir always wants more warm things to swaddle himself in. Written across the chest of the jumper is a double pun, both nerdy and dance related, and Emir loves it immediately. "Theo, this is *incredible*. Where did you even find this?"

There's a picture of four ballerinas dancing the pas de quatre from *Swan Lake*, but on their heads are stormtrooper helmets. Just above the dancers is the phrase *Swan Wars* but in the iconic *Star Wars* font. It's a mashup of the nerdy things they both love and the dance world they share. Emir can already see himself wearing this to and from the studio for weeks until Theo makes him throw it in the laundry to restart the cycle.

"Just on this website I found. There's an artist who makes these sorts of nerd crossover things. And, um, it's already washed so you can wear it if you want, but you don't have to." Theo keeps watching Emir, grinning as he buries his face in the front of it and takes a deep breath in. He'd sprayed a bit of his own cologne on the jumper just before setting it in the box. "Maybe try it on for size? It should fit."

"It's so cosy!" Emir unfolds it to do as Theo suggested, causing the second part of his present to fall out of the middle, just as Theo hoped. "There's more?"

"It sort of goes with the jumper." Theo shrugs, trying to appear casual, but knowing that this is the real gift. He's been waiting to surprise Emir for literally months, since before they were even dating. "You'll see."

Emir slides the swan jumper over his head (on top of the one he's already wearing) before picking up the envelope. His name is written in Theo's handwriting, with "xx" in the bottom right corner. He wants it tattooed, but he'll settle for keeping the envelope somewhere safe.

Inside is the sweetest, most Theo present he could imagine, something they discussed so long ago it's a distant memory. "You got us tickets to go see Trockadero together?"

"For the weekend of your birthday. They leave for South America at the end of January, so the timing was perfect." Theo flushes at the look Emir gives him, his mouth slightly open and eyes sparkling. "I thought we could get all dressed up and have a date night in the city. You said you've never been, so I looked up tickets when I got home that night back in September and then I asked Laurie for your birthday to see if they were in town and...yeah."

"*Theo.*" Emir actually doesn't know what to say. This might be the best present he's ever gotten. "Baby, I - "

"They're not, like, real tickets. They just sent a QR code to my email, but I wanted to give something to you as, like, a souvenir, so I found a template online and added some bits and asked Mum for cardstock to make it look more official and - " Theo gets cut off, Emir throwing himself at Theo and knocking them both to the ground.

"I can't believe you." Emir squeezes Theo tight, kissing the underside of his jaw and nuzzling into his space. "Just know I'd be kissing you so hard right now if we were alone."

"You could kiss me a little, if you want." Theo mumbles, arms going around Emir's back as Bruce jumps down from the couch to join them, paws on Emir's shoulders while he barks excitedly.

"Just a small one then." Emir moves to kiss just the side of Theo's mouth before helping him sit back up, then hugs him again immediately because he's so in love it's hard to contain. Their embrace is awkward with how they're sitting, and Bruce keeps trying to get in the way, but all four of them are laughing, Caroline and George not even trying to calm the dog because they can tell that Emir and Theo love having him bounce around them. His energy is infectious.

"Good present?" Theo asks, holding Emir with a hand on each side of his waist while Emir plays with his hair and toys at the collar of his jumper. Theo's the one who gave the present, but Emir is staring at him with so much love and intensity that Theo can feel the heat in his cheeks, like he's the one being spoiled.

"The best. I'm so excited!" Emir watches Theo's smile continue to grow until it's pure sunshine. "You make me so happy, you know that?"

He's leaning in to whisper to only Theo, needing to convey some fraction of the love he has for his boyfriend. Emir never even dreamed of a gift like this. "You're the sweetest man in the world. So thoughtful."

Theo hides his face against Emir and holds him close for a moment longer. It's just a gift, but it's also a moment for them. This is the first family holiday time they've spent together. It's been lovely and surprising and full of joy, and Theo hasn't even opened whatever gift Emir has for him yet.

Emir gives Theo another kiss on his cheek then sits back in his own space again, turning to Caroline and George with a small container. It's not a Christmas tin, but something similar. Theo will have to ask him about it later, because he's noticed Natalie sending him care packages with similar ones. "Here, before I give Theo his gifts, these are for the both of you."

"Aw, bless you." Caroline leans forward to take the metal box from Emir and holds it between herself and George on her lap. Opening it, she finds a whole collection of homemade sweets that smell like Emir's flat when he's in the mood for his family recipes. George takes one immediately and tosses it into his mouth, giving an appreciative hum then flashing a thumbs up at Emir since he can't speak through his chewing.

"I spent most of Thursday in the kitchen with my mum, and we wanted to make something to say thank you for having me here for a few days and all that." Emir shrugs, leaning into Theo as he gets tugged closer into his space by an arm around his waist.

Bruce can only resist a treat for so long, sniffing excitedly at the sweets until Caroline closes the tiffin again with a laugh, gently pushing his little nose away so he doesn't make himself sick. "Thank you, Emir. They're lovely, dear."

"Amazing." George finishes the bite with a genuine smile, catching Bruce automatically as he climbs across Caroline and into George's lap instead. "Between you and Theo, your kitchen must be a busy place."

"Some days, but not as often as we should." Emir bumps his nose against Theo's jaw fondly then looks back at the others on the sofa with a grin. "We'll have to factor that in for after uni: decent kitchen in whatever flat we find."

"We can make a list. I probably should already have one." Theo fusses at Emir's jumpers until Emir allows him to pull the top one over his head and toss it aside. It's way too warm in the house for Emir to be wearing double jumpers. "Stop with the look. You can put it on later."

Emir sighs, putting the new jumper over his crossed legs and reaching for Theo's presents. "Your turn. Happy Christmas, princess."

"…Which one first?" Theo stares at the gifts in Emir's hands, one a very slim envelope and the other a small, flat box. He's guessing there's art of some kind in the envelope, but he has no clue about the other one.

"Here." Emir decides for Theo, handing over the bulkier of the two and saving the artwork for last. "This one's more, like, cute or whatever."

Theo carefully opens the paper around the box, doing his best not to tear it or possibly damage whatever's inside. But when he gets the paper off he laughs with glee, his face lighting up as he turns the box around to show his parents. It's a Baby Yoda themed spa set, with a Baby Yoda eye mask (that he can wear to sleep), a Baby Yoda terry cloth headband for when they do face masks, an exfoliating face brush, and Baby Yoda fluffy socks that are somehow his size. "It's adorable! Lili's going to make fun of me for days and I don't even care."

"I thought your teddy bear headband could use a friend, and you always need more eye masks for your beauty sleep. Especially when I'm up late with the lamp on." Emir watches as Theo gingerly opens the box and takes out each item, testing them out and showing off the results to his parents as if it's the best present he's ever received. "You're the cutest thing I've ever seen, pumpkin."

"Hold on, let me get a picture." Caroline searches the nearby surfaces until she finds her phone on the edge of the coffee table, Theo smiling with the Baby Yoda ears framing his face and Emir's chin hooked over his shoulder, hugging him from behind. "Oh, that's a nice one. I'll text it to you both."

"Wait, I want one with Bruce!" Theo calls the dog over and waits for him to calm down enough to pose with them, sitting obediently but trying to lick Emir's face every few moments until George distracts him with a treat behind Caroline's phone to hold his attention.

"Just a moment. I want to send that to my mum." Emir takes his phone from his pocket, unlocking it to show Theo the pictures that Caroline's just sent. Theo's grinning with fabric Baby Yoda ears flopping above his soft curls while Emir holds him close and Bruce mostly behaves with a wide doggy smile. "She'll be hanging these on the fridge."

Theo glances at his parents to see them watching on with fond smiles as he and Emir huddle together around the phone. His parents are so genuinely happy for him, for the joy he's found in his relationship, and they appreciate his willingness to trust his parents with this part of his life. Theo knows that some kids get to uni and distance themselves from their family, usually due to lack of support or something even worse. But his parents and his sisters have helped him flourish as a young adult, and bringing Emir into his life is just the next chapter that they've encouraged. They've all welcomed Emir with open arms as if any alternative would be impossible.

"You ready for your other gift?" Emir taps Theo under the chin to get his attention. He's been zoning out, smiling to himself and lost in his thoughts.

In the meantime, Bruce resettled by the tree and a new song started playing softly on the speaker nearby. Emir finds it all very cosy and he's glad he decided to spend a portion of his uni break here, with Theo, getting to know him in this context as well as all the others. He's different at home, like two sides of the same Rubik's Cube.

"Yes!" Theo holds his hand out excitedly, waiting as Emir retrieves it from where he'd set the envelope aside to keep it safe from Bruce's unpredictable paws. "For my collection?"

"I'm not sure they'll fit on your bookshelf, but yes." Emir scoots to the side a bit to give Theo room.

Slowly, Theo removes the stack of paper from the envelope, careful to only touch the edges when possible. He's learned that some of Emir's drawings can smudge if not handled properly, and since they're tiny miracles that sprout from Emir's hands, he wants to avoid that when possible.

"There's three of them in there. Can't remember the order." Emir watches as Theo uncovers the first image, this one of just Theo, all charcoal pencil, shadow and light playing together.

"I'm Batman!" Theo bounces where he sits, staring at the picture before turning it around to show his parents with bright eyes. "Wait, it is me, right?"

"Course it's you." Emir nudges Theo in the side with his elbow, rolling his eyes. He'd used a profile photo of Theo as a reference, and it's pretty spot on, even with the mask over his eyes.

"I look so...rugged." Theo laughs quietly, tracing the drawing with his eyes and trying to find all the tiny details that Emir always includes. The stubble on BatTheo's chin and jawline looks so real. It must've taken hours to get the shading and highlights just right.

"I should still have your cape somewhere around the house. If it's not here it's at your Grandad's." Caroline says over the top of her mug, having handed the phone to George to take over picture duty. He's doing his best, but she knows a good portion will be out of focus or have a finger in the frame.

"Too small." Theo shakes his head with a furrowed brow, as if it was a genuine suggestion. He does miss getting to dress up and play pretend, but now he has his dance performances and his characters, which is sort of scratching the same itch.

"Go on then. Two more." Emir takes the Batman picture from Theo to encourage him to keep going, covering it with the protective paper just in case.

"I'm Batman again and - oh..." Theo flushes, staring at the new picture with an interest that's a bit past platonic. "That's you, yeah?"

"Batman and Catwoman saving the city. I wasn't about to be Robin." Emir scrunches his nose at the thought.

Of course he's Catwoman. Maybe next Halloween he'll get a leather catsuit, especially based on Theo's wide eyes and bright pink cheeks as he continues to stare at the picture.

"It's, um…yeah. Nice, good work - really, yup." Theo looks at the way they're posed, the two of them perched on top of a building with the Bat Signal in the dark sky.

Theo's in the signature Batman suit, cape billowing in the wind, while Emir is crouched beside him. If Emir wasn't so talented at drawing faces, he might be able to imagine it's just a special version of the comic. But instead, his mind is filled with images of Emir in the depicted outfit, with the possibility of Emir stretching and bending and playing with a whip, and that is not a line of thinking he plans to follow in front of his parents.

Emir thought Theo might like the idea, but he didn't expect him to be so obviously flustered just at the concept of Emir in the outfit. Then again, he remembers Theo's reaction to his Halloween costume, so maybe he shouldn't be surprised. "You want to look at the last one, then?"

Theo nods, covering the second drawing as Emir had done with the first and setting it aside. The third picture is so different from the first two that Theo bursts out laughing, immediately throwing his arms around Emir, but careful to keep the picture out of harm's way.

"What is it?" George asks, trying to peer around to see the drawing still held in Theo's hand.

"I drew Theo as the Sam Neill character from Jurassic Park, with the hat and the red bandana." Emir grins, wrapping his arms around Theo for a few moments until he pulls away again and holds the picture in his lap to really look at it.

"And there's a triceratops! And we're sharing a salad! Because we're both vegetarians, I'm guessing." Theo laughs again, Caroline joining in this time. It's a bit absurd, Theo in the denim shirt and khakis, holding a fork while the triceratops sticks its entire tongue into the salad bowl. It's so Emir: silly and perfect and focused on some of Theo's favourite things.

"So *that's* why you needed to know his favourite dinosaur." Caroline knew something was in the works, but she hadn't known exactly what Emir was planning until now. She gets a glimpse of the drawing and keeps laughing along. It reminds her so much of a grown version of that picture of Theo as a kid that she and Emir had briefly discussed that night they were first introduced.

"I need frames. Three of them. And I'll need to colour coordinate with the pictures so like grey for the portrait and maybe red for this one." Theo's brow is furrowed again, very seriously considering how to protect his new additions to his Emir art collection. The spare sheets of paper can only do so much, and he wants them on display in his room. One day he'll have an entire art gallery. "Do we have any, Mum?"

"Not likely, but we could try the craft store in town." Caroline watches as Theo falls back against Emir, like he's melting into him. She's never known Theo to be so easy around another person. Watching them for the past day, she can see how comfortable Theo feels in Emir's presence, how safe and happy he is. "After your visit up North?"

Theo lays his head back on Emir's shoulder, sighing as his hand finds Theo's waist and holds him close. "Suppose it can wait. Dad, you want to come to the shops with us?"

"As long as I'm not at work, I'd be glad to." George shares a glance with Caroline, the same thoughts she's had while hosting Emir in their home reflected back in his eyes.

George has had a beautiful life with Caroline and his three kids. Letting both of his daughters go off to grow and have their own families was hard enough. But Theo's his youngest, his only son, and he didn't think he'd be able to accept the same for Theo without a bit of heartbreak. There's a lingering need to protect Theo in a way he never quite could as he grew up. But Emir is everything George could want for his youngest, especially with the way they both value their family time and relationships.

"Thank you for my presents. You didn't have to, you know." Theo turns his head to look at Emir, getting distracted as always by those gorgeous eyes. They hold so much and showcase his light.

"I know." Emir presses a kiss to Theo's temple and gives him a squeeze. "But it's not just my traditions that need to be shared, princess. I'm here to learn yours, too."

"Theo said he's been invited to your family's celebration for Eid this year?" Caroline asks, taking her husband's hand and gaining that familiar comfort from his thumb brushing across the top, as careful as always. Only as her family grew did she truly appreciate what a gift her gentle husband is, how different to so many of the women in her life with their indifferent, detached, sometimes toxic partners. She sees a lot of George in Theo, the same kindness, the same warmth. It makes her prouder than she could put into words.

"He is, yeah." Emir holds Theo's head against his shoulder with a delicate grasp to let him know he's not asking him to move away, just refocusing his attention so they can share their conversation outside of their bubble. "My parents are really excited to have him."

"Promise to take plenty of pictures for us? It's always in hindsight we wish we had more to remember all the wonderful moments, you know?" Caroline leans her head against George, similar to how Theo leans into Emir.

"Definitely." Emir gives her a genuine smile, Theo sighing again and relaxing against his chest. Usually, when Theo reaches this point, Emir knows he's done talking for a minute and just wants to sit and observe in his happy quiet. It's not that he wants to leave or anything, just let others do the socialising.

It's another part of knowing Theo, recognising his different needs and preferences. And while Theo's learned most of Emir's little quirks and signals, like how he knew to give Emir a half an hour alone in his bedroom this morning so he wouldn't get overwhelmed or anxious, Emir's been doing the same.

There's been a shift ever since that first week of December. They've both been much more intentional about recognising and respecting what they need and setting healthy boundaries around their time and energy. It's a shared path towards long term success and a large part of the reason they're so comfortable around each other. There's a trust that's been earned that weaves them together.

"You two up for a walk? Bruce needs his exercise soon or I'm worried he'll climb the walls." Caroline gives Bruce a head scratch as she asks, his ears having popped up the moment he heard the word *walk*.

"Give us a few minutes to get changed?" Theo asks, thinking for a moment about how this time yesterday was so similar, except without Emir. Adding Emir is wholly positive, and even though it was lovely before, today will be even better.

"Maybe watch a movie when we get back?" Emir mumbles to Theo even as they stand to head upstairs and get ready. He's looking forward to some time outside, needing to move his body before he gets restless.

"Can we watch a Christmas movie? There's so many you haven't seen." Theo's eyes light up again at the thought, wanting Emir to join that part of his traditions too. It wouldn't be the holidays without his favourite movies to set the ambience.

"Only if we have a warm drink and as many blankets as will fit on the sofa." Emir glances around to make sure Theo's parents have left the room before tugging Theo forward for a kiss.

Theo smiles against Emir's lips then holds him by the hips to kiss him again, more, longer, not wanting to stop. But Emir giggles, gently taking Theo's hands and leading him upstairs instead. They can fit a few minutes of snogging into their preparations for their next activity, but he'd rather they do so in the privacy of Theo's room.

***

Theo posts his first true couple photo to his Instagram just after their walk. It doesn't show either of their faces, just their gloved hands intertwined between their bodies on the walk while Emir holds Bruce's lead. It's almost nothing, just nondescript hands and the blurry image of his dog with the pavement beneath their feet, but it means everything to Theo.

He asks Emir's permission before posting, of course, and he doesn't tag his secret account. But he captions the picture: *I've had the best Christmas with Emir by my side. I hope everyone is enjoying the love and light of the season /sparkle emoji/ Emir once told me that autumn would always hold part of our story, and now I know that December will, too.*

Emir gets the notification while laying with his feet in Theo's lap on the sofa. He keeps himself from sniffling, but only just. Since they aren't alone in the room, Emir texts Theo instead of burying him in physical affection, a string of kiss emojis and x's that Theo reads with a pink flush. He darts his eyes over to Emir and responds with an entire story told through emojis, including the gay couple emoji, the heart eyes emoji, a crown emoji, and a few that Emir will have to ask him about later because they seem random, but he's positive they've been chosen for a reason.

Theo doesn't do anything without intention, including his social media posts. Emir feels warm all over, and it's not from the mound of blankets. It's an internal heat, a love that smoulders rather than burns, one that has him changing his position on the sofa to be in Theo's space. Emir gives Theo's crown one soft kiss then settles back in to finish watching the film.

***

"Isn't it stunning?" Theo asks from his spot on Emir's chest, the two of them well and truly moulded into the sofa just as *White Christmas* plays its final scene, the doors of the Inn opening wide to welcome the snow.

"That was cute. I'll give you that." Emir grins, sitting up to make them all a round of tea before they watch another. He could use a few minutes to stretch. "The dance scenes were great, like a historical archive in the middle of a holiday movie."

"That's why I love it!" Theo agrees with excitement, smiling at his mum as she walks past him to use the loo, George also scooting away to the kitchen for a snack. They've all agreed on a quiet afternoon at home before making dinner together in a few hours, which meant holiday movies and relaxing in the living room for now.

Surprisingly, the doorbell rings just as Theo's pausing the telly to search for their next film. They all look around in confusion as if one of the others would know who it is.

"Is Mrs. Alderman coming over today?" Theo asks his mum, but she just shakes her head no before heading up the stairs. George shrugs and keeps moving towards the kitchen, so Theo walks to open the door to see who it is.

Since Emir's already here and his sisters were just over yesterday, he's really not sure this time. Emir follows behind him, stretching out his back as he walks and staying out of the way since this isn't his home.

But it isn't Mrs. Alderman on the other side of the door. It isn't a neighbour at all.

"Jordan?" Theo stares at her in disbelief.

Emir comes up closer behind Theo, setting a hand on the small of his back and tilting his head at their friend unexpectedly waiting on the step.

"You alright?" Emir asks, but he realises the answer is definitely no before he finishes the question. He's never seen her look less like herself. What is she doing here?

"Oh, um...not really." Jordan answers quietly. Theo's fairly sure she's holding back tears. Her eyes are puffy and red and she's clearly distraught, sniffling and trying to hide it.

"Come on in, Jo. It's freezing." Theo steps back, Emir moving with him as Jordan scoots just inside the door like she's worried she's intruding. "Haven't heard much from you or Lili today. I figured you both were busy."

"Actually, I was hoping I could spend a few hours here, if it's not too much of a bother. Lili's on her way to pick me up, but it's a long drive from Wakefield." Jordan shivers and holds her arms tight around her middle.

She has a coat wrapped around herself, but underneath, it looks like she's dressed for some sort of holiday gathering: a red silk dress and skin tone tights with a high heel to match the colour of the dress. She looks every bit the heiress that her upbringing demands. It's certainly not something Jo would choose for herself, her usual fashion much more femme-sporty chic.

"Of course. You can stay for as long as you like." Theo answers just as he hears his mum come back down the stairs behind him, turning to watch her walking towards them with a warm smile. He can always count on his parents to welcome any surprise guests who appear.

"Jordan! What a nice surprise." Caroline sets a hand on Jordan's shoulder before letting it drop, Jordan giving her a weak smile in return. "We were just getting ready to watch another movie. Are you joining us?"

"I don't want to be in the way." Jordan wipes at her eyes, smearing her makeup a bit in the process, as if she's forgotten she's wearing any.

"Nonsense. Theo's friends are always welcome here." Caroline squeezes Theo's bicep in passing before leaving them alone, the three of them still just inside the front door.

"Here, let me get your coat." Theo offers, helping her shrug out of it and confirming that she's dressed very posh, probably designer. It's something she'd wear for a family event at the estate, and not something one wears to casually visit a friend. They never really see this side of her, and the visual is a bit jarring when compared to the Jordan they know and love. It's like a costume, or maybe a uniform.

"I'll, um, be staying with Lili at the N'dri's house for the rest of the break, but it was a bit last minute and your house wasn't far from...from where I was in Birmingham. Lili sent me your address since nothing's open and...there wasn't anywhere to go." Jordan kicks off her heels (Louboutins) near the door and follows after Emir and Theo into the living room, looking like she's on autopilot.

They take back their corner of the sofa, Jo settling herself on the ottoman. She looks ready to bolt, eyes wide and unblinking while staring at nothing. Jordan hasn't actually looked at either of them since she arrived.

"Do you want something to change into?" Theo offers, Emir's hand on his knee as they both wonder how to help their friend. They don't even know what's wrong, but Jo wouldn't just show up out of nowhere without warning if this wasn't some sort of emergency. "I've got clean joggers and some shirts, if nothing else."

"Maybe in a bit. I just...need a minute." Jordan starts taking her hair out of a complicated updo, pins and glittering accessories set carefully to the side until her long blonde hair is flowing past her shoulders. She's starting to look marginally more like her usual self, minus her energy, like she's removing whatever armour got her safely here.

"You want to pick the next movie, Jordan?" George asks as he comes into the room. He and Caroline have met Jordan a few times since she and Lilibet have always been so close, and Lili is essentially an adopted family member to them.

"No, that's alright. You all carry on as you were. I'm sorry to interrupt your family time." Jordan apologises again. Theo really wishes she would stop doing that since her being here would be a lovely surprise if the circumstances weren't so mysteriously negative.

They stew in silence for several moments, none of them quite knowing what to do.

"Jo." Emir finally speaks up, shifting to crouch beside her and setting a gentle hand on her knee. She doesn't look at him but her shoulders shake with withheld tears at the careful gesture. "What's happened?"

Jordan doesn't answer right away, rubbing at her eyes again and tucking her hair behind her ears. Clearing her throat, she admits, "I've been kicked out of the family. Disowned, I suppose. I didn't catch everything that was said, but...well, they dropped me at the edge of the property with my coat and my phone then locked the gate behind me, so the message has been received, even if I missed the details."

"They what?" Theo asks in disbelief, letting Emir stay near Jordan while he keeps himself on the sofa. He doesn't want to crowd her and Emir has it handled for the moment. Theo knew Jordan's family was bad, but he didn't know it could come to this.

"They know...*everything*. They know I'm a lesbian. That I'm living with my girlfriend. That I...that I love Lili." Jordan's voice breaks, the cool detached tone finally shattering as she starts crying, falling forward onto Emir's shoulder and clutching at his back. "I love her so much."

Emir holds her close, rubbing a soothing hand along her bare skin where her outfit leaves her exposed. Her dress is most definitely not suited to being abandoned on the side of the road, even in the middle of the day. Not that any attire would make the situation better, but Theo was right to offer something more comfortable now that she's here.

"How dare they." Caroline's voice gets Theo's attention. She's just walked back in to check on them, joining George at the edge of the room and catching the cause of the breakdown. Theo's never seen his mum look quite so furious. "How absolutely *vile*."

"I always knew. I didn't tell them *because* I knew. I've been waiting for something like this to happen, I just - " Jordan keeps crying on Emir's shoulder as Theo offers her a Kleenex. She takes it and starts wiping at her face, smearing her makeup even further. "How could they?"

"Come on." Emir stands up, taking Jordan with him and moving them over towards the sofa, placing Jo between himself and Theo. She goes easily, leaning onto Theo and letting Emir continue to soothe her, hiding herself in the middle of their comfort huddle. "Do you mind if we call Lili? Let her know you're here, see where she is..."

Jordan shakes her head no, that she doesn't mind, Theo already pulling out his phone to do exactly that. It'd be best to find out how soon she can be here. He's sure she'll be in her own state, with her girlfriend having been turned out by her family the day after Christmas when she's hours away and definitely panicking, a thousand other emotions all overlapping.

"I'll just pop upstairs and see what I can find for you. See what we have to tide you over until tomorrow. Don't you worry, love." Caroline walks over to the three of them, setting a protective hand on Jordan's head and stroking it softly in a way that only a loving guardian ever learns. "We've got you. You're safe here."

"I'll call Yuusuf, and make sure we have you taken care of. Here or at the N'dri's house, you'll be alright." George takes over when Caroline walks away and hurries up the stairs again. He sets his hand in the same spot, Jordan still huddled into Theo while Emir fusses over her, offering Kleenex and what's left of his glass of water from before. "And Jordan?"

"Hm?" Jordan blinks through her tears, unable to stop now that she's started. She's still in a state of shock, but she's safe here. She can fall apart knowing she'll be looked after.

"I'm glad you came here." George reassures her, stroking her hair like he would to comfort his own child. "You stay as long as you need."

She nods, letting herself sob through her pain and shock until there's nothing left. Numb and overwhelmed, she cries herself to sleep on Theo's shoulder.

***

Lili must have driven quite recklessly to get to Theo's house because she shows up only an hour and a half after Jordan. She rushes in the front door and straight past Theo to where Jordan's napping on the sofa, makeup smudged and covered in two oversized blankets, thanks to Emir. Lili immediately takes over as her pillow, laying Jordan's head on her thigh and mumbling reminders of love and calm to Jo even as she sleeps.

At the time of Lilibet's arrival, Caroline and George are at the kitchen table, busy figuring out the logistics of meeting Jordan's immediate needs. They've been on the phone with Lili's parents, even as she drove herself across the country. Yuusuf and Ola are scrambling to do everything they can, from switching the beds around in the house so Lili's room has a double, to Googling to find out what stores might be open to buy her some clothes and be ready for when Lili drives them both north tomorrow. Their preparations are hampered slightly by the fact that Lili had to borrow their car, but they have delivery options and a few shops within walking distance. Thankfully, with Jo's head still cradled in her lap, Lili lets them know that most of Jordan's possessions are still at uni, so she only needs a few things to tide her over until they return to their shared flat in the new year. Assuming that's still the plan.

Jordan sleeps soundly, clearly overwhelmed and exhausted after the day she's had, and likely, the few that preceded it. They all keep their voices low, shuffling around each other and discussing next steps in hushed tones, deciding what they can without Jordan's input and, in Theo's case, making many, detailed, incredibly helpful lists.

What finally wakes Jordan is her phone. She must have the ringer on for some reason, because she jolts awake the moment the tone sounds, rubbing the sleep from her eyes and hugging Lili while staring at the caller ID and trying to wake herself up enough to answer.

"It's my brother." Jordan lets it ring twice while holding on to her girlfriend. "He was running late this morning, so I haven't seen him since yesterday."

"Do you want to talk to him?" Lili asks, brushing Jordan's hair out of her face and focusing on the immediate concern rather than everything else that spirals around them. Theo and Emir watch from their spot on the floor, Theo chewing on the inside of his cheek and Emir fidgeting nervously with the sleeve of his jumper.

Jordan nods, swiping to accept the call and holding the phone up to her ear.

"Cyril?" Her voice is strained from the sleep and the crying, but she clears her throat and sets her shoulders.

The others in the room can't hear the other half of the conversation, but Jordan's portion is mostly unfinished sentences and single word answers. She stays on the call for almost five minutes, starting to pace around the room the longer they talk, the other three watching her and waiting for whatever news there is to share once she's done.

"Thanks, Cy...love you, too...Lili's here, don't worry...I'll send you her parents' address...yeah, call me whenever...I'll be alright...Bye." Jordan hangs up with a sigh and tosses her phone onto the sofa before following it, falling face first into the cushion and letting out a muffled shout.

"Jo?" Lili places a tentative hand on Jordan's shoulder. She's met Cyril before and he seemed alright, but Jordan and her brother have never really been close. Familial affection wasn't exactly encouraged when they were growing up.

Jordan muffles one more scream into the sofa cushion before sitting up again, more uncomfortable in her outfit by the moment, both physically and figuratively. It's just not *her*. "Theo? Did you say you had something I could change into?"

"Yes!" Theo jumps up from the floor, ready to offer Jordan whatever he can. "Mum thought you might fancy a shower, so there's a fresh towel and some basics in the bathroom upstairs, and I've left some old joggers and a jumper that doesn't fit anymore for you to change into. They're yours to keep. And, um, if you're hungry we were going to make something or maybe order takeaway, and Emir is all over the tea situation so we'll have a cuppa ready when you're done getting comfortable, or like, as close as you can, and if there's anything we forgot, Lili can go upstairs with you and shout at me and I'll find whatever it is as quick as I can. Also we have extra phone chargers, which isn't much, but we noticed your phone had low battery and since it's, um…still in service, we thought you may need one. That's also waiting for you upstairs with the clothes."

Theo finishes his impassioned speech with his hands twisting around themselves nervously, waiting for anything else he can do to help.

Jordan stares at him for a moment then grabs Lili's hand and pulls her to her feet. Walking up to Theo, she kisses him sweetly on the cheek then steps away in the direction of the stairs. She looks determined, very different from the disconnected person that arrived at his home just a few hours ago. "I'm on my brother's mobile plan, so that's safe for now, otherwise I'm sure they would've kept my phone when they took everything else, including all my bank cards, so."

"Anything that we can do while you're in the shower?" Emir asks, still on the floor for the moment. It can't hurt to ask, even if Jordan probably isn't sure of what she needs.

"Just let me melt under the water for a bit. I'm sure I'll need food and all the rest, but right now I just feel tired and sore." Jordan pulls at the fabric of her dress with a wrinkled nose. "Thank god I was able to get an Uber from my parents' or I'd probably still be walking. Or worse."

"Come on. Shower." Lili pulls on the hand that Jordan connected them by, heading over towards the stairs to the waiting comfort that Theo detailed. She wants a minute alone to really check in on Jo without anyone else around.

"I'll fill you in when I'm done." Jordan calls down the stairs before disappearing, Lili's hand still interlocked with her own. The phone call with Cyril answered a few questions and gave her a place to start, if nothing else.

"Well, she seems…" Theo turns to Emir, unsure what to do while they wait. His parents essentially have her covered with everything practical.

"Stable." Emir answers for him. He has a fairly good idea how Jordan is feeling right now, and how much that short nap really helped. Emir hasn't been tossed out by his family, but his trauma with his ex was similar in many ways. The shock, the panic, the abandonment, the betrayal.

"Did we think of everything?" Theo sits beside Emir again, taking his hand automatically. They find so much comfort together, just sharing space and providing calm that the other can fall into.

"Everything immediate, yeah. But she'll need to lean on us for a while. Years, maybe." Emir lets his free hand find Theo's face, brushing his thumb over his cheekbone while his fingers curl into the side of his hair. "It'll be up and down. She seemed alright just now, but later, she'll probably break again. Tomorrow, who knows. It's a lot to process and it won't be linear."

"How could anyone do that to their kid? I just don't understand." Theo's eyebrows crease together, his lips thinning as he grows frustrated now that he has a moment to think. They didn't just have a row or say homophobic things (though it sounds like that was included). Jordan's parents took away everything in the blink of an eye, leaving her abandoned, literally, on the side of the road in the middle of nowhere. He shudders thinking about what could have happened to her.

"We can try to understand people's rationale for being cruel, but it won't ever make sense. I learned that the hard way…" Emir keeps caressing Theo's face with his hand, understanding Theo's mood because he's completely right. No parent should ever do what Jordan's parents just did to her. No one should have to go through that, especially when Jo's done nothing wrong. "Sounds like her brother might be decent, which is a lot more than nothing."

"I hope so." Theo leans into Emir's hand, using both of his own to stroke over the one of Emir's that he's claimed in his lap. He feels the bumps and ridges and lines, follows their patterns, lets his eyes lose focus while he tries to put together useful thoughts about the situation.

All he can come up with is thank god she came here, thank the universe she's physically safe, thank his parents for not hesitating for even a moment to take her in. And thank everything that Emir is here, too.

"Let's go fill your parents in, alright? We should let them know Jordan's awake and that we need to figure out food soon." Emir leans in for a quiet kiss before pulling them both up from the ground to walk in the direction of the kitchen. "I was thinking we could make a bit of a blanket fort in the living room and see if Jo wants to watch something with us after we eat? Might be nice for her to have a distraction, maybe a movie she doesn't really need to pay attention to."

"I'm so glad you're my boyfriend." Theo gives Emir another kiss, holding him close and sighing against his solid warmth. Having him here, knowing that they can lean on each other while supporting Jordan and Lili, is making a world of difference. "And I'm sorry if this is bringing up bad memories."

"It is." Emir admits, holding Theo back in an upright cuddle, both of their faces tucked close against the other so their words are muffled. He needs Theo in this situation even more than Theo needs him. He wouldn't want to be alone with his thoughts right now, given the similarities to his own trauma. "But I'm alright. I've got you and my family, and I have Amanda to talk to when we get back to uni. If it gets bad, I'll let you know."

Theo gives Emir a tighter squeeze before releasing him and leading the way out of the room. At the moment, all he can think about is how incredibly lucky he feels to have the parents he does, who welcome his boyfriend and his friends like family, who offer their support and their home without hesitation, who never once made him feel anything less than unconditionally loved his entire life.

As he walks into the kitchen with Emir by his side, Theo pulls both of his parents into a very tight hug. He hopes that someday he'll be able to tell them properly how grateful he is.

***

"So..." Jordan takes a long drag from her mug with her eyes closed, both hands clutching it for warmth. She's wearing the clothes Theo's laid out for her, sleeves and waistband folded several times. Jo hasn't felt this physically comfortable in days.

"You want to tell us?" Theo asks from a few feet away, Emir running his hands through Theo's hair for both of their comfort. The four of them are alone in the living room, Caroline and George giving them space while they take Bruce for another walk.

"You don't have to if it's too much." Lilibet presses a kiss to the top of Jordan's shoulder, koala-ing to her back on the sofa very tightly. She doesn't want to let Jordan out of her grasp for even a moment.

"I'm alright, or at least, I think I'm done crying for the moment." Jo sighs, her legs crossed in front of her where she and Lili face Theo and Emir at the other end of the sofa. It's a tight fit, but they make room. Emir said there could be a blanket fort later, but for now, just after her shower, this works fine. "I haven't told you much about my family, so what happened might seem out of the ordinary to you, but I've always sort of known this would happen...doesn't make it any easier, but I knew how they felt. What they thought."

The four of them sit quietly, sipping at their tea while Jordan finds the path of the story of today. Sometimes, when the roots of pain go this deep, it's hard to find the starting point. "Every year, the extended family gets together on Boxing Day for a sort of unofficial, yet very official family meeting. They talk about land management, connections, investments, that sort of thing. Apparently they consider it crass to discuss those matters on the actual holiday, so..."

"When you say the extended family, you mean...?" Emir asks, wondering exactly how many people allowed Jordan to be thrown out on the street and abandoned by her family without any sort of intervention.

"Cousins, distant uncles, anyone who hasn't been disowned yet, essentially. There's dozens of us. And since my dad is in charge now...well, he has been for a while, which is why we have the house." Jordan frowns down at her tea, thinking about the Harper family estate in Birmingham that she's hated for as long as she can remember. "Anyway, that's why the outfit and all that. Christmas was actually fine. We had our usual 'party' on Christmas Eve then *family time* yesterday. It was exhausting, but it was fine. My brother never stays at the estate anymore, always pretending he has work to deal with, so he only stopped by for a bit each day."

"Just the one brother?" Theo asks to clarify, since Lili's the only one of them with any sort of picture of Jo's family besides what they've learned this afternoon. Jordan doesn't talk about her family when they're at Roseborough.

"Cyril. He's older. Almost a whole decade, and we've never been close. But he's always been nice to me." Jordan shrugs again, leaning back further into Lili and setting her tea aside on the coffee table. "Cyril hates the family as much as I do, but it's not really up to him because he has certain *expectations* as my parent's only son or whatever. He lives in Madrid now, so he only shows up for Christmas when he's required to. He says he won't bother next year with…everything that's happened, but we'll see."

"…And today?" Lili asks, arms still tight around Jordan's middle. She's very protective of those she loves, and panicking from a distance while Jordan was treated so terribly were some of the most frustrating hours of her life.

"It started as it always does. Condescending comments about me needing to start *dating*. Families they approve of, a handful of acceptable men that I could spend time with. People think that's all in the past, like arranged marriages and the old money families setting their offspring up for unhappy, failed partnerships isn't still happening. But my cousin married a Walton last year, and another is engaged to some petroleum company heir, so like…it's not just that it happens, but that it's the norm. The fact I chose Roseborough rather than Oxford like the family tradition, and that I'm not using uni as an excuse to find some rich, white husband, is already a shock to their system."

Jordan twists the ends of her hair around her finger while she talks, not used to sharing this part of her life with her uni friends. But they're not just friends. Not anymore. They're the only safe people in her life.

"I know you know this already, but that's ridiculous." Emir uses his toes to nudge at Jordan's. He has Theo in his lap, so he can't manage anything else. "That must be a heavy burden for you to carry. Especially as a gay woman."

"I sort of…snapped." Jordan admits, glancing up at Emir, then Theo before looking at Lili's arms around her middle and setting her own atop for comfort. "It was just too much. I tried to be polite and tell them no, and I even asked them to let me graduate before any decisions needed to be made, but I'm the oldest of the girl cousins that isn't either married, divorced with a healthy financial severance, or anticipating an engagement. They said I don't have a future, that I'm wasting time and ignoring reality. Apparently, I only have a few years before I'll be considered *past my prime* and if I'm not married by then, I'm useless to the family. Those actual words were used, and...others."

"But how...?" Theo doesn't finish the sentence, letting the question drift through the space between them. He has an idea of the situation Jordan's describing, but he still doesn't see how she ended up kicked out and on the side of the road.

"Everyone was still together at this point, because for some reason, each family member's life needs to be examined and judged by the entire family or some shit. I don't pretend to understand it. The annual Boxing Day meeting is where they decide divorces and business mergers and estate planning. It's awkward and I've no idea why the kids are always involved besides wanting to scare them into acceptance." Jordan scoffs and the others all make suitably disgusted expressions.

"But my uncle made a *joke* about me being a lesbian...and then my mum said it didn't matter if I was going to end up in hell so long as I married the right man and gave her a grandson before I...she said...it was horrible, but I can't stop hearing it. She even laughed after - but she said that if I choose *that life* I should have the decency to kill myself and spare them the shame of anyone finding out." Jordan clears her throat again, picking up her tea and wondering how much longer she can talk before her attempt to do this without crying fails.

The others are sitting in shocked silence, staring at her in horror. Jordan knows the feeling.

"I think it was her calm suggestion that I should kill myself once I was done procreating that finally did it. I didn't want to be in that room or in that family, letting them be horrible to me and to each other, and I was done putting myself through it. I always knew they would try to force me into a marriage and into their lifestyle, but I'd never heard my mum so blatantly say that she would want me to...that I should...who says that to their own child?"

Jordan starts crying again, Theo carefully taking the tea from her hands as Lili turns her around and holds Jo on her chest. Theo grabs the Kleenex and moves them within Lilibet's reach before falling back into Emir.

Emir's quiet, holding onto Theo and letting Lili comfort Jo, wishing that any part of Jordan's story wasn't real because the kind of cruelty and emotional abuse she's endured is so much more than what happened today. They still don't have the entire story, but they've heard enough to know that she's never felt safe a day in her life with a family like that.

"That was just...I didn't care anymore. I don't even remember everything I said." Jordan turns herself around, determined to keep going, facing forward instead of across the sofa like she had been before. She reaches for the Kleenex and blows her nose, taking another long drink from her mug and letting it steady her for a moment. "I just started telling them everything that I've been hiding all at once. That I'm a lesbian. That I already have a girlfriend and we live together. That I'm never going to marry some awful man for his money just to make them happy. And...no one even cared. I always pictured it being dramatic, but it was almost laughably calm."

They wait a moment to see if she's done talking, but she keeps drinking her tea and wiping at her eyes to try to steady herself, so Lili settles on one side with Emir and Theo still cuddled together at the other end of the sofa, patiently giving her time to talk.

"They genuinely didn't care. My dad scoffed and told me it wasn't up to me. I told him he couldn't make me, that I wouldn't break up with Lili or meet with anyone whose name they were tossing around...and that's when he went still, like he finally accepted I was serious. He told me if I was choosing to live *that life* and turning my back on my family, then I'd already made my choice and I should leave. He said it was a family meeting and I was no longer included or welcome in the house."

Emir shuffles out from behind Theo, setting his left hand on top of Jordan's right while pulling Theo into his side with the other. Jo turns her face into his shoulder for a moment and gives his hand a squeeze, her breathing unsteady and laboured as she continues to cry through her words.

"But it wasn't actually an invitation to leave, it was an order. My entire family watched as he walked me to the front door, verifying that everything he'd paid for was safely upstairs in my bedroom...not mine anymore, of course. He said all sorts of things while we walked, but I honestly don't remember most of it. And then he had his personal security literally drive me to the gate and leave me on the other side without another word. My mother didn't even watch as I walked away. I checked, hoping she would say...anything. I was so numb. I think I was in shock. I didn't even yell or raise my voice, I just...let myself be kicked out. And then after, I stood outside in the mud for a while until I realised what happened and texted Lili. She gave me your address and...here I am."

"Here you are." Theo repeats, reaching around Emir to lay his warm hand on her shoulder. "And you're welcome here without needing to ask."

"Thanks, Teddy." Jordan sniffles, giving him an appreciative smile before blowing her nose again. She's always been stubborn, but right now it may serve her well. She's suddenly destitute and without family or any means to make her way in the world, but she has her brother and Lili's family and apparently Theo's too. It could be so much worse.

"...And your brother? When he called?" Lilibet asks, brushing a hand through Jo's hair and hoping that Cyril is at least worth the time he was granted when Jo picked up that phone.

"He's very practical, Cyril. He had a proper row with my dad when he got to the estate and found out why I wasn't there. He even cursed out Mum then stormed out of there, but only after getting a few things answered." Jordan stands up and starts pacing again, a newer habit for her, but it helps to feel like she's moving. "And thank god he did because I hadn't thought of any of it."

"You were in shock, Jo. You still are." Emir sits back on the sofa but watches her with understanding. His need to constantly be moving and running and dancing definitely intensified after what his ex put him through.

"Uni's paid for. Apparently Dad's upset about that, but there's nothing he can do, not that he won't try. The flat is monthly, but Cyril's covering my half until we move. I tried to refuse but he insisted, says he won't let me worry about that on top of everything else. I'm already on his mobile plan, like I mentioned, because my parents have no concept of privacy, so there's that as well." Jordan's talking to Lili now, since it is technically both of their flat, and they have plans to live together past uni. "We graduate in a few months and who knows what then. Cy said he'd keep helping me out as long as I need, but I can't ask him to do that. It's only a matter of time before my parents find out and it becomes an issue. Cyril has the money, more than he knows what to do with, but I need to do what I can for myself."

"That's a huge help, what he's offering. It gives you a few months to figure out what your plan is." Emir is the one who answers again. Of the four of them, he's the one who grew up in a working class family in council housing, and he's very aware of financial stress. It's something Jo's never had to worry about, Lili only sporadically, and Theo hardly at all.

"I'll have to find work. I'll need clothes and food and pointe shoes and all the rest. I try to keep expenses low because I don't need much outside of dance, but still. I was thinking about it in the shower, like what I could do with no work history and no skills. Maybe the library at uni for now? They hire students and they know me from book club, which isn't nothing. But I can't be picky, of course." Jordan starts putting her hair up with an extra satin scrunchie that Lili had with her. The longer she's at Theo's house with her friends, the more like herself she seems, like she's reassembling piece by piece. "I've known this was coming for a while. At least since the row about getting the flat with Lili last year, so I have some ideas but nothing solid. I was...I'm still surprised. But if Cy can help for a few months, I think I'll manage."

"Where is Cyril?" Lili asks, still on the sofa with her legs tucked under her. "You said he left your parent's place."

"On his way back to Madrid." Jordan looks at her phone for a moment to confirm the time. "He has a late flight out of Heathrow, around midnight. He was supposed to leave tomorrow, but he moved it up. He wants to get back to Elena."

When they all give Jordan confused looks, she clarifies, "His girlfriend that my parents don't know about, or at least pretend not to. They've been together for five years. He wants to marry her, have a few kids, but she doesn't meet their guidelines so..."

"Right." Theo acknowledges before they all fall back into silence, Jordan starting to pace again like it's the only thing she remembers how to do. No wonder she's always loved dance. It keeps her moving.

"If you're open to chatting with Sean, there's a fund to help dance students get shoes and tights and all that. He's been making sure I have access since our first year." Emir's never mentioned it before to this group, only Laurie. But Emir didn't come from a household where these things were a given, and dance isn't cheap. "It would only be through June, but it gives you some time to worry about everything else. And there's programmes to help with food and toiletries and all that. It's in the same building I go to for therapy, if you need a buddy."

"I didn't know about the dance fund." Theo turns to Emir, momentarily distracted as he snags Emir's hand in his own and brings it to his mouth for a kiss. He knows Emir's financial situation generally, but not the specifics. It's something they definitely need to discuss soon before they get a flat together.

Emir shrugs. He's not embarrassed, but now is not the time for them to have this particular conversation. "Later."

Theo nods, keeping Emir's hand and turning back to Jordan, looking between her and Lilibet as they have several drawn out moments of silent communication. They stare at each other with head tilts and sighs until Lili stands up from the sofa to walk up to Jordan, who stops pacing to meet her.

"It's done, Jo. You came out. Your parents are abusive and cruel, but it's *done*." Lili takes both of Jordan's hands in her own and waits for her to nod. It's clear this is a conversation they've had many times. "They can't control you anymore."

Jordan nods again, a portion of the tension in her shoulders falling away at Lilibet's words. "I'm on my own. I can do...anything I want. Cut my hair or dye it or get a tattoo or go out to gay bars and not care who might see me."

"I'll help!" Theo answers immediately, ready to support her in whatever her next chapter looks like. Maybe he and Laurie can take her out to a few of the gay pubs near Roseborough. The others would be invited, of course, but it's sort of their thing together, just him and Laurie when they get the urge. "Remember a few months ago I said you could be my sister? I'm ready to be brother Theo. I know you have Cyril, but..."

"Brother Theo? You joining one of them monk houses out in the country?" Emir teases, the four of them cracking a smile for the first time in hours. It's nice to finally have a break in the tension. "I don't know that the haircut would suit you, baby."

"Monastery, and I think the hair may be optional nowadays." Theo pouts, and Emir decides he needs a tickle. His fingers find Theo's sides beneath his jumper and Theo squirms and laughs while Emir tortures him just on the safe side of annoyance.

Before they can realise that nothing's actually very funny, they're all laughing uncontrollably, Theo and Emir rolling around on the sofa with Lili and Jo watching them, Lili holding her stomach and Jo wiping away the last of her tears.

As Emir and Theo attempt to behave themselves, George, Caroline, and Bruce arrive through the front door, glad to see them all in brighter spirits than when they left. The mood had been very sombre and tense, but now the four of them are grinning at each other, sharing looks and small giggles when they catch each other's eyes just right. Emir flattens Theo's hair around his face to demonstrate the hairstyle and they all break out into laughter again, Theo trying to retaliate without success.

"We all ready to order something to eat?" Caroline asks, removing her coat then walking up to Jordan to offer a hug. Jo holds on for several seconds longer than usual, only stepping away when Bruce nudges his way into the middle of them, making Jordan smile and kneel down to give him attention. He's a welcome distraction.

"I'm not very hungry, but I should probably eat." Jordan lets George pull her into another hug, not quite as long as the one from Caroline, but it's very similar to how Theo hugs: warm and gentle, but grounding.

"There's this veggie curry place nearby that's good. We eat there whenever I'm home." Theo suggests, swatting Emir's hands away as they reach to tickle at his sides again.

"Oooo yes. If it's the same place we went last time I visited, then Jo definitely needs to try it." Lili flops onto the sofa, throwing her legs onto Theo's lap and reclining sideways.

"That's settled then." Caroline smiles watching George remove Bruce from his winter walk ensemble. It's chaotically adorable. "Theo, could you order on your laptop? Dad and I will have our usual. Use my card, of course."

"Thanks, Mum." Theo stands up to head towards the stairs, his laptop still up in his bedroom. But Jordan stops him on the way with a soft hand on his forearm.

"I accept." Jordan smiles up at him, hand dropping from his arm and back to her side. "If you're brother Theo, then I'm sister Jordan."

"You'd be an excellent nun, babe." Lili calls over, still laying where she flopped even though Theo's vacated his spot. Emir's back on the floor, of course, a perpetual floor troll. "Except for the chastity bit."

"Thank you?" Jordan laughs, letting Theo go up the stairs before finding her spot back on the sofa. She has to move Lili, but the fact that she gets an annoyed grumble when making Lilibet move is the closest thing to normalcy Jordan's had all day.

"Six samosas enough, you think?" Theo asks as he trots back down the stairs, laptop secure under his arm.

"Better make it eight." George answers from the kitchen. Before the food arrives, he and Caroline need to tidy away all their papers and mugs from earlier when they were in emergency mode.

Foregoing the sofa, Theo takes the bit of floor beside Emir and grins as bright as the sun when Emir kisses the corner of his mouth, resting his head on Theo's shoulder while he hyper-focuses on getting everyone's order entered correctly.

Jordan moves her face from the spot where it's been tucked into Lili's shoulder to give Theo her order, then goes back to cuddling her girlfriend and finding a semblance of calm.

It's a start.

***

"You think we should leave them?" Caroline whispers to George in that liminal space between the kitchen and the open area that contains both the dining and living rooms.

"Probably." George pulls Caroline close to stare at the huddle of young people asleep on the floor in front of the sofas. It's been a while since they've had a full house. "They're exhausted."

"And they have enough blankets? Theo said Emir needs extra." Caroline sets her head on her husband's shoulder, both with an arm around the other's waist.

"Emir looks happy." George can't help the smile that grows as they continue to watch over the others. They all look so peaceful when they're sleeping, the four of them curled into each other with ease.

For the last Christmas movie of the night, *The Muppet Christmas Carol*, they built a sort of blanket fort/nest hybrid on the floor and cuddled up together while Caroline and George took one of the sofas. And when the movie was done they stayed put, talking and planning the rest of their uni break until, one-by-one, they fell asleep. They're in a row, Emir on the far right, closest to the entryway, then Theo as his little spoon, then Lili flat on her back, and on the end nearest the fireplace, Jordan moulds herself to Lili's side, blonde hair fanned around her head like a halo.

"I'm proud of Theo." Caroline adds after a minute. The two of them can't quite leave to head upstairs yet, the panic and stress of the day still making them worriedly hover like the loving parents they are. "He's built this little family for himself. He's got Laurie and his flatmates, and these three. We always worried…"

"He's our special, brave boy." George kisses Caroline's temple and sighs. "Biggest heart of any kid we could've asked for, and a better one than we deserved."

"And Emir…seeing them together makes me so happy, George. Those awful people got in my head and I thought it may never happen for Theo. But he's happier than he's ever been." Caroline drops her arm from George's side to bury her face against his chest and let him fold her into a bear hug.

"I'm glad they found their way together. Emir loves him more than I dared hope." George is still facing the sleeping kids in the living room, watching over them even as he cradles Caroline. She's the best thing that's ever happened to him, and together they've built an incredible life with three independent, kind-hearted children. "I think they'll look after each other. I expect Emir at a lot of our holidays in the future."

"So do I." Caroline moves herself out of the hug to wander into the living room, finally ready to bid them goodnight.

As carefully as she can so she doesn't wake them, Caroline gives each of them a kiss transferred from her warm fingertips to their foreheads, lingering on Theo's a bit longer to brush a few strands of his curls away from his eyes. Her beautiful boy, grown up and in love and almost ready to leave uni for good. His first Christmas feels like yesterday, with so many memories throughout the years, love woven through every moment.

"Carebear…" George mumbles, Bruce waiting for them at the foot of the stairs. He's ready for bed, too.

With a sniffle and the back of her hand wiping at her eyes, Caroline stands up again and walks over to George, taking his hand and letting him lead her upstairs. As they go, George hums for her, a lullaby that they both used to sing for the kids that takes her right back. Today made them reflect and remember how precious their children are, how dearly they still hold them, how loved they will always be.

Someone once told Caroline that having a kid is like half of your heart walking around outside of your body. And that feels almost right, but it's also half of her breath, half of her blood, half of everything she is. She would die for her children, throw herself in harm's way to keep them safe. It's hard for her to imagine one of her kids in Jordan's place. She's always wanted their happiness like it was her own. And Jordan is so lovely. She's smart and determined and, despite her upbringing, incredibly kind. What sort of parent turns their back on such a child? What sort of person decides their prejudice is more important than their child's physical and emotional well being?

George settles into bed, waiting for Caroline to turn off the light and join him. He thinks along the same lines, worrying about his own kids, hoping that if they found themselves alone and lost, or abandoned for some awful reason, that they would have a safe place to go, that they'd find loving people who would put their lives on hold, if only momentarily, to make sure they made it to the next day. For him, there was never an alternative.

Jordan is one of theirs now, invited to holidays and birthday parties and on the receiving end of Sunday phone calls just like their other kids. George won't let her disappear. He and Caroline will step in, along with Lili's parents, and usher Jordan into a safe, loving family that celebrates her. She won't be alone.

"Night, love." Caroline yawns as she snuggles into George's space, kissing his bare bicep and letting her arm fall across his torso.

"Love you." George pulls her close, arms around her back and face pressed into her hair.

CHAPTER TEN

After receiving three rounds of embraces from Lili's parents and brothers, and with leftovers shoved in their hands, Theo and Emir are finally heading back to Theo's car to drive from Lili's parents' house in Wakefield to Emir's in Shipley. They'd stopped in for lunch after escorting their friends safely up North, but lunch turned into tea, and now the afternoon has arrived in force. It really is time to get going towards the Shah house before it gets dark.

Thankfully, there's only a short drive left now. It took more than two hours to get here from the Palmers' house in Stafford, and both Theo and Emir are ready to be done driving for the day.

The couples spent the journey in two separate cars because Lili had to bring hers back to her parents and Theo was driving himself and Emir for the next few days, so Theo followed Lilibet's car at a respectful distance for the sake of directional guidance, Emir and Jo playing passenger princess to their respective partners and texting each other the entire drive. It all felt very *road trip in a coming of age film* in a specifically poignant way, given why the drive was happening in the first place.

"You'll let us know if you need us to come over?" Theo asks Jordan for the second time in as many minutes, hands clutching tight to a Tupperware.

"I promise." Jordan glances over at Emir with a smirk, even as he tries to pull Theo away and in the direction of the car. The fact he got Theo outside was already a victory.

Between Theo's fussing and Yuusuf and Ola's parental hovering, it took a while. Emir and Jordan are on the same page about needing a bit of space after a stressful few days, but their partners are very endearingly velcroed to them and to each other.

"And we'll see you soon." Lili walks right up to Theo and squeezes him in an exceptionally tight hug, almost knocking the wind out of him. "Thanks for inviting us for New Year's."

"Thank T." Emir pries the two apart as they start to tussle, Lili the instigator, as per. How the two of them got by before their partners were here to play referee is a mystery. "When they heard about what happened, they insisted. And Laurie says they can make room for us at his dad's place, so gay night on the town it is."

"I didn't know Darton had a gay scene." Jordan runs a hand through her hair, tilting her head thoughtfully. "Suppose everywhere does, it just might be more underground."

Emir can see wheels turning behind her eyes, but there's plenty of time to talk *after* they finally get to his house, or back at uni.

"It won't be like London, that's for certain." Theo lets himself be moved three steps closer to his car before digging his heels in again. "Wait, should we talk about that now?"

"Princess, you are the light of my days, but if you don't accept that some things will have to be texted and get in your car to drive us to my parents' house, it'll be summer before we leave." Emir tugs unsuccessfully on Theo's waist. Theo's a very strong teddy bear, so he barely moves.

"Just..." Theo is close enough to his car to set the Tupperware on top, despite Emir's dramatics about his hesitancy to leave. He walks up to Jo and folds her back in his arms for one last goodbye hug, feeling like he's abandoning her, even if he knows that she's in exceptionally safe hands at Lili's house. "We're not far. And back at Roseborough we're in the same building. Also, I'm very good at hugs."

Jordan laughs while hugging Theo back, grateful for all the love she's been shown despite the terrible circumstances. "Thanks, Teddy. You're the best."

"Oi." Lili shoves her way between them and latches onto Jordan's front, turning her head around to stare hard at Theo as he backs away with his hands up. "Mine."

"Calm down. I'm all yours." Jordan laughs again, looking down at Lili fondly and letting her arms fall around Lili's small frame. As an aside to Emir, Jordan asks, "Text us when you get home?"

Emir salutes in the affirmative, finally succeeding in getting Theo to open the driver side door, the Tupperware safely set in the back seat. He has no idea what they'll do with it since his mum is sure to be cooking enough to feed a small village, but he's sure someone at his house will enjoy it.

"You have to start the car to make it do the driving, pumpkin." Emir teases when Theo still hasn't made any actual effort to go anywhere. They're sitting in the car but there's no movement, from the car or from Theo. His hands are in his lap, fiddling with the keys and staring straight ahead.

"Just...we need to wait a few minutes. In case Jo forgot something." Theo worries at his bottom lip, letting out a sigh when Emir's hand slides into his and gives it a squeeze. It helps. Emir understands him, even when he's being stubborn.

"Alright, but I'm setting a timer. You get three minutes and then off we go." Emir tries very hard not to melt at Theo's need to protect Jordan with everything he has to offer, but he fails. Theo is too lovely for any other response.

"Five minutes." Theo counters, still watching the front door, ready to spring into action if needed. "Just in case."

"You're so cute when you're focused." Emir leans back against the passenger seat to stare at Theo with the sun in his eyes. He has a perfect view of Theo's side profile, the curls at his temples, the pout of his lips, the perfect shape of his nose. Theo's gorgeous and Emir continues to be in awe of his existence. How he ever pushed Theo away is a mystery. "I'll give you your five minutes, but on one condition."

"Hm?" Theo asks, not turning away from his vantage point, only squeezing Emir's hand back to let him know he heard him.

"I get to kiss you as soon as the alarm goes off." Emir smiles, his tongue poking out between his teeth, knowing how incredibly ridiculous he is, how completely infatuated beyond belief. But those lips, honestly...

"Deal." Theo grins despite himself, still focused, but Emir's doing an excellent job trying to distract him from his worry. "I'm excited to see your family."

"Yeah?" Emir keeps staring shamelessly, taking his fill of Theo from a few feet away. If he had to guess, Theo's feeling more than just excitement. "Nervous?"

"To my core." Theo admits, interlacing his fingers with Emir's and holding their hands on his thigh. "But they're all so nice and you'll be there and you won't let anything happen to me."

"I felt the same a few days ago when I was driving to your place." Emir brushes his thumb along the top of Theo's knuckles and watches the way the light dances through Theo's hazel eyes. "More excited than I knew how to contain, but nervous. But then I'd think of you and how you always look out for me and cuddle yourself into my personal space the moment it's an option and that worry melted into honey until I could relax again. I'm really glad I conspired with your mum to make it happen."

"Me too." Theo finally does turn to look at Emir, surprising him with a kiss across the centre console, his nose brushing the tip of Emir's and their breath fogging the air between them as they pull apart. Winter up North is cold at any time of day. "Four more minutes."

"Can I turn the heat on while we wait?" Emir licks his lips, the hint of Theo left behind like nectar in the desert. He's irredeemably gone for him, but with zero regrets.

Nodding, Theo slides the keys into the ignition and starts the car then claims Emir's hand again. Emir turns the heat to max and brings Theo's hand to his own lap instead to start massaging all the tiny, miraculous muscles it contains, both for something to do while he waits and to soothe the edges of Theo's worry about Jordan.

When the timer goes off, Theo sighs and looks away from Lilibet's front door, turning to Emir for a longer kiss, as promised. Blinking his eyes to refocus on the task at hand, Theo shifts the car in reverse and lets Emir guide him home.

***

Emir groans as he reluctantly wakes up, throwing himself across Theo's warm body and whining at the sun. "No."

"But..." Theo keeps stroking Emir's hair even as he grumbles. He's been awake for a half an hour and he wants to get up, but he's in Emir's house and it's still early and Emir likes to sleep in so Theo doesn't know what he's meant to do. Also, he really needs a wee.

"Sleep." Emir presses a kiss to the side of Theo's neck and gets comfortable on his chest, tugging the blanket back over his body and letting Theo continue to pet his hair. It's very soothing.

"I can't." Theo moves his hand to Emir's back instead, fingertips finding their way beneath the hem of Emir's t-shirt so he can caress the smooth skin beneath. "Been awake for a while."

"Baby..." Emir groans again, squinting his eyes open and pressing his fingertips to Theo's pouted lips. Even in his barely awake state, upon inspection, he can tell Theo's both conflicted and grumpy. He needs something, but he feels bad about waking Emir. "I'm comfy. Do I have to get up right now?"

"No, but...I don't know what I'm supposed to do." Theo stares at a spot near Emir's chest, not meeting his eye because he still gets embarrassed sometimes about this sort of thing. He doesn't want to upset any rules of the Shah house inadvertently. "I'm ready to be up, but I don't want to be a bother. I don't know the squeaky stairs or the thin walls and everyone needs their sleep."

Emir thinks for a minute, trying to wake up enough to be helpful, moving his palm to cradle Theo's face and running his thumb along the top of his cheekbone. Theo's just asking for his reassurance that it's alright to get up without him. "Why don't you go for a wee and freshen up and then make us a cuppa? The girls will still be asleep."

Theo hums because he figured that's what Emir would say. But it's his first morning at the Shahs' house and he doesn't want to be a nuisance. He's trying to be a very polite guest in their home, not an unwelcome alarm clock. "Are you sure? Like...alone?"

"I'm positive. My sisters sleep through anything and my parents won't mind." Emir gives Theo a small smile, rubbing at his tired eyes and laying back against his own pillow with his arms above his head. "But leave your pyjamas on and bring our tea upstairs so we can cuddle."

"Alright." Theo pauses for a moment before leaning forward for a good morning kiss, Emir smiling against his lips before they break apart again. "Sorry I woke you up."

"It's fine, princess." Emir pats Theo on the bum, making him flush as he gets out of Emir's bed. It's a bit early to be naughty, but Theo's bum is just so cute and he likes it when Emir gives him attention. The topic's been discussed at length. "See you in a bit."

Emir rolls over, away from the window and into Theo's vacated spot, hiding his face against Theo's pillow and letting himself fall back into sleep, or the closest he'll get now that he's missing his cuddle bug. With a last glance at Emir's huddled form under the blankets, Theo lets himself out of Emir's bedroom and tiptoes down the hall to the shared bathroom.

Theo relieves himself and washes his hands as quietly as he can, not even daring to turn the tap all the way on. He runs his fingers through his hair, brushes his teeth with his travel toothbrush and Emir's toothpaste. They've been sharing for months now and Theo spends his two minutes of brushing thinking about it. Before he's done, Theo pats a bit of moisturiser under his eyes, then walks back to Emir's room.

He carefully re-opens the door and checks to make sure that Emir is still asleep, leaving it cracked as he walks to the stairs so he can let himself in when his hands will be full with their steaming mugs.

"Oh! I'm sorry, I didn't mean - " Theo pulls up short at the entrance to the kitchen when he sees Natalie in her ankle length dressing gown, petering around near the stove.

"Good morning, Theo. Come on in. I was wondering when you'd wander down." Natalie gives Theo a bright smile, her eyes crinkling as she waves him over.

"You were?" Theo's sock covered feet take their time to cross the room, still feeling like he's intruding despite the warm welcome.

"Emir said you're an early riser." Natalie holds out a measuring spoon for Theo to take without explanation before turning back around to the cupboard. "Unlike my kids who would sleep until noon if left to their own schedules."

Theo fidgets with the measuring spoon, admiring the detail imprinted on the handle. This looks like a well-loved treasure. "I tried to wake Emi but he's a bit grumpy in the mornings, and he sent me away to make tea since I was awake and bored and didn't know what to do, but I don't want to interrupt or get in the way. I can go upstairs and wait for him to wake up again or, like, maybe go for a walk or - "

"I was just making chai for myself and Saleem." Natalie turns back to Theo and gives his forearm a gentle squeeze to calm his nerves. "I don't bother most days, but occasionally I get the urge. Saleem's the same as Emir: impossible to wake up no matter how much he's slept."

"Emir loves your chai!" Theo flushes the moment he's said it, because of course Natalie already knows that. Emir's been her son much longer than he's been Theo's boyfriend.

"He'd better. I know he's moved on to green tea most of the time, but I think it'd be worth it for you to learn how we make it." Natalie taps the side of her nose with a knowing look. "I've heard you'll be getting a flat together after uni, and you'll want to keep the chai blend ready in the cupboard for when he's homesick."

"He really does pull out your recipes when he misses you." Theo scoots a step to the side as Natalie opens yet another cupboard. The Shah spice collection is a thing of beauty. "Even if he doesn't actually say he's homesick, he'll head to the kitchen and start fiddling with measurements and I'll know."

"That's my Emi." Natalie carefully closes all the cupboards and gestures at the assembled jars. None of them are labelled, but she seems very sure of the contents. "I'll write it down before you head home in a few days, but for now I'll just talk you through it. We use milk, but if you need to make it vegan, the plant milks should work fine, they just might taste a bit different. What we make is a masala chai, heavy on the spices, which is one of the reasons it's not an everyday thing. Once you've made it fresh, nothing else will do. You'll see."

"Right...would it be completely strange if I ran to grab a notebook so I could write a few things down?" Theo feels a bit overwhelmed by the task at hand. He had no idea that traditional chai, or maybe specifically masala chai (he'll make a note to learn the difference), had so many ingredients, and he knows that if a single one is out of proportion it won't taste as it should.

"Go on then. I can wait a moment." Natalie gives him another smile, her eyes holding that same depth of kindness that he's always so comforted by in Emir's.

"Thanks, and um...just thanks." Theo darts forward to give her a fleeting kiss on the cheek before hurrying upstairs to his rucksack where he has at least two notebooks and several pens to choose from. He leaves Emir with another forehead kiss then trots back down the stairs, excited and nervous in equal measure. Theo's never spent alone time with any of Emir's family before and Natalie has almost literally been in his place, learning the traditions and culture of her partner with the deepest love in her heart.

Theo spends the next half an hour learning how to make chai from the assembled ingredients, with an CTC Assam black tea base, and so many spices that he does a lot of writing even though Natalie promised to send him the recipe. She's patient and generous, letting Theo do the work himself while she diligently guides his progress, giving him nods of approval as they go along. Natalie sends him away again with a kiss to his cheek, a return for the one he gave earlier, and a request that he remind Emir that his first class is at noon today.

When Theo squeezes himself back into Emir's bedroom, Emir's awake and waiting with a sleepy smile and grabby hands, ready to pull him back into bed for morning cuddles.

"Mmmm, it's perfect. One sip and I'm all cosy." Emir closes his eyes to savour his first mouthful, letting the rich milk coat his tongue as the sweet spices wake him up. Leaning into his boyfriend, he presses a soft kiss to Theo's lips. "Thank you, princess."

"Your mum showed me the recipe. You promise it's alright?" Theo's already tasted from his own mug several times, loving how spicy yet balanced the experience is, especially compared to what passes for chai in the average London cafe. There's an aftertaste of pepper and clove following the sweet cinnamon, layers of flavour mingling in a single cup.

"Promise." Emir's heart constricts picturing his mum and Theo mumbling to each other as they brewed a Shah family recipe. It's just chai, but it's also so much more. Emir loves Theo so intensely that it's hard to contain sometimes, but given the hot beverage in both of their hands, he holds himself back from tackling his partner. Later.

"You want to watch something while we cuddle?" Theo asks, settling into the pillows that Emir's propped against his headboard. "We have a few hours before you teach."

"Hold my mug and I'll get my laptop." Emir gifts Theo another kiss before hopping off the bed, closing his door on the way back. He needs a bit of privacy so he can kiss Theo exactly as much as he wants. Nothing more intimate, but he wants Theo all to himself for a while.

***

Emir needs a break after teaching several classes back-to-back, a task that requires an amount of socialisation that his introverted soul handles best in small doses. Theo came with him to the studio, as he plans to do for all the hours Emir's teaching this week, and mostly did work for their dissertation while Emir was busy. He claims he feels comfort just being near a dance studio, but Emir thinks it's equally his desire to be near his boyfriend, which he definitely doesn't mind.

For the sake of Emir's mental health, he and Theo are currently on a walk with his parents and both of his younger sisters, Amina joining reluctantly and Saima with enough enthusiasm for the both of them. It's rare they do this together as a family, but it's nice. His mum is mostly off work until school starts again, but his baba will have to be back to work tomorrow. And with Theo here, Emir's indulging in all the best parts of his life. Plus, the cold winter air is incredibly refreshing after hours in a sweaty dance studio.

"Emi?" Theo asks from his side, hands shoved in his pockets for warmth. At uni, they hold hands while they walk, but not here. Theo understands, even if his hands feel lonely.

"Princess?" Emir nudges him with an elbow, his hands similarly shielded from the cold, even with gloves to keep them warm.

"Why don't you have a dog? Like, why doesn't your family have a dog? You love them and I know that at least Safiya does too. Is it just too much work? I know your parents are busy." Theo glances up at Emir and moves a step closer so their arms brush occasionally and they can hold a conversation in relative privacy.

"It's the house." Emir shrugs, as if he hasn't been wishing for his own pet his entire life. But he's old enough to understand now. "It's rented. We've always rented, and they've never allowed pets with fur. Like, we had a few fish when Yaya and I were little and shared a room, but nothing since. And you're right about how busy everyone is."

"Oh…guess I've never had to worry about that." Theo furrows his brow and stews in his thoughts for a minute while the walk continues. They're behind the others, Saima and Amina running ahead every few minutes before letting the other four catch up, Saleem and Natalie immersed in their own conversation a few feet ahead of Theo and Emir.

"That's sad, not being allowed a pet. There's so much research that shows children grow up with better mental health with a pet in the house, better marks and healthier relationships, better communication, they're more active and open about their emotions, even accounting for demographic influences. Allergies aside and all that, there's no way pets are more destructive than kids, so like…just seems unfair to say they aren't allowed and not let each family decide that for themselves."

"Hard agree, pumpkin. But." Emir shrugs again and sighs. "Up North, in council housing, especially as a mixed race family…things are just different sometimes. You get used to it, I suppose. Used to there being a different set of rules that usually don't make sense, knowing your home is different from the posh kids at school, hearing the things people will say about you because of where you live, how you look, what your name is. My parents tried to shield us from the worst of it, but there's still things that even kids notice. Not being allowed a pet was one of them."

"Oh." Theo falls silent again, struggling with himself because he wants to comfort Emir, but he knows it's not that simple.

Emir had a wonderful, happy childhood in a loving home. The world is unfair and unjust, but Emir's home is one of the most welcoming, supportive places, so even if he couldn't have a dog and his bedroom is a bit small, that was hardly the biggest worry or what Emir cares most about.

"Lili talks to me about those things sometimes. Less about, like, money and stuff, because she and I are similar in that respect. But there's some of those other things you mentioned that she's shared with me."

Emir nods to encourage Theo to keep talking. He's sure it's nothing new, that whatever Theo's heard are things that Emir's discussed with Lilibet himself at some point. Their experiences being visibly different from their peers in dance was one of the first things that bonded them, even when he and Theo were antagonists for several years.

With Emir's continued attention, Theo goes on, "She said her parents gave her and her brothers English names to make it easier for them at school and how she has complicated feelings about it. Because it did make it easier, but she hates the position it leaves her in. She's proud of her grandparents and her culture and wants to celebrate it, but she also knows her parents made that choice for a reason. Like, she has to decide which sides of herself to share and code switch and all that. Even in London, she deals with racist shit almost every day, and it was worse growing up. Almost all her friends were white, and they didn't even realise what it was like for her or how they sometimes made it worse."

"I think you might understand better than most because you - " Emir glances around to make sure their conversation is still private. It's Theo's information to share if he wants, but they're still by themselves so he finishes the thought. "Because you're autistic and, like, you've told me about masking and all that. You know what it's like to change how you act for your safety or even because of social pressure."

"Right, but it's not the same." Theo walks slower now that he's deep in thought, Emir also slowing to match his pace. "I'll never know what it's like to be treated differently because of my race or my name. I'll never understand what it feels like to be targeted or discriminated against for my religion or my skin colour. And that's just…everyday for you and Lili and, like, a lot of other people. I have my own experiences, but I know it's not the same. Like, I was bullied because I was autistic and queer, but I know it was a fraction of what some of my classmates dealt with."

Theo pauses talking for another minute, Emir walking alongside him in silence. It's a needed conversation, and not the first time they've discussed this, but Theo's right that it's everyday for Emir and this can't be a one time conversation. He needs a partner who engages with him about these topics, who listens when Emir's frustrated or scared or indignant. Emir's very glad to have found that in Theo. No, he'll never quite understand, but Theo tries and he listens, and Emir couldn't be safe in a relationship with anything less.

But Theo's not done talking so Emir tunes back in to the conversation as he starts again.

"Black autistic people and autistic people with higher support needs are targeted by police at a statistically significant rate. There's actual data proving that it's true. They're more likely to experience violence and housing insecurity and general inequity because of their overlapping identities. So while I can understand certain aspects of discrimination, I'll never be in that place. I try to remind myself of that so I don't cause harm unintentionally. But I know I can do more." Theo seems to be talking to himself as much as to Emir, needing to be honest about what he's feeling, but also let Emir know that he's very aware that he'll never actually understand.

He can be empathetic and well educated, but he'll never be in that position, and it would be wrong to claim the false equivalency.

"You're right." Emir stops walking when they pass near an empty bench, sitting down and waiting for Theo to do the same. They can catch up with everyone else in a few minutes, and he wants to make time for both of them to sit with their thoughts. "I don't think there's ever going to be an answer, not in our lifetimes. Sure, we have to do what we can. There's no alternative. But there's…a lot that has to change."

Theo leans his head on Emir's shoulder, hoping it's not too much since they're in public. Emir doesn't usually favour PDA in public and Theo respects those boundaries. He'll move away if Emir shrugs him off.

"Sit here for a minute?" Theo asks, wanting a chance to put his thoughts together because it seems they've reached the end of this conversation for today. Especially outside like this, around other people, he knows there's things Emir won't or can't share.

"And then we can race to meet up with the others. I could use a jog." Emir grins, setting his cheek on top of Theo's beanie for a moment before staring back out at the street. Since it's the week between two major holidays, more people are home and there's kids playing in their gardens and dogs being walked and more life than he would usually get to see on a Monday afternoon.

They sit on the bench together for about five minutes, lost in their thoughts, so the jog to catch up with the others is literal. Arriving out of breath and smiling as they breeze past Emir's parents, they manage to slow before reaching the girls, but only just.

"Easy, kid." Emir's dad laughs when the two of them stop to catch their breath, winded from the combination of the cold and adrenaline. "Just watching you makes me tired."

"We'll be home soon. We'll give you your space before it's time to eat, but maybe we could watch the telly together after?" Natalie asks, leaning into her husband, her eyes moving between her son and her two daughters still a few feet ahead. These moments are increasingly rare as her kids grow up.

"That'd be great." Emir grins, and with a surge of something ineffable, he reaches for Theo's hand and takes it in his own as they fall into step in front of his parents, buffered by his family as they walk along. He's safe and in love and he doesn't want to hide it.

"Emir?" Theo reacts to the sudden gesture in confusion, turning to look at him with a concerned look. When they'd talked about what Emir was comfortable with while they spent time in Shipley, hand holding had been on the list of no's for when they're outside the house.

"Walk home with me?" Emir holds Theo's hand tighter and swings their arms between them, glancing back at his parents to see them watching on. Natalie seems hesitant but understanding while Saleem beams with pride, catching his eye for a moment. They both know what's been taken from Emir to get to this point, how he had to rebuild so much of himself.

"Of course." Theo bumps Emir's shoulder but doesn't disconnect his hand. It's not new for them, but he's aware that two young men holding hands while walking down the street wouldn't have been possible until very recently, and it's still a decision rather than a given because of safety. He knows about Emir's past in this city and the reasons he set those initial boundaries, and they're his to adjust if and when he's ready.

Emir's not entirely sure what came over him. Probably something about wanting to push past a few of those things he and Theo had been talking about. People tend to make assumptions about his family, his sexuality, his core identity, based on how he looks. But Emir's lived reality is that he's a genderqueer bisexual man with loving parents in a mixed race, Muslim, working class household, and none of those things are in conflict.

The last person who tried to shame him into hiding used to walk these same streets with him. They never held hands, not even in private. They weren't affectionate in their relationship. So walking proudly through the neighbourhood with his family, with Theo's hand held boldly in his own, is an act of defiance, a form of resistance towards the homophobic and transphobic parts of this place he called home for most of his life. A way to show that despite his ex's (and others') best efforts, Emir's not ashamed of who he is, who he loves, or how he looks.

A few minutes ago they were discussing all the ways Emir knew he was different as a kid, before he even understood his sexuality or gender. Those were aspects of his identity that he would discover later, after he would be pressured to stay in a cupboard he didn't even realise was built around him. But his youngest memories of school, the times he felt fear and hurt and anger, those were because he had a last name like Shah and a complexion darker than his schoolmates.

And now he's an out and proud queer person, in love with another man, gladly walking through the city that tried to ruin him, living proof that they failed and Emir thrives. He rejected the pain that this place tried to bury within him and rebuilt his life into something far more beautiful with the most incredible people imaginable.

"I'm glad you're here." Emir reaches over to guide Theo's chin in his direction until their eyes meet, keeping their hands connected. It's a gesture he usually reserves for the flat, when they're alone and he wants to get Theo's attention in the softest way possible. "This is a good memory."

"Yeah?" Theo grins so wide that the dimple at the top of his cheek shows up. Seeing Emir this happy and free makes Theo content in a way he didn't know he yearned for before they got together. His happiness isn't only about himself anymore in a very concrete way. "I think we could make a few more."

Emir giggles and flushes slightly, hiding his face by looking down at their feet. He was in love in November, he's in love in December, and he's starting to suspect January as well. Theo's not going anywhere. "I'd like that."

***

Ciaran: Hello lovers
Ciaran: Miss youuuuu
Emi: hello gay people in my phone
Theo: I'm a gay person outside of your phone, too.
Theo: /selfie of himself and Emir on the Shah sofa/
Gabe: How many gay people do you have in your phone, Emi?
Laurie: Not as many as I have /painted nails emoji/
T: Happy Tuesday /Teletubby sunshine gif/
Ciaran: Can't believe you're all having gay new years festivities without us
Ciaran: I forbid it
Laurie: Hop on over from Ireland
Laurie: I hear they even have planes now
Ciaran: Fuck off
Laurie: Hardly the time. I'm waiting for some of the lads to show up for footie at the park like the old days
T: I am also at the park, shivering my entire cock and balls off
Laurie: I love you !!
T: You owe me
T: I can't even wear a cute outfit in this weather
T: What if I'm mistaken for a straight person? /vomiting emoji/
Ciaran: I don't see how being at the park prevents you from fucking off
Laurie: Gabe come get your twink he's being rude
Ciaran: /middle finger emoji/
Laurie: /kissing face emoji/
Theo: Why are we fighting?
T: (they're not actually fighting they're being gay and sarcastic)
Theo: (thank you)
Gabe: We get the flat all to ourselves for a few days before everyone gets back
Gabe: /slumber party gif/
Gabe: Alfie's coming back early to help :) so it'll just be the three of us lounging around naked

Theo: Because of his parents? I know it's been bad and the holidays were probably worse :(
Ciaran: That's one factor but clearly he misses us I mean who wouldn't
T: You think you'll be done with everything by the time we get back? It's a lot of work for three people
T: We can help you know
Laurie: I can enlist the lesbians
Laurie: Not sure what you need help with but they love a project and there isn't another show for a while
Ciaran: We're not moving much honestly
Ciaran: Gabe already listed most of the furniture since we don't have room in the flat
Laurie: Wait...
Emi: what laurie said
Ciaran: What?
Emi: who's moving and to where??
Emi: you said we had until the end of uni to say goodbye
Laurie: ISTG IF ONE OF YOU IS LEAVING US EARLY I WILL RIOT
T: Wow he's just kicked that football so hard that the back of the net is now considered gaping by the local homosexual
T: It's me I'm the local homosexual
T: Laur doesn't want you two to leave. I think he cares about you a little bit
Laurie: DON'T TELL THEM THAT
Ciaran: Calm down Lawrence
Ciaran: Gabe's moving into our flat
Emi: he's what?
Gabe: You both knew this! We've talked about it multiple times!
Laurie: LIES
Laurie: Wait so you aren't leaving early?
T: And now he's pacing with the football under his arm like some sort of frustrated footie coach
T: It's hot
Theo: You think that everything Laurie does is hot, though.
T: And I'm correct /hamster shoving water straw into cheek gif/
Emi: we're getting off topic
T: But I'm BORED and COLD
Laurie: Since when is New York moving into the nerd flat?
T: First of all Emi is also a nerd
Emi: yeah but i practically live there too

Gabe: Ciaran and I barely use my flat and it was either sign for another six months or let the place go and save the money for the international move. We literally talked about this like three family dinners ago.
Theo: You know, this one might be my fault.
Theo: Emir finds me very attractive and I was...distracting him that night.
Ciaran: And what's Laurie's excuse?
Laurie: Mate, odds are I was half asleep at the table. I've been exhausted
Laurie: But now that it's been mentioned I think I might remember a conversation or two
Laurie: Even though Emi and I don't technically live there and obviously the three of you get to make that choice for yourselves
Theo: It's alright, Laurie. You can admit you also find me distractingly attractive.
Emi: ohhhhhhhhhh i knew i missed something that night oops
Emi: teddy's fit and we're boyfriends. sometimes i stare at his boobs and forget to pay attention
Emi: blame the skin-tight vest and diligent weight training
T: /go to horny jail bonk gif/
Emi: you have literally no room to talk
Emi: laurie can't even wear vests around you outside the bedroom
Laurie: Teddy and I just have raw sex appeal
Laurie: Sheer animal magnetism
Ciaran: And if I vomit?
Laurie: Aim for a conservative
T: Lawrence William Tempest.
Laurie: I said what I said
Laurie: How's Jordan?
Emi: depends
Emi: a lot of ups and downs and it's only been like two days
Theo: Lili and her family are taking really good care of her, but it's a lot all at once.
T: I'm really glad she knew to go to your place Theo
Ciaran: Might've saved her life
Ciaran: I can't believe they just...left her there with nothing
Emi: i unfortunately can
Emi: she told us enough to get a good picture of her family and honestly it could've been worse
Theo: You don't think it'll be too much too soon for her to come with us for New Year's?
Gabe: She can always decide to cancel, but it might be good for her
Emi: she's told us a whole list of queer things she's always wanted to do but couldn't and gay clubbing was on the list
Emi: think we might have a bit of a rebel on our hands, but she's earned it

Theo: *I'm not ready to get a tattoo.*
Laurie: *What are you kinky fucks up to?*
T: *This is another one of those times where we have no room to talk*
T: */person wearing a pink frilly collar gif/*
Emi: *jo wants a tattoo*
Emi: *it's on the list*
Emi: *and theo is jo's brother now so he probably feels obligated*
T: *Maybe she could do that with Lilibet?*
Theo: *Lili's terrified of needles! Says she's never getting a tattoo even though she loves the artistic aspect and all that.*
Emi: *wait is lili going to be alright coming out with us?*
Emi: *i know she was fine for halloween but still*
Theo: *She doesn't mind going out sometimes, just not to house parties and not without me, and she won't be drinking.*
Laurie: *Fuck I remember first year*
Laurie: *That was terrifying*
T: *I didn't know Lili then but i'm glad she had you*
Gabe: *I'm glad we all have each other*
Emi: *maybe i'll get another tattoo if jo needs someone to do it with*
Emi: *i sort of liked getting the first one /eggplant emoji; running emoji/*
Theo: *But where would you hide a second one?*
Ciaran: *YOU HAVE A TATTOO WHAT*
Emi: */three running emojis/*
Laurie: *It's next to his cock*
T: *Very tasteful though*
Theo: *I didn't know until we took a shower together. It's very well hidden. Because dance.*
Ciaran: *Can't believe you've hidden a tattoo from me*
Ciaran: *Send me a picture of the tasteful dick tattoo i'm feeling cheated*
Ciaran: *Why's everyone seen it but me ??*
Emi: *it's not a tattoo of a dick it's near my dick*
Emi: *technically it's more hip bone than dick*
Emi: *it's just my name in urdu*
Gabe: *Aw that's beautiful Emi*
Ciaran: *HAS GABRIEL SEEN IT*
Gabe: *Not that I remember /shrug emoji/*
Theo: *Oh, you would remember.*
Emi: *you can see it when we get back to uni i'm not sending you a dick pic*
T: *You could send it to the group*
T: */side eye emoji/*

Emi: *you've seen my dick plenty of times it hasn't changed*
Laurie: *My fiance is such a little cock slut /heart eye emoji/*
Ciaran: *You two are so weird*
Ciaran: *Love you*
Gabe: *I really need to go to bed now it's the middle of the night here*
Gabe: *Text you all when I wake up*
Gabe: *Don't have too much fun without me*
Gabe: *And if you're sending a tasteful dick tattoo pic someone wake me up*
Ciaran: *Love you sweetheart /three heart emojis; three angel emojis/*
Emi: *i'm teaching again today so you'll have to entertain yourselves this afternoon without me*
Theo: *He's so cute with the kids! I get cute aggression. Honestly, I may have to bite him.*
Theo: *The urge to chomp is STRONG.*
Emi: *...why is this the first i'm hearing of this?*
T: */popcorn eating gif/*
Laurie: *Teddy, go bite your boyfriend*
T: *But Theo's the one...*
Theo: *It's not a secret. Literally can't keep a secret from any of you.*
Theo: *Apparently, I'm into biting, both giving and receiving.*
Emi: *and i'm not opposed to it*
Laurie: *Can't believe this is how we find out they both top /writing emoji/*
Theo: *I'm mostly a bottom, but /shrug emoji/ Not ashamed of that.*
Ciaran: *NO SECRETS EH??*
Ciaran: *EXCEPT APPARENTLY WE HAVE SECRET TATTOOS*
Emi: *tattoo singular and as far as i know it's just me*
Emi: *also - eh? has gabe been all canadian with his mama's family visiting? and then rubbing off on you with his canadianisms?*
Ciaran: *Unfortunately he is literally not rubbing off on me due to the ocean in between our bodies*
Laurie: *YOU DIDN'T TELL US GABE WAS MOVING IN EITHER*
T: *We most definitely did Laur you even mentioned a moving in party*
Laurie: *That does sound like me...*
Ciaran: *I'm off to golf with my da you all bite each other and talk about dicks and I'll text you when i'm done*
Emi: */cat biting an arm gif/*

***

It's Emir's third and last class that he's teaching today, and he's lucky enough to be ending the day with the older students. There's almost a dozen of them, all dedicated enough to take daily dance class over their uni break, and glad to have Emir willing to teach. Some of these dancers will be off to uni next year, and he's fondly nostalgic remembering that time in his life: when he was choosing which programmes to apply for, sending audition tapes, attending master classes, whatever it took to turn his passion into a career. It's hard to believe his time at uni is almost over, this new generation ready to take his place.

"Right, let's get the adagio out of the way - " Emir grins at the immediate groans from the dancers, Theo's recognisable among them. Since it's the last class of the day and only the advanced students in attendance, his boss had asked if he'd like to show them part of his dissertation, which meant Theo was warming up by taking his class. Theo's a model student and incredibly respectful of Emir as a teacher, because of course he is. "Stop the grumbling, I'll make it pretty."

"You always do." Theo mumbles, taking a long drink from his water bottle and wiping at his forehead with his vest. There's a series of giggles and Emir rolls his eyes, but secretly he's pleased.

Despite his best efforts to keep their relationship private, the older students had called him out immediately the minute they were introduced. Theo's flush at the teenagers' questions was essentially its own answer, so to avoid hours of distracted students, Emir had quickly verified that yes, Theo was his boyfriend as well as his dance partner, then let them get a majority of the tittering out of the way.

"Behave or I won't be showing off to any of you. You'll have to wait until summer when it's posted to the Roseborough accounts like the rest of the world." Emir has his phone in his hand, switching to a new playlist now that they're working in centre. He sort of loves teaching and he hopes he'll get to continue at whichever company he lands a contract with. Most companies let their dancers teach at their training school unless they're a principal. Since Emir will almost definitely start in the corps, he'll be allowed, and hopefully encouraged, to teach the next generation.

The rest of the advanced class goes smoothly. Emir's been teaching here since he was in sixth form, starting with the toddlers and working his way up until now, when he can teach at all levels. When he was doxxed and outed by his ex, the school director at the time was one of the awful people who shut him out, telling him he was no longer welcome and that she'd call the police if he showed up. But luckily, she left the dance school that same summer and the instructor, Kim, who took over that August, reached out to Emir immediately to welcome him back, letting him know they'd be glad to see him in class or as an instructor. He's been teaching over his uni breaks ever since, earning just enough money to pay for what his parents aren't able to cover. Uni isn't cheap, even with all the assistance he's received.

After grand allegro, when the dancers are out of breath but smiling, his boss sneaks in through the studio door and stands near the corner as Emir finishes class. Kim gives him a subtle thumbs up, not trying to intrude, just wanting to make sure she's here when Emir shares a portion of his dissertation. She proudly talks to her classes about the school's previous students, and Emir is the most successful in recent years.

"Alright, suppose I've made you all wait long enough." Emir gestures for Theo to join him near the front. "You all get back in your warmups and settle in front of the mirror while we get ready. Kim, could you - the music?"

"Gladly." Kim leaves the corner to join him and Theo as the dancers hurry to pull their various layers back on to keep their bodies warm.

Emir's been impressed with all the changes that Kim's made since taking over, educating the dancers on all those things he didn't learn until Sean stepped in: about the healthy approach to taking care of his muscles, properly nourishing his body between classes, the importance of taking breaks, and encouraging having a life outside of the studio. These kids will leave this school much healthier than those who trained here alongside Emir.

"I'm thinking the third section?" Emir turns to Theo, his hand running along Theo's back until he's holding him by the waist as they stare at Emir's phone together. He has the playlist for their dissertation open, ready to hand it over to Kim once they've decided.

"The first section is too slow without the rest, and the others aren't ready." Theo agrees, stepping out of Emir's hold to offer him his hand instead. "But let's practise that lift first. Make sure we're warmed up enough."

Emir gives his phone to Kim, pointing out which song they'll need her to play as he takes Theo's proffered hand and lets himself be walked across the studio. He's aware this may be the first time these students will see non-traditional partner work outside of social media, and he's proud to know he's the reason they're being introduced to the idea as more than just a concept. If he'd seen visibly queer dancers growing up, especially a non-white queer dancer, he would've had a different life.

They practise the lift three times before they both feel comfortable, Emir easily falling back into that space they create for themselves when they're in the studio together. Feeling safe with Theo as a dance partner certainly paved the way for all the rest, and he's not sure where they'd be if not for that first night in the studio, reenacting *Dirty Dancing* and cracking open that wall of contempt. He'd walked Theo home that night because, even then, he knew something had changed.

"Before we start, know this isn't finished and we're only showing you a section from the middle." Emir says to the students who have dutifully seated themselves along the front wall, water bottles in hand while they wait. Emir always experiences a very sharp nostalgia when he's here teaching, thinking about when he was in their place, before his life imploded and he left for uni. It was like a different world, but he wouldn't trade where he is at the moment for anything. He has incredible friends, a loving family, and a devoted partner.

"Just tell me when." Kim stands near the edge, Emir's phone ready in her hand as she flashes him an encouraging smile. He wonders how different his teenage years would've been with her as a mentor, then focuses back on the dissertation.

Theo takes his place beside Emir, curling around him and waiting as their breathing syncs. It always happens when they dance as partners, when they're asleep in the same bed, whenever their bodies are in harmony. And if it doesn't happen, something always feels off, like they're slightly out of rhythm. No such worry today though, Emir's presence in Theo's dance space perfectly familiar. Another deep breath together, positions held and minds focused, two individuals existing as one.

The music starts and they're in their own world. Emir lifts Theo, Theo lifts Emir, they turn and rise and fall and use their bodies to tell a story that they've written together. They have momentum and grace, intention and purpose. It's not a performance and it's not exactly practise either, but some sort of liminal space between the two ends of the spectrum. They haven't had the opportunity to dance together for a few weeks but they fall back into it with ease, like trying on a favourite jumper for the first chilly day of autumn and letting it settle across the frame of their shoulders.

Theo still can't believe that he gets to be with Emir like this. Being his boyfriend is incredible, but being his dance partner in this very specific way is an amount of trust and vulnerability that Theo will never take for granted. Emir is his favourite dancer, someone he admires as an artist, and getting to share in that experience with him, collaborating and pushing each other to be better, it's the most wonderful, validating feeling. Without this connection, they may never have gotten where they are in their personal relationship. Dance gave them the space to know the truest parts of each other that opened the door to all the rest. As Theo cradles Emir in his arms at the end of the section, he feels the moment outside of time, like holding Emir and creating with him exists in its own universe.

But it doesn't, unfortunately. Not that Theo minds the audience, but it's a bit of an awakening whenever they stop moving together and get back to reality. Emir sneaks a kiss behind Theo's ear before stepping away to catch his breath, tossing his arms above his head while Theo places his own on the back of his hips and watches Emir. It's hard not to. He's glowing.

"That was incredible, Emir." Kim breaks the silence several seconds after the music ends and the small audience starts clapping. The dancers take Kim's words as their cue to whisper amongst themselves, darting glances between Emir and Theo with wide, bright eyes. "I can't wait to see the entire piece. You two have really crafted something special. I truly believe that."

"Yeah?" Emir drops his hands to tug Theo into his side for a cuddle. Nothing *inappropriate*, just bringing Theo back into his space like when they'd been dancing. "Theo gets a lot of the credit. It'd just be a mess without him. He's brilliant, honestly."

"Where are you from, Theo?" Kim asks, leaning against the wall for a moment in contemplation. This is a thing dance teachers do, wanting to know where someone trained, what School they studied, what performances they've done, what choreographers they've worked with. Dance is both a very broad world and a very small rumour mill.

"Stafford. I didn't meet Emir until uni, and he's being far too generous. He has more talent than anyone I've ever met." Theo turns his head to give his compliment directly to his partner, smiling when Emir shoves at him playfully. "I spent my term abroad learning about choreography and different genres I hadn't experienced, and, well, I'm sure you all saw Emir's *Firebird*. So when we got back to uni a few months ago and had to start working on our dissertations, it was a good fit. He brings the more creative side of things and I bring the structure."

"What are you two going to do after uni?" One of the dancers asks. She looks a bit like Jordan, and maybe that's just because Jordan is very much on their minds recently, but there is something in the way she holds herself that's reminiscent of their friend.

"Not sure yet. We have to send audition tapes in a few months, and our dissertation will play a role of course." Emir runs a hand through his hair and takes a deep, steadying breath. Going from teaching to full-out partner work then back to standing around is a whirlwind. "We're thinking we might stay in London if we can, but it all depends."

"Did you all want to show Emir and his Theo what you've been working on? You've all got audition tapes of your own to be sent out soon, maybe even to their programme in London." Kim hands Emir back his phone as he walks over to reach his Hydroflask. He noticed the less than subtle attachment of Theo to his name, but she's not wrong. "I'm sure they could offer you valuable feedback."

There's a resounding agreement that yes, they do want to do that. It's clear that the younger dancers look up to Emir, someone who started at their school and has gone on to do great things already, with a whole career still ahead. So many young dancers stop taking class when they leave for uni or to start work, and Emir is a brilliant example of what their future might hold.

"I'll pay you extra if you put up with us a while longer." Kim mumbles to Emir who chuckles and nods, knowing that she's probably just finding an excuse to pay him for the class that had to be cancelled after she'd already promised it to him.

"Do you mind?" Emir turns to check in on Theo. It's not part of what they'd planned for the day and they'll probably be here about an hour longer. And since he's already been here waiting for Emir since about noon, it's not fair to assume.

"Not at all. We've got time." Theo grins, flopping down onto the floor to stretch his body out before it gets cold again. Emir is a tough teacher, not giving the dancers, including Theo, an easy class, even though they're technically on break.

"Who's first?" Kim asks the assembled dancers, several of them already shuffling around the space and thinking through their choreography. Brayden raises his hand and asks to show his *Flames of Paris* variation, wanting their help with the height of his jumps. The others settle again at the front with Emir, Theo, and Kim, waiting their turn for feedback from the experts.

Theo catches Emir's eye to give him a smile, something falling into place this afternoon. He's always thought about teaching, mentoring, being someone like Sean, but he's also not entirely ready to give up his own dance career. Maybe he can find some sort of compromise, a way to do both, and focus on his choreography along the way. But as he and Emir offer guidance and tips and technical pointers as a team, he thinks this should be factored into his next steps after uni. Theo feels like he might have something to offer and this impromptu mentor session is confirmation. He wants to learn how to do this more officially, and he should consider having a chat with Sean about it when he gets the chance.

***

Emir walks quietly down the stairs of his house, Theo already asleep in his bed even though Emir wasn't quite tired enough to join him yet. He's had three days in a row of teaching, with one more before New Year's Eve when they drive to visit Laurie and T. Emir can't go for late night walks here like he can at uni. It wouldn't be safe, and he's honestly not sure what he'll do about that next year when they're destined to be in some tiny flat. But at least for tonight, he can wander around the house.

"Emi?" Saleem looks up at him from the sofa, Natalie seated beside him and nestled under his arm. It's sweet, the way his parents are still so in love and affectionate even decades into their marriage. Emir appreciates the relationship they've modelled for him and his siblings even more now that he has Theo in his life.

"Sorry. Too early to be asleep and I'm restless." Emir scratches at his jawline, his beard starting to grow in after almost two weeks of not shaving. Theo's obsessed with it, hands always fussing at his beard and telling Emir how fit he looks. "Didn't want to wake Theo with my faffing about."

"Come sit with us." Natalie pats the open spot beside her, waiting for Emir to meander over and flop into the corner. He's always been a corner sitter. "Something keeping you up?"

"Not...anything specific." Emir glances at the telly, an ad for some random reality programme he's never watched flashing across the screen. It's just like his mum to immediately know that something's keeping him awake. He had nightmares last night for the first time in months, and it's making him a bit hesitant to force himself to bed, even with Theo there to keep him company.

Emir's dad uses the remote to lower the volume on what they were watching, his parents always willing to give him their full attention, even after their own busy days. "Is this about Theo being here?"

It's just like his dad to read his mind. They're so similar in so many ways that his dad seems to understand his anxieties before he voices them.

"A bit." Emir scratches at his cheek again, the coarse hair a reminder that he's not a kid anymore. He was barely an adult when his last relationship ended traumatically, and he's continued to grow since. "I wasn't really sure what to expect having him here, walking through the neighbourhood and showing him around because, like...the last person I did all that with..."

"Bringing back bad memories?" Natalie leans into her husband, both of them facing Emir with concerned looks. He only comes to them about this when he's struggling, usually coping as best he can on his own until it gets to be too much.

"Yeah. I wish it weren't the case, but every time I'm back home it's just...I worry who I might run into or who might remember me. And I know that's self-centred and people have their own lives to worry about, but I still panic." Emir looks around for a blanket, retrieving one from the pile that his mum keeps in a basket nearby. "It's probably the PTSD and all that, but I don't like how it makes me feel. I don't like feeling scared so often just because of what happened."

"Is it better in London?" Saleem had offered to find a new place for the family to move to after the doxxing, both for Emir's sake and their family's safety.

Unfortunately, it turned out to be almost impossible to find somewhere that didn't require the girls to change schools and Natalie to find a new job, and since Emir was leaving for Roseborough soon anyway, they'd decided together to stay put. But Saleem would revisit the topic if needed, if their family home was a consistent source of anxiety.

"Definitely. There's still triggers and some of those will always follow me wherever I go, but here...I haven't spent much time at home unless I was visiting over break, so my recent memories are still of...then. Of *him*. And having Theo here is so different than returning by myself."

Emir is fully wrapped in the grey blanket, face only barely visible so he can keep talking.

"I really love Theo and I wanted him to spend time with the family, which is why I invited him. But, like, I'll have flashes of what used to be before reality catches up. I'll feel my heart racing and I'll skip a breath before I remember who I'm with and that I'm safe. It's this, like, unstable and shaky feeling, like I'm on a very literal edge...it's worse at night."

"I'm so sorry, Emi. I'm sorry we couldn't protect you. We never wanted you to feel this pain." Saleem scoots out from behind his wife to sit beside his son instead, resting a hand on his cheek and staring into his eyes.

He leans in to leave a kiss on Emir's forehead, something he used to do as he put Emir to sleep each night until he was about thirteen and grew out of it. But sometimes it still seems right, to bless his son and remind Emir that he'll always have Saleem's love.

"You couldn't have known. I certainly didn't." Emir blinks back tears after his dad's caring gesture. As old as he gets, sometimes he just needs to be safe at home with his parents to remind him that he'll be alright and he has somewhere to return. "And I know Theo's different and he'll never hurt me like that, but it's like my body keeps me vigilant just in case. Theo's great about it, very understanding and protective, but it's not fair to him. He hasn't done anything wrong...do you think it might ever go away? All the panic?"

"I think it will." Natalie stands up as well, making the other two scoot down the sofa so she can sit on Emir's other side. He's still cocooned in the blanket, but now he's also got a parent on each side, holding him together. "Until recently, you'd been almost free of it. You still have your triggers, but even those have become more manageable. I don't want to say it takes time as if it's that easy, but it does take time, sunshine. Let Theo love you, and let yourself love him back. You've already built something beautiful."

"Last night I had, um, a bad memory. From that night when...you know. Theo was already asleep, but for some reason it was like I went back in time two and a half years. I swear, I thought I was back in *his* bedroom across town and I could hear him shouting right in my ear. My whole body got sick: chills and sore throat and nauseated. Felt like I couldn't breathe." Even now, Emir feels a tightness in his chest that distracts from his surroundings.

"I must've been crying because Theo woke up to comfort me, even if I couldn't explain what was wrong." Emir wipes at his eyes, fresh tears making their way down his cheeks. "I don't even know what triggered me this time. I wasn't on my phone or even thinking about that night. I was just...drawing."

"What were you drawing?" Natalie uses her sleeve to wipe away more of Emir's tears as he sniffles. Her sweet, sensitive kid, stronger and braver with more resilience than she would have wished for him. There's some wounds Natalie can't heal, but she can offer her shoulder to cry on.

"Last week, Saima drew this like labyrinth spiral pattern thing. Real colourful and intricate. I liked it, so I thought I'd make one for myself, just in my own style." Emir shrugs, but then he realises. Of course. "Wait, actually - when she was drawing it last week, we talked about Theo and a bit about my PTSD because she was curious so like…maybe that was the trigger. I let my brain's defences down and my subconscious brought it up again because it's been more on my mind the past few days."

Taking a deep, shuddering breath, Emir rolls out his shoulders and then his neck, running his palms along his face like a physical reset. He should've seen it. It's not always something obvious that acts as a trigger, especially when he's in a moment of introspection. The brain is a winding, circuitous route and Amanda reminded him that the best way forward is to recognise the path and try to follow a new one.

Healing takes a presence of mind that Emir's been practising the past few years, with his time for quiet and creativity and walks through nature. He always had the tools to rebuild his life, and with the help of family and professionals, as needed, he knows the way to use them. Tonight doesn't have to be like last night, or any other. He'll stay in the present as much as he can. Ground himself. With a few more deep breaths, he settles into his mum's arms. She's always there waiting.

"There we are." Saleem holds his open palm to Emir's cheek again, giving him that proud smile that Emir couldn't live without. He admires his dad more than he may ever be able to explain properly. "You know, there's a part of that night that your mum and I haven't told you about before. I don't know that it will help, but maybe when you think of that summer, you'll have a new story to remember. Or, another one to add that might lower the volume on some of the worst ones. I've been thinking about it since you told us what happened with your friend Jordan."

"Oh…alright." Emir keeps leaning on his mum, sniffling once more and drying his eyes on the blanket while waiting for Saleem to keep talking. He's not sure he wants to hear whatever it is, but he doubts his feelings about that night could get any worse.

"When your mum and I…that night, when we got that phone call from him, your mum answered, but he asked to talk to both of us. It was a short phone call, only a minute or two, but it was like time froze. As soon as he hung up on us, I panicked, worried that you wouldn't make it home. I was scrambling to find the car keys so I could drive around until I found you, but your mum stopped me." Saleem shares a look with Natalie. She nods her permission to continue.

Rambling a bit, because his own memories of that night are scrambled and upsetting, Saleem goes on. "Thing is, all he did on the phone was out you then scream at us, calling us horrible parents, using disgusting language I won't repeat, and he told us how he kicked you out of his house after you two - he was unnecessarily graphic about the details of your relationship, but it wasn't as if we didn't know you two were - we knew you were regularly spending the night, so finding out you were having sex wasn't a shock, even if I think he intended it to be. But he crossed a boundary that wasn't his to cross, telling us things that should've been private between you. Then after all the yelling, when I started running around the house in a panic, your mum thought...she thought..."

Natalie picks up where Saleem leaves off. He's run out of steam as the emotions of that night floods back. Never in his life did he want to worry about his child's safety in such a way.

"Your father kept repeating *I have to find him* over and over again, but he sounded so angry, and I assumed the worst. I thought he was about to be the kind of man I would be ashamed of. I should've known he wanted to bring you home safe, but we were panicked." Natalie kisses Emir's head through the blanket, because the only part of her beloved genderqueer son currently visible is his enraptured face surrounded by soft fabric. "I thought..."

"She thought I didn't want you to come home. That I wanted to find you and stop you from coming back, or worse." Saleem frowns, visibly upset by the memory. He can't imagine a reality where that could have been the case, but they weren't thinking clearly. He doesn't blame Natalie for immediately focusing on protecting Emir. "We usually communicate so well, but in that moment we scattered."

"I stopped him before he could leave to find you and I gave him an ultimatum. I told your baba that if it ever came to it, if it was him or you, I would choose my kids over him in a heartbeat. And if he wasn't going to support you and keep you safe, he may as well leave and never come back." Natalie reaches across Emir for Saleem's hand, glad that Emir is still between them.

"I thought your baba had a problem with your gender or with knowing that you were having sex, since that was most of what was screamed at us over the phone. He didn't tell us much, we just knew you'd come out to him in some way related to your gender and he'd tossed you out for it right after...We didn't know if you'd even had time to get dressed, or - or if you were thrown out literally naked and you were trying to get home somehow, or worse, you were thinking you couldn't come home. Our panic was all consuming. It was just layers of worry, and completely out of the blue."

Saleem nods along, watching Emir and hoping he understands why they're telling him all of this. It's important he understands that the safety of his parents' home was never in question.

"All I could think about was you wandering abandoned through the streets, trying to get home in the middle of the night, and I had no idea what state we might find you in. I could see it so clearly: your shoulders hunched in one of your hoodies, hands hidden away in the front pocket while you tried to find your way back but got lost. Or worse, I would find you hiding, shivering and afraid without your phone or anything to keep you warm and safe until I got there. It was one of the worst things I could imagine, and I was sure something awful would happen to you if I didn't find you immediately. Well, something else on top of what he'd done."

Saleem drops Natalie's hand to place his palm flat against Emir's heart. "When he called us, I wasn't worried about what your mum thought I was. I love you, beta. I just wanted you to be safe. I wasn't even thinking of being upset with you for who you are. It genuinely didn't cross my mind."

"You should've seen him, Emi. I've never seen him so upset, like the panic multiplied when I told him what I'd assumed. We had a proper row, and I'm surprised we didn't wake up the girls with our yelling. He told me you were his most precious gift, and if anything were to happen to you he would never forgive himself. It hurt your dad that I would even consider him putting anything before his children. He said that if I knew him at all, I wouldn't have even thought so." Natalie shifts Emir so she can look at him, even though it moves him from her embrace. He falls into his dad instead, still wrapped up like a very sad burrito, his wide eyes locked with his mum's. "He was right of course. But...we weren't thinking."

"Once we stopped shouting and realised we were on the same team, I ran out to the car. I don't know if you remember that I wasn't there when you came home. Your mum had to call to tell me you were safe, so I could stop looking and hurry back." Saleem wraps his arms around Emir and feels him crying softly through staggered breathing and shaking shoulders, but still so quiet. "I just wanted you to be safe. That's all I ever want. Your mum and I love you so much that we were both ready to throw each other to the wolves if it meant you'd be protected."

"I'm sorry I scared you." Emir's voice is weak and strained, sniffling through his withheld tears. As he ran home that night, frenzied and terrified, Emir realised how lucky he was that he managed to get dressed and find his phone before being shoved and kicked out the door, because the alternative was so much worse. But he didn't know his parents had worried about that, too. They never told him what his ex said to them during that phone call. "I didn't know - I didn't even think to call I just - "

"It's alright. You're alright." Natalie reminds him, running a soothing hand along his back while he cries against his dad's chest. "You had no idea he'd called us and you were completely consumed with what happened. You were deep in survival mode, just trying to get home. We were panicked, but you must have been worse. The relief when you came through that front door is like nothing I ever want to experience again."

Emir nods his understanding and lets himself be held until he cries through the worst of it. He's not upset that his parents decided to tell him about this, but he's already been on edge since arriving home for break, and the memories of those horrible weeks and that horrible night have been closer to the front of his mind. It crashes over him in waves at moments like this, memories stacking on top of each other until he finds his way around them.

Saleem gives Emi a tight squeezing hug and continues. "I wanted to tell you because you should know that I didn't hesitate for a moment to support you. I hate that he hurt you and threatened our family and I wish I could take that away. But I can't, so all I can do is be here when you need me."

He's glad to feel Emir's body relaxing a bit from how it was a minute ago. Saleem regrets that his kid has to hold all this, well aware that none of them had any indication of how Emir's ex would turn out. It's some consolation to know that Emir has wonderful people in his life now who will give him the love he's always deserved, that Saleem can worry less about any sort of repeat in Emir's future.

"I know it's a long journey, but you're not on it alone. Your baba and I are right here, right now. And even when you're away at uni we're only a phone call away." Natalie gets up to bring the Kleenex into reach, Emir's hand sneaking beneath the blanket to take a few and blow his nose. "It still hurts, I know. I think with time and with looking after yourself and seeing someone about it, it will fade away until it's only a memory and not all consuming."

"I just...I really hate that this beautiful thing with Theo has to remind me of all that. Like, I love Theo so much, but I get scared sometimes, and it's usually random. I don't want to be scared anymore. It's not rational and it feels so out of my control." Emir releases a long, shaky breath, leaning forward onto his knees and letting the blanket fall around his waist. "I just want to enjoy my time with Theo, letting you all get to know him and make new memories. I want to show him the neighbourhood without remembering being yelled at down the street. I want to bring him to the charity shop and not think about being kicked out of the cafe next door. I want to hold his hand and not worry that someone's going to hurt us. I'm exhausted and I'm happy and it's a lot all at once."

Emir knows his parents can't protect him from all that, but sometimes he just needs to say it. He needs to be frustrated and scared with people who love him and who were there when it happened. His parents were under attack almost as much as he was that summer. They certainly understand what he's talking about, and the story they've just told him solidly confirms how much he's loved. It's reassuring to know that his queerness wasn't an issue, even in the most stressful moment they've experienced as his parents.

"Could I maybe stay down here and watch something with you for a while longer before I go to sleep?" Emir asks, rubbing at his eyes and wondering if he should get his glasses. His eyes feel so tired all of the sudden.

"Of course you can." Natalie settles in, tucking Emir beside her. Saleem hands Emir the remote, giving him permission to choose what they watch.

"Love you. Both of you." Emir mumbles as he gets comfortable, head on his mum's shoulder and legs pressed against his dad.

Saleem gives his leg a squeeze through the blanket and shares a meaningful look with Natalie once Emir's distracted. There's never been a good time to share their perspective from that night with Emir, but he's glad they did. Emir should know that they would choose him in every lifetime, that they're proud to be his parents, and that they love him for all that he is, even in the worst moments.

Emir falls asleep in between his parents on the sofa, eyes falling shut just minutes after they finish talking. His parents let him sleep until the show is over, glad to have him safe and in reach. It can't always be like this, but sometimes, it's just what they all need.

***

Emir wipes at his eyes as he finally makes his way back into his bedroom. All the crying dried them out, and the discomfort reminds him of their conversation. His parents each gave him a goodnight hug, reiterating that they're just feet away if he needs them, but he thinks he'll be alright tonight. He needed to talk to them about how his PTSD has been the past few days, and now that he has, he feels significantly better.

As quietly as he can, Emir strips down to his boxers and slides into one of Theo's discarded t-shirts, glancing Theo's way every few seconds, overcome with affection. He's never loved anyone more than the curly-haired nerd currently hogging his bed. No one has ever voluntarily loved him so generously, given so much of themselves to him and trusted him with all they are. Theo's one of the most intelligent people Emir knows, always making him laugh and grounding him to his life with cuddles and affection. Also, he's incredibly fit, which Emir tries to remind him on a regular basis because compliments bring a pretty pink tinge to Theo's cheeks.

"Baby..." Emir croons, stroking the hair off Theo's forehead while climbing into bed beside him. He doesn't generally make a habit of waking Theo, but sometimes it's better than the alternative. He wouldn't disrupt his sleep if it wasn't important. "Wake up for me, princess."

Theo scrunches his face and turns into Emir, arms reaching out for him with an almost impressive lack of coordination. He's very asleep, but he knows Emir's there. Somehow, he always knows. Emir thinks back to that night when Theo held his hand in his sleep, sought the comfort of Emir's presence even without knowing, and Emir had kept that moment sacred, treated it like a living relic, drawn their hands and shared the love of that moment in a flash of spontaneity. It's still the only picture on his Instagram account.

It takes a minute of gentle coaxing, but eventually Theo blinks his eyes open to look at Emir, confusion and sleep coating his features. He has the prettiest eyes. Emir knows he's staring without shame, but it's alright. When they're alone they fall into each other and they're not ashamed by the depth of their connection.

"What's wrong?" Theo pets Emir's cheek with one of his warm hands as Emir settles beside him, face to face atop the pillows. Emir doesn't often wake him up in the middle of the night, but last night he'd been upset and Theo had woken up to the sound of Emir's crying. Something important is keeping Emir awake and he might be about to find out what that is.

"Couldn't sleep. I wandered downstairs and talked to my parents." Emir yawns and cuddles himself further into Theo. He's warm and soft and sleepy and Emir wants to be surrounded by him.

He used to wish for the type of security he feels with Theo. Everything about him reminds Emir of safety and comfort: his warm smell, his gentle touch, his kind eyes, his literal physical heat. Despite Emir's past and the echoes of his trauma, Theo is still the most wonderful thing that has ever happened to him, the best decision he ever made, the person who holds his hand while he works through his triggers, and his partner in all things who makes the most gorgeous new memories with him every single day.

Theo lets an arm fall across Emir's waist while their feet find each other beneath the sheets.

"Sad?" He studies Emir's face for clues, but in his own defence, he's barely awake.

"Yes…and no." Emir leans in to press a lingering kiss to Theo's concerned lips, resting their foreheads together and breathing him in. "I've been struggling a bit having you here. I'm so glad you came, it's just been, like, a lot of bad memories trying to fight their way in. It's always like this when I come home to visit, but it's worse than usual."

"Oh." Theo rubs at his eyes, trying to clear them so he can focus. Emir needs him awake even though sleep is trying to drag him back in. "I don't want you to be sad, Emi. If it's too much we can…I don't know, change our plans? I have my car. I can go home tomorrow."

"No!" Emir raises his voice to a normal volume before internally reprimanding himself and going back to mumbling. He doesn't want Theo to think he's upset with him. "Sorry, just, that's not what I meant. I'm tired and I'm not explaining well."

"That's okay. You're, like, really smart, even when you're tired." Theo gives Emir a sleepy smile, glad to hear Emir doesn't want him to leave. He would, of course, if that's what Emir needed. "I'll try to stay awake until you find the words, even though I'm very comfortable and you're an excellent cuddler."

"You're spectacular." Emir sighs, but this time it's happy. Two nights in a row he's woken Theo because of this and he hasn't so much as grumbled about it. "I want you here and I want you in my life, baby. I just need to be honest that I'm struggling a bit. We have to communicate, right? It's important that I make new memories here, happy memories, and I want them to include you. But I can't escape the old ones quite yet and I had a bit of an episode last night, and then nightmares after I fell asleep. So in case it happens again, I wanted you to know. I don't want to scare you or worry you. It's just...it might happen again while we're here, or even back at uni."

Theo waits for Emir to finish sharing, not wanting to cut him off mid-thought. He wondered if that's what was going on last night, but Emir had just sort of frozen while he cried and asked Theo to hold him while he kept drawing until they both eventually fell asleep. But this is the first he's heard about last night's bad dreams. "Is there anything I can do to help?"

"Nothing you aren't already doing. Just having you here is perfect. You keep me grounded and bring me joy and give me kisses and hugs, even when I'm sad." Emir leans forward until Theo gives him another kiss, reassuring him that yes, he will absolutely do that for Emir. "I just...need you to tell me that it's okay to be sad with you sometimes. Like, I know it is, but hearing it helps."

"You can be sad with me. You can be however you need to be with me. I won't hurt you and you won't leave me and we'll keep being honest while we figure it out." Theo slides a warm hand beneath Emir's shirt (technically his shirt, he notices with a grin) to rub soothing circles at the base of his spine. Emir makes a happy little noise and presses his body into Theo, kissing him again and feeling at peace. He needs this, and Theo is so willing to offer comfort.

"It helped to talk to my parents, too. They told me some new things about that night when everything went wrong and, like, they do really love me. It's another one of those things that I feel daft asking for, but it helps to be reminded. I've no idea what I'd do without them." Emir moves them to their familiar spots, laying flat on his back with Theo across his chest, tangled up and relaxed. In any bed, in any room, in any city, they fit together.

"You'll never have to find out." Theo kisses Emir's chest above his heart and presses his ear flat so he can hear that steady beat. It's a habit he's developed, listening for

Emir's heartbeat as he falls asleep, following his breathing and melting against his skin. "You've got your parents and your sisters and me and my family and Laurie and T and Gabe and Ciaran and Lilibet and Jordan and you don't have to pretend with us. If you need to cry, we'll get the Kleenex."

Theo yawns and rubs his face against Emir's chest then resettles before continuing. "I'll always have a warm blanket and a hug, and if you're really lucky, I'll make your green tea just the way you like it and put it in my thermos because I know you like it better than your own, and we can talk or paint or kiss or whatever you need until it passes. I'm here for all of you, babe. Even when you wake me up from a very good dream."

Emir laughs under his breath, stroking along Theo's back out of habit. There's tranquillity in just sharing space with him, in a way he never dared to hope for until they got together. There's no going back to before. He's here, now, with Theo, and it might be scary sometimes and he's going to have bad days, but he won't have to face them alone. There's many things that ground Emir: his art and his dancing, and now, his Theo. He'll be alright.

"Tell me about that dream in the morning?" Emir smiles as Theo grunts his agreement, already half asleep even after that little speech he just gave. He's a remarkable man and Emir loves him to his marshmallow core.

"Goodnight, baby." Emir whispers, laying a kiss on the top of Theo's head before closing his eyes and searching for sleep.

He lets Theo guide him, his warmth like a lantern, his embrace like Ariadne's string, his presence lulling Emir into a dreamless rest that's desperately needed. Sometimes he doesn't need to think, only trust and breathe.

CHAPTER ELEVEN

"Babe?" Theo rustles from his spot leaning against the window as Emir turns the car down a new road, following a different route than he's taken the rest of the week on their way to the studio. They're in Theo's car, but he doesn't mind letting Emir (or T or Gabe or Ciaran, rarely Laurie though) drive it when needed. And since this is Emir's town, he's been the one driving them most of the week.

"Princess?" Emir keeps his eyes on the road, but Theo knows that smile. He's up to something.

"Don't you have an extra class to teach this morning? The studio's the other way." Theo looks around them, not recognising this street at all. He doesn't think they've been here before.

"I don't *technically* have an extra class, but we are going to the studio early after we make a necessary stop. I have another surprise for you, but I promise it's low social energy and you don't need to have anything prepared. We'll be heading to the studio straight after for reasons you'll understand once we get there." Emir considered giving Theo a hint this morning, but Caroline and George are in on the surprise and they assured him that this one is safe enough.

"Oh...not a lot of new people or anything?" Theo asks, his hands twisting around themselves since he doesn't have anything else to fidget with in the car. He's alone with Emir, so he doesn't stop himself.

"Just one new person. Your parents know and they said I should keep it a surprise, but if it's too much, we don't have to stay." Emir always gives Theo that option, especially now that the two of them talk very openly about Theo's autism and what his boundaries and needs are.

"...Alright. Are we almost there, then?" Theo realises he can fidget with his hoodie (technically Emir's, but the two of them essentially share a wardrobe now), tugging on the strings and chewing on the inside of his cheek.

"Almost. You want to give me a few guesses? I'll tell you if you guess right." Emir turns down another side road. He hasn't been here in years, but he'd called ahead and made an appointment for today. Having Theo here is helping him deal with places he's been avoiding, especially the ones that he doesn't *need* to avoid.

"Emir, we can't have a dog yet! We talked about it, remember?" Theo panics, seeing the animal shelter a few buildings down and knowing how much Emir's always wanted one. But they can't, as much as Theo would love that. It's just not an option right now.

"It's alright, princess. We're not getting an animal today." Emir stops at a zebra crossing and glances at Theo, waiting for the panic to dissipate as the pedestrian passes in front of the car with a wave. "That would be way too much of a surprise and not fair to spring on you like this. An animal is a huge commitment. Try again. No new family members involved."

"Thank god. Not that we can't - I mean we *can't*, but - we just have to wait." Despite his knowledge of their limitations, Theo lets his gaze follow the shelter as they drive past. He can't wait until they can pick out a fluffy creature for their flat in a few months, eager for the opportunity to adopt a fur child with Emir and spoil it rotten. That's the plan anyway. "Some sort of restaurant, maybe? It'll be hard to find somewhere better than your house, if I'm honest."

Emir laughs, a sideways smile hiding exactly how fond hearing that makes him feel. The fact that their families like their partners and have gotten to know them over the uni break has been sort of unbelievable in the best way. "Nope. I wouldn't have let you spend all that time cooking with mum this morning if we were going on a food date."

"Are we...getting tattoos?" Theo searches for anything he can remember discussing recently because he's actually run out of ideas and he knew that one would make Emir laugh. Sure enough, beautiful giggles fall past Emir's lips, filling the car and brightening Theo's day. It's such a remarkable sound.

"Nah, but if Jo wants to get one, I'll do it with her. Of course, you can join us, if you like." Emir sees their destination at the end of the block, but he doesn't think Theo's noticed yet. It's sort of nondescript and hasn't changed since the late 90s. He'd be surprised if the sign outside even lights up anymore. "Three guesses and all wrong, pumpkin. But you don't have to guess anymore."

"We're here?" Theo's eyes widen as he looks around again, scanning the names of the shops and trying to piece it together. His gaze lands on a picture of a ballerina in a front window and he assumes that's where they're headed. "Dance shop?"

"Dance shop." Emir confirms, finding a spot to park towards the end of the building so he can talk with Theo before they head inside. If it's truly too much, he doesn't want Theo feeling the pressure of being around someone else when making that decision.

"You need something before we head back to uni? Usually we just order things online." Theo unbuckles his seatbelt as Emir does the same, but Emir doesn't turn the car off yet, so Theo assumes they'll be staying here for a minute. Emir doesn't like to be cold.

"Nope! It's a gift for you, shehzadi. Consider it an overdue birthday present, since we already did the Christmas thing and we missed spending your last birthday together." Emir turns to Theo and takes one of his hands, watching the way their fingers fit together before he continues explaining. "I had help from a few people to make this happen because I knew we needed to do this alone before the store opened for you to be comfortable, and I couldn't figure out a way to make it happen in London so…we're here to get you a pair of pointe shoes. If you want. We have an appointment with a professional fitter since you haven't worn a pair in a really long time."

"For…me?" Theo freezes in place, tears already starting in the back of his eyes because this is potentially the sweetest thing Emir's ever done, and he's done a lot of incredible, romantic things. He could have spent hours guessing what his surprise was and never landed here. Theo never would have done this for himself, which is exactly why Emir chose it.

This opportunity could heal Theo's inner child, patching up the hurt of losing something he was told he shouldn't have, even when he was too young to truly understand. Emir couldn't possibly know what Theo's been feeling when they work together and Emir glides past him en pointe, defying gender expectations and showcasing an entire other side of ballet that Theo can't access. He wants this so badly, but he never thought he could ask. Just hearing those words from Emir feels very surreal.

"An appointment for me?" Theo needs confirmation before allowing himself to feel everything that's barely beneath the surface.

"For you." Emir confirms, watching as Theo's eyes fill with tears and hoping that they're happy tears. He's seen the way Theo watches him tie his ribbons and helps him sew new pairs as needed with incredible care and attention. "I remember that story you told me, the first night we ever worked together. You said you learned a bit of pointe after your injury when you were younger and that you wanted to keep going but your school said no and you had to switch to a new place and everything. And I was sort of hoping…it sounded as if you'd like the chance to try again?"

"Emir!" Theo's throat feels like it's full of sand, trying to swallow past everything he's feeling, but instead just releasing the tears down his cheeks. It's a lot to process, all positive, but *a lot*. He never thought he'd get this chance again. This is more than a surprise present, this is...it's... "Emir, this is...you..."

"I checked with your parents because they were around when all that happened when you were a kid, and they thought you'd like to give it a go. Your mum even called ahead and already paid for you to pick out whatever you like. She said she owed you for all the pairs she couldn't buy you growing up." Emir reaches across the centre console to wipe a few of Theo's tears away. He's definitely overwhelmed, which Emir knew might happen.

Emir has his own complicated feelings about being a generally masculine pointe dancer, and the way that it's not actually about his gender, but if people knew he was genderqueer, they would assign causation. "Thoughts?"

Theo doesn't know what to say. His immediate thought isn't allowed, but it's the only thing in his mind. It's all consuming.

"I can't say what I'm thinking." Theo mumbles, because it's still hard to speak past the lump in his throat, and there really is only one specific thing he can think right now.

Emir tilts his head as his forehead scrunches in confusion. Did he fuck up? "Why not? Is it too much? You can tell me. I won't be mad."

"Not too much." Theo turns away from Emir and faces straight ahead, looking down at his hands in his own lap. There's still a few tears drying on his cheeks and he's practically vibrating from how badly he wants to run inside right now and try on a dozen shoes until he finds the pair that fits just right. "I just can't tell you what I'm thinking because it's a lot and I don't want to make you feel that you have to respond a certain way because it's one of those things that's, like, a reciprocity expectation a lot of the times, but it's sort of overwhelming my system, and all I can think are like two thoughts and that one's at the front."

Emir realised what Theo's rambling about before he found the end of his very long sentence, already reaching out to gently turn his face back to Emir's with a guiding hand under his chin. "You can tell me, but you don't have to."

"It's just...you're so...this is, like, the most incredible gift and only someone who, um...you know...could make this happen for me. This is really special, Emir. Like...it's not just a physical gift. It's validating me and my queerness and my love for ballet, which is a special interest, and giving me a second chance at something that was taken away from me, and it's all bringing me to the same conclusion."

Theo can't stop staring at Emir, because he knows he isn't supposed to say it and break the unspoken rule about giving Emir time to be ready, but also *I love you, Emir Ayan Shah with every molecule of my being* is sort of shutting out every other thought and function.

"If you want to tell me, I'm ready to listen." Emir takes a steadying breath, but he's being completely honest. He's still not ready to say it himself, as true as it is, but he's been finding ways around that mental block. He knows he's getting much closer to saying it and having it be the right time, and he's positive that Theo saying it right now, as it's practically bursting out of him, would also be the right thing. It won't send Emir spiralling. "I can't, um…I'm getting there, baby, I really am. I can even say it out loud when talking about you to my family and only panic a little. But as long as you're alright with saying what I'm positive you're talking around and knowing that I can't say it back right this second, then it's fine. Wonderful actually. If that's how you feel, that's the best thing I've ever heard."

"You're sure?" Theo fully turns his body sideways, his leg closest to Emir folding to join the rest of him in the seat.

He's so very, completely ready to say it, so positive it's true, more sure than anything he's ever felt before. It's not the way he loves his parents or his sisters or his friends. He loves Emir as a romantic and sexual partner, but also as so much more. Emir's his inspiration, his muse, his favourite dancer, his collaborator, the person who makes him feel safe and happy and free. Theo's in love, and it's becoming more difficult by the day not to tell Emir. And now? With this incredible gift?

"I'm sure. As long as you telling me won't make it really hard for you when I can't say it back right away. If you're ready, I don't want to stop you, because you're the only partner who could say that to me and I would believe you, which sort of makes all the difference." Emir reaches for Theo again, cradling his face to kiss him softly across the console. "I'm so glad I decided to bring you here. You're my princess, and I'm here to help you find your glass slippers."

Theo kisses Emir back, one of his hands trailing through the hair at the back of Emir's head to keep him close a moment longer. "Is that a joke because each pointe shoe is unique and moulds to fit the dancer's feet just like Cinderella's slipper?"

Emir giggles and kisses Theo again. He's the perfect man, and somehow they've chosen each other, even after everything they've been through, after everything they've put each other through. Of all the people in this wild, winding world, Emir found Theo. It took him a while, but he finally paid attention and realised what they'd been missing since they met. Thank the thousand strings that pulled them together for bringing them into this moment.

"Emir?" Theo starts again, genuinely feeling like he might split open if he doesn't get this off his chest immediately.

"Theo…" Emir nudges their noses together, glad that they're alone at this end of the car park and can enjoy this milestone alone. He knows what's coming, and instead of feeling anxious or scared, he's so happy he might cry.

"I love you, Emi. I *really* love you. I love you so much I can't stand it. I love that you thought of this and I love that you kept it a surprise and I love that you checked with my parents and I love that you know me so well you brought me here at a special time so I could have my space and be able to focus and be excited and however I need to be. I really, truly love you, Emir."

Theo's smile grows the longer he keeps talking, like the sun is filling him with its light each time he repeats that very special phrase. "That feels so good to finally say, because I mean it so completely, babe. I love you in every way. You doing this for me was just the tipping point. Thank you for letting me say it and I don't need to hear it back right now because, just like you know me, I know you, and I know you feel it even if you can't say it yet. I always know. You show me every day."

Emir's a blubbering mess, the tears hitting him from the first *I love you* and falling steadily while Theo kept talking. He's sniffling and wiping at his eyes and smiling like he's never smiled before all because his favourite person in the entire world loves him, really, truly, deeply loves him, so much that he's telling Emir knowing that his words will come later. He's patient and kind and understanding and *he loves Emir*. Theo's love for him is a miracle; it's the ground beneath his feet, the air in the sky, the salt water falling down his cheeks.

"Happy tears?" Theo asks, wiping them with his sleeve while Emir laughs and gives Theo a blinding smile.

"So happy." Emir sniffs and reaches for the Kleenex, not wanting to be this overly emotional when the two of them walk inside. They have an important task here that he doesn't want to distract from. "You're just so…earnest, you know? You tell me that, and I can *feel it*. You really mean it."

Theo nods, also reaching for the Kleenex and laughing as the two of them blow their noses and wipe at their eyes while crying their way through this milestone together. "You're the first person I've said that to as like - like in the way I mean it: not as a friend or family, but including both of those, you know? You're my first real relationship, so I guess maybe it's not - I don't know - but even so it still feels…"

"It is. It's still a big deal, baby." Emir presses a very wet kiss to Theo's beautiful lips before pulling back to sniffle one last time. "It means the world to me that you feel that way. And I hope you know I do too, and it's sort of huge that I'm ready to hear that and not panic or anything. I'm just happy. All happy all the way through."

"Could we maybe, um…" Theo's eyes drift to the shop, excitement for his new pointe shoes so bright that it's almost competition for his unbridled joy at having told Emir he loves him for the first time. Almost. "I'm just really excited…sorry."

"Don't apologise, pumpkin. That's why we're here!" Emir brushes the hair off Theo's forehead then gives him a final kiss before shifting away and turning off the car. "Before we go inside, I just want to remind you that you can be as excited and curious as you need and ask all your questions and it's not too much, alright? No mask, all Theo."

"All Theo." He echoes, ready to start crying all over again with Emir's reassurance. How did he ever get so lucky? "Love you."

Emir's smile lights up his face again, but now he's shy about it because it's giving him butterflies the way Theo says it so casually. As if it's just a thing they say when they go to sleep, or before heading out for the day, or when one of them makes the other tea. It's achingly lovely and Emir could get used to this. He wants to get used to it.

"You know what all of my colours mean, yeah?" Emir waits for Theo to nod, his own grin stretching his face with joy. He's so pretty Emir may start crying again.

"I'm red." Theo answers proudly, knowing exactly what Emir's telling him. He loves Theo too. "Ooooo do you think they have red shoes?"

Laughing so hard he has to catch himself on the dash, Emir opens his car door and steps out, waiting for Theo to join him before answering. "Probably not, but we can have a pointe shoe night with Lili and Jo and you can learn about pancaking and dyeing them and whatever else. They'll never be just right straight out of the box. But after we're done here, we'll head to the studio and get you set up. Aaaaand you get a private lesson with me to try out your new shoes once classes are over."

"I do?!" Theo hops in place for a moment, because he hadn't realised he'd get a chance to actually wear them so soon. He doesn't care that he's going to get blisters and that his feet will be so sore that he'll feel it for days. Theo's just excited to have the experience. "You're such a good teacher!"

"Thanks, baby. You're a great student." Emir takes Theo's hand for a moment before letting it drop again so he can knock on the door to the shop. It's before business hours so the door's locked, but the fitter is expecting them. "You ready?"

"*So ready.*" Theo peers through the window to look inside, an entire world of possibilities open to him thanks to Emir.

He'll never be a proper pointe dancer, but he just wants the chance to try, to learn the skill, have a bit of fun, and engage with dance on a deeper level. Plus, the shoes are pretty and there's so many pointe variations he's always wanted to learn someday. On the list of great gifts, this one's only slightly below Emir's magic appearance at his home a few days ago. Emir brings so much joy into his life. Of course he loves him. He loves Emir so bright he's ultraviolet.

***

Theo: LOOK
Theo: /picture of new pointe shoes on his feet while he sits on the floor, no ribbons or elastics sewn in, just straight out of the box/
Theo: EMIR IS THE BEST BOYFRIEND IN THE ENTIRE WORLD I LOVE HIM SO MUCH
Lili: OH MY GOD
Theo: I KNOW
Lili: IM SO HAPPY FOR YOU
Lili: YOUVE WANTED POINTE SHOES FOREVER
Emir: making you happy is my favourite thing :)
Theo: Shhhh go teach the little dancers. Let me squeal to Lili and Jo and brag about what a great partner I have. /heart eye emoji, pointe shoe emoji, boyfriends holding hands emoji/

Emir: /as you wish gif from the princess bride/
Jordan: Are you going to learn pointe with us like Emir??
Jordan: Please say yes
Theo: NOT EVEN
Theo: I was allowed to try pointe for only a few weeks as a kid, so I'm basically starting from nothing.
Theo: But Emi is giving me my first lesson once he's done teaching today :):):)
Lili: A private lesson /side eye emoji/
Emir: not that kind of lesson
Emir: behave yourselves while i'm busy
Jordan: Lili's in a mood today, so no guarantees
Lili: It's not a mood
Lili: Someone on the internet was wrong
Theo: Wrong about what?
Lili: Trans people
Theo: GET EM
Lili: I did /painted nails emoji/
Jordan: She definitely did. I'm so proud of my tiny angry sappho.
Lili: /trans rights gif/
Lili: They can catch these hands
Lili: It's on sight
Theo: Damn fucking right /flame emoji/
Theo: Okay, now back to the squealing about how I have the best boyfriend in the entire universe.
Theo: LOOK AT MY POINTE SHOESSSSSS
Theo: /picture of shoes with the elastics pinned in place, ready to be sewn/
Theo: The fitter said I have perfect feet for pointe, even if they're bigger than the average pointe dancer.
Theo: All the years of ankle and arch strengthening have paid off.
Theo: I've never been more excited to have blisters.
Lili: Did you get the beginner toe pads and all that?
Theo: Of course. Emir had me try a few things, and the fitter gave me toe spacers, too. I tried on so many pairs but these were just right :)
Lili: I can't believe Emir did this for you like wow he's really whipped
Theo: I'm a happy Teddy bear :)
Jordan: Have we not already established that the both of you are too far gone for each other? And always were even back when you were fighting?
Theo: I still like having reminders.
Theo: /pouting gif/
Lili: /eye roll emoji/

Theo: *Text you in a bit. I have to sew in the elastics and the ribbons and make sure I have everything just right. I need to be ready for my lesson!*
Jordan: *Have so much fun, Theo /pink heart emoji/*
Lili: *Emir, don't forget to take pictures and videos and whatever. Caroline will want them, and I'm sure Teddy will too. Probably George, even if he forgets to ask.*
Theo: *YES PLEASE I WANT DOCUMENTATION*
Lili: *Go sew*
Theo: *RIGHT YES OKAY BI*

***

"Baby, try to hold still or you won't have an eyebrow left when I'm done with you." Emir giggles at Theo's over exaggerated response, huffing and wriggling around but unable to stop the smile that breaks free. They have so much fun together, always, which is easily one of Emir's favourite aspects of their relationship.

"You sure you've done this before?" Theo teases, knowing very well that Emir used to put a slit in his eyebrow for almost the entirety of his teenage years and has plenty of practice. Theo's seen the pictures. Theo's obsessed over the concept. He trusts Emir.

"If you can't hold still I guess I'll just - " Emir carefully sets the razor down and tackles Theo onto his bedroom floor, tickling at his sides while the two of them tussle and laugh so hard that Emir's glad he doesn't have to worry about waking the rest of the family. They're all still wandering past his open door occasionally as they go about their evenings.

"Emir! Babe - I - hahahahaha." Theo can barely breathe through his laughter, finally managing to get on top of Emir to straddle him, holding his arms safely near his head and away from Theo's tickle spots. "You'll have to fix the tape after all that."

Breathing hard and smiling up at Theo, Emir's heart is more full than he would expect for a Thursday night in. After almost two hours of a private beginner pointe lesson for Theo, they'd returned to the Shah house, enjoyed a meal with the family, and now they're in his room, doing whatever their bi hearts desire to their appearance because the winter show doesn't have strict rules like the others.

Currently, Emir's giving them both eyebrow slits with plans to paint each other's nails later while doing face masks, but next up is their hair. Emir's planning to dye most of his pink and Theo wants to try a strip of purple temporary dye in his own hair to see how he likes it. Jordan and Lili are having a similar night several miles away, the four of them getting ready for a wild New Year's Eve in Darton with Laurie and T.

"I don't think you've ever held me down like this." Emir gives Theo a sideways grin, very pointedly pressing his hips up and into Theo's. He loves that they can play and fuck and laugh and cry and all of it adds up to the most beautiful partnership Emir could imagine.

"Your door's open." Theo laughs again, but he's definitely thought about it. They both generally prefer to have Emir be in charge when they're intimate, physically and mentally guiding them both through their sex life. But they're also both open to trying things the other way around and seeing how it goes. Is now the moment?

"Close it for a few minutes and meet me on the bed." Emir grinds upward into Theo again, which was a bad strategy on his part because it makes him groan and close his eyes when his dick meets a decent amount of friction. It feels way too good to be beneath Theo like this.

"Fine, but *only* for a few minutes. If I don't set a timer we won't end up doing any of the things we've planned, and I'm looking forward to the purple." Theo leans forward for a very quick kiss before climbing off of Emir and doing as requested, quietly closing and locking Emir's bedroom door and rejoining Emir on a much softer surface. "You look so fit with your eyebrow like that. Tough, maybe. Dangerous. But then, you're still you. It's quite a combination."

"Yeah? You will too, once I get to it." Emir pulls Theo in, carefully removing the tape he'd placed against Theo's right eyebrow a few minutes ago because it'll need to be fixed anyway, and he doesn't want any distractions while they indulge in a bit of heated dry humping before returning to their multi-step spa night. "It's so gay. I love queer coding like this."

"One sec." Theo takes his phone from his pocket to actually set a timer. He sets it for ten minutes instead of five like he planned because Emir is *delicious* and Theo loves him and kissing him is one of his favourite activities.

"Now hold my wrists above my head and make me squirm, princess." Emir waits until Theo's able to focus, but once his phone is put away, Emir makes sure they get back to what they were doing. "Get off against me while we kiss. Let me feel you all over even without my hands. I've been craving your mouth against my skin."

Theo doesn't have to be asked twice. He body rolls on top of Emir a few times, keeping himself just out of reach until he finally presses firm against him, taking both of Emir's wrists in his hands and guiding them where they belong. Emir immediately starts moving beneath Theo before their lips even meet again, desperate and horny and ready for Theo to get on with it already. Theo doesn't make him wait long.

Using his free hand, Theo drifts his fingers beneath the hem of Emir's shirt, drawing delicate patterns across his skin near where his boxers rest above his trousers. While his hands are busy, his lips press against Emir's, firm and warm and careful. He may be the one taking control of their movement, but he's still Theo, still soft and gentle and considerate. If Emir wants it rougher, they can try that another time. He's thoroughly enjoying the way Emir moans into his mouth, how he uses Theo's thigh between his legs to rub himself off, how he quivers when Theo trails his fingertips to a new section of Emir's stomach to tease and caress him.

"Fucking hell, baby." Emir groans softly, not wanting to be too loud with so many other people in the house. But Theo being so confident and direct is doing things to him. "You're so fucking good at this."

Smirking then joining Emir in another kiss, Theo doesn't respond right away. He keeps teasing and kissing and licking, biting playfully at Emir's bottom lip, then his chin, and eventually his neck, careful not to leave a mark. Not tonight. "I've had the best teacher."

In another world, Emir may be embarrassed that he's fully hard and very close to an orgasm from a few minutes of Theo on top of him, but this is new, and Theo is so *hot*, literally physically hot, grounding him with the way he presses Emir into the mattress. And with his hands out of commission, Emir can't even get himself off, just frustratedly humping against Theo's dick where he can feel it through their joggers. Knowing Theo's just as aroused while getting Emir worked up like this is incredible.

"Want me to get you off with my hand?" Theo offers, still holding Emir's wrists above his head and waiting for permission to take this a step further.

Emir groans, nodding against the pillow and using the small amount of leverage available to him to bring their mouths back together. He wants a deep, dirty kiss while Theo gets him off, their bodies hot and writhing until he finds his release.

Pressing his tongue confidently inside Emir's mouth, Theo's right hand slides into Emir's boxers, starting with pressure from an open hand for Emir to move against. He knows Emir prefers to take his time, so Theo slowly builds the experience rather than all at once, carefully moving his hand up and down before really going for it in earnest, using every trick he knows Emir likes and kissing him hard while keeping his wrists restrained. He's never had Emir like this but he really likes it. Theo can see why Emir gets so much sexual satisfaction when their roles are reversed because, while his focus is on Emir, his own dick is tenting his joggers, ready for attention at the first opportunity.

Managing to hold off his orgasm for a few minutes (impressive, honestly), Emir lets Theo explore and loses himself in the moment. It's nice to have this, too, to let Theo be so confident and bold and sure while Emir focuses on chasing his own pleasure. Theo's kisses and his bites and the way he takes ownership of Emir's mouth are exactly what he wants, making him chase and squirm and really experience every sensation. He's completely surrounded by Theo, held down and cherished while being brought to the edge.

"You're gorgeous like this." Theo mumbles right by Emir's ear, knowing how close he is to coming. He can feel it in the way Emir's abs contract, how his breathing has changed, the way his hips chase Theo's hand. He's sweaty and his cheeks are pink and Theo adores every single molecule of his existence. "I love you so bad, babe."

"Fuck!" Emir shouts, probably a bit louder than he should, given their surroundings. He comes hard inside his boxers and paints Theo's hand. Apparently declarations of love really do it for him.

He should've known that, now it's an option, Theo will definitely be reminding Emir of that love during intimate moments. Sex for Theo is so much more than just physical intimacy, the emotional and mental pieces equally as important. Of course Theo's love is louder if they're taking things further sexually.

While Emir's body recovers, his heart soars, staring at Theo with a golden intensity as he continues to bring Emir through his orgasm. Theo shifts away and slowly takes his hands back from Emir's body with a grin. That was fun. So much fun. And hot as hell. Watching Emir catch his breath, Theo brings his dirty hand up to his mouth, keeping eye contact as he starts licking up Emir's cum. He doesn't always get the chance, but he's always curious and...a bit into it.

"Theo!" Emir's eyes go wide again, watching him but too worn out to respond at the moment. He needs a few seconds to gather his senses after the scene they just had. How the fuck does he have a boyfriend who brings him to climax with an *I love you* and follows it by licking his spunk of his fingers like it's a little treat he'd been looking forward to? "Fuck."

"What?" Theo reaches to Emir's bedside table for a Kleenex, wiping away what's left and wondering if he should tiptoe to the loo to get something to clean Emir up. But Emir doesn't seem done yet, and Theo doesn't think he looks...composed enough to get away with running into one of Emir's family members.

"You. On your back." Emir sits up suddenly, flipping Theo until he's the one on the pillows and tugging down his joggers. "I'm choking on your dick until you cum down my throat. You've fucking earned the best blowjob of your life, princess."

"Oh! Yeah, that's - please?" Theo's caught off guard by the sudden change, but he has literally zero complaints. Especially because he's *really* hard, and the moment Emir's kiss-bruised lips meet the tip of his dick, his eyes roll to the back of his head and he has to scramble for purchase with his hands against the headboard. "So. Fucking. *Good.*"

Emir's boxers may be a mess and he knows that Theo's phone alarm will be going off any moment, but Theo's dick is hard and hot in his mouth and there's nothing he wants more than to see how quick he can get Theo off like this. He's already so worked up from getting Emir off, and whatever's developing in this impromptu sexual moment is leading them both down an exciting new path.

Theo's babbling incoherently, the words coming out of his mouth making no goddamn sense. They're a combination of love and lust and overwhelm, but in an exquisite way. This is only the second blowjob he's ever received, but Emir isn't holding back like last time. His hands and his mouth are very busy and it's all Theo can do to remember to put a hand in Emir's hair as some sort of grounding. He loves Emir's hair and it's familiar and soft, a reminder of where he is and who he's with even while every nerve ending in his body tingles. When Theo does finally release into Emir's mouth, Emir welcomes it like a trophy, something he's earned after the effort he's put into getting Theo here so quickly.

Literally seconds after Theo's finished, just as Emir is wiping his mouth with the back of his hand, Theo's phone alarm goes off and breaks through the music from the bluetooth speaker. Theo groans in annoyance, flailing his hand around to the bedside table to silence it before pulling at Emir's shoulders to bring him in for a cuddle.

Surprising Emir with a very deep, slow kiss, Theo wraps himself around Emir the moment he's able, continuing the kiss and bringing them both back from their frenzied state. He can taste himself on Emir's tongue and he wonders if it's the same the other way round, both of them with their partner's release fresh in their mouth. Another first that Theo adores, another memory that's equal parts love and attraction.

"You're incredible." Emir has Theo on his chest after several minutes of tender kissing, brushing his hair across his forehead while Theo rises and falls with Emir's breathing. "Few more minutes like this before we get back to your eyebrow slit?"

"Definitely. Need it." Theo kisses Emir's chest through his shirt, cuddling in closer to his neck and breathing him in. "Sorry we made a mess. You'll have to change."

"I don't mind." Emir mumbles, pressing his face into the top of Theo's hair and holding him tight. He needs this too.

"You tasted different this time." Theo has his eyes closed, letting Emir pet him while they relax. It's really nice, the way it's so easy and natural to be together. They can just exist in this serenity they've created, a balance to the adrenaline fueled orgasms of before.

"Hm?" Emir hums, his own eyes shut while his body savours the feeling of Theo so warm on top of him. Theo's need for cuddles post orgasm is one of the best aspects of their sex life.

"When I've tasted you before it was different." Theo shrugs without moving. He's sleepy, but if they have a snack and rehydrate he'll be good as new in no time. "And since I haven't, um...like, you haven't cum in my mouth yet, and I wonder what it'll taste like. Because this time tasted different even though it was on my hand like before."

"That happens. It's always a little different, but the general flavour is the same. When it's during a blowjob, the main difference is the sensation, not the taste." Emir thinks back to their first conversation about this, when Theo had been so embarrassed to even ask what it might taste like to have someone else's spunk in his mouth. To this day, it's one of the most intimate conversations that Emir has ever had and it was so early on. Theo's trust in him has always been so steady and earnest. "How'd you feel about all that? Me swallowing and then tasting yourself after?"

"Loved it." Theo sighs, letting his hand under Emir's jumper again for the comfort of skin-on-skin since they're both still fully clothed. "Love you."

"I like hearing you say that." Emir smiles softly, opening his eyes again to take in the scene.

His bed is wrecked, sheets and pillows all tangled from their writhing, the two of them still clothed but exceptionally rumpled. They'll have to clean themselves up before they can open his door again and several minutes in the loo will be needed. If they wait late enough, they can shower together after everyone goes to bed. He'll ask Theo how he feels about that, since it's not one of their own flats and boundaries might be different.

"I like telling you." Theo could so easily fall asleep like this, but he's not actually tired. He's safe and content and calm. He feels settled when he's with Emir, fulfilled and happy in their relationship. It's a really nice feeling. "Few more minutes."

"We're not setting an alarm this time. You just tell me when you're ready so I can get out of these wet boxers." Emir feels Theo's gentle laugh against his chest, savouring the connection. They'll get up soon, but for now, this is perfect.

***

"You look like a cute little strawberry!" Theo ruffles Emir's newly pink hair, still wet from being rinsed in the sink. They're saving a full shower for after everyone else is asleep so they can discreetly enjoy one together. Theo does *not* want anyone walking in on them.

"You think pink's my colour?" Emir poses for Theo a few times before winking and winding an arm around his waist for a kiss. They lean against the bathroom counter, having just cleaned up after themselves from their admittedly messy hair dye shenanigans. "Purple is definitely yours."

"Mine's just a little strand though." Theo kisses Emir back then twirls him like a music box ballerina. The pink really does suit him. "Nails while our hair dries?"

"Of course." Emir places a comfortable hand on Theo's diaphragm then darts out of the bathroom towards his room, Theo right on his heels.

Picking Emir up gracefully after months of partnering practice, Theo spins them both around while they laugh in the hallway, Natalie and Saleem grinning at the glimpse they get from their spot on the sofa downstairs. It's nice to have so much joy in their house.

"You still want to match your hair to your nails?" Emir takes one of Theo's hands and kisses his knuckles as he's set down in the doorway to his bedroom. They've already borrowed Amina's nail art stash since Emir doesn't paint his nails often enough to need his own and Theo's only done so with friends.

"Yes! Toes first." Theo grins as Emir flips his hand over and places a kiss to the centre of his palm, then the underside of his wrist before pulling Theo into his bedroom again and closing the door almost all the way.

"You like how you look? Eyebrow and purple hair and all that?" Emir asks, sitting cross legged in the centre of his room and waiting for Theo to join him.

"Not sure. It's fun but I think I need a few days with, like, different outfits and things to see if it feels like me." Theo sits facing Emir, legs bracketing him in so they can be close to each other. Emir grins and takes one of Theo's feet in his hand to examine the canvas he'll be working from while Theo keeps talking. He has a few blisters and bruises from his pointe work earlier, so Emir will be sure to carefully avoid those tender spots. He knows all too well the pain of a fresh blister after a long day in the studio.

Watching Emir mentally assemble what they'll need as he examines their supplies is fascinating, but Theo continues his thought aloud while he waits for Emir's hands to cradle his foot again. When he's with Emir, Theo doesn't overthink nearly as much, knowing that Emir is patient and wants to hear what he's thinking.

"I like the colour and the eyebrow slit feels very queer, but like, I'm not sure if this is the kind of queer that I am? Like, not that there's anything wrong with it and I'm having fun, but it's also a lot of maintenance, and you know how hard that can be for me to keep up with. Like, if I have to schedule time to re-dye my hair or carefully re-shave my eyebrow in my already full schedule, it might just be...not the right way for me to express myself?"

Emir finds the soft, pale purple amongst all the rest, not bothering with any sort of base coat because Theo only wants to wear the polish for a day or so and remove it after New Year's.

"That makes sense. Nothing wrong with trying it out. I'm glad you're giving yourself the space to do new things, and letting it be alright if they're temporary." It's a very *Theo* approach. Emir admires the grace he gives himself, and he knows it's been the work of a lifetime for Theo to find those boundaries between his own interests and what the world expects of him.

Theo watches as Emir uncaps the bottle and paints a wet stripe along his pedicured big toe then moves on to the rest. Before they tried the hair dye, they'd cleaned and trimmed hair, nails, facial hair, and whatever else, to have the boring bits out of the way. There's something very domestic and sweet about helping each other express themselves, a shared experience and an excuse to be close.

"You always make me feel like I can, you know? You're so brave with your fashion and your style and, like, you could wear anything at all and look completely at home in your body." Theo grins as Emir uses his thumb nail to remove an errant dash of colour. "I used to envy that so badly before we started working together. Like, I'd see you laughing with Laurie, wearing neon mesh on a Tuesday like it was casual, like that's just…a thing we get to do. And you looked perfect. And there I was in my black t-shirt and the same style I've had for years. I like being comfortable, but you've always inspired me, even before I really knew you."

Carefully recapping the polish and setting it aside with Theo's foot in his hand, Emir pauses, not ready to start on the other one yet even though this set of nails is done. "I've never felt particularly adventurous, but you're right. And it wasn't…it's not that I was trying to be rebellious or anything, but it's never been an accident that I dress loud and queer. But I'm also not just doing it for shock value. I think having ways to express ourselves is really important, but it can look different for everyone. So, like, if hair dye and manicures aren't your thing, that's fine. Don't feel like you have to look a certain way to be queer or interesting or whatever. You're the most interesting person I know, even in your comfortable, consistent outfits. Clothes are just…how we decorate, you know? Same with all this."

Theo nods, reflecting while he watches Emir pick up his other foot and get to decorating. Emir's right, of course, but Theo does think he could push himself slightly out of his comfort zone sometimes. Maybe he could start with borrowing different things from Emir and seeing how they feel. It's not that Theo thinks there's anything wrong with how he dresses or that it makes him any less queer if he sticks to his comfortable outfits, but getting to explore and dress up can be fun, especially if he reminds himself it's fine to try it and decide to go back to what he's already doing.

"Thank you for reminding me. You always do this: comfort me just by being honest and…real. You're such a good partner, and I don't take that for granted. I mean, just look at us."

Pausing to laugh, Theo nudges Emir with the side of his foot, not wanting to annoy him by spilling any polish or disrupting his process. "I never dreamed I'd get to spend this holiday with you, but you made it happen and you gave me the gift of trying pointe again as an adult because you listen and you understand and care about my happiness."

"Of course I do." Emir finishes Theo's toe polish, setting his foot aside with a kiss to the inside of his ankle that makes Theo smile. "It's not one-sided. You care about me more than I know what to do with. I like that we have that balance, especially after my, um, my PTSD episode last month."

"I'm still really proud of you for all that. For seeing Amanda and reaching out to Laurie for help and being honest with me when you're struggling, like when you woke me up to tell me last night. That's so important." Theo places a warm hand on the back of Emir's head and pulls him in for a kiss, careful to keep his wet toes out of harm's way, then takes the polish Emir is holding out to him. Emir's only having Theo paint his fingernails since he dances pointe far too often to paint his toes. "Black nails with the eyebrow slit and pink hair? You're gonna look so punk, babe."

"I'm a bad, bad girl who needs to be punished." Emir cackles at Theo's immediate flush, fumbling the (thankfully still sealed) nail polish while trying to compose himself. "Oh? Have I unlocked another one?"

Theo grumbles something that even he can't decipher, likely something about *Halloween*, tucking his new purple strand behind his ear and trying to will his reaction away. They literally got each other off an hour ago. He needs to behave.

"You're right, I knew from the moment you saw me in drag." Emir lets Theo take his hand in his careful fingertips. Theo isn't very practised at painting nails, so he's very focused despite Emir's recent distraction, willing himself to stay on task. "I'm safe with you, shehzadi. If you'd be open to it, that's something else we could explore. Like, I know drag is separate from being genderqueer, but it's…validating to lean into my feminine side sometimes. So maybe when we get back to uni?"

"Emir." Theo sets Emir's hand down on his knee, recapping the black polish and staring at him very pointedly. He's the one who unintentionally rerouted the conversation, but he's getting very distracted. "I've only managed a single pinky fingernail and my dick is about to bump your hand from my lap."

"I'll take that as a yes." Emir gives Theo a sideways grin and flutters his immaculate eyelashes. Theo rolls his eyes but relents, picking up the bottle of colour again with yet another grumble. Getting Theo flustered tells Emir so much about what he's into, especially since Theo is new to sex and might not know exactly what he likes yet. They're figuring it out together.

After another two fingers have been painted, Theo glances up at Emir to say, "I'm trying to focus, but I need to say that it's important that you feel safe with me and I love you and I would literally jump at the opportunity to involve that in our sex life and also please don't give me any specifics while I'm trying not to spill and permanently stain your bedroom floor because then we'll have to explain to your parents what happened and I don't particularly fancy telling them that I want you to plough me into the mattress while wearing a dress then finish me off with red lipstick smeared around my dick."

"Theo!" Emir's the one flushing now because that was a fairly specific ramble, meaning that Theo has not only thought about this, but in detail. Delicious detail. "We can - *I* can definitely do that someday. Baby, where the hell have you been keeping that fantasy?"

"Carefully tucked away along with a few others." Theo pauses with only Emir's left thumb remaining unpainted on this hand, smirking up at his boyfriend. It's not often he gets to be the one making Emir all hot and bothered, their roles usually reversed. "Just know that I'm quite alright with you expressing your feminine side. Really any side. You're fit from every angle, babe."

Sounding slightly strained, Emir clears his throat before responding. "Same with you. I'm into you in so many different ways. Like, obviously you know how into you I am and how ridiculously easy you turn me on, but maybe we need to explore dirty talk a bit more because you've clearly been holding back."

Emir tries to focus on Theo painting his thumb nail, watching the smooth strokes turning it black. Theo's very good considering he's barely had any practice. As with so many things, Theo hasn't given himself nearly enough credit for his abilities.

"We've got a whole lifetime to try new things together." Theo surprises Emir, setting aside the polish and taking Emir's free hand in his grasp instead. Emir understands why once Theo closes his lips around his pointer and middle finger, pulling them into his mouth, sucking and humming around Emir's fingers like...

"Have you been...practising?" Emir can't believe this is what painting their nails has turned into. First they get each other off with a time limit before dyeing their hair, and now this.

Theo nods, Emir's fingers still in his mouth. He closes his eyes, applying pressure and hoping he's doing this right. He really does want to blow Emir and soon, but he also wants to be as prepared as possible. Theo's still hoping that when the time comes, Emir will guide him and show him the way, as with so much else in their relationship. But right now he likes the look in Emir's eyes, the flush that's so hard to bring to the surface, the shallow breathing and fixated stare on Theo's mouth.

But Theo relents, because it's not actually the time. "I'm ready. Not, like, right this moment, but when it becomes relevant..."

"Do you have any idea what it is you do to me?" Emir uses his slightly dampened fingers to brush Theo's hair fondly across his forehead. There's truly no one else in the world quite like him. "I'm ready for everything with you."

Love, sex, marriage, kids. All of it. Everything. Emir's overwhelmed somewhere in the back of his mind, but somehow, he keeps his composure and manages not to spew those completely ridiculous thoughts into the air between them.

Dropping his naughty behaviour for now after seeing the universe flashing through Emir's eyes, Theo kisses Emir's temple instead. They have nails to finish painting.

Theo gets to work on Emir's other hand, now free of his distracting mouth, and thinks back to before things got heated, when they were having a discussion of something rather different. "What else was it you needed to say? I think I distracted us, but you were saying something about how you like to be loud and queer with your fashion?"

"It's alright, we can talk about that another time." Emir uses his spare hand to change to a new playlist, his bluetooth speaker on the windowsill providing them background noise while they chat. What Theo's asking about is a deeper conversation, more along the lines of what they'd briefly discussed on their walk the other day.

Theo pauses, glancing up at Emir and meeting his soft gaze. He always looks at Theo with so much warmth and open affection, heart eyes and smiling lips constantly drawing Theo in. There's a magic to love, to sharing your heart and your body with someone you trust, and Theo can feel it all around them in the space they're sharing. "We can talk about it right now, if you want. I'm listening."

"Mmm. You always listen. Give me a minute to gather my thoughts, yeah?" Emir tilts his head and waits for Theo to nod his agreement.

Emir would rather Theo not have to split his attention between this conversation and painting Emir's nails. He knows if Theo makes a mess with the nail polish that he'll get upset and apologise and there's no need. Emir's thoughts can definitely wait a few minutes while they gather anyway.

"I think maybe I just want my toes painted. Is that alright?" Theo finishes Emir's black polish and sets it back in the basket with the other colours. "I think I'll chip the colour if we paint my hands and then I'll start picking at it and that doesn't usually end well."

"Whatever you're comfortable with." Emir disentangles their bodies so he can stretch his back out. "Talk while our nails dry?"

With a smile of agreement, Theo rolls out his ankles and leans back on his palms, chest up and stretching his upper body after several minutes hunched forward. Like usual, the playlist Emir's chosen is a lot of music that Theo doesn't recognise, but he likes it. Emir has really eclectic music preferences, but they always fit the mood somehow. Maybe it's part of his synesthesia, associating the music with specific colours or shapes, and his mind matches them up. A question for another time, maybe.

"So, like...the thing about how I dress and the way I do my hair and all that - it's not like a reaction to what happened with my ex or anything, but it became a lot more intentional after that." Emir mirrors Theo's posture, leaning back against his hands so they're facing each other from a few feet away. "It's more complicated than just wanting to be visibly queer, but that part became more important after."

"I've seen pictures of you when you were younger. Seems like you've always been pretty into your own style. Not in, like, a bad way, you were a really cute kid. But like, I didn't really know anyone growing up who really...knew how to dress themself beyond whatever the current trend was." Theo stares at his lilac toes and smiles, moving them up and down to catch the light and appreciating how they look. Emir did a good job.

"I've always found clothes and makeup and all that really interesting, even as a little kid, but I didn't really lean into it until I was a bit older. Around school age, when I started realising other things." Emir sighs, wanting to brush a hand through his hair but stopping himself to avoid ruining his manicure. "I started noticing I was different from the other kids, and not just in one way, right? Like, I wasn't white, I didn't have an English name, I didn't celebrate their holidays - not really - I did ballet instead of football, my family didn't have a lot of money…and this was all before I realised I was bi or genderqueer, but even that young, I had crushes on boys as well as girls, and I learned not to talk about it. So like…"

Theo sits up and crosses his legs carefully. His toes are almost dry but he doesn't want to take any chances. "Were the kids at school mean to you?"

"Not, like, bullying or anything. They were racist and homophobic, and it was all shit they learned from their parents. But no, I wasn't bullied like you, though the same kids that were saying shit to me were definitely bullying some of the other kids." Emir sets a hand on Theo's knee. They're not talking about Theo's childhood right now, but he doesn't want Theo to think he's minimising what he went through. Since the night where he first learned about Theo's school years, they've talked more about the bullying and it was awful. Emir will never understand how kids can be so cruel.

"And that's why you decided to experiment with your clothes? Or maybe not experiment, but like, be creative and not just wear what everyone else was?" Theo appreciates Emir's reassurance, knowing this conversation isn't about him, but recognising it may still hit deep. They both struggled growing up, but for very different reasons.

"It's like this: If a white kid can't focus in class, they need to be challenged. If a brown kid can't focus they have discipline issues. If a white kid has trouble at home, they're offered support. If a brown kid has a complicated family situation, they're expected to sort that out at home and not carry it to school. If a white kid makes a mistake, it's just a mistake. If a Muslim kid makes a mistake, they're dangerous. The Christian kids have all their holidays off, but the Muslim kids, and the Jewish kids, and all the rest? We have to ask for excused absences and get penalised for skipping class. Do you see where I'm going with this?" Emir doesn't know that he's explaining himself well, but it's also a complicated issue. Well, not complicated, because it's bigotry and discrimination which are disgustingly simple, but it's multi-layered and the prejudice compounds through history. He's just dealt with his own small window to it through his own life.

"I'm not sure I see the connection yet, but I'm still listening. If you'd rather me look into this on my own or, like, have me do some reading or something, I can do that. It's not your job to make it make sense to me." Theo never wants Emir to feel like it's his burden to help Theo learn about the injustices of the world, but at the same time he's always willing to listen to Emir's thoughts and let him share whatever it is he needs to.

"I think in this case, I'd rather just explain what I can since it was a personal decision, even if it came from a place that affects way more than just me." Much like the other day on their walk, Emir deeply appreciates that he knows he's safe to have these conversations with Theo, and that even where Theo's knowledge or understanding may be lacking, he's never defensive or anything like that. A lot of people could learn how to be better allies and partners from him.

"So, like, when we were kids, a lot of times we were told, either directly or heavily implied, that it'd be easiest if we kept our heads down, worked hard, didn't attract attention, kept to ourselves. And our families and communities have very good reasons for giving us that advice. For our literal physical safety, sometimes it's necessary, even though it shouldn't be. Like, we grew up in a really Islamophobic society at a very specific time, when anyone with a name like mine who was visibly different was taught to be scared at a very young age, and that can really fuck with a kid's self perception. It can fuck with a lot of things."

Theo doesn't really have anything to say to that. He'll never understand that specific experience, even if he's dealt with his own similar "advice." As an autistic person, he's often been taught ways to fit in or code switch to appease neurotypical ways and systems. What Emir's talking about is different, but there's similarities. But he also knows it's *not* the same, and telling Emir he understands wouldn't be accurate or helpful.

"My parents sort of gave us a choice. They explained what they could about how people might treat us and why, even if it didn't make sense when we were young. Not that it makes sense now, but you know." Emir shrugs, shifting to sit with his legs crossed, his knees matching up to Theo's.

Emir takes one of Theo's hands in his own and interlocks their fingers, comforted by his warmth. His presence soothes Emir to his core. "But they also told us that it was up to us. We're our own people and their job was to protect us and love us and let us make our own decisions. Within reason, like they wouldn't have let us do anything dangerous or illegal. But, like, when I first said I wanted to dye my hair? Mum and Safiya sat me down in the kitchen and helped me bleach a streak near the front that same night. And when I was shopping for clothes, my parents never told me off for choosing something too colourful or *girly* or whatever. I had a few skirts back in sixth form, even if I didn't wear them to school. But there were a few concerts I went to where I wore a mini skirt over skinny jeans and neither of my parents cared or told me I shouldn't. I used to paint my nails and Safiya would help me with makeup sometimes, and my family never even flinched in their support."

"I'm really glad you have the parents you have. And your sisters." Theo takes Emir's free hand to match the other so that they're holding hands atop their knees. It's a reverent pose, like this conversation is a form of prayer. It's certainly a practice in knowing, an exercise in empathy and trust.

"Me too. I love them and I wouldn't be who I am without them." Emir looks up to meet Theo's eyes, but Theo's watching where their hands meet, a very focused expression holding his features. "What I'm trying to explain is that for me, people already pointed out how different I was. There was no fitting in or looking like everyone else, so even as a kid, I just sort of thought…fuck it. If people are going to stare, I may as well like what I'm wearing. If people are going to comment on my hair, I may as well style it the way I want. And I'm not saying that my way is the right way, or anything like that. But being bold and creative with my clothes and my appearance gave me a real sense of identity, and it could be one that I chose for myself. Unlike all the other reasons people would single me out, this one I had some control over. And I know that control is an illusion and I'm fucking lucky to even have the option and the ability to live the way I do. But I still think it matters. It helps me feel at home in myself."

Theo thinks Emir's done talking, so he looks up to see him already staring, waiting for their eyes to meet. Surprising Theo, Emir leans forward for a slow, warm kiss. A kiss for its own sake, just a way to feel connected. Theo smiles after a moment without disconnecting his lips, dropping Emir's hands to hold him instead, one hand in the back of Emir's newly pink hair, the other warm on the small of his back.

"That was all for tonight." Emir stays in Theo's space, foreheads pressed together and eyes closed, mumbling now instead of talking properly. "I'm still adjusting to having a partner who encourages me to talk about these things, but it helps. It really helps. I need to have someone to talk about it with, and I'm happy it's you."

"I'm glad." Theo moves his hand soothingly along Emir's back and holds them in the moment together, finding the words he's looking for. "I appreciate the trust you give me when you tell me about all of this. We have such different backgrounds, and I can love you to the ends of the earth, but I'll never actually know what it's like to be you. I promise to keep listening and learning and giving you space, as trite as that sounds."

"That's all I'm asking." Emir pulls away so he can lay on the floor instead, dragging Theo to lay with him. Theo's head stays on his chest while they move together, sharing peace and quiet and something unnameable, and Theo is exactly who Emir needs. *I love you*, he thinks, cradling Theo's head above his heart and letting them both relax before moving forward with their evening. "You want to watch telly with my parents before we call it a night?"

"Somehow, yes." Theo laughs from his spot on top of Emir. He doesn't know that Emir does it intentionally, but he seems to build in transition time for Theo, which makes everything so much easier. Emir really understands him at the deepest level. He hopes Emir feels the same with him. "Is it weird that I actually like spending time with your family?"

"Maybe it'd be weird for other people, but we're both such family lads, I think it'd be weird if we didn't." Emir breathes in Theo, the smell of his hair, the weight of him, the heat he's always emanating. "Few more minutes of cuddles while our nails finish drying then we can join them on the sofa."

Theo makes a happy noise of agreement and settles in to do exactly that. Emir strokes his hand along Theo's back and grounds himself in the moment. He's feeling so much better than yesterday, and he knows this feeling isn't forever, but for tonight, he's safe and loved and comfortable. As Emir keeps healing, he knows there will be many more nights like this in his future.

CHAPTER TWELVE

It's misty and damp and *winter*. Theo and Emir have only been in Darton for less than an hour, but they've already left the comfort of Laurie's dad's house to make a very important detour. T is standing in front of an open barn, Laurie wrapped around them from behind, pressing a kiss to their neck while they both stare expectantly between their friends. Theo and Emir are here as part of their wedding party, scoping out the venue they've tentatively agreed on and acting as moral support while they finalise such an important decision.

"So...thoughts?" T keeps staring, leaning back against Laurie as much as they can given the many layers of winter coats between them.

"How many people have you invited?" Theo asks, hand held in Emir's because they've been taking a tour of the farm and Emir thought it might be the best way to keep Theo from wandering off. It's an exciting place with a lot of animal distractions. He gets it.

"None yet, technically." Laurie answers, stepping out from behind T but placing a protective arm around their waist. "We wanted all the details decided before we send the invitations, but there'll be at least a hundred."

"It's not a real venue, but we're skint uni students and our parents are already doing too much for us. This place could work, I think. They hold events here sometimes but we'd be the first wedding." T starts gesturing around as they talk, trying to illustrate their vision to the others. "I'm thinking: ceremony over there between those trees, because if we time it right, we'd get the sunset. And we could take pictures with all the animals and the scenic hills and then everything else will happen in the barn with plenty of space for people to walk around and do whatever they want if they don't feel like dancing. If we stick to just the area by the storage barn it won't get too muddy and the owner even said we could come by all week beforehand to decorate so we wouldn't have to hire anyone else to help us. I think that's only because Sara helped deliver their kid last year, but I'll accept the perk if it's offered."

"I think it's perfect." Emir tugs Theo along by his hand and walks towards the barn, waiting for the others to follow. They have a lot of people who want to celebrate their wedding, so a big, open venue like this is ideal. "So what's the plan for in here? Food and dancing?"

T and Laurie spend the next half an hour talking Emir and Theo through their plans for the space: where they want to hang fairy lights, how they plan to arrange the tables they'll need to rent, the way they'll leave room for dancing and how they want their love represented with the decor. They've already decided on the food and basically everything else after months of debate, but it helps to confirm all the details in the space they'll need to assemble. Theo and Emir mostly just listen and let them talk, absorbing their excitement while glad to be included in the process.

"My mum and Suzanne already like the place, but since you're part of the younger crowd and you're our best mates, we wanted your opinion. Gabe and Ciaran are busy being international homosexuals, so I'll just have to send them pictures." Laurie walks them all back out of the barn and closes the door most of the way. The owner said he'll lock everything up again when they're done, but there isn't any rush. It's winter. The farm is quiet.

"What about the ceremony space?" Theo starts wandering towards the aforementioned trees, already assuming what setup they've planned based on what the fiances shared back in the barn. Something simple yet stunning, artistic but grounded.

"Should we?" T mumbles to Laurie, darting their eyes over to their friends but waiting for Laurie's agreement on something.

"Think so, yeah." Laurie gives T a fleeting kiss then waves his hand as if to say *go on then*.

"So...this isn't actually going to be our wedding ceremony." T is rocking on their feet, playing with their hair and looking back and forth between Theo and Emir with bright eyes. Their excitement is nearly tangible, bright energy rolling off of them in sunbeams. "Not technically."

"...What do you mean?" Emir snags Theo by the hand again because he was about to walk over and start examining the trees. But whatever T is telling them is too important for wandering. They can admire the ceremony (or apparently their not-technically-ceremony) space in a minute.

"We're getting married the night before." Laurie's smile is somehow even brighter than T's. It's obvious they created this plan together and are extremely happy to finally share it. "It's a complete secret that only our parents know, but we're waiting until midnight the night before and we're going out in my mum's garden and saying our vows. Lucy is officiating for both and we're doing it the way we want with just you two and our parents and siblings. No one else."

"I'll get to wear what I want and we can say our vows more honestly if it's just our closest people, and it also takes, like, all the pressure off the more traditional ceremony." T glances around at where they are, taking a deep breath before continuing. "The whole big to-do with all the relatives and whoever isn't really our thing, right? But we also want to involve our families and we're not, like, against it. So we'll have our actual wedding privately at Sara's house, and then the next day we'll have our public one with the walking down the aisle and official pictures and a big dance party."

Emir drops Theo's hands to throw himself at Laurie, pulling him into a very tight hug as Laurie immediately holds him back. Theo follows suit, pulling T into an embrace until the couples switch and everyone has had a good cuddle. The moment called for it.

"I can't think of anything more *you* than having a secret wedding under the moonlight at your mum's house." Emir tugs Theo back into his side and snuggles up against him. "And I still think this place is perfect for the big ceremony. Plenty of space for everyone."

"It's relaxed and outdoors and more casual. It's…more you than the traditional wedding venues." Theo confirms, setting his head atop Emir's where it's nestled onto his shoulder. "You two already have your outfits picked out then?"

"I've got some ideas. Making mine myself, of course, but Laurie wants to buy his since I don't really have time to make four to six wedding outfits in between finishing uni and planning the rest of the wedding and all that. Even with help." T purses their lips expectantly until Laurie gives them another quick kiss. They're so in love it's astonishing to anyone who doesn't know them properly.

"Emi, if it's not asking too much, I was thinking you might want to help with some of the decor? You have an artistic eye for that sort of thing and I'd really appreciate the help." T moves over towards the ceremony space and points up towards the trees. "I was thinking of having tapestries or just fabric in our wedding colours sort of draped in the branches with some second set of fabric to accent? Like, it'd be framing where we'll be standing without distracting from the sunset or from us, and we could reuse everything in our flat eventually."

Emir follows T immediately, Theo and Laurie staying where they are several feet away and letting their partners get wrapped up in the planning.

"Not to have you think we only invited the two of you to ask a round of favours, but we'd really appreciate your help with some organising and logistics and that sort of thing. You and your spreadsheets would be a huge help, if you don't mind?" Laurie nudges Theo with his elbow, already positive that he'll agree. "Also, we may want some choreography for the first dance, but that can wait."

"Literally whatever you need. Always." Theo grins down at Laurie, then refocuses towards where Emir is chatting quietly with T under the trees. They're clearly having detailed conversations about exactly what T envisions for the outdoor space. Whatever they decide, it's going to be incredible. "We could sit down when we get back to Bill's house and put some things together on my laptop. Let those two look through sketches and whatever else and maybe we start organising all those details you mentioned earlier? We have an hour or so before the others show up and your dad said we could have the run of his house for the day."

"Thanks. So glad you're my best mate." Laurie puts his hand on Theo's shoulder and gives it a squeeze. "You and Emir, both. It's an entirely new world with you two together, you know? A few months ago you couldn't even be in the same room, and now look at you."

"Suppose it was sort of inevitable. At least, I think it was for me." Theo smiles down at his shoes, trailing the toe of his boot through the mud. When it's time for the actual wedding at the end of June, the weather should be much nicer, but even on a soggy, cloudy day like today, the place has a very specific charm.

"For Emir, too. You were always the direction he was headed, long before he realised." Laurie lets his eyes wander back to his fiance and Emir where they're now laughing about something he could only guess. "You two have your own thing that's nothing like ours, but I can tell you're not temporary. You really love each other, but you love the real person you're with and not some imagined, future partner. Couldn't create anyone better for either of you if I tried."

"That's enough of that." Theo laughs, shoving Laurie playfully but he's smiling so wide it hurts. Laurie knows them both so well that his comment is sincere. Almost too sincere for an offhand moment. "This is your wedding we're here to plan, not ours."

"Damn right it is." Laurie shoves him back until the two of them are engaged in an upright scuffle. T gently scolds them to behave themselves or they won't stop for Nando's on the way back to the house like they promised. Even though Theo's the one who drove, it gets them to pause their wrestling match and rejoin their partners, looking pleasantly dishevelled.

They take their time to finish surveying the barn and surrounding area then head back toward the parked car near the entrance. They have a whole day and a very long New Year's Eve night ahead of them. Laurie catches up to Theo outside the car to mutter, "I don't think your wedding is far off, mate. No rush, you just come talk to me when it's time."

With a wink, Laurie opens the door to the back seat for T and follows behind them. Theo just shakes his head and laughs, but his chest is warm with the certainty that Laurie is probably right. There's Emir in his passenger seat, sticking his tongue out when Theo glances his way and connecting his phone to the car to start a playlist, and Theo is so in love he barely knows what to do with it.

"So. Nando's." Theo starts the car and checks the mirrors before shifting out of park. "Everyone get your orders ready so we don't have a fight when we get there, and someone please text Lili and Jo to find out what they want."

Emir waits until Theo's driving then sneaks his hand over to Theo's where it's resting on his knee and interlocks their fingers. Theo glances his way and mouths *I love you*. Emir grins and watches Theo's profile for the rest of the drive. Laurie and T keep talking about wedding details and Theo contributes an occasional sound of agreement while Emir just takes it all in.

They're a family. That's the feeling settling in his chest and keeping him steady. These beautiful souls are Emir's family as much as the one he was born into.

When the drive is over and they're jumping out of the car towards the promise of food, Emir latches himself against Theo's side without any sort of explanation. Theo just kisses his temple and winds an arm around his waist. He feels that same spark inside. He knows.

***

"You sure about this, babe?" Lilibet is holding firm to Jordan's right hand while her left is carefully placed palm up just inches away from a poised tattoo machine.

"Completely." Jordan grins up at her girlfriend, her eyes sparkling with more than a hint of rebellion. She's doing incredibly well, all things considered, less than a week after her life exploded.

"Just tell me when." Ollie, one of Laurie's mates from growing up in Darton, has been an apprentice at this tattoo shop for about a year now. He's almost ready to be an artist on his own.

Laurie reached out after talking with Jordan and Emir to see if Ollie would be up for some last minute New Year's Eve tattoo work. So here they all are at four in the afternoon, Jo and Emir about to be permanently decorated.

Jordan glances down at the inside of her left wrist, sees the temporary ink of the lesbian symbol waiting to become permanent, and nods her permission, squeezing only a little bit tighter to Lili's hand once the needle first makes contact. She'd chosen that location so it was always in view, but easy enough to cover up for dance performances with a bit of red lipstick and a coat of foundation.

"Could you, um, could you distract me?" Jordan looks around at the rather crowded room, Laurie with T in his lap in the corner, Emir sitting casually on the other bench next to her with Theo pacing the floor behind him, and Lili dutifully at her side. "Tell me about the wedding venue?"

She winces as Ollie works, but follows the conversation, Lilibet reaching over and trailing a soft hand across her cheek when she cringes especially hard for a moment. There's more painful spots to get a tattoo, but the wrist isn't easy, especially for her first. Luckily it's just an outline, meaning only a few minutes of discomfort.

"Done." Ollie sets aside the tattoo machine and waits for Jordan to assess his work. It was a simple enough design, but knowing it was her first tattoo changes how he approaches the interaction.

Jo releases all the air in her lungs and moves her wrist side to side, taking it in as her smile grows. "It's fucking perfect."

There's a quick layer of Saniderm expertly applied by Ollie's steady hands before he stands up to stretch. He peels off his gloves and starts fussing around to change out all of his equipment to get ready to work on Emir's new ink. Luckily, it'll be a similar design. "Let me take care of Emir and then I'll give you both the aftercare instructions and all that."

"Can I see?" T asks, eyes wide from their spot across the small room. Jordan holds her wrist in the air proudly, posing and flipping her hair, her new pink highlights flash through the air with grace. Her wrist stings a bit, but the pain is over. "Nice."

"You happy, Jo?" Lili takes Jordan's hand in her own, palm up like it had been on the table, and really gets a good look at it. She absolutely hates needles, but the tattoo machine looks totally different than medical ones and she doesn't mind watching it happen to other people.

"Definitely." Jordan waits for Lili to glance up then kisses the corner of her mouth, as if it wasn't just days ago that she was thrown out by her parents for being queer. As if she has nothing at all to fear anymore. It's sort of a miracle for her friends, and for Lilibet, to see Jo so openly herself. She's traumatised as hell, but she's also free in a way she's never been. It's a whole new phase of her life.

"Can I know what you're getting now?" Theo turns his attention back to Emir and lets Lili and Jordan have their moment. Laurie and T are busy flipping through Ollie's portfolio because apparently they'll be coming back next week to get something matching before visiting T's family in Middlewich. They just haven't decided what yet. "I've been patient."

"Well...I wasn't positive I was ready and I almost changed my mind and switched to something else. But Jordan inspired me to be brave so..." Emir takes his phone out of his pocket, aware at this point that all eyes are on him. Not that this is really news to most of the people in this room, and he'd sent Ollie the picture yesterday via Laurie. "It's the genderqueer symbol. Or, like, it's one of them. There's not just one but this is the one I use."

Theo looks at the picture Emir's showing him: a circle with an arrow pointing straight out of the top, with a horizontal line through the arrow. He's seen Emir draw this before, sometimes doodling it on his own skin with a pen or incorporating it into one of his art pieces. "On your other hip?"

"Yeah, across from my name." Emir clears his suddenly dry throat and takes his phone back to stow it in his pocket again before realising it will definitely be in the way and sliding it into Theo's jogger pocket instead. Theo just smiles and gives him a hug, holding him close.

"Do you want me to, like, get everyone to leave so you can have a moment? I think they, um, they probably heard that, but still." Theo mumbles, quiet enough that only Emir can decipher his words.

"Nah, it's alright. I'm fine with Lili and Jo knowing, and the others have known for a while." Emir sighs, letting the feeling of being out to two more people - technically three if he includes Ollie - settle into his chest. It feels…fine. Completely fine. "Actually…"

Turning himself so he's still in Theo's grasp but facing the rest of the room again, Emir scratches at his growing beard and waits for the others to stare at him expectantly.

"I'm genderqueer. Like, most of you already know, but I'd rather say it on purpose so you know I've told you and I'm alright with you knowing. But, like…it's just you and my family I've told. I might tell Ciaran and Gabe when we're back at uni, but…yeah. Just seemed like the time to say it out loud since you're all here while I'm getting the symbol inked onto me or whatever."

Theo continues to embrace him from behind while T and Laurie give Emir understanding smiles from across the room. They know what it cost for Emir to get himself to a point of being here: able to come out to new people and not have it be a big deal.

"Does this change anything? I mean like," Jordan drops her hand from Lili's grasp and steps closer to Emir. "Should we use different words for you or anything?"

"No, Emir is great, but Emi is good too. And I don't really care what pronouns people use for me, but to stay private, I just have people use he/him around everyone else and, like, in general. I'm not offended by being called a man or other masculine terms even if it's not, like, the whole truth of me." Emir feels Theo press a gentle kiss on the underside of his jaw, still held in his arms. The safety of Theo's love is an integral part of his certainty in sharing this. "But I appreciate you checking."

"Has Mrs. Shah-Palmer been supportive?" Lilibet asks, tugging Emir out of Theo's arms and into her own for a bracing hug. Her tiny arms are way too strong for her slight build, but it's how he's always known her. "I can fight."

"If you mean me, then yes." Theo huffs and crosses his arms over his chest. "And you can't just steal him from me whenever you like."

"Only borrowing." Lili teases, letting Emir out of the hug and dropping herself into Jordan's vacated chair. Emir will need to lie down on the bench, so she's not contaminating the soon-to-be-work surface.

"For what it's worth, I appreciate you trusting me with this." Ollie's ginger hair bobs up from where he'd been kneeling to fish a few supplies out of the cabinet in the corner. "Figure you trust me cuz of Laurie, which is fair. But I won't post these on Instagram like I normally would. You don't have to worry about that."

"Thanks." Emir gives him a grin and makes his way back over to the bench to lay down, taking Theo with him by the hand. "I'm not stripping in front of all of them, but I'll make sure you have room to work."

Ollie nods and goes back to what he was doing, letting Emir get comfortable as the others move around him.

"Are you finally sending Ciaran a tasteful dick pic after this? Show off the new ink?" T asks with a devious smile, still happy in Laurie's space and with the photo book open across their lap. "I think it's warranted."

"Suppose I might." Emir stretches out with his arms above his head, joggers and boxers pulled so low that the penis in question is literally at risk of peeking out if he scoots even an inch lower on the bench. His toned abs and the hair leading down his stomach are all on full display, and Emir catches Theo staring. "Tease him a bit."

"Maybe while we get ready to go out?" Theo takes the other seat next to the bench, the one not currently occupied by Laurie and T's entwined limbs or Lili's small frame. He *needs* to be close to Emir, especially when he's just *stretched out* like some print model waiting for the camera. "You'll have to be careful what you wear tonight so it won't press against your new tattoo."

"Maybe I'll just borrow a dress for the occasion." Emir laughs as Theo flushes all the way through the roots of his hair. Maroon is such a beautiful colour on him. "Only kidding, princess. I'm going for something high-waisted so the waistband sits well above it. I thought ahead."

"I'll try to match the size and placement of your other hip, but there's still a bit of nuance." Ollie has a few print outs of the genderqueer symbol in his gloved hands, ready to get started when Emir is. "Which of these do you think?"

Emir points to one sort of in the middle of the options, not quite as thin as Jordan's outline had been, but not quite as chunky looking as the thickest option. "Try that one and let me get a look at it?"

Ollie preps Emir's skin and applies the temporary mark, waiting for Theo to take a picture to show Emir so he can evaluate if it's what he wanted. It's a very personal tattoo and Ollie wants to get it exactly right for him.

"Looks great. And, um," Emir sits up on his elbows and leans in so only Ollie and Theo can hear him. "I sort of have a thing for the pain, like, just a bit, so sorry if - "

"It's alright. I appreciate the warning, especially given the location, but you're definitely not the first." Ollie keeps his voice low but darts his eyes over towards Laurie and T for just a moment. "You're not even the only one in this room, but I think you already know that."

"Unfortunately, we all know too much." Emir laughs, laying back down and moving his arms above his head again, but with one palm open. "Pumpkin? Hold one of my hands?"

Theo leans down to kiss Emir so quickly their lips barely brush, then scoots his chair closer so he can be sitting near Emir's head, hand already finding its way to Emir's to interlace their fingers.

"Shouldn't take much longer than Jordan's." Ollie holds his tattoo machine in place and waits for Emir to nod his approval to start. Emir takes a steadying breath then nods and Ollie gets to work.

"Can I take a picture for Gabe and Ciaran while we wait?" Laurie asks, phone already in hand. "I want to watch them gay panic, even from a distance. I'm bored."

"You're always bored." Emir rolls his eyes, settling into the feeling of the needle pressing into his skin. He's only had one other tattoo, but he prefers this experience to his last. He's in a much better mindspace, for one. But he also has Theo and his friends and it's sort of nice. Almost meditative. "But sure. Go ahead."

Then he relaxes back against the bench and shuts his eyes, Theo's other hand brushing across his forehead and into his hair. He'll have to remember this feeling for later, when he can be alone with Theo and whisper all those soft, sappy things that he keeps warm in his heart. He saves it for when he can do something about it, kiss his love into Theo's skin and watch it ripple through his beautiful body.

"Thank you, baby." Emir mumbles, eyes opening just enough to watch Theo smile in response. Theo stares back for a moment then trails his fingers over Emir's eyes, closing them for him. Emir silently wills Ollie to take his time so he can extend this moment a bit longer. Just until he's memorised the shape of it in his soul.

***

Emi: /picture of his hips taken from his own vantage point, boxers so low a good portion of his dick (though not the entire shaft) is showing between his two tattoos/
Emi: as promised
Ciaran: HOLY FUCK
Ciaran: GABE CHECK YOUR PHONE
Ciaran: /three siren emojis/
Ciaran: /screaming gif/
Ciaran: Theo, respectfully, I may have to steal your man.
Ciaran: At the very least drool a bit and whine about how hot he is
Ciaran: Potentially some barking
Gabe: Yeah, I'm not entirely sure I'd be able to handle seeing that in person
Gabe: Theo, where the hell do you find the ability to do anything but stare?
Gabe: Probably best I'm still an ocean away so I have a few days to process because holy fuck
Theo: No stealing, but we could discuss temporary sharing.
Theo: On Emi's terms, of course.
Emi: /side eye emoji/
Laurie: Told you he had a nice cock
T: His dick isn't even in the picture
T: Well...not all of it
Emi: i'm not sending an actual dick pic
Emi: this isn't grindr
Emi: our beloved ciaran heath would never recover
Ciaran: REAL
Emi: you can see it in person when we get back
Emi: if you ask nicely
Theo: Can I see it in person sooner?
Gabe: /two front facing eye emojis/
Gabe: /raising hand gif/
Gabe: Without this sounding like literal porn, I'll show you mine if you show me yours

Emi: If thats your way of asking for a circle jerk when we're back you'll have to check with theo and the others but knowing them they're already on board
T: Obviously yes
Theo: I'll think about it. Maybe in a few months.
Laurie: Did you really take that picture from my bed?
Emi: where else was i supposed to sprawl out and pull my boxers down at bill's house???
Laurie: The mattress that you and Teddy are using tonight???
Emi: there's no sheets on it???
Theo: I'll make it up before we go out so we don't have to worry about a fitted sheet later.
Laurie: Nah it's fine i'll do it in a minute
T: Are you two going to be gone long?
Theo: Just for a few minutes. We needed a walk.
Laurie: You sure you didn't need a wank?
Theo: /gif of a cat flinching away from a squirt bottle/
Laurie: Good try. Still picturing you two in my bed
Emi: surely you two can find a way to entertain yourselves in our absence………
Laurie: I prefer to take my time
Theo: /three side eye emojis/
Gabe: Still can't believe you're all going out without us /crying emoji/
Ciaran: Make it up to us?
T: I think something could be arranged
T: /selfie with Laurie on the same bed as Emi's picture, T laying back against Laurie's chest/
T: Nap time while we wait for our two wanderers to return
T: Lili and Jo are busy getting ready with Ruby's help
Laurie: Casey's helping too
Laurie: But you're right, mostly Ruby
Gabe: Send us pictures tonight? I want to live vicariously
T: Of course :)
T: We miss you two too
T: Hahaha tutu for the ballet boyfriends
T: /ballerina gif/
T: /kiss emoji/

***

"I thought we were going to a gay bar?" Theo asks as they, apparently, approach their destination. Lili drove them all in her parent's car since she won't be drinking, but they're sort of just…in a neighbourhood. They're approaching a corner lot, but still.

Even though it's New Year's Eve, it's half ten and there's hardly any noise to be heard. It's hard to imagine there's a thriving queer scene on this quiet street.

"This is Darton, mate. Jim's is it." Laurie gives Theo a very dry smile, one arm around T's waist, the other waving to someone off to the side of one of the houses. "Trust me. You'll love it."

Emir slides his hand through the hair at the back of Theo's head and pulls him close to press his lips against his jaw. Theo looks incredible in his fitted black t-shirt and snug jeans. His beauty isn't anything new, but to Emir, it's still a revelation. "We can have fun anywhere, baby."

Theo flushes as Emir giggles, all of them following after Laurie and T until they're close enough to the house to hear music. Loud, bright, gay music. It's enough to distract Theo from the feeling of Emir's fingertips sliding beneath his shirt just to be able to touch him. They've been inseparable all day, something about the visit to the wedding venue and it being the second to last night they'll spend together before uni starts back up in a little over a week.

"Alright, Darren?" Laurie keeps T in his grasp but leans forward to give a cheek kiss to the person who'd been standing by the door. T follows suit a moment later. Clearly, they've been here before. "Brought a few mates this time."

Darren gives them all an appraising look before shaking his head fondly and giving Laurie a sideways smile. Their silent conversation addresses everything from their mysterious shared history to a crystal clear, nostalgic pride that Darren directs at Laurie. "Plenty of room for everyone, Laur. Happy New Year."

"See you in there?" Laurie asks, holding open the side door and ushering them in while waiting for an answer. "You still owe me a song."

"Behave, or I'll be ringing your mum." Darren waits for Laurie to disappear inside with the others before turning back to face the street. He's the closest thing to a bouncer this place has ever had.

"Jim's husband." Laurie explains to his waiting friends. Now that they're in the house, it's nothing like any of them had imagined, but it's also exactly what they should have expected when Laurie told them about the place. They've stepped into a very quaint, exceptionally camp, kaleidoscope of small town gay life.

There's a makeshift performance area, with glimmer strands hugging a corner near a platform containing exactly one microphone attached to a stand. The bar is off to the other side, where Laurie waves to another stranger serving a handful of shots, murmuring "Jim" to his friends in explanation. A giant fluorescent arrow points toward the loo at the far end, hidden around another corner, with a sign that reads, *Wash your hands and mind your own business* which makes Emir grin so wide it hurts.

The entire place is wood panelled, likely unchanged for decades, the walls matching the floor and the bar and almost every surface beneath the warm, yellow lighting. There's a smattering of Pride flags (the standard and a handful of specific ones) and rainbow fairy lights as decor, and at least a dozen people in drag, mostly locals chatting easily while much of the younger crowd dances with abandon in the open space between the "stage" and the bar. There's about a hundred people in the space and the fit is comfortable without being stuffy, like everyone who's here is exactly where they're meant to be.

"This is brilliant!" Lili's the first of them to speak, already pulling Jordan by the hand and towards the dance space. "We'll be..."

Laurie just grins and nods, moving himself and T towards the bar. Emir and Theo follow behind because neither are ready to join the girls just yet, and Theo needs a minute to adjust to their environment.

"Look what the cat's dragged in." Jim leans across the bar and gets a cheek kiss from Laurie, just as Darren had. This place is like a time capsule of a different era, when queer life was more underground and places like this were the only option for community.

"Had to show these two the wedding venue this morning." Laurie tilts his head in Theo and Emir's direction. Jim wipes his hand on a nearby towel and offers it across the bar, shaking first Emir and then Theo's hands like he's been waiting to meet them. Maybe he has, if the way Laurie acts around Jim and Darren is any indication. It's clear they have a history.

"Ran into your mum at the market the other day." Jim leans across to embrace T while still talking to Laurie. "She mentioned you might be stopping in."

Jim's voice is lilting and steady with a stronger version of Laurie's accent, like everything a stranger would expect when they take in his rolled sleeves, worn-in trousers, and fantastic magenta platform heels he's chosen for the night.

"New Year's at Jim's is the tradition." Laurie reaches behind himself until he can tug Emir and Theo to stand at the bar beside him instead of hesitantly a few steps away. "Right, what's everyone drinking then? Jim's got it all, and then some."

"Wait, let me guess." Jim looks them over again, one at a time, as if this is a sort of game he likes to play. "Vodka Redbull for Laur, lemon drop for T, gin and tonic for our brown eyed girl," at which point he tilts his head towards Emir, "and a seltzer for Mr. Muscles, but he'll be back later for a beer once you've all settled in."

"You cheated, but I'll allow it." Laurie laughs but turns into T for a kiss as Jim starts fussing around to make their drinks. Of course he knew exactly what each of them wanted without having to ask.

Laurie manages to peel himself away from T's lips with the fondest smile imaginable before turning back to the others. "All good?"

"Perfect." Theo fits himself into Emir's front and melts, but only slightly. He's too excited to cuddle him properly. He doesn't have much experience with a place like this, but it's very much a vibe he wants to fall into. "Can't believe you've never told us about this place."

"If it wasn't obvious already, it's a secret." Laurie leaves the three of them with a grin to meet Jim behind the bar, stopping him from what he's doing to pull him into a proper hug.

"What's the story here?" Emir asks T, taking Laurie's vacated spot and bringing Theo with him. It's loud in here, but not nearly as pounding or sweaty as some club in London. They can still hear each other just fine.

"I'll let Laur tell you the whole thing someday, but Jim and Darren knew his mum before she even had him, when she was just a teenager. Knew his dad, too, but he was gone so much in those days that they're not as close as with Sara and Laurie." T watches Laurie chat quietly with Jim, helping him make the drinks like he works a regular shift here.

"Before Bill's work let him stay in Darton permanently, Jim and Darren were taking care of Laurie as often as Sara or his grandparents, watching baby Laur when she had a late shift at the hospital, walking him to school to let her get some sleep, that sort of thing. Sara and Laurie were technically living with her parents, but this house was their second home. Still is. Jim's run this place since the 90s, so when Laur came out in sixth form...well. Like he said: This is Darton. Jim's is their community space and their gay bar and everything in between."

"That's really fucking sweet." Emir reaches around Theo to set a hand on T's own where it rests on the bar. "I'm glad he has this."

"I'm glad he's sharing it with us." Theo adds, grinning at Laurie when their eyes meet from several feet away. "This place is pretty special. Like, even without his connection, it really means something, you know?"

"Yeah...we considered having the wedding here but Jim said absolutely not, then put Sara and Bill on a three way call to be dramatic about it while Darren added helpful commentary from his side. Apparently we're meant to be doing it *properly* which somehow allows the barn, but not this place." T laughs at the memory of that conversation, holding Emir's hand instead of letting it drift away again. "But if we have some sort of stag night in town, it'll definitely include a trip here."

"What's Sir Lawrence doing behind the bar?" Lilibet shoves her way in between T and the others, rising up on her tiptoes to place her elbows on the counter and breathing heavily after a few minutes of intense dancing. She's recently taken to coming up with increasingly annoying nicknames for Laurie just to watch it bother him, and he's been returning the favour at every opportunity.

"Helping his gay godfather." Emir answers as Jordan slides her arms around Lili from behind and pulls her back enough to let the five of them form a sort of semi-circle. Easier to talk that way.

"You think he'd make us a drink? I'm already beat." Jo keeps herself wrapped around Lili, chin atop her hair puff. It's hard to tell if it's for cuddling or practicality, with the way Lili gets when she's excited. "I have to pace myself or I won't make it to midnight."

"I'm sure I can think of a few ways to reinvigorate you." Lili says in that way that's meant to be a faux whisper, so that all their friends can hear and roll their eyes appropriately.

"Oi. Queenie." Laurie calls over to Lili. She fucking hates when he calls her that, which explains the impish look he's got. He's won this round. "You want a seltzer like Theo or you sharing Jo's usual?"

"I'll have the Palmer special." Lili answers, annoyed, but also loving that Jordan's become an integral enough part of all this to have a usual. "Extra bubbles."

Laurie finishes making their drinks and, with Jim's help, distributes them accordingly. All the glasses are different shapes, clearly purchased at different times and kept until they literally shatter and have to be replaced. Theo's is in an old jam jar, with a wedge of lime on the rim.

"Cough up." Laurie reaches for Jim's tip jar and holds it up between them with a little jingle. "Jim's covered the tab, but those heels deserve at least a quid or two."

"Some things never change." Jim chuckles and steps away again, nudging Laurie towards the direction of the bar exit back into the patron's side of the room. "Kid's been hustling for my tips since his first night out at eighteen. Especially when I perform."

"Is that a hint we'll be seeing Miss Behaviour tonight?" Laurie asks, back at T's side and sneaking a kiss to their waiting lips the second they're in reach.

"She's in retirement, so no." Jim tosses an errant pretzel at Laurie as he picks up a used glass from another patron. "The heels are murder without all the rest."

He turns away from their group to help someone at the other end of the bar, another regular by the looks of it.

"Oh!" Theo suddenly gets very excited and turns into Emir, ignoring his seltzer in favour of holding Emir's cheeks in his hands and staring very brightly into his wide, brown eyes. He gives himself credit for only getting distracted by Emir's *everything* for about three seconds before focusing. "Emir!"

"Shehzadi…" Emir moves his hands to Theo's waist and backs them up a few steps. Sometimes Theo needs a bit of room when he's this excited, regardless of the cause. When they're alone in the dance studio, he gets all the space he likes. But here, there's people that Theo won't want to bump into and need to apologise, especially when he's just excited.

"Um…" Theo glances between Emir's lips and his eyes several times, stealing a kiss before finishing what he wanted to say in a much lower register. "Didn't you say you need a drag mother? Like, back at Halloween?"

With a laugh, Emir nods, tapping Theo beneath the chin and giving him an equally bright look now that he knows what the excitement was about. Theo always does this: remembering things and bringing them up at the right time and validating Emir all at once. "I'll think about it. Jim seems nice enough, even if he'd be far away."

Theo kisses Emir again, because he can, because they're with friends in a safe environment on New Year's Eve and Emir is his favourite person in the entire world. Emir's still got his chin in his hand and his lips taste of gin and the music is coating Theo in a tingle of bliss and everything is *good*. So good. "I completely love you."

Emir melts and drops his hand to slide it beneath Theo's shirt hem instead, needing a hint of his skin in the midst of all the beautiful gay chaos. A moment of unfiltered Theo to ground him. But then he's distracted by a fast moving, quiffed tornado moving their way and he laughs. "Kiss me again while you still can."

"Hm?" Theo's question gets muffled against Emir's lips for approximately five seconds until he feels strong, familiar hands on his shoulders insistently pulling him back.

"Snog later. Dance now." Laurie exchanges a silent conversation with Emir, checking that it's actually alright to steal Theo away like this. Emir shakes his head and rolls his eyes but waves them off with a laugh, Laurie grinning like he's got the world hung on his smile. "Say goodbye to your Emi."

Theo lets himself be led away, giving Emir one of his tiny waves even as Laurie folds him into their familiar rhythm across the room. Emir takes up his drink again, sipping while he watches his friends and everyone else around them. Lili and Jordan have taken the spot next to where Laurie and Theo are now dancing, T is back at the door where they entered, catching up with Darren with an occasional laugh, and Emir just chills at the bar and soaks it all in. Besides their own group, there's several dozen queer people being so completely themselves in a way that they never really get to experience in London.

There's so much more...showing off in the city. So much subtext in those other spaces, like you have to be a specific type of gay, or dress a certain way to announce your identity, or drink a specific thing to show what you want, or whatever the "criteria" is. But here, everyone is dressed in literally whatever they like. There's someone genuinely in their pyjamas, more than one set of joggers, a puppy in a hood, a handful of drag queens decked to the nines, twinks in bootie shorts, butches in leather, and everything in between. Jim's is so much more honest. It's not just something, it's *everything*. For such a small place, it contains the multitudes of the queer experience that those posh, modern places could never even approach.

Emir sips his gin and tonic and grounds himself in the moment, settles into the experience one gay fraction at a time. It'd be easier with Theo to hold, but he knows this is their thing and he couldn't resent them for the joy it brings them. He watches Laurie handling his boyfriend, his love for both of them so intense and so distinctly different. Two of the most important people in his life are completely absorbed in their own moment, and all he can feel is gratitude to know them.

And then his eyes move to T, now behind the bar with Jim like Laurie had been earlier. They're cleaning glassware and talking in low voices, and Emir loves T just as deeply as the others. He can't imagine the absence of knowing them. Where would his life be if he hadn't snogged T at that party their first year before introducing him to Laurie? Where would any of their lives be? Would T and Laurie be engaged right now? Would he have ever really met Ciaran and Gabe? He'd know Theo through dance, but without their friends, would they ever have gotten together?

And then there's Lili and Jo. Lilibet who essentially adopted him their first week of classes, when he took his first Variations class with her and the other girls and out danced them all to prove some sort of point about his belonging in that space. But Lili saw through it, noticed him hiding his injuries, saw he wasn't just pushing himself but truly self-destructive. She knew he was scared and vulnerable and talented, yes, but mostly alone. And Lilibet had invited him over with the excuse of showing him how to pancake his pointe shoes that same night. His friendship with her, such as it was, had been completely separate from her friendship with Theo, but they had found their boundaries and their own sort of thing that worked.

And with Lili came Jordan, since the beginning. The two of them think he only found out about their relationship because he caught them necking in the library, but he'd suspected since they moved in together. He recognised certain things in Jordan, ways she would stare longingly at Lili when she thought no one was looking, inside jokes that seemed far too intimate to be platonic. And like Lili, she'd acted as his appointed extrovert friend, asking him along to that first book club meeting a few weeks into uni their first year because she saw him carrying one of her favourite books: *The Perks of Being A Wallflower*. And everyone in the book club was queer and they only read queer books so he sort of put the pieces together and she became his unofficial lesbian friend, even if they didn't spend much time together and she didn't definitively come out to him until their private library scandal.

And now here they all are: In a hidden bar on New Year's Eve, ready to celebrate the start of another year, knowing that they'll all be going their separate ways far too soon. The reminder of the impermanence of their time together brings a lump to Emir's throat that he takes a sip of gin about, knowing that time only moves forward and it's slipping through their fingers faster than he can try to capture.

If only Ciaran and Gabe were here, then it'd be perfect. There's so few nights like this left and he imagines where they'd be if they weren't plane rides away. Probably up on stage once they had a beer each, then sweating together in the middle of the crowd until T stole Ciaran to go outside and gaze at the universe. If only. They'll have to come back to Jim's when everyone is in Darton for the wedding. He'll make sure of it.

"Alright, doe eyes?" Jim gets Emir's attention from where he's still leaning back against the bar. It's been almost thirty minutes of Emir standing here alone, so it's natural Jim would check in on him. "Need another?"

"No, I'm perfect. Just...swimming in nostalgia. Thinking about what comes next." Emir turns to him and pushes his empty glass away to refuse a refill, needing a break from the sting of alcohol for a while. His emotions are putting him through enough on their own without the assistance. "I'm going to miss them all more than anything. And even if we don't end up too far, it's just...everything's going to change."

"Mmm." Jim agrees, taking Emir's empty glass and replacing it with a seltzer, just like Theo's got sweating in his hand while he grinds against Laurie beneath the lights. Jim had it ready without needing to ask. "New Year's has a way of doing that, I suppose."

"It does. But also..." Emir lets his head drop for a moment, leaning forward over his elbows to take a deep, steadying breath. He trusts Jim, at least with this. "I've lost almost everyone before, but those people weren't...like this. I don't know how to lose this family we've made. I don't know how to rebuild again...I don't want to. They're too important."

"I can't speak for the rest of them, especially your mates who couldn't make it tonight," Jim adds a lemon to the rim of the seltzer glass and pushes it encouragingly in Emir's direction. "But I know Laurie, and I'm getting to know T, and they could be in Antarctica and still find a way to be there for you. There's a lot we can't know, but sometimes we just have to trust in those who love us and know that love will sustain."

"I'm...working on it. Seeing someone about it." Emir admits with a wry smile. Jim has that knack that some of the best people get as they age, of remembering youth while embodying wisdom, all the empathy without the judgement. "But it still helps to have the reminder. So thank you."

"Not to mention that boyfriend of yours. From what Laurie tells me, he's quite dedicated to you and your relationship. Don't take that for granted." Jim smiles at Darren as he comes inside and walks behind the counter. "Hard thing to find."

Jim and Darren are entering the fourth decade of their relationship soon. What started as a tentative teenage flirtation turned into an entire life together, one that never left Darton, but rather grew roots that supported entire generations of queer community.

"I don't take it for granted. Honestly, I don't know that I'll ever deserve him. Theo's the most incredible person I've ever known, and allowing myself to love him and to have it be reciprocated has changed my entire life. I'm a new person, built from the ashes in a way." Emir gives Darren a small wave of acknowledgement as he joins them, one hand sliding onto Jim's lower back. They have that easy comfort of a long established couple, where they bloom into a shared aura regardless of circumstance. It's really fucking sweet and Emir hopes he'll have that someday with Theo. They're on the right path. "Tonight is just…bittersweet. I don't want to leave this year behind yet."

As he's finishing his thought, perfect, warm, sensitive hands slide beneath his shirt and around to his stomach. Theo fits behind Emir with a sigh as they relax into each other's space. Theo is so physically warm, and his presence just *does something* to Emir.

Turning his head to catch sight of his immaculate boyfriend, Emir mumbles, "Hi, baby."

"You looked sad." Theo offers as an explanation for leaving the dance floor and making his way back over here. He knows Emir prefers to spend his nights out with more brooding than dancing, but still. He doesn't want Emir to feel alone. "Everything alright?"

Emir just stares at Theo for a minute, turning the rest of his body around so his back is to the bar while Theo holds him safe and close. He's better now that Theo's here. "Take me for a dance, princess?"

"Thought you'd never ask." Theo sparkles, his eyes shining with love and excitement and joy even while he pulls away to back both of them into the crowd of dancers. Just out of reach, T joined Laurie where Theo left him behind, not that he minded of course, and now the two of them are dancing in their own way, sweet and off tempo, but together. Lili and Jo are a few yards further, completely focused on each other. Jordan's hands hold Lili's smaller frame across her leg so they can grind on each other shamelessly for what is possibly the first time in their lives, definitely the first in their relationship, and Emir gets Theo's attention to appreciate what it means for every single person in this room to be here. There's this collective *feeling* to the night and to this place that can't be captured except in the heart.

When Emir glances back to the bar, Darren and Jim are watching their group with a smile, mumbling between themselves until someone needs them. Together, they watch over and observe this community they've fostered, letting the joy of it all fill their souls. A love that sustains, as Jim would say. They've made a place where people thrive instead of survive, a place for life and love at its most free and uninhibited, and all of it grounded in their relationship, a foundation for everything that's come since they met.

"I'm glad we're here." Emir moves his face next to Theo's ear so he can hear him clearly over everything else, wanting privacy even in the crowd. He leaves a kiss on the side of Theo's neck before laying his head across his shoulder while they continue to dance. Things can get dirty and heated in a minute, but for now, he just wants this. Everything they are together, everything they have been and will be. Tonight is making him maudlin as hell, but he can't find it in himself to care.

"Love you." Theo answers after a minute, mumbling his reply against Emir's cheek while they move together beneath the rainbow of lights.

Midnight's coming up soon, but Emir's done keeping track. He has Theo and he has this moment and it's more than enough.

***

Theo's been carefully watching the clock hidden off to the side since they got here, waiting and biding his time all while dancing, either with Laurie, Emir, or sometimes even Lilibet, and soaking in the atmosphere around them. It's perfect, but now that it's only a few minutes to midnight…

"Take me outside." Theo slides the hand beneath Emir's shirt across his back to squeeze gently at his waist while leaning in for a kiss. "Please."

Emir glances at the clock that Theo's been watching all night. He thinks he's been subtle, but Emir knows him. Usually when they go out, Theo doesn't worry about it much, happy to flow through the night with their mates and with Emir and worry about sleep whenever it comes. But not tonight. "It's almost midnight, pumpkin."

"I knowwww." Theo whines, pressing himself against Emir insistently and grumbling for added effect. "Take me outsiiiide."

"Keep your pants on. I'll take you wherever you ask." Emir laughs, reaching to his right to get Laurie's attention and tilt his head in the direction of the door so he doesn't worry. Laurie nods and goes back to T, so Emir guides Theo away from the crowd and towards the entrance, one hand on his back while Theo holds him close with both arms from the side.

The door creaks as they step through and the noise of the bar shutters almost completely once it closes again. Jim's soundproofed the place well.

"This better?" Emir looks around until he finds a place for them to stand. Jim and Darren's house has a back garden where the windows to the partially underground bar peak out, but it's private enough from the street and open to the fresh air of the still night.

"Much." Theo lets Emir walk him around the house until they're standing beneath the open sky, arms around each other. He can feel his baseline settling, the adrenaline that had been reaching elevated levels falling back into safety, his body relaxing and his mind unfogging. It's not that being inside was *too much* but it's great to get a break, and he asked for space for more than one reason. "I wanted to be alone with you."

"Yeah?" Emir grins, eyes going wide but soft as he presses his lips against Theo's and starts turning them slowly in a circle together.

The music from inside can't be heard, but that hardly matters. Emir wasn't going to pull Theo away from the fun they'd been having, but he also craved some alone time. They're both a bit quieter than their friends. As much as they love a night out, taking a moment alone makes it all even better.

"Thanks for saving me earlier. Jim knew I needed a chat, but you always look out for me. Should've just gone to find you, but." Emir shrugs because the moment's passed and it worked out just fine.

"I'll always be here for that." Theo moves his arms so they're across Emir's shoulders while Emir continues to hold him lower, a bit below his waist. They could be at a prom in some American high school if they weren't in England, outside, and too old for that. But it's sweet. Romantic, like Emir always is. Like they both are. "You want to talk about it?"

"Just feeling a bit broody." Emir takes the chance to twirl Theo by the hand like a music box ballerina before pulling him back in. The giggle Theo gifts him is tucked safely into his memory with all the rest. "About it being the end of the year."

"Seems there's more to it." Theo gives Emir a twirl of his own, watching as he adds a bit of flair, and instead of straight back into their embrace, he dips Emir for a moment just to make him smile. Emir laughs so hard he almost falls to the ground, taking Theo along with him.

Theo waits until they're both upright again before gently nudging Emir to open up. "It's just us, babe. We still have a few minutes to midnight. I'm listening."

"It's just…" Emir kisses Theo again, one arm still around his waist, the other cradling his cheek. "It's been an incredible year. I spent months in America living the life of a professional and loving every second of it. Then I had a few weeks at home with my family, helped Safiya plan the wedding, taught Saima some art, went for a weekend trip with Amina and our cousin, then it was time to head back to Roseborough. And before classes even started, you showed up at that party with Laurie and it was like…clarity. Even though I went home with someone else that night, and even though we kept fighting for a few weeks after, that was the first time I'd seen you in months, and it was like my chest was on fire. I didn't understand it, I just knew that seeing you did something to me."

Theo hums his agreement because his own year has been fairly similar. Their term abroad, family memories, then back to uni, his mates and Emir. And then, of course, everything that came after that they've shared together.

"And then…well, then I found you. The real you. And I let you find me, too." Emir brushes his thumb along Theo's cheekbone while still holding his gaze. He's so beautiful, so handsome, so unguarded right now. "What started as a dance partnership turned into a life partnership. We've been through so much in a short amount of time. We met each other's families, had our first real fight, learned to be friends, fell for each other, took a break for a few days, dealt with our shit. I wouldn't change a single thing about this year. Not one moment. And I'm sure next year will be great too, but so much is about to change, and if I could just...stay for a bit longer..."

"You were the most important part of my year." Theo lets Emir adore him with his careful hands. He's completely on the same page, but he's not quite as hesitant to start the new year. There's a lot to look forward to. "That's why I wanted to come outside and just breathe together."

"I'm glad you did." Emir drops his hand and decides maybe snogging in a garden isn't the worst way to end the year. He presses his body against Theo's, tugs at his hair, bites along his jaw, leaves a bruise low on his neck, everything he knows Theo likes. He could kiss Theo for hours, days, weeks even, with breaks for the necessities. Theo's lips are so plump and his hands are so warm and everything about him settles into Emir's soul and finds a home.

"I think they're counting down..." Theo flutters his eyes back open when the noise from inside manages to make it past the soundproofing of the house. "And since it's about that time, I wanted to tell you that I love you this year and I'll love you in the next one and I probably loved you for the past few but I didn't really understand it and we were both being prats so it's complicated but just know that I'm yours, body and soul, or whatever poetic people say. This year, or next year, or whenever, I'm just glad to be your boyfriend. Because I love you."

"You're so fucking sweet and you're the best thing that's ever happened to me." Emir traces his fingers through Theo's curls until he's gripping the back of his head, already shifting him into a dip of his own and a very deep kiss as the sounds from inside reach an intensity he knows means it's midnight. The new year is starting and it'll be alright. He kisses his love right back to Theo, hoping he can feel everything he's still not quite ready to say, but Emir's positive he'll be ready for it soon. "Happy New Year, baby."

"Happy New Year." Theo drags himself back up to standing and immediately picks Emir up in his arms, just like he has dozens of times before in rehearsal. Emir laughs and wraps himself around Theo, kissing him again, chasing his joy, sharing his excitement, grounding himself in their joint moment. Months from now, when he's tired or sad about leaving uni, he wants to remember that this is how the year started: in Theo's arms, with their friends just inside, pursuing queer joy and love and light. "You know, it won't be so bad."

"I know." Emir steadies himself as Theo sets him back down and takes his hands in both of his own, swinging them between their bodies. It's one of Theo's habits that Emir completely adores. "I'm feeling better about it, thanks to you."

"We've got our dissertation, and Laurie and T's wedding, and moving into our first flat together, and hopefully finding work with a company in London. It's going to be a lot of change, like you said, but I think...it'll be growth." Theo's been gradually thinking more about that first flat together as the holiday has gone on and it's becoming more real. He can't wait. "I'll miss our friends more than anything, but I know they'll still be around. They're family."

"Remember how I told you how much I like your brain?" Emir touches their foreheads together and closes his eyes. "Still true."

"You want to go back inside? I think Laurie said the drag show starts ten minutes after midnight." Theo keeps his eyes shut as well. He's not in a rush to end their solitude, but he knows that Emir *really* wants to watch the drag performers, and he's excited too.

"Few more minutes." Emir thinks about all of what Theo mentioned in the upcoming year. They have so much to look forward to and they get to take on the next chapter together. They're *choosing* to move forward together.

"Is that...it can't be." Theo gasps and pulls back from Emir to look up at the sky in wonder. "Shit. It's snowing!"

"Didn't expect it to snow in Darton." Emir follows Theo's gaze to watch the tiny snowflakes that are forming around them. It's fleeting and barely visible, but it's undeniably snow. "Not properly - at least not while we're here."

"It only slows like you're thinking about five or six days a year, and more often in the springtime." Theo answers readily. He'd done a thorough check of the weather before they drove here. No snow on the forecast, but it's cold enough and the afternoon's sudden temperature drop was the right sort of precursor. "Always loved the snow. I wish we had more in London."

"Me too." Emir sighs, watching the tiny miracles drift along and eventually following one as it lands on Theo's impossibly perfect eyelashes. How is his boyfriend even real? "You're so beautiful in the snow."

Theo looks away from the sky to catch Emir staring, a sort of awe holding his mouth open and his eyes wide. He never knew he could be beautiful before Emir fell in love with him. People had told Theo that he was generally attractive or fit or handsome, but only Emir ever tells him that he's gorgeous and pretty and *beautiful*. Emir, who understands the nuances between the words and delights in the different ways they make Theo melt.

"Only in the snow?"

"No." Emir looks back up at the midnight sky and waits for Theo to do the same. He's thinking about a night in Theo's room, months ago, when he'd first been honest with Theo about his innate importance, the way he cradled the world with his heart. They both frequently return to that night and that conversation, and how it became a foundation for so much of what they've built. "But if you're the sky, then you should know that the snow suits you."

Emir takes a beat, admiring the curve of Theo's throat, the line of his jaw, the shape of his lips as he keeps staring. Sometimes the sky doesn't seem like a big enough metaphor. "You're breathtaking in the sun, gorgeous in the moonlight, and pretty in the rain. Now I know you're beautiful in the snow, too. I appreciate all your seasons."

"You're such a ridiculous sap." Theo chuckles, but Emir knows his flush isn't only from the cold. He cherishes Emir's compliments, internalising how sincerely they're offered. "Kiss me in the snow before someone drags us back inside."

Emir doesn't need to be asked twice.

They get about three minutes of sentimental snogging, mumbled love and laughter included, before they're interrupted by four familiar sets of footsteps coming around the side of the house.

"Told you they'd be shagging in the garden." Lili turns to Jordan with her arms crossed over her chest, shivering slightly. When they left for the night it was about seven degrees warmer and they didn't think they'd be needing layers.

"They haven't even brought their coats." T's forehead is making that concerned scrunch they've all become accustomed to. "None of us have. We shouldn't be outdoors for too long."

"But it's snowing!" Jordan half shrieks as she realises, flinging her arms wide with her face to the sky and twirling in place. Her newfound freedom flows through her like ichor from a fresh wound.

"For the record, I wasn't worried." Laurie has one arm around T and the other still holding what Emir assumes is a beer. "But, like, drag starts in a minute, and also Lilibet wouldn't stop worrying once you were gone past the five minute mark."

"Not true." Lili shoves at Laurie's shoulder then joins Jordan running through the half-hearted snowflakes. Something about nature's surprise is bringing out the youthful spirit of them all, eyes bright and shining with hope. "Do you think we could make a snowman if we wait a few minutes?"

"Not a fucking chance." Laurie laughs, setting his beer on the ground and taking T by the hand until they're both playing in the snow too. "It'll stop in a minute and melt just as quick. Best to enjoy it while you can."

"Can I have this dance, princess?" Emir turns to Theo, dramatically offering his hand and bending a knee. He's Theo's Prince Charming, always.

Theo takes it, bringing them both into a comedic waltz and colliding with their friends every few steps until the six of them are all smiling and out of breath and, as Laurie predicted, no longer experiencing snow. It only lasted a few minutes, but they've built a memory to cherish for life.

"Race you inside." Theo taps Laurie on the shoulder and takes off. It's a very short jog, but it's not about the distance, it's about the game. The rest of them follow after, T holding Emir at the elbow and walking inside with him, Lili and Jo just behind.

The heat of Jim's hits them like a tropical breeze, warming them almost too quickly after their outdoor adventure. But Darren's there waiting, with hot toddies for them all and a gentle scold about catching the sniffles if they aren't careful. He didn't add whiskey to Lili's drink as the designated driver, but the warmth works just as well without it.

They sip from their mugs as they cheer and laugh and admire an hour of drag performances (and tip the queens, of course) before Jim announces last call and tells everyone they have another few songs to dance before they close up.

Emir, Theo, and literally everyone else at the bar stays until the very end, and because Laurie is Laurie, he insists the six of them stay late to help Jim and Darren clear up. It only takes an extra fifteen minutes after everyone else has left, but it saves Jim and Darren hours of cleaning later in the day. None of them mind helping to tidy after the warmth and safety that's been so readily offered to them the past few hours.

By the time Lili drives them all back to Bill's place, they're past exhausted, falling into their respective beds for the night with barely a mumbled goodnight, Lili and Jordan tiptoeing into Ruby and Casey's room and the others piling into Laurie's. Emir lays awake for a while longer, always a night owl. But just before he drifts off, Emir listens to the snores of the other three, the soft, serene sounds of rest, and nuzzles into Theo's neck to mumble, "I love you, too."

***

It's noon on Saturday and none of them are truly hungover, but they also didn't get nearly enough sleep to be dealing with all the energy that runs through Sara's house at any hour of the day. Laurie's mum invited all six of them over for lunch before Theo drives himself and Emir back to the Shah's for one last night together and Lili drives herself and Jordan back to her own parents' place.

"Rosie, get your feet off your sister." Sara calls into the living room, with that knack for knowing when her kids are tussling and need a reminder to behave. Rose and Chloe, while a year apart in age, are at that phase where they're old enough to entertain themselves, but still young enough to need someone to keep an eye on them. "Ruby, could you - "

"On it, mum." Ruby lays down the last fork as she finishes helping Casey set the table. It's a bit cramped with Sara, her new husband Kyle, her ex husband Bill, and all their kids (five, counting Laurie, and not counting the twins growing inside of Sara at the moment, six if you count T which Sara certainly does), plus the four visitors.

"Now, what were you saying, love?" Sara turns back to Laurie where he's helping her in the kitchen while he and T fill her and Bill in on a few more wedding details.

Kyle's busy working on the nursery upstairs because apparently it's the first chance he's had since they got the news about the twins. The babies will be his first biological children, and while he's an adequate stepfather to the children that Sara and Bill share, he's floundering a bit on his way to welcoming the youngest to their world.

"We'll finalise the barn on Monday after the holiday weekend and Teddy's helped me organise some things to make sure we stay on track and on budget. Emir is helping T with the decor, so as long as we can still use the garden the night before, I think...I think it's all set." Laurie reaches around to tighten her apron strings where they've come loose as she's bustled around the kitchen. "It's important to us, but if we need to figure something else out – "

"Absolutely not." Sara grabs for both his and T's hands and gives each of their cheeks a swift kiss. "You won't even let me pay for anything. The least I can do is let you get married in the garden you grew up in, even if you are having two ceremonies. May as well have one here."

"I don't mind paying what I can, and Suzanne and Dean are helping out, too." Bill adds from where he's endeavouring to make a dent on the washing up pile. He may not live in this house anymore, but he and Sara had a very amicable divorce, and with all the kids, there was never going to be a future where they didn't stay in each others' lives. "First kid to get married and I couldn't be more proud. Your mum and I just want you to have a wedding that will make you happy. The both of you."

"We showed the farm to Emir and Theo yesterday." T turns to look at them where they're folding freshly cleaned towels. Theo insisted he needed something to do, and Emir didn't mind helping, so they're standing a few feet away, happily folding linens while the others faff about. "I think we got their approval."

"Definitely. I think it's perfect." Theo grins. He shouldn't be surprised that his and Emir's opinions matter so much to the fiancés because he knows he'd feel similarly if it was the other way around. "Thanks for having us all round, by the way."

"No trouble at all." Sara waves a hand dismissively and reaches for her oven mitts. It's almost time to eat, which means it's time to take everything out of the oven before serving. "Bill, could you go check on the girls? And make sure Lili and Jordan haven't been absolutely covered in glitter? I think Rosie found more somewhere."

"Just finished the washing up." Bill gives her a smile and leaves to join the crowd in the living room. Never a dull moment in this house.

"Make sure you share all this with Suzanne while you're staying with her this week. I don't want her to feel we're forgetting your family, T, what with having the wedding here and you two deciding to move to town for a while afterwards." Sara takes half a dozen trays out of the oven, displaying an impressive amount of coordination and use of counter space. "You seeing Dean when you're there or will he be working?"

"We're going to Dad's house for dinner at least once. I wish I got to see him more." T sighs and leans on Laurie for support. "But he thinks he might have some work in London in the next few months, so it might work out to see him again soon."

"That'd be lovely." Sara rests her hands over her growing baby bump subconsciously. She truly is glowing, and not just from the heat of the kitchen. "Emir, are your parents well?"

"Brilliant." Emir folds the last towel in his hand and moves to help carry things to the table instead, Theo following close behind. "Want me to have my mum give you a ring? I know you work odd hours between the hospital and the kids, but if she misses you, you could just chat her back when you have time."

"Please do! Theo, would you ask your mum as well? I haven't heard from Caroline in a few weeks, what with the holiday and everything." Sara starts handing dishes off to all of them along with oven mitts to protect their hands from the very hot contents. "We can chat more while we eat. I need a wee!"

She rushes away, tugging off her apron and hanging it on the hook near the stove as she goes. Laurie makes sure they get everything on the table then calls the others in to join them. It takes several minutes for everyone to figure out a seat and get assembled, by which time Sara is back and sitting between Kyle and Laurie at the far end of the table.

"Right. Everyone help yourselves." Sara calls out once everyone's seated, the noise never having stopped, not for a single moment, but it's the sound of love and comfort and familiarity.

Emir realises as the food is passed around that this must be what started family dinner at Roseborough. This way that Sara has of bringing her family together must have either inspired Laurie to start one of his own or been so ingrained in him that it just came naturally. The others, Theo and Gabe and Ciaran, who've all been joining since first year, they probably already knew. But to Emir it's a heartfelt revelation that Laurie brought such an important part of his home life to uni and shared it with all of them, creating a new tradition from it. The fact they've all built this found family truly started with Laurie. Theo and T and the others helped it grow, but Laurie was the roots. He still is.

"Emi?" Theo sets a warm hand on his knee and waits for him to look up. "You alright?"

With a sniff, Emir realises he's started tearing up. Only slightly. "Just...family dinner."

Theo understands immediately. He leans in and gives Emir a hug right here at the table, arms wrapping around him as their faces tuck against each other's shoulders. It's not the most natural position, and they're very cramped between T and Lili, but it feels right.

"He really loves us." Theo mumbles to Emir, feeling himself start to tear up as well. Not that he's ever taken their weekly Wednesday night family dinners for granted, but the reminder of where it all started is nostalgic, if nothing else. "Brought us all together."

"Yeah." Emir sniffles again, wiping his eyes on the corner of his own t-shirt, fully aware that he and Theo are crying with zero explanation in the middle of a nice meal with about a dozen other people. But they don't seem to mind, carrying on around them like it's completely ordinary. "I should thank him."

"Later." Theo sneaks a kiss to Emir's cheek before sliding back into his own chair, keeping a hand on Emir's knee under the table. He can eat with just the one hand.

Emir nods, wiping at his eyes again with the back of his hand and giving T a reassuring smile when they shoot him a concerned look. He accepts the plate that's being handed to him, taking a bit of mash to go on the side of everything else before passing it along to Lili as the conversations continue to ebb and flow through the air. Emir suddenly has the urge to break open his heart and leak his feelings all over his loved ones, telling them how much he appreciates them, holding them close and never letting go.

It's good he'll have a week at home with his family after this before uni starts again. It may be the last week he has like that...ever.

"Too much?" Theo leans over to whisper, recognising the signs of overwhelm that Emir's displaying beside him. He's actually doing fine, despite all the chaos, but Emir's been a bit emotionally fragile recently, and maybe this is too much on top of everything else.

"No, just...having a lot of feelings." Emir laughs at himself, scratching at his beard and grasping onto the hand that Theo still has placed on his leg. "All good, though. I'm really lucky."

"For what it's worth," Theo lowers his voice again to keep it below the noise and presses his lips to Emir's cheek to continue, "We're lucky to have you too, babe."

Sometimes he worries that Emir forgets, or that he doesn't realise how appreciated and loved he is by his friends, by his family, by people he doesn't even know. How can someone so remarkable not understand how cherished they are?

"Oi, enough with the secrets you two." Laurie raises his eyebrows at them until they scoff and sit up straight again, but their hands stay linked beneath the table.

After that they rejoin the conversation and enjoy their meal, but their hands never leave their spot atop Emir's knee. It's not until they're helping clean up that they step away from each other, only momentarily, and then they're like velcro again for the rest of the visit. They stay attached even through their drive back to Emir's house, after saying goodbye to everyone at Sara's and huddling up in Theo's car.

They get a warm welcome back from the Shah's, returning for one final night in Shipley before Theo's back to Stafford in the morning. The Shahs enjoy a very different, but no less important, meal together that night. It's hard to reconcile a day that holds so much in just twenty-four hours. Starting with a moonlit kiss in the snow, a beautifully loud feast at Sara's, and ending with a quiet night on the sofa with the Shah family before heading off to Emir's room to be alone, both of them craving it as if they haven't been together the entire day.

"Good start to the year?" Theo asks Emir through a yawn, curled up atop his chest after they've both showered.

"If the rest of the year is anything like today, I think it'll be brilliant." Emir kisses the top of Theo's head and gives him a squeeze with his arms. "Exhausting, but brilliant."

"I'm about to fall asleep if you start playing with my hair again." Theo mostly says it as a subtle request for Emir to trail his perfect fingers through his hair, because it's one of his favourite ways to be adored. Like a lullaby danced across his scalp.

"I'll be right behind you, baby." Emir's already moving a hand into Theo's curls, even as he stifles his own yawn.

"Love you." Theo shuts his eyes and nuzzles against Emir's chest, his leg winding its way between both of Emir's so they're all mixed up and entwined beneath the sheets.

Emir waits for Theo to fall asleep, but then, just like last night, he whispers, "I love you, too."

CHAPTER THIRTEEN

"It's *so good* to be back." Emir has his arms thrown over his head while he catches his breath, his muscles complaining with that comfortable sort of ache that only comes from a few hours well spent in the studio. It's something he hasn't felt in weeks. "That run through was nearly perfect."

"Only nearly?" Theo teases him, reaching for his water bottle and wiping sweat from his brow. They've been working for almost three hours and it's about lunch time, but neither of them is ready to be finished yet, either.

"We can always be better, but that was…it's good to be back." Emir repeats, dropping his arms and wrapping them around Theo instead. They had a week apart before they both got back to uni last night, and the space was needed, but having Theo in his arms is never something he'll take for granted. "Let's plan to film a run-through tomorrow to show Sean on Tuesday."

"Since we're doing so well, you think we could squeeze in a pointe lesson for me some night this week?" Theo manoeuvres himself without dislodging Emir, grabbing Emir's Hydro Flask to encourage him to rehydrate since they're temporarily stationary.

"Mmmm…" Emir pretends to think about it, taking the proffered beverage in his left hand but keeping Theo in his right. "Suppose you might be able to convince me. You could ask Lili and Jo too, you know, in case I'm in rehearsal or something without you. They'd be great teachers."

"I'll stay with you before branching out." Theo laughs, trying to move literally anywhere, but Emir's firmly planted himself (and therefore Theo) right here by the mirror. He's an immovable force when he wants to be. "Not going anywhere, Emi."

"But I had to go without cuddles for a whole *week* princess. A week." Emir drops his water back on top of his rucksack and slackens his entire body against Theo like he's suddenly lost all his bones. "Nearly killed me."

"You're only this dramatic when you're happy, so I'll consider this a win." Theo slides his hands to Emir's face to pull him in for a kiss, smiling when Emir hums his appreciation in response, holding his own weight again. "Can I play something for you before we finish?"

"Oi, I am not getting off in the practice studio." Emir shoves Theo away with a grin, already walking back towards the middle of the room as Theo rolls his eyes. Something's changed over the past few weeks, some sort of certainty in their relationship that was always there, but never quite so instinctual. Being back at uni is an odd sort of litmus test for how much closer they became during their time away from these familiar, mirrored walls.

"Later. And no, not here." Theo reaches down and opens Emir's phone - Emir gave him the passcode months ago - so he can find what he's searching for on Spotify and stream it through the speaker. "Close your eyes for me?"

"This game is more fun horizontal and with less clothing." Emir laughs when Theo scoffs, trying to hold back his own laughter. Sometimes it's nice to have fun like this, to mess around between their hard work and just enjoy each other's company. It's a really satisfying balance that they've found.

"Focus with me for ten more minutes and then we'll go get off together in the shower." Theo promises, smothering another laugh behind his hand as Emir immediately closes his eyes and stills in place. Sometimes he's *too* easy to motivate.

They spent an hour exploring each other's bodies last night when they were reunited before falling asleep in Emir's bed. But what Theo's offering now is a quickie, pure lust and adrenaline and need shooting through them in ecstasy. "Just listen and dance if you want and tell me if you think it makes sense."

Theo finds the song he discovered three days ago and hits play, letting the first few piano notes trill through the air. They haven't used any music with lyrics yet, just the angelic vocalisation that Gabe recorded for them, with Ciaran's help on the production. But Theo heard this song and he could see it immediately, the way they would move together, the tonal shift from the sombre, drawn out notes that would precede it, maybe a short interlude between, and the way the end of the previous section would flow into the third act of their choreography. The reunion that would build to their forever, at least for the story told in their work.

Emir takes a deep breath when he hears the piano, so different from the other music they're using but also feeling *right* in a way that'd be hard to describe. It's sage green with flashes of baby pink and sky blue, a bit of lilac. And when the voice joins in - Birdy if he recognizes that very specific vibe correctly - there's yellow, too. The yellow of a baby duck or the sun soft on the water of a sleepy lake. Like a spring meadow just at sunrise, a field to frolic, a world to explore.

He's dancing by the time the chorus starts, almost automatically. Theo's still standing near the mirrors, but it's like he can feel Theo beside him, a true duet, less lifts than the previous sections, more contemporary technique heavily based in ballet to showcase both of their strengths. Emir's dancing his way through the notes like he's already in the future, on stage, presenting their work and showing the world his love for Theo along with his love for dance and for all that they've built together. There's elongated arabesques, effortless pirouettes, suspended jumps slightly out of synch until their bodies find each other for a dip into a roll over his shoulder.

Emir could improvise his way through the entire song right now, in ten minutes, three weeks down the line, and again on stage, and they'd all be entirely unique versions on the same theme, but completely perfect.

Theo's eyes glaze over, watching Emir dance in awe, his body losing its connection to the earth as Emir's movements carry him away, floating in some liminal space of abject wonder. He'd liked this song before, but now it's taken on an entirely new importance. Emir's his favourite dancer, has been for a while, and getting to watch him work like this, improvised and free and astonishingly beautiful, is a gift that he doesn't know what to do with. The world will never get to see this. It's only for Theo, and it's…it's…

"Come here." Emir carries himself into Theo's space just as the song is ending, pulling him, unresisting, into a passionate kiss. Their bodies collide and Theo's hands are on his waist and for one, glorious, eternal moment it's just them, their connection laid entirely bare, their bodies releasing their souls to share a glimpse at each other in their purest form. Their eyes are closed, their lips are joined, and there's nothing and no one else that exists.

"I love you more than I ever knew I could love anyone." Theo's pressed against Emir and lost in his eyes. He doesn't remember pulling him so close but there's not an inch between them. "That was…I'll never forget that feeling. I'm so proud to love you."

"You're the most important thing that's ever happened to me." Emir brushes his nose along Theo's, arms wrapped around his shoulders while they continue sharing their breath with parted lips and soft eyes. It's not the fullness of his feelings, but it's what translates into words. "And you see me, the real me. I'm just…so grateful for you."

They're quiet for a minute, still and happy, wound up in each other. It's a shared intimacy that's a revelation, new for both of them and so freeing.

"I think we should probably use that song." Theo kisses Emir's top lip without moving away. He's never felt closer to anyone, and in so many distinct, important ways.

"What's it called?" Emir plays with the curls at the back of Theo's head. That purple streak above his eye has faded, just slightly, but it's falling so perfectly right now, like he should be wearing some sort of flower crown but only remembered the first petal.

In an instant, Emir's mind is wandering to painting Theo's portrait with only the softest water colours, all those shades the song had brought to his mind, laying flowers in his hair with the sun across his face. Maybe he can start on it tonight after Theo falls asleep and he has the chance to appreciate Theo's beauty with a paintbrush in hand.

"*Quietly Yours.*" Theo grins, thinking of the conversations they've had about the sort of relationship they want, the quiet, private, lasting sort of love that awakens their souls and inspires their life. He liked the song before he knew the title, but so much about it feels right. "It's by -"

"Birdy?" Emir guesses, kissing Theo again, then twice more, and almost managing to pull himself away until Theo's the one pulling him in. It's ecstasy and certainty and the feeling of forever spreading through his body.

"Can I tell you something embarrassing?" Theo finally does pull himself away, but only because this confession requires props. His phone, specifically. He's been keeping this horrendously sappy, infatuated secret to himself for months, but he thinks it might be the perfect time to share it with the person who inadvertently started the whole thing in the first place.

"Always." Emir starts twirling around himself while he waits for whatever it is Theo needs to tell him. He feels buoyant and light, like he could fly away if only his wings would sprout.

"So...do you remember how you asked me about this playlist? Like...the night of our first kiss? I played it that night and you asked me why it was all love songs and I said I'd tell you about it later?" Theo doesn't know that there's any chance Emir actually does remember that, but he's used the playlist frequently since, so maybe. He's constantly adding to it and it's become the soundtrack to his days.

"Hmmmm a bit." Emir stops twirling and collapses gracefully to the ground instead, laying flat on his back with an arm beneath his head as a cushion, watching Theo join him with stunning clarity. He absolutely adores his boyfriend.

Theo opts for a cross legged seat rather than fully laying down, but he sets one of his warm hands across Emir's diaphragm and lets it rise and fall with the rhythm of Emir's breath.

"The reason it's all love songs is because each one of them is inspired by one of your drawings. Each time you give me another piece of art, I add a song to this playlist that reminds me of it. So by now, there's dozens. And you've been the reason for every single one." Theo offers his phone to Emir with the playlist open, inviting him to scroll. "I listen to it constantly. I was at home in my room, when I played it all the way to the end. I have autoplay active and *Quietly Yours* was what the algorithm chose to play next. And I just sort of had this feeling that we should use it."

"Since...before we were together? You were already feeling...this? Before?" Emir sits up with Theo's phone held in both of his hands, slowly making his way through the song list and once again wondering what in the hell he ever did to deserve Theo.

He remembers some of the songs that played that night, the one where he bit Theo, got embarrassed, and then eventually kissed him like he'd wanted to all along. Even then, when they were ostensibly just friends, the music hadn't been casual or flirty or flippant. When they get back to Theo's flat and his small gallery, Emir wants to know which picture goes with each song, which drawings inspired each choice. And once he knows, Emir wants to relearn the shape of Theo's body beneath his lips while he spends hours anointing his silken skin with his touch.

"I was sure about you, even then." Theo confirms, not shy about the earnest, sincere love he has for Emir. "More sure now."

"I don't think I could possibly have done any of this without you. The choreography or the dancing or even my last year of uni." Emir sets the phone aside, knowing he'll be asking Theo to share the link with him so they can talk about it more, discussing the nuance of each song choice and what certain lyrics mean to Theo. "I don't *want* to do it without you either. Like, it was a choice, I'd choose you a thousand times over. But I also can't imagine where either of us would be right now if we hadn't decided to trust in each other and see where we could go."

Theo takes Emir's hand in his and just stares for a minute. He feels exactly the same way. How did he ever imagine going through this process, one so personal and important and built on a foundation of love, without Emir? He would have, of course, and Emir would've stunned the world with his own dissertation, but neither of them would ever have had this. They've both been changed, and their work along with them.

"Could we head home now? I think we've made decent progress, considering it's still technically during break." Theo stands and brings Emir with him by the hand, pocketing his phone in his joggers. "And I'd like to be alone, like…properly."

"Only have about another hour before Lili and Jo get back and we promised we'd be there." Emir reminds him, dropping Theo's hand with a squeeze so he can pack up their things and carry their bags. Every day, Theo insists he's capable of carrying his own, and every time, Emir kisses him and carries it anyway.

"Shower, then reheat something your mum sent with you for lunch?" Theo takes the water bottle Emir holds out to him, tucking it between his knees so he can pull his hoodie over his head for the walk across campus.

I love you, Emir thinks, but now doesn't seem like the moment to finally say it aloud. He'll know, just like Theo had known that morning in the car. "Sounds perfect."

***

Lili texts Theo when they're a few minutes away from Roseborough, her parents driving both herself and Jordan back after the holiday break. He grabs Emir by the hand and races out of his flat, Emir laughing as he follows along until they're outside.

"Remember: Lili said Jo's been having a hard time the past few days, but she keeps acting like she's fine, so we shouldn't mention her family unless she brings it up." Theo interlaces his fingers with Emir's to walk from his building to where they'll be getting dropped off nearby.

"I remember." Emir boops himself sideways into Theo with a kiss to his temple as they keep walking. "Can't expect any of it to get better so soon."

"I'm glad you're you." Theo sighs, giving Emir a very fond smile. "And I'm glad you have all those muscles to help carry Lili's bags inside."

"How many are we expecting?" Emir gives Theo's hand a squeeze as he laughs. Luckily their flat is as close as anyone could get to the car park, which makes Barbara giving Theo her old car all those months ago that much more convenient, even if he does have to pay an exorbitant fee to park it there.

"You'll see." Theo's focus moves away from Emir as a familiar car pulls up beside them, Lili already rolling down the window to talk at them before the car even stops.

"I need a wee." She shouts, hopping out the second the vehicle's stationary and sprinting past them into the building. "Be right back."

Lili yells at them over her shoulder, Jordan letting herself out of the other rear door at the same time Lili's parents, Yuusuf and Ola, emerge from the front of the car.

"Thanks for helping us get unpacked." Jordan greets Theo with a hug, then Emir with a very European cheek kiss and a side hug that Emir returns automatically.

Theo tilts his head because he hadn't realised that was their greeting. Maybe it's new, now that they're all even closer than before. Maybe he was just always being tackled by Lilibet and hadn't caught it before. It's cute.

"Your hair!" Theo finally notices, her new bob length blonde hair and long fringe swaying as she and Emir step away from each other.

"You like it?" Jordan gives a bit of a twirl, her eyes bright, even though there's a still, sombre air around her. "Thought about going shorter, but it's a start. I was never allowed to have short hair before…"

"It's brilliant." Emir reassures her, tilting his head back and forth then looking her up and down to really get a good look at it. "I think it suits you."

"It definitely suits you." Theo confirms, pulling her in for another hug and mumbling near her ear, "You look fantastic either way, but I'm glad it's making you smile."

Jordan nods before stepping away again, giving Theo a little shrug when he gives her a look that asks *you alright?* She doesn't really have an answer to that right now.

"Elizabeth has managed to bring half the home country back with her." Ola opens the boot of their car to reveal an alarming number of suitcases jammed inside with the skills of a tetris master. "As per."

"You weren't kidding." Emir laughs and sets a hand on Theo's shoulder before letting it drop again.

"How she fits it all in the flat is a miracle." Yuusuf gives them both a hug as well before tugging on the handle of the nearest bag. It barely budges. "Well, it was worth a try."

"Let me grab mine and see if that gives a bit of leverage." Jordan reaches in and removes a sensibly full duffel bag, her rucksack already over her shoulders because it accompanied her on the drive.

"Much better. Thanks, Jo." Yuusuf heaves until one of the bags is free, gingerly setting it down and moving to extricate the next. "Theo, make Lili carry at least one this time."

"I'll probably need to." Theo laughs, taking one that Ola hands over as Emir reaches for yet another. There's at least six bags and they all appear to be bursting at the seams. "She's overdone it a bit, even by her standards."

"I have not!" Lili comes running back to them, and with a confidence that can only come with practice, jumps on Theo's back and wraps her limbs around him as he drops the handle he'd been starting to drag along the pavement. "It's only eight bags and they're not all mine."

"Seven of them are yours, dear." Jo reminds her, causing Lili to dislodge herself from Theo and cross her arms with a pout. There must be one hidden somewhere that Emir and Theo can't see yet. How full is this car?

"If we're staying in London, I'm saving us a trip in the summer. Thinking ahead, like." Lili takes the case her dad hands to her and starts marching away haughtily. You'd think having to move one of her own bags was really putting her out.

"Right. Everyone got something?" Yuusuf has three bags himself, everyone else burdened with as much as they can possibly carry or roll or, in one case, kick, because of course Lili packed one of the bags with no working straps and no wheels.

"I've got it." Emir leans down and adds the sad reject to his pile, struggling to see over top his burden and hoping Theo doesn't let him run into anything important.

After several minutes of helping each other and holding doors and more than one stubbed toe, they're all inside Lilibet and Jo's flat, Lili's belongings finally set down and ready to be unpacked. But this is where Yuusuf and Ola leave their very capable daughter to handle her own mess, with only a few hours left in the day and classes starting up in the morning.

"We'll call when we're back at the house." Ola holds Lili close to her chest, arms wrapped around her protectively and swaying them where they stand. "And we'll see you in a few weeks for the winter show."

Yuusuf is next to hug Lili goodbye, holding her so tight that her feet leave the ground for a moment. "We love you very much. Don't forget to answer your mother when she calls."

They each do the same for Jo, embraces and reminders to call before hurrying back out the door to drive all the way back to Wakefield again.

Lili pretends to be tough and brushes them off to get them going, but she deflates a bit once they're actually gone and it's just the four of them in the flat again. "I'm going to miss them."

"Yeah." Jordan pulls Lili into her for another embrace, allowing Lili to hide her tears from the others. Not that they would judge her. Emir and Theo are also generally weepy when it's time to leave their parents behind.

Rather than unpacking right away, they move Lili's many bags closer to her room and settle on the sofa instead, Theo making everyone tea to fortify them for the rest of their Sunday.

"What's this?" Emir notices a medium-sized brown box left on the kitchen counter when he goes to help Theo carry all the mugs into the living room.

"Must've been delivered while we were away. It was outside our door." Lili answers, head now in Jordan's lap while Jordan trails her fingertips in a circle across Lili's chest, a habit she has from her own self-soothing when her panic about her family would get really bad. At some point she started to do the same when Lili would get worked up, and now it's just a thing she does.

Lili's wearing her hair down today, curls freshly set by her mum just the other day. She doesn't often get to really lean into her natural hair because of ballet, so when she can, she does. And while Jordan would normally bury her fingers in Lili's hair and massage her scalp to soothe away any tension from the day, she knows by now that hair days like this mean hands off. Hence the delicate chest caress.

"You order something and forget about it again?" Jordan teases, but the smile she gives Lili is far too indulgent for such a casual moment with their friends only a few feet away.

"Nah, it's for you." Lili returns the look in equal measure, and Theo almost feels like he's intruding when he joins them back in their miniscule living room. "Saw your name when I chucked it up there on the way to the loo."

"Here." Emir managed to carry both his mug and Jordan's with the mystery package under his other arm, handing Jo first the box then the tea before settling behind Theo and giving him a bit of a nuzzle.

Jordan inspects the package with a confused look because it only has her name and flat number, no proper address, and no return address either. It clearly didn't go through the post. "I'm so genuinely unsure about what this is."

"Only one way to find out?" Theo asks, reaching into the drawer below their coffee table to find the box cutter they keep there for opening packages. Lili has a habit of ordering way too much online about once a month, and keeping one there was easier than always rummaging in the kitchen.

It takes a minute, but Jordan cuts through the tape holding the package together and opens the top to find an envelope with her name on it. But as that doesn't answer any questions, and it seems she's meant to open the letter before the rest of the items, she sets the box aside and carefully tears the paper along the edge to get at whatever message is inside. "Oh...it's from Cyril. I didn't recognise the handwriting."

The other three aren't entirely sure what they're meant to say. Her brother was surprisingly useful and supportive after what happened with her parents, but who knows what that letter might contain. As she reads, Jordan's eyes start to water, a few sniffles escape, and by the time she sets it aside she's fully crying, Lili sitting up to comfort her, unsure of the contents but knowing she's needed.

"Cy, um, he managed to grab a few things from my parent's house. From my old room. He wasn't sure if I'd want them, but he says I deserve to decide for myself. And he's added a few new things as well. Dropped it off on his way to the airport. And he - "

Jordan wipes at her eyes and tucks her hair behind her ears before continuing. She clears her throat and gives Lili a weak smile. "He apologised for being a shit brother and he said he wants to make up for lost time. Invited both of us to visit him and Elena in Madrid this summer, if we can. Also, he wants to watch my dissertation and whatever else family should be invited to, then help us get settled wherever we end up."

"Do you want that?" Lili asks, incredibly carefully, with a hand on the back of Jordan's neck, her thumb rubbing along the soft skin there.

"I...want to let him try." Jordan lets out a sob before catching herself and just letting the tears flow, but quietly. Emir reaches for the Kleenex while Theo holds up her tea, and she laughs in appreciation at their sincere attempts to help while she falls apart. "The thing is...I thought losing my parents meant I didn't have a family anymore. But maybe I can still have Cyril. I just...don't want to be disappointed if he doesn't mean it."

"Whatever you decide, I'm fine with it. Invite him or don't, you won't be alone." Lili kisses the centre of Jordan's forehead before taking a Kleenex from the box Emir still has outstretched and gently wiping away most of Jordan's tears from her cheeks. She's *so gentle* with Jordan. "But to be fair, this does seem like he genuinely wants to try. He came all the way here before he left and put all this together, which is...something. And he's been texting you almost every day to check in."

"Yeah." Jordan agrees, taking the Kleenex from Lili to wipe away her own tears, then accepting the mug from Theo and taking a very deep gulp. "He's trying, so I think I should let him, if he wants. He's not our parents, and I've never really known him as an adult."

"Do you want us to go?" Emir asks, aware that this may be a very private moment for Jordan. They still don't know what Jordan might need to process as she looks through the contents of the box.

"No! Stay, please." Jordan seems to be done crying for now, reaching out a hand first to Emir, then to Theo and waiting for them to take hold. "You're family, remember? Besides, we have to help my tiny overpacker unload all her clothes after I go through this."

"It's not that much stuff!" Lili huffs, picking up her own mug again to hold in her hands. "And we only use one of our bedrooms anyway, so we have plenty of space."

"Just remember we have to downsize in a few months." Jordan is the one to give Lilibet a forehead kiss this time, setting down her cuppa to pick up the box she'd set aside with one last sniffle.

It takes several minutes for Jo to get through everything that Cyril's left for her because some of the items require processing. There's both a baby doll and a teddy bear that used to be Jo's special favourites as a kid, a few personal items of jewellery that she tells them were gifts from now-dead relatives, some family photos with sticky notes covering their parents' faces, which makes Jo laugh, and then the bits Cyril added himself.

At the bottom, there's a Progress Pride flag, a lesbian Pride flag, an assortment of pronoun pins, a stainless steel water bottle that reads "GAY AF" in hot pink, Jo's favourite chocolate bar, and another envelope with over a thousand pounds in cash that she scoffs at but tucks away carefully, knowing it very well might be needed. She can't believe he just left that in the hallway, but since everyone was away for the break, maybe he knew it'd be safe.

After Jordan hangs the two Pride flags in the window with everyone's help and sets the other items aside for later, they do finally get around to helping Lili unpack before they give up for the day and say their goodnights. It's only for a few hours until the morning when classes start up again.

Jordan hugs them both close before they go, Lili thanks them for their help, and the last thing Emir and Theo see before they leave the flat is Jordan staring at her new Pride flags with Lili hugging her from behind.

***

Emir's stowing away his things at the end of rehearsal when he realises it's just him and Sam in the dressing room. It's their second day back from break, and he hasn't had a chance to check in and catch up with him yet, especially because almost all of their classes are separate with Sam being a first year.

"Alright, young Samuel?" Emir drapes his pointe shoes on a hook in his locker, hoping they'll air out a bit tonight since he won't be using them for dissertation work with Theo later. His feet need a night off.

"Yeah. I'm alright. Not as rested as I'd like going into the rest of the year, but good." Sam finishes tugging his jumper over his spiral curls and gives Emir a smile. "You have a nice break?"

"It was real nice, yeah. Had family time, brought Theo to visit Shipley for a bit, saw our friends for a few days, taught class at my old dance school, that sort of thing. The family doesn't really do Christmas, so it was mostly just chilling." Emir sits down on the bench and rolls out his ankles. He has a few minutes to chat and he's grown a bit protective of Sam since their first conversation at the *Alice in Wonderland* pre-show cast party.

"We don't either. And I missed most of Chanukah because of the uni schedule, so until New Year's I was working most days, and then we went to visit my grandparents last week." Sam sits near Emir on the same bench, feet still bare against the linoleum. "I love my family, but, um…some of them are a bit difficult."

"I don't mean this to sound presumptive," Emir thinks for a moment, hoping to find the right words, but there's not really a delicate way to ask. "Are they difficult about you being trans?"

Emir's heard a few comments from Sam before that make him suspect that some of his extended family members might not be as accepting as his parents.

Sam sighs, the sound so heavy that it takes his shoulders with it until he's curled forward into himself. "Yeah. My grandad keeps deadnaming me and my nan made some comment about how I should have *outgrown this phase* which was…I don't always handle it very well. I internalise a lot of it, I suppose."

This conversation is a lot *more* than Emir was anticipating when he started it, but clearly this is something Sam needs to talk about and Emir can be a supportive person if nothing else. "And is it only your grandparents?"

"No." Another sigh from Sam. He brings one of his feet up into his lap and starts massaging the tension away from the arch. "My cousins are alright, but my mum's brother is awful. That sounds harsh, but he is. You'd think after ten years they'd all get over themselves, but."

Sam shrugs, as if to say *it is what it is*.

"I'm really sorry they're treating you that way." Emir reaches out a hand and sets it on Sam's back between his shoulders. He's used to being the big brother, but never in quite this situation. "I know we don't always have a say in who our family turn out to be or how they act or if we have to see them, so I suppose I'll just remind you that you do have people who support you and want to see you thriving as exactly who you are. And if you ever need a reminder, you know at least one person who can always be that."

"Thanks." Sam glances up at Emir with a sideways smile, then stares down at his toes again. "I broke up with Esme, too. We're fine though. Good, actually. When we had space over break, we sort of realised we were much better as friends, like we were before. We don't really have the physical component we used to, you know? We still talk everyday and send each other memes and all that. But the timing with everything else going on with my family...suppose I'm just feeling a bit worn down."

"That's completely understandable." Emir gives Sam's shoulder a squeeze before letting his hand drop back to his own side. "I've noticed you chatting more with the other first year lads. Has that been going better?"

"A bit..." Sam leans forward over his knees, elbows supporting his weight. "Honestly, though, I think I might need more friends outside of dance. You'd think this is where I'd find people who understand and accept me, but mostly they just sort of leave me be. Like, they don't invite me to hang out or anything, but at least they do talk to me now."

"Hm." Emir frowns, unhappy with how the first years are acting, but it's still better than them being outright transphobic. "Most of my best mates aren't dancers, so you could be onto something. Uni events aren't really my scene, but if you're wanting to, like, put yourself out there and meet new people, that might be an idea for a place to start."

"That's a fair point." Sam stands up from the bench and starts sliding his feet into winter boots. No socks, but as they're Sam's feet and Sam's boots to do with as he pleases, Emir doesn't comment. "I have a tendency to wallow and sort of just coast, so could you give me a nudge if you see me sulking for too much longer?"

"I suppose that could be arranged." Emir stands up as well, pulling Sam into a hug and ruffling his messy curls. He releases him, changing his voice to sound like an old Hollywood radio announcer. "Now, off you go. There's a whole world out there waiting for you, young man."

"You're such a nerd." Sam rolls his eyes and gently shoves Emir away, but he's smiling now and it seems genuine. Before he's out the door, he turns back to Emir to add, "But, um...thanks."

And then he's gone. Emir watches the closed door for a few seconds, sitting back down on the bench and thinking. And then it's five minutes later and he's still in the same spot, unmoved and conflicted.

Emi: got a minute?
Theo: For you? Always /kiss emoji/
Emi: i think i need thirty minutes alone in the studio before dinner if that's alright
Emi: does that completely fuck up the schedule?
Theo: Doesn't fuck up anything. But even if it did, you can always ask for some alone time.
Emi: maybe we take the night off dissertation work?
Emi: my head isn't in the right space but i was thinking we could just...have a bit of a lark?
Emi: bring your pointe shoes and i'll bring myself and we'll just dance for the fun of it for tonight? maybe relax together before bed. i could catch up on some reading and you could do whatever it is you fancy?
Theo: That sounds perfect, babe /heart emoji/
Theo: Dinner is just reheated leftovers, so there's no rush.
Theo: I'll get a bit of coursework done while I wait. You take all the time you need!
Emi: have i mentioned recently that i completely adore you?
Theo: You have :)
Theo: And I adore you, too /heart eyes emoji/
Theo: Text me on your way back and I'll walk over to meet you at yours.
Emi: /forehead kiss gif/
Theo: /hug gif/

***

Family dinner has been the same for months now, and yet, somehow, it's their first one after the break and it's different. There are seven people, rather than six, crowded around their table, ready to share a meal. While literally no one is surprised by this development, they're all actively restraining themselves from calling out Gabe and Ciaran for bringing Alfie along.

"So...did one of these two explain how this works?" T is the first to break the barely-held-together silence from Alfie's right; three of them are trying to hold in their comments, two are avoiding eye contact, one is looking between them all in confusion, and T is just...T.

"They've mentioned family dinner once or twice." Alfie sits back in his chair and hides away a smile when he catches Ciaran's eye. He's sitting at the far side of the table beside Gabe, both squished in next to Ciaran, their three sets of legs constantly bumping together, especially with Gabe's extra height. "Or five thousand times."

"Well, it was our turn to cook this week, which means I did everything and Laur looked pretty and figured out a bunch of wedding stuff while the rolls were in the oven." T gives Laurie a very pointed look, clearly asking him to jump into the conversation.

"My beauty is rather integral, as far as contributions go," Laurie leans forward in his chair and grabs one of the aforementioned rolls, "So you're all welcome. Now fucking dig in. Shit's embarrassing. Can't even have a guest without everyone forgetting how to act."

"In my defence," Theo reaches for the roast veg before anyone else can lay claim, "I never knew how in the first place."

T laughs in agreement and catches Theo's eye, the two of them sharing an understanding grin.

"Sorry, just need to..." Emir pulls out his phone right at the table, which he would usually never do, but needs must. He's on the verge of a snarky comment, but he also doesn't want Alfie to feel unwelcome.

Emi: *one of us has to ask them*
Emi: *it stopped being casual ages ago*
Emi: *and like maybe they aren't calling him a boyfriend*
Emi: *but*

"Princess, wasn't there something you needed to check?" Emir kicks Theo's toes beneath the table, distracting him from a mouthful of roast carrots. Very delicious, honey glazed carrots.

"What? No I - " Theo covers his mouth with his hand while answering until he sees Emir's obviously wide eyes looking between his own phone and Theo's face and he understands. "Right, that."

"Christ's sake." Laurie swears, stuffing a bit of roll into his mouth now that it's been buttered. They could at least *attempt* subtlety.

Theo: *Isn't this one of those things we aren't meant to ask them? Like at dinner?*
Theo: *But they wouldn't have invited him if it didn't mean something.*
Theo: *When you started coming it was different. You were already family to everyone but me by then.*
Theo: *NOT that kind of coming.*
Theo: *But now I'm distracted…*

"Easy there, Teddy. You and yours told us not at the table." Ciaran shoves lightly at Theo's shoulder. "I know that face, and last time we all shagged through a meal you got stroppy and Emir threw several cushions at me."

"I was only thinking about it." Theo grumbles, going back to his roast carrots because now he's both a little bit turned on knowing what he and Emir have planned for tonight, and he's genuinely hungry after a very busy day in the studio.

"Right, so, who's going first then?" T gets them back on track, or at least attempts to. "Alfie, you're under no obligation to join, but you're welcome to if you'd like."

"I'll start." Gabe drinks half his glass of water in one go and sets it aside again, sitting up straighter in his chair. "I'm still jet lagged and in a really bizarre sleeping pattern but that actually worked out today because I've been waking up earlier and really settling into my voice before class starts and I got a really nice recording that I'll play for you all later."

Thanks to T and their hosting instincts, dinner is back on track and proceeding almost as usual. Emir and Theo remind everyone about their weekend coming up and how they'll be spending it away to go see Ballet Trockadero together ahead of Emir's birthday. T and Laurie mostly give wedding updates since their courses haven't proven very interesting the past three days. Ciaran talks about his dissertation work a bit and some changes he wants to make. Alfie shares only briefly about visiting his parents over the holidays, on account of how they're both being massive dickheads who insist on putting him in the middle of their divorce. He gets a full kiss from Ciaran, who has to get up out of his chair to do so, and a very loving hand in his hair from Gabe after he's shared. The others very pointedly don't make a big deal out of that.

It's after they've cleared up and everyone's settled haphazardly on the sofas for tea and telly that Emir gets this...feeling. He's already been thinking about bringing this topic up and he doesn't mind telling Alfie who isn't only incredibly decent, but essentially one of them, or well on his way. And it's gone alright the last few times, so...

"Theo?" Emir stands a few feet away from the rest of them, gazing at the scene and needing a hint of reassurance before taking the leap. Theo looks his way with that perfect, warm smile and when Emir holds out a hand in invitation, he stands back up from the sofa to take it and find out what's keeping him.

"You need to go for a run or something?" Theo asks once they're back near the kitchen together, talking in low voices with the excuse of needing extra forks for the tart that T somehow found time to make today.

"No, it's not that, but maybe later before we get to the ravishing." Emir gives Theo a brief, lustful look, knowing that they've planned for Theo to be tied up and whining almost exactly two hours from now back at Emir's flat. But then his mind shifts back to the worry at hand. "I was actually thinking I might - that it's time to - it's just that it went fine with Lili and Jo and I really do need to tell Ciaran and Gabe. I *want* to tell them."

It takes Theo a moment to catch up to the topic because of the sudden shift, but when he does, he understands why Emir's shoulders are tense and he's got that wide-eyed, far away look that means he's nervous and having a hard time grounding himself in the present.

"It doesn't have to be right now, but if it is, you know I'm here no matter what happens or what anyone says, loving you and ready to remind you." Theo pulls Emir close, arms going around his waist until they're essentially moulded together with a bit of useless fabric being suffocated in between. "Also I can fight."

That makes Emir laugh and get out of his head a bit. As if squishy, marshmallow, teddy bear Theodore George Palmer would ever fight anyone. And the fact Lili told him essentially the exact same thing a few weeks ago once she knew his gender identity makes Emir feel this fondness for their friendship that gives him something like courage. "I'm hoping it won't come to that, especially with T being nonbinary and none of them having any issue with it. But...never know, I suppose."

"You don't have to do this tonight, babe." Theo reminds Emir, still holding him tight in a hug. He's sure the others are watching them, but given the Welsh, ginger elephant in the room, he doubts anyone is about to call them out for cuddling near the fridge. "You just tell me what you need."

"Just need you." Emir sighs and nuzzles closer. He's been quite nuzzly in general this week. It goes in phases, like anything else, but there's never really a day where he doesn't want at least morning and nighttime snuggles with Theo. "Thanks. Just needed a moment with you to be sure. I'm ready."

"After you." Theo releases Emir from the embrace and turns him around by the shoulders, reaching behind himself to grab the forks he lied about needing before following after Emir to rejoin the conversation in the next room.

"Welcome back." Laurie gives them a look of gay judgement, waving around the spare forks that were already on the coffee table as they share the spot Theo recently vacated. "We decided on *Derry Girls* since we all have places to be once we've digested."

"Ugh. Digested is *not* a nice word." T looks up from their spot between Laurie's legs with a nose scrunch. "And right in front of my tart."

"Is that what we're calling Laurie now?" Gabe asks with a grin. He's only teasing. Laurie scoffs like he wants to respond, but Emir gets there first.

"Actually, before we watch anything, there was one other thing I wanted to tell everyone." Emir swallows down the lump in his throat. Everything is suddenly grey. Stormy, swirling, stifling grey.

But then Theo's hand is on his thigh and brilliant, warm red starts to clear it away, inch by inch. Why the fuck is this so hard? He just did this a few days ago like it was nothing and he loves these people. This should be easy.

"Why do you look ill?" T asks, concern evident in their voice. They're already halfway out of their seat. "Is everything alright?"

"Fine!" Emir stands up from his spot instead, needing some sort of movement or just…something. He wants to do this, but for some reason he can't get out of the crushing fog of trauma at the moment. "Theo, I need - "

"On it." Theo walks to the kitchen and gets a full glass of water, handing it over to Emir in record time. Emir takes it with shaking hands, needing something to ground him because he doesn't want to panic right now. He doesn't need to. And yet. "Better?"

Emir takes a few sips while the others all watch him in silence. It's rare to see Emir shaken up. But the cold water helped, and so did Theo's hand on his back beneath his shirt, soothing him while he found his footing. He's good. "Sorry, just panicked for a minute."

"Oh..." Laurie realises quietly, but since everyone else is so still, it can be heard through the room. "It's alright, Emi. You're safe here."

T seems to have understood as well, nodding emphatically and watching as Theo guides Emir back to the sofa one step at a time. Alfie looks a bit scared himself, but Ciaran and Gabe mostly just seem curious, with a hint of concern swirling in.

"Right. I'm just going to say it because for some reason my body has decided to do...all this." Emir gestures at the whole of himself with a weak laugh. But it's not a joke and he's only trying to make this easier on himself. Fucking PTSD and its fucking symptoms and his fucking ex who created this situation that Emir has to live with. But focusing on that is not going to help anything. Fuck him. This isn't about him. This is about Emir. Maybe he needs his Friday appointment with Amanda more than he realised.

"Remember the picture of my new tattoo that I sent you?" Emir finally manages to say. It's a place to start.

"Oooo do we get to see the real thing?" Ciaran's eyes sparkle with genuine excitement. But then Gabe slaps him across the chest and says, "Not the time."

"Maybe later." Emir does laugh despite himself. A true laugh this time. It's just chatting with his mates. He's got this. "I never explained what the new one was, but T and Laur already know. Like, you knew about my name in Urdu tattooed on the left hip, but I didn't tell you about the other. Sort of banked on you getting distracted by the dick nearby, if I'm honest."

"I figured it was personal." Gabe shrugs, one hand on Alfie's knee, the other in the back of Ciaran's hair.

"It is." Emir looks between the three of them, glances at T and Laurie who both have encouraging smiles, then up to Theo who mouths *I love you*. So, he sets his shoulders and gets it over with. "It's the genderqueer symbol. Or, like, one of them. Because I'm genderqueer."

"Oh, cool! Makes sense why you'd get it tattooed. Sort of goes with your name then, eh? Like a set." Gabe gives Emir a very genuine smile. "Thanks for telling us and, like, I love you, in case you need the reminder. We all love you, like, maybe a bit too much, but you're a really good person, so you're stuck with us."

Gabe doesn't show a single moment of hesitation in his acceptance. And he's the one who's called Emir a good person, but Gabe's one of the most decent people Emir's ever known.

Realistically Emir knew this would be fine, but yes, he did need the reminder. As he's about to tell Gabe thank you, Gabe tugs on Ciaran's hair and adds, "Also Ciaran *was* distracted by your dick, so you weren't wrong about that. He fully missed seeing the ink for several minutes."

"It's a nice dick!" Ciaran gives them all a vague gesture that mostly communicates they should've all known that already. "Also, it's attached to a very nice person who just came out to us, so maybe we should stop focusing on the penis and more on the person. Hi, hello, sorry we're making your coming out about your dick."

Emir just laughs again, hiding his face against Theo's chest for a moment because he was worried for nothing. Literally nothing has changed now that they know, which is actually entirely perfect.

"For what it's worth, I haven't seen the dick pic in question, so I'm genuinely supportive of you and your coming out regardless of how nice your cock is." Alfie gives Emir an approving nod when their eyes meet. He hadn't planned on Alfie being here for this but he's never had to worry with Alfie. He's chill.

"Also, like, to answer the questions I usually get: Yes, I still use he/him pronouns, and I'm fine with others but only in private. Yes, I'm fine with traditionally masculine words and clothes and all that, I just also like the other words and clothes as well. Yes, me being genderqueer is private information. Only my family and Lili and Jo know, and I intend to keep it that way." Emir ticks them off on his fingers as he goes, Theo pressing a soft kiss beneath his jaw partway through his list. The list he's actually through now, but he feels like being sarcastic. He's earned it. "Yes, it does make me even sexier, thanks for noticing. No, we cannot have a seven person orgy to celebrate my coming out. We all have plans."

"Well there goes my Wednesday night." Laurie leans over and kisses the corner of Emir's lips while Emir is still cuddled up next to Theo. He knows what it takes for Emir to do this, and twice in as many weeks is a lot. "You alright?"

"Yeah, sorry about…all that." Emir waves his hand again, gesturing at where he had been standing a few minutes ago when he was panicking. He knows it's almost entirely out of his control, but he still hates that it happens. At least this time, the trigger was incredibly straight forward.

"Is this the rest of the story with the ex?" Gabe asks, reaching for his portion of the tart now that Emir's gender is out in the open. Given Emir's very visible reaction a few minutes ago and what he already knows, Gabe's making an educated guess. "He's a pile of human shit and I'm glad you've never told me his name because I'd like to do very bad things to him and not in a fun way. Ciaran has connections."

"It's…more of the story. I don't know that I'll ever share all of what happened outside of therapy, but he, um…he threw me out of his house after I told him, and being genderqueer is why he doxxed me, so…" Emir scratches at his stubble. He had to shave the beard he'd been growing for the sake of uni performance guidelines, but he left enough of a shadow to make himself happy. He's been in the mood to be scruffy recently.

"Hold on a moment: your ex did *what*? Was this recently?" Alfie sets aside the plate that T just handed him, looking at Emir in a way he hasn't before. Emir isn't quite sure what Alfie's seeing when he's staring at him.

"No, not really. Summer before we all started here." Emir leans back into Theo, taking hold of Theo's arms and wrapping them around his own middle. Theo kisses his neck again and keeps his head there, a very solid, warm presence that Emir needs even if he's past the worst of it. "And yeah, he was a real prize. He outed me to my family and to everyone I knew, and then he doxxed me and, as you saw a few minutes ago, I'm still a bit fucked about it."

"You're not fucked. You're incredible, you are." Alfie actually stands up and steps over the others until he's crouching in front of Emir, their eyes locked. "You're this amazing person. I've always admired you. And I'm sorry that happened to you. The fact you can tell us at all, that you can come out to us, to *me* who you really don't know very well, even after what he did...I don't mean this to sound so camp, but I'm genuinely proud of you, I am."

And Emir's surprisingly touched. He and Alfie have been casual acquaintances bordering on friends for years, but this is the first time they've ever had a conversation about something real. Well, Alfie's talked about his parents, but even then they've stopped before the conversation reached anything very deep.

"Thanks, Alfie. You're alright, you know?" Emir glances up at Gabe and Ciaran to see them already staring. Maybe Theo was right not to push a conversation with them tonight about their relationship with Alfie. Maybe they're figuring things out in their own way and on their own time. "I'm glad you're one of the people I've told."

Alfie gives his knee a squeeze and stands up to return to his spot with his *not*-boyfriends a few feet away. He's welcomed back like he never left. Like he fits.

"Time for pudding?" T asks, even though half of them already have their allotted portion of tart.

Emir takes a bite, thinking about how much he loves that every piece of this group is a perfect fit. T can tell that Emir is done talking, just like Theo will know he needs a walk before they settle in for the night, and Laurie changes the topic of conversation to something Emir doesn't give a single fuck about while Ciaran starts the show to give them background noise to settle into. Gabe has Alfie in his arms now so that Ciaran can argue with Laurie about football, and it's the antithesis to what Emir's body was preparing him for before he was able to pull himself back from the edge.

"I love you and I'm proud of you." Theo waits until the attention is firmly away from Emir to mumble his own contribution to the moment. The two of them have a way of creating a private bubble for themself, even amongst gay chaos. "If you need space, I can make an excuse to get you out of here."

"You're perfect." Emir turns his upper body so they can talk face to face, just a few inches apart. "I think I'm alright. I'd like a walk on the way back to my flat but I don't need to be alone. It's good I'll be seeing Amanda on Friday. Been a busy few weeks."

"God, it really has. Hard to believe all that's happened." Theo rests their foreheads together and closes his eyes. "If you change your mind about tonight, I won't be upset. I know we planned for sex but, like, plans change."

"I appreciate the reminder, baby, but I think it's passed. I'm good." Emir turns the rest of his body around until he's almost laying on top of Theo, his feet kicking someone that he assumes is Laurie. With this many people and two sofas it's what they can manage. "And I'm looking forward to getting my teeth on my rope bunny, if he's still willing."

"More than." Theo brings Emir closer for a kiss, already anticipating the bite that he gets to his plush bottom lip. He's just *so into* Emir, and all that he is and all that he does. "But we have a tart to eat first."

Emir smiles, pressing his lips to Theo's once more then turning back around to rejoin the rest of the room. Just a typical family dinner after all.

***

Theo's wonderfully sore the next morning as he starts his gym routine. Emir was perfect last night. Stunning, really. Theo begged to be tied up for longer than usual, which meant some bruising, and not only from the ropes, but mostly, it translated to stiff joints and sore muscles from repeatedly straining against the bondage while he whined and moaned. After, Emir had taken him to the shower and massaged every inch of Theo's skin once they were back in Emir's bed, but still. The ache remained.

The thing is, Theo really likes it. He likes the reminder and the feeling that his body was working for the pleasure it received. Not that he always wants it that way, because he's equally as happy when it's all soft kisses and easy hands. But the more he and Emir explore, the deeper Theo understands his own desires.

It's taken them only a few weeks to work their way up from bound wrists to having Theo completely tied, gag included, and it's not an everyday thing, but maybe once a week. It's sort of beautiful in its own way. When Theo woke up this morning, he saw that Emir had left him a drawing of his own naked ass, ropes taut across the skin, Emir's perspective from last night but shared through a new medium.

And they haven't even reached penetration yet, of any kind. Hell, Theo hasn't even given Emir a blowjob despite having received many by now. And he has plans for that. Specific plans that he can't wait to make a reality.

But while he does his cardio warmup before heading for the weights, all Theo can think about is the way his shirt chafes at the rope burn across his chest or how all the tiny muscles in his feet are still tight from the toe-curling double orgasm he'd experienced a few hours ago. He felt so cared for and looked after while he was tied up and for all the time he needed to recover.

Theo lets his mind wander, not really needing to focus because he does this six days a week. There's light variations to work on different muscle groups, but generally his routine is the same.

He's always alone at this hour. The university gym is open twenty-four hours a day, but no one else wakes up this early and comes here unless absolutely necessary, so Theo intentionally planned his mornings to be alone as a result. People don't usually start showing up until he's leaving. At least not until today.

Lilibet shuffles through the door and tosses her bag somewhere random, stepping up and onto the treadmill two down from Theo. She gives him a nod in acknowledgement and, rather than easing herself into a jog, she turns the speed up right away and breaks into a sprint.

Theo's timer goes off soon after, so he silently steps off his machine and closer to Lili, drinking from his water bottle and watching her stare at absolutely nothing out the window like she's trying to run fast enough for her body to catch up to the rest of her. He never really sees her like this, and she's *never* just shown up at the gym, especially first thing in the morning. She's not even usually awake at this hour.

And thank god he's watching Lilibet closely because, after a few minutes of sprinting, she stumbles over her own feet. It could've been really bad with how fast she was going, but Theo catches her on instinct and lifts her up and away from the still moving belt, setting her down on the stationary floor so he can pull the emergency stop. Thankful for their years of partnering work together, Theo tries not to think of what almost happened, what he barely prevented, and mostly by luck.

"Lili, what's happened?" Theo holds her tiny shoulders, just now noticing that she has tears shining all the way down her cheeks. At least that explains the stumble. It's a wonder she can see at all with how hard she's been silently crying.

"I don't know how to fucking do this." Lili wipes at her eyes with the back of her hand, her hoodie sleeve catching a fair bit of the moisture, but more springs up immediately. It's like she's crying a week's worth of tears in a single morning. "But you do, so when I still couldn't sleep, I figured I'd try this and see if it helped."

"Hold on. Back up a minute and let's move away from the equipment." Theo takes Lili carefully by the forearm, picks up her bag from the middle of the floor, and walks the both of them over to one of the benches outside of the changing rooms where his own belongings wait. "Could you fill me in a bit?"

Lili pulls her hood up and over her hair where she's gathered it into a puff at the crown of her head then rests her arms atop it, opening her chest as she leans back. It takes her a minute to settle down, the tears eventually slowing and her breathing calm enough that Theo isn't worried about some form of hyperventilation.

"I'm just so *angry* all the time. I fucking hate Jo's parents and her entire family and the whole fucking world right now. I didn't even know I could be this angry, but it just sits in my chest like a fucking fire and burns me anytime I think about what they did." Lili starts, and Theo realises only a few words in that she has quite a bit to get off her chest.

"And I'm terrified. Jo's so shaky right now. She's unstable in a way I can't pretend is alright. Like, she's doing the best she can, but if one tiny thing goes wrong, I'm worried what she might do. Her mind's real dark right now, and that's only the parts she shows me. Neither of us has been sleeping, and she's so impulsive since they ditched her that I don't even know what to expect from one moment to the next. And then on top of that, I'm worried that we're fucked in a few months because we're both about to be without work, on our own in London, no way to pay for anything, my parents hours away and no one we can lean on until we find our footing. Our relationship is a fucking mess because she won't tell me how bad it is, and I can't make her tell me, and then I can't show her how upset it's all making me feel or how inadequate I am or that I'm unprepared to handle any of it because none of this is actually about me, even though it's affecting me. She needs me to be her fucking rock and I just...I *can't*, Theo. I'm just one person. I don't know how."

"Right." Theo waits, just in case there's more that needs to be let out. But it seems, at least for the moment, she's done. He takes an extra hand towel from his own gym bag and fishes her water bottle out of hers, handing them both over and waiting for her to take them. Lili's not alone. Jo's not alone. But maybe they need the reminder now that they're back at uni. "Let's start with the basics. When's the last time you or Jo ate an actual meal, and how can we get you some sleep?"

Lili drinks from her water bottle for a while without saying anything, eyes closed like she's reminding herself to breathe. "We've been too stressed this week to make anything after rehearsal. It's been burnt toast and jacket potatoes, if we remember at all. At least at my parents they made sure we ate. And...I don't know what to do about the sleep but I know it isn't helping. Jo took melatonin last night, but even then, she barely slept."

"Give me a moment." Theo finds his phone in his bag and he doesn't even bother texting. He dials Emi's number immediately, knowing he'll pick up. And he does, right away. "Yeah, I'm alright. I'm with Lili at the gym...Less alright...No, I don't think it can wait...Could you maybe cut your run short and meet me at their flat?...Wouldn't hurt...We'll be there in a bit...Love you, babe...Bye."

Groaning, Lili thunks her forehead against Theo's shoulder. "You weren't meant to ruin your day for me, I just came here to...I don't know. Try to be you, because you have this all figured out already."

Theo laughs at that, a small, disbelieving sound. "In no universe do I have it all figured out. Emir and I are just going to get you both set up for a few days and make sure you aren't alone since we'll be gone this weekend. And you're not ruining anything. Emir's going to check on Jo while you and I finish our chat."

"What's there to discuss?" Lili stands up and starts stretching and pacing and bouncing, hands in her hoodie pocket and eyes cast down towards her feet. "I'm a terrible girlfriend, and this fucked up society is a cisnormative homophobic hellscape that worships capitalism and hates Black people, in large part because of people like Jordan's family. And I can't do fuck all about any of it."

"Alright, you're not wrong about that, except that part about you being a bad girlfriend because you're not." Theo stays seated, hoping that he at least won't startle Lili because she's exhausted and emotional and came to him for help. "But it's the reality we have and we both know you don't actually believe there's nothing we can do about it. You're just having a really shit time at the moment and, incidentally, all those things you said are true, which is making the shit time even shittier."

"She's not well, Teddy." Lili stops moving and stares at him with wide, concerned eyes. If he had to guess, this is what's really keeping her up at night. "I gave her two weeks before I panicked, but she's not getting better. She's getting worse, but given the circumstances, I don't know that I can blame her."

"Is it past the point you think she can manage?" Theo's never had to worry about this with a partner. Emir's the only one he's had, and even when things have been bad for him, he was never in an acute crisis. It's never been what Lili's describing.

"Yes." Lili keeps staring, like he'll have all the answers. He doesn't, but neither would anyone else.

"Maybe Emir could have a chat with her. He had some pretty intense therapy after what happened to him, and he's good with being realistic when talking about that process or just, like, helping people to get the help they need, himself included." Theo pats the seat beside him, hoping that maybe Lili will come sit down again. It doesn't seem the sprinting on the treadmill or the pacing has helped. She can't outrun this. "And, well, it sounds like you could use someone to talk to for yourself. Maybe someone like Emir's seeing. Someone at the health centre. You don't have to, of course, but I think it might help."

"I think...I was wondering if maybe the two of us should start with Sean?" Lili does take the seat beside him again, tucking one leg beneath herself and leaning sideways against the wall to face him. "He's got resources and all that useful shit and maybe he has some suggestions for Jo. Like a mental health professional he recommends, but also Emir mentioned some sort of dance supply thing and anything like that, we could really use. Especially Jo."

"I think that's a great idea. He's usually got a bit of time after tech hall, and he will *always* make time if there's a need. Sean's, like, a real adult, you know?" Theo pulls her close by the shoulder, holding her to his chest and enveloping her in a hug.

It takes a moment, but she hugs him back, the sort of hug that she doesn't want to admit she needs but falls into the second she allows herself the comfort. "And about after uni - let's figure out the rest of the month and then get back to it. Maybe even get through the winter show first. So much could change in the next few weeks, and getting past these really hard days will seem like forever, but it'll be much more manageable to think about jobs and a flat and all the rest when they calm down. I know the real world is coming soon, but it's not an emergency. Not yet."

"You're right. I'm not handling any of this very well. I just keep thinking about this cliff we're headed for, and I don't want us to be left to jump without a parachute unless absolutely necessary." Lili shifts but doesn't remove herself from the hug, situating herself in a more comfortable position. "How do you do this? With Emir? You make it seem so natural, like you're just this perfect, stable rock for him to lean on when it gets bad."

"This isn't about me and Emir, but we're in no way perfect. You and Jordan are in an entirely different situation and I don't want you comparing yourselves to us or anything like that. And for what it's worth, you do know how to be supportive and loving, even if you've misplaced your confidence at the moment."

Theo rubs his hand along her back, wondering if he could convince her to go for a nap between classes and rehearsal. "Think of all the times you've stood up for me. Finding out about my bullies back home and offering to fight them, for one. Checking in with me when you know I'm getting overstimulated, being my best mate for all these years and never once being anything less than exactly who I needed in my corner. You know how to support Jordan, but you're not her therapist or her parent, you're her girlfriend. You can't be everything to her, especially if you're this stressed and exhausted."

"But she doesn't have anyone else. Not that she ever had her parents, but now it's just...everything's such a mess and I don't even know where to start." Lili sniffles and wipes at her eyes then folds herself into Theo so it's less of a hug and more him holding her together. "I'm so confused all the time, like everything I'm doing is completely wrong."

"Does this, um - " Theo pauses, because he's been meaning to ask about this and hasn't been able to find the right moment yet. But they're alone, so. "I've noticed she doesn't hold back on the PDA anymore. Like, you hold hands and she kisses you goodbye and everyone knows you're together now. And you've always said you were fine with whatever she wanted, but is this what you want? It's a big change."

"I don't mind, but it feels a bit..." Lili's voice is muffled from her spot against his chest but she's making no attempt at moving away. "Like she's overcompensating? Like she's trying to prove how okay she is or something? It's so far the opposite of how she was before, and in private she's either plastered to me or needs complete isolation. I can't keep up - and then she'll go from ignoring me for hours to snogging me while walking on the pavement, and I'm trying to not make this about me, but it's confusing as hell and I never know quite where things stand. Like, I know we're together and I know we love each other, but it's all the rest. She's just all over the place and that includes shagging and everything else. Of course I want to be with her, but nowadays I'm worried if she's on me *and* I'm worried if she's alone. I just...I don't know. I feel a bit used I think, like she's trying to prove a point by being all over me, but I don't think she realises or means it that way. She's the one whose world fell apart, but trying to help her put the pieces back together is like trying to solve a Rubik's Cube on fire."

"That's quite the metaphor." Theo pulls back slightly so he can set his hands on her shoulders and get a proper look at her again. She's definitely calmer than before, but she looks absolutely dreadful, bordering on ill. "How about I walk you home and we can keep talking on the way? And when we get there, the four of us can figure some things out before class. Just because you're back at uni and away from your parents doesn't mean you have to do everything on your own, alright?"

Lili puts her now empty water bottle back in her bag and mumbles something incoherent that Theo doesn't quite catch.

"What was that?" He stands up, taking his own bag and waiting for Lili to do the same.

"I'm just, like, really tired and I sort of want to collapse right here and I'm wondering if maybe I shouldn't go to class this morning." Lili rubs at her eyes with the sleeves of her hoodie. "I don't want to miss rehearsal, but maybe Jo and I will finally be able to get some sleep after figuring things out with the Shahs."

"The Shah-Palmers, but yes. I think it might be best if you give your body a break." Theo tugs her back into his side, arm around her shoulder as he guides her back out of the gym and into the early morning quiet. "And if - like, I know this might not be the issue - but if you're having a sort of mental block preventing you from sleeping in your own bed, you can always borrow mine for a nap today. Offer stands for Jo, too. We can always stay at Emir's tonight, too. The others won't mind."

"How'd you even know we can't sleep in our bed?" Lilibet moves her bag strap from her shoulder to across her body, tugging her hood higher and shivering slightly in the chill. Theo wouldn't be surprised if she is coming down with something, her body's defences lowered from the lack of sleep and general wellbeing.

"Sometimes it's easier to fall asleep on a sofa or a different bed because our brain is out of the spiral it's been stuck in." Theo shrugs, hands in his pockets while they walk. "You know how I do that thing where I purposely get lost when I'm feeling lost? Sort of the same thing. Break the pattern as a sort of reset."

"Why do you get to be all intelligent on top of everything else?" Lili shoves at his shoulder, and the teasing is how he knows she's alright. Nothing's fixed, but she's not panicked at the moment. If all he can do is make this manageable for her, then that's enough for the morning.

"Well, the universe gave me high-masking autism, baby fat during prime bullying years, and disaster bisexuality. Given the fucked up society you reminded us of earlier, I think the universe owed me one." Theo grins, shoving her back, but so gently she barely wobbles.

"Yes, but you also got Emir." Lilibet points out, and she has a point.

"And you got Jo." Theo gives her a careful smile, glad to see it returned.

"Yeah. I did." Lili's quiet the rest of the way back to her flat, linking her arm with Theo's and leaning into his side, grateful for the support.

As they reach their building a few easy minutes later, Theo reminds her, "Just take it one step at a time."

CHAPTER FOURTEEN

"Babyyyy," Emir groans. He's being woken up incredibly gently by Theo's warm, careful hands, but, "Said I could sleep in today."

"It's ten." Theo mumbles, voice so low Emir could sleep through it if those fingertips weren't gliding softly along his stomach and occasionally fiddling with the hair there. He's already let Emir sleep about an hour later than usual, but he also knows Emir was up late drawing again because he found the sketch a few hours ago when he first got up.

"Is it?" Emir sighs but presses himself closer to Theo, eyes still tight shut. Theo cuddles in the morning are worth waking up for, even if he's going to pout about it for a moment.

"Almost. It's three 'til." Theo kisses Emir's forehead and welcomes him into his arms. He's been awake for hours, but Emir can sleep through almost anything. He even dropped his water bottle on the floor a few minutes ago and it definitely could have woken a hibernating bear. "But we need to leave soon."

"Show's not until tonight." Emir grumbles, hiding his face away against Theo's chest and breathing deep. Theo's wearing a soft cotton shirt, so instead of his natural smell, Emir gets a wave of fresh laundry flowing into his consciousness. Honestly, he associates that smell with Theo almost as much as anything else.

Theo doesn't answer right away because he knows if he waits long enough, Emir will keep waking up and eventually realise what he said, and what he's missing. But that doesn't mean he can't keep adoring him and holding whatever version of a conversation sleepy Emir can manage. "Love you..."

Saying it comes so easy to Theo now. It's been a few weeks since the first time, and he doesn't worry about it being too much for Emir anymore. Theo can tell it makes Emir immediately happy to hear it, that he knows it's genuine and accepts it without hesitation, and Theo's proud that they're at this point in their relationship. They've come so far in only a few months.

Emir smiles at Theo's words, pressing a kiss to whatever bit of his boyfriend is closest. There's a trace of hair beneath his lips so Theo must be wearing a v-neck this morning. He loves when Theo wears lower cut tops. They really show off his beautiful chest, his defined pecs and smooth skin that Emir spent last night admiring with his hands and lips and, occasionally, his teeth.

After settling into the cuddle, and with Theo still attempting to get him out of bed, Emir decides he might wake up easier with a kiss, so he reaches his arm up and threads his fingers through Theo's curls, finding them damp. "You showered."

Theo shifts so he can kiss Emir properly, slightly further down the pillows where Emir's made his morning nest. He presses a slow, deep kiss against Emir's waiting lips, letting Emir play with the hair at the back of his head as their noses slide together. "I already went to the gym, and we don't have time to shower together today. We get too distracted."

"Why didn't you wake me before the gym?" Emir asks, kissing him again just because he can. Usually, Theo wakes him up just enough before he slips away on Saturday mornings, even though Emir is very dedicated to his beauty rest on the weekends.

"Babe." Theo chuckles, unable to stop himself as his head falls forward to rest against Emir's shoulder. This isn't the first time this has happened. Emir is adorably clingy when he's still half asleep and he always wants kisses first thing in the morning. "We snogged for five entire minutes when I got up to leave."

"Hm...thought that was a fantastic dream." Emir grins, finally blinking his eyes open so he can have the first sight of the day be his favourite person. The sun is in Theo's eyes and they look wonderfully hazel because of the emerald henley he's wearing. Perfect.

"It was real and you had your hands on my arse the entire time. Thought you were awake." Theo smiles wider once he notices Emir's eyes are open. Progress. They really do have places to be.

Pressing himself further against Theo, Emir wraps his arms around his back and pulls Theo in for another kiss. Theo tastes like toothpaste and tea and home. He won't tire of this for the rest of his life, waking up as many days as possible with these soft lips against his own and Theo's warmth all around him.

As the rest of Emir's body wakes up the longer they kiss, so does his mind. And as it does, "What do you mean we need to leave soon?"

"Knew you'd get there." Theo pulls back from the kiss and sits up enough that he can rest his head on his hand, the other brushing Emir's hair away from his forehead. He has the most gorgeous partner in the entire world. "We have plans, Emi. And we need to be on the train in an hour."

"But the show's -" Emir gets cut off with another kiss before he can continue. He doesn't mind.

"It's a birthday surprise." Theo rolls himself away from Emir until he falls to the floor, careful not to disturb any of Emir's very messy chaos in the process. He's been tidier since Theo's been in his space more often, but his bedroom is still a bit of an artistic hovel. "And you need a shower while I make breakfast *and* you still have to pack."

"Pack what?" Emir rubs the rest of the sleep away from his eyes, no less confused than he was a minute ago. He thought they were going to the show and taking the tube back to stay here tonight. What's there to pack?

"Whatever you're wearing tonight and something to wear tomorrow for the ride home." Theo turns once he reaches Emir's bedroom door and gives him a wink over his shoulder. "No need for pyjamas."

***

Emir carries both of their overnight bags, one over his shoulder and the other in his hand, letting Theo guide him away from the tube and towards wherever it is they're headed. Since the show is across the city, they'd decided not to drive Theo's car and instead take advantage of the full city experience. While they rode, they talked about next year and how they'd probably be on the tube every day just to get around. Sometimes, when they're at uni, it's hard to remember that they won't always have everyone they love and all of their daily needs just a few minutes' walk away.

Theo's watching the map on his phone now that they're out on the pavement. He hasn't been to this part of London before, and even though he looked up the walking route a dozen times, he wants to be sure. They're properly in the city centre and there's more people and more noise and more *everything* than he's really prepared to handle, but according to his phone he'll get a reprieve soon. "Should be just around the corner."

"And you still won't tell me what we're up to all day?" Emir asks, trying to get a peek at Theo's phone even though he's been unsuccessful several times already. He has a hunch there's at least a hotel involved, but that still doesn't explain why they're here so early. The doors to the Peacock Theatre don't even open until seven.

"Don't have to. We're here." Theo stashes his phone in his back pocket and drags Emir suddenly out of the crowd and through an enormous, heavy wooden door that opens into an opulent hotel lobby. An over the top, luxury, borderline museum of a lobby.

"Princess…where are we?" Emir links his fingers with Theo's and leans into his side, staring up at the chandelier in the middle of the foyer in wonder. He's sure he's in the way of other guests, but he doesn't care. He's never even been inside a hotel this nice before.

"London." Theo grins, kissing the side of Emir's mouth and dragging him by their connected hands to the check in area. Emir seems truly in awe of their surroundings, so Theo thinks he's probably done alright. Emir's eyes are sparkling and Theo's glad he decided to make this happen. They could've just stayed at Roseborough tonight, but this is better.

Emir can't even imagine how expensive this place is, but Theo's walking around with that confidence that he used to assume was arrogance before he knew better. Before he knew Theo. Fuck, he loves this man and all the wonder he brings into Emir's life. It's not about the expense, because Theo could bring him to tears in a car park. It's about sharing new experiences together and finding joy along the way.

"Hello, we're here for an early check-in. I called this morning to verify. Reservation for Palmer." Theo drops Emir's hand so he can get out his ID, his credit card, and whatever else he's going to need to get them checked into their room and upstairs for a short rest before Emir's next surprise.

After verifying his identification and clicking a few things on the computer, the front desk agent's face falls from polite geniality to contrition. "I have your reservation, but it looks like there's been an error. You've been booked in a room with a single standard bed and, unfortunately, we don't have any openings for me to be able to move you two to another setup."

"Oh, there's no error. That's the room I booked." Theo takes Emir's hand back at their sides and gives it a squeeze beneath the counter. He doesn't want this to be an issue and a potential trigger for Emir.

"But the room only has the one standard bed. I could call one of our other properties, but as it's the weekend – "

"There's no need. We'll be sharing." Theo slides his credit card across the counter in what he thinks is a very pointed way, trying to end the conversation which was unnecessary to begin with. His first time checking into a hotel on his own, without his parents, and he's having to deal with this? Not that he wasn't prepared for the possibility, but it's the twenty-first century. In central London. Now he's just annoyed.

"...Oh." The employee looks between them three times.

Theo counts as their eyes flick back and forth, putting the gay puzzle pieces together. He lets them sit in their own uncomfortable silence for long enough that he knows his point has been made. Maybe next time they won't make assumptions about their guests based on appearance, or at the very least think before voicing those assumptions. There were kinder ways to ask if a different arrangement would be necessary.

"If we could get into the room soon that would be great, or if the room's unavailable, we could leave our bags somewhere safe until then. We have another appointment in an hour that we can't miss." Theo picks up the credit card this time and uses his left hand to hold it out to them until they get the hint and take it.

Emir's been watching the exchange and letting Theo handle it, because not only is he capable, it's a bit...hot to see him like this. Biting his bottom lip, Emir watches the set of Theo's brow, the confidence in his posture, his refusal to be embarrassed or shy about the nature of their relationship. Anyone who underestimates Theodore George Palmer will rue the day they made that mistake.

"Thank you." Theo gives a curt nod to the front desk agent as he takes their key card, glances at the room number, then brings Emir's hand that's joined with his own up for a brush of a kiss, staring hard into Emir's eyes to make sure he's alright. He seems fine, but very fixated on Theo with a determination he usually only sees in the bedroom. Interesting.

Theo keeps Emir's hand held as he continues to walk across the lobby and towards the lift. He's more than a little overstimulated by the city, and after that interaction, he could use a moment to breathe. "I know this place is magnificent, but we'll have to admire the architecture later tonight. We have places to be."

"Shehzadi?" Emir asks as they stand in front of the lift, waiting for it to make its way down to retrieve them. "Look at me?"

"Hm?" Theo turns his head towards Emir, just in time to see a sideways smirk overtake his face.

Emir drops the bag in his hand so he can lace it through Theo's hair instead, pulling him forward for a kiss right here in front of everyone in the lobby. He's not ashamed, not of loving Theo or their relationship or being queer. Theo gives him the security to be bold like this, to take reasonable chances at PDA or whatever else he's hesitant to allow himself because he knows that even if something goes wrong, they'll handle it together. It's just a chaste kiss. It only lasts for a second, maybe two, but it still matters to be able to share it.

The lift dings upon arrival, so Emir retracts his hand from Theo's hair to pick up the bag again and pulls Theo into the lift, eager to get upstairs. If they have somewhere to be in an hour, he's going to make the most of it.

They kiss in the corner of the (thankfully vacant) lift after Theo presses the necessary button to get them moving, dropping their things so they can grasp onto each other instead. It's a short trip upstairs, but Theo continues to marvel at the way Emir stretches infinities into private moments.

"How in the hell can we afford this?" Emir crowds himself into Theo's space as he lets them into the room. He's excited for today, not knowing what to expect, but positive that Theo's planned something special for his birthday. He should've known that Theo wouldn't consider getting to watch Ballet Trockadero, an actual lifetime dream of Emir's, to be enough. He'll need to spend months planning Theo's next birthday so that Theo doesn't have a single doubt that the love and care is reciprocal.

"Mum let me use most of her reward points from when she travels for work." Theo grins as Emir turns him around in the doorway and starts to walk him backwards into their borrowed room. It's tiny, because even with his mum's help he could only afford something very basic, but it's still new and fun, and it's the first time Theo's ever been able to do something like this. "The rest I paid for myself. I work with my dad in the summers, remember?"

"Get on the bed." Emir tosses both of their overnight bags somewhere near the wardrobe and pushes at Theo's shoulders, already pulling off his own outerwear. They don't have time for sex, but he's spending every available minute kissing Theo boneless against the luxury mattress.

"Could you, um," Theo toes off his shoes but pauses when the backs of his knees hit the mattress and sits automatically. "I'm really overstimulated, so maybe - my sleeping mask is in the front pocket, and I don't want to stop kissing, just..."

"I've got you." Emir fits himself in between Theo's knees where he's sitting at the edge of the bed and takes his face in both of his hands. "How long do we have?"

"Probably thirty minutes. We need to leave in forty-five, but we don't need to change or anything." Theo stares up at Emir and already feels himself relaxing. They're alone, it's finally quiet again, and kissing and cuddling for a while away from it all sounds perfect.

"Leaving our clothes on then. No sex, just more of this, alright?" Emir brushes his thumbs along Theo's cheekbones and waits for him to nod. His eyes have gone soft and sleepy, so Emir kisses him between the eyebrows before stepping away to grab Theo's eye mask.

It's always special when they do this. Sometimes Theo needs to be alone to destimulate, similar to how Emir needs his solitude sometimes. But often, Theo just wants quiet and his eyes covered so he can focus on kissing Emir or holding him close, sometimes both, and grounding himself in their intimacy and connection, grounding himself in Emir.

Theo feels Emir's hair falling beneath his fingertips, his warm lips against his own, his teeth dragging along his jaw, Emir's fingers under his shirt and sliding across his skin. He tastes like green tea and smells like a combination of his shampoo and the city. Emir moans near his ear and giggles when Theo tries to chase his lips, then mumbles sentences in Urdu that Theo doesn't know how to translate. The thirty minutes he's permitted pass in a beautiful haze until his muscles are relaxed and his headache has evaporated. If Emir were to suggest a nap, he'd be asleep almost immediately, so relaxed that it takes him a concerted effort to recompose himself and get ready to leave the room for what comes next.

It may be Emir's pre-birthday weekend, but Theo feels celebrated, too. Like Emir can't bear the thought of Theo going without adoration or praise. He's sharing his light with Theo, like always, like it's automatic, like he doesn't even have to think or try to let Theo in anymore. Theo's just there, in his heart, like he belongs.

***

After the surprise of the hotel, Emir isn't sure what to expect next. The place is architecturally fascinating, and somehow walking distance to the theatre, and he's still not quite sure how Theo managed it, but he's alright with not knowing all the details.

"Have I mentioned how gorgeous you look with your shirt matching your hair?" Theo squeezes Emir's hand as they walk down the pavement, the cafe they're headed towards only a few blocks away, right by the theatre. "Pink is such a good colour on you."

"I look like candy floss." Emir laughs, but he feels himself flushing all the same.

Theo's the only person who's ever made him flush, and it's still a rare occurrence. He only has a few *proper* outfits and he'd saved his nicest for tonight, but the pink button up he'd worn to meet Theo's family is always top of the list when he needs to dress nicer than he normally would.

"Is that why you taste so good today?" Theo manages a cheek kiss that makes Emir roll his eyes and hide his face for a moment. He's really glad that Emir's letting him spoil him for once. Usually he insists on it being the other way around, but he's pretty sure Emir's learned by now that if Theo doesn't have an outlet for all his care and devotion for the loved ones in his life, he gets grumpy.

They fall quiet for the rest of the walk, just holding hands and occasionally sharing smiles while absorbing the city around them. They're not actually very far from Roseborough, all things considered, but it's like a different world.

"In you go." Theo nudges Emir forward as they approach the cafe. Emir insists on holding the door open and *helping* Theo inside with a hand on the small of his back, because he's a gentleman like that. "Order whatever you like, but don't forget we have a reservation for tonight at the hotel's restaurant, so maybe just something light."

"Princess," Emir pulls Theo aside before they can join the short queue to order. It's a private question, but one he needs to ask. "Let me pay for this?"

Theo considers for a moment. He'd planned on paying for the whole weekend. But they had that conversation on their first date about this sort of thing, and they've revisited the topic and confirmed their mutual agreement since, so he nods and leans forward to say, "Thank you."

"After we order our drinks, will you tell me what we're doing here?" Emir keeps a hand on Theo's back as they enter the queue, gentle but protective.

It's not that he's particularly enamoured with the city or anything himself, but he knows it can be a lot for Theo to process. It'd be different if this was a regular spot for them, if Theo was familiar with the surroundings and the menu and was settled into the place. But he's not, so Emir doesn't want anyone bumping into Theo or even getting too close.

"I think you'll figure it out." Theo leans his weight against Emir, enjoying having him this close.

Since the winter break, their comfort level with casual intimacy in public has shifted. Nothing shocking or sexual, just things like this: Emir's hand on his back, holding hands when they feel like it, sharing space in a way that's clearly not platonic, occasional kisses on the temple or cheek, fingers playing with each other's hair. It's been surprisingly easy, something they sort of fell into then acknowledged in soft moments alone.

Emir orders himself a matcha latte and a London fog for Theo, both with oat milk, then an almond croissant for them to share. Theo looks around for a table that will seat them all and steers Emir in the necessary direction once they have their nibbles. Emir lets Theo choose which seat he wants before holding out the chair for him and taking the one beside it.

"Meeting someone, then?" Emir asks, taking a sip of his matcha after snapping a picture to send to their friends. There's a heart in the foam, which is silly and insignificant, but it's cute.

"Three someones." Theo confirms, putting his arm around the back of Emir's chair while sipping his own latte. "We're a few minutes early. I didn't want to be late. Theo Time."

With a smile in acknowledgement of that term he coined several months ago, Emir rests his head against Theo's shoulder and relaxes for a minute. It's actually lovely to be with someone who's so prepared and organised. Not that he's ever been the opposite, but it ensures the enjoyment of moments like this, a quiet bubble alone in the chaos of the city to just be together and appreciate each others' company.

"Theo? That you?" A tall man with artificially tan skin and bright eyes is already holding out his hand for Theo to shake, two other people close behind him.

Standing up from his seat, Theo returns the handshake and lights up into excited extroversion from the relaxed state he'd fallen into. "Jacob! Thanks for meeting us. *This is Emir.*"

"The birthday boy." One of the others grins as he looks between them, Emir having stood up for his own round of greetings. "I'm Mateo. It's good to finally meet you."

"Finally?" Emir looks at Theo with a head tilt, because if the context clues based on their location and the way all three strangers are dressed in dance-related layers add up, Theo's somehow arranged a meeting with a handful of dancers from the company they have tickets to see.

"Theo's been messaging us for weeks. He's told us all about you, honey." The third dancer is noticeably shorter than the others, but he's dressed in some amalgamation of the entire rainbow, multiple patterns and vibrant colours adding up to a very bright first impression. "I'm Chiyo, but you can call me Chi."

"I'm guessing we'll be seeing the three of you on stage later?" Emir pulls Theo into his side with a hand around his waist now that all the handshakes are out of the way. He should've known Theo would manage something like this. He's chosen to love a remarkable man who still manages to amaze him on a regular basis.

"Yes, but we'll be beautiful then. You'll hardly recognise us." Jacob takes off his beanie and ruffles his floppy, sandy coloured hair. "We'll just grab something to drink, then we'll be back."

They're all dressed in enough layers to fill a wardrobe, so there's at least one coat and a scarf tossed on each of their waiting chairs while they go to do just that, leaving Emir and Theo alone for another minute until they return.

"How'd you even manage this?" Emir turns to mumble right next to Theo's ear, giving him a bit of a nuzzle. He definitely plans to wrap himself around his boyfriend like an octopus as soon as they're back at the hotel to get ready for the show.

"I messaged every single Trockadero dancer I could find on social media and these three are the ones who answered and wanted to meet up. We had to wait until they had their rehearsal schedule, but they promised to fit us in during their pre-show break, so here we are." Theo grins as Emir presses a kiss at the corner of his jaw. He can tell Emir's happy with his surprise and trying to tell Theo in his own way. "I know you haven't had a chance to really know dancers like you before, so I thought it might be nice?"

"It's perfect." Emir kisses Theo again, this time at the corner of his mouth, then rests their temples together for a moment just to breathe him in. It's such a thoughtful gift and something he wouldn't have even bothered to ask for. He knows how busy show days can be for the performers, and taking time out of their tour schedule for the sake of a stranger is incredibly generous of them.

"Hope you don't mind. I'm *famished*." Chi returns first with four teetering plates for himself, a can of Redbull appearing out of his pocket and set on the table with a flourish.

"You're going to give yourself a heart attack, darling. What've I told you about drinking that poison after noon?" Jacob glides into the seat beside Chi with two plates of his own and a mug that smells like exceptionally strong coffee. Maybe they're having some sort of caffeine consumption competition.

"Only if it's mixed with vodka." Chi just shrugs and gives Jacob a kiss, fluttering his eyelashes until Jacob rolls his eyes and flicks his wrist as if to say *if you must*.

"Ignore them. Their room has enough low grade stimulants to take down an elephant." Mateo has a sensible cappuccino and a small pie, and he's clearly used to these two. "Annoying as fuck rooming next door when they're *en cuatro* 'til three in the morning and rehearsal starts at eight."

None of the three seem to have any hesitation about being extremely gay and loud around strangers, and Emir's grinning so wide that Theo takes a mental picture. He's stunning when he's this happy.

"You're just jealous because Martina dumped your ass back in New York." Chi takes an enormous bite of pastry and flicks his hair out of his eyes. He's wearing beautiful turquoise eyeshadow with glitter dusted near his temples that catches the light when he moves.

"Martina did not *dump my ass*. She wasn't interested in monogamy and I'm committed to it." Mateo shrugs it off, so it must not be much of a sore spot. At least not anymore.

"Straight people are so boring." Jacob says as an aside to Emir and Theo, letting them in on their conversation with a grin.

"Ay, I am *not* boring!" Mateo does seem to take offence to that, which makes Emir giggle, a flash of a fight he'd had with Theo months ago showing up in his memory. Theo isn't straight, of course, but the sentiment is similar.

"It's fine. Without you around, Jace and I would just be too old queens who can't keep track of a topic long enough to hold a conversation with our new friends." Chi finishes whatever his first plate contained so quickly that Theo never even noticed what was on it.

"You can talk about whatever you want. Just knowing you all exist is an incredible birthday gift." Emir has his leg set on top of Theo's so their knees are connected, almost sharing a chair between them. "It's always been my dream to see your show, but I didn't know I'd get to meet any of you."

"You're giving us way too much credit, vato." Mateo stabs a fork into his pie and grins across the tiny table at Emir. "From the videos Theo sent us, you'll be too busy as the newest muñeca of the dance world to pay us any attention in a few months. Should be snatched up the second you graduate. I'm surprised you aren't already fielding offers."

"I don't know what Theo sent you, but I'll be lucky to end up with a company. I'm talented and I work hard, but so does everyone else." Emir feels Theo huff his disagreement beside him. It's not a new topic for them. "I hope I get a few offers, but I'll just be glad to end up in the corps and work my way up."

"Not with what you have. It might take a few years, but you'll be a principal." Chi cracks open his Redbull and tosses a reusable straw into the opening. He takes a moment to hollow his cheeks and down half of it in one go before continuing. "We're all past our prime, but dancing for Trockadero is the best job I've ever had. Even my mom had to admit I'm happier now."

"Is that what she said the other day?" Jason looks genuinely curious, turning to Chi with his chin in his hand. "I thought she was complaining about the weather again."

"No, she just speaks Japanese around you because you need to learn. Your eyes glaze over while you watch us talk and you follow us like a tennis match, back and forth and back and forth and -" Chi giggles as Jason gasps and clutches at his chest then starts to laugh along.

"It's true. I'm surprised your neck doesn't break. You look like a chicken, bobbing your head around like that." Mateo's pretty focused on his pie at this point, but he's still willing to join in on the teasing. It's clear the three of them have been friends for a long time.

"I don't think we were invited here to discuss how bad I am at Japanese." Jason shakes his head and picks up his coffee again, then gives Emir his full attention. "Theo mentioned that you might have some questions for us?"

"So many. Fuck, I don't even know where to start." Emir glances at Theo and gets trapped in his warm gaze. His hazel eyes, the crinkles beside them as he smiles, the dimple at the top of his cheek that only shows up when he's relaxed and deeply happy.

But Emir can't ignore the lovely people who've taken time out of their busy day to visit with them, so he turns away from Theo to answer the question. "I suppose it's just really nice to see other male dancers on pointe, like, professionally, and to see that so many of you aren't white...sorry Jason."

"No need to apologise. I was the token white guy until Trent joined last year, and I'm still the only American." Jason sets down his mug then puts an arm around Chi. "Trockadero is special for a lot of reasons. I was glad to join a company like this, especially after leaving Chicago. I thought my career was over, but it was really just starting. I never got to tour like this before."

"I've always thought Trockadero is so cool because it's getting to dance in drag, but it's also mixing comedy with technique, and it's international so you're all from...everywhere." Emir pauses to take a drink from his matcha. It's going cold but he doesn't mind. "Like, growing up and training in Shipley - it's up North - I was the only dancer who wasn't white, and definitely the only Muslim kid, and we speak Urdu at home a lot. Shipley's pretty diverse, but ballet isn't. And then on top of all that, I came out pretty young so...yeah. I just don't meet a lot of dancers like me."

"We're not all gay," Chi points a thumb across Jason at Mateo, "But even the straight ones are alright. Mateo came to us from Mexico City, and he'd been dancing for Folklorico since he was like - what were you? Twelve?"

"Thirteen." Mateo confirms, setting aside his fork for a moment. "It was a big deal to dance for them. I grew up in a tiny village with four generations in one house, and now I travel the world as a ballet drag performer. My Mami made me learn English in school because she always wanted me to leave home someday, and I guess it worked. We all basically have stories like that. Different backgrounds and different training before we joined."

"That's incredible, like, just knowing what you've all gone through to dance with the company and to see it all come together. Theo and I talked about Trockadero right at the beginning of us working together - did you tell them about the dissertation?" Emir pauses to get confirmation from Theo. He nods and the others all agree from across the bistro table. "Right, so we've been studying other productions, like the classics and a few more contemporary interpretations, and *Swan Lake* was where we started. Obviously. And we've seen clips of your shows, but this is the first time I'll get to see the whole thing."

"It's sad Bourne was the only one to do a gay ballet like that." Chi's just finished his Redbull, setting the empty can aside and reaching for another one of his plates. "We don't do that same sort of thing, but I remember watching videos of the production in those early days on YouTube and thinking how amazing it was that something like that could exist. An all male *Swan Lake*. Even now it would be a huge deal, and he did it decades ago."

"That's how I feel about what you do." Emir admits. It's still sort of surreal to be sitting here with three dancers from a company he's followed for most of his life. "I've been dancing en pointe since I was about twelve, and I'm the only masc dancer at uni who does. But I think it's becoming more common in some places - and Theo's starting to learn as well."

"I'm truly a beginner. I tried pointe a bit around the same age Emir started, but, um...I wasn't allowed to continue." Theo heats slightly at the sympathetic gazes he's getting from across the table. They can interpret the rest of the story that he's leaving blank. "But I genuinely love pointe as an art form, and Emir got me pointe shoes at Christmas and now he's teaching me the basics. I'll never be at your level, I don't think, but I admire it so much."

"I think that's great, Theo." Mateo sounds sincere, even if his mouth is once again full of chicken pie. "Dancing just for your own joy is important, too."

"Emir once told me that I need to indulge my whimsy, and it changed my life." Theo hooks the ankle of the leg already wrapped around Emir even tighter. Emir gives him his widest smile, tongue poking out like he's trying to contain himself but can't quite manage it. Theo's so in love with him it's like a physical pain in his chest. He never knew he could feel this complete by making someone else happy.

"You two are so cute. And you're both gorgeous. Imagine if you could make babies and give them those genes." Chi pulls another Redbull out of some unnamed location, making Jason audibly scoff and wrestle it from his grasp with a stern, "No. You can have it back tomorrow."

"You been together long?" Mateo ignores their squabble. They must always be like this.

"Only a few months, but...Emir's my favourite person. The best partner in so many ways. My favourite dancer, too. Dancing and creating with him has been an incredible gift." Theo leans his forehead against Emir's for a moment then looks back across the table. "You've seen videos, but Emir on stage is like nothing else I've ever seen. He doesn't even need an audience, though of course he's made for one. I just know I'll be proud of him for the rest of my life."

"Damn. None of my boyfriends were ever like you two. Hold onto that." Jason has the forbidden Redbull behind his back while he distracts Chi by pushing his own coffee in his direction. It's sweet, the clear love and devotion that underlies their bickering.

"Excuse you, I love you that much." Chi takes Jason's coffee begrudgingly and wrinkles his nose as he takes a sip. Theo can't even imagine how awful that combination of flavours must be.

"Yes, darling, but you graduated to husband during that big party we had." Jason hands the Redbull to Mateo instead, who takes it without comment and hides it away in a coat pocket.

The five of them sit around their tiny bistro table in the upscale cafe for two hours until Chi, Jason, and Mateo have to hurry back to the theatre for their call time. They talk about a breadth of topics: ballet, Pride around the world, life as a professional, comic books, growing up in Japan, Mexico, the US, and England, growing old as a dancer, and just before they have to separate, ways to keep in touch since most of them aren't very active on social media. They exchange emails and phone numbers, with promises to catch up when they can, especially as Emir and Theo get ready to leave uni in a few months. It never hurts to have connections.

"Princess?" Emir was quiet for the walk back to the hotel, only breaking the silence once they're alone in their room again. It's a lot for both of them to process even though it was wholly positive.

"Hm?" Theo hangs his coat up and turns around as Emir's hands find his waist, already pulling him towards the bed. Even here, across the city and out of the studio, they move together in graceful harmony.

"You're the best thing that's ever happened to me." Emir waits for Theo's smile before kissing him, wanting to hold the image in his mind a moment longer. He's told Theo this at least a dozen times, but it's still true. He means it anew every single time.

"Your birthday isn't over yet." Theo reminds him as he's carefully guided to lay back against the pillows. "Technically it hasn't even started."

"Shhhh. Just lay with me for a few minutes." Emir arranges them so they can cuddle up facing each other, taking time to recharge and relax before getting dressed up for the show. He has a small surprise of his own for later, nothing like what Theo's already given him, but he's looking forward to it all the same. "Thank you."

"Love you." Theo nuzzles against Emir's neck and takes a slow, deep breath. Here in Emir's arms feels like where he was always meant to be, where he plans to stay for as long as he's allowed.

***

T: *Theo you look so pretty! Did Emi take that picture?*
Ciaran: *Of course Emir took that picture. Theo has heart eyes even though he's trying to smoulder*
Laurie: *Did Emir also do your makeup?*
Gabe: *You look like a doll! I mean that in a good way. Your makeup is flawless!*
Theo: *Yes, Emir did my makeup and took the picture. We took a few silly ones together but I couldn't post them publicly.*
Theo: *What do you mean trying to smoulder? Emir said I successfully smouldered /crying emoji/*
Emi: *you smouldered perfectly baby*
Emi: *you all are allowed to have the outtakes so here fetch*

Emi: /selfie with Emir biting at Theo's neck and smiling while Theo sticks his tongue out at the camera/
Emi: /selfie with Emir's hand in Theo's curls, kissing him, Theo leaning back with the force of it/
Emi: /selfie with them both smiling at the camera, temples rested together as they lean into each other/
T: Awwwww my little gay babies all grown up and on a date
Gabe: Where are your seats?
Theo: Front row of the balcony, right in the middle. Always my favourite /heart emoji/
Emi: my favourite too /heart emoji/
Theo: We match /heart emoji/
Laurie: Disgusting /vomit emoji/
Laurie: Use protection and have fun /water drop emoji/
Theo: We are not shagging at the theatre /eye roll emoji/
Gabe: What are the chances that having sex at a theatre could actually happen? Like just hypothetically...
Ciaran: /writing emoji/
Emi: too many cameras
Emi: but i know of a few places around roseborough if you're wanting to leave the bedroom
Emi: depends if you want an audience /shrug emoji/
Emi: just text me later or tomorrow or whatever
Emi: princess could probably even help me make a map
Theo: CAN WE PLEASE NOT WHILE I'M IN MY BEST SUIT AND IN PUBLIC
Laurie: You're getting a new one for our wedding anyway
Laurie: May as well ruin this one
Emi: i hadn't thought of that but you make a good point
Theo: I BEG YOU TO NOT
Theo: THERE ARE PEOPLE LESS THAN A FOOT AWAY THAT DO NOT NEED TO SEE WHAT'S HAPPENING IN MY TROUSERS
Emi: you're fine it's dim and everyone's gay here
Emi: half the audience is probably high on poppers and waiting for intermission
Ciaran: This is fun /popcorn eating gif/
Ciaran: Rile up the ballet boyfriends from a distance
Gabe: You have a ballet boyfriend right here to rile up
Emi: pause
Laurie: Back up
Gabe: No thank you
Theo: Rewind.
Ciaran: Fast forward

Emi: this feels deliciously like karma
T: Everyone play nice I'm too busy to be mum right now
Laurie: You're such a good mum though
Emi: ballet is going to start in a minute so we're turning off our phones
Theo: WAIT ONE LAST SELFIE
Theo: /selfie of himself and Emir in their seats, the house lights still up, their heads leaning against each other/
Theo: Okay biiiiiiiii
Ciaran: Theo's flushed as pink as Emir's hair
Ciaran: Glad they're staying at the hotel tonight /eggplant emoji; peach emoji; tongue emoji/
Laurie: Good they're gone let's focus back on the ballet boyfriend you two have at home
Ciaran: Error 404 response not found
Laurie: You can't error 404 in a text mate
Gabe: /static gif/
Laurie: Fine but just know we love you
T: We love you sooooo much
Ciaran: Talk later /kiss emoji/
Gabe: We love you too /rainbow emoji/
T: Isn't Laur so cute in his glasses? /heart eye emoji/
T: /picture of Laurie huddled over a mound of fabric, hair sticking up everywhere/
T: Ballet boyfriends: when the show's done, can you let us know what time you'll be home tomorrow? Need to show you some wedding things :)
T: Thank youuuuuuuu
Laurie: And if I quit uni?
Ciaran: I'll quit with you
Gabe: You will not
Gabe: No one is leaving Roseborough before we're done
Gabe: T, do you and Laurie need help with wedding stuff? Too much stress all at once?
T: We might, but I'll let you know
T: Have to go over a few things with the ballet boyfriends and check with Laur's parents
Laurie: We're staying at mine tonight so you two and Alfie can have the other flat to yourselves
Laurie: Same advice as above
Laurie: Use protection and have fun /three eggplant emojis/
Ciaran: /saluting emoji/

***

Theo and Emir were surprised by a text invite from Jason to stay for a few minutes after the show and meet a handful of other dancers before they needed to leave for their dinner reservation. Chi, Jason, and Mateo introduced them to everyone they could in the whirlwind backstage. Emir talked pointe with a dancer named Marc, Theo talked staging with one of their tour choreographers, and by the time they rushed away back to the hotel, they were both glowing and happy, hand in hand.

"Was it everything you thought it would be?" Theo asks, nudging Emir's toe beneath their table. They made it to their reservation exactly on time, shown to their reserved spot and handed their menus with a nod. Theo had spent the performance splitting his attention between the dancers on stage and Emir's enthralled expression from beside him, but now it's all Emir.

"Better. I haven't laughed that hard in ages." Emir forgoes playing footsie to take Theo's hand atop the table instead. They've already ordered, so now they're waiting and chatting. Once they've eaten, Emir plans to whisk them away upstairs so he can have Theo alone again. "Was it everything you remembered?"

"Better." Theo smiles so wide his dimple shows, letting Emir's thumb caress the top of his hand while they stare at each other. "Even if it wasn't your birthday, I'm glad I got the tickets."

"Can't believe you bought them just because I said I've always wanted to see Trockadero. You barely knew me then." Emir still marvels at their relationship sometimes, how they evolved from being unable to hold a conversation to crying because they love each other so deeply it's unbearable.

"I think it's just…who I am. Even if we were only working together, I would've wanted to make you happy if I could. I love seeing you smile." Theo hadn't even hesitated when he'd bought the tickets. He would've gifted them to Emir even if he decided to take someone else; it would have hurt his heart more than a little, but he didn't plan this for himself. It's always been for Emir.

"You're such a special person. Like - I don't want it to sound - I just don't know anyone else like you and I never will." Emir watches the warm, ambient light reflecting in Theo's softened gaze. There's magic in his eyes, always pulling Emir in and guiding him home. "I'm so happy that I get to be your boyfriend. That you chose me."

"It was a mutual choosing." Theo laughs, sliding their hands until their fingers are intertwined instead. It's been a really good day, and it's not quite over. "I'm happy with my choice."

"Me too, baby." Emir lets himself stare for a minute, indulging, his mind filling with the red he sees surrounding them. Red like the wine Theo chose, red like his lips stained from drinking it, red like the apples of his cheeks when Emir makes him flush, red like the bites he leaves behind when they're alone. Red...

***

Back upstairs in their hotel room, Theo gives Emir a kiss at the foot of the bed before hiding himself away in the bathroom to get cleaned up. Emir doesn't know it yet, but Theo has plans for tonight: multiple new sexual experiences he's looking forward to that he's hoping Emir will be alright with trying. He's ready for more with Emir, in so many ways, and he wants to take intentional, thoughtful steps along the way. Which includes tonight, with Theo using the douche kit he'd packed with his things and the tutorial he saved as a bookmark on his phone just in case.

It takes him a while, almost ten minutes, but he feels confident and clean, so Theo tidies everything away after thoroughly sanitising his supplies, and slips back into part of his outfit, knowing it'll be gone again very soon. He likes when Emir takes his clothes off, relishes being carefully unfolded and undone, then held while being put together again. As Theo steps out of the bathroom, he's wearing his tight black boxers and his white dress shirt unbuttoned and falling around his torso, sleeves rolled up to show off his forearms. He knows he looks good.

But then he finds Emir with his gaze and every thought he's ever had leaves in an instant to be replaced with the magnitude of Emir's surprise instead. "Oh my fucking fuck."

Emir smirks from where he's posed on the edge of the bed, looking up at Theo beneath his eyelashes and enjoying every second of his reaction. Theo's frozen, mouth open and eyes wide in shock, arms forgotten at his sides. He looks delectable too, but he didn't know what Emir had planned, so Emir gives Theo a moment to recalibrate before launching himself across the room like he very much wants to right now. "Alright, baby?"

"Nrgh." Theo half groans before clearing his throat and shivering for a moment, like he literally can't believe what he's seeing. In some ways he can't. He's never seen Emir like this, not even that one time a few months ago. That was for the public, this is just for them, another something new for them to share.

"You like the dress, then?" Emir flicks his hair away from his eyes and lets his hands trail down his own body before stopping just long enough to press against his cock through the fabric. He has his legs crossed, so he leans into his hand and moans for effect, watching Theo's eyes go dark and glassy. "It's just something I found online. A little black dress I thought you might fancy."

"I - " Theo can't move, his muscles instantaneously useless for anything besides keeping him upright. He's rarely been this surprised in his life. His mouth has gone completely dry and he can hear his heartbeat in his ears. "You - "

Emir stands up from the bed, barefoot but on his tiptoes as he slowly makes his way to Theo a few feet away. He doesn't want Theo to panic or anything like that. He knows this is something Theo's wanted, probably almost as much as he does, but sometimes Theo needs the reminder that he's allowed to want this and indulge in having it. He's allowed to have Emir. "It's alright, princess. You can touch."

"Emir, please!" Theo reaches for him, hands finding Emir's waist where it's hugged by the satin fabric, so tight it could be a second skin. He's like some sort of dominatrix wet dream, but softer, tempered with intention. The dress falls about mid thigh, short enough for Theo to have already considered both riding Emir and being ridden, which promptly shut down all other thoughts until he had Emir in his hands. And now that he does, "Come here."

"I thought you'd never ask." Emir smiles, nipping at Theo's jaw and letting himself be pulled forward until Theo has himself pressed back against the nearest wall with Emir against his front. He figured they'd be headed the other direction, but they'll get there. May as well start against the wall.

"Fucking use me. Please. I will *beg* if I have to." Theo threads a careful hand into Emir's hair and tugs just enough, their mouths meeting for a warm, deep kiss as he pulls Emir across his thigh, using the wall behind him to hold their weight as he encourages Emir to get off against him. And then he notices what's *not* rubbing against him. "Are you fucking joking?"

"Figured the dress was enough without adding knickers to the situation. Left a few accessories at home." Emir feels Theo's other hand pressing against his lower back, guiding him where he wants him. Theo wants to be used? That can be arranged. "You feel me against your thigh, baby? Feel how you already have me hard and leaking? You look so fucking fit and you feel *even better.*"

Emir lets his voice go quiet and deep, pulling Theo in with all of his senses instead of relying on the visual alone. He bites hard at Theo's shoulder where the skin is exposed, then kisses it slowly and starts a bruise, all while pressing himself into Theo, his dick sliding along Theo's thigh and occasionally brushing his stomach when Theo rolls his hips. He's fucking incredible at this, the upright snogging, the hands beneath Emir's dress, the sounds he makes as they grind against each other. Emir feels so hot, practically burning, as if he's wearing a parka rather than a slip of a dress.

"I'm so into you, babe. You've no idea." Theo groans with his eyes closed, handling Emir and pressing his still covered erection against him while using the wall behind himself as leverage. "Can't believe I'm your boyfriend."

"You're mine, baby. All mine." Emir pulls back enough to run his hands along Theo's toned torso, fingernails catching to scratch at his sides on the way back down, the way Theo likes, just rough enough without being too much. "This is all for you. No one else gets to see this. No one else gets to touch."

"I know, I just - " Theo thunks his head back against the wall and drops his thigh from beneath Emir's legs but pulls him even closer so he can kiss him between the asking. He still wants what he planned, because it wasn't only for himself. And now that he's been given this, he feels a burning need to show Emir exactly how into it he is, preferably with his mouth. "It's your birthday and I was sort of hoping - "

"You can have anything, princess. Spoiling you is my favourite thing to do." Emir takes one of Theo's hands in his own and brings his fingers up for a sweet kiss. They don't need to rush and it's not as if either of them are about to lose interest if they take a pause to breathe.

"Want to blow you." Theo blinks his eyes back open and looks at Emir, hesitant but hopeful. "And, um...I was wondering if - nevermind."

Trailing the fingertips not holding Theo's along his jaw, Emir takes Theo's chin in his hand and presses a very deliberate kiss to his warm lips, holding him in place so he can see how very alright Emir is with whatever he wants. "Of course you can blow me, if you feel ready and all that. What else were you thinking? You can tell me."

"I just - I want you to fuck me but we're not ready yet, so I was thinking..." Theo swallows hard and readjusts himself against the wall. He's not embarrassed or anything, but it's still hard for him to find the words when they're intimate. Emir is all consuming. "I cleaned out in case you might - if you want to - like maybe you could finger me?"

"Shezhadi," Emir grins wide, taking Theo's face in both of his hands to kiss him deep and rough, but still sweet. His tongue swipes along Theo's lips, across the roof of his mouth, behind his teeth, trailing along Theo's own, exploring and dragging filthy moans out of Theo like a song. "I'd fucking love to."

"You're sure?" Theo pulls his mouth away and sets their temples together, faces side by side even as he presses his dick against Emir, the black of his boxers and Emir's dress meeting in the middle with a hush of friction.

"Why don't you let me take you to bed and you can decide which you want to do first, hm?" Emir plays with the curls at the back of Theo's head with his right hand, pressing kisses across his chest while waiting for Theo to calm down enough to keep going. He knew his surprise would knock the wind out of Theo, but he wants him calm and sure before they do anything else.

"Can I blow you with the dress on?" Theo mumbles, both because he's slightly embarrassed to admit just how much he wants this, and he's hoping Emir won't interpret his interest as something fetishzing or, fucking forbid, heterosexually motivated. The truth is closer to him being so in love with Emir and his body and all the different ways it can look that he's never felt gayer in his life.

"I was counting on it." Emir knocks their noses together to give Theo a soft kiss, nudging Theo's leg until his knee is back between Emir's thighs. "But I want it off after. There's a zipper on the back you can enjoy. Maybe undo it with your teeth."

Theo thunks his head back against the wall *again* and he's glad that the room behind is their own bathroom and not another guest. He'd hate to disrupt anyone, even if he can hardly handle everything that's happening tonight in the best way. "Take me, please. I'm ready."

Emir grinds against Theo for a while, snogging him until he's concerned his own lips will bruise before they even make it to the bed. He guides Theo by the waist, hands firm but careful at Theo's sides as he walks backwards across the rug beneath their feet. "Was there anything specific you need to be comfortable?"

"Not sure. Haven't done this before." Theo shrugs, arms draped around Emir's shoulders until the moment they fall back against the mattress together. It takes a minute to tandem crawl their way up to the pillows, Emir pulling aside the sheets and pressing Theo into the soft fabric with a grin. His dress shines in the light of the bedside lamp, but it's nothing compared to the galaxy in his eyes. "You're so beautiful, Emi..."

Flushed slightly, Emir drops his gaze for a moment and sets his hands on Theo's chest even as he brackets his hips with his thighs. Thankfully, the material of the dress has a good amount of stretch. "Probably easiest if I lay down so you have full control of your own body and how you're moving."

"I trust you." Theo means that in so many infinite ways, and he hopes at least a dozen make their way into Emir's awareness. "I've done my research, but I still want you to tell me what you like, what I'm doing wrong, where you want me, whatever I need to know."

Laying himself down beside Theo, Emir continues what they started against the wall, but horizontal, facing each other and rubbing off while kissing and groaning and getting comfortable. Theo looks unfairly debauched with the undone shirt and low slung fitted boxers, and Emir knows Theo well so he knows it was a choice, which makes it somehow even more sexy. Confident Theo is a fucking liability, especially in bed. And while he's thinking of the bed: it's a very nice bed and Emir needs to remember to compliment Theo once again on his choice of venue for the evening. Everything about this weekend has been perfect.

"Touch me, princess. Start with your hand." Emir can walk Theo through this. He *wants* to walk Theo through this. "Just like always. Slow and gentle and kiss me until you're ready."

Theo can absolutely do that. He knows what Emir likes. He lets Emir control the kiss while sliding his hand down Emir's body until he reaches his bare thighs. Using the side of his hand to lift the fabric, Theo pushes up the skirt of the dress just enough to get his hand beneath it.

But Theo also knows that Emir likes to take his time, to have Theo draw out every moment, so he doesn't just move directly to Emir's dick. Instead he whispers his fingers along the inside of his thigh, brushes back between his legs, lifts up his balls in a caress for only a moment before letting his hand move away entirely and grasp Emir at the waist.

"Babyyyy," Emir whines, arching his back and pushing his hips off the mattress. *I love you I love you I love you* he thinks, so loud he wonders if Theo can hear it. "Just like that. Keep going."

"I love you." Theo brings his lips to mumble directly against Emir's ear before leaving a kiss at the hinge of his jaw. He saw Emir mouthing the words, and it's not a new observation. He catches Emir doing it all the time, and occasionally hears it when he's in that intangible space between dozing off and fully asleep, when Emir feels safe enough to voice it aloud. "I hope tonight is worth everything I've made you wait for. If I'm shit at it, or like – "

Emir can't let him think that way. Not when he could never be disappointed in Theo, not when everything Theo does to him drives him wild, not when Theo is all he's ever wanted and so much more that he never even dreamed of. He kisses Theo, hard, grabbing at his wrist and bringing Theo's hand to his dick, groaning when Theo gives him the first stroke. "You're already better than you think, and I'll be right here while you figure this out."

"Thank you." Theo whispers against his lips, moving his hand along Emir slowly and with just enough pressure to keep him interested. He doesn't want this to end before he even gets his mouth on him.

"Open up." Emir has an idea, something he thinks they'll both be into that might also help Theo get more comfortable. Theo pulls his face a few inches away and waits, Emir placing his thumb at the edge of Theo's lips and pausing for him to nod before sliding it inside his mouth. "Practice while you keep my dick entertained with your hand."

Theo stares at Emir, searching his eyes while moving his mouth, suctioning around his thumb and cautiously moving his lips and tongue around it like he's practised. Emir's eyelashes flutter and he curses a few times, the remaining fingers on his hand stroking softly along Theo's jaw. It's nice being able to multitask, to have Emir's thumb in his mouth and his hand around Emir's dick, all while moving along Emir's thigh to work himself up just enough. He's always liked knowing what he's meant to do, and maybe that's why he enjoys submitting to Emir when they have sex. It just...feels right. Everything about them feels right.

Letting Emir's thumb out of his mouth, Theo drops his hand from Emir's dick and straddles his hips to hold Emir's face in both of his palms and kiss him deep. Emir's fingers find his waist, sliding beneath his open shirt and making goosebumps erupt over the entirety of Theo's chest and arms, making him release Emir's face with a sigh. There isn't a feeling in the world like Emir's touch on his flushed skin. "I'm ready, babe. Can I?"

"You can have whatever you want." Emir moves a hand to tuck a curl behind Theo's ear, tilting his own head to the side to get a better look at him. Sex means so much more to Theo than any of Emir's previous partners, and that depth of feeling finds its way into Emir through osmosis or aura or something unnamed that passes between them. "I don't want to finish from your mouth tonight. That's too much pressure on you, so I'll tell you if I get close, alright? And I'll make sure you know how I'm feeling the whole time. Stop or take a break as soon as you need. I won't mind."

Theo nods, nuzzling his cheek into Emir's hand where it's still cradling his face. He feels so cared for, so looked after, even though he's the one who's about to go down on his partner. "I'm not nervous. Not anymore. Just excited."

Emir smiles, rubbing his thumb along Theo's cheekbone before leaning in for a gentle kiss. Theo says he's excited? Maybe that's why Emir's feeling neon orange, a mixture of deep love and feverish excitement, so vibrant it could stop traffic. Tonight feels really special, and not only because Theo's about to blow him for the first time (and he'll get to finger Theo, if that's still what he wants). It's something about this weekend and the way their relationship keeps building, not like a tower but like a garden, care and intention bringing life to their connection the longer they're together.

Theo moves himself down the bed and finally, *finally*, lays down between Emir's legs. In an instant, he realises just how badly he's wanted to do this and for how long. He wasn't actually ready until recently, but *shit* he's wanted to be right here, face inches from Emir's cock, wanted to know what this would feel like and learn how to make Emir come apart by using his mouth. Licking his lips, Theo takes Emir's dick in his hand again, because he knows he won't be able to take him all the way down. There's just no way, not when this is his first time.

Watching Theo focus so intently, his eyes completely trained on his dick, Emir knows he should have been prepared for the moment Theo's lips met his tip. He was not prepared. "Holy fucking - shit, baby - your lips -"

Theo hums, which he's learned can feel really nice as the recipient. But he needs to focus because he's too easily distracted by the reality of Emir and all that he is. So Theo lets his tongue get involved as he takes in more of Emir's incredibly hard, slightly salty, deliciously warm dick, sliding forward until he's worried he'll gag, then backing up to suck around the tip. He's good at suction. He's been practising. He does the exact same thing four or five times before changing it up, trying to gauge Emir's interest. It's surprisingly difficult, even with his dick in his mouth.

"Take your time," Emir hisses as Theo's spare hand hikes up his right knee and presses it off to the side. Their shared flexibility definitely has its perks. "You're doing so fucking good, Teddy."

He can feel himself blushing even as he starts to get into it more. He generally knows what he should be doing, so he focuses on moving his hand with his lips, using his free hand to touch Emir elsewhere, anywhere he can reach, and when he needs a rest to breathe, he asks for another thing he wants. "Pull my hair?"

"You - what?" Emir has been keeping his hands held above his head, not wanting to interfere with whatever Theo needs to do to feel safe and comfortable. Watching him between his legs, seeing his curls below the bunched satin fabric of his dress, listening to him clearly enjoying himself and, more than anything, feeling the wet heat of his perfect mouth around his dick has already been a lot. He didn't want to ask for more.

Theo keeps moving his hand along Emir's dick, stretching out his jaw which is already making itself known even after only a minute of going down on Emir. Taking a break was a good idea. "You're too far away to bite me, but I like when you're sort of...rough? When you remind me I'm yours. So like..."

"I can tug on your hair, but I'm not pulling too hard." Emir lets his right arm float down past his still open knee and into Theo's beautiful curls. *I love you, baby* turns into a gentle tousle of his hair and biting down on his own bottom lip while he lets himself stare shamelessly for a moment. "You feel incredible."

"Use your hand to move me." Theo stares up at Emir, wriggling his own bum a bit in the air while he readjusts his position. He's still figuring out the best way to lay between his legs. Emir cautiously presses Theo back towards his dick, so Theo waits until his lips meet skin again then closes his eyes. He doesn't need to see what he's doing, and having Emir's hand guiding him is actually helpful. Emir shares a rhythm, teaching Theo what he wants and likes, honing what Theo was already doing into something more distinct.

It's not anything like Theo imagined, and he has a very active imagination. Breathing is more difficult than he thought, for one. And he has to be so much more careful with his teeth when it's a real dick and not a finger or a dildo or something, so his jaw is working a lot harder. But the smell and the taste and all that...it's so much better than Theo thought. He's never tasted a dick before, and he knows some people don't take care of their personal hygiene or whatever, but Emir's hair is trimmed just enough and he keeps himself clean and it's the taste and smell of Emir's skin and sweat with something new. Something...more. The feel of his dick on Theo's lips and tongue is like velvet, more give and movement to it than he expected, like no other skin he's felt before. It's not like Emir's lips or his chest or his thighs. Theo's tongue can't get enough and he knows he's drooling, but Emir's hand in his hair is sure and he's cursing and praising Theo and moving his hips just slightly to match Theo's mouth and hand, and Theo is so, so incredibly into this.

"Shehzadi!" Emir half-shouts, using his hand to pull Theo away because he almost came just then when Theo found an extra sensitive spot beneath the head with his tongue. He's way too fucking good at this for his first try and Emir is more than slightly overwhelmed and definitely impressed. He's not used to head meaning something or having it be a relationship milestone. He's not used to weaving so much love into sex. He's still learning. "Up here."

Despite his desire to keep blowing Emir for a while longer, Theo lets Emir tug him back up to kiss him deep, dirty mouth be damned, his hands finding Theo's bum and grinding against him while they snog so rough it's more breathing and tongues than it is a kiss. "Switch places with me."

"Hm?" Emir has a handful of Theo and he's tasting himself on his boyfriend's lips and he'd rather not move, but...

"Lay me against the pillows and paint my face." Theo lets a hand fall back to Emir's dick, starting to jerk him off again even as they keep kissing. He knows what he wants and even though it's really difficult to find words right now, this need is like fire, consuming him until it's shared. Now that he knows what Emir's dick tastes like, he wants his spunk on his tongue as soon as humanly possible. "I can't get enough of you."

"Fuck, alright, I can do that. You're - fuck!" Emir bats Theo's hand away and flips them over with his legs. Theo lets himself be handled then smiles at Emir from the pillows, eyes glassy. He looks so happy and at ease, like they're out under their tree instead of relishing the after effects of a blowjob.

Theo opens his mouth and sticks out his tongue, pulling at Emir's hips until he gets the memo. Emir pauses a moment to brush Theo's hair out of his face so he won't need to clean dried cum out of it later. He knows what a pain that can be. Theo runs his hands along Emir's thighs encouragingly as he pulls himself off, his hand moving fast while he stares down at Theo, which is all the inspiration he could possibly need.

With a groan, Emir unloads across Theo's face, down his eyelashes, dripping on his lips and into his waiting mouth, aiming as best he can while his body shudders. With a hum, Theo licks his lips and swallows, blinking his eyes open again, spunk be damned. It's not a very pleasant taste, but he's ready to burst out of his own boxers at the sensation.

"You alright?" Emir catches his breath, holding himself up with one arm against the wall behind the bed, the other cradling Theo's jaw. That was easily the best blowjob of his life. Not technically, because Theo is still new to this, but his enthusiasm and the love Emir feels for him are worth so much more than the nuances he'll learn as they keep shagging throughout their relationship.

"Perfect." Theo has to close his right eye because there's a significant amount of spunk threatening to fall out of his eyelashes, but he watches Emir with his left, reaching out for him while still swallowing down the taste. "Can I do that again?"

Emir laughs, relieved, as his breath stutters. He didn't know how this would go. He remembers his own first blowjob and how overwhelming it was. He's glad that Theo's experience seems to have been better. "First of all, it's your turn. I know I have stamina, but you'll have to give me a minute to recharge, pumpkin. I'm fresh out."

Pressing gently against Theo's chest, Emir asks him to stay for a moment, rushing into the bathroom to get a soft flannel wet with some lukewarm water. Theo's face needs to be treated gently, and for now, this will have to do. He takes his time softly wiping away anything he left behind - that Theo hasn't already snacked on - pausing for a sweet kiss once he's done. Theo's looking at him with so much love his heart hurts. "There we are, baby. Good as new."

"I really liked that." Theo waits for Emir to toss the flannel to the floor, hands on Emir's waist as he hovers above him. They're far from done, but they're in a sort of interlude, and he wants to process aloud if Emir doesn't mind. "I know I'll get better the more I do it, but it was alright? I was alright?"

"More than alright. One of the most enjoyable blows I've had, and I'm not just saying that. I think it makes a difference that we've taken so much time to learn how we each like to be touched and all that." Emir assures him, sliding his hands up Theo's chest and beneath the shirt still wilting around his back. He's never been so attracted to someone in his life. "Can I get you undressed now? You're so warm all the time, but I don't want you overheating while I finger you. It might be overstimulating."

"Can I take your dress off, too? I want cuddle time when we're done, before we get cleaned up." Theo used to be so self conscious about asking for what he needs, but Emir's always encouraged him to be vocal and honest with him. Having skin-to-skin full body contact after sex has been really important for Theo, especially when he's feeling overwhelmed.

"Find the zipper and take it off while I kiss you." Emir winks at him, tossing his pink hair out of his eyes and leaning forward, legs still straddling Theo's hips. He feels Theo's hands at his back but his eyes are closed. Emir shivers as Theo pulls down the zipper, so very slowly, letting his fingertips trail over his spine in its wake until the dress is open down to his tailbone. The sudden rush of cool air on his back goes to his head, so Emir disconnects their lips and rests their foreheads together, needing a break while Theo carefully slides the fabric up and over his body. He has to disconnect once the dress reaches his chest, but Theo pulls him back in as soon as the dress is discarded gently on the sheets beside them. "Your turn."

Theo sits up so his back is off the mattress, trying to catch Emir's mouth even as he angles away so he can remove Theo's remaining clothes. They end up laughing together, both finally naked and sweaty as they fall back against the mattress. Emir's giggle gets pressed into the skin of Theo's shoulder while they catch their breath and Theo lays a kiss against Emir's soft pink hair. The air is dripping with devotion, landing across their skin with each caress.

"Did you have anything specific in mind for this?" Emir will get up to grab lube and another flannel in a minute. For now he's perfectly content where he is.

"I was thinking maybe start on my hands and knees and if I like it, maybe I could lay down and let you kiss me?" Theo presses his body against Emir's, thinking of all the different scenarios he's imagined and the ways Emir's fingers suddenly became very distracting when performing certain tasks. "Also maybe blow me to finish me off while, um, pressing inside me? Maybe not constantly though. Like you said, it might be overstimulating."

"Can I mention something that we haven't talked much about yet?" Emir carefully catalogues the exact scenario Theo describes, but he does have one more question because he's positive it'll be relevant.

"We can talk about anything." Theo truly means it, too. There's nothing they're too shy or scared to discuss anymore.

"Sometimes you start to hover towards something like subspace, and I'm wondering how you feel about me sort of...tipping you over that edge?" Emir knows Theo well enough by now that he doesn't think it would be out of the question. "Usually I pull you back if I notice you getting too fuzzy, but if you're into it, I think this could be a pretty safe first try at it. But if you'd rather – "

"I've always wanted to. Or, at least, since I learned what it might feel like, and then had someone I trust as much as you to try it with." Theo knows exactly what Emir's talking about, how he starts losing his speech and his muscles start to disconnect from his conscious mind, but Emir always either takes a break or uses some sort of physical stimulus to bring him back from it. "I could easily just fall under if you let me. But like...safe words?"

"I think you should choose a word and some sort of physical stop as well. In case you're too deep to talk to me but need out." Emir hasn't ever had a true BDSM relationship of any kind. He's messed around with bondage a bit before Theo, and he's moderately obsessed with sex positive content on the internet, but he had a few chats with Laurie about it to be sure he'd know how to keep it safe if they ever got to this point. From early on, he had a feeling Theo would be interested, and he trusted Laurie enough for realistic advice, given his experience. Laurie and T have tried nearly everything at least once, determined to have a breadth of sexual experiences within the context of their relationship.

"How about...I like the traffic light system. Having a specific safe word might actually be hard for me to remember in the moment, but I can remember the colours, but then I also thought about how for you red is the best colour, so I'm not sure if that would be confusing?" Theo's also talked to Laurie about this, then later T, too, since they have experience as the submissive partner. Nothing too specific, just general best practices and safety tips, that sort of thing.

"I can actually separate the name of the colour from the experience of it without a problem, which is part of why I didn't realise I have synesthesia for so long." Emir shrugs, leaning onto his hand with his elbow propped against the mattress as he faces Theo. "If the three colours work for you, they work for me. But I still think you should have something physical that isn't words."

"This might sound stupid, but it was Laurie's idea and I think it's actually a good one so long as I can touch your face or your arm or whatever." Theo reaches out his hand to demonstrate as he talks, letting his fingertips rest where he indicates. "So if you're facing me, your forehead is red, your nose is yellow, and your mouth is green. And if I have your forearm because I'm facing away, your wrist is red, your forearm is yellow, and your elbow is green. Like, the same spots as the colours would be on the traffic light, so it's easy to visualise. Also, if I need to push you away because I panic, your forehead and wrists are the safest options."

"That's actually really smart. I'm impressed." Emir grins, practising on Theo with his own fingertips to indicate he's understood and accepted the touch based consent system. "I didn't know you talked to anyone about all this, but I'm glad you had someone to chat with. It's important we have our mates as an external perspective when we need them, you know? Make sure we aren't too codependent, even if we are private about a lot of things."

"I talked to T too. They volunteered more than I asked, but I'm grateful for their honesty." Theo starts tapping at Emir's lips, alternating between his index and middle finger, watching Emir's smile grow as he realises what Theo's telling him. He's green, ready to go, excited and eager. "Love you."

"Let's get you in the position you feel best starting in, then I'll take over, yeah?" Emir sits up, one hand on Theo's waist just because he can, even as Theo sits up as well, dislodging it momentarily.

Theo pulls him into another kiss with a hand on the back of Emir's head. They don't kiss sitting up very often anymore, not when horizontal with full body contact is an option. But it gives Emir the opportunity to lean back, to make Theo work for it and follow his lead.

There's more giggling until Emir decides he doesn't want to wait anymore and shifts his hands to Theo's hips to start turning him around. "Go ahead and face the headboard. I'll help you find a position you can stay in for a while."

Theo does as he's told, hands and knees, tabletop, head falling down already with his eyes closed. Emir's hands start adjusting him, and Theo can already feel himself letting go, the tension leaving his muscles. Emir scoots him back, presses until his face is against the pillow and his forearms are on the mattress, widens his knees then shifts his weight forward so he's not straining his hips or bruising his knees while holding this position and giving him plenty of leverage. It's all so gentle and considerate, and Theo feels so loved and cared for he can't imagine ever wanting to do this with anyone else. Emir is his favourite in every way.

"Could you test out your safety system for me, baby? I'll keep my left forearm where you can reach it, but you might have to shift your weight to get my elbow." Emir slides himself in behind Theo and lets his left arm rest where he plans to keep it. Theo shifts onto his own left arm so he can squeeze Emir's elbow with his right, then drifts his hand down to his smooth forearm, and finally takes a careful hold of Emir's wrist before going back to the position Emir moved him into. "That was perfect. Stay here for just a moment. I'm not leaving, just grabbing what we need."

Unsurprisingly, Theo whines once Emir's body heat moves away from him and his weight shifts from the bed. He knows it's only a minute or so, but it feels like much longer. He's very exposed like this, his skin suddenly shivering without Emir to keep him warm. Ironic since outside of sex, Emir is the one who's always cold and stealing Theo's body heat. It's a nice balance they have, a give and take, and Theo lets himself think of that while he waits patiently for his boyfriend to return from where he's rustling in his overnight bag.

"I'm going to talk you through the whole thing and ask for regular check-ins." Emir doesn't get behind Theo again, instead he kneels on the floor temporarily so he can be eye level with where Theo's resting patiently against the pillow. "Words are already gone, aren't they? Don't try to make yourself talk. I trust you to tap out with your hands, alright? If you're feeling up to talking, go ahead, but you're already fuzzy. You're so beautiful and sweet and you don't need to be anyone or anything besides all that you already are. Just let me take care of you."

Theo smiles at Emir and hums low in his chest, a reverberating sound that earns him a sweet kiss. When Emir pulls back, Theo reaches out his hand to rest his fingertips against Emir's lips, staring with wide eyes. He could stare at Emir forever, but before he's had his fill, Emir is standing up and climbing back up onto the mattress behind him.

"I'll start with my mouth like you're used to and then let you know when I'm switching to lube." Emir sets the bottle nearby where he can reach it with his free hand, sliding into the same position he'd shown Theo earlier with his arm readily available for Theo to communicate.

He takes everything slowly, guiding Theo as much with his voice as with his actions, feeling as he falls deeper and deeper into the safest spaces of his mind by internalising the sensation of Emir's tongue against his hole. He loves when Emir rims him. He loves when Emir does anything, honestly.

After only a minute or two of Emir using his mouth, Theo shut his eyes and started following Emir's voice. Theo may not be speaking, but he is making sounds, and he's made sure to tap Emir's elbow every time he's asked how he's doing. Not having to force himself to find words for all that he's feeling is genuinely helpful, and he already knows he'll be diving headfirst into subspace the moment Emir tells him to. It's like he can feel the water of the ocean lapping at his toes, inviting him to wade in, knowing that he'll be safe because he has his own personal life-guard.

"Time for lube, princess. I'll work around the outside first then start with just the one finger. It shouldn't hurt, so if it does, stop me right away." Emir keeps himself in place, smiling when Theo grasps his elbow and presses his bum higher in the air towards where his face had just been.

With a few drops of his favourite silicone lube on his fingertips, Emir does exactly as promised. Theo moans and presses against him, impatient and needy for Emir to do more. With a few seconds of warning, Emir presses in with his middle finger up to his second knuckle, and Theo's entire body shivers while he says something like, "Emir, yes," but it's muffled against the pillows. Carefully, Emir moves his finger in and out several times, adding a bit more lube and making Theo groan when his hand moves away.

"Patience, baby. I don't want to hurt you." Emir drops a kiss, then a small bite to Theo's right arse cheek, earning another smaller shiver as he presses his finger back inside. He keeps doing much of the same, trying out different speeds and movements to see what Theo responds to until he feels Theo's hand on his forearm. He removes his own hand immediately and sits back. They didn't have a system for yellow, not officially, so Emir will have to try out some yes or no questions and see if that works.

"Need a break?"

Theo shakes his head no and groans.

"New position?"

Theo's response takes longer, probably because he's genuinely considering it, but then that also gets a head shake.

"Did something hurt?"

An immediate no this time, accompanied by Theo scrabbling for Emir's arm and finding his elbow, holding on tight.

"Alright. More, then? You ready for me to use two fingers?"

Theo's hand moves back to Emir's forearm, then up to his elbow, then he twists himself enough that his hand reaches Emir's bicep. What's greener than green? Theo's first two fingers start pressing against Emir's muscle, pulsing, and he thinks he's figured it out.

"You want two fingers and you want me to find your prostate?"

An immediate yes moaned into the pillow as Theo drops his hand from Emir's arm and props himself back into position, widening his legs even more than before. That wasn't so difficult to figure out. Emir's glad they know each other so well.

Still being (probably overly) cautious, Emir drips a bit of lube directly on Theo's hole before pressing in with both his pointer and middle finger, Theo's body trembling again at the new sensation. Emir works on a mark on Theo's left bum cheek while gently fucking his fingers inside of his boyfriend, letting him adjust before he feels around properly. He's done this with probably half a dozen other people so he definitely knows what he's feeling for.

He expected Theo to react, but he didn't expect it to be so loud. Yes, he encourages Theo to let go and make whatever noises he likes, but he's never heard that one before. Emir slowly removes his fingers to give Theo a break just as Theo's hand clamps down hard on Emir's forearm, legs collapsing down against the bed. He looks like he's trying to flip himself over, but his eyes are closed tight and Emir knows he's overstimulated. Hopefully not too far. He doesn't want to overdo it.

With gentle hands, Emir shifts Theo to his back, guiding his knees open and to the side and fitting himself between Theo's legs. Emir takes a moment to fluff the pillows, noticing a bit of makeup from Theo's face left behind. It's fine, he didn't use anything that will stain, but it does remind him to make sure Theo at least washes his face before he falls asleep tonight.

Not entirely sure where his body is, Theo knows Emir is close and he knows he wants more of what he just felt and that's really all he's thinking about. That ecstasy that flooded through him before retreating as quickly as it arrived. More.

"Baby, you're on your back now. Just like you asked earlier. If you want me to keep going, I need a yes or a tap." Emir takes Theo's warm hand in his and brings it up to his face, setting it against his cheek so Theo knows where to find him.

Blinking his eyes open and immediately finding Emir inches away, Theo's vision goes cloudy. He doesn't realise he's crying until Emir wipes away a few of his tears. "You're so beautiful."

"You have no idea, shehzadi. You're a work of art." Emir kisses the inside of Theo's wrist and waits for him to either say more or tap in one of their agreed to spots. Theo licks his lips, tasting the salt of his released emotion, then moves his fingertips to Emir's lips and nods, eyes fluttering closed again and a serene smile taking over his face. He looks so peaceful, Emir almost feels guilty continuing. But Theo said green, so...

"It's going to feel a bit different laying down." Emir warns as he presses both fingers back inside of Theo, watching his smile melt into a gasping release. It only takes him a moment to find Theo's prostate again, so he tries both moving up and down along it then circling directly on top of it, and Theo definitely prefers the latter. There's endless options with prostate play, but Emir doesn't think Theo's first time is the best opportunity to give them all a go.

"If you still want me to blow you until you finish, I need a tap, baby." Emir expects it to take a while to register, and sure enough, it's almost ten seconds before Theo's hand drifts to Emir's mouth, so gentle against his lips, then falling back to his side. His arms are wide open, chest exposed, head thrown back like he's floating on water.

Emir has to shift down the bed, but he has Theo in his mouth soon enough, pressing circles against Theo's prostate and moving his mouth along the portion of his shaft that he can handle while still keeping his left arm within Theo's reach, just in case. He barely has Theo's dick in his mouth for a minute before Theo is moaning, his spunk coating Emir's tongue, on and on and on for so much longer than usual as Emir keeps pressing inside of him, drawing out every last ounce of pleasure as Theo twitches and jerks.

Theo's so far gone, floating and flying and completely free. He's weightless and incorporeal, gone away somewhere new. All he can feel is Emir and bliss and it just keeps going and going and going and -

But then all of a sudden, his body comes back to him, and Emir's mouth is gone but his fingers are still inside Theo, gingerly bringing him through it, and everything is way too fucking much. Way too much. It's too loud and too bright and his mouth is a desert and his skin is crawling so he uses all his energy to grasp Emir's forearm.

Immediately, Emir stops and removes his fingers for the last time tonight, reaching for the flannel to get both of them clean, not loving the expression on Theo's face. "Baby? Are you alright?"

Theo's hand is still on Emir's forearm, so he gives it a squeeze but doesn't move. He's definitely not green anymore but he's also not red. Solidly yellow. It's just...a lot. It's more than a lot. But it's not bad. He can't really say it's good either. It's overwhelmingly everything and he can't process any of it. Theo starts crying quietly, hot tears falling from his eyes. Emir strokes his cheek soothingly but Theo flinches away. Too much.

"Fuck. Did I overdo it?" Emir wonders aloud, mostly to himself. He knows Theo can hear him, but is he even listening? Can he listen right now?

But then Theo covers his ears with his hands and rolls onto his side, curling into himself with his eyes shut tight. *Oh.* He's dropping and he's overstimulated. Even the lightest touch is going to feel like nails on a chalkboard until his nervous system is back closer to a standard level.

"Theo, I'm not going to touch you until you tell me to, alright? Is this quiet enough?" Emir whispers, so quiet Theo probably wouldn't hear him under normal circumstances. But Theo relaxes his shoulders at Emir's words and nods, the tiniest, most careful nod, and Emir knows how to fix this. He knows how to be what Theo needs.

"I'm getting off the bed and turning out the light, and then I'll wait at the edge until you reach for me." Emir does as he promised, stopping to grab both their water bottles as quietly as possible so he won't need to get up again once Theo's back to safety. He's glad he was able to clean up the worst of it before Theo was pushed too far. They'll have to have a chat before they try this again, so Emir knows exactly what made Theo drop and how he can avoid it in the future. Sub drop is sort of inevitable, but it doesn't have to be so intense.

Theo breathes as deep as he can, counting the ins and outs, feeling his diaphragm swell then deflate, searching for each of his muscles one at a time until he thinks he can handle cuddles. He really wants cuddles, Emir's skin warm against his, more than anything, but he needed a moment to find himself first. Tentatively, he reaches out a hand and accidentally finds Emir's wrist, pulling his hand back like he's been shocked, then recalibrating and aiming higher. It takes three tries but he finds Emir's elbow and leaves his hand there.

"Would cuddles with the sheets over you be alright? I'll be quiet and keep the lights off. And you can be little spoon, of course." Emir doesn't move closer until Theo nods, tugging just slightly on his elbow to encourage him to come back into the bed.

Emir climbs carefully over his huddled frame and fits himself behind Theo's back, barely touching at first, then slowly bringing his arms and legs around Theo like he usually prefers after sex. It's not until Emir's settled and done moving that Theo relaxes, letting out a huge sigh and grabbing onto Emir's hand to hold it across his stomach.

"You're incredible, baby." Emir whispers, glad to feel Theo coming back to a safer level. "Could I whisper all the ways you were so incredible for me? Tell you how you were so good? Would you like that?"

"Yes...please." Theo's voice is just as quiet, loud to his own ears, but it's not impossible to speak anymore, which is nice. He misses that perfect, weightless, floating feeling, but he didn't like the crash that came after. He still feels delicate, like he could shatter back down to the bottom if he tries too hard, like he's off balance and needs time to get his bearings.

"I've got you. I'm right here and I'll stay right here until you're ready to move. You have my hand if you need to get my attention." Emir reassures him, pressing the most delicate kiss he can manage against the back of Theo's shoulder. Theo sighs again in response, so Emir starts talking, keeping his voice low. He keeps talking until he hears soft snores, Theo dozing off in his arms, fully relaxed and peaceful in his sleep.

Emir doesn't think that Theo will sleep for too long, likely just a short recovery nap, but he'll stay either way. He promised. It gives him plenty of time to enjoy having Theo curled up in his arms, knowing they've just crossed several new milestones in one evening, and glad to have the time with his own heart to process. He's never loved like this before, but he can't imagine his life any other way. Theo's his match, in everything, and they may still have obstacles they're working through, and they have plenty of discussions and serious conversations to have, but Emir's nearly positive that they have the rest of their lives, so there's no rush.

***

"Your makeup is so completely fucked, princess." Emir grins, muffling a giggle as he brushes a curl away from Theo's gorgeous eyes.

There's barely any space between their warm bodies. He's been staring and admiring Theo while he dozes on and off, shameless and open and infatuated because Theo doesn't mind...and he's been half asleep. But Emir meant what he said: Theo's makeup is smeared all over, mascara smudged, eyeliner smoked out, highlight and blush mostly rubbed off, and everything else that he had meticulously applied hours earlier at least partially left behind on the sheets from when they were having sex. Incredible sex.

"Makeup's not the only thing." Theo's eyes stay closed but he returns Emir's smile and sighs happily. Never has a bed been more comfortable, and he'd love to know whatever magic is in this mattress. Maybe it's the sheets. Most likely, that intoxicating comfort is emanating from Emir in droves. He can smell him nearby, practically taste him still, the traces of Emir lingering on his tongue and the roof of his mouth even ages after they both finished.

"Someday...if you want." Emir presses a kiss to Theo's forehead and breathes him in for a moment. Usually Theo would be hurrying into the shower right about now, but he seems extremely content staying put. Emir's not complaining. He cleaned up the worst of it. "Tonight was more like a preview."

Theo just sighs again and focuses on every bit of skin that touches Emir, moving his awareness from his forehead to his shoulder, all the way down his body until he can feel Emir's toes against his own. Floating away was bliss, and crashing down was unsettling, but being back in his body is like sweet summer rain. He's sore and exhausted, but in a way he's been incrementally learning to love.

"You need a shower or are you alright?" Emir keeps his lips buried in Theo's forehead curls and his voice low, mumbling to maintain this gorgeous feeling they've settled into. He knows they'll get up soon, but these moments are some of his favourites. Just them, away from the world together.

"Should wash the makeup off, I suppose." Theo slides his leg between Emir's and shifts his hips until they're closer on the bed, their stomachs just touching. "In a bit. Still...floaty. Boneless and weak, like I'm swimming in treacle."

Emir has that effect on him, and Theo doesn't want to scrub it away just yet.

"No rush, baby. Never a rush." Emir starts drawing his fingertips along Theo's back again, up and down and up and down and up...Time doesn't feel quite real this weekend, like they're suspended from their timeline and visiting another. "You think you want to try the makeup again sometime?"

"Hmmm..." Theo scrunches up his face to think. He can feel it if he really focuses, but it's not anywhere near as heavy as what he wears on stage. Still not super comfortable, though. He's not against it, per se, but it doesn't feel like something he's into on a regular basis. "Maybe the eyeliner. I like the eyeliner. Always have."

"Shows off those beautiful hazel eyes of yours." Emir confirms. There's never any doubt that Theo will be stunning in whatever clothing or makeup or personal decoration he's in the mood for. The purple streak has already faded out of his hair, but even that was lovely on him.

"Is this what it will be like?" Theo asks a minute later, breathing even and slow, close enough to Emir's neck that he can feel the warmth of it like a summer breeze, tickling at his skin.

"Like what will be like?" Emir closes his eyes for the first time in ages, potentially for the first time since they'd laid down earlier for a rest. Theo's just too pretty to be ignored sometimes, and tonight he's glowing, so Emir's eyes only shut for a few seconds before he's staring again.

"Next year, or like...in a few months." Theo shuffles around under the sheets until his nose is tucked right up against Emir's throat, curled into him completely. This close he can feel Emir's chest rise and fall as he shares the air. This is its own cherished type of intimacy. He's learned so many since he fell in love with Emir. "When we have our flat and we're all grown up. Will this be every night?"

"Not every night, no, and we'll never be all grown up." Emir grins and hugs Theo tighter, arms strong around his back. Theo's out of the clouds and all the way into himself again, so Emir doesn't need to treat him quite as much like glass. "But hopefully we'll have time for this about once a week. Time to enjoy ourselves and each other and just exist for a while. We need it, I think. Both of us."

Theo nods, glad to hear that Emir also needs time like this. It's not only about processing, it's also about appreciating everything they are, finding each other and themselves in the stillness that comes after sex. The quiet that hums with contentment. Satisfaction and joy all wrapped together in the sheets between them. "We should probably have a chat tomorrow."

"Oh?" Emir knows Theo doesn't mean that to sound so ominous, but it's just one of those phrases. Not that he's actually worried. At least not much. "Am I in trouble?"

"Hardly." Theo laughs once then kisses the front of Emir's throat. It's the closest thing he can reach without moving. "I want a spreadsheet for all our company applications so we can keep track of all the audition tapes and deadlines and whatever else. We should start being more intentional about our future. I want to make it happen for us the way we envision."

"We can make a spreadsheet, pumpkin. Let's bring it with us to Sean next time we go, yeah?" Emir shouldn't feel a pang of love at Theo's need for a spreadsheet. And yet. "He's our mentor, or whatever. And we can share it with our other contacts. See if they know anyone or have suggestions."

"Staying in London?" Theo's eyebrows scrunch, and he suddenly needs to itch like...the entirety of his face. Shower soon, then.

"I think so." Emir watches Theo begin to fuss, knowing they both need to get cleaned up and ready for sleep. It's been a great day, but a long one. They need rest. "We should probably talk about backup plans tomorrow, too. Just in case."

"Want to stay together." Theo blinks his eyes open for the first time in a while. The only light in the room is a bedside lamp on its lowest setting, but it feels like the entire sun. "Even as a backup. So if it's Paris for you, I'm following."

"You're the one who knows French." Emir teases, booping Theo on the nose now that he's not the only one staring. Theo's just so fucking cute. "I'll need my translator."

"I like when you use me, so that's agreeable." Theo waits for Emir to roll his eyes fondly, just like he knew he would. He likes knowing someone this well, knowing *Emir* this well. "I'll send you a quote for my services to attach to the spreadsheet. Factor it into the budget."

"You're worth every quid." Emir glances behind Theo at the open door to the bathroom, already dreading the few steps out in the open before they can sink into the hot water together.

"You've never even heard me speak French. Not properly." Theo kicks his legs, restless, until the sheets fall around their waist, their upper halves exposed to the elements. And then his eyes find Emir's bare torso and he's distracted anew. "Christ, you're fit. Remind me how I convinced you to be my boyfriend?"

"Didn't need much convincing." Emir shrugs, reaching out a hand to trace it along Theo's chest now that it's exposed. "I probably told myself you were straight despite the evidence to the contrary just so I didn't have to let myself feel anything real."

"You know...I don't think you ever actually came out to me. Not as bi." Theo lays flat against the mattress so Emir can have easier access to touch his body. Sometimes Emir starts drawing imaginary patterns and shapes on Theo's skin, and Theo is the most willing canvas imaginable. "Just noticed you hooking up with people at parties or whatever and sort of assumed."

"I always knew you noticed. I told myself I just wanted to mess with you, because you'd be with Laurie and you'd be glaring at me whenever I looked and I don't know if you were jealous or anything, but you were definitely annoyed." Emir smiles, a bit sad. "I always wanted your attention, even when I shied away from anyone else and their constant staring. It was different with you. I wanted you to know, even if I didn't think I wanted you."

"I didn't realise I was jealous, but I think I was." Theo threads his fingers into the back of Emir's messy pink hair, pulling him forward for a kiss. "You're my favourite person, and maybe I always knew you would be."

"Mmm." Emir agrees, kissing Theo back for only a moment. The energy's shifted. "Let's get clean. All this talk of our future and then our past is making me too sentimental for someone who just fingered his boyfriend into subspace."

Theo laughs, covering his eyes with his forearm until Emir tickles at his sides and makes him kick and squirm. "Fine! But we're cuddling and watching a sappy movie until we fall asleep. It's required."

"What if I order us room service dessert to share?" Emir climbs over Theo to the edge of the bed, making sure his bum gets very close to Theo's face in passing. He offers a hand and flutters his eyelashes until Theo takes it, yanking him up so quick it makes him laugh again. He loves making Theo laugh.

"I won't stop you. I think I used up all my energy." Theo lets Emir pull him into the bathroom and kiss him against the glass door until the water warms up.

Once they're inside and Emir is rinsing soap suds from his pretty hair, Theo touches him gently at the waist to get his attention, just to remind him he loves him, to tell him thank you, only to have Emir roll his eyes and say he's the one who's grateful. Theo wants to keep him in arms reach, even in this larger than necessary hotel shower, because any further feels like a canyon.

"What am I meant to answer the door in?" Emir ends the call for provisions and turns back to Theo, both of them fully nude and comfortably tangled up at the side of the bed. Theo's been clinging to him like a koala since they dried and moisturised and left the bathroom behind. "You told me not to bring pyjamas."

"I didn't plan for post-coital chocolate." Theo just shrugs, arms still firm around Emir's middle from the side. "You could throw on my hoodie for tomorrow and your joggers, as long as you strip them off as soon as we're alone again."

"Excuse you, I'm more than just a nice arse." Emir crosses his arms over his chest, pretending to be offended. He likes that Theo's so openly attracted to him.

"I know." Theo kisses his bicep and grins up at him, trying not to laugh. "You've also got a nice cock."

Emir tackles him against the pillows then tickles and teases and makes him shriek until they're so distracted that he's still naked when the knock comes at the door a few minutes later, Emir panics, throwing on what Theo suggested and shouting at the employee to wait a second, knowing he sounds out of breath.

"Hush." Emir steals a kiss once he's clothed, throwing the sheets back over Theo and ignoring the way he laughs at the state of him. He answers the door with a hasty apology and a thank you, taking the tray carefully in his hands while Theo whistles from behind the moment the door is closed.

"Strip strip strip strip!" Theo chants, making grabby hands for the tray until Emir hands it over and tugs the hoodie over his head, tossing it aside onto Theo's bag. "That's better. Now the joggers."

"Where was this energy in the shower when you needed me to wash your hair?" Emir turns around to pull down the joggers, leaning forward so Theo can stare at his bum. It's generally effective at distracting him.

"I didn't have chocolate then." Theo lifts the cloche to reveal what Emir's ordered, waiting for him to rejoin him in the bed. "Maybe we should, like, play with food sometime. We could always put a towel down, and I'd really like to find out what caramel tastes like warm from your skin."

"You are *insatiable* sometimes." Emir swipes a bit of whipped cream from the plate and feeds it to himself, then swipes a bit more to feed to Theo. Theo hums and closes his eyes, his lips sucking around Emir's finger far longer than is necessary. "Eat your sugar and I'll find something to watch."

Emir chooses some Meg Ryan film from the 90s, streaming on Theo's laptop at their feet. When the desserts are gone, he carries the tray to wait by the door, then climbs back into bed and pulls Theo to lay on his chest. Theo's asleep before the film is over, happy and refuelled and physically satiated, so Emir lets it play in the background. It's a cute film. He doesn't mind.

When the credits roll, Emir's careful to set Theo back against his pillow before clearing everything away and having a last wee before bed. He fits himself behind Theo's back, wrapping his arms and one leg around his sleeping boyfriend and settling in for the night.

Theo asked if this is what next year would be like, but the truth is that this is what their life is already like. If it all continues into their life in a shared flat, to their relationship beyond uni, Emir wouldn't mind.

CHAPTER FIFTEEN

"Oh thank GAWD." Jordan looks up from her book when she hears the front door to the library open, setting her novel aside and watching as Emir and Theo walk towards her. Theo's carrying the coffee they picked up from Lili on their way when Jordan had texted in a panic realising she left it behind. "I've been literally dying for the past hour."

"You've only been at work for twenty minutes." Theo laughs, handing over the thermos with a grin. Lili had been grumpy and barely awake when she shoved it into his hand, and Jo doesn't seem much better.

"Let me be gay and dramatic. I've earned it." Jo takes a very long drink with her eyes closed, both hands clasped around the travel mug like a lifeline. "Not used to waking up early on a Saturday. Stupid late-stage capitalism."

"At least you only have to deal with us?" Emir suggests, because the library does appear completely empty except for the three of them. He and Theo were headed here anyway to do research, and now that Jordan works the front desk a few shifts a week, they texted to ask if she needed anything. Hence the coffee.

"You're not something that needs dealing with, Emi. I'm only whinging." Jordan has her hair half-up in a messy bun and she looks slightly dishevelled, but otherwise alright. It's been a fortnight since Lili panicked and showed up at the gym to chat with Theo, but Jordan's already made a few changes in that short time.

"We were planning to work in that study room with the big windows, but we could stay down here if you'd rather?" Theo offers. If he were to guess, she's feeling lonely and overtired and, according to Emir, she's going to be in survival mode for a while. If she doesn't want to be alone, he would understand.

"Do you have a few minutes to chat while I let the caffeine enter my bloodstream?" Jordan still has it clutched between her pale hands, looking up at them from her desk, her under eye circles dark, but not quite as concerning as a few weeks ago.

"Course we do." Emir drops his rucksack near his feet and drags a chair over from a nearby study table, Theo following to do the same. There won't be anyone else here for hours to even care about their monopoly on Jordan's attention. "How's the new job so far?"

"It's only been a few shifts, but it's fine. Not much for me to do, honestly, unless someone needs me to look something up or help them with a broken printer, sometimes a bit of cataloguing, so I've been doing a lot of reading." Jordan shrugs and leans back in her chair with a sigh. She's months ahead for book club already. "My coworkers are nice. They're quiet and keep to themselves most of the time. I meet a lot more people this way, especially since Lili and I don't really go out except with you lot. I'd rather be sat here than shelving books, I suppose, but maybe they'll have me do more soon."

"Meet anyone particularly interesting?" Theo stretches his arms up and tilts his head side to side before settling into his seat. This morning at the gym was a lot of upper back and shoulder strengthening, and he should probably stretch more later when they're in the studio. He can feel he's a bit tight.

"Mmmm…might have." Jordan's looking out through the front door thoughtfully, chewing on the inside of her cheek, then starts gesturing with her coffee as she continues. "I was invited to join a queer political group club type thing. They want to host speakers and sign petitions and stuff. Could be interesting."

"The LGBTQ+ Society? Ciaran's met with them a few times." Theo reaches out a hand to play with the loose hair at the back of Emir's neck.

The top of Emir's hair is braided into two adorable pink rows thanks to T's expert hands when they got bored last night, but the back is still loose and begging to be twined around Theo's fingers. Emir looks so cute this morning in his glasses and soft oversized jumper - the one Theo gave him for Christmas - that Theo made him pose for a picture before they left the flat. And since Theo's also wearing his glasses this morning, Emir did the same, positioning Theo against the kitchen counter and making him laugh until his sides hurt, trying to capture his gorgeous smile in an image. Even the best ones don't come close to the real thing.

"But he stopped going?" Jordan's eyes slide over to Theo, pausing for just a moment to smile when she notices his hand in Emir's hair.

"He said it wasn't really his scene, even if he agreed with what they were doing." Theo shrugs. He suspects there was more to it than that, but it was also first year and so much has changed since then, with Ciaran, with their uni, with the whole fucking world.

"You thinking about it?" Emir leans his head just slightly towards Theo, encouraging the attention. Theo's been practically sharing his lap recently, not that he minds, but he's noticed an increase in the physical contact. It used to be frequent, now it's almost constant.

"Lili says I haven't got the time, but like…I could use an outlet for all…this." Jordan waves vaguely at herself, and they get the picture. They both remember what it was like to be newly out and wishing they could take on the whole world.

"I didn't ask what Lili was thinking." Emir isn't rude in the way he says it, but he's been trying to gently remind Jordan that one of the very few benefits of what happened to her is the fact that she gets to take her life back. And her life is hers, not Lili's, not her parents', not anyone else's. Jo has to make the decisions that are right for her, to examine what she needs and wants, then prioritise that over everything else, especially in the direct aftermath of her trauma.

Theo glances at Emir, first in surprise, then in pride. When they got together, he didn't realise what a fantastic friend Emir is. He should've known with how devoted their other friends have always been to him, especially Laurie. But Emir's friendship and support tend to be quieter, more subtle and nuanced. It's moments like this, or like the day Jo showed up at his parents' house and collapsed.

"I think I want to give it a go. I can always try out a meeting and decide it isn't for me, right?" Jordan takes another drink of her coffee, expecting Emir's input. He just stares calmly back and waits for her to think about it without adding his own opinion. She's still adjusting to being allowed to have one. "I want to go. I'm curious but I'm also just…ready to fucking *do* something, you know?"

"Good." Emir's face breaks out into a wide smile, still focused on Jordan. They've definitely grown closer the past few months, but especially since Christmas. "I'm glad you came across something you might connect with. I know you've been feeling…"

"Lost?" Jordan rubs at her eyes. She's exhausted even though she's been sleeping better the past few days. She has *weeks* of insomnia to make up for and it's not gone completely. "I know it takes time. You've told me that often enough. But now that I'm sure dance isn't my endgame, I feel like I need to try a few things while I still can. See what else might fit."

"You've got time. We're still just kids, really." Emir assures her. They're not teenagers anymore, but they're barely adults. They can't be expected to have it all figured out, their whole life charted and wrapped in a neat bow. It doesn't work that way. "It helps that we're at uni where there's a dozen new things to try every day."

"I think you could be really good at that." Theo adds, hand falling from Emir's hair to rest on his knee instead. Emir moved his leg closer a few moments ago, whether consciously or out of instinct, Theo isn't sure. But he gives it a squeeze and Emir glances at him with a private smile before turning back to Jordan. "Part of what makes you a good dancer is your determination. So if you're not using it for dance, I could see you focusing it on community work. Like, rallies and movements and stuff. As long as you want to, of course."

"I think I do want to, actually." Jordan pulls her hands into her knit jumper, one she'd found the other day at the charity shop next to Roseborough. It's this peachy orange colour and it doesn't really celebrate her undertones, but it's cosy and soft and comforting when she's half asleep at her new job. "I've only ever told Lili about this, but I used to have these dreams of working in Parliament. I thought about being a barrister at one point too, but I got older and I think maybe, like, person-to-person work might be more me. Like hands-on type community care. I don't know…"

"You don't have to know, Jo. It's just a meeting." Emir sets his hand atop Theo's and draws nonsense shapes across his skin with his pointer finger. "But if you've been thinking about it, you should listen to yourself. And if you don't have the emotional space, you can always try again later."

Jordan sighs, staring out the front door again as if looking for answers in the clouds. They let her sit in the quiet for a minute, sipping her coffee and thinking while they continue to caress each other's hands on top of Emir's knee. Theo's positive that a majority of their time spent researching for the next few hours will involve at least some point of physical contact, even as they get lost in their own minds for a bit.

"I'll check out their Discord in a minute. They've got their meeting info and all that posted for new people." Jordan looks between them again, posture more relaxed than when they showed up. She's been carrying too much recently, but she's also got plenty of help shouldering her burdens. Jordan has no clue what she would do if she didn't have such wonderful people in her life. "So, why are we at the library today?"

"I need to get some work done on my dissertation. The written part." Emir takes his hand back from Theo so he can reach into his rucksack instead. He pulls out a notebook, one of many, and flips through a few pages before finding what he's looking for. "Looks like today is focusing on ballet as a political device in the court of Louis

XIV. And if I have time, the next hundred years or so. Since my original concept was tracing the story through the progression of dance over time, even though it's modified, I still need to include enough of that history. And I haven't taken all these years of dance history like Theo, so I have some catching up to do."

"And you didn't just want to borrow all the books Theo's already got?" Jordan asks, only slightly teasing. Emir's a nerd, but Theo's on another level when it comes to dance history.

"I brought them with me. I just needed a change of scenery so I don't get too distracted." Emir gives her a sideways smile, then reaches out to pull Theo in for a loud smack of a kiss. "Too many horizontal surfaces at the flat."

"Tell me about it." Jordan laughs, watching as Theo's flush climbs up his face. He goes so soft and squishy for Emir. And not that Emir would admit to it, but he's worse than Theo. "Imagine sharing a flat. I know you practically do, but like, she's always just right there, being perfect and fit and gorgeous. Without flatmates, there's no one else we need to be courteous for. Or quiet."

"I did *not* need to know that." Theo grumbles, shoving Emir off playfully because he's started to blow raspberries on Theo's neck just to watch him squirm. "Not that you asked, but I'm researching different areas we could live in London next year, depending on which companies we might get to work with. I've made a map with links to a bunch of things, but it needs more data. I'll share it with you and Lili once it's done if you need some ideas. It's a lot to figure out."

"Depends where Lili ends up dancing, but yes, we will definitely appreciate any help we can get." Jo stands up from her chair to stretch, groaning when she tilts her head to the left. The stress has really been affecting her physically, especially in the amount of tension she holds onto. "I'll be here most of the day if you need anything."

"Is Lili bringing you lunch?" Theo asks, standing up as well. It's probably a good time to actually get to work since they need to be in the studio in a few hours.

"She said she would, yeah. I get a break around noon. We'll probably go outside for a bit unless it starts raining again." Jordan stifles a yawn and waves goodbye as they start to walk away and towards one of the private study rooms. She's been told by the other library staff that Saturday mornings are very quiet, and normally she wouldn't mind, but this morning she really needed a chat with her friends to remind her she's not alone.

***

After a few hours at the library, lunch shared in Emir's kitchen, and then some time on their own to do as they please, Emir and Theo find each other again just outside the dance building. Emir takes Theo's hand and gives him a twirl then a kiss before holding the door open for him. They don't need to spend much time working on their dissertation today, but there's a few tweaks they both want to take a look at before they move on to choreographing the final section of the piece. So here they are, on a Saturday afternoon, walking casually through the well trod hall towards the practise studio at the far end, unsurprised to hear music already coming from their destination.

Now that it's almost spring, the third years have less than three months to finalise their work. Emir and Theo are sharing the practice studio more often than ever. Third year dance students are permitted use of the other studio spaces when they're available, but after years of habit, most of them still prefer to hide away in the smallest room with the shit speakers and only a single wall of mirrors. Something about that room and all the talent and life that it's seen just...calls to them. A cycle that repeats year in and year out as new dancers come and go through the programme.

Theo and Emir slow down as they get closer to the open door to the practice studio, not wanting to disturb whoever is hard at work inside. But, as a pleasant surprise, it's Alfie they've happened upon today. It's the first time they've caught him at work on his dissertation, and of the other third years, he's definitely at the top of their list for work they can't wait to see.

"Wonder what his is about." Theo mumbles, keeping his eyes on Alfie but moving closer to Emir and pushing him against the doorframe to get a better look.

"We could ask, I suppose." Emir slides an arm around Theo's waist to hold him close. "We'll have to chat about sharing the space anyway."

Alfie stops with his arms above his head only a minute later. He'd noticed them in the doorway and nodded to acknowledge their presence, then finished what he needed to do before turning towards them. "You two need the studio?"

"We could share, or use one of the others. You were here first." Theo steps into the practice studio, Emir following behind with both of their bags. He still refuses to let

Theo carry his own, even if the distance is only from the front of the building to the end of the hall.

"It's fine. I was already almost done for the day." Alfie uses his shirt to wipe at his brow, showing off an impressive set of abs and a toned chest. He's relaxed quite a lot around their friend group as he's spent more time with Ciaran and Gabe, which includes not caring if they see him shirtless; it's happened half a dozen times by now. "You can warm up while I give that another go or two."

"Thanks, mate." Emir smacks Theo lightly on the bum as he walks past, making him yelp and jump nearly a foot in the air. He's allowed. They've discussed it more than once. "Wouldn't mind seeing what you're working on."

Theo pretends to turn around for a moment, but only so he can return the favour and smack Emir on the arse.

Unfortunately, Emir was expecting it, laughing and leaning into him to say, "Later, baby." Which just makes Theo flush and avert his eyes.

"I'll show you mine if you show me yours." Alfie smirks at their antics, drinking from his nearly empty water bottle and waiting for them to get settled along the far wall before starting up again. He remembers all too well how they were before they got together. "Heard from Lilibet that you're about to show us all up at the end of term."

"I don't know about that, but I am genuinely proud of what we've created." Theo strips down to his joggers and a loose vest, Emir doing the same beside him, but leaving his swan jumper on for now. "Give us like ten minutes and we'll be warm enough."

They leave each other be for a while, Alfie playing and replaying the same portion of music while trying out several different versions of choreography, Theo and Emir warming themselves up and stretching off to the side, mumbling amongst themselves. Being at the studio on the weekend is such a specific feeling, different than being there for class, or even at night during the week. It's just a completely different vibe.

"Right. I could actually use the feedback, if you don't mind." Alfie holds his phone in his hand, having just paused his music yet again. "Raphael is great, but you're young and fit and I haven't shown this to anyone in our year yet."

"Tell us what it's about?" Theo tugs on Emir's hand until he sits beside him, their backs to the mirrors while they wait for Alfie to show his work in progress. They'll see everyone's work eventually, of course, but being part of the process for the other third years is another sacred tradition.

"It's not very deep or anything. It's mainly an excuse to show off my technique." Alfie shrugs then holds up the corner of his shirt, silently asking if they mind if he removes it. They just shrug back, so he pulls it up and over his head, dropping it nearby on the floor. The heat in the building must be at max today because even Emir wants to remove his jumper already and they haven't even started. "Mostly writing about my time in Australia and the ways I've developed as a dancer since I got to Roseborough. Not much of a story. I'm starting with some choreo from first year and slowly building to now. One song for each year. Like I said, it's not complicated."

"Doesn't have to be." Emir pushes up his sleeves and settles in with his head against Theo's shoulder, ready to watch Alfie and provide whatever feedback he can. Even dancers like Alfie who are working on their dissertation alone and performing a solo still need some collaboration and input from the others. It's all part of the process. "Ours is a meaningful story, but it's not the only way to do things. You have solid technique. You *should* show it off."

"Thanks, butt." Alfie gives Emir a grin and hands Theo his phone. "It's in order on the playlist, so if you could just start at the top when I tell you. I've only got the first song and part of the second done."

Alfie starts in the corner, a familiar piece of choreography from the corps their first year, something all three of them had done together. Emir and Theo watch, impressed, because they don't often get the chance to just sit and observe Alfie as a dancer. When you're all on stage at the same time or focused on your own technique in class, sometimes it's hard to have perspective. But Alfie truly does have fantastic technique. It's no wonder he has a standing offer to return to Sydney when he graduates. Even if he won't be a soloist, he's incredibly solid and can carry any ballet they give him.

Moving from one song to the next, Alfie gets less sure about a minute into the second song. He has tentative choreography that he tries out until the end of the second piece, but it's clear he's not quite decided, especially near the end. And when the third song starts, he loses steam entirely, groaning and flopping down in the centre of the studio with his arms over his head, his legs spread wide like a starfish.

"You may proceed to berate me now."

Theo stops the music, Alfie's phone still held in his hand, then sets it aside. "Not sure what you're groaning about. I was genuinely impressed by that."

"We never get to watch you on your own." Emir agrees, tucking one leg beneath himself and stretching off to the side. "Didn't know you were such a high jumper. Real soft landings, too."

"Got better when I was abroad. They're fucking giants down there. Gabe sized." Alfie grins, hand still shielding his eyes as his chest heaves. It was only a few minutes, but ballet is a full body workout and he's been in the studio for hours.

"Suppose he and Ciaran would fit right in, wouldn't they?" Theo asks, but he didn't expect Alfie's face to fall immediately. Was that the wrong thing to say? He looks wounded.

"They would love it there." Alfie clears his throat to answer, sitting up but not removing himself from the floor. "Alright, let's hear it. How fucked am I for my dissertation?"

They spend almost an hour helping Alfie work through some of the spots he's been trying to figure out. Sometimes Emir and Theo forget what a huge advantage it is to have a partner to talk through things with, another person to try a position or shape, another mind to fit pieces together. By the end of the hour Alfie is grinning, excited and typing notes to himself on his phone, thanking them over and over again for their help. "I know I can dance, but this dissertation is so much more."

"Definitely. I'm so glad I spent months last year studying choreography. It's made a world of difference." Theo fans his chest with his shirt. Alfie's still shirtless from earlier and Emir stripped out of his jumper a while ago, but the heat of the studio hasn't decreased in the slightest. Just one of those quirks of an older building used for an underfunded programme.

"You need a minute or are you ready to show off your masterpiece?" Alfie asks, reaching for his warmups so his muscles don't get cold while he watches them share what they've been working on. Deal's a deal.

"It's longer than yours, so settle in." Theo walks over to his bag to find his phone, Emir stripping down from his joggers to bike shorts. For some of their lifts, it's easier to have more skin available. Less slipping.

"We still need to fix a few things in the Birdy song and then we'll have one more after that still needs to be choreographed, but the first, like, two-thirds is set. Sean's seen it, of course, and we've shared it with Lili and Jordan." Emir throws himself at Theo out of habit. It's a thing he does every time they start working together for the day, a reminder of that first night alone in the studio, when they'd reenacted *Dirty Dancing* and started a foundation to so much more than a dance partnership.

"Here. We both start off stage." Theo holds Emir against his front with his right arm, offering his phone to Alfie with his left. He's gotten very used to this after months of the two of them climbing all over one another. "Should be in order as well. You'll recognise the voice on the original song."

Alfie tilts his head and looks confused, so maybe Gabe and Ciaran haven't mentioned their contribution to the project. Theo doesn't think about it for too long, Emir tickling him (of course) until he has to drop him again and head to his side of the room. When they're both ready, Emir gives Alfie a nod and sets his shoulders.

Considering it's the first run through of the day, it goes very well. Only one wobble each, perfect musicality, and the work they've put in for almost half a year is evident in the results.

They're too focused to notice, but when Gabe's voice plays through the speakers, Alfie's face completely drains of colour. He's left looking like a ginger ghost, hands shaking while he watches them dance. And by the next song he's crying silently, cheeks blotchy and nose red as he subtly wipes away his tears on the fabric covering his shoulder. Emir and Theo's piece is stunning, haunting and interesting and absolutely technically beautiful, but he's crying for personal reasons. Related reasons, but he wasn't expecting to be weeping just from watching his friends dance.

"So that's about where we've - Alfie?!" Theo still has his hands on Emir's waist, the Birdy song fading away as they reach the end of what they've choreographed. But he pulls away and towards Alfie when he notices the state of him, curled up into himself on the floor with his back to the mirror, scrambling to turn off the music from Theo's phone because he got a bit lost and forgot they'd be done after this song.

"Shit, sorry, I've got it." Alfie finds the pause button on the screen and presses it carefully with his thumb while wiping at his eyes with the sleeve on his free hand. "That was incredible. Lili was right."

"What's going on?" Emir drops himself to his knees beside Alfie, still breathing hard from their performance and waiting for Theo to kneel next to him. They've not gotten particularly close to Alfie, but they're certainly friends after all that's changed this year.

"I just - " Alfie covers his eyes with his hands and starts crying in earnest, sniffling and trying to control it, but failing miserably.

"Hang on." Theo hurries out of the room and down the hall to steal a box of Kleenex from one of the other studios. Unfortunately, the practice studio ran out a few days ago and it won't be restocked until next week. When he gets back, Emir has Alfie's head on his shoulder, one arm around his back while he lets him cry. "Here."

Alfie takes the box without comment, sitting up straighter but not moving away from Emir's zone of comfort. Theo sits cross legged in front of him, setting a warm hand on Alfie's knee and waiting for him to calm down. Neither of them has ever seen Alfie upset like this, not when he mentions his parents and their awful divorce, not when dance is frustrating, not ever.

"It was Gabe's voice." Alfie starts, gesturing in the direction of Theo's phone where it sits a few feet away. "He's so - and Ciaran must've - and then watching your story, it was - Christ, I'm a mess. I'm sorry. That was lovely. You're both going to do such great things, honestly. I'm not crying because - that was lush, but I - "

"Breathe, mate. You've got to fucking breathe before you can do anything else." Emir shakes Alfie a bit where he's still holding him around the shoulders, looking towards Theo and seeing his own grimace returned. It's worrying to see Alfie like this.

"Sorry. You're right, of course." Alfie takes several shaky breaths with concerted effort before they start to even out, blowing his nose into a Kleenex and seeming to recover himself enough to actually talk again.

"You don't have to tell us, but...we're here and we won't judge you." Theo moves his hand from Alfie's knee to reach for the water bottle that's still almost empty, but luckily not entirely. Hopefully that last bit will give Alfie enough to clear his throat, but Theo could always head into the hall again and refill it if needed.

"It's just - it's my own fault. I shouldn't have - " Alfie breaks off with a harsh laugh, running a hand through the red strands that have fallen across his swollen eyes and brushing them off his forehead. His quiff is a disaster of sweat and distress. Alfie may be a good looking lad, but he's not a pretty crier. He seems so forlorn, like a wounded animal who can't find their way home, and it brings out every single one of Theo's protective instincts.

"Shouldn't have what?" Emir pulls Alfie's head back onto his shoulder, glad when Theo starts rubbing his hand soothingly along Alfie's lower leg. Clearly he needs to be comforted right now, even if this is definitely not how either of them saw their afternoon going.

"I love them. I'm in love with them. Both of them." Alfie wipes at his eyes as the tears start up again. "How could I not be? But I'm moving to Australia in a few months and they're not - and I'm not even their boyfriend, so I should never have let this happen. I shouldn't have gotten this invested. I knew this couldn't be forever. I've been daft, but it fucking hurts even though I'm trying to ignore what's coming and just enjoy what we have. But - "

Alfie cuts himself off with a groan, hiding his face against Emir's shoulder.

"You can't help how you feel, mate." Theo catches Emir's eye again, his mouth twisting to the side while he tries to find the right words. But sometimes the situation is what it is and there aren't any right words, only tolerable ones. "Don't be ashamed of loving Ciaran and Gabe. They're easy to love, especially for someone who's spent the sort of time with them that you have. But I'm sorry you're hurting...I don't think they'd want you to be in pain like this."

Alfie nods, giving Theo a weak smile, lip wobbling while he tries to control the tears. He's been holding this in for a while, consciously since Christmas when they were apart, but realistically even longer. He should've known this was where this was always headed, since their first night together. Alfie's never loved any partner like he loves the two of them, and loving them both was less of a revelation than he would've thought. Theo's completely right: they're easy to love.

"Have you talked to them?" Emir asks after giving Alfie a moment of quiet, already suspecting the answer.

"Can't. Not about this." Alfie shrugs his shoulders but somehow he looks even more defeated than before. "They're so excited to start their life after uni, to move somewhere together and take on the world. I'm not upset about that. I'm just crushed I'll be left behind, or like...I'll be alone without them on the other side of the ocean. And I don't want to give up everything I built in Sydney. It's my whole career. I know I can't throw that away, even if I'm so in love with them that I've considered it more than once before my head catches up to my heart...I *need* to go to Sydney, and they won't be."

Emir stares at Theo, both of them still soothing Alfie in whatever ways they can. Being young and in love can be painful. Emir knows that better than most, and Theo can't imagine being in Alfie's place, feeling like he can't talk to the people he loves most about something so important.

Theo and Emir share one of their unspoken conversations. They're both nearly positive that Alfie isn't the only one who's been falling in love the past few months, but it's also not their place to interfere in their relationship, whatever form it may take.

"I think you should talk to them." Emir gently pulls Alfie off of his shoulder because he seems stable enough to sit up on his own again. "They'd want you to talk to them. I know neither of them would be happy that you're this upset, especially if they're the reason. Even inadvertently."

"It doesn't have to be, like, as soon as you leave here." Theo stands up and offers Alfie a hand to help him up as well. Emir keeps his own hand between Alfie's shoulders until he's up to keep him steady. "But I agree with Emir. They're good people, and I know they don't want to hurt you."

"I'll think about it." Alfie says as he gets pulled into one of Theo's warmest hugs, arms so firm and strong around Alfie's back that he lets out a huge sigh and settles into him for an entire minute. He gets a briefer hug from Emir before he's ready to leave, packing up his things but stopping before he walks out. "That really was beautiful. What you two have...it's special. I'm glad I know you. I'm glad we get to dance together."

"I'm glad we're mates." Theo adds for him, smiling once Alfie nods his agreement. "You know where to find us if you need to chat again, yeah?"

"Yeah." Alfie knocks his knuckles against the doorframe to the studio on his way out, waving goodbye as he walks away.

"You think they'll be alright?" Theo waits until he's positive that Alfie's out of ear shot before turning around to face Emir. Emir wrapped his arms around Theo to hug him from behind, but Theo would rather have a full body cuddle for a moment. That was a lot of emotions and things to process that he hadn't been prepared for when they got to the studio.

"I do, actually." Emir tilts Theo's chin with his fingertips and gives him a sentimental kiss. Whatever happens in the next few months, he trusts that they'll all figure it out. "Not sure what the fuck they'll do about Australia, but Ciaran and Gabe definitely love him, too. Their relationship stopped being casual a while ago, and it's hurting all three of them to pretend otherwise."

"It's a big change though." Theo lets Emir play with his curls while they sway on the spot, holding each other just because they can. They'll get to work eventually, but not right this second. "Like, if they've realised they're poly and they decide to be out as partners, that's...it would be a lot. Especially with Ciaran's family and Alfie's parents. I don't think Gabe's family would care. But the world is fucking cruel to relationships like theirs. I'm just...worried about them."

"You can't fix the whole world, baby." Emir slides his arms beneath Theo's vest and holds him close. He's never loved anyone as much as he loves this man, and if what those three are feeling is even a fraction of this, Theo's right. It would be a lot to deal with, knowing they have an expiration date. He had his own worries about that before he and Theo decided to make it official, but they've worked through it and found their way. "We'll just have to be here for them, whatever happens. Whatever they decide."

Theo nods, face tucked into Emir's neck with his eyes closed, letting himself ground into the moment one sensation at a time. He doesn't have any answers, and neither does Emir, but at least he knows that whatever comes next, he'll have Emir. Theo's faith and trust in their partnership has never been more sure, a certainty that's stronger every day. If only everyone could have that sort of security.

There's a fragment of hope that Alfie could find that with Gabe and Ciaran, but there's also dozens of reasons that Alfie's right about what their futures hold: separate because it's what's best for them, not because it's what they want. And that sounds like a very conflicting, painful place to be.

"I love you." Theo purses his lips against Emir's skin, not ready to move out of the hug just yet. Now that he's got Emir and all that they are together, he never wants to let go.

Emir doesn't say it back, but he doesn't have to. Theo knows what his hummed response means and he can feel it in every stroke of Emir's hands along his back. Emir uses his fingertips to write *I love you too* three times over before breaking the hug and giving Theo another kiss. "You ready?"

"Can we go for a walk when we're done? My head's in a funny space now." Theo starts shaking out his muscles, limb by limb, trying to get back to where they'd been before Alfie's understandable breakdown.

"Mine too." Emir reaches for Theo's phone where it's still abandoned on the floor, ready to play the most recent song again so they could smooth out those transitions that still need work. "Let's spend some time under our tree before we go home."

"One more kiss?" Theo shuffles towards Emir, arms out, feeling needy and not ashamed to ask for another quick reassurance. Their dissertation is inherently emotional, and when he's already worked up like this, it helps.

"For you? Always." Emir drops Theo's phone into his jogger pocket while tugging him forward by the waistband, and Theo only swoons a little when he feels the sudden weight against his hip. Emir's smooth as fuck when he wants to be. Theo lets himself be kissed - much more than the once he requested - and it's enough to bring him back to where he needs to be.

Emir runs his hands through Theo's hair while they kiss, massaging his scalp and working away some of the worry that sits so heavy on his frame. He needs this, too, and he's grateful that Theo will always ask. Theo's the reason they have beautiful moments like this scattered throughout their days, and Emir can't imagine his life without him.

***

It's already past eight on a Tuesday night and Theo and Emir are just now leaving the studio. Theo's going to miss his bedtime.

"I could fall asleep right here on the pavement." Theo falls forward against Emir's back, letting Emir hold a majority of his weight while they walk towards his flat. It was a longer than usual night of rehearsal, and even though Emir finished working with Margaret before Theo was done with Sean, he'd waited for his boyfriend before heading home.

"As much as I love carrying you around, could we make it back to your flat before you collapse?" Emir holds onto Theo's arms despite his question, keeping him upright and letting Theo lean on him as they shuffle along in a very absurd sort of rucksack carry. Theo's breath is hot against his neck where he's clearly shut his eyes and nuzzled in. Emir sort of loves that when Theo's sleepy and vulnerable and barely functioning, he clings to Emir like he's the respite amongst the storm. "I'll look after you, but it'd be easier if we were somewhere one of us lives."

"You don't have to look after me." Theo sighs, making absolutely zero attempts to carry any more of his own weight. This is much more comfortable than trying to walk properly. "I'm completely fine."

"You're like Batman after fighting the Joker without Robin." Emir grins when he feels Theo laugh quietly at his joke. They're not actually far from Theo's building, and he is generally used to carrying him by now. They both are.

"It's *so late*. And we haven't even eaten yet." Theo grumbles when they're almost home. He's in no mood to be cooking right now and there's no leftovers waiting for them. They couldn't have predicted that rehearsal would unexpectedly go more than an hour over tonight. It's just a thing that happens sometimes.

"You let me worry about that. I'm not nearly as knackered as you, baby." Emir stops outside the front door to the building, helping Theo to stand properly and giving him a quick kiss. "I said I'll look after you and I meant it. Let me spoil you."

"But - " Theo starts to protest, then gets cut off by his own yawn. It pushes its way out of him without permission, and Emir just smiles and tucks a lock of hair behind his ear. Theo feels disgusting, sweaty and smelly and definitely not worth the way Emir is looking at him right now.

"Inside before I have to carry you again. Go on." Emir turns Theo around and pushes at his back, forcing him to move in a productive direction despite his continuous grumbling.

Emir keeps shuffling Theo along, dropping their bags in the hallway near Theo's bedroom, then redirecting Theo into the bathroom and shutting the door behind them. "I'm drawing you a bath and I don't want to hear any arguing."

"But - " Theo gets cut off by a kiss this time, Emir pressing their lips together as he starts to strip Theo down to nothing. Somehow, he manages to turn on the tap and get him starkers before Theo's really aware that anything at all has happened. Emir's very talented. Also, Theo's very tired.

"Where's the special salt?" Emir knows that Theo has a specific epsom salt blend he uses when he's especially sore and tired, but since Theo's always the one who brings it out, Emir doesn't want to just take apart the drawers trying to find it.

"Are we sharing?" Theo asks, reaching under the sink and towards the back of the cabinet, wondering why Emir is still fully clothed.

"Not tonight. I'll make us something to eat while you relax." Emir takes the jar from Theo but pulls him in by the waist, giving him permission to cuddle.

Theo attaches himself immediately to Emir's side but lets him get the bath ready. He's usually the one trying to take care of people, but Emir always takes care of him, body and soul, like he's making up for lost time. Since the moment they stopped fighting, he's been Theo's guardian angel.

When the tub is filled and the water's just slightly too hot, Emir tries to prod Theo in the direction of the bath. But Theo hesitates, flushing slightly and glancing back at the cabinet again, one arm still clinging to Emir's waist.

"What's wrong, shehzadi?" Emir rubs his hand along Theo's lower back and tilts his head, waiting to find out what's holding him back. Usually he'd be dropping himself into the water before it was even ready for him, especially when he's completely worn out.

"You can't laugh." Theo mumbles, looking at Emir for a moment to make sure he won't mock him for this. It's stupid and childish but Emir gets to see all his most embarrassing habits and idiosyncrasies. "Since you mentioned Batman earlier…"

Theo slides around Emir in the small room and opens the cabinet again, reaching into the same place he'd recently replaced his epsom salt, where his secret comfort is hiding from potentially prying eyes. Standing back up and leaning into Emir, he holds a single rubber duck, very old and well loved, but still discernible as Batman, with the mask and the ears and a cape painted on its back. There's a hint of a logo on the tiny yellow chest, but it's incredibly faded.

"A tiny friend for bath time?" Emir is trying very hard to control his smile. Why would he laugh? This is clearly something that Theo's owned for a very, very long time, something that means infinitely more than its monetary value.

"It's just..." Theo offers the duck to Emir to examine, then steps into the tub since he's starting to get cold. The water is *everything* he needs right now, and he immerses his body completely before continuing. He's so glad Emir thought of this. "When I was really little, I couldn't say Batman right, and it sort of sounded like Bathman, so for my birthday that year, Barbara got me this because...*I'm Bathman.*"

Theo lets his voice go all scratchy and dramatic for the last part, like he's a little kid imitating the character. It's a good thing his body is already flushed from the heat of the water.

"I haven't seen Bathman before." Emir kneels next to the tub, still in his sweaty clothes from the studio. He'll shower after they eat and Theo is all snuggled up cosy in bed. He might even go for a walk after Theo falls asleep, just a quick one to clear his head at the end of a long day. "You keep him hidden away?"

"He's really special to me, so I don't want people making fun of him." Theo watches as Emir sets the little duck in the water, giving it a tiny push in Theo's direction until it bumps against his knee, bouncing off and going on its own little journey around the tub. "I know it's stupid - "

"He's not stupid. *You're* not stupid." Emir pushes up his sleeves and dunks his hands under the water so he can soak Theo's hair, massaging the curls with his fingers for a few moments then moving his attention to Theo's shoulders. He's only planning to make eggs and avocado toast for their dinner. It's minimal effort but should refuel them both, and it won't take longer than Theo will be soaking. "I still have plenty of things from when I was a kid. We all do. Nothing to be ashamed of, baby."

Theo lets Emir keep rubbing his muscles and brushing his curls, closing his eyes and fitting as much of his body as possible into the tub. It's cramped but it's still lovely. He needed this after today. "Thank you."

"You'd do the same for me without even pausing to think." Emir leans forward to press a kiss to Theo's warm forehead, the tiny duck hovering nearby. "Can you relax while I make us food? I'll need about fifteen minutes."

"Could you give me a two minute warning so I can dry off and put some boxers on? It helps if I don't have to think about how long it's been." Theo opens his eyes as Emir pulls his hands away, wiping them on a nearby towel. "And maybe turn the lights off but keep the door cracked open?"

Emir nods, gathering up Theo's dirty clothes to tidy away and blowing Theo a kiss from the doorway as he turns off the overhead light. The thing is, he doesn't think twice about this either. He's never wanted a relationship like this with anyone else, but it's truly everything he never knew he needed. Theo loves him, and even if Emir's not quite saying it aloud yet himself, he loves Theo so deeply that it's instinct.

Loving Theo is just part of his life now, changing Emir and his future in the most remarkable way. The choice of a life partner isn't one he thought he could allow himself to make after what happened with his ex. But he trusted Theo, and thanks to the encouragement of his sister and friends, he trusted himself, and nights like tonight are the result.

Emir's happy with his choice, and even though he and Theo both tell each other so occasionally, it still hits him sometimes when he's contemplative, buttering toast or folding laundry, all those tiny moments that add up to a life. He's never been more sure of anyone or anything before. Emir's still adjusting to the security and safety that define his relationship with Theo, but it's like stretching a muscle that was atrophied from injury. With time, and with care and attention, he's figuring it out. And that beautiful nerd in the bathtub is the reason for it all.

***

Lili: Hello homos
Lili: When are we having another double date?
Theo: Is this you admitting that you actually enjoy spending time with us?
Lili: Of course not
Lili: But Jo likes you or whatever and I live to please my queen
Jordan: She's sick of me saying my new life is only work and uni with no time for fun.
Jordan: But yes, she does please her queen. And quite well /smirk emoji/
Emi: you're welcome
Lili: You only get partial credit

Lili: I've learned plenty on my own
Jordan: I'm not complaining /fire emoji/
Theo: Why is everyone so shamelessly horny? It's literally just a Wednesday evening.
Emi: you're fit and you're my boyfriend and my body likes your body and also we're in like with each other
Emi: i'm not ashamed of my filthy thoughts and where they take us
Theo: I'm still recovering from yesterday. Not enough energy for that tonight, babe.
Lili: What the fuck did you do last night??
Jordan: Why are you asking??
Emi: princess had a nice bath and went to bed early
Theo: IM TIRED FROM REHEARSAL YOU HOMOSEXUAL PERVERTS
Jordan: /shrug emoji/
Lili: First of all i'm bi
Lili: This is bi erasure
Theo: I am literally also bisexual??
Lili: I'm just saying you could've called me a bisexual pervert
Jordan: I don't think that's the hill you want to die on, sweetheart.
Theo: I'd prefer that none of us die on any hills, unless we're old and with our partners and it's like that scene in The Notebook.
Lili: Emi come get your wife he's being maudlin
Jordan: Theo's tired, he gets a pass /heart emoji/
Emir: he's already here
Emir: /selfie with Theo laying with his head in Emir's lap, scrolling Instagram on his phone/
Emir: so double date soon?
Jordan: PLEASE YES
Theo: But it's too cold for a picnic this weekend.
Lili: Not every date has to be a picnic Mrs. Shah
Theo: Mrs. Shah-Palmer
Lili: /eye roll emoji/
Theo: Well, Laur and T are busy all weekend and Ciaran and Gabe are having sad boi hours until further notice, so I think we're available whenever? We can schedule studio time around the double date.
Jordan: What's wrong with the international gays?
Emi: alfalfa related
Lili: What about Alfie?
Lili: I thought they were having fun together?
Jordan: I am so telling Alfie that you called him Alfalfa. He'll turn as red as his hair.

Theo: I don't want to share their personal business, but I think it stopped being only fun a while ago, and now it's almost the end of the year and...Australia and New York and etc.
Jordan: Ouch.
Emi: yes, that
Emi: family dinner was very quiet tonight and asparagus wasn't there and they seemed sad about it so /shrug emoji/
Jordan: ASPARAGUS
Emi: /Veggie Tales gif/
Emi: you can't tell me there's no similarity
Lili: HELP MEEEEEEE
Theo: We could leave Roseborough and walk around London a bit? Try a new cafe and stop wherever looks interesting? I would need a time limit, though. Like maybe three hours before we head back to uni.
Jordan: That could be fun! Are we near anywhere that you have on your spreadsheet?
Theo: Not really, but if we're all going to be living in the city, it might be nice to just spend some time getting used to it properly?
Emi: when we went to see trockadero we got to give it a go (sort of)
Emi: could be a good idea and a small adventure
Lili: Saturday late morning maybe? Jo only works for a bit this Saturday
Jo: I'll be off around noon, if you can wait til then. Or I could meet you I suppose?
Emi: of course we'll wait
Theo: Works for us :)
Jordan: You can send us the calendar invite, Theo. It's nice to have the details!
Theo: Alright! (Thanks)
Lili: Why does this say "A Lesbian and Three Bisexuals: City Life Immersive Experience"
Lili: /screenshot of the calendar invite/
Theo: You got mad when I called you homosexual. I'm just being thorough.
Lili: I WAS TEASING
Theo: HOW WAS I SUPPOSED TO KNOW THAT
Jordan: Lmao not you updating it to "Two Gay Demons and Their Angels On the Prowl"
Emi: do i get to be one of the demons?
Theo: No! You're my angel!
Theo: Wait...do you have wings? Or like...could we acquire wings?
Emi: ....
Lili: BE HORNY ON YOUR OWN TIME
Theo: EMIR MAKES ME HORNY ALL THE TIME
Emi: /painted nails emoji/
Jordan: I'm fairly positive that one of your theatre gays could snag some wings from the costume department. They've got dozens in storage last I checked.

Theo: Why were you in the theatre department's costume storage?
Lili: /three running emojis/
Theo: AND YOU HAVE THE AUDACITY TO CALL ME HORNY FOR WANTING TO SEE EMIR WITH WINGS
Theo: ELIZABETH GRACE GET BACK HERE AND ANSWER FOR YOUR CRIMES
Lili: It's not illegal just frowned upon
Lili: And like our clothes stayed on
Lili: Also we were very much a secret at the time so locations were limited
Theo: You share a flat!
Emi: ohhhhhhh just before the christmas break, right?
Jordan: YOU TOLD EMIR ABOUT IT?!
Lili: I NEEDED SEX ADVICE
Emi: you were doing fine on your own i just helped you focus
Theo: T says they can grab me a pair of old wings for us to borrow, as long as we don't stain them. If they had more time they said they would make some for us to keep, so apparently that's an option in the future.
Emi: /writing emoji/
Lili: I'm hanging up
Theo: We're not on the phone??
Jordan: Babe come see me at work IM BORED
Emi: have fun shagging in the library /rainbow emoji; book emoji; tongue emoji; scarf emoji/
Jordan: YOU TOLD EMIR ABOUT THAT TOO?!
Lili: I love you sooooooo much Jo /three kissy face emojis/
Jordan: /David Rose bewildered gif/
Emi: we're going for a walk
Emi: give us a ring if you need to be bailed out of horny jail after you get caught
Theo: Biiiiiiiiii (and also a lesbian farewell for Jordan)
Lili: IT WAS A JOKE
Theo: I know /smirk emoji/

***

"Are you telling me that we have six gorgeous gay people living in this flat, and none of us are going out on a Friday night? We are a wasteland of homosexual youth and vigour." Laurie turns away from the fridge, beer in hand. No one even bothers to correct him that, technically, he and Emir have their own flat. This is clearly where they all spend a majority of their time.

"We have a day out in the city with Lili and Jo tomorrow." Theo answers from his spot on the floor next to Emir. They're doing face masks, so he's wearing his Baby Yoda headband, and the green goop soothing his skin matches the fabric almost perfectly. "Need to rest up."

"We had sort of a long week." Gabe is busy tuning his guitar, Ciaran watching him from the other end of the sofa. "And I'm playing that open mic tomorrow night. Or are you not all coming to watch anymore?"

"We'll be there. It's, like, walking distance from Roseborough and we'll be back in plenty of time to make it." Theo assures Gabe. He and Ciaran don't have as many performance type events for their friends to support, so when they do, they all move around whatever they can to be able to show up and cheer them on.

"Not like we have any room to talk about staying home, Laur." T waits for Laurie to bring them their glass of chilled chardonnay, taking up most of the middle sofa that's not occupied by the others. Laurie joins them with a kiss, spreading his legs wide and reaching for the remote.

"We have to plan something soon. Otherwise the next time we'll all be out together will be our stag do, and that's ages away." Laurie sips his beer, eyes fixed on the telly while trying to find something worth watching. Re-run of a favourite show? Gay movie they haven't seen yet? If they're all staying in, he'll need to find something they all actually want to watch.

"Maybe the weekend after our winter show?" Emir suggests, scrunching his face because he's got an irritating itch on his nose that he can't scratch for about ten more minutes. "I think we're all around then."

"Teddy, could you add it to the calendar as tentative?" Laurie gives Theo a brief smile before going back to his scrolling. Choosing the entertainment for a house full of opinionated gays is serious business.

Laurie is still browsing when it's time for Emir and Theo to rinse off the face masks and change into their pyjamas for the night. When they're cosy and back in the living room, Gabe's guitar is put aside, Ciaran is scrounging in the kitchen for snacks, and T is snogging Laurie into the sofa, but somehow in the least disgusting way possible. They just really love their fiance.

"What'd you decide?" Emir walks into the kitchen to help Ciaran while Theo scoots past both of them to make himself and Emir tea. If they're getting cosy and settling in, he wants to do it properly.

"*Mamma Mia.*" Laurie gently pulls T away from his lips and settles them into a cuddle instead. T is wearing a very oversized lilac t-shirt and some sort of frilly undergarment situation that looks potentially Victorian, pouting until Laurie slides his hand beneath the loose fabric to hold them around the waist.

"You know who unironically loves ABBA?" T turns their head to Gabe, glances over at Ciaran in the kitchen, then back to Gabe, waiting expectantly for an answer.

"You?" Gabe asks with a grin.

It's not a secret that both T and Laurie are mildly obsessed, drunkenly singing ABBA at every karaoke they've ever attended, and occasionally dancing around the flat to their music. Laurie was half-raised by gays of the 90s. ABBA was required.

"Obviously." T grins back, still staring hard at Gabe, unblinking. "But I meant Alfie. He mentioned it a few weeks ago when we had a chat over breakfast."

"Oh…" Gabe bites his bottom lip and looks down for a moment before searching for Ciaran with his gaze. It's immediately obvious to T the second he finds him because he relaxes into this soft smile that tracks Ciaran's movement back into the living room.

"He does love ABBA." Ciaran confirms as he takes his spot beside Gabe again. He's carrying an odd assortment of everyone's favourite snacks that he drops onto the coffee table, ready to be shared. "He even has it listed on his Grindr profile. Or, at least, he did a few months ago."

"You two seem, um…" T scrunches their face while trying to find the words for what they're trying to say. It's not as if they brought up Alfie by accident. T doesn't meddle as often as Laurie, but they still try to help their friends along sometimes. "Better than you were on Wednesday?"

Emir claims the third sofa for himself and Theo - a more recent charity shop purchase for the flat once it was clear they'd outgrown the previous situation - glancing over his shoulder to make sure that Theo's alright by himself in the kitchen.

He's clearly listening to the conversation while busying himself around the space, in his own little Theo world while waiting for the kettle to be ready.

"About that..." Ciaran straightens up from where he'd been reclining against Gabe's shoulder, reaching for his beer to take a sip before clearing his throat. "We were up most of the night on Wednesday talking with Alfie. We went to see him after family dinner and stayed up having a chat. Like, still awake when the sun came up, and then even longer."

The four of them wait for Ciaran to continue the story, but he runs a hand through his hair and scratches at the scruff on his jaw, looking at the telly where the film is paused at the beginning while they all get settled. He has this thousand yard stare that they can only guess at. The rest of what he's trying to tell them could honestly go either way.

"It hasn't really been working with the three of us recently. But not because we don't like Alfie." Gabe finally contributes to the conversation, picking up where Ciaran got lost.

There's not a single person in this room who hasn't been waiting for this conversation for months. It's been obvious that whatever they intended at the start of the year just isn't where they are anymore.

"Right." Ciaran looks at Gabe and takes his hand, holding it in his lap before turning back to their friends. He has a steely, determined sort of look in his eye, like he's bracing himself for something. "Turns out we want to be with Alfie, like, properly. All three of us. Not just casual shagging or whatever we tried to do for so long. But shit's complicated, right? Like, since when are any of us poly? And we're done at uni in a few months and where does that leave us? We didn't realise we had an end date we were avoiding until we knew we didn't want us to end."

"Is that why Alfie wasn't in class yesterday?" Theo asks from the kitchen, pouring hot water into the two mugs he'd painted at the pottery store back at the beginning of December. They live in these cupboards even though they were technically a gift for Emir. "I figured he was sick. The flu's going around right now. Loads of people are out."

"Wasn't the flu this time. He was too tired after we were up all night, and also we sort of wanted some time together that day, like, as the three of us." Ciaran keeps holding tight to Gabe's hand, pausing again like this conversation is one of the hardest he's ever had. Maybe it is. "He's our boyfriend now, like, we're all each other's partners officially. Decided that early Wednesday night and spent the rest of the time trying to figure out all the rest. We still don't know what it means for the two of us, but...we're considering Australia. Alfie's definitely moving to Sydney, and New York has seemed like the wrong choice for a while now, so..."

"That's a big change." Laurie offers, his tone gentle. He may tease all of them like no other, but he does genuinely want what's best for everyone. "You think you'd stay there long term?"

"Alfie thinks he wants to dance with them for about three years, which is the length of his tentative contract, and after, he plans to find a company closer to home. Not in Wales, because he wants to have some space from his family and make decent money, but probably back in the UK, and we'd return with him. But it's also almost impossible to know what our life will look like even a year from now." Gabe is worrying at his bottom lip with his free hand and looking at Ciaran's side profile while he talks.

"The music industry in Sydney is decent. Gabe and I could both find work, or at least it wouldn't be any more difficult to find work there than anywhere else. The industry is sort of the same anywhere we go, but there's good studios and some potential opportunities for us there, especially if we start looking into it soon." Ciaran stares at Laurie, like he's expecting some sort of judgement about their decision to move so far away for a boy. "I think we just got to the point that losing Alfie was worse than the logistics of moving across the world to be with him. He's worth it."

"Hm." Laurie and Ciaran keep staring at each other for several long moments, looks of understanding and empathy and a true, deep platonic love passing between them. And over their shoulders, T and Gabe are sharing much of the same, T's eyes wide and questioning, Gabe's hesitant but hopeful.

"I know it's a lot to figure out but I'm happy for you." Theo breaks the silence, not wanting the conversation to end before making sure they know they have his support. "If Alfie is a permanent part of your life, I think that's brilliant. He's a top lad, honestly."

"He's perfect for you two and I know he's never been happier since you've been together." Emir smiles between Ciaran and Gabe, letting his hand find Theo's thigh to rest there comfortably. "Seeing him with you always made sense, from that first time at the party. And now I get to tease him properly because he's one of us."

"He did mention what happened at the studio last weekend during our chat." Ciaran shifts his focus from Laurie to Emir and Theo, his face softening into a grateful smile. "Thank you for looking after him. We *never* wanted Alfie to feel like that, but I'm glad he was with you two in that moment."

"I'm glad he was finally honest about what he needs." Theo blows steam off the top of his mug, the demisexual flag-coloured Batman symbol that he'd painted on the front shining in the light of the currently ignored telly. "It's obvious how he feels about you, or at least, it was to us."

"You don't think we're making a horrible mistake?" Gabe asks, looking around at all of them as if expecting a sudden shift in the support they've been receiving the past few minutes, and realistically, all along. But if he needs the reassurance, they don't mind providing it.

"Love, why don't you go get the notebook?" Laurie turns T's chin to him until their eyes meet. T looks confused for a moment but then their face clears and they nod, climbing away from Laurie's embrace to walk towards their bedroom. It only takes a moment for T to return, all of them waiting to see whatever it is Laurie thought was important to include in the conversation.

"Here. This has most of our wedding notes." T hands the book to Gabe and Ciaran, already open to a specific page. "Check the date at the top."

"I don't - " Ciaran takes it carefully, looking at the date as asked, then letting his eyes roam the complicated chart on the page. It's a mess that's written in both of their handwriting, scribbles and arrows and any number of overlapping notes all through the margins.

"Oh!" Gabe lets his finger rest against a point on the page, then takes the book from Ciaran to get a closer look. "All the way back before Christmas?"

"Even before then, actually. But that's when we were starting to finalise the guest list." T sits back next to Laurie and lets Ciaran and Gabe hold onto the book for now. They'll get it back eventually, and they're not doing any wedding planning tonight.

"You included Alfie?" Theo guesses, cuddling closer into Emir but keeping his legs crossed in front of him. Emir kisses him under his jaw as soon as he's in reach, and Theo hopes he never takes these moments of adoration for granted, not tonight and not in fifty years. Hopefully, it'll be the same for everyone in this room: a life of steady love and tempered devotion.

"We had a feeling he'd still be around in the summer, and I didn't want those two to have to ask if he could be invited. I don't want any of you to feel like you're imposing on our wedding day, and we figured Alfie should be included. You four are family, and you should bring who you love with you." Laurie answers, shrugging like it's nothing. "I'm just glad you lot figured it out before June. It'll be mayhem then with the new babies and all that. The wedding has to be ready to go before they're born or it'll be a nightmare."

"We figured out what we wanted a while ago, but we weren't sure Alfie felt the same. Since none of us had ever done anything like this before, we thought he wouldn't want more than what we'd initially agreed to. Like, because of the whole moving across the globe thing, he didn't want a serious relationship this year, but shit happens, right? It's surprisingly difficult to ask your casual friend with benefits to join an already committed and established relationship." Gabe admits, staring at the page for another moment before closing the book and setting it carefully to the side, away from any of the snacks or drinks that could damage its very important contents.

"Alfie busy tonight?" Laurie asks them, tossing his feet up onto the coffee table and tugging T to lay against him. They look so domestic laying there together that it could be a Christmas card.

"Not as far as I know." Ciaran stifles a yawn behind his hand then ruffles the curls at the front of Gabe's forehead fondly. He's always loved those curls, and the fact that Alfie's red hair is so wavy it's borderline curly is not lost on anyone. Ciaran has a type, or at the very least strong preferences, whereas Gabe just likes the guys he likes and there's hardly any pattern to it.

"Then why isn't he here? Invite him over. Movie night." Laurie waves his hand in the air as if it's obvious. It's not technically his flat, but he's inviting Alfie into their found family just as much as any physical space. "All the boyfriends and fiances and et cetera are here. He should be too."

"Yeah?" Ciaran gives Laurie a sideways smile, shifting around to remove his phone from his pocket.

"Which one of us is the et cetera?" Emir asks with a laugh. He's always appreciated Laurie's automatic acceptance of whatever the rest of them identify with, but sometimes he's a bit camp about it.

"All of us." Laurie shrugs again and turns back to Ciaran, waiting for him to text or call or whatever way he wants to invite his new(ish) boyfriend to come round. Some of their relationships, platonic or otherwise, will never quite fit into traditionally accepted definitions, and he tries to leave space for that nuance.

When Ciaran still hesitates with his phone in his hand, the others all agree that Alfie should be here tonight if he wants to be, and that he has a standing invitation to family dinner, but isn't obligated to put up with the rest of them more than he's comfortable with. So Ciaran finally unlocks his phone and brings it to his ear, Gabe grinning beside him, still within kissing distance.

"Hello, darling." Ciaran says, and it's imbued with this gentleness they rarely see from him.

Gabe is Ciaran's sweetheart and angel, and apparently Alfie is his darling. It's obvious from their expressions that they all find it endearing and definitely worth teasing him about later, but in a way that he knows they're genuinely happy for him.

"We're having a quiet movie night, and Laurie decided on *Mamma Mia* so if you're not busy...Yeah, it's everyone...No, you don't need to get dressed. Just come in your joggers or whatever. We're all half dressed as it is...It's not *that* sort of movie night...Yeah, we've just told them...I know...Love you too...Alright, we'll wait until you get here...Love you...Bye."

"He's on his way?" T asks, both to confirm and to get Ciaran out of the infatuated haze he's fallen into just from talking to Alfie on the phone. It's nice to see him relaxing into and accepting this new part of his life after both he and Gabe fought with themselves for months over it. "Will he want anything to drink? If he hasn't eaten, we can put something together, no problem."

"We can ask when he gets here, but he'll be grand. He doesn't like to cause a fuss, you know?" Ciaran relaxes into the sofa, tucking his phone back into his pocket and sliding an arm behind Gabe to give him a squeeze. "I'm aware you all need to get it out of your system, but try to save some for tomorrow. He'll be watching Gabe with us and that should give you plenty of opportunities to tease. Alfie melts for Gabe's singing like you wouldn't believe."

"Oh, I'd believe it." Emir grins, already strategizing when to start in with the nicknames. Maybe aim for Alfalfa tomorrow morning if he wakes up with a predictable amount of bedhead and go from there. "Gabe has that effect on people. So do you, of course, but you're not on stage tomorrow."

"Couldn't talk him into it this time." Gabe lays a hand on Ciaran's chest above his heart. "But I'm hoping we might duet next time. More people should hear Ciaran sing. He's incredible."

"Yes, yes, we're all very lovely and very talented and very gay." Laurie's sarcastic but his tone has absolutely zero bite to it. He loves every single person in this room to their very core. "Do we all need proper food? Should we do a take away?"

"You're such a dad." Theo tosses a pistachio his way that bounces harmlessly off his arm and back onto the coffee table. "But yes."

"What does Alfie like to eat?" T is already pulling out their phone to scroll through all their available options. "We should pick his favourite. Something nice to help him feel included."

"He'll eat anything, but he'll be here soon. We can wait a bit." Gabe grins, standing up from the sofa to stretch for a minute since they won't be starting the movie anytime soon. His neck cracks as he groans and works through the knots from the stress of the week. Ciaran pulls him back to the sofa and starts massaging at his shoulders, Gabe sighing and leaning into him with his eyes closed.

"Yo, it's Emir." Emir has Theo's phone up to his ear, everyone else turning in his direction in surprise.

"What do you want to eat? Gabe said to wait, but you don't know these gays like I do, and by the time you get here and we all faff over you three, it'll take about an hour, so...We'd usually go for a curry...Just text Theo what you want. I'll save your number later..." Emir pauses to laugh freely at something Alfie said, ignoring the exasperated and equally amused looks from the rest of the room.

"Oi, that's our boyfriend!" Ciaran makes a sudden move for the phone, like he's going to end the call or something. There's several feet between them, but Ciaran's spry when he wants to be. "No Emir-ing at him."

"I think he's jealous, mate." Emir launches himself over the end of the sofa and out of Ciaran's grasp, but it's a brief victory because now they're both on equal footing and Ciaran's got the advantage since he's not trying to maintain a phone conversation. "Awww, thanks lad. Theo's especially fond of that as well."

"What's Theo fond of?" Gabe hasn't moved from the sofa, but he's watching Ciaran chase Emir around the dining room table, torn between fondness and concern. He doesn't think Alfie minds this sort of behaviour, and he's likely used to it after three years of sharing studio space with Emir, Theo, and all the rest.

"Emir, mostly." Theo answers, joining the chase and hoping to catch Emir to save his phone from becoming a projectile in the imminent wrestling match once Ciaran finds an opening.

"Do your hair up nice before you leave. Gabe likes it quiffed." Emir manages to smirk at Gabe while still dodging Ciaran, but it costs him a moment and Theo catches him around the waist, picking him up and making him squeal. "Theo's caught me. See you in a few."

Ciaran stops chasing with a huff, hands on his hips while he catches his breath. He's in shape, but he can't keep up with these two and their dedicated training regimens. "You're lucky Theo caught you first."

"I'm aware." Emir kicks his legs in the air as Theo turns them around, but he doesn't actually want to be let down. He's perfectly happy floating through life in Theo's strong arms. Alas, he gets gently dropped beside the table as Theo plucks his phone out of Emir's right hand and tucks it safely back in his jogger pocket. Or as safe as it was before Emir asked to borrow it to "look at the schedule for tomorrow."

Laurie's been laughing with a hand over his mouth while watching the chase, T sipping their wine with raised eyebrows and trying not to giggle. They're like indulgent parents sometimes, observing the antics from their own little bubble. But then other nights they're the worst of them all, causing mayhem and gay chaos like no one else. Tonight is more of the former.

"What are you on about?" Emir flops himself across both T and Laurie, leaving Theo to reclaim their sofa while he spends a few moments being dramatic.

"I'm just remembering a very similar scenario back in September." Laurie shares a look with Theo who flushes fuschia, biting his lip between his teeth and staring at

Emir because he knows exactly what Laurie is talking about. "When two oblivious bisexual bois were mad at me for inviting them both to a party. Even though you dressed nice for each other and spent a good portion of the evening trying to get the other's attention."

"Did Theo chase you around the kitchen?" Emir asks, looking up at Laurie from his lap, like this is just how they always spend their evenings. It used to be a more frequent occurrence, but they're too busy to spend as much time as they like in queer cuddle piles anymore. Tonight's a nice reminder of what first year was like for them, but brought up to match their current realities.

"I might have." Theo picks up his mug again, trying to hide his face behind it with the excuse of taking a long sip. "Things were different then."

"Not by much." Ciaran tosses a pillow at Emir, but it bounces off of him and lands on the floor at T's feet. "You were always obsessed with each other, there was just a bit less shower sex. Same amount of shameless staring though."

"Theo's worth staring at." Emir rolls himself off of Laurie and T and onto the floor, then crawls over to where Theo's waiting for him.

As if to prove his point, he clambers onto Theo's lap instead, legs bracketing Theo's hips as he takes away his mug so he can kiss him without interference. Theo grabs him with a grin, holding him in his lap and letting Emir have his way. When they're at home like this, neither of them cares even a bit about the others seeing them together. There's no hesitation or embarrassment. Plus, they've seen far more intimate moments of the others, so there's really no room for any of them to complain.

"Get it out of your system before Alfie's here. I told him it wasn't that sort of movie night." Ciaran reclines, setting his feet in Gabe's lap and throwing an arm up over his head to be used as a pillow.

Emir flips Ciaran the bird over his shoulder without breaking the kiss, but he smiles against Theo's mouth and Theo laughs before pulling him closer, holding onto Emir like a moving sculpture while they kiss with as much heat as they're in the mood for.

They do manage to stop themselves just before Alfie gets there, Theo readjusting himself in his joggers and Emir fussing with his hair until he's satisfied with its perfectly dishevelled state. Laurie and T are scrolling TikTok videos on T's phone when the door to the flat opens, Alfie flushing slightly when they all turn to stare as he leaves his shoes by the door. He's not quite used to being the centre of attention.

"I've heard there's room for one more?" Alfie asks as he walks over to join them in the living room, gravitating towards Ciaran and Gabe even as he looks around at the others with a shy smile.

"Always room for you, Alfie." Laurie holds a hand up for a fist bump as Alfie walks past to the far sofa, Theo now busy starting their dinner order on his phone while Emir tries his best to distract him.

"Are we sharing everything?" Theo asks without looking up. Alfie settles himself in the middle of the far sofa between Ciaran and Gabe, looking hesitant until Ciaran pulls him in for a hello kiss then nudges him in Gabe's direction.

"Course we are." T sets down their wine glass and switches sofas so they can help Theo with the ordering, gently squishing between him and Emir and ignoring Emir's annoyed huff.

"I don't want any complaints about all the vegetables if we're sharing." Theo grumbles.

Last time he ordered for everyone, they said it was too healthy. What did they expect? Between his vegetarian diet, Gabe's vegan diet, and Emir's dietary restrictions, there's always going to be a lot of vegetables. But there's plenty of options for potatoes and paneer this time, so hopefully they'll all deal with it. He and Gabe gladly take what everyone else doesn't want anyway.

Gabe lays his head against Alfie's shoulder, and then Alfie leans into Ciaran, and within a few moments they've settled into themselves. Emir catches Ciaran's eye and gives him a tiny wink, Ciaran sending him a sideways smile then pressing a kiss to Alfie's temple. He looks happier than he has in weeks.

Emir truly doesn't understand how so many people would see their relationship as any sort of problem. He and Theo have talked at length about their issues with the mono-normative world, even if neither of them identifies as poly. It's like with any other queer identity: if everyone involved is a consenting adult and the relationship is healthy, why does anyone think someone else's romantic or sexual choices are any of their business? Some people fall in love with more than one person, and the way that relationship looks and functions can be completely unique to the circumstances, but why should that matter?

Theo gets properly upset about it sometimes, as he does about other injustices that he just can't process. Not that Emir understands either, but Theo takes it quite personally. He says it's part of his autism, but Emir thinks it's also just part of Theo, with his enormous heart and generous soul. And Emir loves the entirety of him, grateful to have a partner who cares so deeply about his loved ones and the world they all share.

"Could we watch with subtitles?" Alfie asks when he notices Laurie reaching for the remote.

"He can stay." Theo and T say in unison the moment the words are out of Alfie's mouth.

The whole room laughs, Alfie looking incredibly pleased at their reaction. He lets his boyfriends fuss over him while they start the film and wait for the food to arrive, something they've never really been able to do except in the privacy of one of their bedrooms. Alfie eventually joins in on the sing-along about halfway through, and when it's time for the second film, they let him choose with barely any bickering.

Alfie falls asleep on Ciaran's chest halfway through *Handsome Devil*. Ciaran's asleep not long after, leaving Gabe the only person awake in their third of the room. Gabe takes a selfie with his boyfriends in the background, laying one of the many shared blankets across their legs and leaning against the opposite side of the sofa. He keeps staring at the pair of them with hearts in his eyes, so T takes another picture, this time of all three of them from their perspective a sofa away, and sends it to the group chat with a purple heart emoji.

Laurie ends up being the only one still awake by the end of the third film, busy ordering birthday presents for his sisters before he forgets. Starting with T, Laurie wakes everyone up to move to their respective beds for some proper sleep. They all have busy weekends ahead, and like Theo said, he is a bit of a dad. They all grumble at being woken up, but they shuffle away to their rooms soon enough, T staying behind to help Laurie clean up what's left of the mess before being guided to their own bed to settle in.

One flat with seven very tired people. Three rooms with three relationships all at incredibly different stages, but all at home. One found family expanding and evolving between the shared walls and building a foundation that will last far beyond the scope of early adulthood.

"I want toast for breakfast." T mumbles from Laurie's chest, almost asleep, legs wrapped around their fiance as tightly as possible. Laurie's stripped down to his boxers, but T is still in the oversized t-shirt because they get cold some nights, despite being an actual furnace.

"I'll make you toast." Laurie kisses their waiting lips then tucks his chin over their mess of curls. "Goodnight, little love."

"Night." T sighs deeply and closes their eyes, pulling Laurie with them into a deep, restful sleep.

CHAPTER SIXTEEN

Emir wakes up on Monday morning with a groan, but he's not entirely sure he's actually conscious. His eyes are scratchy and swollen, and Theo gives him several concerned looks and many hesitant goodbye kisses before leaving him to go to the gym. Emir would usually be up again almost immediately after Theo leaves, but he ignores his own alarm this morning, huddling under the blankets and feeling like he needs to sleep for about a hundred hours even though he's just woken up.

Laurie shakes him awake hours later, telling him he's going to be late for tech hall if he doesn't get up soon, then rushes away to his own morning: a work shift at the theatre, putting together a set. Emir literally falls out of his bed and onto the floor, rubbing his hands down his face and groaning. He thanks the universe that Theo left him a glass of water on his messy bedside table. Nothing has ever tasted more like nectar as he chugs the entire glass without even stopping for a breath.

The water helps him feel more alive, so Emir checks the clock before dragging himself into the hottest shower he can stand, trying to shake the brain fog and the weight that seems to be coming both from above and within. He feels like absolute shit, but he has no idea why.

Saturday was a busy day in the city with the girls, but he and Theo mostly stayed home yesterday. They only went to the practice studio for about two hours and otherwise enjoyed quiet time beneath their tree, reading and painting and snogging until it was time for dinner. Emir falls back into a memory of yesterday, of soft hands on his waist and warm lips against his skin, eyes closing beneath the water of the shower.

Remembering what time it is with a start, Emir turns off the tap and scrubs his towel across his skin to get dry. He's so sensitive to everything this morning: the overhead light, the fabric of the towel, the rug beneath his feet, the sound of the radiator out in the hall. It's all making his head absolutely pound, so he grabs the paracetamol on his way out of the bathroom and walks naked into the kitchen because he's just so goddamn hot. Maybe he shouldn't have turned the water temperature so high, but it felt too good to consider any alternative.

Emir takes the pills and chases them with another full glass of water while making his morning tea. He usually doesn't take tea with him to tech hall, but he needs the help to wake up this morning. If Georgia can sip on an iced americano every morning during class, he doesn't feel guilty bringing green tea in a thermos just this once when the occasion warrants it.

But when it comes time to get dressed, Emir's suddenly freezing, chilled and wishing he'd had time to dry his hair properly before he's literally running out of the front door of his flat, bag over one shoulder while he jogs to the dance building. Hopefully the paracetamol will kick in soon because he feels like his muscles are made of marshmallow and connected by glass bones, like he might shatter if the wind hits him just slightly too hard.

"Babe!" Theo rushes up to Emir immediately when he makes it to class, hands holding him carefully around the waist. He looks panicked below his wrinkled forehead, eyes roaming every inch of Emir to find what's wrong. "Did you just wake up?"

"Yeah, Laurie woke me up. It's fine. I made it." Emir gives Theo a fleeting kiss at the corner of his mouth and moves to his spot at the barre near Alfie. Lili is watching them with raised eyebrows from the spot she always shares with Theo across the room, stretching but mostly focused on them. Theo's been borderline hysterical the closer it got to class with Emir nowhere to be found.

"You weren't answering your phone." Theo sits down next to Emir while he starts to warm up his feet and stretch. Emir hates feeling this rushed going into a day of class, and Theo can feel how off-kilter he is. He knows Emir must not be feeling well, but if he's here, maybe he's just having a bad day? "Texted you half a dozen times, and I even called once. You sure you're alright?"

"Massive headache and I'm still tired, but I took something. Should be good to go soon, and I brought tea." Emir gives Theo's hand a squeeze and shares a soft smile with him. His head really is pounding, only made worse by all the noise and everything else that comes with class. Sixty students in one room is distracting on his best days, nevermind when he's feeling like this. "Go on, princess. Lili's waiting. We'll have our break together like we planned, yeah?"

"Alright..." Theo doesn't get up just yet, reaching out a hand to Emir's flushed cheek to hold him there for a moment. His eyes are glassy and his hair's still wet from his shower, but he says he's fine. Theo can keep an eye on him from the other side of the room. "Love you."

Emir closes his eyes as Theo walks away then rolls through his neck and shoulders, sitting cross legged on the floor. He's still nearly fully clothed, joggers over his dance tights, a jumper from Theo's wardrobe making him seem small, and a thick winter henley beneath that. He'll warm up soon enough, but for now he needs the comfort.

"You look like shite, butt." Alfie squats down beside Emir, setting the back of a hand against his forehead and frowning when Emir looks up at him. "And I don't fancy your temperature much either."

"I'm fine. Just over-tired or something. Think I have a migraine coming on." Emir takes Alfie's hand in his for a moment, then sets his own on Alfie's knee. "I'm alright, really."

"And you're all flushed." Alfie isn't giving up that easily. Enough of them have been sick recently that he wouldn't be surprised if Emir's the latest to come down with something. "I'm sure Sean would understand if you need a sick day."

"I already took some paracetamol. By rond de jamb, I'll be my usual fit self." Emir shivers involuntarily, the chill rushing through his body and chattering his teeth. A wave of nausea hits him, so he picks up his thermos for a sip to calm his stomach. "Promise."

"You're a stubborn man, Emir Shah." Alfie shakes his head, but he stands up again and goes back to warming up his joints on his own side of the barre, still watching Emir cautiously until Sean gets their attention to start.

Emir honestly has no idea how he makes it through class. His head is spinning, he can barely manage single pirouettes, he bobbles his way through every balance, and the medicine definitely did not kick in at any point. It's almost the end of tech hall and he's put his warm-ups back on, shivering his way through petit allegro and wondering if the world has always been diagonal and very blurry. Probably not, but he can worry about that later.

He knows he's sick. He's not an idiot. But he's been sick before and he's almost always been able to dance through it. But this fever is trying to knock Emir on his arse and he's not sure that he'll make it through the rest of the day with classes and rehearsal. He's not sure he'll even be able to finish tech hall.

Theo's been watching him the entire time, as has Alfie, and Sean has checked on him more than once, but if he can just get through centre, he'll figure it out. Emir can take more medicine and maybe lay down before his next class with Raphael. Theo would probably indulge him in some cuddling if he asked.

Class finally ends with a hasty reverence since they're running slightly over. Everyone starts clapping before heading to gather their things and make their way towards wherever they need to go next. Emir pulls Theo's jumper tighter around himself while removing his technique shoes, then reaches for his water bottle, hoping the cool water will help him feel stable enough that he can walk home with Theo like they planned.

The room empties around him, Lili and Theo chatting near the door to the studio as Emir walks slowly towards where they're waiting for him. Alfie's talking with Sean in the hallway, but otherwise they're the only stragglers left. Even Jordan already rushed away for a short midday shift at the library.

Emir's not sure how he got across the room with his feet like lead and every muscle in his body screaming, but he's swaying and his vision is spinning and there's static in his ears. Everything is narrowing to a very fuzzy, bright point.

The last thing he sees before everything goes black is Theo jumping up towards him, his wide eyes perfect and beautiful and honey hazel, waiting for Emir to fall into them.

So he does.

***

Theo has no idea how he manages it, but he turns his head just in time to watch Emir crumble, eyes fluttering in the most horrendous way as his body goes limp.

He has Emir in his arms before he hits the ground, stunned but able to set him down gently on his back and start checking everything important. Theo knows there's other people nearby, but they don't exist for him right now. It's just Emir and the way his skin is so hot it burns Theo's fingers, how his eyes are still half-open and he's breathing far too shallow, how his skin is a sickly pale colour he's never been before with an unnatural flush colouring his cheeks.

After preliminary evaluations, Theo is confident that Emir's breathing and somewhat conscious, which is better than the dozen scenarios that went through Theo's mind as his arms reached for Emir's falling body.

"Sean? Sean?!" Theo knows that he was nearby a few moments ago, and he needs a second set of hands to carry Emir away from the studio and somewhere with medical assistance. Emir trusts Sean. So does Theo. "Lili, can you elevate his legs?"

She's been standing there in shock since Emir fell, watching as Theo meticulously checked his breathing, his pulse, listened to his chest, everything that he somehow knew to do in an instant. Lilibet rushes forward to do as he asks right as Sean comes in from the hall with Alfie just behind him.

"*Christ.*" Sean squats down beside them, Emir still cradled in Theo's arms where he's kneeling on the studio floor. "It's alright Theo. He'll be alright."

"He needs the hospital. His fever, it's - " Theo pulls back the neck of Emir's many layers to see him visibly sweating. Another thing Emir *never* does. "Fuck, does he need an ambulance?"

"Emi?" Sean puts his hands on both sides of Emir's face, wincing when he feels how hot he is. "Can you squeeze Theo's hand? He's got yours. Go on then, there's a good lad. Just a gentle squeeze."

It takes a moment, but thankfully Emir does squeeze Theo's fingers. It's weak, but definitely there, like doing as Sean asked took all of his remaining energy. It sounds like Emir's trying to say something, but his voice is less than a whisper, more spirit than sound.

"Theo, do you have your car?" Sean asks, already turning to Alfie who's hovering behind them, waiting to be of use. "Between us and Alfie, you think we could get him there? Hospital's not far. I can go with you."

"I could have someone bring my car closer." Theo's glad that Sean also thinks Emir's alright enough to not need an ambulance, even if he's never been more completely terrified in his life. The person he loves most in this world is limp in his arms, mumbling nonsense and barely moving. "Alfie, could you get my phone? Call Laurie. He'll answer."

Alfie's looking before Theo even finishes asking, rifling through Theo's bag for only a moment then holding it up to show the lockscreen. Theo gives him the passcode - his and Emir's anniversary - and starts brushing his hands through Emir's sweaty hair, waiting for the call to connect as Alfie puts it on speaker.

"Laur, it's an emergency." Theo keeps caressing Emir, glad when he makes some sort of effort to nuzzle in closer to him. He may not be able to function properly, but if they can just get him to the A&E, he should be alright. "Emir's collapsed with a fever. Probably the flu."

"Shit, what do you need?" Theo hears Laurie drop whatever it is he's holding and start running, probably out of the theatre where he's been working and down the side stage stairs if he had to guess.

"Grab my keys from the flat and pull the car around to the dance building. I'm driving him to hospital." Theo repositions Emir enough that he can start tugging his own jumper off of Emir's sweltering body. He doesn't have a spare moment to be fond about Emir choosing something of Theo's when he needed extra comfort this morning, but it does momentarily make his heart ache.

"I'm coming with you." Laurie sounds like he's sprinting now, a door closing on his end of the call, but he doesn't hang up. "You alone?"

"No. Sean's here, and we've got Alfie and Lili." Theo glances up at all of them for just a moment before returning his attention where it belongs. Emir's shivering and helpless, curled up against Theo. "Emi's conscious, but - just hurry, please."

"On it." Laurie does hang up this time, probably so he can focus on getting where he needs to be as quickly as possible. Theo wastes only a moment feeling grateful for Laurie, because honestly where would any of them be without him in their lives?

"Right, I can carry him on my own, but I'd rather not have to. Alfie, could you help me up with him?" Theo's already planning a dozen steps ahead, as if he's been preparing for exactly this eventuality. "Sean, could you get the doors and let the other teachers know?"

"Easy." Sean gets up to give Alfie room to help. Alfie supports Theo until he's upright while still holding Emir, careful not to jostle him more than absolutely necessary. Emir's leaning his face against Theo's shoulder and shaking, eyes closed tight.

"Lili, you remember where the spare key to Emir's flat is?" Theo asks, without turning away from Emir. He doesn't need to see her to know she's there. It's one of the many benefits of having their found family around in a moment like this.

"Need me to bring his bag back home?" Lili guesses, already gathering up her stuff along with both Emir's and Theo's things. Thank god Theo is good in an emergency because she would've probably stayed frozen in panic for a while. She's *not* good in any sort of medical situation, especially since their first year when she had her own hospital scare.

"And mine, if you could. I'll just need my phone and my warmups and Emir's phone, but those can go in the car with us for now." Theo hoists Emir fully into his arms in a cradle hold, used to having some sort of help from Emir and missing it. It's entirely different holding his weight like this, limp and largely unresponsive.

Alfie waits until Theo looks at him, then takes Emir's weight under his hips and legs, helping Theo slowly through the studio door and out into the hallway.

Sean's already cleared everyone out of the hall to give them privacy, Lydia closing her studio door behind herself to keep her students in while placing herself near their path in case they need her. Sean had very briefly explained the situation to her and Raphael in a hushed tone that didn't alert the students only a few feet away. Emir's not a spectacle, and Sean knows he would hate to feel like one in this moment.

While they walk, Theo whispers to Emir. His face is close enough that Theo can lean down with very minimal effort and mumble reminders of love and comfort and safety, wanting him to know, even in his fever-addled state, that he's not alone. Theo's right here, taking care of him, loving him, holding him close.

It takes a few minutes for the group of them to reach the outside, but when they get there, Laurie is just pulling Theo's car up to where it really should never be parked, but needs must. He's completely out of breath when he jumps out of the driver's seat, T pulling themself out of the passenger side at the same time. They must've been at the flat when Laurie stopped by for the keys.

"T and I will sit in the back." Laurie runs up to them to take Emir's weight from Alfie, mumbling a quick *thank you* as he does. Lili re-opens the door to the driver seat to drop the items Theo needs, then gets the hell out of their way. It takes both Laurie and Theo to get Emir in the passenger seat and buckled in, but he's slightly more awake with the cool outside air against his feverish skin, eyes blinking a few times and trying to tell them that he's fine and he wants to go home.

"I love you, but you need the hospital. I'll be with you the whole time, Emi." Theo pauses just long enough to press a kiss to his forehead and caress his cheek before he's taking the keys that Laurie holds out to him and hurrying to the drivers side.

"I'll meet you there," Sean waves them off, waiting to run inside for his own keys until he knows they're safely on their way. Theo nods and starts driving, glad to have both T and Laurie in the car just in case. It's a short drive, only five minutes, but five minutes when someone is in Emir's state can be a very long time.

While he drives, Theo notices T laying a damp flannel across Emir's forehead and running soothing fingers through his hair. They must have brought it with them on their way out the door somehow. Laurie is behind Theo, so he sets a hand on Theo's shoulder, keeping it there the entire drive, reminding him he's not alone in much the same way Theo had done for Emir while carrying him outside.

It's possibly the longest five minutes of Theo's life, but they get there, Laurie sprinting inside the A&E the moment the car is parked to grab someone while T and Theo start the process of getting Emir out of the car.

Theo doesn't breathe properly until there's a nurse meeting them outside with a wheelchair, taking over and repeating all of the checks that Theo had done when Emir first collapsed. Emir's still very out of it, but he's aware enough that he can give permission for Theo to come with him as he gets wheeled inside, eyes blinking at Theo while hot tears fall down his cheeks.

This is part of love, Theo thinks as he tosses Laurie the keys again and follows the nurse and Emir inside. This aching worry when your entire heart is another person, and that person is sick or in pain or in any way hurting. Theo didn't have to even think of what to do since the moment Emir fell, his instincts taking over, his priorities crystal fucking clear. Emir is his, in sickness and in health, just like those future vows would have him profess.

But Theo doesn't need any ceremony. He doesn't need to stand up before anyone and declare the love he has for Emir, not that he wouldn't want to. But the truth of it is flowing through him, stronger than ever, guiding him through this emergency as Emir's partner. Did he plan for this to happen? Absolutely not. But he's never been more sure of anything in his life.

Emir is it for him. Emir is his to have and to hold. It'll have to wait a few hours - maybe even days - before he'll be able to share that information with his boyfriend, but Theo guides Emir out of his sweat-soaked clothes and into a hospital gown, helps the nurse lay him in the bed, holds his hand as they hook him up to wires and IVs and take blood samples for testing. He's there through all of it, like a vow, like a promise, like this is his place in the world, here at Emir's side.

Theo stays as T and Laurie catch up with them, bringing along whatever is needed from the car, then sitting in the uncomfortable chairs in the waiting area. Laurie dials Natalie Shah from Emir's phone to fill her in, promising to have Theo call her when he can. T wishes they could be in there, fluffing Emir's pillows while he squirms and tries to get comfortable, but the waiting room is the closest they can get.

Sean shows up shortly after to do anything he can for them, giving his contact number on behalf of the University to Reception, then texting Theo to assure him that he'll take care of getting their absences excused. He reminds Theo that he's only a phone call and a short drive away if he's needed, but then he leaves them to it after sharing that same info with Laurie and T on his way out. Sean knows that Emir is in good hands and he has to get back to all the other students.

Theo sits in a chair at Emir's side like his guardian angel. He holds his hand and brushes his fingers through Emir's hair, watching over him. He panics and he worries and he waits. There's dozens of people bustling around, other patients, their loved ones, and the busy medical staff constantly checking in, but for Theo, it's only Emir.

This is the love of my life, Theo thinks. Then he holds Emir's hand just a little bit tighter.

***

Ciaran: ALFIES JUST CALLED ME
Ciaran: EMIRS IN HOSPITAL???
Ciaran: ALFIE SAID HE COLLAPSED??
Gabe: I know you're busy and you're with Emir but please when any of you get a second can you let us know if he's alright?
Ciaran: It's been an hour and we're trying not to panic but if that gay nerd isn't going to be alright could one of you at least let us know so we can come visit or something
Ciaran: And give Emi our love even if he's asleep or whatever
T: Sorry it's been chaos so I just read these
T: He'll be alright. Scary seeing him like this, but they've got him on fluids and they said he just needs to rest and let the medicine start working and then he can finish healing at home. He'll be in a sort of quarantine for at least a few days
T: Nurse said he's definitely got the flu, and the strain going around right now has been hitting people really fast. That's why Emir was fine yesterday, but also we need to be careful because we've all been sharing a flat

T: They said Emir's extremely contagious, so he's been moved to a private room in an overnight ward and Theo is with him in a fair amount of PPE. They can't have Emi spreading his flu if it can be helped. The hospital reached out to Sean about getting the dance building sanitised, so that's been taken care of. Apparently they already had to go through that last week after a few other dancers got the flu. Emir is just the one who got it worst and last, apparently

T: Theo isn't anywhere near his texts, focusing on Emi of course. Laurie just keeps pacing the room. He's on a video call with Theo, panicking every time a machine beeps to check Emir's alright and ready to storm his way over there if he thinks he should. It's ridiculous but I can't say I blame Laur for being worried

T: Laur and I are going to stay here in the waiting area for another hour or so, but Theo is staying the night. The nurse is being nice and probably realises that getting Theo to leave Emir might be difficult for everyone involved. I honestly wonder if Laurie's mum managed to call in a favour somehow, even in a different hospital in a different city

T: Hopefully Emi can go home tomorrow. Theo drove us all here in his car, so he'll be good to take him home when he's ready

T: I'll fill you all in properly when Laur and I get back. Promise

Gabe: THANK YOU

Gabe: Tell Teddy to give Emir a kiss for us and a good cuddle if he's feeling up to it

Ciaran: TELL EMIR HE'S NEVER ALLOWED TO SCARE US LIKE THIS AGAIN I FORBID IT

T: I'll do all of the above /heart emoji/

T: I would send you a screenshot from Laurie and Teddy's video call so you could see that Emir's sleeping and we're all fine for now but idk how he would feel about this being documented so /shrug emoji/

Ciaran: It's fine we just needed to know he's alright

Ciaran: Alfie's been in a state as well so I'll make sure he knows

T: Thank you /three heart emojis/

***

"But what if Emir needs me?" Theo barely makes it ten steps from Emir's hospital room before he's turning back around.

"Laurie is with him and he'll call if Emir wakes up." T tugs on Theo's arm, trying to at least keep him in the hallway with hopes to persuade him further. "You need food, Theo. It's almost dinner time and you haven't eaten since breakfast."

"Neither have you and Laurie." Theo grumbles, attention still firmly fixed on the door to Emir's room, but he's fighting T slightly less. They have a point.

"Which is why we're going foraging while Laurie sits at his bedside." T moves between Theo and the door, placing their broad hands against his chest and giving him a slight shove. "Don't make me drag you. We'll be back as quick as we can."

"But it's so far away." Theo listened in while T and Laurie asked the (extremely kind) nurse about the hospital cafe after dragging him out of the room, so he knows it's almost at the opposite end of the building. Too far from Emir and where he should be. "If I need to run back -"

"Then I give you permission to sprint, so long as you don't knock anyone over." T starts pushing at Theo's chest again, glad when his feet start walking backwards, albeit reluctantly. "The sooner we go, the sooner we'll be back."

Theo hesitates for several more seconds before sighing and turning around, T's hands dropping as they fall in step beside him. "What if Emir's hungry when he wakes up?"

"He'll probably have to eat whatever the nurses allow." T shrugs, then links their arm through Theo's. "But if he's home tomorrow, you'll be able to nurture him to your heart's content. Not sure if he'll be up to eating, but you're welcome to try while enforcing his quarantine."

It takes them about ten minutes to get to the cafe. As with most hospitals, the hallways make perfect sense to those who work there and are largely incomprehensible to visitors. They only get lost once, but a very nice patient out for their daily rehabilitation walk, caretaker in tow, points them in the correct direction.

"I don't even feel like eating. I need a twelve hour nap and a good cuddle from my boyfriend, and then I'd consider toast." Theo stares blankly at the options in front of him, T already grabbing several prepackaged snacks for themself and Laurie for when they'll be back in the waiting area, and then eventually on the tube to head home.

"I won't force you, but you know you need to try something." T looks around for a moment then shoves a pre-made vegetable wrap into Theo's hands. "Is this a no?"

"Definitely a no." Theo wrinkles his nose and sets it back where it came from, but he appreciates T's attempt. He should probably just grab something shelf stable, some sort of carb that won't upset his anxiety-addled stomach. "I need something bland and boring and predictable. Probably with fiber."

"I can work with that." T nudges Theo with their elbow to give him a smile. It's completely understandable that Theo doesn't have any room to deal with unpredictable foods or textures right now. It might be days before he feels up to anything beyond his safe foods, and all of those are back at the flat.

"Tea. We need tea." Theo swivels when he sees the hot water and neglected tea bags waiting a few feet away. A cuppa sounds like actual heaven right now, and that's something he could bring back for Emir that the nurses might allow. When has tea ever made anything worse with the flu? And he knows Laurie could use the caffeine.

But before Theo can finish fixing the four cups of tea he's started, T's phone rings, startling both of them as T fumbles everything in their hands onto the counter so they can answer.

"Laur, what's - " T gets cut off almost immediately. Laurie is talking loud enough that Theo can hear him from a few inches away, leaning in to find out what's going on.

"Emir's awake. Or like...sort of awake. He's *inconsolable*. He's asking for Theo and crying, but he still has a fever. The nurse said he might be hallucinating or something, then Emir got mad and said he's not hallucinating, that he just needs Teddy. But half of what he's saying isn't English so could you - "

Laurie is still talking when Theo starts running back the way they came, abandoning T in the cafe and shouting to ask them to please bring whatever they can carry as he turns the corner.

It only takes Theo four minutes on his return journey through the hospital, completely out of breath when he finally gets back to Emir's room. Laurie moves away from Emir's side to make space immediately, the nurse already having left to care for other patients once she was sure that Emir was fine, or at least stable, just emotional.

"Babyyyyy." Emir is really, truly crying, hot tears sliding down his cheeks as he whimpers and stares at Theo the moment he arrives in the doorway.

Theo's never seen him like this before, even when he was triggered by his ex, even when he's been injured from dance. The sight would be truly panic-inducing if Theo wasn't positive that the medical staff have already made sure he's not in immediate danger.

"I'm here, babe. I'm right here. You're alright." Theo removes his face mask now that he's back in the privacy of Emir's room. It's not as if Emir is carrying any germs that haven't been pressed deep into Theo's mouth for days. It's one of the reasons he's allowed to be in Emir's physical space for the next several days.

"I'll wait for T in the hall." Laurie gets a nod of acknowledgement from Theo, even as he leans forward to kiss Emir's still hot forehead, trying to calm him down. This is exactly why he didn't want to leave in the first place.

"You were gone forever." Emir's still crying very hard, ugly crying that makes his eyes hurt worse than they already do from the fever. His mind is hazy and confused, and every single inch of his body aches like he's been run over. His throat is so sore it's agony to speak. But he *needs* to talk to Theo. And Theo was gone.

"I was off getting you tea." Theo wipes away a tear of his own on his shoulder, caressing Emir's fiery cheek and brushing his faded pink hair away from his eyes. "Thought you might fancy something warm to drink when you woke up."

"I had a nightmare." Emir's lip wobbles ominously. Theo hates seeing him look so completely helpless and afraid, but he's here now and that's really all he can offer.

Emir's had some bad dreams in his life, but this one was pure terror. He wasn't the one who was in danger, and he couldn't fix it. Everything was broken and wrong, and then that brokenness crept into Emir's heart and shattered.

"Something really bad happened to you in my nightmare, and they said you were gone but they wouldn't let me in to see you, and I never *told* you before it happened. It hurt so bad I couldn't breathe, and then I woke up and you were gone for real and I panicked."

"I'm not gone. I'm not going anywhere." Theo kisses Emir's lips this time, tasting the salt of the tears that pool against them. His heart is aching at the panic in Emir's voice and the plea in his wet eyes. "Do you want cuddles or are you too sore?"

"Now, please." Emir sniffles miserably, unable to move but desperate to be held in the comfort of those arms. He needed Theo here so he could finally tell him, but a physical reminder that he's not gone and very much alive would be perfect. Maybe it would soothe the jagged edges that remain from his horrid dream.

As carefully as he can manage so he doesn't disturb Emir's IV, Theo lifts him enough to slide in the hospital bed beside him, pulling Emir to lay against his chest. Emir shivers but nuzzles against him, closing his eyes again and finally, *finally*, stopping his crying. Theo sighs with relief once they're settled, hospital blanket pulled up to cover Emir's chest. It's a poor substitute for his plush ones at home, but it'll have to do.

"It'll be alright, Emi. You're on all the right medicines and your nurses are looking after you and we'll have you back in your own bed tomorrow as long as you get some rest." Theo keeps trailing his fingers through Emir's hair, his voice low and soothing. Emir relaxes into Theo, and even though every cell in his body aches, he has a direction of hope now.

"I never told you and I thought it was going to kill me that you didn't know. When I woke up it felt real." Emir mumbles, remembering his dream again and why he was so upset when he couldn't find Theo. He's more lucid than he has been for most of the day, but everything is still very fuzzy. The fact that his nightmare is crystal clear because it hurt worse than the physical pain is very telling.

"We can't be having that." Theo shushes Emir for a moment, wrapping an arm around his tired frame to hold him tighter. He can't do much about Emir's physical pain, but he can do his best to soothe his panicked emotions. "What didn't you get to tell me?"

"That I love you." Emir has said it so many times *about* Theo: to Laurie, to his mom, even to Theo himself when he was asleep, but never like this. Never on purpose. Never when Theo would hear him and know.

Emir wasn't ready before, but he's suddenly, overwhelmingly ready now. He doesn't even hesitate. "I couldn't handle thinking about something happening to you and me never having told you. *I love you*, Teddy."

Maybe Theo will think Emir's still hallucinating, that he doesn't know what he's saying or doesn't fully mean it. But that would be so far from reality, because Theo is the truest companion to Emir's heart, and as all-encompassing as the sky. His fever can't manufacture love or dedication or certainty, only focus it.

But Theo's not saying anything and Emir isn't sure why. "Is that alright?"

"Alright?" Theo chuckles through a few happy tears, every positive emotion he's ever learned swirling into a beautiful rainbow directed right at his boyfriend. He's overwhelmed and trying his best to contain it for Emir's sake, but, "Emir, I love you more than I can fit inside my soul."

"You're so good at words." Emir smiles, despite everything, marvelling at the fact that he's not panicked at all anymore and that Theo *knows* without a doubt. The possibility of something happening to Theo and him not knowing with one hundred percent certainty that Emir loves him was the scariest thing his muddled subconscious could imagine.

Saying the words, finally, is a release and a promise, and maybe it shouldn't have taken this context to get to it, but Emir's glad it's been said. Because now he can say it anytime he wants. Like right fucking now, and for the rest of his life. "I love you."

"I love you, too." Theo gives Emir a slight squeeze before relaxing his hold again. He really doesn't want to hurt Emir, even if in different circumstances he'd be snogging him so desperately they'd both be losing oxygen.

"I'm happy now." Emir thinks he might fall asleep again. No nightmares this time, hopefully. He's just so tired and he has his Teddy bear to cuddle, which always helps. If he has to rest to be able to head home tomorrow, this is how it will have to happen. There's no compromise. He needs Theo here with him, as close as possible. "Needed you to know."

"I've known for a long time, babe." Theo smiles so wide his face is starting to ache. He's known for so long that he forgets what it's like to live in a world without Emir's love. "You're not as subtle as you think."

"I'm very subtle." Emir protests, weakly, both from lack of evidence to back up his subtlety, and because now that his greatest fear is behind him, he's slipping back into sleep. This fever is genuinely overwhelming. "Ninja spy."

"A ninja spy?" Theo laughs again, so enamoured he feels his own temperature rising. Emir has that effect on him, always making Theo flush while his heart races and his eyes grow wide with interest. Emir's the most interesting person he'll ever know, the most interesting person he's ever loved, and ever will. "I look forward to the accompanying outfit."

"Shhhhhh." Emir licks his lips, wondering how soon he might feel something resembling human again. He vaguely wishes Theo had brought back that tea he'd left for. It just might be able to revive him. "Love you."

"Get some rest. I'll stay right here unless you or the nurses tell me to move." Theo reassures him, knowing he's already halfway asleep. The telltale signs are the same, even if Emir's very ill.

Theo did already know that Emir loves him, but hearing it has him feeling like he could fly. He'll have to save his own revelation from today for another time. Theo doesn't want to steal any of this moment from Emir, because it means more than it would for most people to be ready to speak truth into those words. Emir's known the pain of a broken love in the most sinister way, and it's not that he needed time to trust Theo, just time to be at home in their relationship and feel secure enough with his place in Theo's life.

Theo watches as T arrives outside the room a few minutes after Emir falls asleep, arms completely full with snacks and a drink carrier containing what he assumes are the four teas he abandoned to sprint back to Emir's side. Laurie waits for Theo's nodded permission, then opens the door to hand over Theo's portion of the food, all three of them speaking in hushed tones to avoid waking Emir.

Theo knows that Laurie and T will be leaving soon to head home, but he's somehow been given permission to stay. Given Emir's panic when he woke up alone, Theo would have to be forcibly removed before he'd even consider going back with the others and leaving his boyfriend behind.

This is where he belongs. Here, with Emir, holding him close and letting Theo be his refuge. This is where he's meant to be.

***

Laurie: ATTENTION
Laurie: EMIR LOVES THEO
Laurie: /three siren emojis/
T: Laurie!!
Ciaran: That's news?
Ciaran: You were meant to text us if there was an update
Laurie: No you don't understand he's out loud in love with Teddy now
Gabe: Awwww that's sweet. I'm happy for them /purple heart emoji/
Laurie: YOU DONT UNDERSTAND
Laurie: THEYRE GOING TO BE UNBEARABLE
Laurie: EMIR KEEPS SAYING IT EVERY OTHER SENTENCE

Laurie: I CAN HEAR THEM SAYING IT OVER THE VIDEO CALL AND IT'S NONSTOP
Laurie: He slept for an entire hour in Theo's fucking arms and then woke up and immediately said it??
Ciaran: Why the fuck are you still on a video call with them? Aren't you getting on the tube? How does Theo's phone have the battery for it? What the hell sort of hospital is this?
T: A very posh one, as it turns out.
T: Laurie always has his charger because his phone is ancient and always dying, so luckily it was in his pocket out of habit. Also Theo had a massive powerbank in his dance bag because he's literally prepared for everything and Lili thought to toss it into the car with their phones because she's smarter than she gives herself credit for
T: Is that a sufficient update?
Laurie: Emir Shah is a SAP
Ciaran: Incredibly unsurprising
Ciaran: You've seen the way he is with Teddy
Ciaran: That's literally his princess /crown emoji/
T: Theo hasn't left his hospital bed in over an hour
T: Emir forbids it
T: It's both very cute and very unhygienic
T: The nurse keeps frowning and shaking her head, but she likes us...I think
Laurie: Our fault for making Theo leave to get food
T: It's alright we fixed it
T: Also I asked permission so here's proof of life (sent the same one to Emir's mum)
T: /picture through the window of Emir's hospital room, Theo and Emir laying together in the bed with a paper cup of tea each/
Gabe: You two coming home tonight?
T: We're staying at the other flat to get Emi's room all ready for him to be a quarantined invalid for a while. It will shock no one that their flat isn't quite ideal for it...yet
Ciaran: Alfie says he's taking videos for Emir and Teddy at rehearsal and he figured neither of them was checking their phones but wanted them to know in case they're worried about falling behind. And he's talked to Sean about how to help them once they're back.
T: That's so thoughtful! I know they'll appreciate it /heart emoji/
Gabe: That's our Alfie /heart eye emoji/
Ciaran: He's going to stay with us while you lot are away, and maybe a bit longer
Ciaran: His flatmate is being a prick and interrupting his sleep EVERY SINGLE FUCKING NIGHT
Gabe: But if it gets to be too much just let us know of course
T: Alfie is almost Teddy-level courteous. If he needs to stay he's more than welcome.
Ciaran: Still...lot of people in one flat, you know?

Ciaran: Shouldn't be for long since he doesn't want to stay over every night but he just needs a bit of space for a few days
Laurie: Emir's just told Teddy he loves him twice more and once was for literally nothing
Ciaran: Let them be /eye roll emoji/
Ciaran: You and T were somehow worse
Gabe: Still are sometimes /blowing kiss emoji/
T: /shrug emoji/
T: Not ashamed of loving my fiance
Laurie: Also the nurse said Emi might be stuck in bed for about a week, even with all the medicines and that
Laurie: Just passing along the update SINCE YOU WERE SO RUDE ABOUT THE LAST ONE
Ciaran: /eye roll emoji/
Laurie: But he won't need like constant care so he'll be fine on his own in a day or two for the rest of us to go to class and not worry too much. Also he shouldn't be contagious after a few days of the meds they're sending him home with.
Ciaran: We can take shifts as needed. Theo is probably already making a schedule
Gabe: Oh Emir's going to HATE being stuck in bed so much, but at least he can read and draw and whatever
T: Theo is in fact making a schedule right now while Emir whines about his sore throat
T: But I think that's actually a good sign because earlier he was barely moving and now he has the energy to complain so /shrug emoji/
Laurie: Mum said she'll send me a list of things to get for Emi to have at the flat, so we'll grab all that on the way back. So lucky that my mum is a nurse, honestly
Laurie: You two need anything from the shops?
Gabe: We're getting low on some things. I can send you a list and transfer you for our share. That would be a huge help if you have time! Save us a trip this week since we couldn't go this weekend
T: You were busy /wink emoji/
Ciaran: /eggplant emoji; water emoji; peach emoji; tongue emoji; boyfriends emoji/
Ciaran: Why isn't there a polycule emoji /angry emoji/
T: Emoji or not, I'm still really happy for the three of you /poly flag gif/
Gabe: We were also busy with my open mic, but you're not wrong /rainbow emoji/
Laurie: We're actually finally on our way back. I'll make sure the princess and his patient have their phones on if you want to send your love
Gabe: This is me sending love from me and Ciaran! And Alfie!

***

Emir's just woken up from another nap, this time warm in the comfort of his own bed. Even though he only got home from the hospital a few hours ago, it could be a different century. His concept of time is so completely fucked when he's this sick.

At least his fever has broken and he's back to a normal dose of paracetamol, on top of the antiviral he has to take for four more days. They make him incredibly nauseous, but he's supposed to take them with food to help with that. If only every food that exists didn't seem impossible to eat right now.

Theo's been absolutely doting on him from the moment they got home. Emir told him he has to go back to class tomorrow, that missing two days to look after him is already too much, and he's pretty sure if he sleeps through the night, Theo might agree. Luckily, it seems he hasn't really infected Theo. He was a bit sniffly last night,, but otherwise fine. Sometimes that's just how it goes. Disease is a fickle bastard.

"Alright, sleepyhead?" Theo heard some rustling in Emir's room from his current place in the kitchen, so he set everything aside and rushed over just in case they had another incident like yesterday. But since Emir's fever cleared, he's been almost his usual self, if significantly more tired.

"You're adorable." Emir stretches his arms above his head and winces. He hates this feeling that comes with bed rest, his body desperate for movement. Maybe he can try a walk tomorrow with Theo's help. "Apron?"

"Called your mum." Theo leans against the doorframe, needing to keep one ear on the stove so nothing burns. "She gave me a few ideas for foods you'll tolerate when you're ill. Sent me the recipes and all that and Lili ran to the shops with my car to get what we needed. You slept through the delivery, but Lili says hello."

"Have I mentioned that I completely love you?" Emir snuggles back under the blankets, frowning when the pillows don't sit right beneath his head.

He takes a moment to turn himself around and reposition them, and unfortunately that minimal effort almost winds him. Emir coughs, once, twice, unable to stop for almost an entire minute. It's awful, the way the cough showed up once the fever finally calmed. And while the nice nurse - he's pretty sure her name was Nani - said it should start improving in a day or two, he hates the way it cramps his muscles and makes his throat even more sore, his head even more achey, and his chest annoyingly tight.

"You have." Theo ignores the kitchen for a moment so he can walk up to Emir's bed and kiss him properly, first on his forehead to check his temperature, then the tip of his nose because it's cute as a button, then on the lips because he pouts otherwise. "I love you more."

"Even when I'm disgusting and sickly?" Emir hides another cough in his elbow, reaching for a Kleenex to wipe at his eyes. They've been so irritated since the fever started, but that's another thing the nurse assured him would clear up as the antivirals kept working.

For the next several days, he has to test himself daily for infection with the kits they sent him home with, but fingers crossed he'll stop being contagious tomorrow or the day after. At which point, Theo is *absolutely* going back to class. Emir will find the energy to literally shove him out of quarantine if he has to.

"In sickness and in health, babe." Theo reaches for a loose terry cloth headband he'd gotten out earlier, sliding it along Emir's forehead to keep his hair out of his face while he rests.

When he's finished cooking and Emir's eaten something, maybe they could shower together so he can hold Emir up under the water. Emir hasn't had a proper shower since yesterday morning, and if Theo were in his place, his skin would be crawling by now.

"You planning to marry me?" Emir asks, only partially teasing. At this rate, he'd marry Theo tomorrow, under their tree all alone, with the lake as their witness. Or maybe wait a few days until he can stand on his own and look more than half-alive in the pictures.

"Mmmm..." Theo looks off to the side, as if he has to really think about it. As if he didn't decide that for certain yesterday at the hospital. "I'll consider it. *If* you eat something for me, then take a shower and sleep through the night."

"And if I don't?" And there's that fucking cough again. Emir leans forward with the force of it, his abdominal muscles protesting at the strain. He hasn't been this sick in years and he absolutely hates it.

"I'll marry Laurie instead." Theo rubs Emir's back, knowing it doesn't actually help one bit with the cough but lacking any other means of soothing him.

"Oi, I claimed him years ago. We had a pact." Emir wipes at his eyes again, but he gives Theo his usual sideways smile when he's making a joke. "And then I introduced him to T three weeks later and got theoretically dumped by my theoretical backup plan."

"Totally fair. I'd theoretically dump almost anyone to be with my actual soulmate." Theo grins, standing up from the bed again because he really does need to get back to the kitchen.

"You mean me, yeah?" Emir grabs at Theo's hand until their fingertips lace together, wanting another moment with him before he's alone again.

"Course I mean you." Theo softens, unwilling to stop himself from leaning forward for another quick kiss. "You need anything while I'm in the kitchen? Maybe another cuppa? I tidied away the last one when it went cold."

"You're perfect, and yes, extra hot with extra honey, please." Emir lays back against his pillows, letting Theo go and reaching for his laptop. Some mindless Netflix viewing is in order. "Thank you, princess. I love you and your perky bum."

"Leave my bum out of this. It's off the menu for at least a week." Theo laughs and shakes his head, leaving Emir behind so he can finish what he started.

About an hour later - and just in time for another hot tea - Theo carefully lays a tray with chicken soup, moong dal khichdi, and besan ka sheera. He knows it won't be the same as Natalie's, but he's hoping bringing some of Emir's home comforts to him will tempt him to eat. Safiya offered to come by and help, but Mihir just got over COVID and Theo figured it might be best to wait until everyone was feeling better. And if Emir doesn't like the way the food's prepared, Theo's tasted enough as he was cooking to know it'll be delicious for any of the rest of them to enjoy. It won't go to waste.

But to Theo's delight, Emir tries a bit of everything and almost finishes the soup, thanking Theo profusely and assuring him it warms his heart as much as his stomach. Emir even sends his mum a cheeky text that Theo's going to give her some competition soon, and then another thanking her for sharing those family recipes with Theo. He knows she wouldn't do so with just anyone.

With a groan, Emir allows Theo to drag him into the shower, the warm water and Theo's hands soothing away another source of discomfort. Once he's clean, Theo deposits him on the sofa so he can change Emir's sheets, stopping his protest with a lingering kiss. He has to bat Emir's hands away from his arse when he insists on carrying him across the flat and back into his bedroom, which Theo takes as a good sign that he's on the mend.

"You're going back to class tomorrow if I'm not contagious when we wake up. I don't want you to miss any more." Emir cuddles on Theo's chest again while they watch some random cooking show they found online. He needs mindless entertainment at the moment.

"If you insist." Theo kisses Emir's temple and keeps playing with his hair. The colour is almost entirely gone now, just phantom strands of pink left behind amongst the artificial blonde. "But we're sticking to the schedule for at least the next two days. I don't like your cough."

Emir agrees, leaning up so he can kiss the underside of Theo's jaw, then settling back where he was, one arm and leg thrown across Theo, as if he had any intention of going anywhere. This is not how he thought he'd be spending his week, but there's a tenderness that's been brought out in Theo that Emir's glad to have seen. Just another layer of his favourite person, uncovered by circumstance and treasured as part of the whole of him.

With a sigh, Emir slides his hand beneath Theo's shirt to rest against his warm stomach. Theo runs his fingertips along Emir's back, scratching gently every so often out of habit. Emir gets bored with the show and decides to switch to something to match his mood, asking Theo to find one of his favourite Bollywood films that he used to watch on the sofa when he was poorly as a kid. A list of sick day films had been sent along with the recipes, because Natalie knows Emir even better than he realises, so Theo opens his texts and asks Emir to choose then gets it queued up.

They settle into another cuddle and start the film, Emir's occasional cough soothed by Theo's careful hands, wrapped up in each other below the cool sheets.

CHAPTER SEVENTEEN

Emir needed over a week to fully recover from the flu. He was back in class the following Monday, but he had to moderate his activity that entire week too. And now it's the end of his first full week back at class and rehearsal and he's feeling fine, albeit exhausted knowing there's five shows to perform next weekend with a busy week of tech in between. But at least his body is nearly back to normal, with an occasional cough that he's been assured will finally go away soon. All things considered, he knows it could have been so much worse.

He glances over at Theo, his absolute angel through it all, and watches as he sets the finishing touches on the decorations for their pre-show party in the student lounge. Theo has no idea he's being watched, and he's scrunching his face in the most adorable way, tongue between his teeth and eyebrows drawn together while draping the fabric across the snack table so it falls just right.

Crossing the room after he's sure Theo's happy with the results so he doesn't interrupt his process, Emir wraps his arms around Theo from behind, laying his cheek against his back and squeezing him tight. He's glad to have a quiet moment alone together. "All done?"

"Think so. I know I didn't choose a theme this time, but the show doesn't have one. Not really." Theo holds Emir's arms across his stomach and closes his eyes. No one else should be showing up for a short while still, which means he gets a few uninterrupted minutes with Emir.

It's been a long week and they've not seen each other much outside the studio or at night in bed, too tired to even consider getting up to anything more heated than some indulgent snogging.

"Looks nice. I like the colours." Emir shifts back so he can turn Theo around in his arms, leaning in for a kiss. Months into their relationship, he still loves the simple pleasure of Theo's lips against his own at least as well as that first night. Possibly more.

"You know..." Theo grins and pulls away, letting his arms slide down Emir's back until he has his hands on Emir's bum, pressing his hips forward because he's beyond subtlety when they're alone. "We have a few minutes before Alfie and the lads show up with the ice."

"Mmm." Emir kisses Theo again, moving his hands into Theo's hair and starting to walk them backwards. "Are you suggesting we get horizontal on the sofa, right here where anyone could walk in?"

"I'm suggesting it *knowing* who's going to be walking in, and not caring that they will." Theo clarifies, letting himself be led and gasping when Emir tugs lightly at his curls. He's so easy for Emir, so willing, always.

"You'll have to be quiet, and we'll have to fix our clothes before everyone else shows up." Emir's knees meet the edge of the sofa, so he turns them around, pushing Theo down against the cushions and climbing on top of him. Theo's already reaching out for him, his eyes wide with anticipation. "And then you'll have to behave until we're home tonight."

"So many hours until then." Theo groans, pressing their bodies together through their clothes and loving every single thing about this borrowed moment. "I've missed this."

"Shhhh." Emir starts marking Theo's neck, beneath his birthmark so it could be covered by his shirt if it really needs to be. "Let me love you until we get interrupted."

"I love you –" Theo had other thoughts, but they flee his mind the moment Emir's hands are on his skin. He sneaks them beneath Theo's shirt while he's distracted, then decides to bite the mark he'd already made, and Theo forgets where they are and what they're doing, completely wound up in *need* and *want* and *Emir*.

Well, not completely. Emir wouldn't even consider bringing him into subspace somewhere public, where they won't have the necessary time and solitude to do it properly. But he does thoroughly distract Theo, enjoying himself and focusing on what he knows will bring Theo the most release without actually being able to let go. It's a balance, but one he's been practising for months. And even though Theo's the one who voiced it, Emir's missed this too.

Emir lets himself indulge in Theo, in everything that he is and all the ways he makes Emir think and feel. His breath, sweet and warm against his cheek, Theo's hair soft against his fingertips, his lips plush and needy. It's a properly intimate kiss, deep and hungry and definitely not quiet, despite Emir's gentle reminder to Theo before they even started. But the way the sofa is positioned means they're almost blocked from view of the door, and it's not as if they're naked or anything like that.

"Excuse the fuck out of me." Ciaran's voice interrupts their (temporarily) private moment, sarcastic and loud and extra Irish because he knows it has a certain effect when he wants it to. "Alfie said it wasn't that sort of party."

"It's not." Alfie's voice joins Ciaran's, and while Emir and Theo have stopped kissing, they're still panting hard against each other while coming back to the present. Alfie rolls his eyes when he sees the state of them, rumpled and worked up. "But last cast party, they snuck away to get off in the hallway, so I suppose this is an improvement. Not abandoning their duties this time."

"And to think of all those times we were scolded for doing this at the flat." Gabe sets down the tub he'd been carrying atop the drinks table, ready to be filled with the ice that Alfie and Ciaran are waiting to drop inside.

"Our clothes are on, and there's no spunk or lube on anything." Emir climbs off of Theo and offers him a hand, helping him up then pulling him into another kiss. A *save it for later* kiss. An *I love you so much* kiss. Theo smiles that angel smile, and Emir's heart twists in his chest.

"Fuck, your hair!" Ciaran is staring at Emir with wide eyes, stuck in place with shock.

"What?" Emir walks their way, bringing Theo with him by the hand. They should get ready for everyone else to show up soon. Private moment over.

"It's...gone!" Ciaran reaches out once they're a few steps away, running his palm over the buzzed top of Emir's head and looking at the others in astonishment. Alfie just shrugs and Gabe doesn't seem too phased either. "You had all this hair yesterday and now you don't."

"Got it cut." Emir lets him get a good feel, chuckling while glancing over at Ciaran's boyfriends. They haven't seen it either, but they don't seem to care much. It's just a haircut, but he knows Ciaran doesn't always do well with change. He needs time to adjust. "Teddy drove me this morning before we went to the charity shop for decorations."

"You look..." Ciaran whistles his appreciation, finally dropping his hand and stepping back. "Now I see why Theo couldn't wait until you got home. Your cheekbones are so...And your jaw...Your eyelashes look enormous now!"

"Doesn't this one belong to both of you?" Emir smirks at Ciaran's compliments and waves him off in the direction of the others. He knows he looks fit, but he's had short hair before. It's not that much of a revelation.

"Sorry, he's not meant to be off his leash." Alfie jokes, pulling Ciaran in to give him a sweet kiss at his temple. They all laugh rather harder than the joke earned, but since they know someone who does actively enjoy leashes in the right context, namely with a collar and fully in Laurie's control... "But you told me to invite him."

"Course we did. He and Gabe are your partners, so if you want them here, they should be here." Theo runs his own hand along Emir's hair. He loves the way it feels against his palm, and Ciaran's not wrong about how fit Emir looks with the new style. He's all edgy but soft, hard lines and delicate angles. Emir's the most beautiful contradiction and Theo was glad to support his new hair era. He'll support Emir's appearance in any era, especially because he can stare at him as much as he wants. "I'll try to keep Georgia away from you three, but you know how she is."

"Oh, we've heard about Georgia." Gabe scoffs, arranging the ice in the bucket so it can hold whatever drinks the others signed up to bring. He hadn't even opened Theo's spreadsheet, just brought whatever Alfie told him to.

Lili and Jordan arrive next, so it becomes a miniature family reunion before the party actually begins. Theo's back to fussing at the decor nervously, so Emir pulls Theo into his side and kisses the underside of his jaw, mumbling, "Good job, baby."

Theo looks away from their friends to meet Emir's eyes. He knows that Emir understands the work and the thought that goes into something as seemingly simple as this party, and he genuinely appreciates that Emir takes the time to tell him. He'd plan these gatherings anyways, but knowing the effort is recognised makes it feel worth it, like he accomplished what he set out to do. "Love you. Thanks for helping."

"And just so you know..." Emir turns his head so he can whisper near Theo's ear properly, "When we get home tonight, I'm tying you up and rewarding you with as many orgasms as you can handle before you collapse. Been looking forward to it all week."

"You're incorrigible." Theo's hold on Emir's waist tightens as he swallows down the saliva that just pooled in his mouth at the thought of sucking Emir off while tied up. He'll beg Emir to let him, but he's hoping it won't come to that...not that he minds begging. Not with Emir.

"Go greet your guests, princess." Emir kisses Theo once more then nudges him in the direction of the entrance as a gaggle of first years walk through, Sam and Esme laughing about something together, as per usual.

Emir loves watching Theo in these moments, when he's happy and vibrant and floating around between everyone. His social battery is limited, much like Emir's, but when he uses it like this, to lead a crowd, even in this sort of context, he's magnetic. Even back before they were together, back before they were anything, Emir recognised the beauty in it, the beauty in Theo.

And now, Emir gets to hold his hand through it, to kiss him on the cheek when he's being sweet and then remove himself to a quiet corner while Theo does his thing.

Theo catches sight of Emir, Sam, and Gabe at the games table about an hour in, talking animatedly about something he can't decipher, so he lets himself enjoy the sight for a moment before being pulled away again. He'll only have one more of these. Maybe two if he decides to do something for the third years before their dissertations. He'd like to pass off the tradition to someone because it seems to be a genuinely popular and wholesome way to get everyone together. Maybe Sam. Maybe Esme. Maybe the both of them together. They'd be excellent hosts.

Emir finds Theo every so often, floating back into his space and either teasing him with naughty ideas, making him flush with compliments about the party, or just silently squeezing his hand and laying his head on Theo's shoulder. They don't leave to have a moment in the hallway this time, both because they're saving that energy for later and because there's no way anyone would let them get away with it. But Theo doesn't need a stolen hallway moment today. All he needs is Emir and the way they fit together, harmoniously aligned.

***

Predictably, Sean is late to their Tuesday meeting, rushing inside his office where his four dissertation students are waiting, but they've amused themselves thoroughly in his absence. Emir has Theo in his lap, despite there being a completely empty chair off to his side, and Lili and Jo seem to be in some sort of costume debate, scrolling through their phones and showing the others to get their thoughts before sticking with what they'd already decided on anyway.

"Sorry, got a call from Darian's school." Sean drops everything on his desk and falls into his swivel chair, waking up his computer as he turns to face them all. "Apparently, my kid staged some sort of mutiny over one of the lessons and demanded to speak to me on the phone before he would go back to class."

"Isn't Darian like eight?" Emir doesn't move Theo off of his lap. If Theo wants to move, he will. "How'd he arrange a mutiny?"

"Honestly? I don't even want to know." Sean runs a hand through his hair and laughs. "That kid is already smarter than my Claire and I combined. Sometimes it's best not to know."

"But Darian's alright though?" Theo stops moving to focus on Sean's kid's safety. He'd been wriggling around and fidgeting in Emir's lap, but Sean distracted him.

"Fine. Completely fine." Sean looks back at his computer monitor to type in his password. "Darian believes in nonviolent protest, so he just led a bunch of children in feminist chants. I don't even know where he learned how to do that, but."

"According to Ciaran, it's in the Irish blood." Emir smirks, knowing that Sean misses his home back in Bray, even though he loves his life here in London.

"Alfie's Ciaran?" Sean glances across the desk, not familiar with all of their friends, especially those outside the dance programme. He does know Laurie and T because of their involvement with the stage crew, but the others he's only heard mentioned.

"How is it you know about Alfie and Ciaran?" Theo resettles on Emir's lap, folding Emir's arms around his middle to keep him in place. Emir's not complaining and he doesn't feel like moving at the moment. "You know about Gabe as well?"

"Is Gabe the American one? Voice of an angel? Real tall?" Sean hovers his hand as high above his head as he can manage to demonstrate Gabe's remarkable height.

"Who is telling you all the gossip and why aren't they sharing with the rest of us?" Lili crosses her arms over her chest and huffs, leaning back in her seat.

"Can't reveal my sources." Sean laughs, because really all he had to do was pay attention at any point during the year to know about Alfie's partners. These kids all share far more than they realise while casually chatting in the studio, and since Sean is a nonthreatening, safe presence, they don't moderate their conversations much when he's around. "Right, who's first? And sorry we had to all meet at once. Busy week, as you know."

"Me!" Jordan speaks up for the first time since Sean sat down, tossing her hair out of her face and squaring her shoulders. She looks determined, even as she says, "I'm going to fail. Massive disaster. May as well kick me out of the programme."

"You're not going to fail." Sean frowns and leans forward over his desk with his hands folded together. He watches as her face starts to crumble, lip trembling and eyes filling with tears. "What's happened?"

And then Jordan's crying. Her tolerance is so short recently. Jo's stress levels are at a peak, and all it takes some mornings is the wrong temperature to set her off. "I only have half the choreography done, and I'm never going to finish the written portion. If I fail out of uni I'm going to be destitute and alone so I may as well quit now."

"Jordan, I am *not* going to let that happen." Sean lets Lili reassure her, arms wrapping around Jordan from the side while Theo finds the Kleenex and hands it over. "You have plenty of time to finish the choreography and you can always set up an appointment with any of the teachers to give you a hand."

Jordan nods after a moment, Kleenex in hand, so Sean continues. "The written portion is daunting, but you could maybe ask one of the librarians to help you with the research? Now that you know them better with your new job, you might be able to research while you work."

"That sounds...alright." Jordan sniffles, her voice small and vulnerable, about an octave higher than usual.

"Did you want me to find a time for you to work with me and Margaret? Bit busy still next week with auditions, but I'm positive we could spend a few hours with you and whoever else needs a boost the week after." Sean has done everything in his power to support Jordan since he found out about what happened with her family, but there's only so much he can do as her mentor and advisor.

"I don't have my work schedule for that week yet." Jordan wipes at her eyes with a fresh Kleenex, smearing the minimal makeup she'd applied that morning.

"That's alright, we can work around it." Sean reassures her again, glad that she's accepting the help being offered. Not everyone, notably Emir, is always so easy to convince.

"And maybe until then I could try to ask around at the library?" Jordan suggests extremely tentatively, Lili still holding her close.

"See? Less than a minute and we've already got a plan for you." Sean gives her a smile then sits back in his chair again. She'll be alright. "And I'll send you all those reminder emails about scheduling with the costuming department since they'll need to get started soon if you're expecting their help."

"We already met with T about it, and we have another meeting scheduled soon." Theo finally gets up from Emir's lap to sit in the chair to his right, but he takes his hand and interlaces their fingers to maintain a physical connection. "With their wedding coming up, we wanted to have our costumes off their to-do list earlier if possible."

"I'm still using my own clothes, but T is giving me some advice as I put it together. I might need help from the costume department for the other dancers, but I'm not at that point yet." Lili gives Jordan one last squeeze then sits back in her own seat. "Since it's a sort of visual auto-ethnography, it's all part of it. I can't remember if you've read the version of my paper that includes that bit or not, but I've added it."

"Send me what you have. I don't think I got around to finishing my edits, so I may as well read the newest you've got." Sean turns to Jordan again. "Do you have an idea for your costumes? If not, the costume department always has a backlog, and that may give you some ideas to work with, especially if you're looking for faux vintage."

"Oh…" Jordan wipes at her eyes but she seems better. Sometimes she just needs that release of emotion then she's alright to go on. "That would be a huge help, actually. I'm having a hard time deciding."

"T and Laurie are around all weekend for the winter show. Why not ask T to walk you through there?" Theo leans around Emir to chat with Jo. "They love that sort of thing, and it might be fun."

"Do you four even need me?" Sean laughs to himself again, picking up his water for a drink. "Not that I have favourites, of course, but you four have made this a very easy year for me. You could run this place yourself one day, Theo."

"We could make it a difficult year if you'd like." Emir gives Sean that same challenging smile with warm eyes that Sean's grown very accustomed to the past few years.

"I'd rather you didn't, sleeping beauty." Sean rolls his eyes at Emir's comment, glad that they're far enough past Emir's scare with the flu to make jokes about it.

"See? Very interesting year we've been having." Emir takes his hand out of Theo's grasp and lays his arm around the back of his chair instead. He's not quite claiming Theo, but in every interaction, their body posture is clear that they belong to each other, whether intentional or not. "Also, you got stuck with Lili so…"

"Oi!" Lili bristles in his direction, but Emir starts laughing immediately, leaning into Theo as much as he can given the circumstances. Lili scoffs but seems to accept the teasing for what it is.

"Only joking. You're essentially our only competition. Well," Emir rubs at his chin thoughtfully. "You and Alfie. But he's leaving this mess of an island, so mostly just you."

"Sometimes I think Alfie's got the right idea." Jo laughs, but it's sad and heartless.

One of the things she's mourned hardest recently is the fact she may never get to travel like she did before. As much as she hates her family, she did have the means to visit wherever she wanted, within reason, and it was one of the aspects of her life that gave it meaning.

"Before you all leave, I want a quick rundown on your progress." Sean waits for a break in the bickering before making them focus again. "Even you, Jordan. I think it'll help you realise how much you've already done."

"Me first this time." Lilibet cuts in the moment he's done, because she's been getting steadily more excited about her dissertation as the year went on, to the point that she's counting down the days to their performance date.

They don't use the full hour for their group meeting, which means a welcome break to relax before it's back to class and then straight across to the theatre for another day of tech rehearsals.

***

Theo: Hypothetically, will you all be out of the flat until it's time for family dinner?
Theo: Because, as you know, it's my turn to cook, with Emir's help.
Theo: And I'm already done with tech for today, so I'll be in the kitchen.
T: Laur and I will be at the theatre an hour (ish) past when Emir is done, so probably won't make it back until family dinner.
T: Something wrong? Do you need one of us to come home?
Theo: No! Please stay at the theatre!
Laurie: Wait.......
Ciaran: Alfie's joining tonight, as long as that's alright
Theo: I planned for it! We'll have plenty to share.
Emi: going into my last thirty minutes or so
Emi: be home soon princess /heart emoji; peach emoji/
T: OH
Laurie: /smirk emoji/
Gabe: T, will you grab Alfie on your way back? He'll be there as late as you two. Ciaran may reach him first, but just in case.
Laurie: We will gather the ginger otter and ensure the flat remains empty since the ballet boyfriends will be so busy "cooking"
Theo: There will be cooking! Look!
Theo: /picture of about a dozen ingredients laid out on the counter/
Theo: I'm making vegan pho with mushrooms. It's a new recipe but it sounds so good! It won't be like restaurant quality but I thought it was worth a try. Something different /shrug emoji/
Laurie: So it's a recipe that requires a lot of sitting around and waiting time, is it?
Laurie: /sipping tea gif/
Theo: /hiding gif/
T: Have to run. Ripped seam on one of the second year's tunics /crying emoji/

***

Emir walks in through the flat's front door without knocking, excited to spend some domestic boyfriend time with Theo before the others get home. He stopped knocking at the flat months ago after Laurie laughed the last time he tried. "Princess? You here?"

"In the kitchen." Theo calls back, his skin starting to prickle with anticipation. He's really hoping he's timed this correctly, otherwise everything could go disastrously wrong.

Pausing for only a moment when his eyes find his boyfriend, Emir smirks, dropping his things in the middle of the floor and sliding himself in behind Theo, hands wrapping around his torso the moment he's in reach. "What's all this, baby?"

"Just...a little something." Theo stays facing the stove, naked except for the apron he's tied around his front. He didn't want to risk any burns while waiting because that truly would have derailed the whole night.

"Hmmm." Emir's hands smooth down Theo's skin until they reach his thighs, encouraging them apart and pressing himself into his bum from behind. It's a shame his own clothes haven't evaporated. "Feels like a big something."

"Not that big." Theo flushes, stirring the vermicelli noodles once more then setting the spoon on the rest. They'll be done in a minute or so and then they'll be put aside until it's time to eat.

"I very much beg to differ." Emir mouths at Theo's neck, one hand still on the inside of Theo's thigh, the other starting to remove some of his own clothes. "Tell me what you want, pumpkin. I know you've planned it all out."

"We have to wait until the noodles are done, and then I need to add the stock to the vegetables. After that, we can have fun." Theo groans as Emir bites his shoulder carefully. They can't have any marks with the shows only a few days away. "I was hoping you could be distracting until I can, maybe..."

"Yes?" Emir stops undressing himself because he has a feeling Theo wants to be the one to do that tonight. He's gotten pretty good at knowing what Theo's in the mood for.

"I want to press you up against the counter and blow you until your knees give out." Theo steadies himself against the stove, careful not to cause any mishaps, and rolls his body against Emir's. He loves knowing he can affect Emir like this. It's powerful to know he makes his favourite person feel *so good*, and it's fulfilling some sort of internal need he's still learning to access.

"You want my clothes to stay on?" Emir gives Theo enough room to turn his attention back to the food. He knows Theo has to be sure the meal won't be ruined before they can have fun. Otherwise, he'll be distracted or distressed while attempting to be intimate.

"Yes, I'd prefer it." Theo doesn't shift Emir away, but he turns to the sink and sets the strainer inside before leaning back towards the hob for the noodles, which need to stop cooking before they become mush. He has a whole system, carefully planned and timed out. "Stay here, just let me..."

"Not going anywhere." Emir mumbles an *I love you* into the skin of Theo's shoulder while following him through the space, letting him get on with whatever he needs to. It seems like once the stock is going, they'll have a while to explore each other. As always, he marvels at Theo's ability to plan and factor in variables like that so they can just live in a moment and not have to worry.

"That can all rest for now." Theo unties the strings around his neck, then shifts Emir's hands to those around his waist to encourage him to free Theo of the last of his clothing.

Once he's fully naked, Theo turns himself around and kisses Emir, immediately earnest and deep, like he's been waiting for hours. Which he has, of course, but Emir loves that he can feel that anticipation in every press of Theo's tongue against his own.

"Can I blow you in the kitchen? Been wanting to for ages."

"Definitely." Emir lets Theo back him up against a counter, Theo's hands on his hips like sunbeams.

Theo doesn't want Emir undressed until he's come at least once. Something about it seems so debauched, like Theo couldn't wait for the inconvenience of clothing to be removed before devouring his boyfriend.

He kneels at Emir's feet, completely naked and vulnerable, ready to make a mess and savour every sensation as his emotions start to float him away. "I want you to finish in my mouth, if you can."

"Oh that will *not* be an issue, baby." Emir smirks as Theo sinks to his knees, already working at Emir's waistband to untie his joggers and yank them down. But, "Wait."

Dropping his hands, Theo glances up at Emir with a tilt of his head. He looks like a confused puppy, so Emir sets a hand on his cheek to caress it for a moment, needing Theo to know he's very on board with this, just looking after him.

"Your knees, princess. Let's set something under them, yeah?" Emir waits for Theo to nod, then leans down for a quick kiss. He's so sweet and he's all Emir's. "Be right back."

Hurrying to the sofa, Emir finds one of his plushest blankets and starts folding it as he walks back towards where Theo is waiting for him, still kneeling exactly in the same spot. Carefully, he lets Theo hold onto his shoulder so he can shift the blanket beneath him, then kisses him again once he's settled with his cushion. "Better?"

"I would've been fine." Theo waits for Emir to lean back against the counter, pretending to be annoyed. But he's actually much more comfortable now and he knows he'll be grateful tomorrow when he's trying to dance for a million and a half hours.

"Love you too." Emir traces a hand through Theo's hair, knowing that he appreciates it even though he's trying to be stubborn about it. Theo's not very good at faking stubbornness, but Emir wouldn't want him to learn. He's his sensitive, sweet Theo and that's all he ever needs to be.

Theo moves his hands back to Emir's body, sliding his fingers beneath Emir's shirt to trail across the skin of his torso and waist, waiting until Emir leans his head back and closes his eyes before pulling down his joggers and boxers to about mid-thigh. Out of the way, but still clearly being worn. Just how he's pictured it.

Emir lets Theo have his way, uses his hand to encourage him and mumbles reminders of appreciation and love the entire time, letting them fall against Theo while he moans deep, gagging and drooling onto his own chest. Theo's first blowjob a few weeks ago was incredible enough, but he's really improved already, knowing exactly when to slow down, when to pull off and use his hand, when to take Emir as far as he can, when to groan and let Emir feel it through his skin. He looks gorgeous, deeply flushed, his lips puffy and eyes glassy whenever he looks up to check on Emir.

It's a drawn out blowjob, but even so, Emir only lasts a few minutes, releasing into Theo's mouth, one hand in the back of his curls as Theo keeps moving around him. He has to tug Theo off when it becomes too much, guiding him up and into his arms even as Theo is tucking him back into his boxers. Why have they never done this before?

"Shower with me." Emir bites Theo high on his neck beneath his ear, just hard enough to sting. He can already feel Theo's semi against his leg, and he'd really like to return the favour. But he's still covered in residual sweat from dance, and now Theo is covered in his own saliva, so they could both use a hot shower to compose themselves before their friends show up.

Theo checks on their food before allowing Emir to lead him down the hall and into the shower. They won't have gotten away with anything if there's no meal waiting for everyone at the end of all this. And based on Laurie's texts from earlier, they may not get away with it at all.

Emir holds off until Theo's done shampooing before he presses him against the tile, kissing him hard while pulling him off and praising him through every moment. He knows by now that Theo has a thing for affirmation during sex, and it's just *so easy* to find reasons to fulfil that need. Emir could keep a running list for hours and hours, but they don't have that sort of time tonight. Theo's knees buckle as he comes, but Emir's there to catch him, rubbing awareness back into his muscles as his adrenaline regulates itself, tingling through his body long after the water is turned off.

Even with all their fun, they manage to get dressed and make it back to the kitchen before anyone else is home, dressed in what they'll be sleeping in and not bothering to dry their hair. Gabe is the first one home, giving them a knowing look as he heads toward his shared room with Ciaran, and then everyone else shows up within a minute of each other, Alfie scurrying away to find Gabe because he hasn't seen him in hours and he misses him. He already spent a few minutes with Ciaran on the way here, so Alfie's content to leave him on the sofa for now.

"I see you gave the innocent pedestrians a nice show." Laurie comments aloud without looking up from his phone. He has his feet in T's lap on their sofa while they both rest as Theo finishes family dinner, Emir very helpfully encouraging him with kisses and cuddles.

"What show?" Theo turns, panicked, to look at Laurie who just smiles, still scrolling through his messages as if he isn't an agent of chaos with distractingly blue eyes.

"Left the curtains open." Laurie points in the direction of the living room windows as T starts to giggle, their hands busy working a few knots out of Laurie's tired feet.

"Fuck, Emir I didn't – " Theo turns to Emir, already reaching for him in a panic. They *always* discuss that sort of thing before starting. Theo fucked up. They didn't plan on being watched this time, and he meant to close those before Emir got home.

"Shhhhh, it's alright princess." Emir lets Theo grab onto him, waiting until Theo hides against his shoulder to add, "I knew and I was fine with it. No one could see anything except my chest and face. You were hidden by the counter and I still had my kit on…it was sort of hot, actually."

"…Oh." Theo shifts himself in Emir's hold, no longer panicking about it, pressing their middles together and moving his face so he can mumble very quietly, "I wouldn't mind, um…we should talk about that later. But I'm sorry I forgot to close the curtains."

"We'll talk. Also I love you." Emir kisses the hinge of Theo's jaw and steps away because he knows they're being observed, and he also knows Theo would prefer to have that conversation in private. Louder, to the rest of the room, he says, "So, food should be ready in about ten minutes. Who wants to help me set the table?"

"Me." Alfie sticks his head back out of Gabe and Ciaran's room, looking slightly more rumpled than he had a minute before and with Gabe following behind him. "Also, can I cook next week? I haven't had a turn yet."

"Course you can." Ciaran answers from the sofa, watching as Gabe disconnects his hand from Alfie's so they can go their separate ways: Gabe to join Ciaran in the living room, Alfie to follow Emir into the kitchen. "It was supposed to be Laurie's turn, but I'd prefer something edible."

Laurie hits Ciaran with a cushion, but it bounces off onto the floor while Ciaran cackles before tossing it back.

"Your hair's a bit fucked, Alfalfa." Emir reaches out and rumples Alfie's hair so it's even worse than before. Now that Alfie's part of their gay family, their friendship has been transforming to include a lot more teasing in between their usual conversations.

Alfie just shrugs Emir's hand off and opens the cupboard to take out a stack of plates. "Gabe never gets to mess up Ciaran's because he's a diva about his hair, so I think he overcompensates with mine."

"He does." Theo stirs the pot with intention, both literally and figuratively. "Told me so himself."

"I knew it." Alfie grins, bumping Theo with his hip on his way back out of the kitchen and towards the table. He's really settled in recently, into his new relationship and into everything that comes with it. Like family dinner.

"Right. Everyone sit and I'll bring you your bowls." Theo calls out once everything's ready. The thing about pho is it has to be basically boiling when it's served and it's easiest if he just handles that on his own. Emir helps him, of course, but Theo's the one who gets to excitedly tell everyone about the recipe, why he chose it, how he prepared everything, and to their credit they all seem genuinely interested.

Emir sparkles across from him, heart eyes so bright the others can't even mock him for it. He keeps hold of Theo's ankle beneath the table the entire meal, Theo occasionally leaning over for a kiss. Everyone helps clean up, Ciaran kissing Alfie gratuitously on the sofa as soon as they're done. Emir tosses another pillow their way, but they just laugh and go back to it as the others settle around the room, Gabe claiming Alfie, then Ciaran until the three of them seem content with the amount of spit swapping and just lay together.

No one's heading back out tonight, so they settle in with their individual work and extend family dinner well into the evening.

***

"I cannot believe we've managed to find a restaurant that can fit all of us." Emir is towel drying his buzzed hair in the dressing room mirror while Theo gets dressed beside him. They didn't technically require showers after the show like Emir had after the *Alice* performances, but there's five shows this weekend, and after two in a row, they both felt decidedly rank.

"I can't believe our families chose the same night without our input." Theo works on the buttons of his shirt, fingers fumbling more than once. He's exhausted, and wondering how any of them will make it through two more shows tomorrow. But tonight it's all about family and celebration, and he needs to find a second (or third) wind.

"Our mums talk now." Emir watches Theo's fingers carefully going through the process of dressing, finding himself getting far too distracted when they only have about five minutes until they're surrounded by a majority of their relatives. "I'm sure it wasn't an accident."

"My eyes are up here." Theo smirks, catching Emir staring at his chest just before it's covered with pressed blue cotton. If he wasn't wearing an undershirt, Emir would probably have him pushed against the counter, regardless of the others still in the dressing room with them.

"You sure your family's fine with tandoori? You think the kids will eat?" Emir's already asked Theo this same question at least twice, but he knows that Theo's nephews aren't as accustomed to Desi food as the rest of the Palmers. And certainly less than the Shahs.

"I'm positive. Both Boo and Jayna love a curry, and I know they try to get the kids to eat the grown up food, even if they still prefer chicken nuggets most days." Theo starts packing up his things now that he's dressed, able to leave most of it here overnight since they have their last two shows tomorrow.

"I'm glad they were able to bring the kids, you know? I haven't met them yet." Emir pulls a soft red jumper over his head, letting it drape over his black jeans. Hopefully with his hat and a bit of heat stolen from Theo, Emir won't freeze tonight, even though it's beyond chilly outside.

"They've heard all about you, though. I talked about you at Christmas when they were at the house." Theo double checks everything, then tucks his phone into his back pocket and reaches for Emir's hand with his own.

They're not the last ones leaving the dressing room this time. Alfie is primping a few yards away, presumably ready to be taken on a date by his boyfriends, because he asked his parents not to come watch this show for the sake of his own mental health. Sam is near the corner scrolling through something on his phone, adding offhand comments to the other first years' conversation nearby. There's a handful of other dancers in various stages of post show exhaustion trying to put themselves together to leave for the night. Somehow, Emir and Theo are actually some of the first dancers ready to leave.

"Come on then." Emir lets Theo glance around for a few moments, but they really do need to get going. Since they have such a large group as compared to their separate family dinners for *Alice in Wonderland*, they had to make a reservation a bit further from campus than last time. "Kiss?"

Theo refocuses on Emir and pulls him in without hesitation, closing his eyes as he gives him a plush, lingering kiss. They won't be alone again for hours, and they're both already very low on energy to be dealing with whatever chaos awaits them upstairs.

Leading Theo with a hand at the small of his back, Emir guides them both out of the dressing room, down the hallway, up the hidden stairs, and through the backstage area, pausing once more for an embrace before he lets them out into the lobby.

Emir needs a moment in the quiet, a *private* moment to hold Theo close and prepare himself. And if the way Theo clings to him is any indication, he does too. "You ready, baby?"

Laughing just once, Theo shakes his head no, still cuddled up into Emir because he needs more time than he has to recharge. "We might actually need to sleep in tomorrow."

"I'm so glad we have Monday off." Emir breathes in the smell of Theo, warm where his nose is tucked against his neck. He smells like soap and laundry, and there's a new cologne he's been trying that Emir really fancies. It smells clean and crisp, but not sharp. It suits him.

With a heavy sigh, Theo leans out of the hug, resting their foreheads together then stepping to the side so Emir can bring them out to their families.

They're barely ten steps into the foyer when there's a shriek of "Emiiii!" followed by a Saima-sized wrecking ball colliding hard with Emir's middle.

He disconnects from Theo to return Saima's hug, one hand on the back of her head, the other around her shoulders. Two months is a long time, even if it passed so quickly that Emir can't fathom where it went. He swears Saima's grown another inch since he was home.

Theo steps away from Emir with a fond smile then turns towards where his parents are waiting, but -

"Grandad?!" Theo freezes in place, because behind his dad is his Grandad Robert, smiling and opening his arms for Theo to rush to him. Once the initial shock wears off, Theo walks straight up to him and into a warm hug, holding tight to make sure this is real. His Grandad hasn't been able to make the trip for any of his performances since early last year. "I didn't know you'd be here."

"I've missed too many of these, lad. Wasn't about to miss another. You've grown so much." Robert has to hold back tears at the way Theo's flung himself into his embrace with so much love. And watching him on stage like that, seeing him perform...he's never been more proud of his grandson. "You were spectacular tonight."

"I'm so happy you're here." Theo steps back from the hug to wipe at his eyes with the palms of his hands, looking towards his parents who are watching on with wide smiles. They must have planned this as a surprise for him. They know how much it's always mattered to Theo that his Grandad Robert is one of his biggest supporters and favourite people. "You're coming to dinner with us? All of us?"

"I have to meet the boyfriend, don't I? You told me all about him over Christmas and your mum sent me a few pictures of you two." Robert pulls Theo in by the shoulders and into a side hug, turning them both so they can watch where Emir now has all three of his sisters clambering for his attention at once. "He's quite talented, isn't he?"

"He's my favourite dancer. I still can't believe I get to work with him everyday." Theo moves his eyes away from Emir to look at his grandad with a huge, easy smile. He's missed having him in the audience for his shows. Grandad Robert used to sit front row and take dozens of pictures, giving Theo standing ovations, even when he was a tiny kid. And, like he said, he finally gets to meet Emir. "Emir's the best person I've ever known. You'll love him."

"Go say hello to your parents and the kids. They've been going on about Uncle Teddy for hours. You've got quite the fan club." Robert lets Theo out of his grasp so he can greet the rest of his family, waiting behind him to be introduced to Emir once all the rounds of embraces have been shared. He doesn't want to interrupt a very sweet reunion and he's happy to just watch his son's family having their moment.

Emir steps away from his dad as the group resettles from their arrival and sets a careful hand on Robert's elbow to get his attention. Robert's been chatting with George while Theo is absorbed with the kids, but Emir doesn't want to wait to introduce himself until Theo's untangled from his nephews. He knows it may take a while.

"Are you Theo's grandad? I'm Emir."

"The boyfriend, of course." Robert takes Emir's proffered hand and gives it a firm shake. He's inclined to like him already and he's impressed that Emir took the initiative to introduce himself. "I've heard a lot about you. George says you've been good to my grandson, and I can see clear enough that Theo adores you."

"I promise it's very mutual." Emir drops Robert's hand and darts his eyes over to Theo who's finally noticed their interaction. He seems content to let it play out while he keeps twirling the kids one at a time, Saima joining in with his nephews. "Theo's told me so many memories and you're exactly as he's described. I suppose I introduced myself on my own so I could thank you."

"What for?" Robert furrows his brow, and it's so similar to the way Theo does when he's confused that Emir has to hide away a smile.

"Well, not all grandparents are as…accepting as you've been his entire life. Theo is unique, the most brilliant man, of course, and he has this incredibly generous heart but…" Emir runs his hand across his head and shoves the other into the front pocket of his jeans, trying to find the right phrasing. Theo is often an entity beyond words, a soul too precious to fit into the English language. "I know how much it means to him that you've always been there. You showed up at his ballet when he was little, and you were there for him when he was harassed at school, and you walked with him at Pride when he came out. Most grandparents wouldn't have done any of that. You've set a wonderful example. So I wanted to thank you for loving him in his entirety instead of by halves."

Staring at Emir for a long moment, Robert seems to decide something with a nod and a smile. "You are exactly the way Barbara described. I'm glad she was right."

He claps a hand on Emir's shoulder and gives it a brief squeeze then he turns and beckons Theo over with his free hand. "Teddy, why don't you let the kids climb all over Emir, hm? He seems up for the challenge."

"Maybe after dinner. We need to leave, like, right now or we'll miss our reservation." Theo carefully sets Barbara's son Ron down to join Emir and his Grandad, taking Emir's hand again like it's the easiest thing in the world. So much has changed, including their comfort with each other. A few months ago, neither of them would have been so bold.

It takes longer than any of them would admit to get out of the foyer, into the tube, ride past three stops, then head out and into the city about a block from the restaurant. Amina and Saima run ahead with the other kids just behind, the adults watching their every move to make sure they don't run anyone off the pavement or get too far away.

"Mihir's sitting next to you, mum." Safiya squeezes herself between her brother and her mom, her husband chatting quietly with Saleem a few feet behind them. "The girls are already yapping his ears off."

"As long as I'm next to my Emi, I don't care who sits on my other side." Natalie links her arm with her son's and pulls him into her side. Theo is similarly claimed by his own mum just ahead of them, glancing back at Emir every few steps as if he'd have gone somewhere in the intervening moments. As if he's ever going to leave Theo. As if he'd ever want to.

Once they're shown to their enormous table at the restaurant, Theo and Emir take their seats in the middle, Natalie on Emir's right and George on Theo's left, everyone else settling around them, a mixture of both families blending seamlessly together.

Mihir chats quietly with Jayna, Saima complains about school with George and Ron, Robert laughs with Saleem about something the rest of them miss, and it may be chaos, but it's family.

***

"Well, that was exhausting." Emir waves as his parents drive away, Theo at his side after saying goodbye to his own parents and grandad only a few minutes before.

Both of their families stayed the night in London and returned to watch the matinee show on Sunday, except for Barbara, Jayna, and the kids who had to head home mid morning.

"Funny you should say that…" Theo pulls Emir into him for a warm kiss, both of them melting into it as if they haven't had the pleasure all day. In reality it's only been about twenty minutes since they were snogging, hidden in the stairwell at the theatre for a few borrowed moments.

"I'm happy they're all getting along and all that, but my introverted arse is done. Running on empty." Emir closes his eyes and hides his face against Theo's neck, nuzzling into his scarf and throwing his arms over Theo's broad shoulders. He's not above dramatic embraces.

"I'm not as overstimulated as I thought I'd be, actually." Theo rubs Emir's back with his gloved hands, pulling him up and away from the hug so they can walk home. "But I had a plan for how we could spend the next two hours until we have to be back at the theatre."

"I'm too tired to lick chocolate off your cock, pumpkin." Emir lets Theo drag him away from the car park and towards the flat, hoping he can collapse on the sofa for a few minutes. And despite his exhaustion, he'd always find energy for a quick afternoon delight if Theo was in the mood.

"Where did that even come from?" Theo laughs, sliding an arm around Emir's waist as their steps fall into sync. It's nice to be reminded that Emir is extremely attracted to him, but they're both in need of a significant amount of rest.

"You had chocolate last night and there was a bit I got to lick off the corner of your mouth." Emir shrugs, snuggling up against Theo to avoid the cold. "Consider me a sure thing. I see you with chocolate, get a taste, and want the whole meal."

"You are absolutely ridiculous, but I'll make sure we have plenty of chocolate for next weekend. Maybe caramel too." Theo really doesn't know where Emir finds his endless inspiration for their sex life, but he's certainly not complaining. He gets plenty of his own inspiration from Emir in so many ways. "We're taking a nap when we get back to the flat. The international gays are at Alfie's while his flatmate is away for the weekend and Laurie and T are at your flat, so we'll have two hours of blissful, silent, private space to snore on each other until we have to wake up, cram food in our mouths, and run back in time for call."

Emir stares shamelessly as Theo explains their afternoon plans, leaning in to kiss him the moment he's done. Even without the chocolate, that particular corner of his lips is enticing. "I've never loved you more than the moment you said nap."

Laughing loud, Theo almost falls over with the force of it, Emir catching him at the small of his back and smiling so wide his cheeks ache. Theo is the only person who's ever made him this effortlessly happy.

"Come on, babe. You'll love me even more when you're under your four different blankets and I turn on that new noise machine we got." Theo takes Emir by the hand this time so they can walk easier, glad it's only a few more buildings to pass before they can cuddle up in his bed.

"I take it back. *Now* I've never loved you more." Emir twirls Theo in place just to make him laugh again. It's his favourite sound in the world. "And I want five blankets because we're sleeping naked."

"I suppose that could be arranged." Theo sighs, dramatic and loud, like he's really being put out by the request. "I'll just have to deal with my sexy boyfriend, naked in my bed, wrapped around me like we're trying to fuse together."

"If you want to see fusion, you'll have to wait til next weekend, princess." Emir leans over to nip at the bit of Theo's neck that's exposed above his scarf. "Once I get that chocolate on and then off of you, I have a few other ideas for ways to *get under your skin*."

"I love you and I need you to shut all the way up, because if you keep talking like that, there is no way we'll be sleeping when we're back to the flat." Theo feels himself flushing, glad that the pavement is abandoned and they can banter easily without being worried about being overheard.

"I think you should make me." Emir steers Theo off the path and near a tree, grinning as Theo presses him against it and kisses him hard.

The nap can wait a few more minutes.

***

"Personally, I think nine is stretching the limits of our dining situation." Ciaran is standing at the head of the table, the gifts that he and Gabe would normally bring to the theatre for their friends' performances waiting at their usual spots.

They attended the final show, as always, but now that Alfie's their boyfriend, it was just too much to fucking carry…especially since they'd gotten a full bouquet for Alfie and a stuffed kangaroo holding an Australian flag. Ciaran still has no clue how Gabe found that at the charity shop, but it's perfect.

"Should we like…on the sofas instead?" Theo suggests from the opposite end of the table. Everyone except Lili and Jo have already made it back to the flat, but Emir's in the shower, Gabe and Alfie are up to something quite loud in the bedroom, and T and Laurie are taking a quick walk to decompress after dropping their things in T's room and scurrying away.

"Still not enough room for the girls though." Ciaran starts moving chairs again, but they're already so squished together, and that's without the extra that Lili and Jo are bringing with them because the flat only has eight chairs, and only half of them match.

"We can squeeze. It'll be cosy and we'll all be bumping into each other, but we'll make it work." Theo moves his chair closer to Ciaran's usual spot, then shifts Emir's closer to Laurie's, and he's pretty sure they can fit both Lili and Jo cramped together around the end between him and Emir, opposite Alfie.

"Princess!" Emir calls to Theo as he opens the bathroom door, steam billowing around him like some sort of Hollywood heart-throb. "I'm wearing your clothes."

"You don't need to ask." Theo reminds him, watching as Emir crosses the short hallway between the loo and Theo's bedroom in only a towel. His thoughts veer entirely off course at the sight. There's just something about Emir, clean and warm and pink from a hot shower that calls to Theo like a siren song, shutting out all other input.

"Wasn't asking, only telling." Emir ignores his own half of the drawers that have remained stocked with his things since December and focuses on Theo's share of the contents. He wants something comfy and slightly oversized, and it's always better if it belongs to his boyfriend.

"Go on then." Ciaran nudges Theo who's been staring blankly at his open bedroom door for several long seconds. He's nice enough not to make a whole thing of it. They've all had a long weekend. "Go have fun with your Emi. I'll finish setting the table."

"You're sure?" Theo asks, but he's already moving away towards his room. That nap they had earlier really gave him back his energy for the rest of the night, and he'd like to use up a bit of what's left.

"Might even have time for some fun of my own." Ciaran tilts his head in the direction of his and Gabe's bedroom and gives Theo a wink, then laughs as Theo literally jogs the last few steps to his room. Ciaran hear's Emir's happy shriek a moment later, then a thump as they both fall on the bed.

***

Post show family dinner is long over, but they're all still chilling around the table. As it turns out, nine fit just right when it's this exact combination of lovely people. There's been laughter and memories shared and a bit of wine for those who were interested, but mostly it's been just bursting with love.

"Sneak away with me soon?" Emir leans into Theo to mumble near his ear, his hand already high on Theo's thigh. He and Lili switched spots after a few minutes because he kept staring at Theo longingly, and apparently, it was distracting everyone else from their meal. "I have somewhere I want to take you."

Theo turns his head to look at Emir while he considers it, the rest of the room falling away as he looks between his lips and eyes, trying to decide which needs his attention at the moment. Somehow, both. "Alright. But not just yet."

As much as they're all enjoying their casual celebration, every single one of them is exhausted, and only the dancers have classes cancelled for tomorrow. So after roughly fifteen more minutes of family time, Jordan and Lilibet decide to head out, which sends everyone else on their way like a ripple effect.

Theo and Alfie clear the table, but Theo keeps his focus partially on Emir, wondering what he has planned. Which is how he catches Emir following Laurie into T's room for a moment before reappearing, tucking something into the pocket of his borrowed joggers. Interesting...

That could be something sex related, weed related, or just something gay and chaotic that has nothing to do with them sneaking away somewhere mysterious. Having Emir as a boyfriend and Laurie as a best mate is never a boring combination.

The clean up from dinner goes rather quickly with so many hands helping out. Emir and Theo only get two suggestive comments tossed their way - from Laurie and Ciaran, of course - when they head towards the front door with their hands linked, offering their flatmates zero explanation.

"Don't get too excited. We'll be back later. We're staying here tonight." Emir slides into his trainers while Theo gathers both of their coats. "But feel free to indulge in our absence. Just text one of us so we can decide if we're joining in."

"Is that an option?" Alfie asks from where he's cradled in Ciaran's arms in the kitchen, the remaining plates forgotten for the moment.

"Someday." Theo answers with a grin. It's one of those things he and Emir have talked about often enough. They've mutually decided they want to try as much as they can on their own before involving anyone else in their sex life. But with how they've been progressing, that opportunity could be any day now. "You'll have your hands full enough tonight without us."

"I've got my hands full every night." Alfie laughs, turning his head for a kiss from Ciaran. "Actually, not just my hands."

Laurie makes an exaggerated gagging sound as if that was somehow too much information. As if they aren't in the middle of a conversation about the five of them having group sex once Emir and Theo are out the front door. As if there's anything related to sex or sexuality that Laurie could possibly find scandalous.

"Don't worry. We'll make sure Alfie makes it to the morning in one piece." Gabe tries to shoo Emir and Theo out the door, which definitely means that Emir's assumption about the next hour or so of activities at the flat wasn't hyperbole.

Theo frowns down at his phone when he sees Laurie's name with a notification just as he's about to put it in his pocket. He opens their group chat while Emir leads him out through the front door and stops to laugh, immediately falling into the wall of the corridor. How is this his life?

Laurie: Consider this your warning text /five eggplant emojis/

"Well, you did ask them to text." Theo shows his phone to a confused Emir who lets out a giggle of his own then tugs Theo forward into a kiss.

"Mmm." Emir hums against Theo's lips before pulling away. He likes having Theo so close. "Missed you. We've been too busy. I wanted some time just the two of us."

"You're being very mysterious and sexy, so I assume you have something devious planned." Theo holds open Emir's coat for him to slide his arms into before they reach the outside. It's been unusually cold this past week, even for February. And since he's not sure how long they'll be outside, he wants to be prepared.

Surprisingly, Emir guides Theo back along the exact path they've trod multiple times this past week. They're walking back to the theatre that they'd only left behind a few hours ago, and they aren't due back for months.

"Babe?" Theo tugs on Emir's hand to ask him to stop when they're almost at the side entrance. He can't imagine what they're doing back here so soon.

"Trust me." Emir sparkles at him beneath the light of the streetlamp, waiting for Theo to agree, then walking him the last few feet to the door. He finds the keys he borrowed from Laurie in his pocket and easily unlocks the side door, ready to bring Theo inside.

But Theo hesitates, because of course he does. Emir knew he would.

"I don't want us to get in trouble. Trespassing or whatever." Theo disconnects from Emir and steps a few feet away from the open door, crossing his arms over his chest.

"Thought you might be worried about that." Emir takes his phone out of his pocket, tugging off his gloves to scroll until he finds what he's looking for. "Here. I asked permission and Sean gave it. But don't look at the email I sent him, it'll ruin the surprise."

Theo holds Emir's phone and reads Sean's reply twice through. It's exactly as Emir said. They have permission to be here, and Sean even mentioned borrowing keys from Laurie, or if he couldn't spare them, they could borrow Sean's own. It's not that Theo didn't trust Emir, he just needed to read it for himself. Which Emir understood, otherwise he wouldn't have already taken all these steps.

He hands back Emir's phone with a small kiss, finally letting Emir drag him inside well after hours. Emir doesn't stop leading him until they're backstage, every movement they make magnified to echo through the empty theatre. They step out of their shoes and strip out of their over layers before touching the Marley, so automatic they don't even pause to think. The floor will be stored away tomorrow by the stage crew, with Laurie as their fearless leader, but for tonight, it belongs to them.

"Wait here. I'll be right back." Emir brings Theo to centre stage, only the ghost light illuminating the space, then dashes towards the side stage stairs and down to the dressing rooms. He'd stashed what he needed here earlier, letting Lili distract Theo so he wouldn't notice. She needed very little encouragement to annoy her best friend.

While he waits for Emir, Theo starts rolling through his feet and ankles, settling into his body and staring out into the dark void of the theatre where he can just barely make out the first row of empty seats. There's always something so reverent, and more than slightly spooky, about being here alone, especially so late at night.

"Close your eyes." Emir stays hidden behind one of the wings until he knows Theo is listening to his request, a soft smile across his beautiful lips when he hears Emir's voice.

Walking quietly to the very edge of the stage, Emir sets down his bluetooth speaker then strips out of his shirt and socks so he's left in only his joggers - borrowed from Theo, of course. He takes out his phone again, finds the playlist, makes sure it's queued, then slides himself into Theo's space. Emir holds him at the waist before moving his hands up under his shirt, along his spine, caressing his smooth skin.

"You can open."

"I am *not* having sex on the stage." Theo scrunches his forehead in confusion when he notices Emir's bare chest, scandalised that Emir would even suggest it. There's cameras everywhere, for a start.

"Well, I know where your mind is." Emir teases, biting Theo's bottom lip between his teeth then kissing him properly. He could kiss Theo for hours, days, centuries if they could figure out how to freeze time. "We're here to dance, baby. After last weekend in the studio, I was feeling inspired. And then I remembered T and Laurie's little post show tradition and asked Laurie how it works. I emailed Sean, borrowed the keys, and here we are."

"You want to dance through our dissertation? Now?" Theo looks at Emir with a healthy scepticism. They've just put themselves through five shows in three days and it's nearing midnight on a Sunday. Has Emir temporarily forgotten...all of that?

"It's the only chance we'll have before the real thing. The spring show isn't until after our dissertations, and even though we'll have tech here, I wanted us to have a chance on our own. I think we could use a feel for the experience, knowing how different the space is from the practice studio." Emir keeps Theo in his embrace, swaying them on the spot while he wins him over to the idea. He can tell that the more he talks, the more Theo understands why they're here, tonight of all nights.

"Is that your speaker?" Theo glances to the front of the stage and Emir's discarded belongings. Emir does have a few very good points. After so many months in a relationship, that shouldn't be a revelation. But Emir surprises Theo every single day.

"Is that you agreeing?" Emir toys with the curls at the back of Theo's head with his right hand while his left stays warm on Theo's back.

He's so in love, right now, yesterday, a month ago, that first night together in the practice studio. Dance brought them together, and he can't stop himself from making that connection in moments like this. Nothing about their work would be the same if they hadn't fallen arse over elbows for each other during the process of its creation.

"Well, we don't even need to warm up. Not really. And you've thought of everything." Theo shrugs out of Emir's hold so he can strip out of his own shirt. They haven't finalised their costumes, but for certain lifts, it helps their stability to have more of their skin available. Skin doesn't slide out of a hold as easily as fabric.

"I love you." Emir reminds Theo for the hundredth time, taking Theo's discarded shirt to join his clothes near the front, laughing as Theo kicks his socks in Emir's direction with a sideways smile. It's definitely chilly in here without most of their clothes, but they'll warm up soon enough.

"Want me to press start since you dance first?" Theo asks, waiting for an answer before heading off stage right.

"I added a countdown track to the top of the playlist for this sort of thing, so I'll just use that." Emir rushes back to Theo and jumps into his arms without warning, planting a very firm kiss on his lips even as he's set back down on the Marley. He was just so cute, standing there, waiting for Emir, being perfect. Being Theo.

"Save it for later." Theo gives Emir a kiss of his own, shaking his head and smiling fondly. He loves that Emir can never get his fill. "I was brought here for dance and I'd like to sleep before the next century."

"So bossy." Emir teases with a pinch to Theo's bum, but he steps away and lets Theo walk to where he belongs: across from him in the wings on stage right.

It's incredible how quickly they settle into an entirely different space the moment the music starts, a transformation that rolls over them like fog. Theo gets caught up watching Emir from his hidden spot for the first few minutes, realising the brilliance of Emir's plan for tonight. He listens to Emir's feet against the stage, watches his fluid form catch the yellow light, observes how the abyss of the empty audience almost swallows him entirely before he's back in Theo's purview. Theo's so distracted that he almost misses his own queue, so enthralled by the spell of it. But he doesn't, months of rehearsal taking over even if his mind has started to wander.

Emir welcomes Theo onto the stage in some infinitesimal, indescribable way. Something only a nuanced, intentional performer could manage. They dance without interacting for the entire first song, but any audience will see the pull between them, that magnetism that keeps them in orbit, the connective thread they dance along even before they meet.

They're so lost in their work that by the time they get to *Quietly Yours*, Theo is actually crying. Tears of joy slide down his cheeks, Emir wiping them away in a moment of inspiration when Theo pulls him into a lift. It's added something to the performance, being here alone on this stage. For tonight it's only for them, but they find sparks of inspiration they would've missed if they'd stayed in their usual surroundings.

There's no fifth and final song yet, so as Birdy's voice fades away, Emir and Theo fade into each other, wrapped in an embrace at centre stage that feels so natural and fated that the universe pauses to collect the memory of it.

"I love you." Theo mumbles into the silence of the abandoned space, not wholly convinced their souls haven't somehow inextricably linked. It's more than a feeling, it's a physical manifestation he can't ignore. "You're the most brilliant person. So much more than a dance partner, but the best one I'll ever have."

"I love you more than life, shehzadi." Emir lets out a heavy sigh, then repeats it in Urdu, letting the words encase them in their truth.

"This was your best idea yet. Well…equal to Christmas. And my pointe shoes." Theo wipes away another round of happy tears with the back of his hand then leans out of the embrace to hold Emir's face. He'll never tire of looking into the eyes of the man he loves. "I'm so lucky to know you. Sometimes I still can't believe this is all real, that I get to have you and this and everything we create together."

"You told me you wanted to create the sunrise." Emir remembers that night beneath their tree. They've had so many wonderful hours there since then, but that memory will stay with him for the rest of his life. "I may not be able to create a universe with you, but we can keep trying."

Theo grins, leaning forward to kiss Emir, hands moving from his cheeks to the sides of his head as Emir's hands find his waist. Emir kisses Theo carefully, like he's made of flower petals or stained glass, his world turning red the longer they kiss as Theo consumes all that he is. Everything is Theo and love, and maybe that's its own sunrise. A brilliant red wave that crashes over him and into infinity.

"We should practise a few more times before calling it a night." Theo rests their foreheads together like always, one of his habits that Emir absolutely indulges at every opportunity. "But then, when we're home, more of this, too."

"Baby," Emir trails his fingertips through Theo's forehead curls then tucks them out of the way while they share a sparkling smile. He was already planning exactly what Theo's asking for. It's nice how often they're on the same page. "We have so much more to look forward to."

Acknowledgements

The titles for each individual book, as well as the series title, were inspired by the song *Latch (Acoustic)* by Sam Smith, from their *In the Lonely Hour* album. Back in my days as a dance professional, I once choreographed a performance to this song. The story I imagined behind that choreography has stuck with me ever since. While it's expanded from a short dance to a three book series, the heart remains the same. Thank you to Sam and to everyone else who created that song.

Thank you to my editors, J and E. J helped with clarity and consistency, while E helped me sound less American for the sake of my British and Irish characters. Both of your work has been invaluable to the final product.

Thank you to Hannah for the incredible cover art. From the first sketch, you drew Theo and Emir exactly as I pictured. Thank you for giving them life in an entirely new medium.

Thank you to Ashley, who has been the first reader for this series, almost since its conception. Your encouragement has been more necessary than you will ever understand. There were days I wanted to give in and shelve the entire project, but your faith in my writing, and my characters, saw me through.

Thank you to Shriya for having dozens of conversations about Emir's character, including, but not limited to, his use of Urdu and his experience as a Desi individual in England. Your feedback, and your friendship, have been integral to the process.

Thank you to my other early readers and sensitivity readers. Your feedback and commentary were extremely valuable.

And a last thank you to every single reader who has supported my work, in any format. I would not be the writer or the person I am today without the online communities who have shaped me, and for that, I will always be grateful.

BT

About the Author

Briar Townsend is a writer, a reader, and about a dozen other things. Mostly, they are a human who is doing their best. Briar is unapologetically queer and neurodivergent. They find value in writing the stories they always wished to read and representing identities that often go unacknowledged by the mainstream.

Contact: briar.townsend.official@gmail.com

Website: briartownsend.com

www.ingramcontent.com/pod-product-compliance
Lightning Source LLC
LaVergne TN
LVHW091652070526
838199LV00050B/2151